Praise for H.

'An exciting and oddly hopeful look into what feels, smells, and sounds very much like life in today's South Africa . . . dark, explosive . . . full of love for the vast beauty of the country but also riddled by the anger of South Africa's recent racial and political struggles' *Chicago Tribune*

'A rip-roaring adventure' *Washington Post*

'A new book by Deon Meyer is a cause for celebration. *Heart of the Hunter* is not just an exciting story of a pursuit; it paints a thought-provoking picture of today's South Africa' *Sunday Telegraph*

'First-rate, worthy to be on a bestseller list' *Bookreporter.com*

'A terrific thriller of the first order and highly recommended' *Shots magazine*

'Out of post-apartheid South Africa comes a thriller good enough to nip at the heels of le Carré . . . Wonderful setting; rich, colourful cast' *Kirkus Reviews* (starred review)

'Outstanding . . . one of the most original heroes in recent fiction. A must read' *mysteryone.com*

'Moves at a breathtaking pace that will carry readers away . . . Highly recommended' *Library Journal* (starred review)

'Like John le Carré's *The Taylor of Panama*, this novel examines the rippling horrors too often caused by so-called intelligence agents working for foreign masters . . . South Africa should prove fertile ground for many fine spy thrillers to come. Don't be surprised if quite a few of them are written by Meyer' *Booklist* (starred review)

Deon Meyer lives in Melkbosstrand on the South African West Coast with his wife, Anita, and four children. Other than his family, Deon's big passions are motorcycling, music (he is a Mozart fanatic, but loves rock 'n' roll too), reading, cooking and rugby. When he isn't writing novels, he consults on brand strategy for BMW Motorrad.

Deon Meyer's books have attracted worldwide critical acclaim and a growing international fanbase. Originally written in Afrikaans, they have now been translated into several languages, including English, French, Italian, Spanish, German, Dutch, Bulgarian, Czech, Danish and Norwegian.

Heart of the Hunter won Germany's Deutsche Krimi Preis in 2006, and South Africa's ATKV Prose Prize in 2003.

Also by Deon Meyer

Dead Before Dying

Dead at Daybreak

Devil's Peak

Heart of the Hunter

Deon Meyer

Translated by K L Seegers

HODDER

Copyright © 2003 by Deon Meyer

Translation copyright © 2003 by K L Seegers

First published in Great Britain in 2003 by Hodder & Stoughton
A division of Hodder Headline

This paperback edition published in 2007

The right of Deon Meyer to be identified as the Author
of the Work has been asserted by him in accordance with the
Copyright, Designs and Patents Act 1988.

A Hodder paperback

5

A CIP catalogue record for this title
is available from the British Library

ISBN 978-0-340-82198-5

Printed and bound in the UK by CPI Mackays, Chatham ME5 8TD

Hodder Headline's policy is to use papers that are natural, renewable
and recyclable products and made from wood grown in sustainable
forests. The logging and manufacturing processes are expected to
conform to the environmental regulations of the country of origin.

Hodder and Stoughton Ltd
A division of Hodder Headline
338 Euston Road
London NW1 3BH

For Anita

1984

He stood behind the American, almost pressed against him by the crush of *le Métro*. His soul was far away at a place on the Transkei coast where giant waves broke in thunder.

He thought of the rocky point where he could sit and watch the swells approaching in ranks across the Indian Ocean, in awe at their epic journey over the long, lonely distance to hurl and break themselves against the rocks of the Dark Continent.

Between each set of waves there was a time of perfect silence, seconds of absolute calm. So quiet that he could hear the voices of his ancestors – Phalo and Rharhabe, Nqika and Maqoma, his bloodline, source and refuge. He knew that was where he would go when his time came, when he felt the long blade and the life ran out of him. He would return to those moments between the explosions of sound.

He came back to himself slowly, almost carefully. He saw that they were only minutes from the St Michel *Métro* station. He leant down, only half a head's length, to the ear of the American. His lips were close like those of a lover.

'Do you know where you are going when you die?' he asked in a voice as deep as a cello, the English heavy with an accent of Africa.

The tendons in the back of the enemy's neck pulled taut, big shoulders tilted forward.

He waited calmly for the man to turn in the overfilled crush of the carriage. He waited to see the eyes. This was the

moment he thirsted for. Confrontation, the throwing down of
the gauntlet. This was his calling – instinctive, fulfilling him.
He was a warrior from the plains of Africa, every sinew and
muscle knitted and woven for this moment. His heart began
to race, the sap of war coursed through his blood, he was
possessed by the divine madness of battle.

The American's body turned first, unhurried, then the
head, then the eyes. He saw a hawk there, a predator without
fear, self-assured, amused even, the corners of the thin lips
lifting. Centimetres apart, theirs was a strange intimacy.

'Do you know?'

Just the eyes staring back.

'Because soon you will be there, Dorffling.' He used the
name contemptuously, the final declaration of war that said
he knew his enemy – the assignment accepted, the dossier
studied and committed to memory.

He saw no reaction in the lazy eyes. The train slowed and
stopped at St Michel. 'This is our station,' he said. The
American nodded and went, with him just a step behind, up
the stairs into the summer-night bustle of the Latin Quarter.
Then Dorffling took off. Along the Boulevard San Michel
towards the Sorbonne. He knew that prey chose familiar ter-
ritory. Dorffling's den was there, just around the corner from
the Place du Pantheon, his arsenal of blades and garrottes and
firearms. But he hadn't expected flight; he'd thought that the
ego would be too big. His respect for the ex-Marine turned
CIA assassin deepened.

His body had reacted instinctively; the dammed-up adrenalin
exploding, long legs powering the big body forward rhythmically, ten, twelve strides behind the fugitive. Parisian heads
turned. White man pursued by black man. An atavistic fear
flared in their eyes.

The American spun off into the Rue des Ecoles, right
into the Rue St Jaques and now they were in the alleys

of the University, almost deserted in the student-holidays August, the age-old buildings sombre onlookers, the night shadows deep. With long sure strides he caught up with Dorffling and shouldered him. The American fell silently to the pavement, rolled forward and stood up in one sinuous movement, ready.

He reached over his shoulder for the cut-down assegai in the scabbard that lay snug against his back. Short handle, long blade.

'*Mayibuye*,' he said softly.

'What fucking language is that, nigger?' Hoarse voice without inflection.

'Xhosa,' he said, the click of his tongue echoing sharply off the alley walls. Dorffling moved with confidence, a lifetime of practice in every shift of his feet. Watching, measuring, testing, round and round, the diminishing circles of a rhythmic death dance.

Attack, immeasurably fast and before the knee could drive into his belly – his arm was around the American's neck and the long thin blade through the breastbone. He held him close against his own body as the pale blue eyes stared into his.

'Uhm-sing-gelli,' said the ex-Marine.

'*Umzingeli*.' He nodded, correcting the pronunciation softly, politely. With respect for the process, for the absence of pleading, for the quiet acceptance of death. He saw the life fade from the eyes, the heartbeat slowing, the breathing jerky, then still.

He lowered the body, felt the big, hard muscles of the back soften, and laid him gently down.

'Where are you going? Do you know?'

He wiped the assegai on the man's T-shirt. Slid it slowly back into the scabbard.

Then he turned away.

March

I

Transcript of interview with Ismail Mohammed by
A.J.M. Williams, 17 March, 17:52, South African
Police Services offices, Gardens, Cape Town.

W: You wanted to talk to someone from Intelligence?
M: Are you?
W: I am, Mr Mohammed.
M: How do I know that?
W: You take my word for it.
M: That's not good enough.
W: What would be good enough for you, Mr Mohammed?
M: Have you got identification?
W: You can check this out if you want to.
M: Department of Defence?
W: Mr Mohammed, I represent the State Intelligence
   Service.
M: NIA?
W: No.
M: Secret Service?
W: No.
M: What, then?
W: The one that matters.
M: Military Intelligence?
W: There seems to be some misunderstanding, Mr
   Mohammed. The message I got was that you are in
   trouble and you want to improve your position by
   providing certain information. Is that correct?

[Inaudible.]

W: Mr Mohammed?

M: Yes?

W: Is that correct?

M: Yes.

W: You told the police you would only give the information to someone from the Intelligence Services?

M: Yes.

W: Well, this is your chance.

M: How do I know they are not listening to us?

W: According to the Criminal Procedures Act the police must advise you before they may make a recording of an interview.

M: Ha!

W: Mr Mohammed, do you have something to tell me?

M: I want immunity.

W: Oh?

M: And guaranteed confidentiality.

W: You don't want Pagad to know you've been talking?

M: I am not a member of Pagad.

W: Are you a member of Muslims Against Illegitimate Leaders?

M: *Illegal* Leaders.

W: Are you a member of MAIL?

M: I want immunity.

W: Are you a member of Qibla?

[Inaudible]

W: I can try to negotiate on your behalf, Mr Mohamed, but there can be no guarantees. I understand the case against you is watertight. If your information is worth anything, I can't promise you more than that I do my best . . .

M: I want a guarantee.

W: Then we must say goodbye, Mr Mohamed. Good luck in court.

M: Just give me—

W: I'm calling the detectives.

M: Wait . . .

W: Goodbye, Mr Mohammed.

M: Inkululeko.

W: Sorry?

M: Inkululeko.

W: Inkululeko?

M: He exists.

W: I don't know what you're talking about.

M: Then why are you sitting down again?

October

2

A young man stuck his head out of a minibus taxi, wagging a mocking finger and laughing with a wide white-toothed grin at Thobela Mpayipheli.

He knew why. Often enough he had seen his reflection in the big shop windows – a huge black man, tall and broad, on the tiny Honda Benly, the 200cc engine ineffectively but bravely putt-putting under his weight. His knees almost touching the handlebars, long arms at sharp angles, the full-face crash helmet incongruously top heavy.

Something of a spectacle. A caricature.

He had been self-conscious too during those first weeks when, to add to it all, he had had to learn to ride the thing. Going to work or home, every morning and afternoon in the rush-hour traffic of the N2, he'd been awkward and unsure. But once he'd learned the skills, learned to dodge the vans and 4×4s and buses, learned to slip between the gaps in the cars, learned to turn the pitiful horsepower to his advantage, the pointing mocking fingers had ceased to trouble him.

And later he began to revel in it: while the larger vehicles sat trapped and frustrated in the gridlocked traffic, he and his Benly buzzed between them, down the long valleys that opened up between the rows of cars.

On the road to Guguletu and Miriam Nzululwazi.

And Pakamile who would wait for him on the street corner, then run alongside the Benly the last thirty metres to the driveway. Silent, seven-year-old solemnity on the wide-eyed face, serious like his mother, patiently waiting till Thobela took off the helmet and lifted down the tin workbox, swept his big hand over the boy's head and said, 'Good afternoon, Pakamile'. The child would overwhelm him with his smile and throw his arms around him, a magic moment in every day, and he would walk in to Miriam who would be busy already with cooking or washing or cleaning. The tall, lean, strong and beautiful woman would kiss him and ask about his day.

The child would wait patiently for him to finish talking and change his clothes. Then the magic words: 'Let's go farm.'

He and Pakamile would stroll down the yard to inspect and discuss the growth of the last twenty-four hours. The sweetcorn that was making cobs, the runner beans ('Lazy Housewife – what are you hinting at?' asked Miriam), the carrots, the squashes and butternuts and watermelons trailing along the beds. They would pull an experimental carrot. 'Too small.' Pakamile would rinse it off later to show to his mother and then crunch the raw and glowing orange root. They would check for insects and study the leaves for fungus or disease. He would do the talking and Pakamile would nod seriously and absorb the knowledge with big eyes.

'The child is mad about you,' Miriam had said on more than one occasion.

Mpayipheli knew. And he was mad about the child. About her. About them.

But first he had to navigate the obstacle course of the rush hour, the kamikaze taxis, the pushy four-by-fours, the buses belching diesel exhaust, the darting Audis of the yuppies switching lanes without checking their rear-view mirrors, the wounded rusty bakkies of the townships.

First to Pick 'n Pay to buy the fungicide for the butternuts. Then home.

★ ★ ★

The Director smiled. Janina Mentz had never seen him without a smile.

'What kind of trouble?'

'Johnny Kleintjes, Mr Director, but you need to hear this yourself.' Mentz placed the laptop on the Director's desk.

'Sit, Janina.' Still he smiled his hearty, charming smile, eyes soft as if gazing on a favourite child. He is so small, she thought, small for a Zulu, small for a man bearing such a great responsibility. But impeccably dressed, the white shirt a shout in contrast to the dark skin, the dark grey suit an expression of good taste, somehow just right. When he sat like that the hump, the small deformity of back and neck could barely be seen. Mentz manoeuvred the cursor on the screen to activate the replay.

'Johnny Kleintjes,' said the Director. 'That old rogue.'

He tapped on the computer keyboard. The sound came tinnily through the small speakers.

'*Is this Monica?*' Unaccented. Dark voice.

'*Yes.*'

'*Johnny Kleintjes's daughter?*'

'*Yes.*'

'*Then I need you to listen very carefully. Your Daddy is in a bit of trouble.*'

'*What kind of trouble?*' Immediate worry.

'*Let's just say he promised, but he couldn't deliver.*'

'*Who are you?*'

'*That I am not going to tell you. But I do have a message for you. Are you listening?*'

'*Yes.*'

'*It is very important that you get this right, Monica. Are you calm?*'

'*Yes.*'

Silence, for a moment. Mentz looked up at the Director.

His eyes were still soft, his body still relaxed behind the wide, tidy desk.

'Daddy says there is a hard-disk drive in the safe in his study.'

Silence.

'Are you getting this, Monica?'

'Yes.'

'He says you know the combination.'

'Yes.'

'Good.'

'Where is my father?'

'He is here. With me. And if you don't work with us, we will kill him.'

A catch of breath. *'I . . . please . . .'*

'Stay calm, Monica. If you stay calm, you can save him.'

'Please . . . Who are you?'

'A businessman, Monica. Your Daddy tried to trick me. Now you have to put things right.'

The Director shook his head ruefully. 'Ai, Johnny,' he said.

'You will kill him anyway.'

'Not if you cooperate.'

'How can I believe you?'

'Do you have a choice?'

'No.'

'Good. We are making progress. Now go to the safe and get the disk.'

'Please stay on the line.'

'I'll be right here.'

The hiss of the electronics. Some static interference on the line.

'When did this conversation take place, Janina?'

'An hour ago, Mr Director.'

'You were quick, Janina. That is good.'

'Thank you, sir, but it was the surveillance team. They're on the ball.'

'The call was to Monica's house?'

'Yes, sir.'

'What data do you think they are referring to here, Janina?'

'Sir, there are many possibilities?'

The Director smiled sympathetically. There were wrinkles around his eyes, regular, dignified. 'But we must assume the worst?'

'Yes, sir. We must assume the worst.' Mentz saw no panic. Only calmness.

'I . . . I have the disk.'

'Wonderful. Now we have just one more problem, Monica.'

'What?'

'You are in Cape Town, and I am not.'

'I will bring it.'

'You will?' A laugh, muffled.

'Yes. Just tell me where.'

'I will, my dear, but I want you to know. I cannot wait for ever.'

'I understand.'

'I don't think so. You have seventy-two hours, Monica. And it is a long way.'

'Where must I take it?'

'Are you very sure about this?'

'Yes.'

Another pause, long-drawn-out.

'Meet me in the Republican Hotel, Monica. In the foyer. In seventy-two hours.'

'The Republican Hotel?'

'In Lusaka, Monica. Lusaka in Zambia.'

They could hear the indrawn breath.

'Have you got that?'

'Yes.'

'Don't be late, Monica. And don't be stupid. He is not a young man, you know. Old men die easily.'

The line went dead.

The Director nodded. 'That's not all.' He knew.

'Yes, sir.'

She tapped again. The sound of dialling. A phone rang.

'Yes?'

'Could I talk to Tiny?'

'Who's speaking?'

'Monica.'

'Hold on.' Muffled, as though someone was holding a hand over the receiver. *'One of Tiny's girlfriends looking for him.'*

Then a new voice. *'Who's this?'*

'Monica.'

'Tiny doesn't work here any more. Nearly two years now.'

'Where is he now?'

'Try Mother City Motorrad. In the city.'

'Thank you.'

'Tiny?' asked the Director.

'Sir, we're working on that one. There's nothing on the priority list, sir. The number Monica phoned belongs to one Orlando Arendse. Also unknown. But we're following it up.'

'There's more.'

Mentz nodded. She set the program running again.

'Motorrad.'

'Could I speak to Tiny, please?'

'Tiny?'

'Yes.'

'I think you have the wrong number.'

'Tiny Mpayipheli?'

'Oh. Thobela. He's gone home already.'

'I need to get hold of him urgently.'

'Hold on.' Papers rustled. Someone cursed softly.

'Here's a number. Just try it. 555–7970.'

'*Thank you so much.*' The line was already dead.

New call.

'*Hello.*'

'*Could I speak to Tiny Mpayipheli, please?*'

'*Tiny?*'

'*Thobela?*'

'*He is not home yet.*'

'*When do you expect him?*'

'*Who is calling?*'

'*My name is Monica Kleintjes. I . . . he knows my father.*'

'*Thobela is usually home by a quarter to six.*'

'*I must speak to him. It's very urgent. Can you give me your address? I must see him.*'

'*We're in Guguletu. 21 Govan Mbeki.*'

'*Thank you.*'

'There is a team following her and we've sent another team to Guguletu, sir. The house belongs to a Mrs Miriam Nzululwazi and I expect that was her on the phone. We will find out what her relationship with Mpayipheli is.'

'Thobela Mpayipheli, also known as Tiny. And what are you going to do, Janina?'

'The tail reports that she is travelling in the direction of the airport. She could be on her way to Guguletu. A soon as we're sure, sir, we'll bring her in.'

The Director folded his delicate hands on the shiny desktop.

'I want you to hang back a bit.'

'Yes, sir.'

'Let's see how this unfolds.'

Mentz nodded.

'And I think you had better call Mazibuko.'

'Sir?'

'Get the RU on a plane, Mentz. A fast one.'

'But, sir . . . I've got this under control.'

'I know. I have absolute confidence in you, but when you

buy a Rolls-Royce sometime or other you must take it for a test drive. See if it is worth all the expense.'

'Sir, the Reaction Unit . . .'

He raised a small, fine-boned hand. 'Even should they do nothing, I think Mazibuko needs to get out a bit. And you never know.'

'Yes, sir.'

'And we know where the data is going. The destination is known. This creates a safe test environment. A controllable environment.'

'Yes, sir.'

'They can be here in –' the Director examined his stainless steel watch '– a hundred and forty minutes.'

'I'll do as you say, sir.'

'And I assume the Ops Room will get up and running?'

'That was next on my agenda.'

'You're in charge, Janina. And I want to be kept up to date, but I'm leaving it entirely in your hands.'

'Thank you, sir.' Mentz knew that she was being put to the test. She and her team and Mazibuko and the RU. She had been waiting a long time for this.

3

The boy was not waiting on the street corner and unease crept over Thobela Mpayipheli. Then he saw the taxi in front of Miriam's house. Not a minibus – a sedan, a Toyota Cressida with the yellow light on the roof: 'Peninsula Taxis', hopelessly out of place here. He turned up the dirt driveway and dismounted – more a case of careful disentanglement of his limbs from the motorbike – loosened the ties that held his tin box and the packet with the fungicide on the seat behind him, rolled the cords carefully in his hand and walked in. The front door was standing open.

Miriam rose from the armchair as he entered. He kissed her cheek but there was tension in her. He saw the other woman in the small room, still seated.

'Miss Kleintjes is here to see you,' said Miriam.

He put down his parcel, turned to her and put out his hand. 'Monica Kleintjes,' she said.

'Pleased to meet you.' He could wait no longer and looked to Miriam. 'Where is Pakamile?'

'In his room. I told him to wait there.'

'I'm sorry,' said Monica Kleintjes.

'What can I do for you?' Mpayipheli looked at her, slightly plump in her loose, expensive clothes, blouse, skirt, stockings and low-heeled shoes. He struggled to keep the irritation out of his voice.

'I am Johnny Kleintjes's daughter. I need to talk to you privately.'

His heart sank. *Johnny Kleintjes*. After all these years.

Miriam's back straightened. 'I will be in the kitchen.'

'No,' he said. 'I have no secrets from Miriam.'

But Miriam walked out anyway.

'I really am sorry,' said Monica again.

'What does Johnny Kleintjes want?'

'He's in trouble.'

'Johnny Kleintjes,' he said mechanically as the memories returned. Johnny Kleintjes would choose him. It made sense.

'Please,' Monica said.

He jerked back to the present. 'First, I must say hello to Pakamile,' he said. 'Back in a minute.'

Mpayipheli went through to the kitchen. Miriam stood by the stove, her gaze directed outside. He touched her shoulder but got no reaction. He walked down the short passage and pushed open the door of the child's room. Pakamile lay on the little bed with a schoolbook. He looked up. 'Aren't we going to farm today?'

'Afternoon, Pakamile.'

'Afternoon, Thobela.'

'We will go farming today. After I have talked to our visitor.'

The boy nodded solemnly.

'Have you had a nice day?'

'It was OK. At break we played soccer.'

'Did you score a goal?'

'No. Only the big boys kick goals.'

'But you are a big boy.'

Pakamile just smiled.

'I'm going to talk to our guest. Then we'll go farm.' Mpayipheli rubbed his hand over the boy's hair and went out, his unease now increasing. Johnny Kleintjes – this meant trouble, and he had brought it to this house.

*   *   *

They strode in time across the Parachute Battalion parade ground, Captain Tiger Mazibuko one step ahead of Little Joe Moroka.

'Is it him?' asked Mazibuko and pointed to the small group. Four Parabats sat in the shade under the wide umbrella of the thorn tree. A German Shepherd lay at the feet of the stocky lieutenant, its tongue lolling, panting in the Bloemfontein heat. It was a big, confident animal.

'That's him, captain.'

Mazibuko nodded and picked up the pace. Red dust puffed up at each footfall. The Bats, three whites and one coloured, were talking rugby, the lieutenant holding forth with authority. Mazibuko was there, stepped between them and kicked the dog hard on the side of the head with his steel-toed combat boot. It gave one yelp and staggered against the sergeant's legs.

'Fuck,' said the Bat lieutenant, dumbfounded.

'Is this your dog?' asked Mazibuko. The soldiers' faces expressed total disbelief.

'What the hell did you do that for?' A trickle of blood ran out of the dog's nose. It leant dazedly against the sergeant's leg. Mazibuko lashed out again, this time kicking the animal in the side. The sound of breaking ribs was overlaid by the cries of all four Parabats.

'You fucker . . .' screamed the lieutenant and hit out, a wild swing that caught the back of Mazibuko's neck. He took one step back. He smiled. 'You are all my witnesses. The lieutenant hit me first.'

Then Mazibuko moved in, free and easy, unhurried. A straight right to the face to draw attention upwards. A kick deftly and agonizingly to the kneecap. As the Parabat toppled forwards, Mazibuko brought up his knee into the white man's face. The lieutenant flipped over backwards, blood streaming from a broken nose.

Mazibuko stepped back, hands hanging relaxed at his sides. 'This morning you messed with one of my men, lieutenant.' He jabbed his thumb over his shoulder at Little Joe Moroka. 'You set your fucking little dog on him.'

The man had one hand over his bloody nose, the other on the ground trying to prop himself up. Two Bats came closer, the sergeant kneeling by the dog, which lay still. 'Uh . . .' said the lieutenant looking down at the blood on his hand.

'*Nobody* fucks with my people,' said Mazibuko.

'He wouldn't salute,' said the lieutenant reproachfully and stood up, shaky on his feet, the brown shirt stained darkly with his blood.

'So you set the dog on him?' Mazibuko strode forward. The Parabat raised his hands reflexively. Mazibuko grabbed him by the collar, jerked him forward and smashed his forehead into the broken nose. The man fell backwards again. Red dust billowed in the midday sun.

The cell phone in Mazibuko's breast pocket began to chirp.

'Jissis,' said the sergeant. 'You're gonna kill him.' He knelt down beside his mate.

'Not today . . .'

The ringing got louder, a penetrating noise.

'Nobody fucks with my people.' He unbuttoned the pocket and activated the phone.

'Captain Mazibuko.'

It was the voice of Janina Mentz.

'Activation call, captain. At 18:15 there will be a Falcon 900 from 21 Squadron standing by at Bloemspruit. Please confirm.'

'Confirmed,' Mazibuko said, his eyes on the two Parabats still standing. But there was no fight in the men, only bewilderment.

'18:15. Bloemspruit,' Mentz said.

'Confirmed,' he said once more.

The connection was cut. Mazibuko folded the phone and returned it to his pocket. 'Joe. Come,' he said. 'We've got things to do.' He walked past the sergeant, treading on the hind leg of the German Shepherd as he went. There was no reaction.

'My father said – more than once – that if anything ever happened to him I should get you, because you are the only man that he trusts.'

Thobela Mpayipheli only nodded. Monica Kleintjes spoke hesitantly; he could see that she was extremely uncomfortable, deeply aware of her invasion of his life, of the atmosphere that she had created here.

'And now he's done a stupid thing. I . . . we . . .'

She searched for the right words. He recognized her tension, but didn't want to know. Didn't want it to affect the life he had here.

'Did you know what he was involved with after '92?'

'I last saw your father in '86.'

'They . . . He had to . . . everything was so mixed up then, after the elections. They brought him back to help . . . the integration of the Intelligence Services was difficult. We had two, three branches and the apartheid regime had even more. The people wouldn't work together. They covered up and lied and competed with each other. It was costing a lot more money than they had made provision for. They had to consolidate. Create some order. The only way was to split everything up into projects, to compartmentalize. So they put him in charge of the project to combine all the computer records. It was almost impossible: there was so much – the stuff at Infoplan in Pretoria alone would take years to process, not to mention Denel and the Security Police and the Secret Service, Military Intelligence and the

ANC's systems in Lusaka and London, four hundred, five hundred gigabytes of information, anything from personal information on members of the public to weapons systems to informants and double agents. My father had to handle it all, erase the stuff that could cause trouble and save the useful material, create a central, uniform, single-platform database. He . . . I kept house for him during that time, my mother was sick. He said it upset him so much, the information on the systems . . .'

Monica was quiet for a while, then opened her big black leather handbag and took out a tissue as if to prepare herself.

'He said there were some strange orders, things that Mandela and Nzo would not approve, and he was worried. He didn't know what to do, at first. Then he decided to make back-ups of some of the material. He was scared, Mr Mpayipheli, those were such chaotic times, you understand. There was so much insecurity and people trying to block him and some trying to save their careers and others trying to make theirs. ANCs and whites, both sides of the fence. So he brought some stuff home, data, on hard disks. Sometimes he worked through the night on it. I kept out of it. I suspect that he . . .'

She dabbed at her nose with the tissue.

'I don't know what was on the disks and I don't know what he meant to do with the data. But it looks as if he never handed it in. It looks as if he was trying to sell the data. And then they phoned me and I lied because—'

'Selling it?'

'I . . .'

'To whom?'

'I don't know.' There was despair in Monica's voice, whether for the deed or for her father he couldn't say.

'Why?'

'Why did he try to sell it? I don't know.'

Mpayipheli raised his eyebrows.

'They pushed him out. After the project. Said he should go on pension. I don't think he wanted that. He wasn't ready for that.'

He shook his head. There had to be more to it.

'Mr Mpayipheli, I don't know why he did it. Since my mother died . . . I was living with him but I had my own life – I think he got lonely. I don't know what goes on in an old man's head when he sits at home all day and reads the white men's newspapers. This man, who played such a major role in the Struggle, pushed aside now. This man, who was once a player. He was respected, in Europe. He was somebody and now he is nothing. Maybe he wanted, just one more time, to be a player again. I was aware of his bitterness. And his weariness. But I didn't think . . . Perhaps . . . to be noticed? I don't know. I just don't know.'

'The information. Did he say what was so upsetting?'

Monica shifted uneasily in the chair and her gaze slid away from his. 'No. Just that there were terrible things . . .'

'How terrible?'

She just looked at him.

'Now what?' Mpayipheli asked.

'They phoned. From Lusaka, I think. They have some disks, but that is not what they want. I had to get another disk from my father's safe.'

He looked her in the eye. This was it.

'In seventy-two hours I must deliver another disk in Lusaka. That's all the time they gave me.'

'Not a lot of time.'

'No.'

'Why are you wasting time sitting here?'

'I need your help. To deliver the data. To save my father, because they will kill him anyway. And I –' she raised the hem of her long wide skirt, '– am a little slow.' He saw the wood and metal, the artificial legs. 'And not very effective.'

Tiger Mazibuko stood under the wing of the Condor in his camouflage uniform and black beret, feet planted wide, hands behind his back, his eyes on the twelve men loading ammunition boxes.

He had waited thirty-eight months for this. More than three years since Janina Mentz, dossier in hand, had come to fetch him, a one-pip lieutenant, out of the Recces.

'You're a hard man, Mazibuko. But are you hard enough?'

Fuck, it was hard to take her seriously. A chick. A white woman who marched into the Recces and sent everyone back and forth with that soft voice and way too much self-assurance. And a way of playing with his head. 'Isn't it time to get out of your father's shadow?' Mazibuko had been ready to go from the first question. The follow-up was just Mentz showing that she could read between the lines in those official files.

'Why me?' he had asked anyway, on the plane to Cape Town.

Mentz had looked at him with those piercing eyes and said, 'Mazibuko, you know.'

He hadn't answered, but still he had wondered. Was it because of his . . . talents? Or because of his father? He found the answer progressively in the stack of files (forty-four of them) that he had to go through to choose the twenty-four members of the Reaction Unit. He began to see what Mentz must have known from the start. When he read the reports and interviewed the guys, looked into their eyes and saw the ruthlessness. And the hunger.

The ties that bound them.

The self-hatred that was always there had found a form, had become a *thing*.

'We're ready, captain,' said Da Costa.

Mazibuko came out from under the wing. 'Get up. Let's go to work.'

Yes, they were ready. As ready as nearly three years of tempering could make them. Four months to put the team together, to hand-pick them one by one. The winnowing of the chaff from the grain, over and over, till there were only twenty-four, two teams of a dozen each, the perfect number for 'my RU', as the Director referred to them possessively, *Aar-you*, the Hunchback's English abbreviation for Reaction Unit. Only then did the real honing begin.

Now Mazibuko pulled the door of the Condor shut behind this half of the Dirty Double Dozen. The Twenty-four Blackbirds, the Ama-killa-killa and other names they had made up for themselves in the twenty-six months since the best instructors that money and diplomatic goodwill could buy had taken them in hand and remodelled them. Driven them to extremes that physically and psychologically they were not supposed to withstand. Half of them, because of the two teams of twelve, one was continuously on standby for two weeks as Team Alpha, while the other as Team Bravo worked on refining their skills. Then Team Alpha would become Team Bravo, the members shuffled around, but still they were a unit. A Un-it. The ties that bind. The blood and sweat, the intensity of physical hardship. And that extra dimension – a psychological itch, a communal psychosis, that shared curse.

They sat in the plane, watching him; their faces bright with expectation, absolute trust and total admiration.

'Time to kick butt!' he said.

In unison, they roared.

4

Through the kitchen window they could see the child standing in the vegetable garden. 'I never told him that men go away. Now he will learn for himself.'

'I am coming back,' Mpayipheli said.

She just shook her head.

'Miriam, I swear . . .'

'Don't,' she said.

'I . . . it's . . . I owe Johnny Kleintjes, Miriam . . .'

Her voice was soft. It always was when she was angry. 'Remember what you said?'

'I remember.'

'What did you say, Thobela?'

'I said I am not a deserter.'

'And now?'

'It's only for one or two days. Then I'll be back.'

She shook her head again, filled with foreboding.

'I have to do this.'

'You have to do this? You don't have to. Just say "no". Let them sort out their own trouble. You owe them nothing.'

'I owe Johnny Kleintjes,' he repeated.

'You told me you can't live that life any more. You said you had finished with it.'

Mpayipheli sighed deeply. He turned around in the kitchen, turned back to Miriam, his hands and voice pleading. 'It's true. I did say that. And I meant it. Nothing has changed. You're right – I can say "no". It's a choice, my choice. I have to choose the right way. I must do the right thing, Miriam, the thing that makes me an honourable man. Those are the difficult choices. They are always the most difficult choices.'

He saw that she was listening and he hoped for understanding. 'My debt to Johnny Kleintjes is a man's debt; a debt of honour. Honour is not only caring for you and Pakamile, coming home every afternoon, doing a job that is within the law and non-violent. Honour also means that I must pay my debts.'

She said nothing.

'Can you understand?'

'I don't want to lose you.' Almost too soft to hear. 'And I don't think he can afford to lose you.' Her gaze indicated the boy outdoors.

'You won't lose me. I promise you. I will come back. Sooner than you think.'

She turned to him, her arms around his waist, held him with a fierce desperation.

'Sooner than you think,' he said again.

The biggest room on the sixth floor of Wale Street Chambers was known as the Ops Room and had only been used eight times in twenty-four months – for 'readiness testing', the term Mentz used for the quarterly trials to test the systems and the standards of her team. The bank of twelve television screens against the east wall was connected to digital and analog satellite TV, closed-circuit TV and video-conferencing facilities. The six desktop PCs against the north wall were connected by optic fibre to the local network and the Internet backbone. Next to the double doors on the west side were the digital tuner and receiver for the radio network and the cellular and landline exchange with eighteen secure lines and telephone-conferencing facilities. On the south wall was the big white screen for the video projector, which was suspended from the ceiling. The oval table with seating for twenty people occupied the centre of the room.

The sixteen now seated around the table had a strong feeling that this late-afternoon call to the Ops Room was not a practice run. The atmosphere in the room was electric when Janina Mentz walked in; their gazes followed her with restrained anticipation. There would already have been rumours. The phone tappers would have hinted at superior knowledge, acceded with vague nods that something was developing, while their envious colleagues could only make guesses and use old favours as leverage to try and get information.

That was why the sixteen pairs of eyes focused on Mentz. In the past there had been different kinds of unspoken questions. At first, when she had been assembling the team for the Director, they had been gauging her skills, her ability to wield authority, because the group was predominantly male and its members came from backgrounds where their gender reigned supreme. They put her to the test and they learned that crude language and boorish behaviour wouldn't put her off her stride: aggression left her calm and cold, thinly disguised anti-feminism would not provoke her. Piece by piece they reconstructed her history so that they could know their new master: the rural upbringing, the brilliant academic career, the political activity, the climb through the Party ranks, slow because she was white and Afrikaans and somewhere along the way had been married and divorced. A gradual progress – until the Director had sought her out.

Really they respected her for what she had accomplished and the way in which she had done it.

That was why she could enter the room with muted confidence. She checked her watch before she said 'Evening, everyone.'

'Good evening, Mrs Mentz.' It was a jovial chorus, obedient

to the Director's wishes for formal address. She was relaxed, unobtrusively in control.

She tucked her grey skirt under her with deft hands as she took the seat at the head of the long table, next to the laptop plugged into the port of the video projector. She switched it on.

'Let us begin with one sure thing: from this moment the Ops Room is officially operational. This is not a test.' There was a tingling atmosphere in the room.

'Let there be no doubt that this is the real thing. We have worked hard to get here and now our skills and abilities will be put to the test. I am depending on you.'

Heads nodded eagerly.

Mentz turned on the laptop and opened Microsoft Power-Point. 'This photo was taken nineteen days ago at the entrance to the American Embassy as part of our routine surveillance. The man exiting the door is Johnny Kleintjes, a former leader in the intelligence services of the Struggle. He studied mathematics and applied mathematics at the University of the Western Cape, but due to political activity, restrictions and extreme pressure from the Security Police of the previous regime, he never obtained his degree. He was an exile from 1972, too late to be one of the *mgwenya* of the Sixties. He quickly made a name for himself at the ANC and MK offices in London. Married in 1973. He was East German-trained at Odessa from 1976 and specialized in Intelligence, where he earned the nickname *Umthakathi*, meaning wizard, thanks to his skill with computers. Kleintjes was responsible for establishing the ANC's computer systems in London, Lusaka and Quibaxe in Angola in the Eighties and, more importantly, the project leader for the integration of Struggle and Regime computer systems and databases since 1995. He retired at the age of sixty-two in 1997, after his wife died of cancer, and shares a house with their only daughter, Monica.'

She looked up. She had their attention still.

'The question is: what was Johnny Kleintjes doing at the American Embassy? And the answer is that we don't know. Telephone monitoring of the Kleintjes household was initiated the same evening.'

Mentz clicked the mouse. Another photo, black and white, of a woman, slightly plump, at the open door of a car. The coarse grain of the photo indicated it was taken at a distance with a telephoto lens.

'This is Monica Kleintjes, daughter of Johnny Kleintjes. A typical child of exiles. Born in London in 1974, went to school there and stayed on to complete her studies in computer science in 1995. In 1980 she was the victim of a motor accident outside Manchester that cost her both legs. She gets around with prosthetic limbs and refuses to use crutches or any other aids. She is any personnel manager's affirmative-action dream and currently works for the technology division of Sanlam as senior manager.'

Mentz tapped at the keyboard. 'These are the major players that we have pictures of. The following conversations were recorded by our voice-monitoring team this afternoon.'

Mpayipheli sat with Pakamile at the kitchen table with the big blue atlas and a copy of *National Geographic* magazine, just as they did every evening. Miriam's chair was, as always, a little further back, her needlework on her lap. Tonight they were reading about Chile, about an island on the west coast of South America where wind and rain had eroded fantastical shapes out of the rock, where unique plants had created a false paradise and animal life was almost non-existent. He read in English as it was printed, for that way the child would learn the language better, but translated paragraph by paragraph into Xhosa. Then they would open the atlas and look for Chile on the world map before turning the pages to a smaller-scale map of the country itself.

They never read more than two pages in a session, because Pakamile's concentration faded quickly, unless the article dealt with a terrifying snake or some other predator. But tonight it was more difficult than usual to keep the boy's attention. His gaze kept darting to the blue sports bag resting by the door. Eventually Mpayipheli gave up.

'I've got to go away for a day or two, Pakamile. I have some work to do. I have to help an old friend.'

'Where are you going?'

'First, you must promise to tell nobody.'

'Why?'

'Because I want to give my friend a surprise.'

'Is it his birthday?'

'Something like that.'

'Can't I even tell Johnson?'

'Johnson might tell his father and his father might phone my old friend. It must be a secret between us three.'

'I won't tell anyone.'

'Do you know where Zambia is on the map?'

'Is it in – eee – Mpumalanga?'

Miriam would have smiled, in normal circumstances, at her son's wild guess. Not tonight.

'Zambia is a country, Pakamile. Let me show you.' Mpayipheli paged through the atlas to a map of Southern Africa. 'Here we are.' He pointed with his finger.

'Cape Town.'

'Yes. And up here is Zambia.'

'How are you going to get there, Thobela?'

'I am going to fly on an aeroplane to here, in Johannesburg. Then I will get on another plane that is going to fly here, over Zimbabwe, or maybe here, over Botswana, to this place. It's called Lusaka. It's a city, like Cape Town. That's where my old friend is.'

'Will there be cake? And cold drinks?'

'I hope so.'

'I want to come too.'

Mpayipheli laughed and looked at Miriam. She just shook her head.

'One day, Pakamile, I will take you. I promise.'

'Bedtime,' said Miriam.

'When are you going to fly?'

'Soon, when you are sleeping.'

'And when are you coming back?'

'Only about two sleeps. Look after your mother, Pakamile. And the vegetable garden.'

'I will. Will you bring me back some cake?'

'The wild card is Thobela Mpayipheli,' said Janina Mentz. 'We don't know why Monica Kleintjes went to him. You heard the conversations – he is also known as "Tiny", works at Mother City Motorrad, a BMW motorbike dealership, and lives with Miriam Nzululwazi in Guguletu. We know she is the registered owner of the house, nothing else. Kleintjes went by taxi to the house, stayed just over forty minutes and went straight home. Since then neither Mpayipheli nor Kleintjes have moved.

'There are two surveillance teams with her and one in Guguletu, with him. The Reaction Unit is on its way from Bloemfontein and should land at Ysterplaat any minute now. They will stay there until we have more information. That, people, is how things stand.'

She turned off the video.

'Now we must jump to it. Radebe, we have only one man in Lusaka. I want four more. With experience. The Gauteng office is closest and they have enough of the right kind of people. Preferably two men and two women who can book into the Republican Hotel as couples. Discreetly and certainly not at the same time, but I'll leave that to you. Get your phone systems running. Quinn, we need to intercept the calls to the Nzululwazi home in Guguletu. Urgently. Rajkumar, bring in your team. I want to know who Thobela Mpayipheli is. I don't care what database you fish in; this is absolute priority. Right, people – go, go, go. Twenty minutes, please, then we are rolling.'

Tiger Mazibuko was the last one off the Condor. He let the members of Team Alpha go first, watching them, white, black, brown, each with his own story. Da Costa, sinewy descendant of Angolan refugees, with the knife scar on his cheek and a five o'clock shadow on his jaw. Weyers, the Afrikaner from Germiston, with bodybuilder's arms. Little Joe Moroka, a Tswana raised on a maize farm at Bothaville, who spoke seven of the country's eleven official languages. Cupido, the shortest, the most talkative, a coloured town boy from Ashton with a Technikon diploma in electronic engineering. Even a 'token Royal', as Zwelitini, the tall, lean Zulu, liked to call himself, although he was not a member of the King's family.

They stood in line on the runway. The Cape summer breeze blew softly against Mazibuko's cheek as he dropped to the tar.

'Offload now. Hurry up and wait. You know the drill.'

At the front door Mpayipheli put his arms around Miriam, pressed her slender body against him, smelt the woman smell, the faint remains of shampoo and scent after a long day, the aromas of the kitchen and that unique warmth that was special to her.

'I will have to stay over in Johannesburg,' he said softly into her ear. 'I can only catch a plane to Lusaka tomorrow.'

'How much money did she give you?'

'Plenty.'

Miriam did not comment, just held him tight.

'I'll phone as soon as I get to the hotel.'

Still she stood with her face pressed against his neck and her arms around him. At last she stepped back and kissed him quickly on the mouth. 'Come back, Thobela.'

Janina Mentz phoned home from the privacy of her office. Lien, the oldest, picked up. 'Hello, mamma.'

'I have to work late, sweetie.'

'Maaa . . . You promised to help me with Biology.'

'Lien, you're fifteen. You know when you know your subject well enough.'

'I'll wait up.'

'Let me talk to Suthu. She must sleep over, because I won't get home tonight.'

'Ma-aa. My hair – tomorrow morning.'

'I'm sorry, Lien. It's an emergency. I need you to help out there. You're my big girl. Did Lizette do her homework?'

'She was on the phone the whole afternoon, Ma, and you know how those Grade Sevens are. "Did Kosie say anything about me? Do you think Pietie likes me?" It's so childish. It's *gross*.'

Mentz laughed. 'You were in Grade Seven once yourself.'

'I can't bear to think of it. Was I ever like that?'

'You were. Let me talk to Lizette. You must get some sleep, sweetie. You need to be fresh for the exam. I'll phone tomorrow, I promise.'

5

The taxi dropped Mpayipheli off outside Departures; he paid, took his bag and got out. How long since he had last flown? Things had changed; everything was new and shiny to make a good impression on the overseas tourists.

At ComAir he bought a ticket with the cash that Monica Kleintjes had handed him in a stack of new hundred-rand notes. 'That's too much,' he had said. 'You can bring me the change,' had been her response. Now he wondered where the money had come from. Did she have time to go and draw the cash? Or did the Kleintjes keep that much in the house?

He sent the bag through the X-ray machine. Two pairs of trousers, two shirts, two pairs of socks, his black shoes, a jersey, his toilet bag, the remaining cash. And the hard disk, small and flat, technology that was beyond him. And somewhere in the electronic innards were unmentionable facts about this country's past.

He didn't want to think about it, didn't want to be involved, he just wanted to give the stuff to Johnny Kleintjes, see him safe, come home and get on with his life. So many plans for himself and Miriam and Pakamile . . . and then he became aware of the two grey suits behind him, the instinct a relic from another life, a muted warning in the back of his mind. He looked back but it was just his imagination. He took his bag and checked his watch. Thirty-three minutes to boarding.

*　　*　　*

'What should we do?' asked Quinn, looking expectantly at Mentz with his headphones pulled down.

'First I want to know where he's headed.'

'They're finding out. He bought a ticket with ComAir.'

'Keep me informed.'

Quinn nodded, shifted the earphones back and spoke quietly into the mike at his mouth.

'Rahjev, anything?' Mentz asked the extremely fat Indian seated behind his computer.

'National Population Register lists nine Thobela Mpayiphelis. I'm checking birth dates. Give me ten.'

She nodded.

Why had Monica Kleintjes chosen Mpayipheli? Who was he?

Mentz stepped over to Radebe who was on the phone talking to the Gauteng office. Someone had brought coffee and sandwiches. She didn't want coffee yet and she wasn't hungry. She went back to Quinn. He was just listening, and glanced up at her, calm and competent.

An unbelievable team, she thought. This thing will be over before it has begun.

'He's flying to Johannesburg,' said Quinn.

'He has only one bag with him?'

'Just the one.'

'And we are absolutely sure that Monica Kleintjes is at her house?'

'She's sitting in front of the TV in the sitting room. They can see her through the lace curtain.'

Mentz considered the possibilities, running through all the implications and scenarios. Mpayipheli must have the data. They could take it now and send their own team to Lusaka. Better control; with the RU as back-up. Perhaps. Because it would be difficult to get Mazibuko and company into Zambia. Too many diplomatic favours. Too much exposure.

The Director might have to test his reaction unit some other time. The main issue: keep it in the family. Keep it safe and under control.

'How good is the team at the airport?'

'Good enough. Experienced,' said Quinn.

She nodded. 'I want them to bring Mpayipheli in, Quinn. Low profile – I don't want a confrontation at the airport. Discreet and fast. Get him and his bag in a car and bring them here.'

Mpayipheli sat with his bag on his lap and the awareness of isolation crept over him. He had been living with Miriam for more than a year now, more than a year of family evenings, and suddenly here he was alone again, like he had been in the old days.

He searched for a reaction in himself. Did he miss it? The answer surprised him, as he found no satisfaction in this privacy. After a lifetime of depending on himself, in twelve months Miriam and Pakamile had changed his life. He wanted to be there, not here.

But he had to complete this task.

Johnny Kleintjes. The Johnny Kleintjes he knew would never have sold out. Something must have happened to change the old man. Who knew what was happening in the inner circles and walkways of the new government and the new intelligence services? It wasn't impossible, just improbable. Johnny Kleintjes was a man of integrity. And loyalty. A strong man with character. Mpayipheli would ask him when he saw him, when the data was handed over and Johnny had got his money. If everything went off OK. It had to. He didn't feel like trouble, not any more.

And then they were next to him, two grey suits. He hadn't seen them coming and as they appeared beside him he started at the depth of his thoughts, the blunting of old skills.

'Mr Mpayipheli,' said one.

'Yes.' He was surprised that they knew his name. They were right against him, preventing him from getting up.

'We want you to come with us.'

'What for?'

'We represent the State,' said the second, holding a plastic ID up to his eyes – photo and national coat of arms.

'I have to catch a plane,' he said. His head was clear now, his body reacting.

'Not tonight,' said Number One.

'I don't want to hurt anybody,' said Thobela Mpayipheli.

Two laughed: he-he, amused. 'Is that so?'

'Please.'

'I am afraid you don't have a choice, Mr Mpayipheli.' He tapped the blue bag. 'The contents . . .'

What did they know? 'Please listen,' he said. 'I don't want trouble.'

The agent heard the note of pleading in the big Xhosa's voice. *He's afraid*, he thought. *Use it.* 'We could give you more trouble than you would ever imagine, big fellow,' he said and pushed back the lapel of his jacket to display the pistol, steel grip in a black shoulder holster. He stretched out his hand for the sports bag. 'Come,' he said.

'Ai, ai,' said Thobela Mpayipheli. In the time it took for the agent's hand to reach the sports bag he had to make a decision. He had gleaned something from their behaviour: they didn't want to cause a scene. They wanted to get him out of here quietly. He must use that. He saw One's jacket gaping as his arm reached for the bag. He saw the pistol grip, reached up and took it, turned it, stood up. One had the bag in his hand, his eyes wide with shock. Mpayipheli leaned into him with the pistol barrel pointed at his heart. Two was behind Number One. Other passengers here and there had not seen anything amiss.

'I don't want trouble. Just give me my bag.'

'What are you doing?' asked Two.

'He's got my pistol,' hissed One.

'You take the bag,' Mpayipheli told Two.

'What?'

'Take the bag from him and put your pistol in it.' He shoved the pistol in his own hand hard against One's chest, keeping him between himself and Two.

'Do what he says,' said One softly.

Two was uncertain, eyes darting from them to the passengers waiting in the departure hall, trying to decide. He made up his mind.

'No,' he said drawing his pistol and keeping it under his jacket.

'Do what he says,' One whispered urgently, with authority.

'Fuck, Willem.'

Mpayipheli kept his voice reasonable, calm. 'I just want my bag. I am not good with revolvers. There are lots of people here. Someone might get hurt.'

Stalemate. Mpayipheli and Willem intimately close, Two a metre away.

'Jissis, Alfred, do what the fucker says. Where can he go?'

At last: 'You can explain to the boss.' Alfred took the bag slowly from Willem's grip, unzipped it and slipped his pistol inside, zipped it back up and deposited it carefully on the floor as if the contents were breakable.

'Now both of you sit down.'

The agents moved slowly and sat.

Mpayipheli took the bag, Willem's pistol in his trouser pocket with his hand still on it and walked, jogged to the passenger exit, turning to check. One and Two, Willem and Alfred, one white, one brown, staring at him with unreadable faces.

'Sir, you can't . . .' said the woman at the exit but he was past her, outside, onto the runway. A security man shouted something, waving, but he ran out of the ring of light from the building into the dark.

A bellow from the fat Indian: 'I've got him.' Mentz strode over to his computer monitor.

'Thobela Mpayipheli, born 10 October 1962 in Alice in the Eastern Cape, father is Lawrence Mpayipheli, mother is Catherine Zongu, his ID number is 621010 5122 004. Registered address is 45, 17th Avenue, Mitchell's Plain.' Rajkumar leaned back triumphantly and took another sandwich from the tray.

Mentz stood behind his chair reading off the screen.

'We know he was born, Rahjev. We need more than that.'

'Well, I had to start somewhere.' He sounded wounded at the dearth of praise.

'I hope his birthday isn't an omen,' she said.

Rajkumar glanced from the screen to her. 'I don't get it.'

'Heroes Day, Raj. In the old days the tenth of October was Heroes Day. That address is old. Find out who lived there. He's forty years old. Too old to be Monica's contemporary. Old enough to have been involved with Johnny Kleintjes . . .'

'Ma'am,' called Quinn, but Mentz would not be interrupted.

'. . . I want to know what that connection with Kleintjes is, Rahjev. I want to know if he served and how. I need to know why Monica Kleintjes went to *him* with her little problem.'

'Ma'am,' Quinn called again with great urgency. She looked up.

'We have a fugitive.'

* * *

Mpayipheli aimed for the darkest area of the airport and kept running. His ears expected sirens and shouts and shots. He was angry, with Monica and Johnny Kleintjes and himself. How did the authorities suddenly know about Johnny Kleintjes's little deal?

They had known his name, the two grey suits. Had tapped a finger on the blue bag. They knew what was in there. Had been watching him since he'd walked into the airport, knew about him; must have followed Monica to his house, so they knew about her, about Johnny Kleintjes, bloody Johnny Kleintjes. They knew everything. He ran, looking over his shoulder. No one was behind him. He had sworn to himself: no more violence. For two years he had been true to his vow. Had not shot, beaten or even threatened anyone. He had promised Miriam that those days were gone but within thirty seconds since the grey suits had reached him it was if all the promises were in the water and he knew how these things worked, they just got worse. Once the cycle began it couldn't be stopped: what he should do now was take the bag back to the woman and tell her that Johnny Kleintjes could sort out his own mess. Stop the cycle before it went any further. Stop it now.

Mpayipheli pulled up at the wire boundary fence. Beyond it was Borchards Quarry Road. He was breathing hard, his body no longer used to the exertion. Sweat ran down his cheek. He checked behind again: the building was too far away to distinguish the people in it but all was quiet, no big fuss.

Which meant that it wasn't a police or Customs operation. If it had been, the place would have been crawling.

That meant . . .

Spooks.

It made sense, if you took into account what was on the hard drive.

Fuck them. He was not afraid of spooks. He jumped for the fence.

'Put them on speaker,' said Janina Mentz and Quinn pressed the button.

'. . . He was just lucky, Control, that's all.'

'You're on speaker, Willem.'

'Oh.'

'I want to know what happened,' said Janina Mentz.

'He got away, ma'am, but—'

'I know he got away. How did it happen?'

'We had everything under control, ma'am' said the voice in awe. 'We waited until he sat down in the departure hall. We identified ourselves and asked the target to accompany us. Control said we must keep it low-profile. He's only a motorbike mechanic, he sat there with the bag on his lap like a farm boy, he looked so shy and lonely. He said he didn't want any trouble. It was obvious he was scared. It's my fault, ma'am. I wanted to take the bag and he got hold of my firearm . . .'

'He got hold of it?'

'Yes, ma'am. He grabbed it. I . . . um . . . his actions were . . . I didn't expect it.'

'And then?'

'Then he took the bag, with Alfred's firearm in it, and ran away.'

Silence.

'So, now he has two firearms?'

'I don't think he knows what to do with them, ma'am. He called my pistol a revolver.'

'Well, *that*'s a relief.'

Willem did not respond.

Quinn sighed despondently and said in a quiet aside to Mentz: 'I thought they could handle it'.

'Ma'am, he just got lucky. Judging by his reaction we'll get him easily,' said Willem over the ether.

Mentz did not answer.

'He even said "please".'

'Please?'

'Yes, ma'am. And we know he's not on a plane.'

Mentz pondered the information. The room was very quiet.

'Ma'am?' said the voice on the radio.

'Yes?'

'What do we do now?'

6

There comes a time to show anger, controlled but with purpose, rejection not of your people but of their actions.

Mentz turned off the speakerphone angrily and walked over to her computer. 'We were in control of this thing. We knew where she was, where he was, where he was going, how he was going to get there. Absolute control.'

Her voice carried across the room, the anger barely submerged. Everyone was looking at her, but no one made eye contact.

'So why did we lose control? Lack of information. Lack of intelligence. Lack of judgement. Here and at the airport. Now we are at a disadvantage. We have no idea where he is. At least we know where he is going and we know the quickest way to get there. But that is not enough. I want to know who Thobela Mpayipheli is and I want to know now. I want to know why Monica Kleintjes went to him. And I want to know where he is. I want to know where the disk is. Everything. And I don't care what you must do to get that information.'

She looked for eyes, but they were looking at the floor.

'And those two clowns, Quinn.'

'Yes, ma'am?'

'Let them write a report. And when that's done . . .'

'Yes, ma'am,'

'Let them go. They don't belong on this team.'

She walked out of the room, wishing that there was a door to slam, down the passage, into her office – where there was a door to slam – and dropped into her black leather chair.

Let the fools sweat.

Let them understand in the first place that if you can't take the heat, Janina Mentz will remove you from the kitchen. Because, Lord knew, this was no place for failure. She would live up to her promises.

The Director knew. He sat there in his office in his snow-white shirt and he knew because he was listening. He heard every word spoken in the Ops room – and judged it: her actions and reactions, her leadership.

It seemed a lifetime ago that he had asked her at their first interview concerning the job: 'Do you want it, Janina?'

And she had said 'Yes', because as a white woman in a Black administration there were only so many opportunities, never mind that your IQ was 147 and your record one faultless minor success after the other – with the emphasis on 'minor', because the big chance had not yet come. Until the Director had taken her to lunch at Bukhara's in the Church Street Mall and laid out his vision to her: 'An intelligence service that is outstanding, Janina, that is what the Vice-President wants. A new intelligence service, without a past. Next year he will be President and he knows that he doesn't have the Madiba Magic, the charisma of Nelson Mandela. He knows it will be hard work against every form of resistance and undermining that you can think of, nationally and internationally. I have carte blanche and I have a budget, Janina, and I believe I have the architect here in front of me this afternoon. You have the profile, the brainpower, you have no baggage, you have the loyalty, and you have the persistence. But the question is: "Do you want it?"'

Oh yes, she wanted it, more than he realized. Because it was eleven months since her husband had developed an itch for young things and had told her 'the marriage is not working for me', as if it was her fault, as if she and the children were not enough fulfilment for him any more, whereas the only fulfilment truly in question was the space between Cindy's legs. Cindy. The pseudo-artist with dirty feet who flogged her fabrics to German tourists from her stall in Greenmarket Square and fluttered her big brown eyes at married men until she caught one in the snare of her firm, free, braless breasts. And then the happy couple moved to Pilgrim's Rest to 'open a studio for Cindy'.

So, Mr Director, she wanted it. She *hungered* for it. Because she was consumed by an anger that was fed by the rejection, oh yes, let there be no doubt. Fed by ambition too, make no mistake, as the only child of poor Afrikaners, who would pay any price to rise above the soul-destroying, pointless existence of her parents. Fed by the frustration of a decade in the Struggle and the fact that all she had to show for it despite her talents was a deputy directorship when she could do so much more; she could fly, she knew the landscape of her psyche, knew where the valleys were and where the peaks were, she was impartial in her self-awareness. She could fly; what did it matter where they came from, the winds that blew beneath her wings?

Janina Mentz had not said that. She had listened and spoken coolly and calmly at lunch and had answered, with quiet assurance, 'Yes, I want it' and then had begun the very next week to work out their vision: a first-world intelligence unit in a country trying to drag itself up by the straps of its third-world boots, a new independent unit with a clean sheet.

And she still wanted it. No matter what price must be paid.

Her phone rang with the single ring of an internal a call.

'Mentz.'

'Pop in for a moment, Janina, would you,' said the Director.

*   *   *

Mpayipheli took a minibus to Bellville – the first opportunity that came up. He was driven to put distance between himself and the airport regardless of the direction; implications were coming through to him one after the other. He could not go back to Monica Kleintjes; they were surely watching her. He couldn't phone her. He could not go home. He could not go back to the airport – by now there would be swarms of spooks there. And if they were at all awake, they would be watching the station – bus or train travel was also out of the question.

Which left him with the big question: how to get to Lusaka?

He sat in the dark between the other passengers – domestics and security guards and factory workers on their way home who talked about the rise in the price of bread and the soccer results and politics – and he longed to be one of them. He wanted to leave the hard disk on Monica's lap and say 'There is one thing that you didn't take into account' and then he would go to Miriam and Pakamile and tomorrow he would ride to work on his Honda Benly and during lunch he would walk up St Georges to Immanuel the shoeshine man and play a game of chess with him in between his taking care of his cellphone-talking, wealth-chasing clients and all the while they would good-naturedly mock the whites in Xhosa.

But right now he had two Z88 pistols and a flat hard disk in a blue sports bag standing between him and that life.

'And what do you do for a living?' asked the woman next to him.

He sighed. 'At the moment, I'm travelling,' he said.

How was he to get to Lusaka?

You wouldn't know that he was in the office by six every morning – here it was nearly half past eight in the evening and the Director, in his early fifties, looked fresh, rested and alert.

'I had an interesting call, Janina. This afternoon our Tiger assaulted a Parabat at Tempe.'

'Assaulted?'

'Landed him in hospital and the commanding officer started phoning higher up. He wants justice.'

'I am sure there was good reason for the fight, sir.'

'I am, too, Janina. I just want to keep you informed.'

'I appreciate that, sir.'

'Ask him about it when you see him.'

'I will.'

'Is that all, Mr Director?'

'That is all, Janina. I know you are busy,' and he smiled in a fatherly way. Mentz hesitated a moment before turning away, willing him to say something about the happenings in the Ops Room. He must bring it up so that she could assure him that everything was under control. But he just sat there with his smile.

She took the stairs and stopped halfway.

I know you are busy.

He was weighing her, testing her; she knew it as an absolute truth.

She laughed softly. If only he knew. She took a deep breath and took the last steps one by one, measuring, as if enumerating a strategic plan.

Radebe began reporting the minute she walked into the Ops Room, his voice softly apologetic, explaining the redeployments of the teams – six of the best at the airport, six at Cape Town station, in two teams of three each to watch the trains and the bus terminal. His three team-mates beside him were busy contacting every car rental business in the city with instructions to let them know if someone of Mpayipheli's description tried to hire a vehicle. They would also contact every private plane charter service. Three more teams of two each were in their cars awaiting instructions, down below in

Wale Street. There was no activity at Monica Kleintjes's place or at Miriam Nzululwazi's.

Mentz nodded. Quinn confirmed the monitoring of the Nzululwazi phone. There had been no calls yet.

Rajkumar, ever sensitive, had a bearing of injured pride as he gave his report: 'No record of Thobela Mpayipheli in the Umkhonto we Sizwe files. Mpayipheli's registered home address is Mitchell's Plain – the property belongs to one Orlando Arendse. Probably the same Arendse that Monica phoned this afternoon when she was looking for Mpayipheli. But Arendse's registered home address is in Milnerton Ridge.' The obese body shifted subtly, self-confidence returning. 'The interesting thing is Arendse's criminal record – twice served time for dealing in stolen goods, in 1975 and 1982 to 1984, once charged and found not guilty of dealing in unlicensed weapons in 1989, twice arrested for dealing in drugs, in 1992 and 1995, but the cases were never brought to trial. One thing is certain: Orlando Arendse is organized crime. Drugs. Big time. Prostitution, gambling, stolen property. The usual protection racket. And if I read the signs correctly, the Scorpions are looking very closely at his dealings. That Mitchell's Plain address could be a drugs house, seems to me.' Rahjev Rajkumar leant back in satisfaction.

'Good work,' Mentz said. She paced up and down behind the Indian, her arms folded.

Organized crime? She grasped at possibilities, but it wouldn't make sense.

'Organized crime?' She spoke aloud. 'I don't see it.'

'Money makes strange bedfellows,' said Rajkumar. 'And if it's drugs, it's money. Big money.'

'Mpayipheli could be a dealer,' said Quinn.

'He's a motorbike mechanic,' said Radebe. 'It doesn't fit.'

Mentz stopped her pacing, nodding. 'Rahjev, find out who the owner of the bike shop is.'

'Company registrations are not up to date. I can poke around, but . . .'

Radebe: 'I'll send a car over there. Sometimes there are emergency numbers on the doors.'

'Do it.'

She tried to analyse the known facts, angles and different points of perspective, stumbling on the crime bits of the jigsaw puzzle.

'No record of Mpayipheli with the ANC, MK, PAC or Apla?' she asked.

'Nothing. But of course the ANC systems have had a few knocks. They are not complete. And the PAC and Apla never really had anything. All the PAC info came from the Boers. And there's nothing on Mpayipheli.'

'There must be a connection between Mpayipheli and the Kleintjes.'

'Hell,' said Quinn, 'he could have been their gardener.'

Radebe, always careful with what he said, frowned deeply as if he had strong doubts. 'She phoned the Arendse number to find Mpayipheli. Maybe Arendse is the connection.'

'Could be.' Mentz was walking up and down again, digesting the input, weighing up possibilities. Her thirst for information all-encompassing, she knew that they had to make a breakthrough and shine a bright light into the haze of ignorance. But how did you get a drug baron to talk?

Another cycle in her traverse of the room.

'OK,' she said. 'This is what we are going to do.'

In the dirty toilets of Bellville Station, behind a closed door, Mpayipheli took the pistols out of the rolled-up magazines. Then he went out and placed the different guns in separate dustbins. He began to walk towards Durban Road. He still had no idea where he was going. He was aware of the minutes ticking by and knew that he was only ten kilometres closer to

Lusaka than when he'd been at the airport. The temptation to drop the whole mess and go home lay like yearning on him. But the question kept returning to him: was that what Johnny Kleintjes did when Thobela needed him? And the answer was always no, no matter how many times he thought about it, no matter how little he wanted to be here, no matter how little he wanted the urgency and tension growing in his belly. He owed Johnny Kleintjes and he would have to move his butt as he turned the corner of Voortrekker and Durban Road and saw the vehicles at the traffic lights and a light came on in his head hurrying up the tempo of his footsteps as he moved towards the office of the Revenue Services.

There was a taxi rank there. He had to get back to the city. Quickly.

For the second time that day Captain Tiger Mazibuko cut his cellphone connection with Janina Mentz and began barking out orders to Team Alpha: 'Let's get these boxes open, there's work to be done. Hecklers, handguns, smoke grenades, bulletproof vests, and night sights. And paint your faces.'

They sprang into action with a will and snapped open the equipment cases, flicking glances at him, curious about the order, but Mazibuko gave nothing away while he reflected on his conversation with Mentz. Why had he assaulted an officer this afternoon? Because the fucker had set his German Shepherd on Little Joe Moroka. What had Little Joe done? Hadn't saluted the little lieutenant. Why not? Because Little Joe was Little Joe. So busy inside his head sometimes that he didn't know what was going on around him. In-a-fog negligence was all that it was. And when the lieutenant confronted him with a stream of obscenities the outcome had been inevitable. Little Joe took shit from only one person and that person was Mazibuko. *That's why we fetched Little Joe out of the MP cells in the first place.* Little Joe told the lieutenant to go do an unmentionable deed with himself or his dog and the lieutenant encouraged the dog to bite him. Which in any case, militarily speaking, was a contravention of the worst degree. Did the dog bite Little Joe? Yes, the dog bit him in the trousers. Was Little Joe hurt? No. The lieutenant and the dog embarrassed Little Joe. And that was as bad as a bite that drew blood. Worse, in his case. An injustice had been perpetrated, however you looked at it. Tiger Mazibuko chose not to work through channels to restore the balance because then others would start taking chances with the RU. A point had to be made. And now the Bats were crying.

'Yes, indeed they are crying. They want disciplinary action.'

'Then discipline me.' Challenging, because he knew that the RU was untouchable before he beat up the Bat.

'Not before you've earned your keep.' And Metz gave him the background, the task.

His team handed Mazibuko his jacket and weapons, the night-sight headset and camouflage paint last. He prepared with deft, practised movements till they stood in line in front of him and he walked down the row, plucking here at a belt or there straightening a piece of equipment.

'I have a new name for the Amakillakilla,' he said. 'After tonight you will be known as the Gangsta Busters.'

7

Mpayipheli asked the taxi driver to drop him off in front of the Media24 building in the Heerengracht. He chose to go east through the Nico Malan, turning left into Hertzog. Traffic at this time of evening was light. He deliberately walked without urgency, like a man going nowhere in particular, turned left again into Oswald Pirow and as he passed between the petrol pumps, greeting the petrol jockeys through the window of their night room, he saw the car in front of Mother City Motorrad. The lights were on, the engine idling and he saw the intelligence officers in the front seat and his heart sank.

Spooks. They were watching the place.

He opened the door of the petrol attendants' room and went inside, knowing that he would be spotted if he stayed outside.

The idling engine was a good sign. If they were keeping the place under surveillance they would be parked in the cross street with lights and engine off. The attendants were glad to see him; any distraction at this time of night was welcome. What was he doing here, what was in the bag? He made up an answer: a client's motorbike had not been returned after servicing and now he, Mpayipheli, had to sort out the Whiteys' problems. He kept an eye on the car outside, saw it pull away, and tried to keep track of it without raising the suspicions of the petrol jockeys

Did he have to deliver the bike at this time of night?

Yes, the guy was angry, he needed the motorbike tomorrow morning and the Whitey boss was too lazy to go out, so the Xhosa was called out, you know the story. What are you guys watching on TV, a competition? Yes, see, every guy has to pick one of three girls, but he can't see them, he can only ask them questions . . .

The car had gone. Mpayipheli listened politely to the attendants for a minute or two, then excused himself and left, looking up and down the street, but there was nothing. He crossed the road and went behind the building into the service alley. He took his wallet from the blue bag, sorting through the leather folds. The silver key to the wooden door lay flat and shiny where he always left it. He was the first one here every morning to sweep up half an hour before the mechanics arrived. He had to put on the kettle and the lights and make sure that the display windows were clean. He unlocked the door and typed in the code on the alarm panel. He had to decide whether to switch on the lights or not. The guys at the garage would wonder if he didn't, but he decided against it – he mustn't attract attention.

Next decision: which bike? Lord, the things were big. Would he be able to manage with his Honda 200 experience? He had never been allowed to ride them: he had to push them outside, wash and polish, rub till they shone, push them back in again. Tonight he must get onto one and ride to Johannesburg. But which one?

He felt the weight of the bag dragging at his hand.

The 1200 RS was the fastest, but what about the bag? The LT had packing space but it was gigantic. The GS demonstration model in the display room had fixed baggage cases either side of the rear wheel. The machine stood there, chunky and crouching, orangey-yellow. The key, he knew, hung in the spares room.

Lord, they were so big.

★   ★   ★

Despite the concrete walls topped with razor wire and the high gate, despite the early-warning system of human eyes all down the street, and despite the eight men with their collection of weapons inside, it took only seven minutes for Tiger Mazibuko and his Reaction Unit to take the house.

They came through the darkness in three teams of four, four, and five. The two unmarked cars dropped them one block south of the house and they moved unerringly through gardens and over walls until they could scale the wall of the yard on three sides, quietly and easily cutting the rusty razor wire, their hand signals visible in the light from the street.

The windows were burglar-proofed but the large panes were unprotected and that was how they entered. With smooth practised movements of break, dive and roll, in three separate places, within seconds of each other. When the people inside scrambled to react, panic-stricken, it was too late. Fearful figures with thick welts of camouflage paint, in battledress, forced them adroitly to the floor, pressing chunky Heckler & Koch machine pistols to their temples. Moments of chaos and confusion suddenly turned to quiet till only one man's voice was heard, clear and in control.

Mazibuko had the captives brought into the front room and forced down on their bellies on the floor with their hands behind their heads.

'Weyers, Zongu, watch the street.' Then Mazibuko focused on the bundle of bodies on the floor. 'Who's in charge here?' he asked.

Face down, one or two of the bodies trembled slightly. Seconds passed with no answer.

'Shoot one, Da Costa,' said Mazibuko.

'Which one, captain?'

'Start there. Shoot him in the knee. Fuck up his leg.'

'Right, captain.'

Da Costa loudly pulled back the slide of the H & K and pressed the barrel against a leg.

'You can't shoot,' said a voice in the bundle.

'Why not?'

'There are rules for the SAPS.'

Mazibuko laughed. 'Shoot, Da Costa.'

The shot was a thunderbolt in the confined space; the man made a deep, curious noise. The smell of cordite filled the room.

'Here's some bad news, arseholes. We are not police,' said Mazibuko. 'Let me ask you again: who is the chief gangsta here?'

'I am,' said the man in the middle, anxiety creasing his face.

'Stand up.'

'Are you going to shoot me too?'

'That depends, gangsta. That depends.'

Janina Mentz developed her policy on transcripts systematically.

The challenge was to secure information, which in this country leaked like water from an earth dam, through the cracks of old loyalties and new aspirations, filtering away through a sandy bottom of corruption and petty avarice. If something gave off the smell of money, scavengers would emerge from the oddest holes.

From the beginning her method had been to trust nobody too much, to lead no one into temptation, to dampen the smell of the money.

Rahjev Rajkumar had coached her in the vulnerabilities of electronic information. Easy to copy, easy to distribute: stiffies, zip disks, CD-ROM, FTP, hard disks smaller than half a cigarette box, e-mail, hacking, because if it was linked it was crackable. If they could get into other's databases, sooner or later with some new ingenious programming others would get into theirs.

There was only one way to secure information. One copy, on paper: fileable, controllable, limited.

That was why Rajkumar had an extra section to manage. The typists. Four women who played their old-fashioned electric IBM typewriters like virtuosos. Who fingered the keys at the speed of light in a single video-monitored room on the sixth floor. Who would sign out each digital and magnetic tape, transcribe it and sign it back in with the single copy on white paper. Paper that would not yellow or decay. So that Radebe and his team could analyse it and then file it away in the access- and temperature-controlled document library, together with the magnetic tapes. The digital tapes were deleted.

By the time the transcript of the interview with Orlando Arendse reached her, forty-seven minutes after it had taken place in Milnerton Ridge, Janina was already familiar with the crucial content.

```
Transcript of interview by A.J.M. Williams
with Mr Orlando Arendse, 23 October, 21:25, 55
Milnerton Avenue, Milnerton Ridge.

W:   I represent the State, Mr Arendse. I have a few
     questions about Mr Thobela Mpayipheli and a Miss
     Monica Kleintjes . . .
A:   I don't work from home. Come and see me at my
     office in the morning.
W:   I am afraid it can't wait that long, Mr Arendse.
A:   Where are your credentials?
W:   Here, Mr Arendse.
A:   Drop the 'mister'; I can see you don't mean
```

it. This card says nothing. Come see me in the
morning, thank you.

W: Maybe you should—

A: Maybe nothing. It's outside my office hours and
you don't have a warrant.

W: I do.

A: Then where is it?

W: Here.

A: That's a cellphone.

W: Just take the call.

A: Goodbye, my brother.

W: It's from a house in Mitchell's Plain that
belongs to you.

A: What?

W: Take the call.

A: Hello. Yes . . . Yes . . . The bastards . . .
Yes . . . Williams, who the hell are you?

W: Is there somewhere we can talk in private, Mr
Arendse?

A: What do you want?

W: Just some information.

A: Said the spider to the fly. Come through, we
will sit in the back.

W: Thank you.

A: You shot my man, Williams.

W: We wanted to get your attention.

A: You can't just shoot someone. There are rules of
engagement.

W: I am sure that most of the government departments
would agree with you.

A: So who are you?

W: We need some information about a Mr Thobela
Mpayipheli and a Miss Monica Kleintjes.

A: I don't know the lady.

W: And Mr Mpayipheli?

A: He no longer works for me. Not for two years . . .

W: What sort of work did he do?

A: Now I must ask you to excuse me while I phone my lawyer.

W: I am afraid that will not be possible.

A: Do you imagine, my brown bro, that I will sit here and feed you incriminating evidence because you hold a barrel to my troops' heads? My men know the score; they know they can get hurt in our line of work.

W: Mr Arendse, we know that you are involved in organized crime and the fact of the matter is that we don't care. That is the problem of the SAPS. Do you really think that our actions in Mitchell's Plain, which are hardly in line with the laws of criminal procedure, are part of a plan to bring you to justice?

A: Why do you talk like a Whitey? Where are your roots, my bro?

W: Mpayipheli. What did he do for you?

A: Go fuck yourself.

W: Mr Arendse, my people at the Mitchell's Plain house say there are 200 kilogrammes of cocaine in various stages of processing. I am sure that's worth something to you, even if your personnel are not.
     [Inaudible]

W: Mr Arendse?

A: What is your problem with Tiny?

W: Who?

A: Mpayipheli.

W: We just need some background.

A: Why?

W: Routine investigations, Mr Arendse.

A: At ten o'clock at night? Pull the other one.

W: I am not in a position to discuss our interest in Mr Mpayipheli with you.

A: Did he go into business for himself?

W: How do you mean?

A: He must have done something to attract your
     attention.

W: What did he do for you?

A: He was my enforcer.

W: Enforcer?

A: Yes.

W: Could you describe that more fully?

A: Jirre, you talk fancy. The government has taught
     you well.

W: Mr Arendse . . .

A: OK, OK, but don't expect a saga, it's more of
     a short story. Tiny was firepower and physical
     intimidation, that's all. He rode shotgun.
     Sharpshooter, like you wouldn't believe. And
     he was big and strong and he was a mean bastard.
     You could see it in his eyes – there was a hawk
     there, he would watch you and look for weakness.

W: How long did he work for you?

A: Six years? I think it was six years.

W: And before that?

A: You should know. He was a soldier in the
     Struggle.

W: Umkhonto we Sizwe?

A: Exactly.

W: With respect, Mr Arendse, there aren't many MK
     soldiers in Mitchell's Plain.

A: Too true, my bro, they stick to their own. But I
     got lucky. There was a vacancy and you know how
     it is – word gets out and the next I know this
     huge Xhosa is standing at the door and he says
     the vacancy is now filled. Best appointment I
     ever made.

W: And he told you he was ex-MK.

A: Exactly. I was a bit sceptical, so we drove down

to Strandfontein for a proper job interview
and we gave him an old AK47 and a lot of
Castle beer bottles at two hundred yards.
It may not sound far to you, my brother, but
those dumpies were small and he blew them
apart with monotonous regularity till the
other troops gave him a standing ovation, you
understand me?

W: Has he ever used his talents in your service?

A: Speak plain, my bro. Do you want to know if he
ever shot someone?

W: Yes.

A: It was never necessary. His hawk look was
enough. His mother loved him, but everyone else
was shit-scared of him.

W: Where did he serve with MK?

A: How would I know? He never talked about it.

W: Never?

A: Hardly a word. Six years and I never knew him.
Kept to himself, always a bit apart like Colin
Wilson's Outsider, but who cares, he was a jewel
in my crown.

W: Colin who?

A: Literary reference, my bro. You wouldn't
understand.

W: And then he left your service?

A: Two years ago, he came in and said he was
finished. I thought he was playing me for an
increase, but he wasn't interested. Next thing
we know he was working in a motorbike shop,
dogsbody and general cleaner, can you believe
it? Works for peanuts – he earned a small
fortune with me. But now it seems he was busy
with something on the side.

W: So you have had no contact with him during the
last two years?

A: Sweet Fanny Adams.

W: I won't take up your time any longer, Mr
    Arendse.

A: Now there's a relief.

W: You can send medical back-up to Mitchell's
    Plain. We will withdraw from the property.

A: Mister Williams, you know nothing about Tiny
    Mpayipheli, am I right?

W: Why do you say that, Mr Arendse?

A: Just call it a sneaking suspicion. So let me
    give you some advice: start ordering the body
    bags now.

8

Janina Mentz went quickly to phone from her office. The maid said Lizette was asleep already. She thanked Suthu for the extra bother of sleeping over and asked to talk to Lien.

'I know my work now, ma, even though you weren't here to help me.'

'I knew you could handle it.'

'Can I watch Big Brother on DSTV, Ma? Till ten?'

Kids. Tried to manipulate every situation to maximum advantage. She wanted to be angry and laugh at the same time.

'You know the rules, Lien. The age restriction is sixteen,' and even as she said it she knew exactly what the response would be.

'All my friends watch it, ma. I'm nearly sixteen. I'm not a child any more.' All three basic arguments in one breath.

'I know you're not a child any more. You are a wonderful, lovable fifteen-year-old who only needs to wait a couple more months. Then you can watch with your undisciplined friends. Get enough sleep – you need it for the exam.'

'Maa-aa . . .'

'And tell Lizette I was just too late to say good night. Tell her I love both of you very much – and I'm very proud of you too.'

'Don't work too hard, ma.'

'I won't.'

'We love you, too.'

'I know, kid. Sleep well.'

'Night, ma.'

Mentz hurried back to the Ops Room, impatience gnawing at her.

'Look again, Rahjev. If he was MK there must be something,' she said as she entered.

'Yes, ma'am.' But the Indian's body language said that he knew what the result would be.

'You don't believe we will find anything?'

'Ma'am, the methodology we use to search the known data is very refined. There was nothing. I can run it again, but the result will be the same.'

'He could have lied to Arendse about his background,' said Quinn. 'Work was very scarce in the early nineties, people were prepared to say anything.'

'Things don't change much,' said Radebe dryly.

'And now we have a fugitive sharpshooter with two pistols,' said Mentz.

Rajkumar's brain was working overtime: 'The ANC had a paper filing system, too: for Umkhonto we Sizwe. Isn't it on Robben Island?'

'Pretoria,' said Radebe. 'The MK files are at Voortrekkerhoogte.'

'What can you tell us about it?'

'It was never much of a system. With the big influx of recruits after '76 there was too much paper and too few administrators. But it could be worth looking.'

'What about the old National Intelligence Service's microfiche library? The Boers computerized the index but it's a secure unconnected system. It's still active, in Pretoria. We can put in a request,' said Rajkumar.

It was Radebe who made a disparaging noise and Mentz knew why. Her colleagues at the new National Intelligence Service did not command much respect from her and her people. But she liked the idea.

'If the request comes from high enough up they will jump to it,' she said. 'I'm going to talk to the Director.'

'Ma'am,' said Quinn, holding up his hand to stop her.

'What is it?'

'Listen to this.' He selected keys and the electronic hissing of the speakerphone filled the room.

'Tell us again, Nathan.'

'We managed to track down the owner of Mother City Motorrad. His name is Bodenstein and he lives in Welgelegen. He says Mpayipheli isn't a mechanic, just a gofer. Quiet man, hard worker, punctual and trustworthy. Bodenstein knows nothing about a military background.'

'Tell us about the alarm again, Nathan.'

'While we were busy with the interview the phone rang. Bodenstein's security company reported that the bike shop's alarm was turned off more than an hour ago and hasn't been reactivated. He said he must go immediately and we are following him there.'

'And what did he say about the key, Nathan?'

'Oh, yes. He says Mpayipheli has a key to the place and he knows the alarm code, because Mpayipheli is the one who opens up in the morning.'

Mpayipheli almost fell before he was properly on his way. The power of the huge bike caught him totally unaware as he turned into Oswald Pirow and turned the throttle. The reaction of this bike was so different from his little Honda Benly that he nearly lost it. And the size – the GS felt massive, heavy and high and unmanageable. He was shocked – adrenalin made his hands tremble, his breath misting the visor of his helmet. He wrestled the bike back in line and this time twisted the throttle with great care and progressed to the traffic lights at the N1. He pulled the front brakes and nearly tipped again, the ABS kicking in hard and urgent. He stopped, breathing heavily, knees trembling, not willing to die on this German machine. The lights turned to green. He pulled away slowly, turning gently to the right with an over-wide arc and exaggerated care, keeping the revs low, through the gears – bloody hell, the thing had power, he was at 100 kilometres per hour before he was properly in third gear, that would be just about the Benly's top speed.

The traffic on the freeway was light, but he was painfully aware of the cars around him. He was riding slower than the flow of traffic, cringing in the left lane, trying to get a feel for the GS – once you were going the balance was easier, but the handlebars felt too wide, the tank in front of him impossibly big.

He checked again where the flickers were, how the dims and brights worked, his eyes flicking between the switches and the road ahead: his following distance was long, his speed just under a hundred. He had made a mistake, he had thought this was the way to get a long way from Cape Town very fast – if he could make Bloemfontein tonight still he would be away because he could catch a plane there, they wouldn't be watching Bloemfontein airport. But this thing was practically unrideable, he had made a mistake, it would have been quicker to take a minibus taxi and it was dark too, the lights of Century City reflected off the helmet. Maybe he should ride to Worcester, or only as far as Paarl and ditch the bloody bike, what could he have been thinking of?

At the N7 off ramp Mpayipheli had to change lanes to let a lorry come past and he accelerated slowly, using the flickers, changed lanes, swung back into the left one, relaxed a little. Through the long uphill turn at Parow, up the Tygerberg, he knew his body was leaning to the wrong side in the turn, but the bike was so unwieldy, the bend uncomfortable, if only there was less traffic, where were all these people going at this time of night? Down the hill to Bellville's off ramps and then the street lights on the freeway became fewer, the traffic dropped off, he saw the signs at the one-stop petrol station beckoning and glanced at the fuel gauge. The tank was full. Thank God. How far could he go on one tank?

His eye caught the speedometer, 110, he throttled back, felt out of control again – this machine had a life of its own, a wild mustang. All his senses intensely engaged, he knew he must plan ahead, what to do? The toll gate was up ahead, thirty kilometres. What should he do? Avoid the toll gate, go to Paarl, abandon the bike, catch a taxi?

There must be taxis running to Worcester, but it was already very late. And if he stuck with the GS? Take on the Du Toits Kloof Pass with this monster?

The toll gate was a spoor that he would leave: people would remember a big black man on a motorbike, wouldn't they? Lord, he feared the pass in the dark on this thing. But beyond were more passes, more dark roads with sharp turns and oncoming freight trucks. What had possessed him?

What was he going to do?

A taxi was not going to work, not at this time of night.

Look at this positively. He was on the move, on his way. Suppress the desire to get rid of the bike. Use the dark. Use the lead he had. Use the element of surprise. They had no idea, despite the two Spooks in the car at the motorbike shop, it would be tomorrow morning before someone realised the GS was gone, he had . . .

He hadn't reset the alarm. That knowledge came out of the back of his head like a hammer blow. In his hurry and wrestling with the GS he had forgotten to switch on the alarm.

Jissis, he had gotten sloppy.

By the time he passed the Stellenbosch turn-off, his anger at Johnny Kleintjes and the Spooks and at his own stupidity had grown greater than his fear of the motorbike and he cursed inside the helmet, in all the languages he knew.

'I don't believe it,' said Bodenstein. 'I bloody don't believe it.' They were standing in the showroom of Mother City Motorrad, the two agents and the owner. Bodenstein held out the piece of paper. 'Read what he's written. Can you believe this?'

Nathan took the note.

Mr Bodenstein

I am borrowing the GS demonstration model for two or three days. I also took a suit and helmet and gloves, that is what the money is for that I left in your desk drawer. Unfortunately I have to urgently help a friend and I had no other choice. Wear and tear and any damage to the motorbike will be paid in full.

Thobela Mpayipheli.

'You think you know someone. You think you know who to trust,' said Bodenstein.

'Which one is the GS?' asked Johnny.

'It's that fuckin' huge thing, only yellow,' said Bodenstein, pointing to a silver motorbike on the showroom floor. 'He's going to fall. Fuckin' hard. It's not a toy. Can you believe it?'

'See reality the way things are, not as you want them to be' was one of the principles of Janina Mentz.

That was why she accepted the developments calmly.

She thought through the happenings while the Ops Room buzzed around her. She stood still at the end of the long table with one hand on her chin, her elbow propped on her other hand, head bowed, a study in calm thoughtfulness. Aware that the Director would hear every word, aware that the way she responded and the decisions she made, her tone of voice and body language would all create an impression on her team.

Vision: in her mind's eye she saw the road that the evasive persona of Thobela Mpayipheli must travel. He was headed north and the N1 lay like a fat, twisted artery stretching out ahead to the heart of Africa. The reason for his single-mindedness, the source of his motivation was unplumbed and now irrelevant. She focused on the route: the implications, the countermeasures, the preventative and limiting steps.

In a soft and even voice Mentz ordered the big map of the country to be put up on the wall.

With red ink she drew in the likely route. She defined the role of the Reaction Unit: they would be her net, the welcoming party seventy-seven kilometres north of Beaufort West, where the route forked and the possibilities doubled – Kimberley to Johannesburg left, or Bloemfontein to Johannesburg right.

She asked Quinn and Radebe's teams to alert the police stations and traffic authorities along the route, to warn them merely to gather intelligence and not to act, because their armed fugitive was still largely an unknown factor. But they knew he could shoot.

Their ignorance of this factor lay heavily on her and the next round of instructions had to set that right: investigative teams to Miriam Nzululwazi, to Monica Kleintjes. The gloves were off now. Track down the fugitive's family. His parents. His friends. Get information. Who? What? Where? Why? How? She needed to know him, this ghost with the elusive face.

Mentz had the power. She would use it.

Extract from transcript of interview by J.
Wilkinson with Mr André Bodenstein, owner of Mother
City Motorrad, 23 October, 21:55, Oswald Pirow
Boulevard, Cape Town:

W: What do you know of Mr Mpayipheli's previous
    employments?
B: He was a gofer.
W: Gofer?
B: Yes. For a car dealer in Somerset West.
W: How do you know this?
B: He told me.
W: What kind of gofer?
B: A gofer is a gofer. It means you do all the shit
    jobs that nobody else will.
W: That's all you know?
B: Listen, I don't need a man with a bloody degree
    to wash the motorbikes.
W: And you trusted him with a key?
B: Not the first day, I'm not a moron.
W: But later on.
B: Hell, he was here on the doorstep every morning
    when I arrived. Every bloody morning, never
    sick, never late, never cheeky. He worked, hell,
    that man can work. Last winter I told him he must
    open up, he can't stand in the rain like that,
    he could sweep out so long and put the kettle
    on, by the time we arrive, the coffee is made,
    every fucking morning, the place shines like a
    new penny, you think you can trust someone. You
    think you know people . . .

Twice Mpayipheli was gofer at Killarney when the BMW
Rider Academy had been coaching well-off middle-aged white
men in the art of motorcycle riding and now he regretted that

he hadn't paid attention, that he hadn't absorbed all that knowledge.

Du Toits Kloof Pass in the dark and he was aware that he was a caricature of how it should not be done. Riding jerkily, brakes and throttle and brakes and throttle and switching the light between bright and dim in a battle between good vision and the oncoming traffic, massive, snorting trucks avoiding the toll fees by using the long route and taking the sharp turns wide or chugging along at a snail's pace ahead of him. He sweated inside the expensive efficient bikers suit, his body heat steaming up the shield with water vapour so that time and again he had to clip it open, always aware of the drop on the left side, the lights very far down below.

Brake, turn, brake, turn, ride, struggling and swearing to the highest point and then the road swung abruptly east and the lights were gone. For the first time the darkness was complete and the road suddenly quiet and he became aware of the tremendous tension in his torso, muscles like strung wires and he pulled to the side, stopped, pulled the helmet from his head, put the clutch in neutral, took his hands from the handlebars and stretched, taking in a deep breath.

He must relax, he had to, he was tired already and there were hundreds of kilometres ahead. He had made progress. He had come this far, navigated half the pass in the dark. Despite his hamfistedness the monster bike was not impossible. It was being patient with him as though it was waiting for him to try a lighter touch.

Deep breaths, in and out, a certain satisfaction, he had reached this milestone, he was at the top. He had a story to tell Pakamile and Miriam. He wondered if she was asleep: the digital clock on the instrument panel said Miriam had laid out the boy's school things, clothes and lunch box. If he had been home, his lunch tin would have been packed, the house tidy, the sheets of their bed folded back and she would come and lie down with the wonderful smells of the oils and soaps of the bathroom, the alarm set for five o'clock, the light off and her breathing immediately deep and peaceful, the sleep of the innocent, the sleep of the worker.

Behind him Mpayipheli heard a lorry approaching the turn and he stretched one last time, savouring the night air, clipped the shield down and pulled away with the knowledge that he had at least mastered the throttle. He turned it deliberately open, felt the power beneath him and then he was in the next turn and he concentrated on keeping his body relaxed, to lean into the turn as he did with the Benly, carefully, unskilled, but a lot better, more comfortable, more natural, accelerated slowly out of the turn, aimed for the next, through the old tunnel, another curve and another, down, down to the valley of the Meulenaars River, down, fighting the urge to stiffen up, keeping himself loose and light, feeling the personality of the bike through his limbs, turn and straighten, over and over, joining up with the toll road suddenly impossibly luxurious and three lanes wide, the curves broad. The relief was tremendous.

As he looked down at the speedo he saw that it read 130 and then he smiled inside his helmet at the sensation and the amazing thing that he had accomplished.

9

'This is not what we were trained to do,' said Tiger Mazibuko over the cellphone. He was standing outside, next to the runway. He could see his men through the window: they were still pumped after the action they had seen, they talked of nothing else, living it over in the finest detail on the way to the air force base, teasing each other, even him, begging their commander to let them all have a chance to shoot, why only Da Costa? Zwelitini said he was going to send a strongly worded letter to the Zulu king to complain that even in the country's most elite unit there was racial discrimination – only the colonials were allowed to fire, the poor ole blacks could only watch – and the twelve roared with mirth. But Tiger Mazibuko did not.

'I know, Tiger, but it was very valuable.'

'We are not the SAPS. Give us something proper to do. Give us a challenge.'

'Does a man who can pick off beer bottles with an AK at 200 metres sound like a challenge?'

'Only one man?'

'Unfortunately just one, Tiger.'

'No, that doesn't sound like a challenge.'

'Well, that's the best I can do. Stand by for an Oryx from 23 Squadron. We are going to pursue the fugitive, you will go on ahead and wait for him.'

His quietness indicated his disgruntlement.

When Mentz realized what he was up to her voice grew angry.

'If the challenge is not big enough for you, you can always go back to Tempe. I am sure I can find another alternative.'

'What do we know about this great shooter of beer bottles?'

'Too little. He might or might not have been MK, he was a sort of bodyguard for organized crime, and nowadays he is a gofer at a motorbike dealer.'

'Was he MK or wasn't he?'

'We are working on it, Tiger. We are working on it.'

Transcript of interview by A.J.M. Williams with Mrs Miriam Nzululwazi, 23 October, 22:51, 21 Govan Mbeki Avenue, Guguletu.

W: I represent the State, Mrs Nzululwazi. I have a few questions about Mr Thobela Mpayipheli and a Miss Monica Kleintjes.

N: I don't know her.

W: But you do know Mr Mpayipheli.

N: Yes. He is a good man.

W: How long have you known him?

N: Two years.

W: How did you meet?

N: At my work.

W: What work do you do, Mrs Nzululwazi?

N: I am a tea lady at Absa.

W: Which branch of Absa?

N: The Heerengracht.

W: And how did you come to meet him?

N: He is a client.

W: Yes?

N: He came to see one of the consultants and I brought him tea. When he was finished he came to look for me.

W: And asked for a date?

N: Yes.

W: And you said 'Yes'.

N: No. Only later.

W: So he came back again, after the first time.

N: Yes.

W: Why did you refuse him at first?

N: I don't understand why you wake me up to ask me questions like this.

W: Mr Mpayipheli is in trouble, Mrs Nzululwazi, and you can help him by answering the questions.

N: What kind of trouble?

W: He unlawfully took an object that belongs to the State and—

N: He took nothing. That woman gave it to him.

W: Miss Kleintjes?

N: Yes.

W: Why did she give it to him?

N: So that he could take it to her father.

W: But why did she choose him to do this?

N: He owes her father a favour.

W: What kind of favour?

N: I don't know.

W: He didn't tell you?

N: I didn't ask.

W: Do you and Mr Mpayipheli live together?

N: Yes.

W: As man and wife?

N: Yes.

W: And you didn't ask him why he was receiving stolen property and agreeing to take it to Lusaka?

N: How do you know he is going to Lusaka?

W: We know everything.

N: If you know everything why are you sitting here asking me questions in the middle of the night?

W: Do you know what Mr Mpayipheli was involved with before his present work?

N: I thought you knew everything?

W: Mrs Nzululwazi, there are gaps in our knowledge. I have already apologized for disturbing you so late. As I have explained it is an emergency and Mr Mpayipheli is in big trouble. You can help us by filling in the gaps.

N: I don't know what he did.

W: Did you know that he worked for organized crime?

N: I don't want to know. He said he had another life, he said he did things that he wants to forget. In this country it wasn't very hard to get involved in such matters. He would have told me if I had asked him. But I didn't. He is a good man. There is love in this house. He is good to me and to my son. That is all I need to know.

W: Do you know if he was a member of Umkhonto we Sizwe?

N: Yes.

W: Was he?

N: Yes.

W: Did he tell you that?

N: In a way.

W: Did you know where he served?

N: He was in Tanzania and Angola and in Europe and Russia.

W: Do you know when?

N: That is all that I know.

W: But he told you that as a member of MK he—

N: No. He never told stories. I worked it out myself.

W: What do you mean?

N: Like when he talked to Pakamile about other countries.

W: Pakamile is your son?

N: Yes.

W: And this is all you had to go on?

N: Yes.

W: He never actually said he was with MK?

N: No.

[Silence – 8 seconds]

W: Mrs Nzululwazi, the favour he owed to Johnny Kleintjes . . .

N: I have already told you I don't know.

W: You didn't find it strange that Miss Kleintjes came in here and Mr Mpayipheli immediately agrees to undertake a long and dangerous journey on her behalf?

N: Why would it be dangerous to go to Lusaka?

W: You are not aware of the data on the disk?

N: What data?

W: The stolen data that he has with him.

N: Why should it be dangerous?

W: There are people who want to stop him. And there are—

N: People like you?

W: No, Mrs Nzululwazi.

N: You want to stop him.

W: We want to help. We tried at the airport, but he ran away.

N: You wanted to help.

W: We did.

N: You must leave. Now.

W: Madam . . .

N: Get out of my house.

There is a plaque at the entrance to the Air Force base at Bloemspruit. In military terms it is a new plaque, being scarcely three years old. On the plaque is the legend '16 Squadron' and below that 'Hlaselani'. Black inhabitants of Bloemfontein know what 'hlaselani' means, but just to be sure that everyone understands, in brackets at the bottom of the plaque is the word 'Attack'.

It is the pilots of 16 Squadron in particular who look at those words with satisfaction. It defines their purpose, separating them from the winged-bus drivers and freight carriers of other squadrons, especially the other helicopter jockeys. They are an attack unit. For the first time in nearly sixty-five years of existence. Forget the quasi-bombers like the Marylands, Beauforts and Beaufighters of the Second World War. Forget the Alouette III helicopters of the bad 1980s.

Their satisfaction is due in large part to the contents of the giant hangars: twelve almost brand new Rooivalk AH-2A attack helicopters, impressive air platforms with nose-mounted 20mm cannon that can fire 740 rounds per minute, and the capacity to carry up to sixteen air-to-ground missiles such as the ZT-35 laser-guided anti-tank missile. And on the wing-tips are fittings for the Darter air-to-air missiles to lie snug. Add the Rooivalk's electronic warfare capability, the fully integrated HEWSPS (Helicopter Electronic Warfare Self-protection Suite) with radar warning, laser warning and countermeasures systems and the pilots feel they are the only ones in the South African Air Force with twenty-first-century technology between their legs – which is their regular joke in the officers' club over their Red Heart rum and Coke.

The call came at 21:59 from General Ben van Rooyen at Air Force Headquarters for two Rooivalk helicopters with extra fuel tanks for an extended operating range of 1260 kilometres to take off for Beaufort West as part of a real-life operation (and not the simulated warfare of the last thirty-six months). The biggest dilemma of the commander of 16 Squadron was how to explain to the pilots and gunners who were not chosen how he had made his choice.

'How is it possible that MK has no record of him, Rahjev? If she is right and he was in Russia and Angola, how is that possible?'

'Ma'am, we don't know. We can only look at what is in the databases and analyse that, that's all.'

'What is the probability that a MK member is not on record?'

Rajkumar pulled with a plump hand at his ponytail hanging over his shoulder. 'Hell, ma'am . . . fifteen per cent?'

'Fifteen per cent.'

'Round about.'

'If there were ten thousand MK soldiers, as many as one and a half thousand are not on record?'

'Not on *electronic* record.'

'If there were fifty thousand, could seven and a half thousand just be missing?'

'Yes, ma'am.'

'But they might be in the files in Voortrekkerhoogte?'

Radebe answered: 'I think the odds are greater that they will find him in the Voortrekkerhoogte files.'

'How long before we hear?'

'An hour or two. They have three people searching the archives.'

'And the Boers' microfiche library?'

Radebe shrugged his shoulders. 'It depends how strongly the orders from above came through.'

Mentz did a circuit of the room. To be dependent on others was a great frustration. She shook it off.

'What is a motorcycle gofer doing with a consultant at Absa?' she asked the Ops Room at large.

'Tell me I can scratch around in the Absa system, ma'am. Please?' Rajkumar stretched his interlaced plump fingers in front of him, cracking his joints in anticipation.

'How much time do you need?'

'Give me an hour.'

'Go for it.'

'Yeah, yeah, yeah!'

'What is the situation on the road?' she asked Radebe.

'The toll gate says no big bikes have gone north tonight – a few came in South, but no Black man. We are working through Police Head Office. They say the local law enforcement and petrol stations as far as Touws River are alerted. They are phoning Laingsburg, Leeu-Gamka and Beaufort-West now. But if he doesn't take the N1 . . .'

'He will.'

He nodded.

Mentz looked at them. They were keen to please.

'Are we making progress with the people who helped Kleintjes with the computer integration?'

'There is a transcript coming, ma'am.'

'Thank you.'

This is the one, she thought. The one she was waiting for. She looked over the room. They didn't know everything. Only she held all the pieces to this particular jigsaw.

So much careful planning. So much exception management. Long careful months of fitting the gears one by one into this clock. And now it must all change, thanks to one middle-aged motorbike gofer.

10

Miriam Nzululwazi lay on the double bed in the dark room, hands folded on her chest, gaze turned to the ceiling. She did not hear the familiar sounds of Guguletu at night: the eternal barking of dogs, the shouts of groups going home from the shebeen, their last fling before the week began again, the revving of a car engine in a backyard repair shop, the insects, music somewhere only audible in bass, the sigh and creak of their house settling for the night.

Her thoughts sought out Thobela and came back every time to the same conclusion: he was a good man.

Why were they chasing him? He was doing nothing wrong.

This country. Would it never stop banging on your door in the middle of the night? Would the ledger of the past never be closed?

Was he doing a wrong thing?

Was Thobela someone else than the man she knew?

'I was different,' he had said one afternoon, when their relationship was young, when he had to fight to win her trust. 'I had another life. I am not ashamed. I did what I believed in. It is over. Here I am now. Just as you see me.'

That first day in the consultant's office she had not even noticed him – just another client. She had transferred the tea from the trolley onto the tray and slid the tray onto the desk and nodded when the consultant and his client thanked her and she had pulled the door closed behind her, little knowing that that mundane task would change her life. He had come right into the kitchen looking for her, apparently had told the consultant's secretary that he wanted to tell her how good the tea was, he had put out his hand to her and said 'My name is Thobela Mpayipheli.' She thought it was a nice name, an honest name,

'Thobela' meant 'with respect', but she wondered what he wanted. 'I saw you in Van der Linde's office. I want to talk with you.'

'What about?'

'Anything.'

'Are you asking me out?'

'Yes, I am.'

'No.'

'Am I too ugly?' – with his smile and broad shoulders.

'I have a child.'

'A boy or a girl?'

'I haven't got time to talk. I have work to do.'

'Just tell me your name, please.'

'Miriam.'

'Thank you.' He had not used any of the popular slang, none of the quasi-American *cool* of the township rakes, he had left and she had gone on with her work. Two days later there was a phone call for her. No one phoned her at work, so she feared someone had died. He had to remind her who he was, he asked her when she took her lunch break, she answered evasively and asked him not to phone her at work, there was no outside line to the kitchen and reception didn't like it if the staff kept the lines busy.

The next day Mpayipheli was waiting outside, not leaning against a wall somewhere, but standing right in front of the entrance, his legs planted wide and his arms folded on his chest and when she sought the sunshine in Thibault Square he was there. 'May I walk with you?'

'What do you want?'

'I want to talk to you.'

'Why?'

'Because you are a lovely woman and I want to know you.'

'I know enough people, thank you.'

'You never told me if you had a son or a daughter.'

'That's right.' He walked beside her, she sat down on a step and opened the waxed paper wrapping of her sandwich.

'Can I sit here?'

'It's a public place. You can sit where you like.'

'I am not a *tsotsi*.'

'I can see that.'

'I just want to talk.'

Miriam let him talk. She was in a dilemma – fear on one hand, loneliness on the other. The experiences behind her argued with the possibilities that lay ahead. She had to shield her child and her heart from the big, handsome, gentle, proper man sitting in the spring sunshine alongside her. Her solution was to wait and see, to be passive. Let him talk – and he did. Every other day he was outside, sometimes he brought something to eat, never luxuries: bunny rolls, hot chips with the irresistible flavour of salt and vinegar, sometimes a little bowl of curry and rice or his favourite, a chilli bite from the Muslim takeaway in Adderley Street, fresh and fragrant and sharp, and let her taste it. He shared his lunch with her and slowly she began to melt. Relaxing, she told him about Pakamile and her house for which she had worked so long, how hard it had been to pay it off and one day he brought a gift for the boy, a jigsaw puzzle, and she said no, that's it, she wouldn't see him any more, she would not expose Pakamile to disappointment, men always left. Men never stayed, he was a good man but she thought men couldn't help it. That was how life was: men were temporary. Undependable. Unnecessary. Unnecessary for Pakamile.

Not all men, he had said and it was on the tip of her tongue to say 'That is what you all say', but there was something in his eyes, in his look, in the set of his mouth and the clenching of his teeth that stopped her, that touched her and she let it go and then he said 'I had a wild life. I did things . . .'

'What things?'

'Things in the name of the Struggle. I was different. I had another life. I am not ashamed. I did what I believed in. It is over. Here I am now. Just as you see me.'

'We all did things in the name of the Struggle.' She was relieved.

'Yes,' he said. 'I was searching for myself. Now I have found myself. I know who I am and I know what I want. I am not a deserter.'

She had believed him. He had looked into her eyes and she had believed him.

'Rooivalk One, we have a weather situation,' said the tower at Bloemspruit. 'Trough developing in the west, all the way from Verneukpan to Somerset East and a weak frontal system on the way. It could get wet.'

The pilot looked at his flight plan. 'Can we get through?'

'Affirmative, Rooivalk, but you had better shake ass,' said the tower, knowing that the Rooivalk's operational ceiling was just under twenty thousand feet.

'Rooivalk One ready for take-off.'

'Rooivalk Two ready for take-off.'

'Rooivalk One and Two cleared for take-off. Make some thunder.'

The noise of the double Topaz turboshaft engines was deafening.

Mpayipheli mastered the R1150 GS just before the Hex River valley. He knew it when he came out of a bend and opened the throttle and there was pleasure in the power. The exhaust pipe snorted softly behind him and he kicked back one gear, chose the line for the curve, tilted the bike, his shoulder dipping into the turn, and there was no discomfort, no fear of the angle between machine and road, just the tingling of pride for a small victory, skills acquired, satisfaction in control of power. He accelerated out of the turn, eyes focused on the next one, taking in the red lights a kilometre ahead, a lorry, aware, in control, bits and pieces, the instructor's voice at the Advanced Riding School slowly making sense now. He could get to like this, a little adrenalin, a little more skill, lorry ahead, manipulate clutch and gears and accelerator, a whisper of the front brakes, shoot past and then he looked up and the moon broke away from the mountain peaks, full and bright and in that moment he knew that it was going to work: the trouble lay behind him, just the twisty, open road ahead and he opened the taps and the valley lay spread out ahead of him, a fairyland in the silvery light of the moon.

Monica Kleintjes sat hunched in the sitting-room chair in her father's house, the lines of suppressed tears down her cheeks. Opposite her Williams sat on the edge of his chair, as if he would reach out to her in empathy. 'Miss Kleintjes, I would have done precisely the same if it was my father. It was a noble action,' he said softly. 'We are here to support you.'

She nodded, biting her lower lip, hands clenched in her lap, her eyes large and teary behind the spectacles.

'There are just two things we need to shed light on: your father's relationship with Mr Mpayipheli and the character of the data that he has with him.'

'I don't know what is on the hard disk.'

'No idea?'

'Names. Records. Numbers. Information. When I asked my father what it was all about he said it was better if I

didn't know. I think . . . Names . . .' Her gaze wandered
over the wall next to the mantelpiece. There were photos
hanging, black and white, colour. People.

'What names?' Williams followed her gaze, stood up.

'Well-known ones.'

'Which?' He looked over the photos. A coloured family
in Trafalgar Square, Johnny Kleintjes, Monica, perhaps five
years old, her little legs stout and very present.

'ANC. The Regime . . .'

'Can you remember any specific names?' There were
photos of Kleintjes and people now in positions in the government. Red Square, East Berlin, Checkpoint Charlie and the
Wall in the background. Prague. The tourist spots of the
Cold War.

'He didn't say.'

'Nothing at all?' Williams stared at Johnny Kleintjes's
wedding picture. Monica's mother in white, not a beautiful
woman but proud.

'Nothing.'

Williams looked away from the pictures, to her. 'Miss
Kleintjes, it is essential that we know what is in that data.
This is in the interests of the country.'

Her hands sprang loose from her lap, the tears finally spilled
over the dam wall. 'I didn't want to know and my father didn't
want to say. Please . . .'

'I understand, Miss Kleintjes.'

'Thanks.'

He allowed her a moment to calm down. She reached for
her tissues and blew delicately.

'And Mr Mpayipheli?'

'My father knew him in the Struggle.'

'Could you be more specific?'

Another tissue. Monica Kleintjes removed her spectacles
and wiped carefully under her eyes. 'Three weeks . . . two

or three weeks ago my father came to me at work. He had never done that before. He had a piece of paper with him. He said it was the name and contact number of someone he trusted completely. If anything should happen to him I must phone Tiny Mpayipheli.'

'Tiny?'

'That was what was on the paper.'

'Were you surprised?'

'I was disturbed. I asked him why something should happen to him. He said nothing was going to happen, it was just insurance, like we work with at Sanlam. Then I asked him who Tiny Mpayipheli was and he said a phenomenon.'

'A phenomenon?'

She nodded. 'Then he said a comrade, Tiny was a comrade, they served together. He saw Tiny grow up in the Struggle.'

'Your father was in Europe during the Struggle?'

'Yes.'

'And that was where he got to know Mpayipheli?'

'I assume so.'

'And?'

'And should anything go wrong, I should contact Tiny. Then I asked him again what would go wrong. I was worried, but he would say nothing, he wanted to talk about how nice my office was.'

'And then, when you got the calls from Lusaka, you phoned Mpayipheli?'

'First I opened the safe to get the hard disk. On top of it was a note. Tiny Mpayipheli's name and phone number. So I phoned him.'

'And then you took the hard disk to him in Guguletu?'

'Yes.'

'And you asked him to take it to Lusaka for you?'

'Yes.'

'And he agreed?'

'I owe your father, he said.'

'I owe your father.'

'Yes.'

'Is his photo here?'

Monica Kleintjes looked at the row of portraits as if seeing them for the first time. She pulled her crutches closer, stood up with difficulty. Williams wanted to stop her, sorry he had asked. 'I don't think so.' She looked over the photos. The liquid welled up in her eyes again.

'Have you had any contact with Mr Mpayipheli since then?'

'You listen to my phone. You know.'

'Miss Kleintjes, have you any idea where Mr Mpayipheli is now?'

'No.'

Radebe called Janina Mentz to the Ops Room.

'Yes?'

'The team searching the files in Pretoria, ma'am . . .'

'Yes?'

'There's nothing. They can't find Thobela Mpayipheli.'

11

The agent was from the Eastern Cape Bureau in Bisho. She knew, operationally speaking, that it was the backwoods of South Africa, a professional quicksand where nothing ever happened to give you a chance to rise above the routine, to propel yourself to Headquarters. The longer you remained there, the more you suffocated in the sands of mediocrity.

When Radebe phoned from HQ to order you to interview a Subject in Alice, you didn't moan about the lack of information, you put zeal in your voice and hid the gratitude and climbed into the grimy, juddering Volkswagen Golf Chico with 174,000 km on the clock and you seized the day, because this could be your passport to higher honours.

Then you focused on the questions you were going to ask, the tone of voice to maintain, you prepared until your thoughts began to wander, when you began to daydream about the possibilities this could bring, you saw in your mind's eye Mrs Mentz reading the report (not knowing what her office looks like, you filled it with chrome and glass) and calling Radebe in to say 'This agent is brilliant, Radebe. What is she doing in Bisho? She belongs here with us.'

Before the fantasy could properly take shape, before she could furnish the dream apartment in Sea Point and picture the view, she had arrived. She parked in front of the house in Alice, just a kilometre or so from the lovely new buildings on the Fort Hare campus. There was a light still burning and she knocked politely, her tape recorder and notebook in her handbag, her weapon in the leather holster in the small of her back.

The hair of the man who opened the door was silver-grey, the wrinkles on his face deep and multiple, the tall body bowed with age, but his 'Good evening' conveyed only patience.

'Reverend Lawrence Mpayipheli?'

'That is correct.'

'My name is Dalindyebo. I need some help.'

'You have come to the right place, sister.' A strong voice. The minister stepped back and held the door open. Two veined bare feet showed under the burgundy dressing gown.

The agent stepped inside, swept her gaze over the room, the bookshelves along two walls, hundreds of books, the other walls hung with black and white and colour photos. The room had simplicity, no luxuries, an aura of restfulness and warmth.

'Please sit down. I just want to tell my wife she can go to sleep.'

'I apologize for the late hour, Reverend.'

'Don't be sorry.' The minister disappeared down the passage, bare feet silent on the carpet. The agent attempted to see the photos from her chair. The minister and his wife in the middle, with bridal couples, at synod, with amorphous groups of people. At one side, a family photo, the minister young, tall and straight. In front of him stood a boy of six or seven, a serious frown on his face, an overbite of new front teeth. The agent wondered if that was Thobela Mpayipheli.

The old man appeared from the passage again. 'I have put the kettle on. What do you bring to my house, Miss Dalindyebo?'

For a moment she hesitated, suddenly doubting the prepared phrase on the tip of her tongue. There is something shining out of the old man, a love, compassion.

'Reverend, I work for the State . . .'

He was about to sit down opposite Dalindyebo when he saw her hesitation. 'Carry on, my child, don't be afraid.'

'Reverend, we need information about your son. Thobela Mpayipheli.'

Deep emotion moved over the old man's face, across his mouth and eyes. He stood still for long moments as if turned to stone, long enough for her to feel anxiety. Then slowly he sat, as if his legs were in pain, and his sigh was deep and heavy.

'My son?' One hand touched the grey temple, just the fingertips; the other gripped the arm of the chair, eyes unseeing. A reaction she had not expected. She must adjust her timescale and review her questions. But for now she must remain quiet.

'My son,' he said, this time not a question, the hand coming loose from the chair and floating to his mouth as if weightless, his gaze focused somewhere, but not in this room.

'Thobela,' he said as if remembering the name.

It took nearly fifteen minutes for the old man to begin his story. He first asked after the welfare of his son, which Dalindyebo answered with vague lies to spare him anguish. He excused himself to make coffee, treading like a sleepwalker. He brought the tray, which he had arranged with a plate of rusks and biscuits, he dithered about where to begin the chronicle of Thobela Mpayipheli and then it came out, at first haltingly, a struggle for the right words, the right expression, till it began to flow, to make a stream of words and emotions, as if he were confessing and seeking her absolution.

To understand you needed to go back to the previous generation. To his generation. To him and his brother. Lawrence and Senzeni. The dove and the falcon. Jacob and Esau, if you would forgive the comparison. Children of the Kat River, of poverty, yes, simplicity but pride, sons of a tribal chief who had to do herd duty with the cattle, who learned the Xhosa culture around the fire at night, who learned the history of the People at the feet of the Grey-Haired Ones, who went through the Xhosa initiation before it became an exploitation of the poor. The difference between them was there from the early days. Lawrence, the elder, the dreamer, the tall lean boy, the clever one who was always one step ahead of the others at the Mission school with its single classroom, the peacemaker. Senzeni, shorter, muscular, a fighter, a born soldier, impatient, short-tempered, fiery, his attention only fully engaged when the battles were retold, his eyes glittering with fighting spirit.

There had been a defining moment, so many years ago, when he, Lawrence, had had to defend his honour in a senseless adolescent fist fight with another boy, a troublemaker who was jealous of Lawrence's status as chief's offspring. He was baited with cutting ridicule and within the circle of screaming children had to defend his dignity with his fists. It was as if he was raised above the two boys facing each other in ever-diminishing circles, as if he floated, as if he was not really there. And when the blows began to rain down he could not lift his hand against the other boy. He could not ball his hands into fists, could not find the hate or anger to break skin or draw blood. It was a divine moment, the knowledge that he could feel his opponent's pain before it existed, the urge to assuage it, to heal.

Senzeni came to his aid, his little brother. Lawrence was staggering and bleeding in the ring of boys, head singing from the blows, blood in his eyes and his nose and then Senzeni was there, a black tornado of rage ruthlessly thrashing the other boy with frightful purpose.

When it was over Senzeni had turned to Lawrence with disdain, even a degree of hate, reluctant to accept this new responsibility and questioning without words how they could be brothers.

Lawrence found the Lord at the Missions school. He found in Christ all the things he had felt within him that day. Senzeni said it was the white man's religion.

Lawrence received a bursary through the church and their mother encouraged him. He studied and married and began the long eternal journey as disciple here among his own people in the Kat River valley. And his brother was always there, a counterweight, by default the next tribal chief, the warrior, who fastened on the rumours of a new movement from the North, who read every word on the Rivonia trials over and over, who became another kind of disciple – a disciple of Freedom.

And then there was Thobela.

The Lord made the boy with a purpose, He looked at the ancestors and took a bit here and a little there and sent the child into the world with the presence of his grandfather Mpayipheli, the ability to lead, to make decisions, to see past the angles and sides of a matter and make a judgement. The Lord gave him the body of his father, tall, the same limbs that could run the Ciskei Hills with characteristic rhythmic stride, the same facial features so that many, including Thobela's own father, would mistakenly assume that the same peace-maker was inside.

But God created a predator in him, a Xhosa warrior, the Lord went far back in the bloodline, to Phalo, Rharhabe, Nquika en Maqoma, as he did with Senzeni, and gave Thobela Mpayipheli the heart of the hunter.

In early years his likeness to Lawrence fooled everyone. 'His father's son,' they said. But the son grew and the truth emerged. His father was the first to know, because he was brother to Senzeni. He knew the signs and he prayed for mercy, because he feared the consequences. He enveloped the boy with love, to create a cocoon to wrap him safely in, but that was not the Lord's will. Too late he came to realize that this was his test, this child – too late, because he failed, his wisdom and compassion failed him, his deep love for his son made him blind.

The strife began insignificantly, domestic differences between father and son, and from there, as the years advanced, it expanded like the ripples from a pebble dropped in a still pool.

And Senzeni came home to verify the rumours and their fierce hearts recognized each other, Thobela and his uncle, their mouths spoke the same language, their bodies thirsted for the same battlefields, their heads rejected the way of peace and love. And Lawrence Mpayipheli lost his only son.

'In 1976, at the time of the Soweto Riots, Thobela was fourteen years old. Senzeni came for him in the night. My brother was forbidden the house because of his influence but he crept in like a thief and took the child and phoned later to say that he would bring Thobela home when he had become a man. He had him initiated somewhere, and then took him to every place where Xhosa blood was shed. He filled his head with hate. They were away a long time, three months, and when they returned I did not know my son and he did not know me. Two years we lived like this in the rectory, strangers. He walked his own paths, quiet and secretive, as if tolerating me, waiting.

'In 1979 he was gone. The evening before he left he said goodnight, a rare occurrence, and in the morning his room was empty. The bed unslept in, some clothes missing from the wardrobe. Senzeni came and said my son had gone to the war. There was a terrible row that day. Hard words were spoken. I forgot myself. I was wounded because I could not be a father, because my brother had stolen my son. My words were to Senzeni, but I raged with God. The Lord had let my son leave me. He had drawn the dividing lines of this land and this family in strange places. He made me a man of peace and love, called me to be a shepherd and then He placed a wolf in the fold, so that I was ridiculed, so that the apostate could scorn Him – and that I could not understand.

'Only later did I see that it was my test. It was the Lord's way to humble me, to strip me of the illusion that I was more holy than others, to show me my feet of clay. But by then it was too late to save my son, too late to bring him home. Sometimes we had news, sometimes Senzeni would send a message about Thobela, how well he was, that he had been noticed, that the leaders of the Struggle recognized his character, that he had gone to foreign parts to learn to fight for his country.

'Then one evening the message came. The Security Police had taken Senzeni – to Grahamstown. For eight days they beat the life out of him and left his body as rubbish beside the road. And we never heard of our son again.'

Beyond Touws River the road shrugged off its bends and for the first time Thobela's thoughts drifted from the motorbike. He took stock of his position – the implications and what alternatives were available to him. The LCD stripes of the petrol gauge indicated that he must refuel. At Laingsburg. After that it was 200 kilometres to Beaufort West, a deadly stretch of highway through the Great Karoo, wide and straight, oppressively hot in daytime, soul-destroying at night. Expected time of arrival approximately midnight.

From Beaufort West it was another 500 or 550 to Bloemfontein – too far to reach before sunrise? Maybe not, if he pushed on, if he could manage the refuelling stops quickly.

He would have to sleep in Bloemfontein, ride into the Black township and rest somewhere while the sun shone.

The big question remained: did they know yet that he had taken the bike? Had his error of not turning off the alarm already had consequences? If the answer was 'no' he had until eight, nine o'clock tomorrow morning before the message went out. And they would have to guess his route.

But if they already knew . . .

He knew the game. He knew how fast the variables multiplied for the hunters and the prey. He knew how they would reason if they already knew. Put their money on the main route, the fastest, shortest road, use resources there because that was where the highest percentage probability lay, even if it was not more than fifty per cent. There were too many longer, lesser routes; the possibilities would drive you out of your mind.

If they knew, the N1 would be their candidate. That was why he needed to use the darkness and the lead he had on them.

He switched the beam of the lights on high, the black ribbon strung out before him, opened the throttle, the needle crept past 140, up the long gradients, 150, his eyes measuring the lighted course in front of him. How fast could he safely go at night?

Just over the crest of the next rise a valley opened up before him and the GS moved past the 160 mark. He saw the blue and red revolving lights of the law far ahead in the distance.

He grabbed at the front brakes, kicked the back brake, the ABS shuddered, intense pressure crushed his arms, kept the clutch in, for a moment he thought he would lose control, and then he had stopped in the middle of the road and there was something he still had to do, what was it, the lights, turn off the lights, searching for the switch in panic, got it, switched it off with his right thumb and suddenly he was night blind, all dark, just himself and the knowledge that they knew, that they were waiting for him, everything had changed.

Again.

12

The crime reporter of the *Cape Times* didn't know that the call would be a turning point in her life.

She would never know whether the loss of life would have been less and the outcome very different if had she taken her bag and left for home one minute earlier

She was by nature a plump woman with wide soft curves, cheerful with a broad quick smile and a hearty laugh, jolly dimples in her cheeks. If she had been more introspective, she might have wondered if she got on with people so easily because she presented no threat.

Her name was Allison Healy and when the phone rang on her desk late on a Sunday night, she answered with her usual cheery voice.

'*Times*,' she said.

'Allison, this is Erasmus from Laingsburg.' Slightly muffled, as if he didn't want his colleagues to hear. 'I don't know if you remember me.'

She remembered. The policeman had worked at the Sea Point office. They called him 'Rassie'. Burned out at twenty-eight in the fight against a declining suburb, he had transferred to more restful pastures. She greeted him happily, asking how he was. As well, he replied, as you could be in a place where the sweet blow all grew a metre high. She laughed her throaty laugh. Then the voice on the line became serious.

'Do you know about the Xhosa on the BMW?'

'No,' she said.

'Then I've got a story for you.'

*** Classified Grade One ***

Memorandum

17 November 1984 *** 19:32

Status: Urgent

From: Derek Lategan, legal attaché, Embassy,
Washington.

To: Quartus Naudé

Urgent request from CIA, Langley, Virginia:
Any possible information and /or photographic
material:

Thobela Mpayipheli, alias Tiny, alias Umzingeli.
Suspected previously Umkhonto we Sizwe,
probably current operator, Stasi/KGB.
Probably operational in UK/Europe. Black male,
2.1 m, 100 – 120 kg. No further intelligence
available.

End

Janina Mentz looked at the fax, the poor reproduction –
the handwritten note in the upper right corner was barely
legible: 'Our help with this matter could open doors. Regards.
Derek.'

She checked the cover page. 'Attachments: 1.'

'Is this all?' she asked.

'Yes, ma'am, that's all,' said Radebe.

'Where's the follow-up? Where's the answer?'

'They say that is the only reference on the microfiche, ma'am. Just that.'

'They're lying. Send a request for the follow-up correspondence. And contact details for the sender and addressee of the memorandum: Lategan and Naudé.'

Why did they have to struggle for cooperation? Why the endless rivalry and politicking? Mentz was angry and frustrated. She knew the real source was the new information, the calibre of their fugitive and their underestimation of him. This meant escalation. It meant trouble. For her and the project. And if the NIA wanted to play games, she had to get a bigger stick.

She reached for the phone and dialled an internal number. The Director answered.

'Sir,' she said, 'We need help with the NIA. They are not playing ball. Can you use NICoC influence?'

The Director, together with the Director-General of the National Intelligence Agency, the head of Military Intelligence, the head of the Police National Investigation Service and the Director-General of the Secret Service, was a member of the National Intelligence Coordinating Committee, under the chairmanship of the Minister.

'Let me phone the DG direct,' said the Director.

'Thank you, sir.'

'I am happy to help, Janina.'

She took up the fax again. In 1984 the CIA suspected that Mpayipheli was working for the KGB? In Europe?

The CIA?

Urgent request . . . Our help with this matter could open doors.

This man? This middle-aged gofer? The coward from the airport?

She pulled the transcript of the Orlando Arendse interview

from the pile in front of her. *So let me give you some advice: Start ordering the body bags now.*

Mertz took a deep breath. No reason to worry. It meant that Johnny Kleintjes knew what he was doing. He would not put his safety in amateur hands. They had underestimated Mpayipheli. She would not make that mistake again.

She used the new intelligence, ran through her strategy. More sure than ever that Mpayipheli would use the N1. A cool cat, this, self-assured, his display at the airport calculated to mislead, the smooth disarming of the agents was explained, the choice of motorbike in perspective, very clever.

But still they had the upper hand. Mpayipheli did not know that they knew.

Add to that, if things went wrong – there was always the leverage of Miriam Nzululwazi. And the child.

Mpayipheli knew that he had to get off the road. He couldn't stay where he was in the dark. Or he must turn back, find another route, but he was unwilling, his entire being rejected retreat, he must move on, to the north.

Gradually, his eyes adjusted to the darkness. He switched the motorbike on, slowly rode to the side of the highway, looked at the moonlit veld, the wire fence straight as an arrow parallel with the N1. He was looking for a farm gate or a wash under the wire and kept glancing back, unwilling to be caught in the glare of oncoming headlights. He wanted to get off and have a stretch and think.

How far ahead was that roadblock? Four or five kilometres. Closer. Three?

Thank God the GS's exhaust noise was soft. He kept the revs low, scanning the fences, and saw promise on the opposite side of the road – a gate and a two-track road into the veld. He rode over, tyres crunching on the gravel, stopped, put the bike on the stand, pulled off his gloves and checked the fastening of the gate. No padlock. He pulled the gate open, rode the bike in and closed the gate behind him.

He must get far off the road, but close enough to still see the lights.

He realized his good fortune: the GS was dual-purpose, made for tar and dirt road, the so-called adventure touring bike, spoke wheels, high and well sprung. He turned in the veld so that the bike's nose faced the highway, stopped, got off. He pulled the helmet off his head, stuffed the gloves inside, placed it on the saddle, stretched his arms and legs, felt the night breeze on his face; heard the noises of the Karoo in the night.

Blue and red and orange lights.

He heard an oncoming vehicle, from the Cape side, saw the lights, counted the seconds from when it flashed past, watching the red tail lights, trying to estimate the distance to the roadblock but it got lost in the distance, melting into the hazard lights.

He would have to turn back. Take another route.

He needed a road map. Where did his other choices lie? Somewhere there was a turn-off to Sutherland, but where? He did not know that region well. It was on the road to nowhere. A long detour? Tried to recall what lay behind him. A road sign on the left had indicated Ceres, before Touws River even, but it would take him almost back to Cape Town.

He breathed in deeply. If he must, he would go back, whether he wanted to or not. Rather a step backwards than wasting his time here.

Stretched, bent his back, touched toes, stretched his long arms skywards, cracked his shoulder joints backwards and took up the helmet. Time to go.

Then he saw the orange flashing lights from the blockade coming closer. Stared rigidly at them. Yellow? That was not the Law. A possibility whispered, he watched, filling up with hope as the vehicle approached, the noise reaching him and then it took shape, rumbled past sixty metres from where he stood and he saw the trailer clearly, the wreck being towed, a car that had rolled over and he knew it was not a roadblock, they were not looking for him.

An accident. A temporary hurdle.

Relief.

He would just have to wait.

'The problem,' said Rahjev Rajkumar, 'is that Absa only keeps the last two months' statements immediately accessible for any account. The rest are backed up on an off-line mainframe and there is no way to get in there. The good news is that that is the only bad news. Our Thobela had a transmission-savings account and a bond on a property. This is where it gets interesting. The balance in the savings account is R52, 341.89, which is quite a sum for a labourer. The only income the last two months was from Mother City Motorrad, a weekly payment of R572.72, or R2,290.88 per month – and the interest on the account, just over R440 per month. The debit order from the savings account for the bond repayment is R1,181.59. There is another debit order, for R129 per month, but I can't work out what that is for. That leaves him with R1,385.29 per month to live off. He draws R300 a week from an autobank, usually the one at Thibault Square, and it seems like the remaining R189.29 is saved. A disciplined man, this Thobela.'

'The property?' Janina prodded.

'That's the funny thing,' said Rajkumar. 'It's not a house. It's a farm.' He raised his head, looking for a reaction from the audience.

'You have our attention, Rahjev.'

'Eighteen months ago Mpayipheli bought 800 hectares near Keiskammahoek. The farm's name is *Cala*, after the river that runs there. The bond, listen to this, is just over R100,000, but the original purchase price was nearly half a million.'

'Keiskammahoek?' said Quinn. 'Where the hell is that?'

'Far away in the old Ciskei, not too far from King William's Town. Seems he wants to go back to his *roots*.'

'And the thing is, where did he get the other R400,000?' said Janina Mentz.

'Precisely, ma'am. Precisely.'

'Good work, Rahjev.'

'No, no,' said the fat Indian. 'Brilliant work.'

Thobela Mpayipheli sat with his back against a rock, watching the lights on the N1.

The night had turned cool, the moon was high, a small round ball on its way, unmarked, to score the goal of the night in the west. His gaze wandered over the desolate ridges, followed the contours of the strange landscape. They said that there had been rainforests here long ago. Somewhere around here, he had read, they had dug up the bones of giant dinosaurs that had lived between the ferns and short stubby trees, a green pleasure garden of silver waterfalls and thunderstorms that watered the reptilian world with fat drops. Weird sounds must have risen with the vapour from the proto-jungle: bellows, bugling, clamour. And the eternal battle of life and death, a frightful food chain, terrifying predators with rows of teeth and small, evil eyes hunting down the herbivores. Blood had flowed here, in the lakes and on the plains.

He shifted against the chilly stone. Blood had always flowed on this continent. Here, where man at last had shrugged off the ape, where he left his first tracks on two feet in mud that later turned to stone. Not even the glaciers, those great ice rivers that transformed the landscape, that left heaps of unsuspecting rocks in grotesque formations, could staunch the flow of blood. The ground was drenched with it. Africa. Not the Dark Continent. The *Red* Continent. The Mother. That gave life in abundance. And death as counterweight, creating predators to keep the balance, predators in all their forms, through the millennia.

And then She created the perfect hunter, the predator that upset the balance, that could not be controlled by ice ages and droughts and disease, that kept on sowing destruction, rejecting Her power and might. The two-legged predators carried out the Great Coup, the cosmic *coup d'état*, conquered all and then turned on each other, white against white, black against black, white against black.

He wondered if there was hope. For Africa. For this land.

Johnny Kleintjes – if steadfast Johnny Kleintjes could bow to temptation, led astray by the rotten stink of money, merely one of the lures of this continent, could there be hope?

He sighed deeply. More lights broke away from the cluster in the darkness, an ambulance siren wailed through the night, coming closer, gone along the road.

Not long now.

It became gradually still again. He heard a jackal howl, far over the ridges, a mockery of the ambulance.

Predators and scavengers and prey.

He was the former. *Was.*

Maybe. Perhaps there was hope. If he had looked in the mirror of his life and found it abhorrent, he who had lived his carnivore vocation so mercilessly, then there could be others like him. And perhaps that was all that was needed, one person, at first only one. Then two, four, and a handful of people to shift the scales, just a fraction of a millimetre, to reclaim Mother Africa piece by piece, foot by foot, rebuild, to give a glimmer of hope.

Maybe, if he and Miriam could take Pakamile Nzululwazi away to the Cala River, make a new beginning, away from the cycle of poverty and soulless travail, the crime, the corruption of empty foreign cultures.

Maybe.

Because nothing in this world could make Mpayipheli as he once was.

The Rooivalk helicopters chose their flight path through the tops of the cumulonimbus, the white towers majestic in the moonlight, lightning striking silver tentacles kilometres long through the system, turbulence jerking and shaking them, the green, orange and red flickering of the weather-radar screens confirming the pattern.

'Another ten minutes, then we're through,' said the pilot of Rooivalk One. 'ETA twenty-two minutes.'

'Roger, One,' answered the other.

Just over 160 kilometres east of the two attack helicopters the flight engineer of the Oryx clicked on the intercom.

'Better buckle up, Mazibuko.'

'What's up?'

'Weather system. And it looks bad.'

'How long still?' asked Tiger Mazibuko.

'Just over an hour. I hope you brought raincoats in those crates.'

'We're not scared of a little rain.'

Just wait, thought the flight engineer. *Wait till the winds begin tossing us around.*

13

Allison Healy, crime reporter for the *Cape Times*, wrote the story immediately, because the official deadline was already past.

CAPE TOWN – A manhunt for an armed and dangerous fugitive is under way after an unknown government intelligence agency alerted local police and traffic authorities along the N1 to be on the lookout for a Xhosa man travelling on a big BMW motorcycle.

No, she thought. *Too formal, too official, too crime-reporter. There's a lighter element in this story, something unique.*

CAPE TOWN – A big, bad Xhosa biker on a huge BMW motorcycle is the subject of a province-wide manhunt, after an undisclosed and top-secret government intelligence agency alerted police and traffic officials along the N1 to be on the lookout for what they called 'an armed and dangerous fugitive'.

Reliable sources told the Cape Times *the alert was posted around 22:00 last night, but the directive did not provide details about the reason Mr Thobela Mpayipheli was sought so desperately by what is rumoured to be the Presidential Intelligence Unit (PIU).*

The fugitive is allegedly in possession of two firearms and one BMW R 1150 GS, all illegally obtained. 'But

*apparently that's not the reason they want to apprehend
him,' the source said.*

Now she had to spin another paragraph or two out of the
meagre details. That was all the front page would have
room for.

The news editor stood impatiently in the doorway. 'Almost
done,' Healy said. 'Almost done.' But she knew he would wait,
because this was news, good front-page material. 'With legs,'
he had said in his cubicle when she had told him about it.
'Nice little scoop, Alli, very nice.'

When she had scurried out to begin writing he had called
after her: 'We've got a head start. When you're done, go get
us more. *Who* is this guy? Why do they want him? And what
the hell is he doing on a BMW bike, for God's sake?'

'The Rooivalks are in Beaufort West, ma'am,' said Quinn.
'They are waiting for your instructions.'

'Tell them to get some sleep. If we have heard nothing by
dawn they can start patrolling the N1 southwards. But they
must talk with us before they take off. I don't want contact
with the fugitive before we are ready.'

'Very well, ma'am.'

Janina Mentz gave him time to relay the message. She
counted hours. Mpayipheli couldn't be close yet – too early. If
he made good time on the BMW, he would be somewhere on
the other side of Laingsburg. Another two hours to Beaufort
West. Not a great deal of time.

'Is the roadblock ready at Three Sisters?'

'The police and traffic people are there already, ma'am.
They are moaning. It's raining in the Karoo.'

'They'll grumble about anything, Quinn. They know they
have to check all vehicles?'

'They know, ma'am.'

'How long before Mazibuko gets there?'
'Any time now, ma'am. Ten minutes, not longer.'

Captain Tiger Mazibuko sat with folded hands, eyes closed in the yellow-lit vibrating interior of the Oryx, but he did not sleep.

It was the dawning realization that the Reaction Unit would never come into its own that kept him awake. His team-mates were asleep. They were accustomed to the cramped uncomfortable conditions, able to snatch a few minutes or an occasional hour of sleep between events. Mazibuko too. But rest eluded him; the germ of unease over their deployment had grown since his last exchange with Mentz. He had never thought about it this way before: they were somewhere between a counter-terrorist instrument and a hostage-rescue unit, cast in the mould of the FBI Hostage-Rescue Team and the similar British group, the Special Air Service, the SAS. The Reaction Unit had been operational for thirteen months and had done nothing more than simulations and training exercises. Until now. Till they'd had to invade a drugs den like fucking blue-trouser cops and now they were to man a roadblock in this godforsaken desert to wait for a middle-aged fugitive who might once have been an MK soldier.

Maybe he should go and see his father and ask him whether, before he sold out to the Boers, before he sang his cowardly song of treason, he had known someone called Thobela Mpayipheli.

His father. The great hero of many kitchen battles with his mother. His father who beat his wife and who beat his children to breaking point because he could not live with his humiliation. Because in a Security Police cell he had broken and the names and places, the methods and the targets had bubbled out over the floor along with the spit and the blood and the vomit. And then, deliberately released, the shame shackled to his ankles defined the shuffling course of his life.

His father.

Isn't it time to move out from your father's shadow? Janina Mentz's words could not be blocked out.

Did you know Mpayipheli, father? Was he one of those you betrayed?

Since the beginning he had had visions, dreams at night and fantasies in his solitary moments. Fired up by the training and Mentz's propaganda, prospects of micro-battles, of lightning raids in dark passages, shots cracking, grenades exploding, smoke and cordite and life and death, bullets ripping through him, bursting his head, spattering his rage against the walls. He lived for that, lusted after it. It was the fuel of his zeal, his salvation, the ripping-loose from the sins of his father, the destruction of the cells of his brain with the memories, and now he wondered if it ever would happen. Mentz telling him so seriously that the world had become an evil place, presidents and countries not knowing who was friend or foe, wars that would no longer be fought with armies, but at the front of secret rooms, the mini-activities of abduction and occupation, suicide attacks and pipe bombs. September 11 was water to her mill, every statement of every radical group she held up as watertight evidence. And where did they find themselves now?

He heard a change in the note of the engines.

Nearly there.

Now they sat in a land that the world passed by. Even the terrorists were no longer interested in Africa.

The Reaction Unit, sent to man a roadblock. The world's best-trained traffic officers.

A good thing the fucker had two pistols. A pity he was alone.

*   *   *

Just after two a.m. Mpayipheli swept easily around the last bend and saw Laingsburg brightly lit ahead of him. His heart beat beneath his ribs, conscious that the dark blanket of the night was lifted. The reserve-tank light shone bright orange, leaving him no choice. He slowed down to the legal sixty, saw the big petrol station logo on the left, time to get it over with, turned in, stopped at a pump, the only vehicle at this time of night.

The petrol jockey came slowly out of the night room, rubbing his eyes.

Thobela put the motorbike on the main stand, climbed off and removed the gloves. He must get money out.

The jockey was at his side. He saw the man's eyes widen.

'Can you fill it up? With unleaded?'

The man nodded too eagerly. Something was not right.

Thobela unlocked the tank, lifted the valve.

'They are looking for you,' said the jockey, his head conspiratorially close, his voice a hoarse whisper as he placed the spout in the tank.

'Who?'

'Police.'

'How do you know?'

'They were here. Said we must look for a Xhosa on a motorbike. A Bee-Em-Double-you.'

'So what are you supposed to do?'

'I have to phone them.'

'And will you?'

'They say you are armed and dangerous.'

He looked at the man, into his eyes. 'What are you going to do?'

The attendant shrugged his shoulders, staring into the tank.

Just the noise of the fuel running in, the sweet aroma of petrol.

Eventually: 'It's full.'

The digital figures on the pump read R77.32. Mpayipheli took out two hundred-rand notes. The attendant pulled only one from his fingers.

'I don't take bribes.' He took a last look at the man in the helmet, turned on his heel and walked away.

'Masethla. NIA. I understand you need our assistance,' said the voice on the phone without friendliness or subservience.

You need our assistance. 'I appreciate you calling,' said Janina Mentz without appreciation. 'We enquired about any references to a Thobela Mpayipheli in the microfiche library and you sent a fax with a 1984 memorandum from Washington.'

'That is correct.'

'I can't believe that that is the only reference. There must have been a response.'

'Possibly. What is it about?'

'Mr Masethla, I don't see the necessity to explain that. It was an urgent official request in the national interest. We are all working for the same interest. Why can't we get the other documentation?'

'There isn't any.'

'What?'

'There isn't any other documentation.'

'You say this memorandum is all?'

'Yes.'

'I can't believe that.'

'You will have to.'

She pondered this for a moment. 'Mr Masethla, is your library complete?'

He was silent at the other end.

'Mr Masethla?'

'It is not my library. It was the Boers'. In the old South Africa.'

'But is it complete?'

'We have reason to believe that some films were removed.'

'Which films?'

'Here and there.'

'By who?'

'Who do you think, Mrs Mentz? Your people.'

'The PIU?'

He laughed at her. 'No. The Whites.'

Rage swept over her. She gripped the receiver with whitened knuckles, fighting it back, swallowing it, waiting till her voice would not betray her.

'The sender and receiver of the memorandum. I want their contact details.'

'They have left the Service.'

'I want their details.'

'I will see what I can do.'

Then she unleashed her rage. 'No, Mr Masethla. You will *not* see what you can do. You will have their details with me in sixty minutes. You will get rid of your attitude and you and your people will get to work if you don't want to become another unemployed statistic tomorrow. Do you understand?'

He took just long enough to answer for her to think that she had won this round. 'Fuck you, you white bitch,' he said. Then he put the phone down.

Captain Tiger Mazibuko was first out of the Oryx, a hand on his hat so that the rotor blast would not blow it away.

In the pitch dark he saw one white van from the SAPS and one blue and white Toyota Corolla from the Provincial traffic authority, their blue lights revolving. They were parked beside the road and a single traffic officer with a torch in his hand stood on the N1 road surface. A few orange traffic cones indicated a parking area for vehicles. The officer was flagging down an eighteen-wheeler truck.

Mazibuko swore and strode over to the police van. He saw one of the occupants opening the door. He stood directly in the opening, one hand on the roof, and leant in.

'What is going on here?' He had to shout as the engines of the Oryx were still winding down.

There were two men inside, a sergeant and a constable; each had a coffee mug. A flask stood on the dashboard. Faces looked back at him guiltily.

'We are drinking coffee – what does it look like?' the sergeant shouted back.

'Is this your idea of a roadblock?'

The two policemen looked at each other. 'We haven't got a torch,' said the sergeant.

Mazibuko shook his head in disbelief. 'You haven't got a torch?'

'That's right.'

The helicopter's motors wound down gradually. He waited until he no longer needed to shout. 'And what are you going to do when an armed fugitive on a motorbike races through here? Throw the flask at him?'

'There've been no motorbikes so far,' said the constable.

'Lord help us.' Mazibuko shook his head from side to side. Then he slammed the van's door and walked back to the helicopter. The men had disembarked and were standing waiting, their faces shining in the reflected blue lights. He barked orders about weapons and equipment and their deployment. Four men must take over from the traffic officer, four must walk a hundred metres up the road as back-up, four must put up two tents next to the road as shelter from the rain.

The truck crawled past him. The officer had not even looked in the back. Mazibuko walked to the dark figure with the torch. He saw that the two policemen were now out of the van, standing around aimlessly.

'What is your name?' he asked the traffic officer.

'Wilson, sir.'

'Wilson, would a motorbike fit in the back of that truck?'

The traffic officer was tall and impossibly thin. A floppy fringe hung over his eyes. 'Uh . . . er . . . possibly, but . . .'

'Wilson, I want you to pull your Corolla into the road here. Block off this lane. Understand?'

'Yes, sir.' Wilson's eyes glanced from Mazibuko to the helicopter and back, deeply impressed by the importance of the arrivals.

'Then tell your friends to pull their van in there, in the other lane, about ten metres further on.'

'Right, sir.'

'And then you sit in your vehicles and start the engines every fifteen minutes to keep them warm, do you understand me?'

'Yes, sir.'

'Have you got a road map of this area?'

'Yes, sir.'

'Can I look at it?'

'Yes, sir.'

Pulsating white light suddenly lit up the night around them. Thunder grumbled above, a deep sound rolling from east to west. A few drops of rain plopped on the tarred road.

'It's getting closer, sir. It's going to be a mother of a storm.'

Mazibuko sighed. 'Wilson.'

'Yes, sir?'

'You don't have to "sir" me. Call me "captain" instead.'

'Right, captain.' And Wilson saluted him with the wrong hand.

Thobela Mpayipheli saw the far-off flashes of light on the

northern horizon, but he didn't know it was the dance of light-ning. Above him the starry heavens were clear, but he didn't see them – he rode at 150 kilometres per hour, the headlights lighting the road straight ahead of him, a bright cocoon in the night, but his gaze was on the rear-view mirrors.

What had the petrol attendant done?

There was nothing behind him. They would have to drive fast to catch him. At 160 or 180 and even then the gap would not close quickly. Or they would radio ahead, to Leeu-Gamka or Beaufort West.

Probably both – a pincer movement, with him in the middle.

They knew. The Spooks from the Cape knew about him and the GS. They had guessed his route correctly.

Not bad.

And if the pump jockey had reported him, they would know he knew they knew. If the man had reported him. He hadn't been able to read his expression, that nothing-to-do-with-me attitude could have been a smokescreen.

They say you're armed and dangerous.

The pistols. That he didn't even have. Well, let them mis-calculate. But *dangerous*? What did they know? Possibilities danced through his head and he felt the tension run through his body and then Otto Müller came to visit. In the night on a Karoo road he heard the voice of the Odessa instructor, the East German with the fine, almost feminine features below a grotesque bald head, nearly twenty years past. He heard the heavy Germanic accent, the stilted English. *It is game theory; it is referred to as the Nash equilibrium. When two players have no reason to change from their chosen strategies, they continue with those strategies. The equilibrium. How do you break the equilibrium, that is the question. Not by second-guessing, because that is part of the strategy and therefore part of the equilibrium. In a game of chess, you will lose if you think only of your opponent,*

think of every option, think of every possibility. You will go crazy.
Think what you will do. Think about your strategy. Think how
you can change it. How you can dominate. How you can break
the equilibrium. Be the actor, not the reaction. That is the key.

Otto Müller. There was a bond between them; Mpayipheli
was only one of ten operators, the rest came from the Eastern
Bloc – Poland, Czechoslovakia, Romania. He was one of
the chosen and he fascinated Müller. *I have never taught a*
schwarzer *before.*

So he said *I haff never taken orders from ze whitezer before.*
Lord, he was full of fire, in those days. Müller laughed at his
put-on German accent. *You have the right – what is the words*
– attitude?

He didn't tell the Stasi man that he had been born with that
attitude, he didn't have the self-knowledge then: his *attitude*
engulfed him, his *attitude* was him, his complete being.

A month or so ago he had read in a textbook about
enzymes, very large molecules in the living cell that elicited a
chemical reaction by presenting a surface that encouraged that
particular reaction. He pondered this and found in himself
the metaphor of this biology. His whole life he had floated
through the bloodstream of the world with a surface that
encouraged violence as a reaction, until that moment when
it had made him sick, that moment when, for the first time
in thirty-seven years, he could step back from himself and see
and find it repugnant.

The difference was that enzymes could not change their
nature.

People could. Sometimes people had to.

In a game of chess, your opponent is looking for patterns of
play. Give him the pattern. Give him the Nash equilibrium. Then
change it.

But to do that he needed information.

They expected him to follow the N1. He could only change

this pattern if he knew what his options were. He needed a good road map. But where on earth could he get one?

Janina Mentz's first impulse after replacing the phone was to be with her children.

She fought it, understanding the need, understanding that Masethla's cutting words made her look for comfort, but her head said that she must get used to it, she should have known that Masethla would not like being leant on from above, would be incapable too, given their relative positions of power, of taking orders from a strong woman.

They were all like that.

Lord, why did there have to be men, why did she have to fight against their weak, brittle, fragile egos? That and the sex thing, the one-way traffic of their thoughts – if you were a woman you were prey. If you didn't give in and jump into bed you were a lesbian, if you were a woman in authority, you had slept your way to the top, if he was a man with more authority then you were screwable.

She had learned these lessons the hard way. A decade ago, after a long, frustrating and even painful realization that she would have to live with a constant stream of overt and covert innuendo and sexual advances, she had taken stock of herself and pinpointed her two major physical assets. Her large mouth, wide and full-lipped with white and regular teeth, and her bust, impressive without being excessive. She had developed a deliberate style, no lipstick, small severe steel-rimmed spectacles and hair always drawn back and fastened, outfits never too form-fitting, neutral colours – mostly grey, white and black. And her actions, interactions, communications were refined until eventually the volume of erotic interest was turned down to acceptable, manageable levels.

But about the other thing, the male ego, she could do nothing.

That was why she forced her thoughts away from her children, stood up and straightened, brushing the wrinkles from her skirt, smoothing her hair.

Rajkumar brought her a result. 'The other debit order, ma'am, the R129 per month?'

'What?' she said, not in the present right then.

'The other debit order on Mpayipheli's bank account. The clearance code . . . I ran it down. We know where the money is going.'

'Yes?'

'To the CCE. The Cape College of Education.'

'For the child?'

'No. It's a correspondence college. For adults.'

'Oh.'

'High-school education. Grades ten to twelve. Someone is doing a course with them.'

There was little new in the information. 'Thanks, Rahjev.'

Her cellphone rang. She checked the screen, which read 'Mazibuko'.

'Tiger?'

'I am letting Bravo come down from Bloemfontein. In our vehicles.'

'What for?'

'There's nothing happening here. Two policemen and a speed cop with two vehicles. There's a big thunderstorm on the way that looks bad and there are two or three roads off the N1 between here and Beaufort West and who knows how many farm roads.'

'He's on a motorcycle, Tiger.'

'I know. But if he spots the blockade and turns back, how do we pursue him?'

'With the Rooivalks.'

'In the rain?'

'How sure are you that it will rain?'

'Ma'am, it's raining already.'

'It's a five-hour drive from Bloemfontein, Tiger.'

'That's why I want them to leave at once.'

She decided. 'OK, let them come.'

'Mazibuko out.'

'Tiger?' she asked quickly.

'I'm still here.'

'Mpayipheli. He might have been more than MK.'

'More?'

'Don't underestimate him.'

'What do you mean? What have you found?'

'He . . . We don't know enough yet. Just don't underestimate him.'

'He's still only one man.'

'That's true.'

'Mazibuko out,' he said again.

Mentz pressed the 'end' button on the cellphone. Her gaze caught the fax machine printing out a document. Stepping up to it she read the heading as she waited for it to finish. *NIA.*

'Well, well,' she said softly keeping her fingertips on the paper till it finished scrolling and then picking it up.

Last known address – Derek Lategan: Orange River Wine Exports, P.O. Box 1798, Upington, Northern Cape.

Last known address – Quartus Naudé: 28 14th Avenue, Kleinmond, Western Cape.

Masethla had supplied the information. She could imagine his internal struggle, his reluctance, irritation and fear that his outburst would be reported. A small victory for her. She found no pleasure in it.

Radebe, frowning, came over the floor to her with another document in his hand. 'Here's an odd one, ma'am. This report came in from Pretoria, but we hadn't given instructions.'

She took it from him.

```
Transcript of interview by V. Pillay with Mr
Gerhardus Johannes Groenewald, 23 October, 21:18,
807 Dallas Flats, De Kock Street, Sunnyside,
Pretoria.
P:  You were on the integration team with Johnny
    Kleintjes?
G:  I was second in command.
```

'It was on my orders, Vincent.'

'Ma'am?'

'I phoned Pillay direct. Groenewald was on our records.'

Radebe looked at her, still frowning.

'I'm sorry, Vincent. I ought to have told you.'

'Ma'am, that's not it . . .'

'What is it, then?'

'I thought I knew all our agents.'

She held eye contact with him, smiling reassuringly. 'Pillay doesn't work full-time for us, Vincent. I don't want to interfere with your people.'

The frown lifted.

'Ma'am, there's something else . . .' His voice was soft, as if he didn't want the others to hear.

'Talk to me.'

'Mpayipheli, ma'am. We are treating him as a criminal.'

'He *is* one, Vincent.'

It seemed that he wanted to contradict her, but thought better of it.

'He disarmed two of our agents, refusing a legal request to hand over state property, and he stole a motorcycle.'

Radebe's gaze was distant. He nodded, but Mentz did not feel that he agreed. He turned around. She watched him thoughtfully until he sat down.

Transcript of interview by V. Pillay with Mr
Gerhardus Johannes Groenewald, 23 October, 21:18,
807 Dallas Flats, De Kock Street, Sunnyside,
Pretoria.

P: You were on the integration team with Johnny
    Kleintjes?
G: I was second in command.
P: Did you have access to the same material?
G: Yes.
P: Did you know Mr Kleintjes had made back-ups of
    certain sensitive records?
G: Yes.
P: Tell me about it, please.
G: It's ten years ago.
P: I know, Mr Groenewald.
G: Most of that data is useless now. The people . . .
    Things have changed.
P: We need to know.
G: Those were strange times. It was . . . To
    suddenly see what the enemy had on you, to show
    them what we had, it was surreal. Your enemy was
    no longer your enemy. After all those years. To
    work with them, it was difficult. For everyone.
    Both sides.
P: You worked for the National Party government,
    before 1992?
G: Yes.
P: Proceed, Mr Groenewald.
G: Some people on the team couldn't handle it. It
    was conditioning, hammered into you for so many
    years, the secretiveness, the idea of us against
    them. Stuff disappeared.
P: What sort of stuff?
G: Operational records. The kind of stuff that

individuals didn't want counting against them.
When Johnny Kleintjes realized people were
deleting stuff he began to make back-ups. We
worked together, as fast as we could. And when
one of the back-up tapes disappeared he started
taking work home.

P: Did you know what material he took home?

G: He never hid anything from me.

P: What was it?

G: There were the X-lists of the politicians,
judges and intelligence people. You know –
who is sleeping with whom, who has financial
troubles, who's in league with the opposition.
And the E-lists. 'E' for elimination. Who was
killed. Who was to be taken out next. And the
Zulu Dossier.

P: The Zulu Dossier?

G: You know, the Zulu nationalists.

P: I don't know, Mr Groenewald.

G: You must know that in the Zulu ranks there is a
conservative nucleus that still dreams of Zulu
independence?

P: Proceed, Mr Groenewald.

G: They supported the former regime's policy of
separate development. They saw it as the way
to their own sovereign Zulu state. Elements
in the old regime were only too eager to help
– promises were made, they worked intimately
together. And then F. W. de Klerk went and
cheated them by unbanning the ANC and allowing
free elections.

P: Yes?

G: The Zulu Dossier contains names of members of
the secret Organization for Zulu Independence,
the OZI. There are politicians, businessmen and

a lot of academics. The University of Zululand
was a breeding ground. If I remember rightly,
the head of the History Department was the head
of OZI for years.

P: Is that all? Just a list of OZI members?

G: No, there was more. Weapons caches, strategy,
plans. And the name of Inkululeko.

P: You'll have to explain.

G: Inkululeko. A code name. It's the Zulu word
for 'Freedom'. A member of OZI who infiltrated
the ANC years back. A mole. But high up. There
was talk that he also worked for the CIA during
the Cold War. Lately I heard a rumour that –
considering the present government's attitude
to Libya and Cuba, for example – he was still
helping the Americans.

P: Do you know who it is?

G: No.

P: But Johnny Kleintjes knows?

G: Johnny knew. He saw the list.

P: Why did he never expose it?

G: I don't know. I wondered about that. Remember
the violence in Kwa Zulu, Pillay? Remember the
political murders, the intimidation?

P: I remember.

G: I wondered if he didn't use the list as a trump
card in negotiations. You know, a sort of 'Stop
your nonsense or I will leak the list' type of
thing. The unrest decreased, later.

P: But that is rather unlikely, isn't it?

G: Yes. It is.

P: What do you think the real reason is?

G: I think Johnny Kleintjes knew Inkululeko
personally. I think he was a friend.

14

Through the lens of a hidden camera or the eyes of a voyeur the scene would have been sensual. Allison Healy sat in front of the music centre in her restored semi-detached in Gardens. She was naked. Her plump body glowed from the hot bath, the creams and oils she was massaging into her skin. The CD playing was *Women of Chicago* – Bonnie Lee, Karen Carroll, Shirley Johnson and her favourite, Lynne Jordan. Music about women's trouble with men. There was a cigarette in the ashtray on the small table next to the navy-blue easy chair, smoke trailing upwards in a tall thin column. The room was softly lit by one table lamp beside the small television.

Despite the potential an eye could find in this scene, her thoughts were far from sexual. She was considering a motorcyclist speeding through the night, a mysterious man hunted by law enforcement and intelligence officers. She wondered why.

Before Healy had left the office she had phoned Rassie Erasmus of the Laingsburg police again. Asked questions. There was mischief in their talk, as if they were co-conspirators against the Secret Forces of the state, but the chat had yielded little new information.

Yes, the request to be on the lookout had come from the regional Police Head Office. And the order to report there if they spotted something. No, it was never explicitly stated that it was the Presidential Intelligence Unit looking for Mpayipheli, but the police had their own language, their own references, their jealousies and envy. Erasmus was fairly certain that it was the PIU. And, from what he could gather, the fugitive had something the PIU were after.

'Any news on Mpayipheli, Rassie?'

'No. Not a word.'

Healy reached for the journalist's study bible – the telephone directory. There were three Mpayipelis and four Mpayiphelis listed. All in Khayalitsha or Macassar, but none had the initial 'T'. She phoned every number, aware of the late hour, knowing she would be disturbing hard working people in their sleep, but she had a job to do too.

'I am so sorry to bother you so late, but can I speak to Thobela, please?'

Every time the same response. A sleepy voice saying 'Who?'

Just to be sure, she had searched with Ananzi and Google on the Internet, typed in 'Thobela Mpayipheli' and to be thorough, 'Thobela Mpayipeli' and clicked on 'Search'.

Your search – Thobela Mpayipheli – does not appear in any documents.

So she had turned off the computer, taken her handbag, said goodbye to the few colleagues still at work and come home to a long hot bath, half a glass of red wine, her skincare routine, music and a last cigarette.

Healy rose to pack away the bottles and jars in the bathroom and returned to lie back in the chair, drawing deeply on the tobacco, closed her eyes to let Johnson's 'As the Years Go Passing By' flow over her. It evoked nostalgia in her, for Nic, for the intensity of those moments. No. Longing for a journey. To the smoky Blues bars of Chicago. To a world of pulsing, moaning rhythms, sensual voices and strange new experiences, a new uncontaminated life.

Focused on the music. Sleep was near. The prospect of a long well-deserved rest. She wasn't due back at work until noon.

Where was he now, the big, bad Xhosa biker?

Mpayipheli was two kilometres from Leeu-Gamka, the head-lights turned off, the GS standing in the veld a few hundred metres from the road. He stripped off the suit, locked it in one luggage case, put the helmet in the other and began walking towards the lights.

The night air was sharp and cool, carrying the pungent scents of Karoo shrubs crushed under his boots. The weari-ness of the last fifty or sixty kilometres had invaded his body, his eyes were red and scratchy, he was thirsty and sleepy.

No longer twenty, his body complained. He knew that he had been running on adrenalin but the levels were running low. He knew the next few hours till dawn would be the most difficult. He walked briskly to get his circulation going and his boots crunched gravel on the road verge, rhythmically. Lights from the petrol station on the right and the police station on the left of the highway came steadily closer. There was no movement, no sign of life, no roadblock or other indications of a search. Had the petrol jockey in Laingsburg said nothing? He owed him, Mpayipheli thought. It was so difficult to read people, how oddly they behaved. Why had the man not told him that he would keep quiet? Why keep him worrying? Was he still making up his mind?

He walked into the petrol station. There was a twenty-four-hour kiosk, a tiny café. Behind the counter was a black woman, fast asleep with her chin dropped onto her chest, mouth half open. He took two cans of Coca-Cola from the fridge, a few chocolate bars from the shelf. Behind her on the wall he saw the rack of road-map books.

Mpayipheli cleared his throat. The woman's eyes opened.

'Sorry, sister,' he said softly, smiling sympathetically at her.

'Was I asleep?' she asked, baffled.

'Just resting a bit,' he said.

'What time is it?'

'Just after three,' he said.

She took the cool drinks and chocolate and rang them up. He asked for a map book.

'Are you lost?'

'No, sister, we are looking for a short cut.'

'From here? There are no short cuts here.' But she took the book down from the shelf and put it in the plastic bag with the other things.

He paid and left.

'Drive safely,' she called after him and settled back on her chair.

Mpayipheli looked back once he was a little way off. He could see through the window that her head had dropped forward again. He wondered if she would remember that he'd been there, should anyone ask.

Halfway back to the bike he popped open the can of Coke, drank deeply, burped the gas, drank again. The sugar would do him good. He emptied the can and opened a Milo bar, pushing the chunks into his mouth. A white Mercedes flashed past on the highway, spoiling his night vision for a while. He put the empty can and sweet papers back into the plastic packet.

He would have to inspect the map book. He had no torch. The moon gave less light now, almost setting in the west. He should have bought a torch.

Perhaps the moonlight would be sufficient. Mpayipheli left the road, cutting across the veld, for the first time thinking of puff adders. The night was cold, so they shouldn't be active. He reached the GS and took the book out of the bag.

The routes and roads were a spider web of alternatives, spooky-looking in the dim light. He strained to see – the moon cast a shadow of his head over the page, forcing him to shift around, his eyes irritatingly close to the page. He found the right page.

There was a road from here, from Leeu-Gamka to Fraserburg.

Fraserburg?

The direction was wrong – too far west, too few possibilities. He would have to go north.

He saw that there were two additional routes from Beaufort West, snaking threads to Aberdeen in the east and Loxton approximately north-north-west. That might do. He turned to the next page to follow it. Loxton, Carnarvon, Prieska. Too far west.

Paging back, he followed the N1 to Three Sisters. The road forked there. To Bloemfontein or Kimberley. Paging on he found the Kimberley route and traced it with his finger. Promising. Many more options.

In a game of chess, your opponent is looking for patterns of play. Give him the pattern. Then change it.

'We will change it at Three Sisters, Herr Obergruppenführer,' he said softly.

He would have to fill up in Beaufort West. He would ask how far it was to Bloemfontein, what the road was like. Hopefully the Spooks would hear about it. And at Three Sisters he would take the road to Kimberley.

He took out the second can of Coke.

It was raining in the Great Karoo. The weather had rolled in over the plains, rumbling and spitting like some giant primordial predator, only visible in the night sky when lightning came searching in fantastic forms and now here it was above them, the rains of Africa, extravagant and pitiless.

Captain Tiger Mazibuko cursed, splashing through ankle-deep puddles, wiping water from his face. The rain fell in dark sheets and thunder growled continuously.

He had been checking the maps in the traffic officer's car. There were at least two side roads they would have to block. Halfway between the roadblock and Beaufort West one turned east to Nelspoort, the other was closer, forking west to Wagenaarskraal. Unfamiliar routes, but alternatives available to a fugitive. And they had too few men and too few vehicles. He would have to deploy four RU members; the police van would have to drop them off, minimizing the effect of his roadblock here. They would have to guard the roads in pairs. They would be on foot, while Mpayipheli had a motorbike. Visibility was terrible in this weather. It was a fucking fiasco. But that was typical. Backward. Everything was backward. You could say what you liked about the Americans, but if the FBI Hostage unit had been here, it would have been four-wheel drives and armoured vehicles and helicopters. He knew because he had been there, in Quantico, Virginia, for four months, he had seen it with his own eyes. But no, in Africa things worked differently, here we fucked up. *Here we potter around with a bloody bakkie and a Corolla and a frightened traffic cop and two Boers who worry about their caps getting rained on and just one fucking middle-aged Xhosa on a motorbike, jissis, couldn't the fucker get a more respectable form of transport, even the bad guys are backward in Africa.*

Mazibuko shook his fist at the heavens, which for a moment were still. He screamed his frustration, an uncanny sound, but the rain drowned it.

He pushed his head into the tent. Four soldiers looked dumbstruck at him.

'I have to send you out,' he said, calm and under control.

The early hours began to take their toll in the Ops Room, urgency had leaked away.

Janina Mentz struggled to decide whether or not to send people to Derek Lategan and Quartus Naudé tonight.

They didn't have to cooperate. They were retired agents, had taken the package, were probably not well disposed to the present Government. A visit at this time of night would just complicate matters. She weighed that against the need for information. What could they contribute? Could they confirm that Mpayipheli had worked for the KGB? What difference would that make to the investigation?

Let it wait, she thought. She looked up at the big chart of Southern Africa on the wall.

Where are you, Mpayipheli?

Are you on the N1? How strong is your motivation? Are you sleeping somewhere in a hotel room while we make the wrong assumptions about you?

No. He was out there, somewhere; he couldn't be far from Mazibuko now. Contact. That was what they needed to shake off the lethargy, to regain momentum, to be in control again.

Contact. Action. Control.

Where was Thobela Mpayipheli?

She stood up. There was another job to do.

'May I have your attention, everyone,' she said.

Unhurried, they turned to her.

'This time of night is always the worst,' she said. 'I know you've had a long day and a long night, but if our calculations are right, we can finish this before eight o' clock.'

There was little response. Blank faces gazed back at her.

'I think we must see how many people we can relieve for an hour or two. But before we decide who is going to take a nap, there are some who wonder why we regard this fugitive as a criminal. I can understand why.'

Bloodshot eyes looked back at her. She knew that she was making no impression.

'But we must also wonder where all that money came from. We must remember that he worked for organized crime.

Remember that he hired out his talents for the purpose of violence and intimidation. That he stole two firearms, after rejecting the chance to work with the State. See the nature of the man.'

Here and there a head nodded.

'We must be professional. There are too many gaps in our knowledge, too many questions unanswered. We have a very good idea now of what is on that hard disk. And that news is not good. We are talking about information on a mole at the highest level, code name "Inkululeko". We are talking about very, very sensitive information that can cause untold damage in the wrong hands. Our job is to protect the State. Sympathy has no place in this. If we put everything into the balance, there is only one choice: be professional. Keep focused. Look at the facts, not at the people behind them.'

Mentz looked over the room.

'Have you any questions?'

No reaction.

But no matter. She had planted the seed. She had to force herself not to look up at the ceiling where she knew the microphones were hidden.

15

Mpayipheli's thoughts roamed freely, for this road did not require much concentration. He thought of this and that, knowing he must get some sleep but not wanting to waste the darkness. Somewhere beyond Three Sisters, once the sun was up, he would find a screened and shaded place in the veld for a few hours' rest. He was familiar with the landscape of sleep deprivation, knew that the greatest danger was poor judgement, bad decisions. His thoughts jumped around – who were the Spooks pursuing him, how desperate were they, what was the whole purpose, the stuff on the disk that cast a hex over him?

In one month's time Pakamile would be finished with Grade One. They could leave the township – how long had they been talking of this?

Miriam didn't want to. She always wanted to stick to the known, afraid of change. Like she had been with him, when he had started courting her. When he had first seen her, that time in the investment consultant's office, her hands, such deft, slim hands, her grace and pride had been like a beacon to him. She wasn't even aware of him, but he could barely hear what the man was saying, so strongly had she consumed him. He had been in love before, now and then, sometimes lust, sometimes more than that but never absolutely right, never like it was with Miriam and she wanted nothing to do with him at first. The father of her child had put her off men, but he couldn't think of anything but her, lord, to be in love like a teenager at his age, sweaty palms and heart beating haywire when he sat with her in Thibault Square in the bright sun and watched the cloud on the mountain grow and shrink and grow and tried to hide the longing, afraid to scare her, his desire to touch her, to hold her hand, to press her against him and say 'I love you, you belong to me, let me keep you safe, I will chase away your fears like an evil spirit, I will cherish you, hold you and honour you'.

He had to wait a year before he could make love to her, a year, twelve months of sighs and dreams, not at all what he had expected, soft and slow, quenching, and later his fingers on her body, no longer a young woman's body, found the traces of motherhood and he was overwhelmed with compassion, his hands traced the marks in awe at this thing that she had accomplished, the life she had created and carried and borne, in her and on her she carried the fullness of her vocation and he could only trace it with his fingertips, so conscious of his incompleteness, so filled with the urge to find his own.

How would he tell her of the land that he had bought? He already knew how she would react, how she clung to the things she had control over, because there was so much she could not control. The battle she had fought to get where she was, in her house with her son, had been so long, so hard in a world of poverty and violence. Her work, her house, her daily routine, it was her sanctum, her shield, her very survival.

One Saturday he had looked up from the mathematics textbook he was studying and decided that today was the day. She had her needlework in her hands, he had turned down the radio and told her that in that time when he had stared into his own eyes his urge had been to get away, to go back to where he came from, to continue his life's journey back to the source, to begin again, a new life. To build something with his own hands – hands that had broken – perhaps a house, with his sweat and muscle and concentration, a place to live.

To dig his fingers into the ground, to turn the earth and to plant and grow. He began to search and weeks later he found it in the Cala Valley, a beautiful place where the mist rose up against the mountain slopes in winter, where as far as the eye could see the veld was an undulating green of fertility, Xhosa country, the landscape of his youth and his people.

He had been on his way, busy with the final arrangements, when Miriam had crossed his path, and now, months later the urge remained. But he could no longer do it alone, for he no longer was alone. He asked her to come with him. Her and Pakamile. They would take the child out of this harsh world and show him his heritage, let him learn other values, give him a carefree youth. There were schools there, in town, where he would get his education. She wouldn't have to work. It would be just the three of them – he could provide, he *would* provide, he would build this new life for them.

Miriam was quiet for a long time, the needle and thread moving rhythmically in her hands. Then she said she needed to think about it, it was a big decision and he nodded, grateful that she would at least consider it, that her first answer had not been 'no'.

The lightning brought Mpayipheli back – it seemed that there was rain up ahead. He looked at the odometer: another sixty to Beaufort West. The fuel gauge was below half. The eastern horizon was changing colour, he had to make town before daybreak to refuel. He opened the throttle, 160, feeling the tiredness in his body, 170, he checked the figures on his digital watch, 04:43, the night was nearly over, he had not come very far and there was a long way to go today. Kimberley – if he could get there he could get a plane, 180, perhaps to Durban, to break the pattern, from Durban to Maputo, Maputo to Lusaka or something, but keeping flexible, 190, be adaptable, get this thing over and then go back, so Miriam would see that he would never desert her, 200, the white lines on the road flew past, too fast, he had never gone so fast. Yes, the new day was a red ribbon in the east.

Two more vehicles arrived, an Opel Corsa and an Izuzu bakkie, policemen climbing out stiff-legged, pulling their raincoats tight around their bodies, irritated by the early call-out and the rain. They walked over to Mazibuko.

'The sergeant called over the radio to say that he has dropped off your men.'

'I know. We have radio contact. Where's the sergeant now?'

'They have gone home. Their shift is over.'

'Oh.'

'The road will get very busy once it's light – are you stopping everything?'

'Just the necessary. Are you here to help?'

'Yes.'

'Then you must shift your vehicles.'

'How?'

He directed them. He wanted a formation that would make running the roadblock impossible. They followed his instructions, pulling their vehicles into the road, while he waded through puddles to the helicopter and pulled open the door. The flight engineer lay asleep in the back with his mouth agape. The pilot was up front, awake.

'Do you have a weather report?' asked Mazibuko.

'Yes,' said the pilot. 'Rain. Any minute now.' He smiled broadly at his own joke.

'The rest of the day?'

'The system will move east. It will clear in the afternoon.'

'Fuck.'

'You can say that again.'

Mazibuko pulled his cellphone from under his jacket and punched in a number.

'How far are you?' he asked.

'Just beyond Richmond,' said Lieutenant Penrose, second in command of the Reaction Unit.

'You must shift.'

'We are driving as fast as we can, captain.'

'Is it raining there?'

'Not yet, but we can see it coming.'

'Fuck,' said Tiger Mazibuko.

'You can say that again,' mumbled the pilot in the Oryx.

The consignment of Cape newspapers landed in a pile on the desk of the news editor of the SABC's morning television programme in Auckland Park, Johannesburg – yesterday's *Argus* and this morning's *Burger* and *Cape Times*. It was one of his moments of truth every morning: how well the news team in the south had fared against the opposition, but also a window to another strange world: ships sinking in storms, Muslim extremists, gangs in the Cape Flats, the ongoing political circus.

More NNP leaders cross over read the *Burger*'s headline in Afrikaans. No surprises there. Nor in the rugby analysis: *Skinstad: We have no excuse*. He overlooked the usual manipulative Christmas Fund article and skipped to the last front-page story, of a thirteen-year-old cricket protégé. Mmmm. Country story, from Barrydale. He circled it with a thick red marker for follow-up.

Pulled the *Times* from the stack. *New alliance for province?* the headlines cried. And *There goes the Rand again*. Then his eye fell on the third front-page story. *Spooks seek big bad BMW biker. By Allison Healy*. He read it.

'Molly,' he called, but there was no response.

'Molly!'

A face appeared at the door.

'Get that asshole in the Cape on the line. Right now.'

'Rooivalk One, this is Ops Control, come in, over.' There was urgency in Quinn's voice. He waited for a moment, had no reaction. He made sure that the frequency on the digital panel was correct, called again. 'Rooivalk One, this is Ops Control, come in, over.'

'This is Rooivalk One, Ops Control. What have you got for us? Over.' The voice was a little sleepy.

'We have contact, Rooivalk One. Repeat, we have contact. Subject is four minutes out of Beaufort West on the N1 on the way to Three Sisters. We want you in the air. Do you read me? Over.'

'We read you, Ops Control, we read you. Rooivalk One and Two operational. Over.'

'What is your expected time of interception, Rooivalk One? Over.'

'Expected time of contact ten minutes, Ops Control, repeat, ten minutes. Over.'

Quinn clearly heard the big engines being started up in the background. He spoke louder automatically. 'We just want to chase him on to Three Sisters, Rooivalk One. We want presence, but no contact. Do you understand? Over.'

'No contact, Rooivalk One confirming, no contact.'

The pitch of the engines hit high. 'Are you aware of the weather status, Ops Control? Over.'

'We know it's raining at Three Sisters, Rooivalk One. What is your situation? Over.'

'The rain is threatening, Ops Control, there's a helluva system up north. Over.'

'Rooivalk One and Rooivalk Two on the way, Ops Control. Over.'

'We will keep contact, Rooivalk One, the channels stay

open. Report when you intercept. Ops Control over and out.'

'Roger, Ops Control. Rooivalk One over and out.'

Quinn leaned back and looked around. Janina Mentz was busy on the cellphone with Tiger Mazibuko. The few people who had rested since four a.m. were back at their posts. There was a tingling in the air. The Ops Room was awake.

Allison Healy was dreaming of her mother when the phone rang. The dream was an argument, a never-ending disconnected fight over nothing, and she was relieved by the sound. In her dream she lifted the instrument to answer but it continued ringing.

She made a noise, a groan of reluctance to rise out of her deep sleep, sitting half upright in bed, the sheet falling away to reveal her rounded nakedness to the room.

'Hello.'

'Allison?' It was the voice of a colleague, she couldn't place which one.

'What?'

'Are you awake?'

'Sort of.'

'You had better come down here.'

'What's going on?'

'There's a shoeshine man downstairs. He wants to talk to you.'

'A shoeshine man?' She wondered if she was awake.

'He's a friend of your big bad Xhosa biker.'

'Oh shit,' she said. 'I'm coming.'

16

Mpayipheli had drunk coffee and swallowed an uninteresting sandwich at the petrol station while the attendant had filled up the GS and he had asked how far it was to Bloemfontein and if there were police on the road. He had tried to look like an 'armed and dangerous' fugitive but had no idea if anyone would take the bait. The jockey was as jumpy as a cat in a dog run, but that meant nothing and now the dark bank of clouds hung in front of him, twenty, thirty kilometres away and the road stretched out ahead of him, the light washing the Karoo in pastels. He rode fast, 185, because he wanted to pass Three Sisters on his way to Kimberley before they could react and the caffeine had awakened anxiety that he should have felt since Laingsburg. If they knew he had taken the motorbike and knew he was on the N1, why had there been no attempt to stop him, why were they not waiting for him?

Never mind, he thought, never mind. He was here and he had done all he could to establish Bloemfontein as his destination and all he could do now was ride as hard as he could, try 200 kilometres per hour, in daylight perhaps it would be less terrifying. He kicked down to fifth and twisted the ear of the great machine, feeling the vibration of the two flat cylinders, the Boxer engine, strange name. He was consumed with urgency, anxiety – where were they, what were they up to, what were they thinking? And when he heard the thunder, his first instinct was that it came from the heavy clouds up ahead but the noise was continuous and his heart turned cold. It was an unnatural thunder and then a dark thing swept over him, a huge shadow whose noise drowned out the Boxer beneath him and he knew they were here; he knew what they were up to.

Miriam Nzululwazi was rinsing Pakamile's porridge bowl in the kitchen. She missed Thobela, he was the one who brought good humour to the morning, before him it had been a silent, almost morbid rush to be ready before the school bus came and she had to catch the Golden Arrow to the city. Then the man had come, the man who swung his feet off the bed at the crack of dawn with a lust for life, who made the coffee and carried the fragrant steaming mugs to the bedrooms, singing all the way, not always in tune, but his deep voice buoyed up the house in the morning.

She had said that the boy was too young for coffee but Thobela had said he would make it especially weak. She knew that hadn't lasted long. She had said she didn't want to hear that Afrikaans radio announcer in her house, but he'd said that he and Pakamile couldn't learn to be farmers by listening to the music of Radio Metro every morning. They listened to the weather forecast and the market prices and talks on farming topics and the child was learning another language too. He kept Pakamile on the go with RSG when the boy dawdled, saying, 'Pakamile, it's raining on the farm,' or 'The sun is shining on the farm today, Pakamile, you know what that means?' And the boy would say, 'Yes, Thobela, the plants are growing with chlorophyll' and he would laugh and say, 'That's right, the grass is getting green and sweet and fat and the cattle are going to swish their tails.'

This morning Miriam had switched on the radio to compensate for Thobela's absence, to restore normality. She listened to the weather forecast from habit, wanting to shake her head, here was Miriam Nzululwazi listening to Afrikaans, Thobela had changed so many things, she must go and see how far along with his preparations Pakamile was. 'Pakamile, have you brushed your teeth?'

'No, ma.'

'It's going to be hot on the farm today.'

'Oh.' Uninterested. He too was missing Thobela. The time signal sounded on the radio, time for the news, she must hurry. The newsreader's sombre voice sounded through the house: America in Afghanistan, Mbeki in England. The Rand had dropped again.

'Don't dawdle, Pakamile.'

'Yes, ma.'

Petrol was going up. Thobela would always talk back to the announcers and newsreaders, would always say when petrol prices were announced each month, 'Get to the diesel price, Pakamile and I have a tractor to run' and then he and the boy would grin at each other and Pakamile would mimic the Afrikaans word *trekker*, rolling the 'r's that drew out each end of the word.

'According to a Cape newspaper intelligence authorities are hot on the trail of a fugitive, Mr Thobela Mpayipheli, who allegedly stole a motorcycle in Cape Town and is thought to be heading—' She ran to the kitchen and snapped off the radio before Pakamile could hear. Stole a motorcycle, stole a motorcycle, Thobela? Her hands trembled; her heart beat in her throat.

What had he done?

In the Ops Room the voice of the pilot came clearly over the speakers. 'Rooivalk One to Ops Control. We have intercepted. Thirty kilometres outside Beaufort West, fugitive on a yellow motorcycle, estimated speed 200 kilometres per hour, this guy is sending it. Over.'

They applauded, the entire room, punching the air, shouting. Janina Mentz smiled broadly. She had been right, but mostly she felt relief more than anything else – enormous relief.

'Ops Control to Rooivalk One, we hear you, interception verified. Just stay behind him, Rooivalk One. Do not attempt contact.'

'Confirm no contact, Ops Control. We are just chasing him on.'

'Ma'am . . .' said Radebe, but over the applause she couldn't hear him.

'Ma'am?'

'Vincent?'

'The vehicle team say we must get hold of a *Cape Times*.'

'Why?'

'They say there are posters all over town, ma'am.'

It took an effort to change gears, to make the shift and understand what he was saying. 'What do they say, Vincent?' the anxiety in her voice quickly silenced the entire room, only the radio static hissed.

'They say *Spooks Seek Big Bad Biker*.'

It was like a blow to her chest.

'Will you get us a paper, Vincent?'

'Yes, ma'am.'

'Quinn, tell Mazibuko the Subject is on his way, he must confirm contact with him. Rahjev . . .'

'Yes, ma'am?'

She looked up at the bank of television screens on the wall. 'Put on TV2 for us. And eTV. And please ask someone to monitor the radio news.'

'OK, ma'am.'

The police. She knew the leak came from the police.

Luckily this thing was almost over.

*   *   *

The helicopter flew low over Mpayipheli, its dark belly scarcely a hundred metres above his head, and then it swooped back behind him and when he looked around he saw that there were two of them, side by side, predatory birds biding their time behind him. He could feel the vibrations of their great engines in his body, the adrenalin ran thickly in his veins, the accelerator was fully open but he knew it was in vain, these things were much faster. A truck came from ahead. The driver, his eyes disbelieving, nearly swerved in front of him. Why were they hanging back?

The speedo pointer was just beyond 200, the cloud bank loomed. Oncoming traffic had windscreen wipers and lights on, he began to hope – how deep was this weather, how hard was it raining, would the helicopters follow him in? He wanted to pass a car, the driver confused by the tremendous noise from above, brake lights, oh God, here's trouble, he swerved just in time, spray hit the helmet visor, shit, he was going too fast, he saw the rain ahead, a dense curtain, spatter became drops, hard to see, dying to lift a hand and wipe but at this speed . . . A truck in front of him, he couldn't maintain this speed, couldn't see, he braked, closed the throttle, then the rain hit, sheets, gusts, the drops hard and stinging on his body, the truck's tyres spurting up plumes of mist, he couldn't see oncoming cars, slower, slower, at last wiped his visor, just rearranging the water patterns. The rain was harder now, African rain, the lorry moved over, he went down a gear, accelerated, past but not fast, visibility was terrible, what to do, and then he realized the helicopter's noise was fading, they were no longer with him.

'My name is Immanuel,' he said to Allison Healy. 'I'm the shoeshine man.'

She put out her hand to him. 'Hullo, Immanuel.'

'I get the *Cape Times* every morning. I fetch my lot at the back here, I sell them. And when I have set out all my stuff, then I read it because there are not many clients so early.'

'I understand,' she said patiently.

'So this morning I read about Thobela.'

'Mpayipheli?'

'He is my friend. And the things you wrote about him are not right.'

'What do you mean?'

'He is not a *big bad biker*.'

'Uh . . . It's just a way of writing, Immanuel.'

'But it's not true. He's a good man. He's a war veteran.'

'A veteran?'

'That's right. He was a soldier in the Struggle. He fought in lands far away. Russia and Germany.'

'MK?'

'He fought for all of us.'

'You say he was an MK fighter?' This was news. Big News.

Immanuel just nodded.

'Why did he steal the motorcycle?'

'That's not true. Thobela doesn't steal.'

'How do you know, Immanuel?'

'I know him. He's my friend. We talk three, four times a week. He is an honest man. A family man.'

'He has a family?'

'It's the most important thing in his life. Why would he steal?'

'Where can I find his family?'

'It's impossible, Ops Control, visibility is too poor. Heavy turbulence. We have to turn back. Over.' Static crackled on the radio connection, the voice breaking up.

Quinn looked to Janina Mentz. She shook her head, he translated. 'Negative, Rooivalk One, stay with him. Over.'

'Ops Control, visibility is zero. We don't know where "with him" is. We don't even have visual contact with each other. These are non-operational conditions. Over.'

Quinn looked at Janina. She stood with folded arms, her lips thin. 'How many million rand did it cost to develop these machines? And they can't fly through rain.'

Quinn waited.

'Tell them to turn around. Tell them to make sure he doesn't go back.'

Her cellphone rang in her pocket. She looked over the bank of televisions where the country's channels were flickering, early-morning cartoons, local news, sport, CNN, the voices and music whispering. On TV2 the newsreader was talking. Behind him was a graphic of a man on a motorbike.

Cellphone rang.

Rahjev Rajkumar touched a panel and the sound filled the room . . . *Somewhere in the Western Cape on a stolen motorcycle. Considered to be armed and dangerous, it is not clear why authorities are seeking Mr Mpayipheli at this time.*

She felt like swearing. She picked up her phone.

'Mentz,' she said grimly.

'Ma, Lien says I'm fat,' said her daughter in a whingeing tone.

Mpayipheli crept forward at fifty kilometres per hour, the leather gloves were sodden, his hands cold although he had turned on the electric heaters in the handgrips. His biggest problem was seeing the road ahead, the inside of his helmet steamed up and rain poured down the outside, the road was slippery. How to see the traffic ahead in time, the urge for speed and distance gnawing at him, at least the helicopters were quiet, but he knew they were out there somewhere, he had to get away.

They must want him very badly to use that sort of technology.

Johnny Kleintjes, what is on that hard disk?

They had waited for daylight, patient and easy, like a cat for a mouse, waited for the early morning, knowing he would be tired, knowing the helicopters were excessive, that they would intimidate and conquer.

They were not fools.

The helicopters had stayed behind him.

Like dogs herding a sheep.

Into the pen.

They were waiting for him. Somewhere up ahead they were waiting.

Allison Healy's finger ran down the pages of the phone book, found *Nzululwazi*, found *M. Nzululwazi, 21 Govan Mbeki Avenue*, scribbled the number down in her notebook, pulled the phone closer and dialled.

It rang.

A war veteran. A family man. A good man.

Still rang.

What was going on here? Why were they after him?

Ring, ring, ring. There was nobody home.

Time to ring Laingsburg again. Perhaps there was news.

17

Seventeen kilometres south of the Three Sisters roadblock the gravel road turned west off the N1, an insignificant branch going nowhere, merely a connection that ended in a T-junction at the normally dusty route between the forgotten villages of Sneeukraal and Wagenaarskraal.

Two soldiers were standing nearly 300 metres from the tar road where the police van had dropped them off at the bend of the first turn. Little Joe Moroka and Koos Weyers were dry under their plastic raincoats but the cold had seeped through their camouflage uniforms. Their faces were wet; water ran down the barrels of the R6 assault rifles and from there streamed down to the ground.

In the hour before dawn they had talked about sunrise and the light that would bring relief, but the rain still poured down. The only improvement was the visibility extending another forty or fifty metres to expose the low thorn trees and Karoo veld, the stony ridges and pools of mud.

It was twenty-four hours since they had slept, if you could even count that restless dozing on the Oryx. Their exhaustion was showing in the feebleness of their legs and the red scratchiness of their eyes, in the dull throbbing in their temples. They were hungry. Conversation ran to a fantasy of hot, sweet coffee, sausage, egg and bacon and toast with melting butter. They could not agree on the necessity for fried mushrooms. Moroka said fungus was snail food; Weyers responded that when taste was at issue sixty million Frenchies couldn't be wrong.

They did not hear the motorbike.

The rain was a soundproof blanket. The exhaust of the GS fluttered softly at the low revs needed for the muddy road. The soldiers' senses were dulled by weariness and tedium and their voices drowned the last chance of warning.

Later, when Little Joe Moroka gave his full report in the face of the spitting fury of Captain Tiger Mazibuko, he would attempt to break down and reconstruct each moment. They should not have stood so close to each other. They should not have been talking, should have been more alert.

But there were some things you could not plan for, such as the fact that the fugitive had lost control. The straight just before the corner had a good surface where the bike would have accelerated; the turn would have been sudden and unexpectedly sharp. And just in front of them it was muddy, thick snotty porridge where a boot would sink twenty centimetres deep. The rider had followed the contour of the road formed by the regular traffic but in the mud the front wheel had lost its grip at the critical moment.

They saw him – saw the light over the predatory beak of the monster machine and heard the engine when it was right in front of them, an apparition. Moments, fractions of moments within which the senses register, signals are sent, the brain interprets and searches via a network of tired synapses for the right reaction in the memory banks of endless training.

On reflection Little Joe Moroka would will himself to react faster, but in the real moment he registered the simultaneous snicking of safety catches as he and Weyers reacted in unison, conditioned by training, the motorbike sliding, iron and steel colliding with Weyers. The rider falling away from the machine, Moroka staggering, slipping, falling on his back, finger in the guard of the R6 pulling the trigger unwilled, shots in the air, rolling, jumping up. The shoulder of the Fugitive driving into his midriff, falling again, winded. 'Captain, that man, I don't know how he did it, I saw him fall, I saw him falling over the front of the bike on the right of Weyers, but when I stood up he hit me, he was so fast . . .'

'He's fucking forty years old,' Mazibuko would scream at him, the commander's face centimetres from his.

Rain in Moroka's eyes, gasping for air, boots kicking for grip to get up, the rider on top of him, bashing him in the face with the helmet, pain coursing through him. The man grabbed Moroka's firearm, pulled, jerked and twisted it from his grip. Blood, his blood against the front of the helmet, then the barrel of the R6 in his eye and he could only lie there in the mud until the man pushed up the helmet visor and said 'Look what you're making me do.' He heard Weyers groaning, 'Joe.' Weyers calling him but he could not turn his head to his mate. 'Joe?' A weird expression on the face of the man above him, not anger – sorrow, almost. 'Joe, I think my leg is broken'.

'Look what you made me do.'

The digital radio at Tiger Mazibuko's hip came to life and he heard an unexpected word: 'Hello.' Immediately temper flamed up in the tinder of his frustration and discomfort and exhaustion.

'Alpha One receiving and why the fuck aren't you using radio protocol? Over.'

'What is your name, Alpha One?' He didn't know this voice. It was deep, strange.

'This is a military frequency. Please get off the air immediately, over.'

'My name is Thobela Mpayipheli. I am the man you are looking for. Who are you?'

It was a bizarre moment, because there was joy in it, tempered with a sudden deep apprehension. He knew something had happened to one of his teams, but that would take some level of skill. It would take a worthy opponent.

'My name is Captain Tiger Mazibuko,' he said. 'And I am talking to a dead man. Over.'

'No one needs to die, Captain Tiger Mazibuko. Tell your masters I will do what I have to do and if they leave me alone there will be no blood. That is my promise.'

'Who did you steal that radio from, you bastard?'

'They need medical help here, west of the N1, the Sneeukraal turn-off. Your men will tell you that the serious injury was an accident. I am sorry for it. The only way to avoid that is to avoid confrontation. I am asking you nicely. I don't want trouble.'

A wonderful thing happened in Tiger Mazibuko's head as the meaning of the man's words was assimilated and processed, like tumblers falling into place. The end result was the synaptic equivalent of an explosion of white fire. 'You're dead. You hear me, you're dead.' He ran towards the nearest vehicle. 'You hear me, you cunt, you fuckin' shit.' No, the helicopter. He spun around. 'If it's the last thing I do, you're gone, you cunt, you fuckin' dog.' The helplessness of the distance between them was driving him insane. 'Get this thing going, now,' he told the pilot. 'Da Costa, Zongu, get everybody,' he shouted, 'now.' Back to the pilot: 'Get this fucking chopper in the air.' He touched the weapon at his belt, the Z88 pistol, jumped out of the helicopter again, ran to the tent, pulled open a chest, grabbed the R6 and two spare magazines, ran back, the Oryx engines were turning, Team Alpha came running, he held the radio to his lips. 'I'm going to kill you, I swear as God is my witness I'm going to kill you, you fucking piece of shit.'

Like a condemned man, Rahjev Rajkumar read the words on www.bmwmotorrad.co.za to the whole room, knowing that the tidings he brought would not be welcome. 'At home all around the world. Adventures are limitless with the BMW R 1150 GS, whether on hard surfaces, pistes or gravel tracks. Uphill and downhill, through valleys and plateaus, forests and deserts – the R 1150 GS is the perfect motorcycle for every adventure.'

'He can ride dirt roads,' said Janina.

The people in the Ops Room were quiet, the murmur of voices from the television bank suddenly audible.

'It's my fault,' she said. 'I take responsibility for this one.'

She ought to have made sure. She should have had questions asked. Should never have accepted the conventional idea.

She walked over to the big map of the country hanging on the wall, she checked the distance between the turn-off and the roadblock. It was so near. She had been right. About everything. Mpayipheli had taken the N1. He was an hour later than she had predicted but he was there. But for the rain . . .

She looked at the great stretches of the North-West Province.

What now? Mpayipheli's choices multiplied with every thin red stripe that represented a road, no matter what the surface. Even with Team Bravo in action there were simply too many holes, too many cross roads and junctions and turnoffs and options to cover.

What to do now?

She needed a hot bath, needed to wash the night out of her hair and scrub it from her body. She needed new clothes and fresh make-up. A good breakfast.

Her gaze wandered to the final destination. Lusaka.

She knew one thing. He had turned west. Written off the direct route through Bloemfontein. She traced a new line. Through Gaborone, Mmabatho, Vryburg and Kimberley.

That was the strongest possibility.

The storm had saved Mpayipheli, but now it was his enemy. They knew the weather system was 200 kilometres wide but he could only guess. He had fallen on the gravel road, not too skilled. He would have to ride slowly in the mud, carefully. He would consider his choices. He would wonder where they were. He would look over his shoulder for the helicopters; check the road ahead for soldiers. He was tired and cold and wet. Sore from the fall.

Five, six hundred kilometres to Kimberley. How fast could he go?

Mentz checked her watch. Of the seventy-two hours twelve had passed. Sixty remaining. Six, seven, eight hours to reach Kimberley. A lot could happen in that time.

She looked around at the waiting faces throughout the room. Anxious. Tired. Chagrined. They needed rest, to regain their courage. A hot shower and a hot breakfast. Perspective.

She smiled at the Ops Room. 'We know where he is, people. And he has only one place to go. We'll get him.'

At the T-junction Mpayipheli nearly fell again. As he braked sharply the motorbike slid and he had to wrench his body to stay upright. Pain focused in his shoulder. The signpost opposite him said Loxton to the left, Victoria West to the right. He hesitated for long seconds, wavering. Instinct made him turn left because it was the only unpredictable option he had, kept moving, the events that lay behind him rested heavily on him, he would have to check the map again.

He would have to sleep.

But it was raining, he couldn't just park in the veld and lay his head down, he needed a tent.

The dirt road was bad, the surface unpredictable, where it dipped it was easy to expect the soft mud, he kept to the middle. His hands were freezing, his head dull now that the adrenalin had worked out of his system. He wanted to defer thinking about the two soldiers and his own deep disappointment when he picked up the motorbike and got going again, fleetingly surprised at the lack of damage, at the engine that sprang to life at the first turn, taking off with back wheel waggling in the sodden ground. He was disappointed with himself, about the incredible hatred that had come over the radio but he didn't want to think of that now.

Mpayipheli made a list of his problems. They knew where he was. They would count his options on a map. They were using the army, unlimited manpower, helicopters. Vehicles? He was weary, a deep fatigue, his shoulder muscles were damaged or badly bruised, his knee less so. He had been driven from the highway, the fast route was denied. It was raining.

Lord, Johnny Kleintjes, what have you got me into? I want to go home. Add that to the list, he had no stomach for it; he wanted to go home to Miriam and Pakamile.

He saw the homestead from the corner of his eye. To the left of the road, a ruin between stony ridges and thorn trees that suddenly made sense. It altered the predictable, offered a solution and rest. He pulled at the brakes carefully, turned around slowly and rode back to the two-track turn-off. The gate lay open, ramshackle and neglected. He went slowly up the rocky track, the handlebars jerking in his grip. He saw the cement reservoir and the windmill, the old house, windows filled with cardboard, walls faded by the Karoo sun, tin roof without guttering, the water running off in streams. He rode round to the back and stopped.

Did anyone live here? No sign of life, but he remained on the bike, hand on the accelerator. No washing on a line, no tracks, no vehicle.

He turned the key, switched off the engine and clipped open the helmet.

'Hullooooo . . .'

Just the sound of rain on the roof.

He climbed stiffly off and put the bike on the stand, careful to prevent it tipping over in the soft ground. Pulled off the sodden gloves and the helmet.

There was a back door, paint long since peeled away. He knocked, the sound was hollow, 'Hello,' an antique doorknob, he turned it, was the door locked, put his good shoulder to it, pushed, no luck.

He walked around, checking the road, no sound or sign of traffic.

No door on that side, walked back, tried to peer through a window, through a crack between cardboard and frame but it was too dark inside. He went back to the door, turning the knob, bumped hard with his shoulder again, a bang and it swung wide open. A field mouse scurried across the floor, disappearing into a corner; the smell was of abandonment, musty.

The small coal stove against the wall had once been black, was now dull grey, the handle of the coal scuttle broken off. A dilapidated cupboard, an iron bedstead with a coir mattress. An ancient wooden table, two plastic milk crates, an enamel basin, dust and spider webs.

For a moment Mpayipheli stood there, considering. The motorbike could not be seen from the road. Nobody had been here in weeks.

He made up his mind. He fetched his bag from the bike, closed the door properly and sat down on the mattress.

Just for an hour or two. Just for the worst fatigue.

He pulled off the leathers and boots, found warm clothes in his bag, shook the worst dust from the mattress and lay down with the bag as his pillow.

Just an hour or two.

Then he would study the map and define his options.

The news that the fugitive had outmanoeuvred the helicopters and the roadblock, that one Special Forces soldier was being flown to Bloemfontein by helicopter spread through the law-enforcement community like a bushfire. By the time Allison Healy contacted her source in Laingsburg it had garnered the baroque embellishments of a legend in the making.

'And he is ex-MK,' Erasmus told her with relish. 'He's a forty-year-old has-been, fucking up the spies left, right and centre.' His tone was such that she could have no doubt that the police were enjoying every minute of the drama.

'I know he's a war veteran,' she said, 'but why are they after him?'

'How did you know that?' Erasmus was hungry for more gossip.

'I had a visitor. An old friend. Why are they chasing him?'

'They won't say. That's the one thing the fuckers won't say.'

'Thanks, Rassie, I have to go.'

'I'll phone you if I hear something more.'

Allison put the phone back in her bag and walked in to the Absa offices in the Heerengracht. At the Enquiries desk she had to wait in line. The newest information milled in her head. The phone rang again.

'Allison.'

'Hi, Allison, my name is John Modise. I do a talk show for SAFM.'

'Hi, John.'

'You broke the story about the black guy on a motor-cycle.'

'Yes.'

'How would you like to be on the show this morning? Telephone interview.'

She hesitated. 'I can't.'

'Why not?'

'It would compromise my position, John. You are opposition media.'

'I understand, but your next edition is only tomorrow morning, a lot can happen . . .'

'I can't.'

'Did you know this guy was Umkhonto we Sizwe?'

'I did,' she said with a sinking heart. Her lead was disappearing. 'How did you find out?'

'My producer got it from the Beaufort West police. He slipped through their fingers just an hour ago.'

Now they were all singing like canaries.

'I know.'

'You see? It's public knowledge. So there's no harm in being on the show.'

'Thanks, but no, thanks.'

'OK, but if you change your mind before eleven, you call me.'

'I will.'

It was Allison's turn at the desk. 'Hi,' she said. 'I'm looking for a Ms Miriam Nzululwazi. She works here.'

18

'I am finished with all these things. I am finished with fighting, with the violence, with shooting and beating and hate. Especially the hate. Finished,' Mpayipheli said.

That was in the hospital in Milnerton, beside the bed of his white friend Zatopek van Heerden, the two of them swathed in bandages, full of medication and pain and the shared trauma of a strange and violent experience that he and the ex-policeman had gone through together by sheer chance. That was while he worked for Orlando Arendse. He had felt an inner glow, a Damascus experience of a new life vision, pumped up by the *lucidum intervallum*. Van Heerden had stared expressionless at him, just his eyes betraying a hint of empathy.

'You don't believe I can change?'

'Tiny, it's hard.'

Tiny. That was his name. He had rejected it in the metamorphosis, part of the process of killing off the past, like a snake shedding its skin and leaving it behind as a ghostly reminder. He had become Thobela. It was his christening name.

'If you can dream it, you can do it.'

'Where do you get that populist crap?'

'Read it somewhere. It's true.'

'That's Norman Vincent Peale or Steven Covey, one of those false prophets. Great White witch doctors.'

'I don't know them.'

'We are programmed, Tiny. Wired. What we are, we are, in sinew and bone.'

'We are growing older and wiser. The world is changing around us.'

Van Heerden was always excruciatingly honest. 'I don't believe a man can change his inherent nature. The best we can do is to acknowledge the balance of good and evil in ourselves. And accept. Because it's there. Or at least the potential for it. We live in a world where the good is glorified and the bad misunderstood. What you can do is to alter the perspective. Not the nature.'

'No,' he had said.

They left it there, agreeing to differ.

When he was discharged and left the white man behind in the hospital, he said goodbye with so much enthusiasm for reinventing himself, on fire for the new Thobela Mpayipheli, that Zatopek had taken his hands and said 'If anyone can do it, you can.' There was urgency in his voice, as if he had a personal stake in the outcome.

And now he was lying on a dusty, musty coir mattress in the middle of the Karoo and sleep eluded him because the scene with the two soldiers played over and over in his head. He sought the singularity, the moment when he had regressed, when that which he wanted to be had fallen away. The high blood of battle risen so quickly in his head, his hands so terribly ready to kill, his brain clattering out the knowledge of the vital points on the soldier's body like machine-gun fire, despairing, *don't, don't, don't,* fighting with himself, such deep disappointment. If Pakamile could see him, Miriam, how shocked she would be.

'Look what you made me do.' The words had come out before they were formed; now he knew it was displacement of blame – he needed a sinner, but the sinner lay within. Wired.

What could you do?

If Van Heerden was right, what could you do?

They went to visit Van Heerden once, he and Miriam and Pakamile, on a smallholding beyond Table View, at a small white house – his mother lived in the big white house. A Saturday afternoon, the family from the townships picked up at the taxi rank in Killarney, Van Heerden and Thobela chatting straight off, the bond between them as strong as it always is for people who have faced death together. Miriam was quiet, uncomfortable, Pakamile's eyes wide and interested. When they arrived Van Heerden's mother was there to sweep the child away: 'I've got a pony just for you.' Hours later when he came back the boy's eyes were shining with excitement, 'Can we have horses on the farm, Thobela, please, Thobela?'

The attorney, Beneke, was also there. She and Miriam had spoken English, but it wouldn't work, lawyer and tea lady, the gulf of colour and culture and three hundred years of African history gaped in the uneasy silences between them.

Van Heerden and Mpayipheli had made the fire for the braai outside. He stood by the fire, he told stories of his new job, of motorbike clients, middle-aged men looking for remedies for male menopause and they had laughed by the burning *rooikrans* logs, because Thobela had a talent for mimicry. Later, when the coals were glowing and Van Heerden was turning the sausages and chops with a practised hand, he had said to his friend, 'I am a new man, Van Heerden.'

'I'm glad.'

He laughed at the other man. 'You don't believe me.'

'It's not me who must believe, it's you.'

They hadn't visited like that again. Rather he and Van Heerden went somewhere to eat and talk once a month. About life. People. About race and colour, politics and aspirations, about the psychology that Van Heerden had begun studying intensely to try and tame his own devils.

He sighed, turned onto his back, the shoulder aching more now. He had to sleep; he had to get his head clear.

What could you do?

You could walk away from circumstances that brought out the worst in you. You could isolate yourself from them.

The hatred in Captain Tiger Mazibuko's voice over the radio. Pure, clear, sheer hate. He had recognized it. For nearly forty years it had been his closest companion.

It's not me who must believe, it's you.

It took Allison nearly fifteen minutes to convince the Xhosa woman that she was on Thobela's side. The set of Miriam's mouth remained stern, her words few, she evaded questions with a shake of the head, but finally gave in: 'He's helping a friend, that's what. And now look what they're doing.'

'Helping a friend?'

'Johnny Kleintjes.'

'Is that the friend's name?' Allison did not write it down, afraid to intimidate the woman. Instead she memorized it feverishly, repeating the name in her head.

Miriam nodded. 'They were together in the Struggle.'

'How is he helping him?'

'Kleintjes's daughter came around yesterday evening to ask Thobela to take something to him. In Lusaka.'

'What did she want him to take?'

'I don't know.'

'Was it a document?'

'No.'

'What did it look like?'

'I didn't see it.'

'Why didn't she take it herself?'

'Kleintjes is in trouble.'

'What sort of trouble?'

'I don't know.'

Allison drew a deep breath. 'Mrs Nzululwazi, I want be sure I've got this straight, because if I make a mistake and write something that is not true, then I and the newspaper are in trouble and that won't help Thobela. Kleintjes's daughter came to your house yesterday evening, you say, and asked him to take something to her father in Lusaka?'

'Yes.'

'Because her father is in trouble?'

'Yes.'

'And Thobela agreed because they are old comrades?'

'Yes.'

'And so he took the motorcycle . . .'

The tension and confusion was too much for Miriam. Her voice broke. 'No, he was going to take the plane, but they stopped him.'

For the first time the reporter saw the stubbornness in the light of deep worry and put her hand on the other woman's thin shoulder. For a moment Miriam stood, stiff and humiliated, before leaning against Allison, letting her arms fold around her. And then the tears ran freely.

For two hours Janina Mentz slept on the sofa in her office, a deep dreamless sleep until the cellphone's alarm went off. Her feet swung to the ground immediately and she stood up with purpose, the brief rest a thin buffer against fatigue and tension, but it would have to suffice. She showered in the big bathroom on the tenth floor, enjoying the tingling water, the scent of soap and shampoo, her thoughts going on to the next steps, laying out the day like a map.

She pulled on black trousers and a white blouse, black shoes, wiped the steam from the mirror, brushed her hair, made up her face with deft movements of fingers and hands and walked first to her office for the dossiers and then to the Director's door.

She knocked.

'Come in, Janina,' he called, as if he had been waiting for her.

She opened the door and entered. He was standing at the window, looking out over Wale Street towards the provincial government buildings and Table Mountain behind. It was a clear and sunny morning with the flags across the street waltzing lazily in the breeze.

'I have something to confess, sir.'

He did not turn. 'No need, Janina. It was the rain.'

'Not about that, sir.'

When he stood etched against the sky like that his hunchback was obvious. It was like a burden that he carried. He stood so still as if too tired to move.

'The minister has phoned twice already. She wants to know if this thing will become an embarrassment to us.'

'I am sorry, sir.'

'Don't be, Janina. I am not. We are doing our job. The minister must do hers. She is paid to handle embarrassments.'

She placed the dossiers on the desk. 'Sir, I involved Johnny Kleintjes in this.'

He did not move. The silence stretched out between them.

'On March seventeenth this year a Muslim extremist was arrested by the police on charges of possession of unlicensed firearms. One Ismail Mohammed, a leading player, probably a member of Pagad, Quibla and/or MAIL. He repeatedly requested a meeting with a representative of the intelligence services. We were fortunate that the police approached us first. I sent Williams.'

The Director turned slowly. Mentz wondered if he had slept last night. She wondered if it was the same shirt he was wearing yesterday. His face betrayed no weariness.

He walked over to the chair behind his desk, not meeting her eyes.

'Here is the full transcript of the interview. Only Williams, the typist and myself know about this.'

'I am sure you had a reason for not showing me this, Janina.' Now for the first time she could see that he was tired, the combination of inflection and body language and the dullness in his eyes.

'Sir, I made a choice. I think you will eventually agree that it was a reasonable choice.'

'Tell me.'

'Mohammed had information about Inkululeko.'

It was a moment she had waited a long time for. He showed no reaction, said nothing.

'You know there have been speculations and suspicions for years.'

The Director seemed to sigh as if releasing internal tension. He leaned back in his chair. 'Do sit down, Janina.'

'Thank you, sir.'

She pulled the chair closer, drawing a breath before proceeding. But he held up a small hand, the palm rose-coloured, the nails perfectly manicured.

'You kept this from me because I am under suspicion.' Not a question, a mild statement.

'Yes, sir.'

'Was that the right thing to do, Janina?'

'Yes, sir.'

'I think so, too.'

'Thank you, sir.'

'No need to thank me, Janina. It is what I expect from you. That is how I have taught you. Trust no one.'

She smiled. It was true.

'Do you think it necessary now for me to know everything?'

'I think you need to know about Johnny Kleintjes.'

'Then you may tell me.'

Janina Mentz considered a while, collecting her thoughts. The Director would know of Inkululeko's history back through the 1980s when the rumours in the leaders' circle of the ANC were put down to counter-intelligence maliciously planted by the Regime to damage the unity between Xhosa and Zulus in the organization. But even after 1992 the rumours persisted, the violence in Kwa-Zulu, the Third Force. And since the '94 elections there'd been the feeling that the CIA were too well informed.

She tapped the dossier in front of her. 'Ismail Mohammed says in the interview that Inkululeko is a senior member of the Intelligence arm. He says he has proof. He says Inkululeko is working for the CIA. Has been for years.'

'What proof?'

'Not one big thing. Many small ones. You know the Cape Muslim extremists have connections with Ghadaffi and Arafat and Bin Laden. He says they deliberately fed disinformation into the system here and watched things unfold in the Middle East. He says there is no doubt.'

'And we must assume that they have decided to remove Inkululeko by giving us information.'

'We must consider that possibility at least, sir.'

He smoothed his tie slowly as if removing imagined wrinkles. 'I think I understand now, Janina. You fetched Johnny Kleintjes out of retirement.'

'Yes, sir. I needed someone credible. Someone who would have had access to the data.'

'You sent him to the American consulate.'

'Yes, sir.'

'He was to tell them that he had data he wanted to sell. And if it had been me I would have told Johnny to use the September 11 attacks as motivation. Something like "I can no longer sit back and watch these things happen while I have information that can help you."'

'Something like that.'

'And the name of Inkululeko as an afterthought, an incidental extra?'

She merely nodded.

'So that they can know we know. Clever, Janina.'

'Apparently not clever enough, sir. It may have backfired on us.'

'I would guess that you had a few names you wanted to experiment with, a few possible Inkululekos? To test reactions?'

'Three names. And a lot of harmless information. If the Americans said the data was nonsense we would know that he was not one of those three. If they paid, we would know we were on target.'

'And my name was one of them.'

'Yes, sir. After Johnny's visit to the consulate, the CIA reacted as we expected. They told Johnny not to make direct contact again, that the building was being watched. *Don't call us, we'll call you.* I arranged for his phone to be monitored. A week ago they called, a smokescreen for a meeting in the Gardens at the Art Museum. There they asked Johnny to take the info to Lusaka.'

'What went wrong, Janina?'

'We think Johnny used his own initiative, sir. We think the hard disk he took was empty. Or filled with pointless data.'

'Johnny Kleintjes,' said the Director with nostalgia. 'I think he did not completely trust you, Janina.'

'It's possible. It took a lot of persuading to get him to go along. The three names . . .'

'He knows all three.'

'Yes, sir.'

'And he does not believe any one of the three is Inkululeko.'

'That's right.'

'Typical of Johnny. He would want to check things through first. But with an escape route if the Yanks got serious.'

'I suspect Thobela Mpayipheli has the real hard disk.'

'The one you prepared.'

'Yes, sir.'

'And you do not want that data to reach Lusaka.'

'I thought we would stop Mpayipheli at the airport. I wanted to send the disk with one of my own people. That is still the plan.'

'More control.'

Mentz nodded. 'More control.'

The Director pulled open a drawer in the big desk. 'I too have a confession, Janina,' he said lifting out a photograph, a dog-eared colour snapshot. He held it out to her. She took it carefully, holding it up to her eyes with her fingertips gripping lightly the edge of the faded card. The Director, young – easily twenty years ago. He had his arm around a tall broad-shouldered black youth, supple and muscular, regular features, a strong line to mouth and chin, determined. In the background was a military vehicle.

'Dar es Salaam,' said the Director. '1984.'

'I don't understand, sir.'

'The other man in the photo is Thobela Mpayipheli. He was my friend.' There was a faint smile lingering on the small Zulu's mouth.

A chill swept over her. 'That is why you let the Reaction Unit come.'

He looked up at the ceiling, his thoughts in another time. She waited patiently.

'He is a ruthless man, Janina. A freak of nature. He is . . . he was only seventeen when he enlisted. But they picked him out from the start. While the others had general infantry training in Tanzania and Angola he was sent with the elite to the Soviet Union. And East Germany. The KGB fell in love first, and kept us up to date with his training. The Germans pinched him. They knew . . .'

'That's why there is no record.'

The Director was still somewhere in the past. 'He was everything they needed. Dedicated, intelligent, strong, mentally too. Fast . . . He could shoot, ah, Tiny could shoot . . .'

'Tiny?'

A dismissive gesture. 'That is a story in itself. But above all he was unknown in their world, a wild card that the Americans and Brits and even Mossad knew nothing of. A Black unknown, a brand new player, an unrecorded assassin with the hunger . . .' The Director pulled himself back to the present and his eyes focused slowly on hers.

'They bought him from us, Janina. With weapons and explosives and training. There was one small problem. He was unwilling. He wanted to come back to South Africa, to shoot Boers and blow up the SADF. His hate was focused. They sat with him for nearly two weeks, trying to explain that he would make a contribution, that the CIA and MI5 were hand in glove with the Boers, that war against one was war against the others. Two weeks . . . until they turned his head.'

Mentz pushed the photo back across the desk. She met the Director's gaze and they sat, staring, testing, and waiting.

'He makes me think of Mazibuko,' she said.

'Yes.'

'Was he the so-called "Umzingeli"?'

'I don't know the whole story, Janina.'

She stood up. 'I can't afford to let him reach Lusaka.'

The Director nodded. 'He is the sort of man who will retrieve Johnny and the data.'

'And that would not do.'

'No, that would not do.'"

Silence descended between them as each considered the implications, till the Director said: 'I want you to know that

I am going home for some rest. I will be back later. Will you be sending the usual team to watch me?'

'It will be the usual team, sir.'

He nodded wearily.

'That is good.'

19

The editor of the *Cape Times* looked at the rounded figure of Allison Healy and thought once more: if she could lose ten or fifteen kilograms . . . She had a sensuality about her. He wondered if it was the curves, or the personality. But there was a beautiful slender woman somewhere inside there.

'. . . And nobody else knows about this Johnny Kleintjes, which gives us a great angle for tomorrow's story. I've got his address, and I will get an interview with the daughter. And this afternoon, we'll get a pic of Mrs Nzululwazi and the boy. Exclusive.'

'Right,' said the editor, wondering if she was a virgin.

'But there's more, chief. I know it. And I want to use this radio show to put some bait in the water. Stir the pot.'

'You're not going to leak our scoop, are you?'

'I'm going to be all coy and clever, chief.'

'You're always coy and clever, Allison.'

'Fair enough,' she said and he laughed.

'Just make sure you plug the newspaper. And if you can let it slip that we will be revealing a lot more tomorrow morning . . .'

Self-assured, at ease, Janina Mentz sat at the big table.

'Can you hear us, Tiger?' she asked.

The entire room listened to the captain's voice as it came over the speakerphone. 'I can hear you.'

'Good. What is your status?'

'Team Bravo has arrived with our vehicles. We expect the Oryx back any moment and another is on the way from Bloemfontein.' She could hear the impatience in Mazibuko's voice, the suppressed anger.

'What's the weather doing, captain?'

'It's not raining so hard any more – the Air Force says the system is moving east.'

'Thank you, Tiger.' She went to stand alongside Vincent Radebe. 'We have established beyond reasonable doubt that Thobela Mpayipheli was an MK member who received specialized training in the Eastern Bloc. There are still some details outstanding but he is a worthy opponent, Tiger. Don't be too hard on your team.'

Just hissing on the line, no response.

'The point is, he is not an innocent citizen.' Mentz looked pointedly at Radebe, who boldly met her stare.

'He knows how serious we are about that data and he did not scruple to use violence. He chose confrontation. He is dangerous and he is determined. I hope we all understand this.'

Some heads nodded.

'We also know now that the data he is carrying is of an extremely sensitive nature for this government and especially for us as an intelligence service. So sensitive that you have the right to use any necessary force to stop him, Tiger. I repeat: any necessary force.'

'I hear you,' said Captain Tiger Mazibuko.

'In the next half-hour I shall be requesting the mobilization of the available manpower from the army bases at De Aar, Kimberley and Jan Kempdorp. We need more feet on the ground. There are too many possible routes to watch. Tiger, I want you centred in Kimberley, so that you can respond quickly. Given the background of the Fugitive, we will need a concentration of highly mobile well-trained men when he makes contact again. Let the police and the army watch the roads. I will ask that the entire Rooivalk Squadron be moved to Kimberley on standby.'

'How certain are you of Kimberley?' Mazibuko's voice came back over the ether.

She thought a little before answering. 'It's an informed guess. He's tired, he's wet, hungry and the rain is slowing him down. He hears the clock ticking and his time running away. Kimberley is the closest to a straight line between him and Botswana and he will see Botswana as freedom and success.'

She saw one of Rahjev Rajkumar's people whispering in his ear.

'Is there something, Raj?'

'Radio programme, ma'am. SAFM.'

'Any questions?' She waited for reaction from Radebe and Mazibuko.

'Mazibuko out,' said the captain over the speakerphone. Radebe sat and stared at the digital instruments before him.

'Switch on, Raj,' she said.

. . . Joined by Allison Healy, crime reporter from a Cape Town newspaper, who broke the saga of the big, bad Xhosa biker in her newspaper this morning. Welcome to the show, Allison.

Thanks, John, it is a privilege to participate.

You have interesting new information about our fugitive motorcyclist?

I have, John. We have information that casts a new light on Mr Mpayipheli's motivation, and it seems this is something of a mercy mission. His motive, it seems, might just be noble.

Please go on.

I'm afraid that's about all I can say, John.

And how did you get that information, Allison?

From a source very close to him. Let's call it a love interest.

'Quinn,' said Janina Mentz with suppressed rage.

'Yes, ma'am?'

'Bring her in.'

He looked bewildered.

'Miriam Nzululwazi. Bring her in.'

'Very well, ma'am.'

. . . On the side of the fugitive?

It is not for me to choose sides here, John, but there are two things that I find puzzling. According to information provided to the police by what is allegedly the Presidential Intelligence Unit, Mr Mpayipheli stole the BMW motorcycle. But that seems to be untrue. No charges were laid with the police, there is no theft investigation and I spoke to the owner of the dealership just five minutes ago, and the truth is that Mr Mpayipheli left a note behind, saying he had no choice but to borrow the machine, and will pay for the privilege. That does not sound like theft to me.

And the second thing, Allison?

The Cape Times *broke the story more than five hours ago, John. If the fugitive is guilty of anything, why has the government not stepped forward to set the record straight?*

I see where you are going. What do you think is happening here?

I think the Government is once again trying to cover up, John. I wouldn't be surprised if some form of corruption or something similar is involved. I'm not saying that's it. I'm just saying I will not be surprised. I'm working on several new leads, and the Cape Times *will have a full story tomorrow morning.*

Thank you very much, Allison Healy, crime reporter of a Cape-based newspaper. This is John Modise and you are turned to SAFM. The lines are open now, if you have an opinion on the matter, please call us. And remember, the subject this morning is the fugitive motorcyclist, so let's stick to that . . .

'Monica Kleintjes,' said Janina. 'We will have to bring her in, too. Before the media flock to her door.'

'Right, ma'am,' said Quinn. 'But what about her telephone, if they call again from Lusaka?'

'Can you redirect the line here?'

'I can.'

Janina's thoughts were jumping around. How had the Healy woman got that information? How had she made the connection between Mpayipheli and Nzululwazi? What could be done to slow her down?

. . . Pretoria Chapter of the Hell's Angels. Good morning, Burt.

Good morning, John. What we want to know is where the man is. Do you have information?

We know he was in the vicinity of Three Sisters at six o'clock this morning, Burt. Where he is now is anybody's guess. Why are you asking?

Because he's our brother, man. And he's in trouble.

Your brother?

All bikers are part of a greater brotherhood, John. Now, you may have heard a lot of untruths about the Angels, but I can tell you, when one of our brothers is in trouble, we help.

And how do you think you will be able to help?

Any way we can.

Rajkumar made a deprecating sound and turned the volume down. 'All the worms are creeping out of the woodwork,' he said.

'No,' said Janina. 'Leave it on.'

Mpayipheli dozed shallowly, fitfully crossing the border of sleep, dreams and reality mixing. He was riding the GS down infinite roads, feeling the faint vibration of the bike in his legs, talking to Pakamile, hearing the rain on the roof of the cottage and then the sucking sound of tyres in the mud, an engine at low revs, but only really woke to the bang of a car door. He rolled off the mattress and continued rolling up to the wall beneath the window.

★　　★　　★

Anonymous from Mitchell's Plain, go ahead, you are on the air.

Hello, John, can you hear me?

You are on the air, go ahead.

I'm on the air?

Yes, anonymous, the whole country can hear you.

Oh. Well. I just wanted to say this Mpayipheli is not the hero you make him out to be.

We are not making him into a hero. We are letting the facts speak for themselves. What have you got for us?

I don't know if it is the same guy, but there was a Thobela Mpayipheli working for a drug dealer in Mitchell's Plain. Big black man. Mean as a scrapyard dog. And they were saying he was ex-MK. They used to call him 'Tiny'.

Working for a drug gang?

Yes, John. He was what we call an 'enforcer'.

'We', anonymous? Who are 'we'?

I used to be a drug dealer in the Cape Flats.

You were a drug dealer?

Yes.

In Mitchell's Plain?

No. I worked from the Southern Suburbs.

Sounds like a franchise business. And what does an 'enforcer' do, anonymous?

He makes sure the dealers pay the supplier. By beating them up or shooting them. Or their families.

And Mpayipheli worked as an enforcer for a supplier?

He worked for the biggest supplier in the Peninsula at the time. That was before the Nigerian Mafia came to town. These days, they run the show.

The Nigerian Mafia? We must have you back for a radio show all of your own, anonymous. So what made you quit dealing?

I did time. I'm rehabilitated now.

There you have it. Strange but true.

This is a strange country, John, believe me.
Amen, brother.

Mpayipheli lay on the floor, breathing the dust. Footsteps sounded as if they were circling the motorbike. Then a voice called.

'Helloooo . . .'

Instinctively he looked around for a weapon, cursing himself for not keeping the soldier's assault rifle. He could break a leg off the table. He stopped one stride away. No more violence, no more fighting. Implications ran through his mind. Did this mean that the journey was over – could he go home? It meant that Johnny Kleintjes was fucked; he stood in limbo between instinct and desire.

'Hello the house . . .' A man's voice. Afrikaans. Was it the farmer?

His hands hung by his sides, but were clenching open and shut.

'Thobela?' He heard the voice say his name. 'Thobela Mpayipheli?'

Soldiers, he thought. Adrenalin flowed in his veins. One step to the table. He grabbed one wooden leg in his hands and pressed his foot against the table top. *No*, said his mind, *no, let it be over.*

Go ahead, Elise, what is your take on this unfolding drama?

Two things, John. Firstly, I don't believe this drug business at all. Why is it that people always want to drag someone down the moment they hit the limelight? Secondly, I am the secretary of the Pretoria BMW motorcycle club, and I just want to say we don't need the Hell's Angels to act on our behalf. Mr Mpayipheli is riding a BMW, and if anybody helps him, it will be the BMW motorcycle fraternity. I don't know how the Hell's Angels with their Harleys are going to travel on the gravel roads of the Northern Cape.

So the fugitive is a member of a BMW club?

No, John, but he rides a BMW.

And that gives you ownership.

We don't own him, John. But neither do the Hell's Angels.

What's this about gravel roads?

Mr Mpayipheli slipped through the roadblocks by travelling on gravel roads. He's on a GS, you know.

And what is a GS?

It's an on-road/off-road motorcycle.

Like a scrambler?

No. Yes, I suppose you could call it a scrambler with a thyroid condition.

Ha. Now there's *the quote of the day. How do you know he slipped through a roadblock?*

It is all on our website, John.

Your website?

Yes. www.bmwmotorrad.co.za. We have inside information.

And just how is your website getting inside information?

Oh, policemen ride BMWs too, you know.

'I'm coming inside, Thobela – don't shoot. I'm your friend.'

Don't shoot. They still thought he was armed.

'I'm on my own, Thobela, be nice.'

The door opened.

'I'm on your side, my brother.'

He waited the space of a single heartbeat and dropped his shoulder in readiness.

'I can't get it,' said Rahjev Rajkumar. The web browser showed an error message: *The page cannot be displayed. The page you are looking for is currently unavailable. The Web site might be experiencing technical difficulties, or you may need to adjust your browser settings.*

'Motorrad has two "r"s,' said Vincent Radebe softly.

'How do you know?' said Rajkumar nastily.

'It's German for "motorcycle".'

Rajkumar typed in the new address. This time the website loaded. At the top, under the page title, were the words: 'FOLLOW THE GS FUGITIVE – AN INSIDE STORY'.

Mpayipheli stood with his feet apart, shoulder lowered, the internal battle raging, knowing it was his moment of truth, knowing that this was where he would win or lose – on so many levels.

The door swung slowly wider. The voice was soft and soothing. 'I am a man of peace.'

A coloured man, dressed in tattered suit, anonymous grey shirt and a bowtie that could have been red in a previous era. His eyes were wide and his hands held up in front of him protectively.

'Who are you?'

'I am Koos Kok,' he said very carefully. 'You won't kill me now, hey?'

'How do you know my name?'

'Just one look at that big motorbike. You are all over the radio. The *big, bad Xhosa biker*.'

'What?'

'Everyone is very excitable about you.'

'What are you doing here?' Mpayipheli straightened up.

'I was lonely for my winter house,' Koos Kok said, motioning at the cottage. 'I came to keep myself warm.'

They had a roadblock at Three Sisters, manned by an army unit, some SAP and traffic authorities, and a big helicopter. They also had some Rooivalk attack helicopters at Beaufort West, who tried to follow the GS, but the rain forced them back, Rajkumar read aloud from the website and he wondered why fate had singled him out to be the bearer of bad news.

'Shit,' said Quinn.

'Go on,' said Janina.

Apparently, the GS took a side road, presumably the Sneeukraal turn-off, and went through a two-soldier roadblock, hurting one badly. Then he disappeared. That is all I have at the moment.

The only way we can help this guy is if all BMW owners in the country unite. We must all gather at Three Sisters and try to find him. That way, we can help him get through to wherever he is going.

'They want to help him,' said Quinn.

'Who wrote that?' asked Janina.

'*An Insider.* That is all they say.'

'Fucking policeman,' said Quinn and saw Janina's disapproving eye. 'I beg your pardon, ma'am.'

'Is there any more?' she asked Rajkumar.

'There are a few messages from guys who say they are going to help.'

'How many?'

He counted. 'Eleven. Twelve.'

'Not many,' said Quinn.

'Too many,' said Janina. 'They'll get in the way.'

'Ma'am,' said Vincent Radebe.

'Yes?'

He held out the phone to her. 'The Director.'

She took the receiver. 'Sir?'

'The Minister wants to see us, Janina.'

'In her office?'

'Yes.'

'Shall I meet you there, sir?'

We have time for one more call. Burt from the Hell's Angels, you back again?

Yes, John. Two things. We don't ride Harleys. Well, a few

members do, but only a few. And this thing that the black guy belongs to the BMW people is bullshit.

Let's watch the language, Burt. This is a family show.

I'm sorry, but they're nothing but a bunch of fair-weather, breakfast-run weekend wannabe bikers.

What happened to the great brotherhood of motorcycle riders, Burt?

Real bikers, John. Not these Beemer sissies. That Mpheli . . . Mpayi . . . that guy out there is a real biker. A war veteran, a warrior of the road. Like us.

And you can't even say his name.

20

They got two ministers for the price of one.

The Minister of Intelligence was a woman, lean, as fitted her office, a 43-year-old Tswana from the North-West province. The Minister of Water Affairs and Forestry sat in the corner, a grey-haired white man, an icon of the Struggle. He said not a word. Janina Mentz did not know why he was there.

The Director and Mentz sat down in front of the desk. Janina glanced briefly at the Director before she began to speak. He indicated with a minimal nod that she must hold nothing back. She filled in the background first: the Ismail Mohammed interview, the counter-intelligence operation, and the things that had gone wrong.

'Have you seen the TV news?' asked the Intelligence Minister coldly.

'Yes, Minister.' Resignedly. Not for the first time did Janina wonder why politicians were more sensitive about TV than newspapers.

'Every half-hour there is something new over the radio. And the more they talk, the more he becomes a hero. And we look like the Gestapo.' A dainty fist emphasized the words on the wood of the desktop, her voice rising half an octave. 'This cannot continue. I want solutions. We have a public-relations crisis. What do I tell the President when he calls? And he will call. What do I say?'

'Minister . . .' said Janina.

'Two agents at the airport. Two Rooivalk helicopters and a whole brigade at Three Sisters and you don't even know where he is.'

Janina had no answer.

'And everyone wonders why the Rand falls and the world laughs. At Africa. At bungling, backward Africa. I am tired of that attitude. Sick to death of it. This cabinet –' the Minister stood up, too angry to sit, her hands bracketing the words '– labours night and day, battling the odds, and what support do we get from the civil service? Bungling. Lame excuses. Is that good enough?'

Janina stared at the carpet. The Minister drew a deep breath, collected herself and sat down again.

'Minister,' said the Director in his soft, diplomatic tones, 'while we are speaking frankly, may I place a few points on the record? This is the first well-planned counter-intelligence operation we have attempted and may I say it is high time. It is not only necessary, but also ingenious. Creative. Nothing that has happened has jeopardized the purpose of the mission. On the countrary, the longer this develops, the more genuine it will look to the CIA. Granted, things haven't unfolded as planned, but that is the way life goes.'

'Is that what I must say to the President, Mr Director? That is the way life goes?' Her tone was sarcastic and cold.

The Director's tone echoed hers: 'Minister, you know that shifting blame is not my style, but if the members of the police service were loyal to the collective State, the media would not be having a field day. Perhaps we should place the blame where it belongs: at the door of the Minister of Safety and Security. It is high time he sorted this out.'

'This operation is my responsibility. My portfolio.' The Minister had calmed down, but the mood was fragile.

'But the behaviour of another Department is jeopardizing

the operation. Undermining it. We don't shrink from taking our punishment, but it must be deserved. The circumstances at the airport were such that we wanted to avoid an incident. Our people acted with circumspection. As for the weather: our influence does not stretch that far.' Janina had never heard the Director speak with such passion.

The Minister was silenced. The Director continued: 'Consider for a moment the possibility that we can make a fool of the mighty CIA. Think what it would be worth on every conceivable level. Let them laugh at Africa. We will laugh last.'

'Will we?'

'We will conclude the operation successfully. And speedily. But someone must deal severely with the police.'

'How quickly can you conclude this operation?'

Janina knew it was her call: 'Two days, Minister. No more.'

'Are you sure?'

'Minister, if the Department of Defence and the police work together, I will stake my professional reputation on it.' Janina heard herself say it and wondered if she believed it.

'They will cooperate,' said the Minister fiercely. 'What do I tell the media?'

Janina had the answer. 'There are two possibilities. One is to say nothing.'

'Nothing? Have you any idea how many phone calls this office has had this morning?'

'Minister, no country in the world allows the media to interfere with covert operations. Why should we allow it here? Whatever you say, the media will write and broadcast what they wish; they will twist your words or use them against us. Ignore them; show them we will not be intimidated. Tomorrow, the day after, there will be some other event to attract their attention.'

The Minister thought a long time. 'And the second possibility?'

'We use the media to our advantage.'

'Explain.'

'The line between hero and villain is very narrow, Minister. It often depends on how the facts are interpreted.'

'Go on.'

'The fugitive was previously a member of a drugs network that contributed to the collapse of the social structure and ruined the children on the Cape Flats. He misused his MK training for intimidation and violence. We suspect that he is still involved – there are large unexplained sums of money in his bank account. He is a man who does not hesitate to parasitize an innocent woman and her child; he does not even have his own house. A reckless man who has seriously injured a young white soldier with deliberate intent, a man who twice chose to obstruct the purposes of the State when he had the chance to surrender himself. Innocent people, good citizens or heroes do not become fugitives. There are many ex-MK who followed another path. Who chose to build this nation, not break it down. Who even now fight the good fight in the midst of unemployment and poverty. And all we need to do is turn the facts over to the media.'

The Minister of Intelligence nudged the gold-rimmed spectacles further up the bridge of her nose, thoughtful.

'It can work,' she said.

'You prefer the second option?'

'It is more . . . practical.'

From the corner sounded the melodious voice of the Minister of Water Affairs and Forestry. 'We must remember one thing,' he said.

All the heads turned.

'We are talking about Umzingeli.'

*   *   *

Talking non-stop, Koos Kok had unloaded two chairs from the back of his dilapidated 25-year old Chevrolet El Camino van and now he and Mpayipheli were seated at the table, eating bread and tinned pilchards in rich chilli tomato sauce and drinking cheap brandy out of enamel mugs.

'I am the great Griqua troubadour,' Koos Kok introduced himself in his Griqua dialect. 'The guitar player that David Kramer overlooked, *skeefbroer* by birth, hardly *voorlopig* a child, always *vooraan* since I was little, *norring* crazy for music, *langtanne* to go to school . . .'

'I can't understand what you're saying.' Thobela halted him.

'I don't speak Xhosa, my brother, *sôrrie*, it's a *skanne*, and great-granpa Adam Kok went to live with you and all.'

'You're not speaking Afrikaans, either.'

'Dutchman Afrikaans? Well, I can.' And Koos Kok's story emerged on a flood of shamelessly self-centred words, the wrinkled, weathered face animated with the telling in conventional language until he reverted to the tongue of his people and Thobela had to frown and put up his hand to get a translation. Here was the Troubadour of the Northern Cape, the entertainer of the 'townies' who frequented the dance halls where he sang of the landscape and the people with his guitar and his verses. 'But I don't see chance for the *drukmekaar* squeeze, I travel in summer, in winter this is my home, I make a fire and write more songs and now and again when the feeling is too strong I will go *jongman-jongman* with the girls in Beaufort West.'

This morning he had had the radio on in his rusty old Chev bakkie when he had heard the news and later listened to John Modise, so he knew about the *big bad Xhosa biker* running around loose in the area and when he saw the motorbike behind his winter quarters, he knew straight away. It was the work of the Lord, it was divine guidance and he was not going to look on with *paphanne*, no, he was going to help.

'You are going to help me?' asked Thobela, his belly properly full and the brandy in his blood.

'*Ja*, my brother. Koos Kok has a plan.'

Tiger Mazibuko called Team Alpha together at the open door of the Oryx helicopter. The rain had diminished; blue cracks shone through the clouds, the drops were fine and the wind restless.

'This morning I crapped out Little Joe in front of you all and I want to apologize. I was wrong. I was angry. I should have stayed calm. Joe, it wasn't your fault.'

Little Joe Moroka nodded silently.

'I just can't handle it when something happens to one of my men,' Mazibuko said uncomfortably. He could see the fatigue drawn on their faces.

'We are going to Kimberley. Anti-Aircraft School. There will be hot food and warm beds. Team Bravo will do first standby. The army and police will do the roadblocks.'

A few faint smiles. Mazibuko wanted to say more, to restore the bond and minimize the damage. The words would not come.

'Climb up,' he said.' Let's get some sleep.'

Allison Healy drove to the Southern Suburbs, to Johnny Kleintjes's house as it was in the telephone book. She used the hands-free cellphone attachment to call the office for a photographer, and then dialled Absa's number. She wanted to ask Miriam about Thobela's alleged drugs involvement. She did not believe it. The radio contribution was thin on facts, heavy on insinuation.

'Mrs Nzululwazi is not here,' said the receptionist.

'Can you tell me where she is?'

'They came to fetch her.'

'Who did?'

'The police.'

'Police?'

'Can I take a message?'

'No.' She felt like pulling over but she was on De Waal Drive with the Cape stretched spectacularly before her. There was no road shoulder, she had to keep going, but her hands began to tremble. She searched for the number of the SAPS liaison officer and pressed the button.

'Nic, this is Allison. I need to know if you have taken Mrs Miriam Nzululwazi in for questioning.'

'I wondered when you would phone.'

'So you have got her?'

'I don't know what you're talking about, Allison.'

'She is the common-law wife of Thobela Mpayipheli, the man on the motorcycle. Her employers said the police fetched her at work.'

'I know about him, but I don't know about her.'

'Can you find out?'

'I don't know . . .'

'Nic, I'm asking nicely . . .'

'I'll look into it. And get back to you.'

'Another thing. There are rumours that Mpayipheli was involved with drugs on the Cape Flats . . .'

'Yes?'

'Who would know?'

'Richter. At Narcotics.'

'Would you?'

'OK.'

'Thanks, Nic.'

'Till the day I die I shall feel responsible for that man,' said the Minister of Water Affairs and Forestry. He sat silhouetted against the window, the late-morning light forming a halo around him. Janina wondered if it was sorrow that made his voice so heavy.

'I was Chief of Staff: Operations. I had to make the decision. We owed the Germans so much.'

He rubbed his hands over his broad face, as if he could wipe something away. 'That's not relevant now,' he said, leaning forward with his elbow on his knees. He folded his hands as if to pray.

'Once every six months I had a visitor from Berlin. A good-will visit, you might say. A verbal progress report, nothing on paper, a diplomatic gesture to let me know how Tiny was getting on. How pleased they were with him: "He is a credit to your country." It was always a tall, lean German. They were all lean. *Yon Cassius has a lean and hungry look; He thinks too much: such men are dangerous.* Every time they would update the score. Like a sport. "He has done six." Or nine. Or twelve.'

The Minister of Water Affairs and Forestry unfolded his hands and crossed his arms on his chest.

'They used him seventeen times. Seventeen.' His gaze leapt from the Minister to the Director to Janina. 'The one they couldn't talk enough about was Marion Dorffling. CIA. A legend. Thirty or forty eliminations – it boggles the mind. Those were strange times, a strange war. And Umzingeli got him. Smelt him out, tracked him for weeks.'

He smiled with fond nostalgia. 'That was my suggestion. Umzingeli. The hunter. That was his code name.'

He shook his head slowly from side to side – the memories were incredible. He had forgotten them, for a minute or longer he was absent from the room. When he began to speak again his voice was lighter.

'He came to see me. Two months before the '94 elections. My secretary, well, there were so many people wanting to talk to me, she didn't tell me. She thought she was doing right to keep them away. Late one afternoon she came in and said "There's this big guy who won't go away" and when I went to see there he was, looking apologetic and saying he was sorry to bother me.'

The head shook again. 'Sorry to bother me.'

Janina Mentz wondered where this was leading, whether there was a point to all this meandering. Impatience welled up in her.

'I was ashamed that day. He told me what had happened since the fall of the Wall. His German masters had disappeared overnight. His pay had dried up. He didn't know where to turn. And he was crown game, because the West had got hold of the Stasi dossiers and he knew that they would come after him. It was a new world and everyone wanted to forget, except the ones who were hunting him. No one at our London office knew him; they were new personnel, knew nothing about him and didn't want to know. He lay low for a while and when he eventually came home and came to me for work, I said I would help. But the elections came and the new government and I forgot about him. I simply forgot.'

The Minister of Water Affairs and Forestry stood up suddenly, giving Janina a fright. 'I am wasting your time,' he said. 'It is my fault, I must take the blame. It is my fault that he found another livelihood. But I want to say this. Something happened to that man, because if he were still Umzingeli, there would be at least four dead bodies for you to explain. If you can work out why he spared them, you have a chance of bringing him in.'

21

'Thank you, sir,' Janina Mentz said outside on the stairs to the small Zulu.

He stopped, a serious frown on his face. 'Not at all, Janina. I was just being honest. I really do think it is an ingenious operation.'

'Thank you, sir,' she said again.

'Why didn't you say anything?'

'About your name being on the list?'

He nodded.

'I didn't think it relevant to the purpose of the meeting.'

He nodded again and walked slowly down the steps. She stayed where she was.

'Are *you* Inkululeko, sir?'

He walked to the bottom, turned and looked up at her with a faint smile before setting off on the long walk back to the office.

Mpayipheli lay in the back of the El Camino on an old mattress alongside the R 1150 GS that was lying incongruously on its side. The baggage cases had been removed and it lay next to the carton of stolen mutton ('A little something towards redistribution of wealth, I'm a *skorrie-morrie*,' Koos Kok had said), between bits of rickety furniture – two chairs, a coffee table with three legs, and the headboard of a bed. Four tatty suitcases were filled with clothes and documents. All this under a paint-flecked dirty canvas tarpaulin. The bakkie's shock absorbers were gone, the dirt road was very bumpy, but the mattress made it bearable. He lay curled in a foetal position in the cramped space. The rain was almost over, just the occasional shower against the tarp and the water dripping through holes.

He was thinking of the moment when the door had opened, thinking of his self-control, his victory of reason over instinct, suppressing the almost irresistible impulse and he was filled with satisfaction. He felt like telling Miriam. Sometime he would phone her and tell he was OK. She would be worried. But what tales he would have to tell Pakamile in the evenings. Koos Kok the Griqua. 'Don't you know about Adam Kok, Xhosa? He went to live with you guys.' And he heard the short version of that history.

The brandy had made Mpayipheli drowsy and as they turned towards Loxton on the tar road between Rosedene and Slangfontein, the soft rocking of the Chev lulled him to sleep. His last thoughts were of a river god. Otto Müller had told him about the theory of two British scientists that animals deliberately behave unpredictably in order to survive, as the hare flees from the dog. *Does it run in a straight line? Of course not. If it runs in a straight line it will be caught. So it zigzags. But not predictably. Now zigging, then zagging, the dog always guessing, never knowing. The British scientists called it protean behaviour.* After the Greek god Proteus who could change his form at will from a stone to a tree, from a tree to an animal, in order to confound his enemies.

The *big, bad Xhosa biker* had become the *big, bad Xhosa passenger*. Müller would have approved of the change of form to avoid the opponent.

His last conscious thought as he slipped into a deep, restful, satisfying sleep was of his friend Zatopek van Heerden who would not believe that he had become the Proteus of his inherent nature.

*   *   *

Allison Healy had knocked, walked around the house, knocked again, but there was no life there. She leaned against her car in the driveway and waited. Perhaps Monica Kleintjes had gone out for a while. The photographer had come and left again, saying he could not wait, he had to get to the airport – Bobby Skinstad was arriving after the losing rugby tour to Europe. He took some pictures of the house, just in case. It was not an unusually large house – pretty garden, big trees, tranquilly unaware of the drama that surrounded the occupants.

Allison lit a cigarette. She was comfortable with her habit, ten a day, sometimes less. Nowadays there were few places where one could smoke. It was her appetite suppressant, her consolation prize, an escape to small oases through the day.

She had learnt it from Nic.

Nic had seduced her while he was still married.

Nic said he'd had the hots for her from day one when she had walked into the SAPS office to introduce herself. He said he couldn't help it.

The affair had lasted sixteen months. An uncomplicated, chain-smoking man, a good man, basically, if you left his unfaithfulness to his wife out of the equation. Emotionally needy, not very attractive, an unexceptional lover. But then, she was no great judge of that. Five men, since that first time at university.

She and Nic in her flat once or twice a week. Why had she let it happen?

Because she'd been lonely.

A thousand acquaintances and not one bosom friend. This was the lot of the fat girl in a world of skinny standards. Or was that just her excuse?

The truth was that she could not find her place. She was a round peg in a world of square holes. She could not find a group where she felt at home among friends.

Not even with Nic.

It felt better after he left, lying naked alone on the bed and sexually sated, with music and a cigarette, than it did in the moment of passion, the peak of orgasm.

She did not love him. Just liked him a lot. She did still, but after the divorce and the guilt he carried around like a ball and chain she had ended the relationship.

He still asked every now and then: 'Could we start again? Just one more time?' She considered it. Sometimes seriously, because of the desire to be held, to be caressed . . . He had liked her body. 'You are sexy, Allison. Your breasts . . .' Maybe that was the thing, he had accepted her body. Because she could not change it, the curves were genetic, passed on from grandmother to mother to daughter in an unbroken succession, stout people, plump women, regardless of the best efforts of diets and exercise programmes.

She crushed the cigarette into the grass with the tip of her shoe. The stub lay there like a reproach. She picked it up and threw it behind a shrub in a bed of daisies.

Where was Monica Kleintjes?

Her cellphone rang.

'It's the boss, Allison. Where are you?'

'Newlands.'

'You had better get back. The Minister is doing a press conference in fifteen minutes.'

'Which one?'

'Intelligence.'

'I'm on my way.'

During the design and equipping of the interview/interrogation room of the Presidential Intelligence Unit Janina Mentz had asked why a table was necessary. Nobody could give her an answer. That was why there was none. She had asked why the chairs should be hard and uncomfortable. Why the walls had to be bare except for the one with the one-way mirror.

She asked whether a stripped, unpleasant, chilly room yielded better results than a comfortable one. Nobody could answer that. 'We are not running a police station,' was her argument. So there were three easy chairs of the sort that Lewis Stores or Star Furnishers sold in their hundreds for people's sitting rooms. They were upholstered in practical brown and treated with stain-resistant chemicals. The only difference was that these chairs could not be moved, so that no one could prevent or delay entry to the room by pushing the chairs under the door handle. The chairs were bolted down in an intimate triangle. The floor was covered in wall-to-wall carpet, uniform *beige* – not khaki, not pumpkin, but exactly to Janina's specification: *beige*. The microphone was concealed behind the fluorescent light in the ceiling and the closed-circuit television camera was in the adjoining observation room, pointing its cyclopean eye through the one-way glass.

Janina stood by the camera and looked at the woman seated in one of the chairs. Interesting that everyone brought in chose the chair half turned away from the window. As if they could sense it.

Was this the result of too many television serials?

The woman was Miriam Nzululwazi, common-law wife of Thobela Mpayipheli.

What had Umzingeli seen in her?

She did not seem a cheerful type. She looked like someone who was chronically unhappy, the permanent lines of unhappiness around her mouth. No laugh lines.

She predicted that the woman would not cooperate. She expected her to be tense and hostile. Janina sighed. It had to be done.

Allison's phone rang as she climbed the stairs.

'It's Nic.'

'Any news?'

'We don't have your Mrs Nzululwazi.'

'Well, who has?'

'I don't know.'

'Can the Intelligence services detain people? Without trial?'

'There are laws that are supposed to regulate them, but the Intelligence people do as they please, because it is in the interest of the State and the people they work with are not the sort who run to the courts over irregular treatment.'

'And the drugs angle?'

'I talked to Richter. He says Mpayipheli is well known. He worked for Orlando Arendse when he was Prince of the Cape Flats. No arrests, no record, but they were aware of him.'

'And Orlando Arendse was a dealer?'

'An importer and distributor. A wholesaler. Mpayipheli was a deterrent for dealers who would not pay. Or who did not reach their targets. It's another kind of business, that.'

'Where do I get hold of Arendse?'

'Allison, these are dangerous people.'

'Nic . . .'

'I'll find out.'

'Thanks, Nic.'

'There's something else.'

'Not now, Nic.'

'It's not about us.'

'What is it?'

'Memo from the Minister. Strong steps if they catch anyone leaking information on the Mpayipheli affair to the media. Full cooperation with our Intelligence colleagues, big mobilization in the Northern Cape.'

'You were not supposed to tell me that.'

'No.'

'I appreciate it.'

'I want to see you, Allison.'

'Goodbye, Nic.'

'Please,' he begged in a little-boy voice.

'Nic . . .'

'Please, just once.'

And she weakened in the face of . . . everything.

'Maybe.'

'Tonight?'

'No.'

'When, then?'

'The weekend, Nic. Coffee somewhere.'

'Thanks.' And he sounded so sincere that she felt guilty.

It was fifteen years since Miriam Nzululwazi's terrible night in the Caledon Plain cells, but the fear she had felt then made the jump to the present, here to the interrogation room. Her hands gripped the arms of the chair, but her eyes were blind to the wall they faced. She remembered, one woman in the cell kept screaming, screaming, a sound that penetrated marrow and bone, never-ending lament. The red-faced policeman, who opened the cell door and cleared a way through the perspiring bodies to the screaming one with his truncheon, raised the blunt object high above his head.

She was seventeen, on her way home to the thrown-together wooden hut on an overpopulated dune at Khayalitsha, her week's wages clasped in her handbag, on the way to the buses at the Parade when the mass of demonstrators blocked the road. A seething mass like a noisy pregnant python curling past the town hall, banners waving, whistles, chanting, toyi-toyi-ing, shouts, a swinging carnival of protest over pay in the clothing industry or something. She had joined in, as they were flowing in her direction, laughed at the young men cavorting like monkeys and suddenly the police were there, the tear gas, the charge, the water cannon, the pregnant python had borne chaos.

They pushed her into the back of a big yellow lorry, pulled her out at the cells with the rest of the horde, shoved them into a cell, too full, nobody could sit and the screaming woman, moaning, something about a child, she must go to her sick child, the red-faced white man threatening with the truncheon above his head, shouting, voice lost in the din, the arm dropping, again and again and terror had overwhelmed Miriam, she needed to escape, she pushed against the others, through the screaming women till she reached the bars, put her hands through them and there were more policemen shouting too, faces wild, till someone pulled her back, the lamenting voice was suddenly quiet.

She felt the same fear now, in this closed space, the locked door, the locking-up without reason, without guilt. She jumped as the door opened. A white woman entered and went to sit opposite her.

'How can I convince you that we want to help Thobela?' Janina Mentz used his first name deliberately.

'You can't keep me here.' Miriam heard the fear in her own voice.

'Ma'am, these people are misusing him. They are putting him in unnecessary danger. They have lied and misled him. They are not good people.'

'I don't believe you. He was Thobela's friend.'

'He was. Years ago. But he has gone bad. He wants to sell us out. Our country. He wants to hurt us and he is using Thobela.'

She could see uncertainty in Miriam's face – she would capitalize on it. 'We know Thobela is a good man. We know he was a hero of the Struggle. We know he wouldn't have got involved if he knew the whole story. We can sort this out and bring him home safely, but we need your help.'

'My help?'

'You talked to the media . . .'

'She also wanted to help. She too was on Thobela's side.'

'They are manipulating you, ma'am.'

'And you?'

'How will the media be able to bring Thobela home? We can. With your help.'

'There is nothing I can do.'

'Do you expect Thobela to phone?'

'Why do you want to know?'

'If we could just give him a message.'

Miriam glanced sharply at Janina, at her eyes, her mouth, her hands.

'I don't trust you.'

Janina sighed. 'Because I am white?'

'Yes. Because you are white.'

Captain Tiger Mazibuko could not get to sleep. He rolled about on the army bed. It was muggy in Kimberley, not too hot, still overcast, but the humidity was high and the room poorly ventilated.

What was this hate that he felt for Mpayipheli?

The man had been in the Struggle. This man had not sold out his comrades.

Where did this hate come from? It consumed Mazibuko, it influenced his behaviour; he had not treated Little Joe well. He had always had the anger but it had never before affected his leadership.

Why?

This was just a poor middle-aged man who had had a moment of glory a long time ago.

Why?

Outside there was a rumbling that grew louder and louder.

How was he supposed to sleep?

It was the Rooivalks. The windows shook in their frames, the deep bass note of the motors reverberated in his chest.

Earlier it had been the trucks, departing one after the other with single-minded purpose. Soldiers were being deployed to set up the roadblocks on dirt roads and tar roads. The net was cast wider to catch a single fish.

He turned over again.

Did it matter where the hate came from? As long as he could control it. Channel it.

Any necessary action, Janina Mentz had said. In other words, shoot the fucker if you like.

Lord, he looked forward to it.

22

The six-man team searched the house in Guguletu with professional skill.

They took video footage and digital stills before they began, so that everything could be replaced exactly where it had been. Then the methodical laborious search began. They knew the hidey-holes of amateurs and professional frauds: no nook or cranny was left unsearched. Stethoscopes were used on walls and floors, powerful torches in the spaces between roof and ceiling. The master keys they had brought for cupboards and doors were not required. One of the six men was master of the inventory. He murmured into a palm-sized tape recorder like a businessman dictating a letter.

It was a small house with not much inside. The search took 130 minutes. Then they were gone in the microbus they had arrived in. The master of the inventory phoned his boss, Vincent Radebe.

'Nothing,' he said.

'Nothing at all?' asked Radebe.

'No weapons, no drugs, no cash. A few bank statements. The usual documentation. Mpayipheli is writing Matric, there is correspondence and books. Magazines, cards – sentimental love notes to the woman in her clothes drawer. "From Thobela. To Miriam. I love you this, I love you that." Nothing else. Ordinary people.'

In the Ops Room Vincent shook his head. He had thought so.

'Oh, one other thing. A veggie garden out the back. Very neat. Best tomatoes I have seen in years.'

The trick at a news conference was to phrase your questions in such a way as to not disclose the information you had to the other media.

That was why, after the Minister had read the prepared statement on the stormy life and violent criminal times of Thobela Mpayipheli and had responded to a horde of questions from radio, newspaper and television journalists almost without exception with 'I am not in a position to answer that question, due to the sensitive nature of the operation', Allison Healy asked: 'Is anybody else connected with this operation being detained at the moment?'

And because the Minister did not know, she hesitated. Then she gave an answer that would cover her if the opposite were true. 'Not to my knowledge,' she said.

It was an answer that she would later wish with all her heart she had never uttered.

They brought Miriam coffee and sandwiches in the interrogation room. She asked when they would let her go. The food bearer did not know. He said he would ask.

She did not eat or drink. She tried to overcome her fear. The walls suffocated her, the windowless room pressed down on her. Tonight it was she who needed to go to her child, tonight it was she who wanted to cry out in a high frightened voice, 'Let me out'. She must go and fetch Pakamile. Her child, her child. Her work. What were the bank people thinking? Did they think she was a criminal? Were they going to release her? Would someone here go and explain to the bank people why they had come to fetch her?

She needed to get out.

She had to get out.

And what about Thobela? Where was he now? Was it true what the white woman said, that he was in danger?

She had not asked for this.

Janina Mentz waited until everyone who had been resting was back before she gathered them around the table.

Then she told them almost the whole story. She did not mention that the Director's name was on the list, but she confessed that she had set up the operation from the start. She did not apologize for keeping them in the dark. She said they should understand why she had done it this way.

She described the meeting with the Minister, the confirmation that Thobela Mpayipheli, code name Umzingeli, was a former MK operative, that he had received advanced training, that he was a dangerous opponent and that it was of cardinal importance that he be stopped.

'We will waste no more time finding out who he was. We are going to focus on finding out who he is *now*. With his background, his behaviour during the last eighteen hours makes no sense. He has deliberately refrained from violence. At the airport he said, I quote: "I don't want to hurt anybody." In the confrontation with two Reaction Unit members he said, "Look what you made me do." But on neither of these occasions did he give himself up. It doesn't make sense to me. Does anyone here have an opinion?'

She knew Rajkumar would have an opinion. He always did. 'Escalation,' he said. 'He's not a moron. He knows that if he shoots someone things will escalate out of his control.'

Radebe said nothing, but she had her suspicions. So she drew him out. 'Vincent?'

Radebe sat with his palms over his cheeks, fingertips on his temples and his eyes on the big table. 'I think not.'

'What do you mean?' asked Rajkumar irritably.

'Put everything together,' said Radebe. 'He left the drugs work. Of his own free will. Orlando Arendse said he just left without any explanation. He deliberately chose an occupation without violence, probably at a much reduced salary. He begins a relationship with a single mother, lives with her and her child, enrols in correspondence Matric, buys a farm. What does that tell us?'

'Smokescreen,' said Rajkumar. 'What about all the money?'

'He worked for six years in the lucrative drugs industry. What could he spend his money on?'

'A thousand things. Wine, women, song, gambling.'

'No,' said Radebe.

'What do you think, Vincent?' asked Mentz softly.

'I think he began a new life.'

She watched the faces around the table. She wanted to test the support for Radebe. She saw none.

'Why not give himself up, then, Vincent?' Rajkumar asked with a flamboyant gesture.

'I don't know,' said Radebe. 'I just don't know.'

Rajkumar leaned back as if he had won the argument.

'A leopard doesn't change its spots,' said Janina. 'He was out of the big game for ten years. But now he's back. I think he is enjoying it.'

Mpayipheli woke with a start, immediately aware that the El Camino was no longer moving and the engine was off. He heard voices.

'Koos Kok, get out.'

'Why?'

'We want to see if you are smuggling a man with a motorbike.'

Under the tarpaulin, he was blind to the action.

'*Ja*, OK, you got me. Have mercy, it's just a dwarf on a 50cc.'

Roadblock. Mpayipheli's heart thundered in his ears, his breathing sounded very loud, he wondered if he had made any noise waking up.

'You always were a smooth-mouthed bastard, Koos, all your life.'

'And you are a *ghwar*, sarge, even for a Dutchman.'

'*Ghwar*? What's a *ghwar*?'

'Just playing, sarge – what's with you today?'

'How many sheep have you got in the back, Koos?'

'I'm not in that business any more, Sarge.'

'You lie, Koos Kok, you will be a sheep stealer till the day you die. Lift up that sail.'

How many men were there? Would he be able to . . . ?

'Leave the man, Gerber, we've got more important things to do.'

'He's a thief. I bet you there's meat here.'

Thobela Mpayipheli heard the man's voice right by him, heard the rustle of a hand over the canvas. Lord, he was helpless, weaponless, he was lying down without a chance.

'You can look, it's just my furniture,' said Koos Kok.

'Where are you moving to?'

'Bloemfontein. I'm looking for a proper job.'

'Ha! You lie like a dentist!'

'Let him go, Gerber, he's blocking the road.'

'I tell you there are sheep here . . .'

'Let him go.'

'Okay, Koos, get your *skedonk* out of the road.'

'But what about the dwarf with the motorbike? He can't ride in the back there all the way.'

'Fuck off, Koos, before you get in trouble.'

'OK, OK, sarge, I'm going.' And the springs of the bakkie

shifted as Koos Kok got in and then the engine fired and the big six-cylinder rumbled.

'Jissis, Koos, you must work on that exhaust.'

'Just as soon as I've dropped off the motorbike,' said Koos Kok and pulled away with spinning tyres.

Quinn set the first issue of the *Argus* carefully in front of Janina Mentz.

Fugitive biker was MK hero.

Main headline.

The fugitive motorcyclist now hunted nationally by Intelligence agencies, the military and the South African Police Service was a top Umkhonto we Sizwe soldier who served the Struggle with great distinction, says a former SANDF colonel and comrade of Mr Thobela Mpayipheli.

'Although I lost track of Thobela's military career during the latter part of the struggle against apartheid, there is no doubt that he was an honourable soldier,' says Colonel 'Lucky' Luke Mahlape who retired as second in command at 1 Infantry Battalion in Bloemfontein last year.

Col. Mahlape, now living in Hout Bay, called The Argus *to set the record straight after news of Mr Mpayipheli's high-speed cross-country dash on a big BMW motorcycle caught local head-lines earlier today.*

They would have to change their tune now, she thought. If the Minister did her part thoroughly.

Mpayipheli did not sleep again, but shook on the mattress, the adrenalin dammed up, wondering if there would be more roadblocks – he felt that his nerves could not take it. He wanted to get out from under the tarpaulin, wanted to get on the bike and have control: he could not be this helpless, wondering where they were, how long he had been sleeping.

It was practically dark where he lay, the hands of his watch invisible. He turned so he could lift the canvas, realized it had stopped raining, and managed an opening. Twenty past twelve. Lowered the sail again.

Two hours on the road at an average of ninety or a hundred kilometres per hour. Richmond, that was where he guessed the roadblock had been. It was one of the danger spots that they had discussed in the house when they had hunched over the map. He wanted to go to De Aar, Koos Kok had said no, the army was there, let's go through Merriman to Richmond and then take the back roads to Philipstown and there you'd be through the worst, Petrusville, Luckhoff, Koffiefontein, perhaps some danger at Petrusburg because it was on the main route between Kimberley and Bloemfontein, but after that it was a straight run, Dealesville, Bloemhof, Mafikeng and Botswana and nobody would be any the wiser.

He was not so sure. Kimberley was the straight line. And that was where they would wait for him. Expecting him to be on a motorbike, not in the back of an El Camino.

And eventually he decided that the risk was too high.

The bakkie lost speed.

What now?

Stopped.

Lord.

'Xhosa,' said Koos Kok.

'What?'

'Don't worry. I have to fill up.'

'Where?'

'Richmond. It's just here.'

Lord.

'Okay, fine.'

Koos Kok pulled away again.

He should have added: 'No jokes about the man on the motorbike.'

But it probably would have made no difference.

23

Allison Healy was naive when she joined the *Cape Times*, an alumnus of Rhodes University's school of journalism with stars in her eyes and a burning desire to live out her romance with words at *Cosmo* or *Fair Lady*, but prepared to work out her apprenticeship at a daily. She trusted everyone, believed them, looked with wide-eyed wonder at the famous with whom she came into contact on her daily round.

But disillusionment followed, not suddenly or dramatically – the small realities slowly took over uninvited. The realization that people were an unreliable, dishonest, self-centred, self-absorbed, backstabbing, violent, sly species that lies, cheats, murders, rapes and steals, regardless of status, nationality or colour. It was a gradual but often traumatic process for someone who wished only to see good and beauty.

Miriam Nzululwazi and Immanuel the shoeshine man had argued with such conviction that Mpayipheli was a good man. The minister had sketched another picture, the tragedy of the once trustworthy soldier gone bad. Very bad.

Where was truth?

Will the real Thobela Mpayipheli please stand up?

The only way to find the truth, she knew, was to keep on digging. Keep asking questions and sift the grain from the chaff.

Eventually Nic phoned through Orlando Arendse's contact numbers. 'You can try, but it won't be easy,' he said.

Allison began phoning, one number after another.

'Orlando who?' was the reaction, with no exception. She would tell her story in a breathless hurry before they broke the connection: it was about Thobela Mpayipheli, she just wanted background, she would protect her source.

'You have the wrong number, lady.'

'So what is the right number?'

Then the line would go dead and she would ring the next one. 'My name is Allison Healy, I'm with the *Cape Times*, I would really like to talk to Mr Orlando Arendse in absolute, guaranteed confidence . . .'

'Where did you get this number?'

She was taken unawares. 'From the police' was on the tip of her tongue but she bit the words back. 'I'm a reporter, it's my job to find people, but please, it's about Thobela Mpayipheli . . .'

'Sorry, wrong number.'

She rang all five numbers without success and slammed the flat of her hand down on the desk in frustration and then went to have a smoke on the pavement outside – short, angry drags on the cigarette. Maybe she should threaten: 'If Arendse does not speak to me, I will put his name and occupation in every article I write about this. Take your choice.'

No. Better to try again.

When she pulled the notebook of numbers towards her the phone rang.

'You want to speak to Mr O?'

For a second she was lost. 'Who?' she said. And then, hurriedly, 'Oh, yes, yes, I do.'

'There's a blue-whale skeleton in the museum. Be there at one o' clock.'

Before she could respond the phone went dead.

The big whale hall was in twilight, dim blue light that repre-sented the Deep. The taped sounds of the massive mammals lent a surreal atmosphere to the place as the coloured couple, a young man and girl, wandered hand in hand from one display to the next. Allison did not take any notice of them until they were right next to her, when the man spoke her name.

'Yes?' she answered.

'I have to search your handbag,' he said apologetically and she stood rooted until insight caught up with her.

'Oh.' She handed over the bag.

'And I have to frisk you,' said the girl, with a suggestion of a smile. She was nineteen or twenty, with long pitch-black hair, full lips and tasteful but heavy make-up. 'Please raise your arms.'

Allison reacted automatically, feeling the hands sliding skilfully over her body; then the girl stepped back.

'I'm going to keep this until after,' said the man, holding up her tape recorder. 'Now, please come with us.'

Outside, the sunlight was blinding. Ahead lay the Kompanje gardens, pigeons and fountains and squirrels. The couple walked wordlessly, one on either side of her, leading her to the tea garden, where two coloured men, somewhat older, sat, their faces stern.

Heads nodded, the two men stood, and the girl indicated that Allison should sit. 'Nice meeting you,' she said and they were gone. Allison sat with her handbag tucked under her arm, feeling that she would not be surprised if Pierce Brosnan loomed up beside her and said 'Bond. James Bond.'

She waited. Nothing happened. Families and business folk sat at the other tables. Which of them were Orlando Arendse's people? She took out her cigarettes and put one to her lips.

'Allow me,' said a voice beside her and a lighter appeared. She looked up. He looked like a schoolmaster in his tailored suit, blue shirt, red-spotted bow tie, his hair greying at the temples. But the long brown face was etched with the lines of a hard life.

While she held the tip of her cigarette in the flame he said: 'Please forgive the cloak and dagger. But we needed to be sure.' He sat down opposite her and said, 'Rubens.'

'I beg your pardon?'

'A game, Miss Healy. Rubens would have painted you. I like Rubens.'

'He's the one who liked fat women.' Allison felt insulted.

'No,' said Arendse. 'He is the one who painted *perfect* women.'

She was off balance. 'Mr Arendse . . .'

He pulled out the chair opposite her. 'You may call me Orlando. Or Uncle Orlando. I have a daughter your age.'

'Is she also in the . . .'

'Drugs business? No, Miss Healy. My Julie is a copywriter at Ogilvie. Last year she won a Pendoring award for her work with the Volkswagen Golf campaign.'

Allison blushed deeply. 'Please excuse me. I had the wrong impression.'

'I know,' he said. 'What will you drink?'

'Tea, please.'

With the air of a man accustomed to giving orders he gestured to a waiter. He ordered tea for her, coffee for himself. 'One condition, Miss Healy. You will not mention my name.'

Her raised eyebrows asked the question.

'To throw my weight around in the newspapers is one way to draw the attention of the SAPS,' he said. 'I can't afford that.'

'Are you really a drug baron?' He did not look like one. He did not speak like one.

'I always found that name amusing. Baron.'

'Are you?'

'There was a time in my life – when I was young – that I would have answered that with a long rationalization, Miss

Healy. How I merely met people's need to escape. That I was merely a businessman supplying a product greatly in demand. But with age comes realism. I am, among other things, a supplier. An illegal importer and distributor of banned substances. I am a parasite living off the weakness of humanity.' He spoke softly, without regret, merely stating the facts. Allison was amazed.

'But why?'

Arendse smiled at her in a grandfatherly way at the predictable question. 'Let us blame apartheid,' he said. Then he laughed softly and privately and switched to a Cape Flats accent and nuances like speaking another language. 'Crime of opportunity, *mêrrim, djy vat wat djy kan kry, verstaa' djy.*'

Allison shook her head in wonder. 'The stories you could tell,' she said.

'One day, in my memoirs. But let us talk about the man of the moment, Miss Healy. What do you want to know about Tiny Mpayipheli?'

She opened her notebook. She explained about the Minister's declaration, the allegations that Mpayipheli was a fallen hero, misusing his skill. She was interrupted by the arrival of the tea and coffee. He asked her if she took milk and poured for her. He put milk and three spoons of sugar with his coffee and sipped it.

'The Spooks came to me, last night. Asking questions – they had that attitude: "We have the power and the right . . ." It is interesting to me, the way everything changes but nothing changes. Instead of chasing the Nigerians who are taking over here. How is one supposed to make a living? Nevertheless, it made me think, last night and this morning, when Tiny was in the news. I thought a lot about him. In my line you see all kinds. You learn to recognize people for what they are, not for what they are trying to show you. And Tiny . . . I knew he was different from the moment he walked in my door. I knew he was just passing through. It was as if he was there, but not his spirit. For years I thought it was because he was a Xhosa in a coloured people's world, a fish out of water. But now I know that was not so. He was never an enforcer at heart. He is a warrior. A fighter. Three hundred years ago he would have been the one in front, charging the enemy with spear and shield, the one who reached the lines while his comrades fell around him, the one who kept stabbing until there was only blood and sweat and death.'

Arendse came back to reality. 'I am a romantic at heart, my dear. You must excuse me.'

'Was he violent?'

'*Now there's a question.* What is "violent"? We are all violent, as a species. It simmers just below the surface like a volcano. The lucky ones go through their entire lives without an eruption.'

'Was Thobela Mpayipheli more inclined to violence than the average person?'

'What are we trying to prove here?' he said with some anger.

'Have you seen today's *Argus*?'

'Yes. They say that he is a war hero.'

'Mr Arendse . . .'

'Orlando.'

'Orlando, the intelligence services are pursuing this man over the length and breadth of the country. If he is a violent and criminal man, it places a whole different perspective on what they are doing. And how they are doing it. The public needs to know.'

Orlando Arendse grimaced until the lines of his face creased even more deeply.

'That is my problem with the media, Miss Healy. You want to press people into packages, that is all there is time and space for. Labels. But you can't label people. We are not good or bad. There is a bit of both in all of us. No. There is a *lot* of both in all of us.'

'But we don't all become murderers or rapists.'

'Granted.' He took a packet of sugar in his fingers, twirling it around and round. 'He never sought violence. You must understand that he was big. Six foot five. If you are a dealer on the Flats and this big black bugger walks in the door and looks you in the eyes, you see your future and it doesn't look good. Violence is the last thing you want to provoke. He carried the threat of violence in him.'

'Did he resort to violence sometimes?'

'Lord, you won't give up until you have the answer, the sensation that you are looking for.'

Allison shook her head, but Arendse continued before she could protest.

'Yes, sometimes he did use violence. What do you expect, in my line of business? But remember, he was provoked. In the days before the Nigerians started messing us around, it was the Russians who tried to get control of the trade. And they were racist. Tiny worked a couple of them over, right into intensive care. I wasn't there, but the men told me, whispering, their eyes big as if they had seen something otherworldly. The intensity was awesome. Raw. What frightened them most – they said he enjoyed it. It was as if a light shone out from him.'

She scribbled in her notebook, hurrying to keep up.

'But if you want to define him like that, you will make a mistake. He has a lot of good in him. One bad winter we were in the city late at night, the other side of Strand Street in the red-light district, collecting protection money and he was watching the street kids. And then he went over and collected them up, there must have been twenty or thirty and he took them to the Spur Steakhouse and told the management that it was their birthday, all and each of them must get a plate of food and a sparkler and the waiters must sing Happy Birthday. That was a party for you.'

She glanced up from her writing. 'He made a choice in those days. He came to work for you. I can't understand why an MK veteran would go to work for a drug baron.'

'That is because you were never an MK veteran out of work in the new South Africa.'

'Touché.'

'If you had committed your life to the Struggle and won, you would expect some kind of reward. It's human, an inherent expectation. Freedom is an ephemeral reward. You can't grasp it in your hand. One morning you wake up and you are free. But your township is just as much a ghetto as it was yesterday, you are just as poor, your people are as burdened as before. You can't eat freedom. You can't buy a house or a car with it.'

Arendse took a big swallow of coffee. 'Madiba was Moses and he led us to the Promised Land, but there was no milk or honey.'

He put his cup down.

'Or something like that.' And he smiled gently. 'I don't know what to say to you. You are looking for the real Tiny and I don't think anyone knows who that is. What I can say is that in the years he worked for me he was never late, he was never sick; he did not drink or sample the produce of the trade. Women? Tiny is a man. He had his needs. And the girls were mad about him, the young ones – seventeen, eighteen – they ran after him, pursued him with open desire. But there was never any trouble. I can tell you his body was in the work, but his mind was elsewhere.'

Orlando Arendse shook his head in recall. 'Let me tell you about the thing with the French. One day we were walking in the city, down St George's, and there were these tourists, French, standing with a map and wondering and they called me over in their bad English and they were looking for a place. The next thing, big black Tiny starts babbling in French like you won't believe. There in front of my eyes he became another person – different body, different eyes, another language, another land. Suddenly he was alive, his body and mind were in one place together, he was alive.'

The material in Arendse's memory banks made him laugh. 'You should have seen their faces – those tourists nearly hugged him, they chattered like starlings. And when we walked away I asked him what was that? And he said, "My previous life", that's all. "My previous life." But he said it with longing that I can still feel today and that was when I realized that I didn't know him. I would never know him. Some more tea?'

'Thank you,' Allison said and he did the honours. 'And then he left your service?'

Orlando Arendse drank the last of his coffee. 'Tiny and I . . . There was respect. We looked each other in the eye and let me tell you it doesn't often happen in my business. Part of that respect was that we both knew the day would come.'

'Why did he leave?'

'Why? Because the time had come, that is probably the simplest answer, but not the whole truth. The thing is: I loaned him out, just before he resigned. Long story. Just call it business, a transaction. There was shooting and a fight. Tiny landed in hospital. When he came out, he said he was finished.'

'Loaned him out?'

'I'm honour bound, my dear. You will have to ask Van Heerden.'

'Van Heerden?'

'Zatopek van Heerden. Former policeman, former private eye, now he's like a professor of psychology at the university.'

'The University of Cape Town?'

'The Lord works in mysterious ways, *verstaa' djy*,' said Orlando Arendse with a twinkle in his eye and beckoned the waiter to bring the check.

Vincent Radebe closed the door of the interview room behind him. Miriam Nzululwazi stood by the one-way mirror, a deep frown on her face.

'When can I go home?' she asked in Xhosa.

'Won't you sit down, sister?' Soft, sympathetic, serious.

'Don't *sister* me.'

'I understand.'

'You understand nothing. What have I done? Why are you keeping me here?'

'To protect you and Thobela.'

'You lie. You are a black man and you lie to your own people.'

Radebe sat down. 'Please, ma'am, let us talk. Please.'

Miriam turned her back on him.

'Ma'am, of all the people here I am about the only one who thinks that Thobela is a good man. I think I understand what happened. I am on your side. There must be some way I can make you believe that.'

'There is. Let me go. I am going to lose my job. I have to look after my child. I am not a criminal. I never did anything to anyone. Let me go.'

'You won't lose your job. I promise you.'

'How will you manage that?'

'I will talk to the bank. Explain to them.'

She turned around. 'How can I believe you?'

'I am telling you. I am on your side.'

'That is exactly what the white woman said.'

Mentz was right, Radebe thought. It was not easy. He had offered to come and talk to Miriam. He was uneasy that she was here, that she was detained. His thoughts were with her, his empathy, but the damage had already been done. He let the silence grow.

She gave him an opening: 'What can I say to you? What can I do so that you will let me go?'

'There are two things. This morning you spoke to the newspapers . . .'

'What did you expect me to do? They come to my work. They also say they are on my side.'

'It was not wrong. Just dangerous. They write crazy things. We—'

'You are afraid they will write the truth.'

He suppressed his frustration, kept his head cool. 'Ma'am, Thobela Mpayipheli is out there somewhere with a lot of information that a few people want very badly. Some of them will do anything to stop him. The more the papers write, the more dangerous the things that they will do. Is that what you want?'

'I won't talk to them again. Is that what you want?'

'Yes, that is what I want.'

'What else?'

'We need to know why he has not given himself up yet.'

'That you must ask him yourself.' Because if everything was as they said then she did not understand either.

'We would dearly love to. We hoped that you would help us to get him to understand.'

'How can I? I don't know what he thinks. I don't know what happened.'

'But you know him.'

'He went to help a friend, that is all I know.'

'What did he say before he left?'

'I have already told the coloured man who came to my house. Why must I say it again? There is nothing more.

Nothing. I will keep quiet, I will talk to nobody, I swear it
to you, but you must let me go now.'

He saw that she was close to breaking – he knew that she was
telling the truth. He wanted to reach out and comfort her. He
also knew that she would not tolerate it. Radebe stood. 'You
are right, ma'am,' he said. 'I will see to it.'

24

Mpayipheli had to stretch his legs – the cramps were creeping up on him and his shoulder throbbed. The nest under the tarpaulin was too small now, too hot, too dusty. The rattling over the dirt roads – how far still to go? – he needed air, to get out, it was going too slowly, the hours disappearing in the monotonous drone of the Chev. Every time Koos Kok reduced speed Mpayipheli thought that they had arrived, but it was just another turn, another connection. His impatience and discomfort were nearly irrepressible and then the Griqua stopped and lifted the sail with a theatrical gesture and said 'The road is clear, Xhosa, *laat jou voete raas.*'

He was blinded by the sudden midday sun. He straightened stiffly, allowing his eyes to adjust. The landscape was different, less Karoo. He saw grass veld, hills, a town in the distance.

'That's Philipstown.' Koos Kok followed his gaze.

The road stretched out ahead of them, directly north.

They wrestled the GS off the El Camino, using two planks as a ramp that bent deeply under its weight, but it was easier than the loading. They worked hurriedly, worried about the possibility of passing traffic.

'You must wait until sunset,' said Koos Kok.

'There's no time.'

The GS stood ready on its stand; Thobela pulled on the rider's suit, opened the sports bag and counted out some notes, offering them to Koos Kok.

'I don't want your money. You paid for the petrol already.'

'I owe you.'

'You owe me nothing. You gave me the music.'

'What music?'

'I am going to write a song about you.'

'Is that why you helped me?'

'Sort of.'

'Sort of?'

'You have two choices in life, Xhosa. You can be a victim. Or not.' Koos Kok's smile was barely discernible.

'Oh.'

'You will understand one day.'

Mpayipheli hesitated a moment and then pushed the cash back into his top pocket. 'Take this for wear and tear,' he said handing over a couple of hundred rand.

'Ride like the wind, Xhosa.'

'Go well, Griqua.'

They stood facing each other uncomfortably. Then Thobela Mpayipheli put out his hand to Koos Kok. 'Thank you.'

The Griqua shook his hand and smiled with a big gap-tooth smile.

Mpayipheli put the bag in the side case, pushed his hands into the gloves and mounted. Pushed the starter. The GS hesitated a second before it took and then he raised his hand and rode, accelerating gradually through the gears, giving the engine time to warm up. It felt good, it felt right, because he was in control again, on the road, fourth, fifth, sixth, a hundred and forty kilometres per hour, shifted into position, found the right angle with most of his torso behind the windshield, bent slightly forward and then he let the needle creep up and looked in the rear-view mirror to see that Koos Kok and the El Camino had become very small behind in the road.

The digital clock read 15:06 and he made some calculations,

visualizing the road map in his mind, 200 kilometres of tar road to Petrusburg – that was the dangerous part, in daylight on the R48 – but it was a quiet road. Petrusburg by half-past four, five o' clock. Refuel and if he was reported then there was the network of dirt roads to the north, too many for them to patrol and he would have choices, to go through Dealesville or Boshof and his choices would multiply and by then it would be dark and all going well he could cross the border at Mafeking before midnight. Then he would be away, safe, and he would phone Miriam from Lobatse, tell her he was safe, regardless of what they said over the radio.

But first he had to pass Petrusville and cross the Orange River.

If he were setting up a roadblock it would be at the Big River, as Koos Kok called it. Close the bridge. There were no other options, according to the map – unless you were willing to chance your luck in Orania.

The thought made him smile.

Odd country, this.

What would the Boers of Orania think if he pulled up in a cloud of dust and said 'I am Thobela Mpayipheli, chaps, and the ANC government would love to get their hands on me'? Would it be a case of 'If you are against the government, you are with us'? Probably not.

He had to pass a sheep lorry, slowed down using his flickers like a law-abiding citizen, sped up again, leaning the bike into the turns where the road twisted between the hills, aware of the landscape. Beautiful country this. Colourful. That is the difference, the major difference between this landscape and the Karoo. More colour, as if God's palette was increasingly used up on the way south. Here the green was greener, the ridges browner, the grass more yellow, the sky more blue.

Colour had messed up this land. The difference in colour.

The road grew straight again, a black ribbon stretching out

ahead, grass veld and thorn bush. Cumulus clouds in line, a
war host marching across the heavens. This was the face of
Africa. Unmistakable.

Zatopek van Heerden said it was not colour, it was genes.
Van Heerden was big on genes. Genes that caused the Boers
of Orania to pull into the defensive *laager*. Van Heerden said
racism was inherent, the human urge to protect his genes, to
seek out his own so the genes could persist.

Thobela had argued because Van Heerden's philosophy
was too empty. Too damning. Too easy.

'So, I can do as I please and shrug my shoulders and say
"it's genes"?'

'You must differentiate between genetic programming and
morality, Thobela.'

'I don't know what you mean.'

Van Heerden had bowed his shoulders as if the weight of
knowledge was too heavy to bear.

'There is no easy way to explain it.'

'That is usually the case with absolute drivel.'

Laughing: 'That's fucking true. But not in this case. The
problem is that most people won't accept the big truths. You
should see them fighting in the letters page of the *Burger* over
evolution. And not just here. In America they don't want to
allow evolution into the classroom even. In the twenty-first
century. The evidence is overwhelming, but they fight to the
bitter end.'

Van Heerden said that accepting evolution was the first
step. People are formed through natural selection, their bodies
and thoughts and behaviour. Programmed. For one thing
alone: the survival of the species. The preservation of the
gene pool. The white man had laid down evidence in front
of Mpayipheli in one motivated layer after another, but
eventually, though he had conceded that there was some
truth in what Van Heerden said, it could not be the whole

truth. He knew that, he felt it in his bones. What of God, what of love, what of all the strange, wonderful things that people were capable of, things we did and experienced and thought?

Van Heerden waved his hand and said, 'Let's forget about it.'

And Mpayipheli had said: 'You know, Whitey, it sounds like The New Excuse to me. All the great troubles of the world have been done in the name of one or other Excuse. Christianization, Colonialism, *Herrenvolk*, Communism, Apartheid, Democracy and now Evolution. Or is it Genetics? Excuses, just another reason to do as we wish. I am tired of it all. Finished with that. I am tired of my own excuses and the excuses of other people. I am taking responsibility for what I do now. Without excuse. I have choices, you have choices. About how we will live. That's all. That's all we can choose. Fuck excuses. Live right or get lost.'

He spoke with fervour, and with conviction. He had been loud and heads had turned in the coffee shop where they sat, but he didn't care. And now, in this desolate piece of Africa, at 160 kilometres per hour, he knew that he was right and it filled him with elation for what he must do. Not just the thing in the bag, but afterwards. To live a life of responsibility, a life that said if you want change, start here, inside yourself.

'Ma'am, let us let her go.' Vincent Radebe sat next to Janina Mentz, speaking softly to keep the potential for conflict between them low-key. He knew that she was keeping an eye on him, knew that she had doubts about his attitude and his support for her. But he had to do what he must do.

She sat at the big table at her laptop. She finished typing but did not turn to him.

'Ai, Vincent,' she said.

'She knows nothing. She can't add value,' he said.

'But she can do damage.'

'Ma'am, she understands that she must not talk to the media.'

Janina put her hand on Vincent Radebe's arm compassionately. 'It is good that you are part of the team, Vincent. You bring balance. I respect and value your contribution. And your honesty.'

He had not expected that. 'Can I go and tell her?'

'Let me give you a scenario to think over. We drop Mrs Nzululwazi at her house. She fetches her child and a photographer from the *Cape Times* photographs them standing hand in hand in front of their little house. Tomorrow the picture is on the front page. With the caption "Mother and child wait anxiously for fugitive's return" – or something like that. Do we need that? While the minister works to explain Mpayipheli's true colours to the media? She has already done damage. You heard the reporter on the radio. "His common-law wife says he is a good man."'

He could see what she meant.

'In any case, Vincent, what guarantee do you have that she will not talk to the media again? What happens when they start pulling out their chequebooks?'

'I have summed her up differently,' he said.

She nodded thoughtfully. 'Perhaps you are in a better position to make this decision, Vincent.'

'Ma'am?'

'The decision is yours.'

'You mean that I can decide if she can go or not?'

'Yes, Vincent, just you. But you must bear the responsibility. And the consequences.'

He looked at her, searching for clues in her eyes, suddenly wary.

'I will have to think about it,' he said.

'That is the right thing to do.'

Thobela Mpayipheli slowed down when he saw Petrusville. He had hoped that the road would bypass the town but it ran directly through. Koos Kok was right, it would have been better at night, but there was no help for it now, he must face it out. He checked the fuel meter – still over half. Keeping the needle on sixty he rode into town, one-and two-storey buildings, bleached signboards, old-world architecture. From the corner of his eye his could see black faces from the lower town turning, staring. He was colourless, without identity under the helmet, thankfully. He halted at the four-way stop. A car pulled up alongside him, driven by a woman, fat and forty. She stared at the bike, at him. He kept his gaze forward, pulled away, excruciatingly aware of the attention. There was a sprinkling of activity in the hot, sleepy afternoon. Pedestrians. Cars, bakkies, bicycles. He rode with his ears pricked for alarm signals, his back tense as if waiting for a bullet. Kept to sixty, revs low, trying not to make a racket, to be invisible, something impossible on this vehicle. He passed houses and children by the road, a few fingers pointed, did they recognize him or was it the motorbike? Town boundary, a sign saying he could ride at 120 again. He accelerated slowly, uncertain, keeping watch in the rear-view mirror.

Nothing.

Was it possible?

A car beside the road. White people under a thorn tree, a flask of coffee on the concrete table. They waved. He lifted his left hand.

Signboard saying *Vanderkloof Dam*, to the right.

He carried straight on

Somewhere up ahead was the turn-off to Luckhoff – and the bridge over the Orange.

Trouble must be waiting there.

Fourteen kilometres south of Koffiefontein the official of the Free State Provincial Traffic Authority sat at his speed trap.

'Department of Psychology,' said the woman's voice over the phone.

'Hi. May I speak to Mr van Heerden?'

'You mean Doctor Van Heerden?'

'Oh. Zatopek van Heerden?'

'I'm afraid Dr Van Heerden isn't in. May I take a message?'

'This is Allison Healy of the *Cape Times*. Do you know how I can get hold of him?'

'I'm afraid I'm not at liberty to provide his home number.'

'Does he have a cellphone number?'

The woman laughed. 'Dr Van Heerden is not keen on cellphones, I'm afraid.'

'May I leave my number? Will he call me back?'

'He will be in again tomorrow.'

Thobela Mpayipheli knew that the bridge must be within a kilometre or two, according to the map.

A Volkswagen Kombi approached from the front. He watched the driver, looking for signs of blockades, the law or soldiers.

Nothing.

He saw the green seam of the river, knew the crossing was just ahead but there was no sign of activity.

Was he far enough east? Was that why they were not here?

The road straightened and the bridge came into view – two white railings, double lane, open, clear.

He accelerated, leaving the Northern Cape, looked down at the brown waters flowing strongly, the midday sun reflecting brightly off the ripples. The sluices of the dam must be open, he surmised. Probably because of the rain. Over the bridge, over the Orange.

Free State.

Relief flooded through him. They had slipped up.

What about . . . His head jerked up to the sky, searching for the specks of helicopters, ears straining for their rumble above the noise of the motorbike.

Nothing.

Had the ride in the back of the El Camino slipped him through the net?

It didn't matter. The initiative was with him now; he had the lead and the advantage.

He must use it.

He used the torque purposefully, felt the power flow to the rear wheel, how the steering rod got lighter.

He wanted to laugh.

Fucking beautiful German machine.

Fourteen kilometres south of Koffiefontein the official of the Free State Traffic Authority sat reading.

The white patrol car was behind the thorn trees that grew by the dry wash, his canvas chair was positioned so that he could see the reading on the Gatsometer and the road stretching out to the south. The book was balanced on his lap.

So far it had been an average day. Two minibus taxis for speeding, three lorries from Gauteng for lesser offences. They thought that if they came through here avoiding the main routes they could overload, or get away with poor tyres, but they were wrong. He was not over-zealous. He enjoyed his work, especially the part that allowed him to sit in the shade of an acacia on a perfect summer's day, listening to the birds chattering and reading Ed McBain. But when it came to enforcing traffic ordinances, he was probably a tad stricter with vehicles from other provinces.

He had pulled over a few farmers in their bakkies. One hadn't had his driver's licence with him, but you couldn't just write a ticket for these gentlemen, they had influence. You gave them a warning.

Two tourists, Danes, had stopped to ask directions.

An average day.

He checked his watch again. At a quarter to five he would start rolling up the wires of the Gatsometer. Not a minute later.

He looked up the road. No traffic. His eyes dropped back to the book. Some of his colleagues from other towns listened to the radio. Where there were two officers stationed together they talked rubbish from morning to night, but he preferred this. Alone, just him and McBain's characters, Caralla and Hawes and the big black cop, Brown and Oliver Weeks and their things.

An average day.

25

Everything happened at once.

The Director walked into the Ops Room and everyone was astounded. Janina Mentz's cellphone rang and Quinn, earphones on his ears, suddenly started making wild gestures to get her attention.

She took the call because she could see from the little screen who it was.

'It's Tiger,' said Mazibuko. 'I am awake.'

'Captain, I will phone you back now,' she said and cut the connection. 'What have you got, Rudewaan?' she asked Quinn.

'Johnny Kleintjes's house number. We relayed it here.'

'Yes?'

'It's ringing. Continuously. Every few minutes they phone again.'

'Where is Monica Kleintjes? Bring her down.'

'In my office. Is she going to answer?'

A nervous question because of the Director's presence – the figure at the margins, the big boss that they almost never saw. They couldn't afford a mess-up now.

Mentz's voice was reassuring. 'Perhaps it's nothing. Maybe it's the media. Even if it is the people in Lusaka – by now they must know something is going on, what with all the media coverage.'

Quinn nodded to one of his people to go and fetch Monica Kleintjes.

Mentz turned to the Director and stood up. 'Good afternoon, sir.'

'Afternoon, everyone,' said the small Zulu and smiled like a politician on voting day. 'Don't stand up, Janina. I know you are busy.' He came and stood by her. 'I have a message from the Minister. So I thought I would come down. To show my solidarity.'

'Thank you, sir. We appreciate it.'

'The Minister has asked the Department of Defence to track down people who worked with Mpayipheli in the old days and, shall we say, do not have fond memories of him.'

'She is a woman of initiative, sir.'

'That she is, Janina.'

'And did she find someone?'

'She did. A Brigadier in Pretoria. Lucas Morape. They trained together in Russia and Morape describes our fugitive as, I quote, "an aggressive troublemaker, perhaps a psychopath, who was a continuous embarrassment to his comrades and the Movement".'

'That is good news indeed, sir. From a public-relations angle, of course.'

'It is. In the course of the afternoon the Brigadier will release a short report to the media.' The Director prepared to leave. 'That is all I have at the moment, Janina. I won't disturb you further.'

'I truly appreciate it, sir. But may I ask one more favour? Could you pass on this news to Radebe personally?'

'Is he somewhat sceptical, Janina?'

'One could say that, sir.'

The Director turned and walked over to where Radebe was sitting at the communication banks. Mentz concentrated on her cellphone getting Mazibuko on the air.

'You must know that we are working with a bunch of morons here,' said Tiger Mazibuko.

'How so?'

'Jissis,' he said. 'So many egos. So much politicking. Free State Command want to run the show and so do Northern Cape. They don't even have enough radios for all the road-blocks and Groblershoop is not covered because the trucks have broken down.'

'Slow down, Tiger. Where are you?'

'Anti-Aircraft School. Kimberley.'

'Is that where the Rooivalks are?'

'Yes. They are waiting in a row here. My people too.'

'Tiger, according to my information Free State Command is covering the N8 from Bloemfontein to Perdeberg and Northern Cape is responsible for the rest, up to Groblershoop. With the police as back-up.'

'In theory.'

'What do you mean, in theory?'

'In the Free State things look OK, they have fourteen road-blocks and things look all right on the map. But between us and Groblershoop there are about twenty roads that cross the N8. The little colonel here says they have only sixteen road-blocks, and four of them have not reported back yet because either they haven't received radios or they don't work.'

'Do you include the police in that?'

'The police are using their own network. The coordination stinks.'

'You would expect that, Tiger. This thing came down on them out of the blue.'

'They are going to let the fucker slip through, ma'am.'

'Captain . . .'

'Sorry.'

She saw Monica Kleintjes coming in, limping urgently, Quinn's assistant behind her.

'Let me see what I can do, Tiger – I'll phone you back.'

She stood up and went to Quinn. 'Are they still ringing?'

'Not at the moment.'

'How are you feeling, Monica?'

'Scared.'

'There is nothing to be afraid of. Our people are already in Lusaka and we will handle this thing.'

The coloured woman looked at her with hope.

'If it is the media, say you don't know what they are talking about. If it is the people from Lusaka, tell them the truth. With one exception, tell them you are at home. Don't tell them we brought you here. Understand?'

'I must say I gave the hard disk to Tiny?'

'The whole truth. Tell them why you gave it to him, when you gave it to him, everything. If they ask you if it is the man who is so much in the news say yes. Keep to the truth. If they ask you if we have contacted you, say yes, there was a man who came to question you. Admit you told him everything. If they ask how we knew, tell them you suspect your phone was tapped. Keep to the truth. Just don't tell them you are here.'

'But my father . . .'

'They are after the data, Monica. Never forget that. Your father is safe as long as that is the case. And moreover, we have teams in Lusaka. Everything is under control.'

Monica's eyes stayed wide, but she nodded.

You are not your father's child, thought Janina. There was nothing of Johnny Kleintjes's quiet strength. *Perhaps that will work in our favour.*

'Ma'am,' said Rahjev Rajkumar, 'something is brewing.'

She looked at the Indian tapping a fat finger on the computer screen of one his assistants.

'I'm coming,' she said. 'Quinn, let Monica answer if they phone again.'

'Very good, ma'am.'

As she moved towards Rajkumar, she could see the Director and Radebe deep in conversation in the corner at the radio panel. She could see Radebe talking fervently, waving his hands, the Director small and defenceless against the onslaught, but she could not hear a single word. Let him see what she had to deal with. Let him see how she was undermined. Then there would be no trouble when she transferred Vincent Radebe to lighter duties.

The Indian shifted his considerable bulk to make room for her. On the screen was the BMW motorcycle website.

'Look at this,' he said. 'We have been monitoring them all afternoon.'

She read. Messages, one after another.

This is going to be better than the annual gathering. We are four guys, leaving at 13:00. See you in Kimberley.
—John S, Johannesburg.
I'm leaving now, will take the N3 to Bethlehem, then Bloemfontein and on to Kimberley. I'm on a red K 1200 RS. If there's anybody who wants to come along for the ride, just fall in behind me. If you can keep up, of course.
—Peter Strauss, Durban.
See you at Pietermaritzburg, Peter. We are on two R 1150's, an F 650 and a new RT.
—Dasher, PM.
We are three guys on 1150 GS's, just like the Big Bad Biker. We will meet you at the Big Hole, will keep the beers cold, it's just over the hill for us.
—Johan Wasserman, Klerksdorp.

'How many are there?' asked Janina.

'Twenty-two messages,' said Rajkumar's assistant. 'More than seventy bikers who say they are on the way.'

'That doesn't bother me.'

Rajkumar and his assistant looked at her questioningly.

'It's just a lot of men looking for an excuse to drink,' she said. 'Seventy? What are they going to do? Carry out a *coup d' état* at Northern Cape Command with their scooters?'

'Department of Psychology.'

'This is Allison Healy of the *Cape Times* again. I wonder if—'

'I told you Dr Van Heerden would be in tomorrow.'

'You did. But I was wondering if you could call him at home and tell him it is in connection with Thobela Mpayipheli.'

'Who?'

'Thobela Mpayipheli. Dr Van Heerden knows him well. The man is in trouble, and if you could call him and tell him, I can leave you my number.'

'Dr Van Heerden does not like to be disturbed at home.'

'Please.'

There was silence on the other end of the line followed by a dramatic sigh. 'What is your number?'

Allison gave it.

'And your name again?'

The Reaction Unit's members sat around in groups defined by the shade of the acacias next to the hard-baked red and white parade ground of the Anti-Aircraft School, between the vehicles and boxes. The row of trees provided ever-shifting shelter from the merciless sun and dominating heat of thirty-four degrees Celsius. Two tents had been erected, just the roof sections like enormous umbrellas. Shirts were off, torsos glistening with sweat, weapons were being cleaned, a few of Team Alpha lay sleeping, others chatted, here and there a muffled laugh. A radio was playing.

As Captain Tiger Mazibuko approached, he heard them fall silent as a news bulletin was announced. He checked his watch. Where had the day gone?

Four o'clock on Diamond City Radio and here is the news, read by René Grobbelaar. Kimberley is the focal point of a country-wide search for MK veteran Thobela Mpayipheli, who evaded law enforcers yesterday evening in Cape Town on a stolen motorcycle. According to Inspector Tappe Terblanche, local Liaison Officer for the police, a joint operation between the army and SAPS has been launched to intercept the fugitive. He is probably somewhere in the Northern Cape. A similar operation is underway n the Free State.

During a news conference earlier today the Minister of National Intelligence revealed that Mpayipheli, who is armed and considered dangerous, is in possession of extremely sensitive classified information that he has illegally obtained. In reply to a question on the nature of the information the Minister replied that it was not in the interest of national security to reveal details.

Members of the public who have contact with Mpayipheli, or who have information that could lead to his arrest, are advised to ring the following toll-free number . . .

With my luck, thought Tiger Mazibuko, *some idiot or other will force Mpayipheli off the road with his souped-up Opel and demand the reward too.*

He sat down beside Lieutenant Penrose. 'Is Bravo ready?'

'When the signal comes, we can be rolling in five minutes, captain.'

'*If* the signal comes.' Mazibuko motioned towards the building behind him where the operation was being coordinated. 'This lot of monkeys couldn't find a turd in a toilet.'

The lieutenant laughed. 'We will get him, captain. You'll see.'

Fourteen kilometres south of Koffiefontein the Gatsometer gave its shrill electronic scream and the officer closed his book in one fluid motion, checked the speed reading, stood up and walked into the road. It was a white Mercedes Benz, six or seven years old. He held up his hand and the car began immediately to brake, stopping just next to him. He walked around to the driver's side.

'Afternoon, Mr Franzen,' he greeted the driver.

'You got me again,' said the farmer.

'A hundred and thirty-two, Mr Franzen.'

'I was in a bit of a hurry. The kids forgot half their stuff on the farm and tomorrow is rugby practice. You know how it is.'

'Speed kills, Mr Franzen.'

'I know, I know, it's a terrible thing.'

'We'll look the other way this time, but you must please respect the speed limit, Mr Franzen.'

'I promise you it won't happen again.'

'You can go.'

'Thank you. Cheers, boet.'

He doesn't even know my name, the officer thought. *Until I write him a ticket.*

Quinn motioned for everyone to keep quiet before he allowed Monica Kleintjes to answer. She had a headset on, earphones and microphone, and then he pressed the button and nodded to her.

'Monica Kleintjes,' she said in a shaky voice.

'You have a lot of explaining to do, young lady.' Lusaka. The same unaccented voice of the first call.

'Please,' she said.

'You gave the disk to the guy on the motorbike?'

'Yes, I—'

'That was a very stupid thing to do, Monica.'

'I had no choice. I . . . I couldn't do it on my own.'

'Oh, no, Monica. You were just plain stupid. And now we have a real problem.'

'I'm sorry. Please . . .'

'How did the Spooks find out, Monica?'

'They . . . the phone. It was tapped.'

'That's what we thought. And they're listening right now.'

'No.'

'Of course they are. They are probably standing right next to you.'

'What are you going to do?'

The voice was still calm. 'Unlike you, my dear, we are sticking to the original deal. With maybe a few codicils. You have forty-eight of the seventy-two hours left. If the disk isn't here by then, we will kill your father. If we see anything that looks like an agent in Lusaka, we will kill your father. If the disk gets here and it is more bullshit, we will kill your father.'

Monica Kleintjes's body jerked slightly. 'Please,' she said despairingly.

'You should know, Monica, that your daddy is not a nice man. He talked to us – with a little encouragement, of course. We know that he is working with the intelligence people. We know he tried to palm off bullshit data. That's why we ordered the real stuff. So here's the deal for you and your friends from Presidential Intelligence: if the motorbike man does not make it, we kill Kleintjes. And we'll give the bullshit disks and the whole story of how they abused a pensioner to the press. Can you imagine the headlines, Monica? Can you?'

She was crying now, her shoulders shaking, her mouth forming words that could not escape her lips.

And then everyone realized that the connection was broken and the Director was looking at Janina Mentz with a strange expression on his face.

26

Mpayipheli was doing nearly 180 when he saw the double tubes of the Gatsometer on the road in front of him and grabbed a handful of brakes and pulled hard, a purely instinctive reaction. The ABS brakes kicked in, moaned, one eye on the instrument panel, one eye on the tubes, still too fast, somewhere around 140 and he saw the man run over the road, hand raised and he had to brake again to avoid contact, realizing it was traffic police, one man, just one man, a speed trap. He must decide whether to run or to stop, the choice too suddenly on him, the causality too wide, he chose to run, he twisted the throttle, passed the traffic officer and one car on the right, under the tree, only one car, he made up his mind, heart in his throat and he pulled the brake again, bringing the motorbike to a standstill on the gravel verge. It didn't make sense, a lone traffic cop, one car and he turned to see the man jogging towards him, half apologetic and then he was standing there and saying, 'Mister, for a minute there I thought you were going to run away.'

For the first time Janina Mentz felt fear as she climbed the stairs with the Director to his office.

In that moment when he had looked at her in the Ops Room something had altered between them, some balance. He had made a small movement with his head and she knew what he meant and had followed, her staff unknowing but silently watching them.

It was not the change in the balance of power between her and the Zulu that clamped around her heart, it was the knowledge that she was no longer in control; that perception and reality had drifted apart like two moving targets.

He waited until she was inside, closed the door and stood still. He looked unblinkingly at her. 'That is not the CIA, Janina,' he said.

'I know.'

'Who is it?'

She sat down, although he had not invited her to do so. 'I don't know.'

'And the disk that Mpayipheli has?'

She shook her head.

He walked slowly through the room, around the desk. She saw his calm. He did not sit, but stood behind his chair and looked down at her.

'Have you told me everything, Janina?'

One man – the situation was surreal. Mpayipheli was moving in a dream world as he climbed off the motorbike and pulled off his gloves and helmet. 'That's a beautiful bike,' said the traffic officer.

For a moment he considered the irony: the traffic cop saw the removal of his accessories as submission, he knew that he did it for ease of movement should he need to react. Retreating from the threat of violence, he forced himself into pacifist mode. He could see the weapon in the shiny leather holster on the officer's hip.

'We don't see many of those around here.'

The blood was pulsing through him – he was aware of his readiness. As long as he recognized it he could control it. He still felt unreal: the conversation was impossibly banal. 'It is the biggest-selling bike bigger than 750cc in the country,' he said, keeping his voice even with difficulty.

'You don't say?'

He didn't know how to answer. The motorbike was between them: he wanted to reduce the gap, but also maintain it.

'You were going quite fast.'

'I was.' Was he going to get a ticket? Would it be as ridiculous as that?

'Let me see your driver's licence.'

Suspicion – the traffic cop must know something, he could not be that isolated. 'Of course.' Mpayipheli took the key from the ignition, unlocked the luggage case, tried to scan the line of thorn trees and bushes surreptitiously: where were the others?

'Lots of packing space, hey?' There was an ingenuous quality in the officer and the question loosened something in Mpayipheli's belly, a strange feeling.

He unzipped the blue sports bag, looking for his wallet, took out the card and handed it over. He kept a vigilant watch on the officer's face, looking for signs of covertness or deceit.

'Mpay—'

'Mpayipheli.' He helped the man pronounce it.

'Is this your motorbike, Mr Mpayipheli?'

Then he knew what was happening and the urge to giggle became overwhelming, pushing up in him without warning as his brain grasped the possibility that this provincial representative had absolutely no idea. It almost overcame him. He allowed it to bubble up modestly, careful not to lose it, but suddenly relaxing, laughing heartily. 'I could never afford one of these.'

The officer laughed along with him, bonding, two middle-class men admiring the toys of the rich. 'What do these things cost?'

'Just over ninety thousand.'

The man whistled through his teeth. 'Whose is it?'

'My boss's. He has an agency in the Cape. For BMW.'

And again the laugh bubbled up in him, any minute now he was going to wake up under the tarpaulin of the El Camino – these moments of drama could not be real.

The traffic officer handed back Mpayipheli's driver's licence. 'I rode a Kawasaki when I did traffic in Bloemfontein. A seven-fifty. Big. I don't see a chance for that any more.' Trying to strengthen the bond.

'I've got a Honda Benly at home.'

'Those things last for ever.'

They both knew that the moment of truth was coming, a defining factor in the budding relationship. It hung in a moment of silence between them. The officer shrugged his shoulders, apologetically. 'I really should ticket you.'

Fuck – he could not hold it in. It was filling his body with the urgency of a call of nature. 'I know,' was all he could manage.

'You better go, before I change my mind.'

He smiled, perhaps too widely, and put out his hand. 'Thank you,' he said and turned quickly away, putting away the licence in the wallet, wallet in the bag, bag in the motor-bike.

'And take it easy,' came the voice over his shoulder. 'Speed kills.'

Mpayipheli nodded, put on the helmet and pulled on his gloves.

'You know all that I know,' said Janina Mentz. But she lied. 'I planned the operation on Ismail Mohammed's testimony. I recruited Johnny Kleintjes. I alone. No one else knew anything. We compiled the data together. It is false, but credible, I am sure of that. He contacted the Americans. They showed interest. They invited him to Lusaka. He went and then the call came to his house.'

'And his daughter got Mpayipheli.'

'Unforeseen.'

'Unforeseen, Janina? According to the transcript of Monica's interview, Johnny came to her place of work two weeks before he left for Lusaka and said that if something happened to him, Mpayipheli was the man to contact. And, moreover, on top of the hard disk in his safe was a note with Mpayipheli's phone number.'

Then she saw what the Director saw and the hand around her heart squeezed a little tighter. 'He knew.'

The Director nodded.

She saw from a wider perspective. 'Johnny Kleintjes sold us out.'

'Us and the Americans, Janina.'

'But why, sir?'

'What do you know of Johnny Kleintjes?'

She threw up her hands. 'I studied his file. Activist, exile, ANC member, computers . . .'

'Johnny is a communist, Janina.'

Mentz sprang up – frustration and fear were the goads. 'Mr Director, with respect, what does that mean? We were all communists when it suited us to have the help of the Eastern Bloc. Where are the communists now? Marginalized dreamers who no longer have a significant influence in the government.'

She stood with her hands on the desktop and became conscious of the distaste in the Zulu's demeanour. When he eventually answered his voice was soft. 'Johnny Kleintjes may be a dreamer, but you were the one who marginalized him.'

'I don't understand,' she said, removing her hands and stepping back.

'What don't you understand, Janina?'

'Sir,' she said, sinking slowly into the chair. 'To whom could he go? To whom did he sell us out?'

'That is what we must find out.'

'But it makes no sense. Communism . . . There's nothing left. There's no one any more.'

'You are too literal, Janina. I suspect it is more a question of "the enemy of my enemy".'

'You must explain.'

'Johnny always had a special hatred for the Americans.'

Insight came slowly to her, reluctant. 'You mean . . .'

'Who does the CIA currently view as threat number one?'

'Oh my God,' said Janina.

A bespectacled black soldier with the epaulettes of the Anti-Aircraft School on his shoulders came to call Captain Tiger Mazibuko under the tree. 'The colonel asks the captain to come quickly.'

Mazibuko jumped up. 'Have they got him?' He ran ahead, aware of the expectations of the RU behind him.

'I don't think so, captain.'

'You don't think so?'

'The colonel will tell you, captain.' He jogged into the building. The colonel stood at the radio, microphone in hand.

'We have a situation.'

'What?'

'There are thirty-nine Hell's Angels on motorbikes at the Windsorton Road roadblock. They want to come through.'

'Where the hell is Windsorton Road?'

'Forty-five kilometres north, on the N12.'

'The Johannesburg road?'

The colonel nodded.

'Fuck them. Send them home.'

'It's not that simple.'

'Why?'

'They say there are another fifty on the way. And when those arrive they are going through and if we want to stop them we will have to shoot them.'

Tiger Mazibuko reconsidered. 'Let them through.'

'Are you sure?'

'Mazibuko smiled. 'Very.'

The colonel hesitated a moment and then depressed the 'send' button on the microphone. 'Sergeant, let them through whenever they want.'

'Roger and out,' came the response.

'What is your plan, captain?' the colonel asked just before Mazibuko walked out with a certain zip in his step.

Mazibuko did not look up, but kept walking. 'Diversion, colonel. Nothing like a bit of diversion for a bunch of frustrated soldiers,' he said.

The traffic officer was carefully rolling up the tubes of the Gatsometer. It was a tedious job on his own, but he did it mechanically, without bitterness, just another part of his easy routine. His thoughts were occupied with the black motorcyclist.

Strange, that. A first. Black man on a big motorbike. You don't see many of those.

But that wasn't all.

The thing was, when he rode off, the BMW's flat, two-cylinder engine made a nice muffled sound. The cop could have sworn he had heard the man laugh – a deep, thundering, infectious, paralysing laugh.

Must have been his imagination.

'Who?' asked Janina Mentz. 'Al Qaeda? How, sir? How?'

'My personal feeling is Tehran. I suspect that Johnny had made a contact or two by some way or other. Perhaps through the local extremists. But in my opinion, that is not the burning question, Janina.'

She drew a deep breath to damp her growing unease. She was watchful for what would follow.

'The question that we must ask ourselves now is, what is on the hard disk?'

She knew why the balance had shifted. He was not the Zulu source, he was not Inkululeko. He was free. Of suspicion, misunderstanding, circumstantial evidence. He was pure.

The Director leaned towards her and said, with great tenderness: 'I had hoped you would have some ideas.'

The lieutenant of One Infantry Battalion had put a lot of thought into the roadblock at Petrusburg. His problem was that the place had a proliferation of roads leading like arteries out of the heart of the town in every direction – three dirt roads north, the east-west route of the N8 to Kimberley and Bloemfontein, the R48 to Koffiefontein, another dirt road south and then the tar road to the black township, Bolokaneng.

Where to put up the blockade?

His eventual decision was based on the available intelligence: the fugitive was heading for Kimberley. That was why the roadblock was just 400 metres outside the town boundary on the Kimberley side, on the N8. For extra insurance, the SAPS, who provided two vans and four policemen, according to the agreement, were sitting on the gravel road that ran parallel east/west and joined the N8 further along towards the city of diamonds.

Now the lieutenant had a more difficult decision to make. One thing was for sure, if you were a member of the military faced with a complicated choice, your first option was to pass the decision up the chain of command. That was how you covered your back.

So he did not hesitate to resort to the radio.

'Oscar Hotel,' he said to the ops commander at the Anti-Aircraft School. 'I have stopped nineteen riders on BMW motorbikes here. One says he is a lawyer and will get an urgent interdict against us if we don't let them through. Over.'

He could have sworn that he heard the colonel say 'Fuck,' but perhaps the radio reception was not clear.

'Stand by, Papa Bravo.' *Papa Bravo*. Military abbreviation for Petrusburg. There was once a time when the lieutenant had felt like a clown using these terms, but it had passed. He waited, looking out of the tent that stood beside the road. The BMWs stood in ranks of two, all with headlights on and engines idling. Where the fuck were they going? His men stood with their assault rifles over their shoulders, looking on curiously. There was something about a group of bikers. Like one of Genghis Khan's Mongol hordes on the way to cause desolation . . .

'Papa Bravo, this is Oscar Hotel Quebec, come in, over.'

'Papa Bravo in, over.'

'Are you sure there are no black guys on any of the BMWs? Over.'

'We are sure, Oscar Hotel, over.'

'Let them through, Papa Bravo. Let them through. Over.'

'Roger, Papa Bravo. Over and out.'

27

In the editorial office of the *Cape Times* Allison Healy read the story that had come in from *The Star*'s offices in Johannesburg.

'A violent man, a troublemaker and most probably a psychopath' is how a former comrade-in-arms of the fugitive Thobela Mpayipheli describes the man now being sought across three provinces by Intelligence authorities, the SA National Defence Force and the SAPS.

According to Brigadier Lucas Morape, a senior member of the Supply and Transport Unit at SANDF Headquarters in Pretoria, he served with Mpayipheli in Tanzania and at a Kazakhstan military base in the former USSR, where Umkhonto we Sizwe soldiers were trained as part of Eastern Bloc support for the Struggle in the Eighties.

'In one instance, he almost beat a Russian soldier to death in a mess-room fist fight. It took the leadership weeks to repair the diplomatic damage done by this senseless act of brutality.'

Mpayipheli allegedly received sensitive intelligence data from his Cape Town employer, and is heading north. He slipped through a military cordon at Three Sisters early this morning during a heavy thunderstorm. His current whereabouts are unknown.

In an issued statement, Brigadier Morape goes on to describe Mpayipheli as a compulsive brawler who became such a problem to the ANC that he was removed from the training programme. 'I am not surprised by allegations that he worked for a drug syndicate in the Cape. It fits his psychopathic profile perfectly.'

★   ★   ★

'Psychopathic profile,' Allison said softly to herself and shook her head. Suddenly everyone was a psychiatrist.

How well the brigadier's opinion fitted in with the efforts of the Minister.

The wheels were rolling, the great engine of the State was building up steam. Mpayipheli did not stand a chance.

And then her cellphone rang.

'Allison Healy.'

'This is Zatopek van Heerden. You were looking for me.' The tone was belligerent.

'Thank you for returning my call, doctor.' She kept her tone cheery. 'It is in connection with Mr Thobela Mpayipheli. I would like to ask a few—'

'No.' The voice was brusque and irritable.

'Doctor, please . . .'

'Don't "doctor" me.'

'Please help, I—'

'Where did you hear that I know him?'

'Orlando Arendse told me.'

Van Heerden was silent for so long that Allison thought that he had hung up on her. She wanted to say 'doctor' or something again and was wondering how to address him when he asked: 'Did you say Orlando Arendse?'

'That's right, the . . . um . . .'

'The Drug Baron.'

'Yes . . .'

'Orlando talked to you?'

'Yes . . .'

'You have guts, Allison Healy.'

'Um . . .'

'Where do you want to meet?'

Thirty minutes south of Petrusburg, just across the Riet River, the road curved lazily between the Free State koppies, a few wide sweeping curves before it returned to running straight as a die. Enough to draw Mpayipheli's concentration back to the motorbike again – the engine was running optimally in the heat, a reassuring constant, tangible heartbeat beneath him. This extension of his body lent him security. It was the moment when he realized that he could keep riding, past Lusaka, continuing north, day after day, he and the machine and the road to the horizon. It was the moment when he understood the addiction the white clients had spoken of.

It was that time of day.

The sun shone with a benign orange as if it knew that the day's task was nearly done.

Mpayipheli had discovered the magic of late afternoon in Paris, during his two years of desolation after the Wall had fallen. He had fallen too, his lot inextricably entangled with the Berlin barrier, from celebrated assassin, the darling of the Stasi and the KGB, to uneducated and unemployed. From wealthy man of the world to the disillusionment of knowing that the thirty dollars in his account were the last and that there would be no more income from that source. From arrogance to depression, angrily and reluctantly accepting the new reality in between. Until he picked himself up from self-pity and went door-to-door, looking for work like any lowly labourer. Monsieur Merceron had asked to see his hands: 'These hands have never worked, but they are built to work.' And he had got the job, just west of the Gare du Nord in Montmartre, gofer at the bakery, sweeper of floury floors, bearer of sacks and boxes, scrubber of the big mechanical blenders, early-morning deliverer of baguettes, with arms full of loaves. In the winter the steam rising from the warm bread into his nostrils had become the fragrance of Paris, fresh, exotic and wonderful. And in the late afternoon when the sun angled down and the whole city was in transition between work and home he would go back to his first-storey apartment near the Salvador Dali Museum. Every day he walked the long route, first up the steps on the hill to the Sacré Coeur, the Basilica of the Sacred Heart, and went to sit right at the top, his body delightfully weary, and watched the evening claim the city like a jealous lover. The sounds rose up, the shadings slowly shifting to greys – the crouching mass of Notre Dame, the twisting Seine, the sun sparking gold off the dome of Les Invalides, the dignified loneliness of the Eiffel Tower and in the east the Arc de Triomphe. He sat till every landmark disappeared in the dark and the lights flickered like stars in the city firmament, the scene changing to a wonder world without dimension.

Then he would rise and go into the church, allowing the peace of the interior to fill him before lighting a candle for each of his victims.

The memory filled him with a deep nostalgia for the simplicity of those two years and he thought that with the money in the sports bag, if he kept the nose pointing north, he could be there in a month.

He smiled sardonically inside the helmet: how ironic, now he wished to be there. When the one thing, the single lack, the great desire when he *had* been there was this very landscape that now stretched out ahead of him. How many times had he wished he could see the umbrella of a thorn tree against the grey veld, how he had longed for the earth-shaking rumble of a thunderhead, the dark grey anvil shape, the lightning of a storm over the wide open, endless plains of Africa.

Vincent Radebe was waiting for Janina Metz at the door of the Ops Room and said, 'Ma'am, I will bring in a camp bed for Mrs Nzululwazi, I realize now that we can't let her go.' And Janina put her hand on the black man's shoulder and said, 'Vincent, I know it wasn't an easy decision. That's the trouble with our work: the decisions are never easy.'

She walked to the centre of the room. She said that every team must decide who would handle the night watch and who would go home to sleep, so that there would be a fresh shift to start the day in the morning. She said that she was going out for an hour or two to see her children. If anything happened, they had her cellphone number.

Radebe waited until she had gone before slowly and unwillingly walking to the interview room. He knew what he must say to the woman, he needed to find the right words.

When he unlocked the door and entered, Miriam Nzululwazi sprang up urgently.

'I have to go,' she said.

'Ma'am . . .'

'My child,' she said. 'I have to fetch my child.'

'Ma'am, it is safer to stay here. Just one night . . .' He saw the fear in her face, the panic in her eyes.

'No,' she said. 'My child . . .'

'Slow down, ma'am. Where is he?'

'At the day-care. He is waiting for me. I am already late – please, I beg you, you can't do this to my child.'

'They will take care of him, ma'am.'

She wept and sank to her knees, clutching at his leg. Her voice was dangerously shrill, 'Please, my brother, please . . .'

'Just one night, ma'am, they will look after him, I will make sure, it is safer this way.'

'Please. Please.'

Thobela Mpayipheli saw the sign beside the road that said only ten kilometres to Petrusburg. He drew a deep breath, steeling himself for what lay ahead, the next obstacle in his path. There was a main route that he had to cross, another barrier before he could spill over into the next section of countryside with its dirt roads and extended farms. It was the last hurdle before the world between him and the Botswana border lay open.

And he needed petrol.

The traffic officer of the Free State Provincial Administration stopped at the office in Koffiefontein. He opened the boot of the patrol car, removed the Gatsometer in its case, carried it inside with difficulty, put it down and closed the door.

His two colleagues from admin were ready to leave. 'You're late,' said one, a white woman in her fifties.

'You didn't catch the biker, did you?' asked the other, a young Sotho with spectacles and a fashionable haircut.

'What biker?' asked the traffic officer.

Allison Healy found the plot at Morning Star with difficulty. She did not know this area of the Cape; no one knew this area of the Cape.

'When you drive through the gate, the road forks. Keep left, it's the small white house,' Dr Zatopek van Heerden had said.

She found it, with Table Mountain as a distant backdrop. And far out to sea a wall of clouds, stretching as far as the eye could see, hung like a long grey banner in front of the setting sun.

Lizette ran out the house before Janina Mentz had stopped the car and when she opened the car door, her daughter threw her arms around her theatrically. 'Mamma,' a dramatic cry with the embrace and she felt like laughing at this child of hers in that uncomfortable stage of self-consciousness. With the girl's arms around her neck she felt the warmth of her daughter's body, smelt the fragrance of her hair.

'Hello, my girl.'

'I missed you.' An exaggerated exclamation.

'I missed you too.' Knowing the hug would go on too long, that it was as it should be, she would have to say, 'Wait, let me get out' and Lizette would ask, 'Aren't you going to put the car away?' and she would say 'No, I have to go back soon.' She looked up and Lien stood on the steps of the veranda, still and dignified just to make the point that she could control her emotions, that she was the older, stronger one and Janina felt her heart was full.

'Mamma,' Lien called from the veranda, 'You forgot to put off your flicker light again.'

Vincent Radebe carefully closed the door of the interview room behind him. He could no longer hear the sobs.

He knew that he had made the wrong decision. He had realized it inside there, with the woman's face against his knees. She was just a mother, not a Player, she had one desire and that was to be with her child.

He stood still a second to analyse his feelings, because they were new and unfamiliar to him, and then he understood what had happened. The completion of the circle – he had finally become what he did not want to be and just now realized that he must get out of here, away from this job, this was not what he wanted to do. Perhaps it was something he could not do. His ideal was to serve his country, this new fragile infant democracy, to raise up and build, not to break down, and look at him now. He made up his mind to write his letter of resignation now and put it into Janina Mentz's hand, pack his things and leave. He expected to feel relief but it was absent. He went over to the stairs, the darkness still in his mind.

Later Radebe would wonder if his subconscious had made him leave the door unlocked.

Later he would run through his exit of the room in his head and every time he would turn the key.

But it would be too late.

Captain Tiger Mazibuko put away the gun cloths and oil in the olive-green canvas bag and stood up. He walked purposefully over to where Little Joe was sitting with Zongu and Da Costa. He still felt guilty about shouting at Moroka.

'Do you feel like a bit of fun?' he asked.

They looked up at him, nodding and expectant.

'How many of us do we need to take on forty Hell's Angels?' he asked.

Da Costa got it immediately and laughed: 'Hu-hu'.

'Just one or two,' said Little Joe, looking for his approval.

'Take the whole of Alpha, captain,' said Zongu. 'We deserve it.'

'Right,' said Mazibuko. 'Don't make a big issue of it. Get the men together quietly.'

That was when they heard running footsteps and turned around. It was the bespectacled soldier, the colonel's messenger.

'Captain, the colonel . . .' he said, out of breath.

'What now? Guys on Hondas?'

'No, no, captain, it's Mpayipheli.' And Mazibuko felt that internal shock.

'What?' Too nervous to hope.

'The colonel will tell you . . .'

Mazibuko grabbed the soldier by the shirt. 'Tell me now.'

The eyes were frightened behind the spectacles, the voice shook. 'They know where he is.'

28

Mpayipheli recognized the symptoms – the heart rate increasing steadily, the soft glow of heat, the fine perspiration on palms and forehead and the vague light-headedness of a brain that could not keep up with the oversupply of oxygen. He reacted out of habit, drew a deep breath and kept it all under control. He pulled in at the first petrol station in the main street of Petrusburg and watched two F 650 GS riders pull away. He stopped at the pumps, the engine still running when the petrol jockey said, 'Can you believe it? Black like me.'

He did not react.

'Do you know what Bee-em-double-you stands for?' asked the jockey, a young black guy of eighteen or nineteen.

'What?'

'*Bankrot maar windgat* – that's what the Boers say. Bankrupt but boastful.'

He tried to laugh and switched off the bike.

'Fill up?'

'Please.' He unlocked the fuel cap.

'What are you going to do when you find the Xhosa biker?' the jockey asked in Tswana as he pushed his electronic key against the petrol pump. The figures turned back to zeroes.

'Excuse me?'

'You guys are just going to be in the way. That man needs a clear road.'

'The Xhosa biker,' he repeated and understanding came to him slowly. He watched the tumbling numbers on the pump. Eventually the attendant asked: 'So, where are you from?'

The pump showed nineteen litres and the petrol was still running.

'From the Cape.'

'The Cape?'

'I am the Xhosa biker,' he said on impulse.

'In your dreams, brother.' Twenty-one litres and the tank was full. 'The real one is at Kimberley and they are never going to catch him. And you know what? I say good luck to him, because it's high time somebody stopped the gravy train.'

'Oh?'

'It doesn't take a rocket scientist to work out what he's got. It's the numbers of the government's Swiss bank accounts. Maybe he will draw the money and give it to the people. That would be *real* redistribution of wealth. You owe me R74.65.'

Thobela Mpayipheli handed over the money. 'Where's the roadblock?'

'There are two, but the BMWs can go through. They shouldn't, because you guys are just going to get in the way.'

He put away the wallet and locked the case. 'Where?' His voice was serious.

The jockey's eyes narrowed. 'The Kimberley side. Turn left at the four-way stop.' He indicated up the street.

'And the other one?'

'On the Paardeberg gravel road. It's further on, other side the Co-op, then left.'

'And if I want to go to Boshof?'

'What is your name?' asked the young man in Xhosa.

'Nelson Mandela.'

The pump jockey looked at him and then the smile spread broadly across his face. 'I know what you are planning.'

'What?'

'You want to wait for him other side Kimberley.'

'You are too clever for me.'

'Boshof is straight ahead via Poplar Grove for about twenty kilometres, then turn left other side the Modder and right again at the next bridge.'

'The Modder?'

'The Mighty Modder, Capie, the Modder River.'

'Thank you.' He already had the helmet on, just pushed his fingers into the gloves.

'If you see him, tell him "sharp, sharp".'

'*Sharpzinto, muhle, stereke.*' Mpayipheli pulled away.

'You speak the language, my bro, you speak the language,' he heard the jockey calling after him.

Miriam Nzululwazi knelt by the chair in the interview room and she wept. Her tears began with the fear that had grown too big, the weight of the walls too heavy so that she slid from the chair, her eyes shut so that she could not see them closing in on her, the memories of the Caledon Square cells that echoed in her head. The fear had grown too great and with it the knowledge that Pakamile would wait and wait and wait for his mother to fetch him, for the first time he would wait in vain because she was never late, in six years she had always been there to pick him up. But today he would not know what was wrong, the other children would be fetched, one after the other except him, please God, she could see him, she could feel her child's fear and it crushed her heart. Gradually her weeping included the wider loss of her life with Thobela, the lost perfection of it, the love, the security in every day, the predictability of a man who came home evening after evening and held her tight and whispered his love to her. The scene of him and her son in the vegetable garden behind the house, the block of man on his haunches by the small figure of the boy, close together, and her Pakamile's undisguised hero-worship. The loss of those evenings when they sat in the kitchen, he with his books that he had studied and read with a thirst and a dedication that was scary. She had sat and watched him, her big, lovely man who now and again would look up with that light of new knowledge in his eyes and say 'Did you know . . .' and express his wonderment of the new world that he was discovering. She would want to stand up and throw herself down before him and say, 'You can't be real.' When they lay in bed and he shifted his body close to hers and with his arm over her pulled her possessively tight against himself, his voice would travel wide paths. He would share with her what was in his heart, so many things, the future, the three of them and a new beginning on a farm that lay waiting green and misty and beautiful. About their country and politics and people, his often weird observations at work, his worry over the violence and poverty of the townships, the filtering away of Xhosa culture in the desert sands of wannabe American. And sometimes, in the moments before they drifted into sleep, he would speak of his mother and father. How he wished to make peace, how he wished to do penance and now she wept because it was all gone, lost, nothing would ever be the same. The sobs shook her and the tears dampened the seat of the chair. Eventually she calmed, emptied of crying – but one thing remained: the impulse to get out.

She did not know why she stood up and tried the door. Maybe her subconscious had registered no sound of a key turning with that last exit, maybe she was merely desperate. But when she turned the handle and the door gave to her fingers, she was shocked and pushed it shut again. She went back and sat in the chair, on the edge and stared at the door, her heart beating wildly at the possibilities awaiting her.

Allison sat on the veranda of the little white house with its green roof. She sat in a green plastic garden chair opposite Dr Zatopek van Heerden, captivated by his lean body and his intense eyes and the energy locked up in him like a compressed spring – plus something indefinable, unrecognizable but familiar.

It was hot and the light was soft in the transition from afternoon to evening. Van Heerden had a beer and she drank water with tinkling ice cubes. He had cross-examined her for everything she knew, hovering like a falcon over her words, ready to swoop on nonsense and now he had heard her chronological story and he asked, 'What now? What do you want?'

Allison was discomfited by the intensity of his gaze – he looked right inside her, those eyes never still, over her and on her, searching and measuring, evaluating. With his psychological expertise, could he multiply the fractions of her voice and body language to form a sum of her very thoughts? Strangely, there was a sexuality in him that reached out and lured an involuntary response from deep in her body.

'The truth,' she said.

'The truth.' Cynical. 'Do you believe there is such a thing?' He did not look away, as other people did when they talked. His eyes never left her face. What was it, this thing she felt?

'Truth is a moving target,' she admitted.

'My dilemma,' he said, 'is loyalty. Thobela Mpayipheli is my friend.'

Four Rooivalk attack helicopters flew low over the flat earth, crossing the boundary between Northern Cape and the Free State province. Behind flew two Oryx, slow and cumbersome by comparison, each carrying four members of the RU's Team Alpha in their constricted interiors. The men were fully kitted out for the job: bulletproof vests, steel helmets mounted with infra-red night sights, weapons held comfortably clasped

with both hands between knees. In the leading Oryx Tiger
Mazibuko tried to conduct a cellphone conversation over the
roar of the engines.

Janina Mentz was in the dining room of her house, her
head lowered between the school homework books of her
daughters. She could barely make out Mazibuko's words.

'Where, Tiger? Where?'

'Somewhere near Pe—'

'I can't hear you,' she was practically shouting.

'Petrusburg.'

Petrusburg? She had no idea where that was.

'I'm going back to the Ops Room, Tiger. We will try
the radio.'

'. . . Get him . . .'

'What?'

The signal was gone.

'What's that about Petrusburg, Ma?' asked Lien.

'It's work, sweetie. I've got to go.'

The tension that Mpayipheli had felt going into the petrol
station had resurrected a memory, brought it back from the
past, the same trembling in his hands and the perspiration on
his face during that first time, that first assassination. He was
in Munich with the SVD in his hands, the long sharpshooter's
weapon, the latest model with the synthetic non-folding stock,
a weapon whose deadly reach was 3,800 metres. The cross-
hairs searched for Klemperer, the double agent who should
come out through a door a kilometre away.

He felt as if Evgeniy Fedorovich Dragunov himself was
lying beside him, the legendary modest Russian weapons
developer. He had met him briefly in East Germany when he
and the other students of the Stasi sharpshooters school were
helping to test an experimental SVDS. Comrade Evgeniy

Fedorovich was fascinated by the black student with the impossible groupings. At 2,000 metres with a crosswind of seventeen kilometres per hour and the poor light of an overcast winter's day, Thobela Mpayipheli had shot a R100 factor of less than 400mm. The stocky ageing Russian had said something in his mother tongue and pushed up his black-framed spectacles onto his forehead before reaching out and gripping the Xhosa's shoulder – to feel if he was real, perhaps.

He wanted to dedicate this one to Dragunov, but dear God, his heart bounced so in his ribs on this, his first blooding, his fingers and palms were wet with sweat. On the practice range it was the testosterone of competition but this was real, a man of flesh and blood, a bald middle-aged West German who was feeding on both sides of the fence. The KGB had earmarked him for elimination and it was time for the ANC's exchange student to earn his keep. There was steam on the telescope lens; he dared not take his concentration from the door. It opened.

Miriam sat on the chair, staring at the door, trying to recall the route that they had followed bringing her here. Was there another way out? It was so quiet in the building, just the soft sound of the air-conditioner and now and then the creak of metal expanding or contracting. She could not wait much longer.

'I don't want to be on record,' said Dr Zatopek van Heerden. 'That is the condition.'

'I will show my story to you first.' Allison hoped for a compromise, but he shook his head.

'I am not anti-media,' he said. 'I believe every country gets the media they deserve. But Thobela is my friend.'

Allison had to make a decision. Eventually she said, 'It's a deal.' And then Van Heerden began to speak, his gaze never leaving her face.

Tiger Mazibuko held the light of the little torch to the map in front of him. The fucking problem was that the R48 forked beyond Koffiefontein, the R705 went to Jacobsdal, the R48 carried on to Petrusburg. He had ordered four Rooivalks south to Jacobsdal, the other four with the two Oryx to the more likely east, but the problem was that the damn traffic officer had alerted them too late. By Mazibuko's reckoning the Fugitive could be past Petrusburg but where, where the fuck? Because the roadblocks, two bloody roadblocks said a horde of BMWs had gone through, but not one had seen a black guy and the possibilities were legion. Where are you going, you dog? Dealesville or Boshof, Mazibuko's finger traced the routes further and he gambled on Mafekeng and the Botswana border. That made it Boshof. But had he crossed the Modder River yet? The Rooivalks would each have to follow a dirt road; there were too many alternatives.

'He is not a complex man, but that is precisely where you can make a mistake,' said Van Heerden. 'Too many people equate "uncomplicated" with "simple" or a lack of intelligence. Thobela's non-complexity lies in his decision-making abilities: he is a man of action, he examines the facts, he accepts or rejects, he does not worry or agonize over it. If Miriam told you that he was helping a friend by taking something to Lusaka then he took the decision that his loyalty lay with his friend, regardless of the consequences. Finished and *klaar*. They are going to battle to get him to stop. They are going to have their hands full.'

Only part of Mpayipheli's attention was on the long lighted path that the double lamps of the GS cut through the growing dark. The dirt road was a good one, reddish brown and hard-surfaced. He kept his speed down to sixty or seventy. That fall in the Karoo storm still bothered him. The rest of his mind was in Munich, on his first assassination. Somewhere in the back of his consciousness he was aware that during the last twenty-four hours he was reliving the past, as if he was somehow reactivated, he let it flow, let it out, perhaps it was part of a healing process, a changeover, a closure so that he could shake it off, a point at the end of a paragraph in his metamorphosis.

The door had opened and his finger had curled around the trigger, the SVD became an extension of his being. In his mind's eye he could see the bullet waiting for metal to hit the percussion cap, the 9.8-gram steel of the 7.62-millimetre bullet waiting to be spun through the grooved tunnel of the 24-inch barrel, through the silencer and then in a curved trajectory, irrevocably on its way. Pressure on the trigger increased – a woman and child appeared in the sniperscope lens, freezing him, the junction of the cross-hairs rested on her forehead, right below the band of the blue wool cap, he saw the smoothness of her face, the bright, healthy skin, laugh lines at her eyes and he blew out his breath and the tempo of his heart accelerated some more.

Tiger Mazibuko screamed orders into the microphone. There were three routes to Boshof, from Paardeberg, Poplar Grove and Wolwespruit. Two Rooivalks on the first, his primary choice, one each on the other two, fly north, he wanted them to start searching from Seretse.

'I am putting the TDATS on infra-red,' said the pilot over the radio and Mazibuko had no idea what he was talking about. 'That means we will see him even if his lights are off.'

29

Miriam Nzululwazi stood up suddenly, opened the door and went out, closing it quietly behind her.

The passage was empty. Grey cold tiled floor stretched left and right. She had come from the left; there were offices and people that way. She turned right, the flat heels of her shoes audible, tip-tap, tip-tap. She walked purposefully until she saw another door at the end of the passage.

Faded peeling red paint – she could just make out the letters. *Fire Escape.*

'How well was he trained as a soldier?' asked Allison.

'Soldier? He was never a soldier.'

'But he was in Umkhonto.'

Van Heerden looked at her in surprise. 'You don't know?'

'Don't know what?'

'He was an assassin. For the KGB.'

She knew that her face betrayed her shock and dismay.

'And now you are going to judge him. You think that changes everything?'

'It's just . . .'

'Less honourable?'

She searched for the right words: 'No, no, I . . .' But he did not give her time.

'You formed a picture in your head of a foot soldier of the Struggle, a relatively simple man, maybe something of a rebel who broke out now and again, but nothing more than that. Just an ordinary soldier.'

'Well, yes. No. I didn't think him ordinary . . .'

'I don't know the whole story. The Russians discovered him. Shooting competition in Kazakhstan, some base in the mountains where the ANC men were trained. Probably he shot the hell out of the Commies and they saw possibilities. He had two years of training in East Germany, at some special spy school.'

'How many people did he—'

'I don't remember precisely. Ten, fifteen . . .'

'My God.' She blew out a breath. 'Are we still off the record here?'

'Yes, Allison Healy, we are.'

'My God.' She would not be able to write this.

Mpayipheli had given the sniperscope lens a quick wipe with the soft cloth and lined up his eye behind it again. Not too close, just the right focus length, checked his adjustments again and waited for the door. Beads of sweat ran down his forehead, he would have to get a sweatband; it was going to sting his eyes. The door, dark wood, was shut again, his palms were wet and the temperature inside the warm clothes still rising. He became aware of a distaste for what he was doing. This was not the way to wage war, it was not right; this was not the way of his people.

There was a bar on the door, white letters on a green background that read 'Push/Druk' and Miriam obeyed. They was a snap as the lock disconnected and the door creaked and groaned as the unused hinges protested and she saw that she was outside, she saw the night and she heard the city sounds and stepped forward and closed the door behind her. She looked down and far below there was an alley but right here in front of her was a metal rail and the rusty wounds of a sawn-off metal stairway. She realized she was in a dead end. The door had clicked shut behind her and there was no handle on the outside.

The light flashed on the Access Control panel and the official picked up the internal phone and called the Ops Room.

It was Quinn who answered.

'Fire door on the seventh floor. The alarm has been activated,' said the official.

Quinn raised his voice. 'Who is on the seventh floor? The fire door has been activated.'

Six metres from him Vincent Radebe sat listening to the crackle of the Rooivalk radios more than a thousand kilometres north. He only half registered what Quinn had said, but the hair rose on his neck.

'What?' he said.

'Someone has opened the fire door on seven.' Quinn and Radebe looked at each other and understood and Radebe felt an icy hand knot his innards.

'You are a journalist. You should know that concepts of good and bad are relative,' said Zatopek van Heerden. He was up and moving to the edge of the veranda, looking out at the night sky. 'No, not relative. Clumsy. Insufficient. You want to take sides. You want to be for him or against him. You need someone to be right, on the side of justice.'

'You sound like Orlando Arendse,' Allison Healy said.

'Orlando is not a fool.'

'How many people did he murder?'

'Listen to yourself. *Murder.* He murdered no one. He fought a war. And I don't know how many of the enemy died at his hand, but it must have been many, because he was good. He never actually said, but I saw him in action and his ability was impressive.'

'And then he became a gofer at a motorbike dealership?'

Van Heerden moved again, this time closer to her and for Allison it was equally stimulating and threatening. He passed close by her, leaned back on the white plastic garden table and sat on it. She smelt him; she swore she could smell him.

'I wondered when you would get to the crux of the matter.'

'What do you mean?'

'The question that you and the Spooks must ask is why Thobela left Orlando. What changed? What happened?'

'And the answer is?'

'That is his Achilles heel. You see, his loyalty was always total. First it was the Business. The ANC. The Fight. And when it was all over and they left him high and dry he took his talents and found someone who could use them. He served Orlando with an irreproachable work ethic. And then something happened, something inside him. I don't know what it was, I have my suspicions, but I don't know precisely. We were in hospital, he and I, beaten and shot up, and one day just before six he came to my bed and said he'd finished with violence and fighting. I still wanted to chat, to pull his leg, the way we did, but he was serious, emotional, I could see it was something to him. Something big.'

'And that is his Achilles heel?'

Van Heerden leaned forward and she wanted to retreat from him.

'He thinks he can change. He thinks he *has* changed.'

Allison heard the words, registered the meaning, overwhelmingly aware too of the subtext between them and in that moment she understood the attraction, the invisible bond: he was like her, somewhere inside there was something missing, something out of place, not quite at

home in this world, just like her – as if they didn't belong
here.

And then the door opened and the bald man appeared,
eyes blinking in the bright light of the street outside and
Mpayipheli's finger caressed the trigger and the long black
weapon jerked in his hands and coughed in his ears and a
heartbeat later the blood made a pretty pattern on the wood.
In the forty-seven seconds it took to dismantle the weapon
and pack it away in the bag he knew that he could not wage
war like this. There was no honour in it.

The enemy must see him. The enemy must be able to
fight back.

Miriam Nzululwazi knew that there was only one way out of
here. She had to climb, she had to get over the railing and hang
from the lowest bar and then let herself drop the extra metre to
the lower-storey fire escape and then repeat the process till she
was there where the sawn-off stairs resumed and zigzagged
down to the ground.

She pulled herself up over the rail. She did not look down
but swung her leg over, then her body – seven floors above
the dirty smelly alley.

'Ma, you're never at home any more,' said Lien, outside by
the car.

'Ai, my child, it's not because I *want* to be at work. You
know I sometimes have to work extra hours.'

'Is it the motorbike man, mamma?' asked Lizette.

'You watch too much television.' Stern.

'But is it, mamma?'

She started the car and said softly: 'You know I can't talk
about it.'

'Some people say he's a hero, mamma.'

'Suthu says she battles to get you to go to bed. You must listen to her. You hear?'

'When will we see you again, ma?'

'Tomorrow, I promise.' She put the car in reverse and released the clutch. 'Sleep tight.'

'Is he, mamma? Is he a hero?' But she reversed in a hurry and did not answer.

Quinn and Radebe ran, the black man ahead, up the stairs, their footfalls loud in the quiet passage. How was it possible, how could Miriam have escaped, it could not be her. They ran past the door of the interview room, Radebe saw it was shut and it gave him courage, she must be there, but his priority was the fire-escape door. He bumped it open and at first saw nothing and relief flooded over him. Quinn's breath was at his neck and they both stepped out onto the small steel platform.

'Thank God,' he heard Quinn say behind him.

'As long as he believes it,' said Zatopek van Heerden, 'things shouldn't get out of hand. They even have a chance to persuade him to turn back. If they approach him correctly.'

'You sound sceptical,' said Allison.

'Have you heard of chaos theory?'

She shook her head. The moon lay in the east, a big round light shining down on them. She saw his hand lift from the table and hang in the air, for a moment she thought he was going to touch her and she wanted it, but the hand hung there, an aid in the search for an explanation. 'Basically it says that a minute change in a small local system can expand to upset the balance in another larger system, far removed from it. It is a mathematical model – they replicate it with computers.'

'You've lost me.'

Van Heerden's hand dropped back and supported his posture on the table. 'It's difficult. First you have to understand who he is. What his nature is. Some people, most people, are passive bending reeds in the winds of life. Resignedly accepting changes in their environment. Oh yes, they will moan and complain and threaten, but eventually they will adjust and be sucked along by the stream. Thobela belongs to the other group, the minority – the doers, the activators and the catalysts. When apartheid threatened his genetic fitness index, he resolved to change that environment. The apparent impossibility of the challenge was irrelevant. You follow?'

'I think so.'

'Now, at this moment, he is suppressing that natural behaviour. He thinks he can be a bending reed. And as long as the equilibrium of his own system is undisturbed, he can do it. So far it has been easy. Just his job and Miriam and Pakamile. A safe, closed system. He wants to keep it like that. The problem is that life is never like that. The real world is not in balance. Chaos theory says that in the balance of probability something should happen somewhere to ultimately change that environment.'

Vincent Radebe looked down just before he was about to go back through the fire door and that was when he saw Miriam. She was suspended between heaven and earth below him. Their stares met and hers was full of fear. Her legs were a pendulum swinging out over the drop, and back over the lower platform.

'Miriam,' he cried in utter despair and bent to grab her arms, to save her.

'And then what?' asked Allison. 'If this theoretical thing happens and he comes back to what he is?'

'Then all hell will break loose,' said Dr Zatopek van Heerden pensively.

Miriam's reaction was to let go, to open her cramping fingers.

The pendulum swing of her body took her past the platform of the sixth floor. She fell. She made no sound.

Vincent Radebe saw it all, saw the twist of her body as it slowly revolved on its way to the bottom. He thought he heard the soft noise when she hit the dirty stone paving of the alley far below.

He cried once, in his mother tongue, desperately to Heaven.

Thobela Mpayipheli absorbed the world around him, the moon big and beautiful in the black heaven, the Free State plains, grass veld stretching in the lovely light as far as the eye could see, here and there dark patches of thorn trees, the path that the headlights threw out ahead of him. He felt the machine and he felt his own body and he felt his place on this continent and he saw himself and he felt life coursing through him, a full, flooding river, it swept him along and he knew that he must cherish this moment, store it somewhere secure because it was fleeting and rare, this intense and perfect unity with the universe.

30

Janina Mentz's cellphone rang twice as she drove back to Wale Street Chambers. The first caller was the Director.

'I know you are enjoying a well-earned rest, Janina, but I have some interesting news for you. But not over the phone.'

'I'm on my way back now, sir.' They were both aware of the bad security of the cellular network. 'There are other things happening too.'

'Oh?'

'I will fill you in.'

'That is good, Janina,' said the Director.

'I will be there in ten minutes.'

Barely three minutes later it was Quinn. 'Ma'am, we need you.'

She did not pick up the depression in his voice at first. 'I know, Rudewaan, I am on the way.'

'No. It's something else,' he said and now she registered his tone. Worry and frustration coloured her answer. 'I am coming. The Director wants me too.'

'Thank you, ma'am,' he said.

She ended the call.

The children, the job. Eternal pressure. Everyone wanted something from her and she had to give. It was always that way. Ever since she could remember. Demands. Her father and mother. Her husband. And then single parenthood and more pressure, more people, all saying, 'Give.

More.' There were moments when she wanted to stand up and scream, 'Fuck you all!' and pack her bags and leave because what was the use? Everyone just wanted more. Her parents and her ex-husband and the Director and her colleagues. They demanded, they took and she must keep giving and the emotions built up in her, anger and self-pity and she looked for comfort where she always found it, in the secret places, the clandestine refuge where no one else went.

Mpayipheli saw the helicopter silhouetted against the moon, just for a moment, a pure fluke, so quick that he thought that he had imagined it and then his finger reached feverishly for the headlight switch, found it and switched off.

He pulled up in the middle of the dirt road and killed the engine, struggled with the helmet buckle, took the gloves off first and then pulled off the helmet. Listened.

Nothing.

They had searchlights on those things. Perhaps some form of night vision. They would follow the roads.

He heard the deep rumble, somewhere ahead. They had found him and he felt naked and vulnerable and he must find a place to hide. He wondered what had happened, what had tipped them off to look for him here. The petrol jockey? The traffic officer? Or something else?

Where do you hide from a helicopter at night? Out in the open plains of the Free State?

His eyes searched for the lights of a farmhouse in the dark, hoping for sheds and outbuildings but there was nothing. A feeling of urgency grew in him, he couldn't stay here, he had to do something and then he thought of the river and the bridge, the Mighty Modder, it must be somewhere up ahead – and its bridge.

Under the bridge would be the place to shelter, to hide away.

He had to get *there* before they got *here*.

Quinn and Radebe waited for Janina Mentz at the lift and Quinn said, 'Can we talk in your office, ma'am?' and she knew that there was something wrong somewhere because they were grim, especially Radebe, he looked crushed. She walked ahead, opened the office door, went in and waited for them to close the door behind them.

They stood, conventions of sitting irrelevant now. The two began to speak simultaneously, stopped, looked at each other. Radebe held up his hand. 'It is my responsibility,' he said to Quinn and he looked at Janina with difficulty, his voice monotone, his eyes dead, as if there was no one inside his skull any more. 'Ma'am, due to my neglect Miriam Nzululwazi escaped from the interview room.' She went cold.

'She reached the exterior fire escape and tried to climb down. She fell. Six floors down. It is my fault, I take full responsibility.'

She drew breath to ask questions but Radebe forged ahead. 'I offer my resignation. I will not be an embarrassment to this department any more.' He was finished and the last vestige of dignity left his body with those words.

Eventually Janina said, 'She is dead.'

Quinn nodded. 'We carried her up to the interview room.'

'How did she get out?'

Radebe stared at the carpet, unseeing. Quinn said, 'Vincent thinks he did not lock the door behind him.'

Rage welled up in her, and suspicion. 'You *think*? You *think* you didn't?'

There was no reaction from him and that fuelled her rage. She wanted to snarl at him, to punish him, it was too easy to stand lifelessly and say that he thought he hadn't locked the door; she had to deal with the consequences. She bit back a flood of bitter words.

'You may go, Vincent. I accept your resignation.'

He turned around slowly but she was not finished. 'There will be an inquiry. A disciplinary hearing.'

He nodded.

'See that we know where to find you.'

Radebe looked back at Janina and she saw that he had nothing left, nowhere to go.

Dr Zatopek van Heerden walked Allison to her car.

She was reluctant to leave – the nearing deadlines called, but she did not want to be finished here.

'I don't entirely agree,' she said as they reached the car.

'About what?'

'Good and evil. They are very often absolute concepts.'

She watched him in the moonlight. There was too much thought in him: perhaps he knew too much, as if the ideas and knowledge built up pressure behind his mouth, and the outlet was too small for the volume behind. It caused strange expressions to cross his face, but found some release in the movements of his body. As if he wrestled to keep it all under control.

Why did he turn her on?

Ten to one he was a bastard – so sure of himself.

Or was he?

Allison had always been sensual, deep inside. She saw herself that way. But a woman learned with the years that that was only a part of the truth. The other part lay outside, in the way men saw you. And women too, who measured and compared and helped to put you in your place in the long food chain of love play. You learned to live with that, adjusting your expectations and dreams and fantasies to protect a sensitive heart whose wounds of disappointment healed slowly. Until you were content with the now-and-then, the sometimes-reasonable intensity of stolen moments with a bleached policeman, someone else's husband. And here tonight, she wished she were tall and slim and blonde and beautiful, with big breasts and full lips and a cute bottom, so that this man would propose something improper.

And what did she do?

She challenged him intellectually. She who was so average – in everything.

'Name me someone evil,' he said.

'Hitler.'

'Hitler is the stereotypical example,' he said. 'But let me ask you: was he worse than Queen Victoria?'

'I beg your pardon?'

'Who fed Boer women and children porridge with glass in it? What about the scorched-earth policy? Maybe it was her generals. Maybe she had no idea. Just like P.W. Botha. Denying all knowledge and therefore good? What of Joseph Stalin? Idi Amin? How do we measure? Are numbers the ultimate measure? Is a sliding scale of the numbers of victims the way we determine good or evil?'

'The question is not who is the worst. The question is are there people who are absolutely evil.'

'Let me tell you about Jeffrey Dahmer. The serial murderer. Do you know who he is?'

'The Butcher of Milwaukee.'

'Was he evil?'

'Yes.' But there was less assurance in her voice.

'The literature says that for seven or nine years, I can't remember, let's say seven years, Dahmer suppressed the urge to kill. This broken, fucked-up, pathetic wreck of a man kept the nearly inhuman drive bottled up for seven years. Does that make him bad? Or heroic? How many of us know that sort of drive, that intensity? We who can't even control basic, simple urges like jealousy or envy.'

'No,' she said. 'I can't agree. He murdered. Repeatedly. He did terrible things. It does not matter how long he held out.'

Zatopek smiled at her. 'I give in. It is an endless argument. It rests ultimately on so many personal things. I suspect it rests ultimately on the undebatable. Like religion. Norms, values. They way you see yourself, the way you see others and what we are. And what you have experienced.'

Allison had no answer to that and just stood there. Her face was expressionless but her body felt too small to contain all she felt.

'Thank you,' she said to break the silence.

'Thobela Mpayipheli is a good man. As good as the world allows him to be. Remember that.'

Mpayipheli was busy putting the R 1150 GS down when he heard the drone of the helicopter coming closer.

He had battled to negotiate the steep bank of the river down towards the water, then he had ridden the motorbike up with spinning rear wheel through the grass and bushes directly under the concrete of the bridge. It would be difficult to spot there. Neither the side stand nor the main stand would work there and he had to lay the bike on its side. It was difficult – the secret was to turn the handles up and hold the end, let your knees do the work, not your back. The big engines of the helicopter came ever nearer. Somehow or other they must have spotted him.

He placed the helmet on the petrol tank and removed the jacket and trousers: they were too lightly coloured for the night. He tried to see where the aircraft was and when he looked around the edge of the bridge he saw that it was only thirty or forty metres away, not far off the ground. He could feel the wind of the great rotors against his face, saw the red and white revolving lights and saw too, through the open door of the Oryx, four faces, each one beneath an infra-red night sight.

★　　★　　★

Da Costa, Little Joe Moroka, Cupido and Zwelitini waited till the Oryx landed and the great engines had quieted before jumping down.

The helicopter had landed in a piece of open veld, bordered by the river and road and thorn trees. The first thing they did was to walk to the river, drawn by the ancient magnetism of water. Behind them the main rotor turned ever slower and eventually stopped. The night sounds took over: frogs that had until now been still, insects, somewhere far away a dog barked.

Da Costa walked to the water, opened his fly and urinated an impressive shiny stream in the moonlight.

'Hey, the farmers have to drink that fucking water,' said Cupido.

'The Boers drink brandy and Coke,' said Da Costa and spat his chewing gum in an impressive arc.

'Not bad,' said Zwelitini. 'For a Whitey.'

'So, can you do better?'

'Naturally. Didn't you know that we Zulus have lips like these so we can spit on Whiteys and Xhosas?'

'Put your money where your lips are, your highness.'

'Ten rand says I can do better than that.'

'Best of three.'

'Fair enough.'

'Hey, what about us?' asked Cupido.

'This is the RU, my bru'. Come and spit with us.'

'Wait,' said Da Costa. 'I must radio the captain first. Tell him we are in position.'

'Take your time. The night is young.'

And so they bantered and teased and spat, ignorant of their prey only twelve metres away, unaware that one of them would not see the sun rise.

31

Janina Mentz told the Director in his office about Miriam Nzululwazi's death and she could see how the news upset him, how the stress of the whole affair slowly crept up on him. The little smile was gone, the compassion and consideration for her was less, the cheerfulness had been swept away.

He was feeling the strain, she thought. The snow-white shirt had lost its gleam; the wrinkles were like cracks in his armour, barely visible.

'And Vincent?' he asked in a weary voice.

'He offered his resignation.'

'You accepted it.'

'Yes, sir.' There was finality in her voice.

The Zulu closed his eyes. He sat motionless, hands on his lap, and for a moment she wondered if he was praying. But she knew really that it was just his manner. Other people would make gestures or blow out their breath or their shoulders would sag. His way was to shut out the world briefly.

'There are always casualties in our work,' he said softly.

She did not think that he expected her to respond. She waited for his eyes to open but it did not happen.

'This is the part I don't like. It is the part I hate. But it is inevitable.'

The eyes opened. 'Vincent.' A hand gesture at last, a vague wave. 'He is too idealistic. Too soft and emotional. I will get him a transfer. Somewhere we can channel that dedication.'

She still had no idea what to say for her opinion differed. Vincent had failed. For her he no longer existed.

'What are we going to do with . . . Mrs Nzululwazi?'

With the body? Why didn't he say it? Mentz was learning a lot tonight. She saw weakness.

'I will arrange to have her sent to the mortuary, sir. No questions asked.'

'And the child?'

She had forgotten the child.

'Sir, the best would be for family to look after him. We are not . . . we don't have the facilities.'

'That is true,' he said.

'You said over the phone that you had some interesting news.'

'Oh. Yes, I have. I had a call from Luke Powell.'

It took a while to sink in. 'Luke Powell?' she repeated, mainly to gain time, to make the necessary mental adjustments.

'He wants to meet us. He wants to talk.'

She smiled at the Director. 'This is unexpected, sir. But not an unpleasant prospect.'

He answered her smile with one of his own. 'It is, Janina. He is waiting for us. At the Spur on the Waterfront.'

'Oh, he wants to play a home game,' she said and waited for the Director to acknowledge the joke. But he did not.

Allison Healy made two calls before she began to type the lead story for the *Cape Times* of the following day. The first was to Rassie Erasmus of the Laingsburg police.

'I tried twice this afternoon but your cellphone was off,' he said reproachfully.

'I had an interview with a difficult man,' she said. 'Sorry.'

'Three things,' he said. 'The thing this morning at Beaufort West. They say the biker held a gun to one soldier's head, he could have shot them both to hell, but he let them go and said something like "I don't want to hurt anybody".'

'I don't want to hurt anybody,' she repeated as she made frantic notes.

'Number two: it's a rumour but the source is good, an old pal of mine in Pretoria. That brigadier who said over the news that the Biker was such a fuck-up in the Struggle – you know who I mean, the one in the army?'

'Yes?' She sifted through the documents on her desk for the fax.

'Apparently there's a case pending against him. Sexual harassment or something. They say he's talking now, because the sexual harassment thing against him may just go away if he's helpful enough.'

'Wait, wait, wait, Rassie.' Allison found the paper and ran her finger down it. 'You say the brigadier, here it is, Lucas Morape, you say he's lying about this to save his own skin?'

'I'm not saying he's lying. I'm saying he's helping them. And that's not a fact, it's a rumour.'

'So what's the third thing?'

'They've cornered the Biker in the Free State.'

'Where in the Free State?'

'Petrusburg.'

'Petrusburg?'

'I know, I know, between bugger-all and nowhere, but that's what the guy says.'

'You said they've cornered him.'

'Wait, let me explain. This afternoon he went through a speed trap this side of Petrusburg and the speed cop wrote him a fucking ticket without a clue who he was and then let him go. When the poor fool got back to the office the bomb exploded. They thought he must have slipped through Petrusburg because of all the other BMW motor-bikes, but now they've blocked all the holes. Apparently there's a whole squadron of Rooivalks waiting for him with guided missiles.'

'Rassie, don't be ridiculous.'

'Sweetness, have I ever lied to you?'

'No . . .'

'I tell you like I hear it, Allison. You know that. And I've never let you down.'

'That's true.'

'You owe me.'

'Yes, I owe you, Rassie.' She disconnected and shouted at the news editor: 'I'm going to need some help on this one, chief.'

'What do you need?'

'People to make some calls.'

'You've got it,' he said and crossed over to her desk.

She had already dialled the next number. It was to the house of Miriam Nzululwazi in Guguletu. 'I need someone to call Defence Force Media Relations and ask them to confirm or deny the fact that Brigadier Lucas Morape has a sexual harassment case pending.'

The phone rang in Guguletu.

'What brigadier?'

'The guy who put out the press release about how bad the biker really is.'

'Check,' said the news editor.

'And I need someone to call that Kimberley number and ask them to confirm or deny that Thobela Mpayipheli has been trapped near Petrusburg.'

'Good girl,' said the news editor.

The phone kept on ringing.

'And I need someone to try and find a list of child day-care centres in Guguletu and start calling. We need to know if a Pakamile Nzululwazi has been picked up by his mom today.'

'It's eight-thirty.'

'It's Guguletu, chief. Not some cosy white suburb where everybody goes home at five o' clock. We might get lucky. Please.'

The phone rang and rang.

Tiger Mazibuko sat in the co-pilot's seat of the Oryx. It had landed beside the R64, halfway between Dealesville and Boshof.

He had the radio headset on, listening to the Rooivalk pilots calling in from each sector they had searched as clear. He marked them off on a chart.

Could the Dog be through already, beyond Boshof?

He shook his head.

Impossible. Mpayipheli couldn't ride that fast.

They would get him. Even if he got lucky, there was a last resort. Beyond Mafeking there were only two roads over the Botswana border. Just two. And he would close them off.

But it would probably not be necessary.

At first there was relief. It was not because they had spotted him that the Oryx had not landed here. But now there was the frustration of being trapped.

Mpayipheli lay beside the GS under the bridge and he dared not move, he dared not make a sound, they were too close, the four romping young soldiers. The co-pilot had come down too and now they were skipping flat stones over the water. The one with the most skips before the stone sank would be the champion.

He had recognized one of the soldiers, the young black fellow. This morning he had held a rifle to his head.

He saw himself in them. Twenty years ago. Young, so very young, boys in men's bodies, competitive, idealistic and so ready to play soldiers.

It was always so, through the ages – the children went to war. Van Heerden said it was the age to show off what you had, to make your mark so you could take your place in the hierarchy.

He had been even younger when he had left home: seventeen. He could remember it well, in his uncle Senzeni's car, the night-time journey, Queenstown, East London, Umtata, they had talked endlessly, without stopping, about the long road that lay ahead. Senzeni had repeated over and over that it was his right and his privilege, that the ancestors would smile on him, the revolution was coming, injustice would be swept away. He remembered, but as he lay here now, he could not recall the fire that had burned in his soul. He searched for that zeal, that *sturm und drang* that he had felt, he knew it had been there, but as he tried to taste it, it was only cold ash. He had caught the bus in Umtata, Senzeni had hugged him long and hard and there had been tears in his uncle's eyes and his farewell was 'Mayibuye'. It was the last time he had seen him – had Senzeni known? Had he known that his own battle would be even more dangerous than Mpayipheli's, working inside the lion's den, with even greater risks? Was the desperation of Senzeni's embrace because of a foreboding that he would die in the war on the home front?

The bus ride to Durban, to Empangeni, was a journey into the unknown; in the earliest hours before dawn, the enormity of that journey ahead became a worm in his heart that brought with it the corruption of insecurity.

Seventeen.

Old enough to go to war, young enough to lie awake in the night and fear, to long for the bed in his room and the reassurance of his father in the rectory, young enough to wonder if he would ever feel his mother's arms around him again.

But the sun rose and burnt away the fears, it brought bravado, and when he got off at Pongola he was fine. The next night they smuggled him over the border to Swaziland and the following night he was in Mozambique and his life was irrevocably changed.

And here he was now, using a skill the East Germans had taught him. To lie still, that was the art of the assassin and sniper, to lie motionless and invisible for hours, but he had been a younger man, this one was forty years old and his body complained. One leg was asleep, the stones under the other hip were sharp and unbearably uncomfortable, the fire in his belly was quenched and his zeal was gone. It was fifteen hundred kilometres south in a small house on the Cape Flats beside the peaceful sleeping body of a tall slim woman and he smiled to himself in the dark, despite his discomfort, he smiled at the way things change, nothing ever stays the same and it was good, life goes on.

And with the smile came the realization, the suspicion that this journey would change his life too. He was on the way to more than Lusaka.

Where would it take him?

How could anyone know?

Allison Healy worked on the lead story, knowing it was going to be a difficult job tonight.

A squadron of Rooivalk attack helicopters cornered the fugitive motorcyclist Thobela Mpayipheli near the Free State town of Petrusburg late last night amidst conflicting reports from both military and unofficial sources.

She read her introductory paragraph. Not bad. But not quite right. The *Burger* and television and radio could have the same information. And by tomorrow morning Mpayipheli might have been arrested.

She placed the computer-screen cursor on the end of the

paragraph and deleted it. She thought, she rephrased, she tested sentences and construction in her mind.

A new drama surrounding the fugitive motorcyclist Thobela Mpayipheli unfolded late last night with the mysterious disappearance of his common-law wife, Mrs Miriam Nzululwazi.

This was where her scoop lay. She went on.

Authorities, including the SAPS and the office of the Intelligence Ministry, strongly denied that Mrs Nzululwazi was in government custody. Yet colleagues say the Absa employee was apprehended by unidentified law-enforcement officials at the Heerengracht branch yesterday.

The military reaction to persistent rumours that a squadron of Rooivalk attack helicopters had cornered Mpayipheli near the Free State town of Petrusburg after sunset yesterday was 'no comment'.

That's better, she thought. *Two flies with one swat.*

'Allison . . .'

She looked up. A black colleague stood beside her.

'. . . I've got something.'

'Shoot.'

'The kid. I found him. Sort of.'

'You did!'

'A woman at the Guguletu Pre-school and Child Care Centre says he's a regular there. And the mother never turned up tonight.'

'Shit.'

'But some sort of government guy did.' The man looked at his notes. 'Said his name was Radebe, flashed a card at her and said there had been some sort of accident and he was there to take the kid into his care.'

'Ohmigod. Did he say who he worked for? Where was he taking the kid?'

'She says the card he showed her just said he was Department of Defence.'

'And she let the kid go?'

'He was the last one left.'

'The last one left?'

'He was the last kid to be fetched and I think the lady just wanted to go home.'

Vincent Radebe could not tell the boy that his mother was dead. He did not know how.

'Your mother has to work late.' That was the best he could do, in the car. 'She asked me to look after you.'

'Do you work with her?'

'You could say that.'

'Do you know Thobela?'

'Yes, I do.'

'Thobela has gone somewhere and it's our secret.'

'I know.'

'And I'm not going to tell anybody.'

'That's good.'

'And he's coming back tomorrow.'

'Yes, he's coming back tomorrow,' Radebe had said on the way to Green Point where his flat was. There were moments in the car that his guilt, the heaviness of spirit became nearly too much for him, but now in McDonald's opposite the Green Point athletics stadium he had control of himself. He watched Pakamile devour a Big Mac and asked: 'Have you got other family here in the Cape?'

'No,' said the boy. There was tomato sauce on his forehead. Radebe took a serviette and wiped it off.

'Nobody?'

'My granny lived in Port Elizabeth, but she's dead.'

'Have you got uncles or aunts?'

'No. Just Thobela and my mother. Thobela says there are dolphins in Port Elizabeth and he is going to show us at the end of the year.'

'Oh.'

'I know where Lusaka is. Do you?'

'I know.'

'Thobela showed me. In the atlas. Did you know that Thobela is the cleverest man in the world?'

32

Luke Powell's official title was Economic Attaché of the American consulate in Cape Town.

But his unofficial function, as everyone in the intelligence community was well aware, had little to do with the economy. His actual rank was Senior Special Agent in charge of the CIA in Southern Africa, which included everything this side of the Sahara.

In the politically correct terminology of his country, Luke Powell was an *African-American*, a jovial, somewhat plump figure with a round kind face who wore (to the great mortification of his teenage daughter) large gold-rimmed spectacles that had gone out of fashion ten years ago. He was no longer young, there was grey at his temples and his accent was heavy with the nuances of the Mississippi.

'I'll have a Cheddamelt and fries,' said Powell to the young waiter with the acne problem.

'Excuse me?' said the waiter.

'A Cheddamelt steak, well done. And fries.'

The frown had not disappeared from the waiter's forehead. Every year they were younger. *And dimmer*, thought Janina Mentz. 'Chips,' she said in explanation.

'You only want chips?' the waiter asked her.

'No, I only want an orange juice. He wants a Cheddamelt steak and chips. Americans refer to chips as fries.'

'That's right. French fries,' said Luke Powell jovially and

smiled broadly at the waiter who was properly confused now, the pen poised over the order book.

'Oh,' said the waiter.

'But it's not French, it's American,' said Powell with a measure of pride.

'Oh,' said the waiter again.

'I'm just going to have a plate of salad,' said the Director.

'OK,' said the waiter, relieved, and scribbled something down. He hovered a moment longer but as no one said anything more he left.

'How are y'all?' asked Luke Powell, smiling.

'Not bad for a developing, third-world nation,' said Janina and opened her handbag, taking out a photograph and handing it to Powell.

'We'll get right to the point, Mr Powell,' she said.

'Please,' he said. 'Call me Luke.'

The American took the black-and-white photo. He saw the front door of the American consulate in it, and the unmistakable face of Johnny Kleintjes who was leaving the building.

'Ah,' he said.

'Ah, indeed,' said Janina.

Powell removed his gold-rimmed spectacles and tapped them on the photo.

'We might have something in common on this one?'

'We might,' said the Director softly.

He's good, this American, thought Janina Mentz, registering Powell's lightning adaptation to changes, his poker face.

An innocent six-year-old boy from Guguletu has become a pawn in the nationwide manhunt for Thobela Mpayipheli, the fugitive motorcyclist being sought by intelligence agencies, the military and police.

'Now you're cooking,' said the news editor, tramping around nervously behind Allison as the deadline loomed.

Pakamile Nzululwazi was taken from a day-care centre for pre-schoolers late last night by an official from the 'Department of Defence'. He is the son of Mpayipheli's common-law wife, Miriam Nzululwazi, who also mysteriously disappeared from the Heerengracht branch of Absa, where she is an employee.

'Cooking with gas,' said the news editor and she wished he would sit down so she could concentrate in peace.

'What happened in Lusaka?' asked Janina Mentz.

Luke Powell looked at her and then he looked at the Director and then he replaced the glasses on his face.

What a strange game this is, thought Janina. He knew they knew and they knew he knew they knew.

'We're still trying to find out,' said Powell.

'So you got stung?'

Luke Powell's kind face betrayed nothing of the inner battle, of the humiliation of admitting that the superpower's little African expedition had gone wrong. As always he was the professional spy.

'Yes, we got stung,' he said evenly.

Now the four soldiers, the pilot and co-pilot sat in a circle on the grass, chatting.

Thobela Mpayipheli was relieved because now they were at a safer distance. He could hear their voices but not their words. He could hear laughter bursting out so he assumed that they were telling jokes. He heard the periodic crackle of the radio that would hush them every time until they were certain the message was not for them.

The adrenalin had left his body slowly, discomfort had increased, but at least he could move now, shift his limbs and work away the stones and grass tufts that bothered him.

But he had a new worry now: how long?

They were obviously waiting for a signal or an alarm. And

he knew he was the object of that alarm. The problem was, as long as he lay penned under this bridge, there would be no call. Which meant they would not leave. Which meant it would be a long night.

But more crucial were the hours lost, hours in which he should have been burning up the kilometres to Lusaka. Not yet a crisis, still enough time, but better to have time in the bank, because who knew what lay ahead? There were at least two national borders to cross and although he had his passport in the bag he did not have papers for the GS. The African way would be to put a few hundred-rand notes in the pages of the passport and hope it would do the trick, but the bribery game took time for haggling and you could run up against the wrong Customs man on the wrong day – it was a risk. Better to find a hole in the border fence, or make one and go your way. The Zambezi River, however, was not so easy to cross.

He would need those hours.

And then, of course, the other little problem. As long as it was dark he was safe. But tomorrow morning, when the sun came up, this hiding place in the deep shadow of the bridge would be useless.

He had to get out.

He needed a plan.

'There is one thing that I have a problem understanding, Luke,' said the Director. 'Inkululeko, the alleged South African double agent, works for you. So why offer to buy the intelligence off Johnny Kleintjes?'

Powell merely shook his head.

'What do you care if we think we know who he is?' asked the Director and Janina was surprised at the direction the questions had taken. The Director had confessed nothing to her of his suspicions.

'I don't think that is a sensible line of questioning, Mr Director,' said Powell.

'I think it is because the smell of rat is fairly strong in this vicinity.'

'I have no comment. I am willing to discuss our mutual Lusaka problem, but that's it, I'm afraid.'

'It does not make sense, Luke. Why would you take the risk? You knew it was there, from the moment when Kleintjes walked into the Consulate. You know we have a photographer outside.'

Powell was spared for a moment by the waiter who brought the food – a Cheddamelt steak for the American, a plate of chips for Janina and an orange juice for the Director.

'I did not—' Janina began and then decided to let it go, it would not help to correct the waiter. She took the orange juice and placed it in front of her.

'I'm going to get some salad,' said the Director and stood up.

'May I have some catsup?' asked Powell.

'Excuse me?' said the waiter.

'He wants tomato sauce,' Janina said, irritated.

'Oh. Yes. Sure.'

'Why do you do that?' she asked Powell.

'Do what?'

'Use the Americanisms?'

'Oh, just spreading a little culture,' he said.

'Culture?'

He just smiled. The waiter brought the tomato sauce and Powell poured a liberal amount over his chips, took his fork and stabbed some and put them in his mouth.

'Great fries,' Powell said and she watched him eat until the Director returned with a full plate of salad.

'Have you any idea who burned you in Lusaka?' Janina asked.

'No, ma'am,' said Powell through a mouthful of steak.

The waiter materialized at the table. 'Is everything all right?'

Janina wanted to snap at the pimpled face that all was *not* right, that she had not ordered chips, that he'd better not come flirting for a tip, leave them in peace instead, but she did not.

'Steak's fantastic,' said Powell. The waiter grinned, relieved, and went away.

'How's your salad, Mr Director?' asked Powell.

The Director placed his knife and fork precisely and neatly on his plate. 'Luke, we have people in place in Zambia. The last thing we need is to run into a team of yours.'

'That would be unfortunate.'

'So you have a team there too?'

'I am not at liberty to say.'

'You said you were willing to discuss our mutual Lusaka problem.'

'I was hoping that you had information for me.'

'All we know is that Thobela Mpayipheli is on his way there with a hard drive full of who knows what. You are the one who knows what happened there. With Johnny.'

'He was, shall we say, intercepted.'

'By parties unknown?'

'Exactly.'

'And you don't even have a suspicion?'

'I wouldn't say that.'

'Enlighten us.'

'Well, frankly, I suspected that you were the fly in the ointment.'

'It's not us.'

'Maybe. And maybe not.'

'I give you my personal guarantee that it was not my people,' said Janina Mentz.

'Your personal guarantee,' said Powell, smiling through a mouthful of food.

'It's going to get crowded in Lusaka, Luke,' said the Director.

'Yes, it is.'

'I am asking you, as a personal favour, to stay away.'

'Why, Mr Director, I did not know that South Africa had right of way in Lusaka.'

There was a chill in the Director's voice. 'You have botched the job already. Now get out of the way.'

'Or what, Mr Director?'

'Or we will take you out.'

'Like you're taking out the big bad BMW biker?' asked Powell and put another piece of steak loaded with cheese and mushroom into his mouth.

The big bad BMW biker had his plan thrust upon him.

Fate played an odd card beside the Mighty Modder.

33

Had it not been for the singing, Little Joe Moroka might never have stood up from the ring of jokers.

Cupido started the whole thing with one of those teasing statements: 'You Whiteys can't . . .' and it ended up eventually with a sing-song and that was when the pilot and co-pilot, white as lilies, burst forth with 'On a Bicycle Made for Two' in perfect harmony, *a cappella*, and filled the night with melody.

'Jissis,' said Cupido when they had finished and the rowdy applause had faded. 'Where the fuck did you learn to sing like that?'

'The Air Force has culture,' said the pilot, acting superior.

'In striking contrast with the other branches of the SANDF,' confirmed his colleague.

'All sophisticated people know this.'

'No, seriously,' said Da Costa. 'Where does it come from?'

'If you spend enough time in the mess, you discover strange things.'

'It wasn't bad,' said Little Joe. 'For Whitey harmony.'

'Ooh, damning with faint praise,' said the pilot.

'But can the Darkie sing?' asked the co-pilot.

'Of course,' said Little Joe. And that was how it began, because the pilot said, 'Prove it', and Little Joe Moroka smiled at them, white teeth in the darkness. He stretched his throat, tilted his head up as if his vocal cords needed free rein and then it came, warm and strong, *Shosholoza*, the four notes in pure bravura baritone.

Thobela Mpayipheli could not hear the conversation from under the bridge, but the first song of the two pilots had reached him and although he did not consider himself a music fanatic he found pleasure in it despite his position, despite the circumstances. And now he heard the first phrase of the African song and his ears pricked, he knew this was something rare.

He heard Little Joe toss the notes into the night like a challenge. He heard two voices join in without knowing whose they were, the song gained meaning and emotion, longing. And then another voice, Cupido's tenor, round and high as a flute it hung for a moment above the melody and then dived in. The final ingredient when Zwelitini added his bass softly and carefully so that the four voices formed a velvet foundation for Moroka's melody, the voices intertwining, dancing up and down the scales. They sang without haste, carried by the restful rhythms of a whole continent and the night sounds stopped, the Free State veld was silent to receive the song, Africa opened her arms.

The notes filled Thobela, lifted him up from under that bridge and raised him to the patch of stars in his sight, he saw a vision of black and white and brown in a greater perfect harmony, magical possibilities, and the emotion in him was at first small and controllable, but he allowed it to bloom as the music filled his soul.

And another awareness grew, it had been hiding somewhere, waiting for a receptive spirit and now his head cleared and he felt for the first time in more than a decade the umbilical drawing him back to his origin, deeper and farther, back through his life and the lives of those before him, till he could see all, till he could see himself and know himself.

As the last note died away over the plains, too soon, there

was a breathless quiet as if time stood still for a heart-beat.

Thobela discovered the wetness in his eyes, the moisture running in a long silver thread down his cheek and he was amazed.

The night sounds returned, soft and respectful, as if nature knew she could not compete now.

Wordlessly, Little Joe Moroka stood up from the circle of man at the helicopter.

From habit he slung the Heckler & Koch UMP sub-machine pistol over his shoulder and he walked.

No one said a word. They knew.

Little Joe walked down the bank. It had been a bitter-sweet day and he wanted to cherish the sweet part of it a little longer, taste the emotions a little more. He walked down to the river, stood gazing into the dark water, the H&K harmlessly behind his back. He did not want to stand still, but walked towards the bridge, thinking of everything, thinking of nothing, the sounds reverberating in his head, damn, it was good, like when he was a kid, aimlessly wandered into the dark under the bridge. He saw the dull gleam of the stainless steel exhaust pipe but it did not register because it did not belong, he looked away, looked again, a surreal moment with a tiny wedge of reason, a light coming on in his brain, one step closer, another, the shiny object took shape, lines, tank and wheel and handlebars and he made a noise, surprised, reached for his weapon, swung it around, but it was too late. Out of the moon shadow came a terrifyingly fast movement, a shoulder hit him for the second time that day, but his finger was inside the trigger guard, his thumb already off the safety and as his breath exploded over his lips and he tumbled backwards, the weapon stuttered out on full automatic, loosing seven of its nineteen rounds.

Five hit the concrete and steel, whining away into the night. Two found the right hip of Thobela Mpayipheli.

He felt the 9mm bullets jerk his body sideways, he felt the immediate shock; he knew he was in trouble but he followed the fall of Moroka, down the steep bank to the river. He heard the shouts of the group at the helicopter, but focused on the weapon, Little Joe was winded, he landed on top of him, his hand over the firearm, jerked it, got it loose, his fingers sought the butt, his other forearm against the soldier's throat, face to face, heard the approaching steps, comrades shouting queries, pressed the barrel of the H&K against Moroka's cheek.

'I don't want to kill you,' he said.

'Joe?' called Da Costa from above.

Moroka struggled. The barrel pressed harder, the weight of the Fugitive heavy on him, the man hissed 'Shhh' in his face and Little Joe submitted because where could the fucker go, there were six of them against one.

'Joe?'

Mpayipheli rolled off Moroka, moved around behind him, pulled him up by the collar to use him as a shield.

'Let's all stay calm,' said Thobela. The adrenalin made the world move in slow motion. His hip was wet, blood running in a stream down his leg.

'Jissis,' said Cupido above. They could see now. Little Joe with the gun to his head, the big fucker behind him.

'Put down your weapons,' said Mpayipheli. The shock of the two 9mm rounds combined with the chemistry of his body to make him shake.

They just stood there.

'Shoot him,' said Little Joe.

'No one is getting hurt,' said Thobela.

'Kill the dog,' said Little Joe.

'Wait,' said Da Costa.

'Put it down,' said Mpayipheli.

'Please, man, shoot him,' Little Joe pleaded – he could not face Tiger Mazibuko's anger again, no more humiliation. He writhed and struggled in the grip of the Fugitive and then Thobela Mpayipheli hit him with the butt of the H&K where the nerves bunch between back and head and his knees sagged, but the arm locked around his throat and held him up.

'I will count to ten,' said Mpayipheli, 'and then all the weapons will be on the ground,' and his voice sounded hoarse and strange and distant, a desperate man. His mind was on the helicopter, where was the pilot, where were the men who could use the radio to send a warning?

They put their weapons down, Da Costa and Zwelitini and Cupido.

'Where are the other two?'

Da Costa looked around, betraying their position.

'Get them here. Now,' said Mpayipheli.

'Just stay calm,' said Da Costa.

Little Joe was beginning to come round and started wriggling under his arm. 'I am calm, but if those two don't get here now . . .'

'Captain,' Da Costa called over his shoulder.

No answer.

He's using the radio, Mpayipheli knew – he was calling in reinforcements.

'One, two, three . . .'

'Captain!' There was panic in Da Costa's shout.

'Four, five, six . . .'

'Shit, captain, he's going to shoot him.'

'I will. Seven, eight . . .'

'OK, OK,' said the pilot as he and his colleague walked over the rim of the river bank with their hands up.

'Stand away from the weapons,' said Mpayipheli and they all moved back a few steps. He shoved Little Joe up the bank, so that he could see the helicopter better. The soldier was unsteady on his feet, but still mumbled, 'Shoot him,' and

Mpayipheli said, 'You don't want me to hit you again,' and the mumbling stopped.

They stood, the fugitive with his hostage, the other five in a bunch.

In Mpayipheli's head a clock ticked.

Had the pilot got a message out? How much blood had he lost? When would he feel the light-headedness, the loss of concentration, and the loss of control?

'Listen carefully,' he said. 'We have a bad situation. Don't make it worse.'

No response.

'Is his name Joe?'

Da Costa was the one to nod.

He felt the armour of the Kevlar vest under Little Joe's shirt. He chose the words carefully. 'The first shot goes in Joe's shoulder. The second in his leg. You understand?'

They did not answer.

'You three.' He gestured with the barrel. 'Get the motorbike.'

They just stood there.

'Hurry up,' he said and pressed the barrel against Little Joe's shoulder joint.

The soldiers moved down to the bottom of the bridge.

'You haven't got a chance,' said the pilot and Mpayipheli knew then for sure that the man had used the radio.

'You have thirty seconds,' he screamed at the three by the motorbike. 'You.' He motioned at the co-pilot. 'Fetch the helmet and my suit. They are over there. And if I think you are wasting time . . .'

The man's eyes were wide; he jogged off, past the men struggling to push the motorbike up the incline.

'Help them to get it in the helicopter,' he said to the pilot.

'You're fucking insane, man. I'm not flying you anywhere.' And that was when Little Joe suddenly jerked out of his grasp with a drop and a twist of the shoulders and dived towards the pile of weapons on the ground. Thobela followed him with the Heckler's barrel as if in slow motion, saw him grab a machine pistol, roll over, fingers working the mechanisms with consummate skill. He saw the barrel turn towards him, saw everyone else frozen and he said softly, to himself, once, 'No' – and then his finger pressed the trigger since the choice was no longer to shoot or not, but to live, to survive. The shots cracked, he aimed for the bulletproof vest and Little Joe jerked backwards, Mpayipheli moved, right leg trailing (how much damage?), towards Little Joe and jerked the weapon out of the young soldier's hands, threw his own down, looked up. The others still stood transfixed, he looked down, three shots had harmlessly hit the chest, and one was in the neck, ugly, blood spurting.

He took a deep breath; he must control himself. And them.

'He needs to get to hospital. You determine how fast,' he said. 'Load the bike.'

They were shocked now.

'Move. He will die.'

Little Joe groaned.

The GS was at the open door of the Oryx

'Help them,' he said to the pilot.

'Don't shoot,' said the co-pilot, coming up the bank with the helmet and clothes.

'Put it in.'

The four men battled with the heavy machine, but the adrenalin in their arteries helped them lift first the front and then the back.

'Do you have first-aid equipment?'

Cupido nodded.

'Put a pressure bandage on his neck. Tight.'

Mpayipheli walked to the Oryx, his steps wobbly and the pain in his hip throbbing and sharp, demanding. He knew that he was nearly out of time.

'We must go,' he said looking at the two Air Force pilots.

34

In the second Oryx, which stood beside the R64 halfway between Dealesville and Boshoff, Captain Tiger Mazibuko was the one who heard the emergency signal. 'Mayday, mayday, mayday, they are shooting here below, I think we've found him . . .'

And then it went quiet.

First he shouted outside where the helicopter crew stood around smoking and chatting to the other members of Team Alpha. 'Come!' he screamed and then, over the radio, 'Where are you? Come in. Where are you?' But there was silence and his heart began to race and frustration was the bellows of his rage.

'What?' said the pilot, now beside him.

'They've found him, someone called in mayday,' Mazibuko said. 'Come in, mayday, where are you, who signalled?'

The officer had his headset on in the control cabin.

'Rooivalk One to Oryx, we heard it too.'

'Who was it?' asked Mazibuko.

'Sounded like Kotze, over.'

'Who the fuck is Kotze?'

'The pilot of the other Oryx.'

'Come,' yelled Tiger Mazibuko again but his pilot had the engines running already. 'I want all the Rooivalks, too,' he said into the mouthpiece. 'Do you know where they and Kotze are?'

'Negative, Oryx, over.'

'Fuck,' said Mazibuko and struggled with the map in the dark cabin.

'Show me,' said the co-pilot. 'Then I'll give the coordinates.'

'Here.' He jabbed the map with his index finger. 'Right here.'

They tore over the landscape and the pilot shouted, 'Where?' and Mpayipheli shouted back above the racket, 'Botswana' and the captain shook his head.

'I can't cross the border.'

'You can. If we keep low, the radar won't pick us up.'

'What?'

The pain in his hip was terrible, throbbing; his trousers were soaked in blood. He had to have a look. But there were more urgent things.

'I want a headset,' he said and gestured.

The co-pilot got it, hands trembling, eyes on the H&K in Mpayipheli's hands. He got earphones and passed them over, plugging the wire in somewhere. Hissing, voices, the Rooivalks were talking to each other.

'Tell them about the wounded man,' said Thobela Mpayipheli into the microphone to the co-pilot, 'and nothing else. Understand?'

The man nodded.

Thobela searched the instrument panel for the compass. He knew Lobatse was north, almost directly north. 'Where's your compass?'

'Here,' said the pilot.

'You lie.'

Their gazes met, the pilot assessing him, glancing down at his wounds and his trembling hands, like a predator eyeing its prey. Mpayipheli listened while the co-pilot called in the news about the wounded soldier. 'Oryx Two to Oryx One, we have a casualty, repeat, we have a casualty, we need help immediately.'

'Where are you, Oryx Two?' Mpayipheli recognized the voice. It was the one from this morning, the crazy guy.

'That's enough,' he said to the co-pilot who nodded enthusiastically.

'Listen carefully,' he said to the pilot. 'I only need one pilot. You saw what happened to the soldier. Do you want me to shoot your partner too?'

The man shook his head.

'I want to see the compass. And I want to see the ground, all the time, understand?'

'Yes.'

'Show me.'

The pilot touched the top of the instrument. It read *270*.

'Do you think I am a stupid *kaffir*?'

Voices talked on the radio, Mazibuko's incessant calling, 'Oryx Two, come in. Oryx One to Oryx Two, come in.' The pilot said nothing.

'You have ten seconds to turn north.'

A moment of hesitation, then the pilot turned the helicopter, 280, 290, 300, 310, 320, the instrument swung under its cover, white letters on a black background, 330, 340, 350, 355.

'Keep it there.'

He had to take care of his wounds. Stop the bleeding. He must drink something, the thirst made his mouth like chalk, he had to stay awake, he must stay ready.

'How long to Lobatse?'

'Hour, hour and a quarter.'

The atmosphere in the Ops Room was morbid.

Janina Mentz sat at the big table, trying to keep the tension off her face. They were listening to the cacophony over the radios. It was chaos up there, she thought, chaos everywhere, the meeting with the American had been chaos, the ride back with the Director had not been good and what she had found back here was a demoralized team.

Everyone knew of the death of Miriam Nzululwazi now, everyone knew that Radebe had gone, everyone knew that one of the RU members had been badly wounded and the Fugitive – no one knew where the Fugitive was.

Chaos. And she had no idea what to do.

In the car she had tried to talk to the Director, but there had been distance between them, a breakdown of confidence and she couldn't understand it. Why had his circle of suspicion extended to include her? Or was it a case of killing the bearer of bad news?

Or did the Director see all this chaos as a threat to his own career? Was he thinking ahead, to explaining this mess to the Minister?

She heard the first Rooivalk arriving where the wounded soldier was.

She heard Da Costa report in over the radio of the Rooivalk.

Thobela Mpayipheli had hijacked the Oryx.

Her heart sank.

She heard Tiger Mazibuko's reaction, the cursing tirade.

He was not the right man for the situation, she thought. Rage would not help now. She would have to step in. She was about to get up when she heard Mazibuko call the other Rooivalks. 'The dog is going to Botswana. You must stop him. Get that Oryx.'

One by one the attack helicopters confirmed their new bearings.

What are you thinking, Tiger? Are we going to shoot the Oryx down, with our people and all?

A terrible choice.

'And get Little Joe to hospital,' said Mazibuko over the radio.

'Too late, captain,' said Da Costa.

'What?' said Mazibuko.

'He's dead, captain.'

For the first time the ether was still.

Vincent Radebe looked at the sleeping child in the sitting room of his Sea Point flat. He had made up a bed on the sofa and put the TV on, skipping through the channels for something suitable.

'I don't want to watch TV,' said Pakamile, but he couldn't keep his eyes off the screen.

'Why not?'

'I don't want to go stupid.'

'Stupid?'

'Thobela says it makes people stupid. He says if you want to be clever you must read.'

'He's right. But it's too much television that makes you stupid. We are just going to watch a little bit.' *Please, Lord*, he prayed silently, *let me keep the child occupied, let him go to sleep so I can think.*

'Just a little?'

'Just until you go to sleep.'

'That must be OK.'

'I promise you it will be OK.'

But what do you let a child watch?

And there, on one of the SABC channels was a series on a pride of lions in the Kalahari and he said 'This will make you clever too, because it's about nature' and Pakamile nodded happily and rearranged himself. Vincent had watched as sleep drew an invisible veil over the boy's face, slowly and softly, till the eyes fell shut.

Radebe switched the TV off, and the sitting-room light.

The one in the open-plan kitchen he left on so that the child would not be bewildered if he woke up in the night. He stood on the balcony and thought, because it was a horrible mess.

He would have to tell him that his mother was dead.

Some time or other. It was not right to lie to him.

He had to get the boy clothes. And a toothbrush.

They couldn't stay here. Mentz would find out that he had collected the child and she would take him away to that little room.

Where could they go?

Family was no good. That was the first place Mentz would look. Friends were also dangerous.

So where?

Allison Healy lit a cigarette in her car before turning the key. She inhaled the smoke and blew a stream at the windscreen, watching the smoke dissipate against it.

A long day. A strange day.

Woke up and looked for a story and found a complication.

Moments of truth. Tonight she had wanted to write another intro.

Thobela Mpayipheli, the fugitive motorcyclist, is a former KGB hit man.

No. *Thobela Mpayipheli, the man the media has dubbed the 'Big Bad BMW Biker', is a former KGB assassin.*

She had broken 'off the record' agreements before.

It was a nebulous agreement at best. People didn't always mean what they said. The source talked and talked and talked and somewhere along the way said 'You can't write that' and in the end no one remembered what was on the record and what was off. Of course the really juicy bits, the real news, lay in those areas. Some people used it as a 'cover my ass' mechanism but actually wanted you to write it as long as they could protest, 'I told her it was off the record'.

Sometimes you wrote regardless.

Sometimes you trespassed knowingly, weighing up the consequences and *publish and be damned* and if people were angry – they would get over it, because they needed you, you were the media. With others it didn't matter, let them be angry, they got what they deserved.

Tonight the temptation was exceedingly strong.

What had prevented her?

Allison took out her cellphone. She felt her heart bump in her chest.

She searched for the number under received calls. Pressed the button and put the phone to her ear.

Three, four, five rings. 'Van Heerden.'

'There is something you said that I don't understand.'

He did not answer immediately. In the silence there was meaning.

'Where are you?'

'On the way home.'

'Where do you live?'

She gave the address.

'I'll be there in half an hour.'

She put the phone back in her bag and pulled deeply on the cigarette.

Dear God, what am I doing?

35

It was difficult to watch the compass, to gauge their altitude, keep an eye on the crew and get the sports bag out of the luggage case while juggling the H&K in one hand.

Mpayipheli did it step by step, aware of the need to concentrate. Nothing need happen quickly, he just had to stay alert and monitor all the variables. He placed the bag next to him.

He pulled up the shirt to get at the wound. It did not look good.

He heard the first Rooivalk arriving at the scene and listened to the reports. Heard the Rooivalk's orders to come after them.

They knew he was going to Botswana.

It was the voice from this morning.

My name is Captain Tiger Mazibuko. And I am talking to a dead man.

Not yet, Captain Mazibuko. Not yet.

Mazibuko barking out, *And get Little Joe to a hospital.*

Too late, captain.

What?

He's dead, captain.

It was the pilot who looked around, disgusted at Mpayipheli's presence here. The injustice registered with Thobela, but that was irrelevant now.

But his status was relevant. And that had changed dramatically. From illegal courier, in their perspective, to murderer.

Although it was in self-defence, they would not see it like that.

He looked down at the wound.

He must concentrate on survival.

Now more than ever.

He could see now that it was more than one bullet: one had taken out a chunk of flesh just below the hip bone, the other had gone in and out on a skewed trajectory, it must have struck the hip bone. Blood was thick over the wounds. He pulled a shirt from the bag and began to clean them up, first looking up to see the co-pilot watching him, seeing the wounds, the man was pale. Checked the compass, looked outside – down below he could see the landscape flashing by in the moonlight.

He looked around the interior. Some of the soldiers' gear had been left inside: backpacks, two metal trunks, a paperback. He pushed the backpacks around with his left foot. Got hold of two water bottles and loosened them from the packs.

'I need bandages,' he said. The co-pilot pointed. At the back was a metal case, a red cross painted on it, screwed to the body of the helicopter. Sealed.

Mpayipheli stood up and unplugged the headset. He broke the seal of the case and opened it. The contents were old, but there were bandages, painkillers, ointment, antiseptic, syringes of drugs he did not recognize, everything in a removable canvas bag. He took it out and moved back to his seat, replaced the headset, went through the checklist of crew, altitude and direction. He placed the bandages aside, trying to make out the labels of the tubes of ointment and packets of pills in the poor light. He put what he needed to one side.

He had never been wounded before.

The physical reaction was new to him but he vaguely recalled the expected pathology: there would be shock, tremors and dizziness, then the pain, fatigue, the dangers of blood loss, thirst, faintness, poor concentration. The important thing was to stop the bleeding and take in enough water: dehydration was the big enemy.

He heard his mother's voice in his head. He was fourteen: they were playing by the river, chasing lizards, and the sharp edge of a reed had sliced open his leg like a knife. At first, all he felt was the stinging. When he looked down there was a deep wound to the bone – he could see it, above the kneecap, pure white against the dark skin, he could see the blood that instantaneously began seeping from all sides likes soldiers charging the front lines. 'Look,' he said proudly to his friends, hands around the leg, the wound long and very impressive, 'I'm going home – so long,' limping back to his mother, watching the progression of blood down his leg with detached curiosity as if it wasn't his. His mother was in the kitchen, he needed to say nothing, just grinned. She had a shock – 'Thobela,' her cry of worry. She let him sit on the edge of the bath and with soft hands and clicking tongue disinfected the wound with snow-white cotton wool, the smell of Dettol, the sting, the bandages and plaster, his mother's voice, soothing, loving, caressing hands, the longing welled up in him, for her, for that carefree time, for his father. He jerked back to the present – the compass was still at 355.

Mpayipheli got to his feet and pressed the H&K against the co-pilot's neck. 'Those helicopters. How fast can they fly?'

'Aah . . . uum . . .'

'How fast?' and he jabbed the weapon into the man's cheek.

'About two-eighty,' said the pilot.

'And how fast are we going?'

'One-sixty.'

'Can't we go faster?'

'No,' said the pilot. 'We can't go faster.' Unconvincingly.

'Are you lying to me?'

'Look at the fucking aircraft. Does it look like a greyhound to you?'

He sagged back to his seat.

The man was lying. But what could he do about it?

They wouldn't make it; the border was too far away.

What would the Rooivalks do when they intercepted?

He unclipped another water bottle from one of the rucksacks and opened the cap, brought it to his lips and drank deeply. The water tasted of copper, strange on his tongue, but he gulped greedily, swallowing plenty. How the bottle shook in his big hand, hell, he trembled, trembled. He breathed in slowly, slowly breathed out. If he could just make it to Botswana. Then he had a chance.

He began to clean the wound slowly and meticulously.

Because if he was still Umzingeli, there would be at least four bodies for you to explain.

That was what the Minister of Water Affairs and Forestry had said and now there was one body and Janina Mentz wondered if the gods had conspired against her. For what were the odds that the perfect operation, so well planned and seamlessly executed would draw in a retired assassin?

And in that moment of self-pity she found the truth. The foundation of reason that she could build upon.

It was not by chance.

Johnny Kleintjes had instructed his daughter to involve Thobela Mpayipheli if something happened to him. Was it a premonition? Did the old man expect things to go wrong? Or was he playing some other game? Someone had known about the whole thing, someone had waited in Lusaka and taken the CIA out of the game and the question, the first big question was: who?

The possibilities – that was what drove her out of her head, the multiple possibilities. It could be this own country's

National Intelligence Agency, it could be the Secret Service, or Military Intelligence, the rivalry, the spite and corruption were tragic in their extent.

The content of the hard disk was the second Big Question, because that was a clue to the 'who'.

If Johnny Kleintjes had contacted someone else . . . An old colleague now at the NIA or SS or MI who'd said 'This is what the people at PIA are planning, but I have other data.'

Impossible.

Because then this thing of the phone calls to Monica Kleintjes, the threats to kill Johnny Kleintjes, would never have happened. Why complicate it so? Why endanger his own daughter?

Johnny could just have given copies of the data to the NIA.

It had to be someone else.

Mentz had recruited Kleintjes, she had explained the operation to him, she had seen his eagerness, estimated his loyalty and patriotism. They had watched him in those weeks, listened to his calls and followed him, knew what he did, where he was. It made no sense. Kleintjes could not be the leak.

Where then? With the CIA?

Perhaps a year or two ago, but not since September 11. The Americans had retreated into the *laager*, they played a serious, pitiless game, cards close to the chest. Took no chances.

Where was the leak?

Here she was the only one who knew.

Here. Quinn and his teams had trailed Kleintjes and tapped his phone without being briefed with the whole picture. Only she knew the whole story. Everything.

Who? Who, who, who?

Her cellphone rang and she saw that it was Tiger. She did not want to speak to him right now.

'Tiger?'

'Ma'am, he's on the way . . .'

'Not now, Tiger, I'll call you back.'

'Ma'am . . .' Desperation, she could understand that. One of his men was dead, murder burned in his heart, someone had to pay. First, though, she had to think. She pressed the button, cutting him off.

When Mentz entered the Ops Room she felt despair. She no longer felt up to the task. She recognized the feelings of self-pity. The Director was the source of that. He had withdrawn his support and trust and now she felt suddenly alone and aware of her lack of experience. She was a planner, a strategist and a manipulator. Her skill was in organization, not crisis management. Not violence and guns and helicopters.

But the fact remained, this was not about the crisis of the Fugitive and a dead soldier.

Don't get caught up in the drama. Maintain perspective. Think. Reason. Let your strong points count.

The hard disk.

Johnny Kleintjes had done what any player with a lifetime of sanctioned fraud behind him would do: left an escape route, a bit of insurance. Thobela Mpayipheli was that insurance, but Kleintjes had not even left the man's proper address or telephone number with Monica, it had been out of date. If he had really expected trouble, he would have taken more trouble, probably gone to see Mpayipheli himself. At least made sure where his old friend was.

No, it was out of habit, not foreknowledge.

The same went for the hard disk. It was a piece of insurance from the days when he'd been coordinator for the integration of the awful stuff. Old forgotten intelligence on political leaders' sexual preferences and suspected traitors and double agents. Negligible. Irrelevant, just something that Kleintjes had thought of when he was knee-deep in trouble, a way of using his insurance. *Don't focus on the hard disk; don't be misled by it*. She felt relief growing, because she knew she was right.

But she did not need to disregard it; she could play more than one game.

She had to concentrate on Lusaka. She had to find out who was holding Johnny Kleintjes. If she knew that, she would know where the leak was and in that knowledge lay the real power.

Forget the Director. Forget Thobela Mpayipheli. Focus.

'Quinn,' she called out. He sat hunched over his panel and jumped when he heard his name.

'Rahjev.'

'Ma'am?'

'Don't look so depressed. Come, walk with me.' There was strength in Mentz's voice and they heard it. They looked to her, all of them.

By the time Van Heerden knocked on the door, Allison had showered, dressed, put on music, agonized over the brightness of the lights, lit a cigarette and sat down in her chair in the sitting room, trying to attain a measure of calm.

But the moment she heard the soft knock, she lost it.

Janina Mentz walked in the middle, the two men flanking her: Quinn the brown man, lean and athletic, Rajkumar impossibly fat – a pair of unmatched bookends. They walked down Wale Street without speaking, round the corner at the church towards the Supreme Court. The only sound was Rajkumar's gasping as he struggled to keep up. The two men knew that she had got them out to avoid listening ears. As participants in the plot they accepted her lead.

They crossed Queen Victoria Street and went into the Botanical Gardens, now dark and full of shadows of historic trees and shrubs, the pigeons and squirrels quiet. She had brought her children here with her ex-husband on days of bright sunshine, but even in daylight the gardens whispered, the dark corners created small oases of complicity and secretiveness. She walked to one of the wooden benches and looked at the lights of Parliament on the other side, and at the homeless figure of a *Bergie* on the grass.

Ironic.

'Good,' she said as they sat. 'Let me tell you how things stand.'

Zatopek van Heerden had brought wine that he opened and poured into the glasses that Allison provided.

They were uneasy with each other, their roles now so different from this afternoon – the awareness they shared was avoided, sidestepped, ignored like a social disease.

'What is it that you don't understand?' he asked as they sat.

'You talked of genetic fitness indicators.'

'Oh. That.'

He studied his glass, the red wine glowing between his hands. Then he looked up and she saw that he wanted her to say something else, to open a door for him and she could not help herself, she asked the question of her fears. 'Are you involved?' Realized that was not clear enough. 'With someone?'

36

'No,' Van Heerden said and the corners of his mouth turned up.

'What?' Allison asked unnecessarily because she knew.

'The difference between us. Between man and woman. For me it is still . . . enigmatic.'

She smiled with him.

He looked at his glass as she spoke, his voice quiet. 'How many times in one person's life will you know that the attraction is mutual? In equal measure?'

'I don't know.'

'Too few,' he said.

'And I need to know if there is someone else.'

He shrugged. 'I understand.'

'Doesn't it matter to you?'

'Not now. Later. Definitely later.'

'Odd,' she said, drawing on her cigarette, taking a swallow of wine, waiting. He stood up, placed his glass on the coffee table and came to her. She waited a moment then bent down to stub out her cigarette.

Tiger Mazibuko sat in the Oryx, alone. Outside at the bridge where Little Joe had died the men stood waiting, but he did not think of them. He had the charts with him, maps of Botswana. He hummed softly as his fingers ran over them, an unrecognizable, monotonous refrain – busy, busy – when the phone rang. He knew who it would be.

'What I really want to do,' he said straight away, 'is to blow the fucker out of the sky with a missile, preferably this side of the border.' His voice was easy, his choice of words deliberate. 'But I know that's not an option.'

'That's right,' said Janina Mentz.

'I take it we are not going to call in the help of our neighbours.'

'Right again.'

'National pride and the small problem of sensitive data in strange hands.'

'Yes.'

'I want to ambush him, ma'am.'

'Tiger, that's not necessary.'

'What do you mean, not necessary?'

'This line is not secure, take my word for it. Priorities have changed.'

Mazibuko nearly lost it, right there, the rage pushed up from below like lava, *priorities have changed*, jissis, he had lost a man, he'd been humiliated and sent from pillar to post, he had endured the chaos and the fucking lack of professionalism and now someone in a fucking office had changed the fucking priorities. His anger wanted to explode out violently but he held it in, choked it back, because he had to.

'Are you there?'

'I am here. Ma'am, I know what route he will use.'

'And?'

'He's going to Kazungula.'

'Kazungula?'

'On the Zambian border. He won't go through Zimbabwe, too many border posts, too much trouble. I know this.'

'It doesn't help us. That's in Botswana. Even if it comes from the top, official channels will take too long.'

'I didn't have anything official in mind.'

'No, Tiger.'

'Ma'am, he's wounded. The way Da Costa talks—'

'Wounded, you say?'

'Yes. Da Costa says it's serious, his stomach or his leg. Little Joe got shots off before he was shot himself. It will slow him down. He has to rest. And drink. That gives us time.'

'Tiger . . .'

'Ma'am, just me. Alone. I can be in Ellisras in two hours. In three hours at Mahalapye. All I need is a vehicle . . .'

'Tiger . . .'

'It gives you an extra option.' He played his trump card.

Mentz vacillated and he saw opportunity in that. 'I swear I will keep a low profile. No international incident. I swear.'

Still she hesitated and he drew breath to say more but stopped. *Fuck her* – he would not plead.

'On your own?'

'Yes. In every way.'

'Without back-up and communications and official approval?'

'Yes.' He had her; he knew that he had her. 'Just a car. That's all I ask.'

'Oryx Two, this is Rooivalk Three. We are two hundred metres behind you with missiles locked on. Land, please – there's lots of places down below.'

Mpayipheli had swallowed the painkillers with lukewarm water but they had not kicked in yet. The wound was clean now, the bandage stretched tight around his middle, pulling heavily on his side. It was still bleeding in there, he did not know how to stop it, hoped it would just happen. The pilot asked, 'What now?'

'Stay on course.'

'Oryx Two, this is Rooivalk Three. Confirm contact, please.'

'How far are we from the Botswana border?'

The two officers merely stared ahead. He cursed quietly

and stood up, feeling the wounds, Lord, he should keep still. He hit the co-pilot against the forehead with the barrel of the Heckler, drew blood and shook the man who raised his hands protectively. 'I am tired of this.'

'Seventy kilometres,' said the pilot hurriedly.

Mpayipheli checked his watch. It could be true. Another half-hour.

'Oryx Two, this is Rooivalk Three. We have you in our sights – you have ninety seconds to respond.'

'They are going to shoot us down,' said the co-pilot. He had wiped his forehead and was looking at the blood on his hand now, then at Mpayipheli, like a faithful dog that has been kicked.

'They won't,' Mpayipheli said.

'How do you know?'

'Sixty seconds, Oryx Two. We have permission to fire.'

'I'm going down,' said the pilot, fear in his voice.

'You will not land,' said Thobela Mpayipheli, the H&K against the co-pilot's neck.

'Do you want to die?'

'They won't fire.'

'You can't say that.'

'If you do anything but fly straight, I will shoot off your friend's head.'

'Please, no,' said the co-pilot, his eyes screwed shut.

'Thirty seconds, Oryx Two.'

'You're fucking crazy, man,' said the pilot.

'Stay calm.'

The co-pilot made a strangled noise.

'Oryx Two, fifteen seconds before missile launch, confirm instruction – I know you can hear me.'

Two innocent lives and a helicopter worth millions of rand, they would not shoot, they would not shoot, they would have heard an official order over the radio, this kind of decision was not made at operational level, they could not shoot. The seconds ticked by and they waited for the impact, all three rigid, instinctively bracing for the bang, for a sign, waiting. They heard the Rooivalk pilot. 'Fuck,' he said.

Relief.

'You've got balls, you black bastard, I'll give you that,' said the Rooivalk pilot.

37

Mpayipheli made the Oryx land near a road sign to make sure that they were over the border. The Rooivalks had turned back and the main route between Lobatse and Gaborone was quiet. The night was warm. He made the men lie face down on the tarred road while he struggled mightily to get the big GS up from the floor of the helicopter. There was no help for it, he would have to start it and ride it out, hoping not to fall in the jump from the aircraft to the ground half a metre down. He had a slight fever that created a thin invisible membrane between him and reality. The painkillers had kicked in and he moved studiously, every step ticked off against a checklist in his mind lest he forget something.

If he fell they would leap up: the pilot was the danger, the officer's hate for him was like a beacon.

He got the motorbike on the side stand and checked that the sports bag was in the luggage case, locked. What was he forgetting? He mounted and pressed the starter. The engine turned and turned, but would not take.

He pressed the choke up and tried again. This time it took with a roar and a shudder. He lifted the side stand with a foot and turned the steering. He couldn't ride out slowly; he would accelerate powerfully and let momentum carry him out. The helicopter was beside the road, engines still on, the blades sweeping up a whirlwind around the resting bird. He had to be sure that the GS's engine was warmed up enough and he revved.

The pilot lay watching, his face expressionless.

Mpayipheli drew a breath – now or never – clutch in, first gear, turned the throttle and released the clutch. The GS shot forward and out, the front wheel dropped, hit the ground, shocks banging, the force shooting up his arms and making him lose balance, then the rear wheel came down and with the throttle still wide open he shot forward, straight across the road, braked to stop going into the veld and came to a halt. His heart pounded, dear Lord, he looked around, the pilot had leapt up and was running to the helicopter, the Heckler lay there inside, *that* was what his head had been trying to tell him, *don't forget the machine pistol*, but now it was too late, there was only one option. He rode as fast as the motorbike would accelerate, lying flat without looking back, a smaller target, ears pricked, second, third, fourth gear, something struck the bike, fifth, a hundred and sixty kilometres per hour, still accelerating, what had the pilot hit?

Then he knew that he was out of range and kept the speed there and he wondered if the pilot's hate was great enough to follow him with the Oryx.

Janina Mentz carried out her plan meticulously.

She fetched the Director from his office. She could see he was tired now; his whole body expressed it. 'I want to talk, sir, but not here.'

He nodded and stood up, taking his jacket from where it hung neatly on a hanger, took his time putting it on and then held the door for her. They rode down in the lift and left the building, he a courteous step behind her. She led him up Long Street knowing the Long Street Café would still be open. This part of the city was still alive, young people, tourists with backpacks, Rikki taxis, scooters. Nightclub music pounded from an upper floor. The Director was short and bowed beside her and she was once again conscious of the spectacle they presented: what would people think, seeing the white woman in a business suit walking with the little hunchbacked black man?

There was a vacant table at the back near the cake display.

He held the chair for her and for an instant she found his courtesy irritating – she wanted simply to be accepted or rejected, not live in this no man's land.

He did not look at the menu. 'You believe we are being bugged?'

'Sir, I have considered all the evidence and somewhere there is a leak. With us, or with Luke Powell.'

'And you don't believe it is with them?'

'It's not impossible, just improbable.'

'What has happened to our Johnny-the-Communist theory?'

'The more I think about it the less it makes sense.'

'Why, Janina?'

'He would not endanger his own daughter. He would not leave an outdated address and phone number for Mpayipheli with her. If he wanted to threaten the CIA there are other ways. To tell the truth, nothing about it makes sense.'

'I see.'

'You still think it's Johnny?'

'I no longer know what to think.' The weariness in his voice was undisguised and she saw him with greater clarity then. What was he? Somewhere on the shady side of fifty, the Director carried the burden of the invisible, endless decades of intrigue that were now behind him. While a young waitress with dark secret eyes took their order, Janina Mentz studied him. Did he once have dreams and ambitions for greater things? Had he seen himself as material for the inner circle, to wear the head ring of the stalwart? Had he been on the verge of that once in his wanderings during the Struggle? He was a clever man whose potential they would have recognized.

What had held him back, kept him out, so that now he sat here, a worn-out old man holding on to his status as a senior civil servant with titles and white silk shirts?

He misinterpreted her examination. 'Do you really suspect me, Janina?'

She sighed deeply. 'Sir . . .'

There was compassion in the set of her mouth.

'. . . I had to consider it.'

'And what was your conclusion?'

'Another improbable.'

'Why?'

'All you could know was that Johnny Kleintjes was one of a large number of people we were keeping tabs on. I was the only one who knew why.'

The Director nodded slowly, without satisfaction; he knew that would be the result. 'That goes for all of us, Janina.'

'That is what puzzles me.'

'Then the leak is not with us.'

'I don't know . . .'

'Unless, of course, it is *you*.'

'That's true. Unless I am the one.'

'And that couldn't be, Janina.'

'Sir, let me speak frankly. I feel that our relationship has altered.'

The coffee arrived and her words hung in the air until the waitress left.

'Earlier today when we met Powell, after that,' she said.

He took his time, tore open the sugar packet and stirred the sugar into his coffee. He looked up at her. 'I don't know who to trust any more, Janina.'

'Why, sir? What has changed?'

The Director brought the cup to his lips, testing the heat carefully, sipped and replaced the porcelain cup carefully back in the saucer. 'I don't have an empirical answer to that. I can't set out the points one by one. It is a feeling, Janina, and I am sorry that you felt it includes you too, because that is not necessarily the case.'

'A feeling?'

'That I am being led up the garden path.'

When Thobela Mpayipheli dismounted from the R 1150 GS in front of the Livingstone Hotel in Gaborone he could barely stand. At first he held on to the saddle with a thousand stars swimming in his vision, bending over it until balance and sight returned.

When he moved around the bike, he saw the damage for the first time.

The 9mm bullets had struck the right-hand luggage case, making two small neat holes in the black polyvinyl. The sports bag was in there.

He unclipped the case and took out the bag. Two holes, perfectly round.

He locked everything, crossed the pavement and entered the hotel.

The night porter sat sleeping in his chair. Thobela had to ding the bell with his palm before the man stood up groggily and pushed the register over the desk. He filled in his particulars.

'Will you take South African rand?'

'Yes.'

'Can I still get something to eat?'

'Ring room service. Nine one. Passport, please.'

Thobela passed it over. The man's bloodshot eyes barely looked at it, just checking the number against the one he had written down. Then he pulled a key out of the lock-up cupboard behind him and passed it over.

Before the rattling lift had reached the ground floor and opened for Umzingeli, the night porter was asleep again.

The room was large, the bed heavenly under its multicoloured spread and the pillows billowy and tempting.

First, a shower. Re-dress the wound. Eat, drink.

And then sleep – dear God, how he would sleep.

He unzipped the sports bag. Time to review the damage. He shook the contents onto the double bed. Nothing to mention, even his toilet bag was unscathed. Then he picked up the hard drive and held it in his hands – and he saw that it was destroyed. The Heckler & Koch rounds had hit the middle of the almost square box, where metal and plastic and integrated circuits came together. The data was lost for ever.

No wonder the bang had been so loud.

Heads together, voices low, Janina Mentz and the Director looked like lovers in the Long Street Café. She said that the hard disk was the wrong focus, containing nothing of importance, stale old intelligence locked up in a safe by an old man who wanted to feel he still had a part in the Game, suddenly dug up when he was in trouble. Thobela Mpayipheli was no longer important; he had become a marginal figure, an irritation at worst. Let him go, the action was in Lusaka, the answers lay waiting there.

'We already have four operatives there. We are going to send another twelve, the best we have. We want to know who is holding Johnny Kleintjes hostage and we want to know how they knew about this operation. I considered sending the RU to Lusaka but we don't want an incident, we need a low profile, to work subtly. We need silent numbers, not fireworks.'

'And what about the leak?'

'I am only involving four people here – myself, you, sir, Quinn and Rajkumar. We will keep it small, we keep it intimate and we get the answers.'

'Does Tiger know?'

'Tiger only knows that priorities have changed. Anyway, he is on a mission of his own. Apparently he is going to stop Mpayipheli. In Botswana.'

'And you let him go?'

Mentz thought this over before answering carefully. 'Tiger has earned his chance, sir. He is alone.'

The Director shook his head. 'Tiger has the wrong motives, Janina.'

'He has always had the wrong motives, Mr Director. That is why he is such an asset.'

They lay beside each other in the dark, she on her back, he on his side next to her, stroking her body, getting to know it from her neck to her toes. His touch was paradise, absolute acceptance. She had asked him, when the perspiration and the passion had cooled and his palm was absently stroking over her full breasts and she felt the warmth of his breath on her nipples, she had asked him if he liked her body and he had said, 'More than you will ever know' and that had been the end of her fears for that night. She knew there was one more up ahead, but that could wait until tomorrow, she wanted to experience this moment without anxiety. His voice was gentle, his head nestling against her neck, his hand never stopped stroking and he spoke to her, told her everything, opening a new world to her.

Captain Tiger Mazibuko crossed the border an hour after midnight. He was driving a 1.8-litre GTI Turbo Volkswagen Golf. He had no idea how Janina Mentz had organized it – it had been waiting for him at the police station at Ellisras and the keys were handed to him at the desk of the charge office once he had shown his passport. Now he was in Botswana and he drove as fast as the narrow road and the darkness allowed in this other country, with cattle and goats grazing beside the

road. He had made his calculations. Everything depended on
the Dog's progress but his injuries would hold him up. The
pilot of the Oryx had spoken with him over the cellphone;
they had their hate for Mpayipheli in common. The pilot
said that the wound was bad and the fugitive would not last
the night on the motorbike. He was close to falling when he
came out of the helicopter and there were more shots fired,
perhaps he had taken another bullet or two.

*Let's say the fucker was tougher than they thought; let's say
he kept going . . .*

Then Mpayipheli would be ahead of him. At least two
hours ahead.

Would he be able to catch him?

It depended how fast the bugger could ride: he had to eat,
he had to rest, he had to drink and fill up with petrol.

It was possible.

Maybe he was sleeping somewhere – then Tiger would wait
for him. At the bridge over the Zambezi, just beyond the place
where the waters of the great river and the Chobe merged.

A good place for a death in Africa.

Before Mpayipheli turned off the light and sank into the
softness of the double bed, he sat staring at the telephone. His
longing for Miriam and Pakamile was overwhelming, just one
call, 'Don't worry about the reports over the radio, I am OK,
I am nearly there, I love you', that was all he wanted to say,
but if they had tapped the line they would know immediately
where he was and they would come and get him.

If only he could contact someone and say the terrible information on your piece of computer equipment is destroyed,
your dark secrets are safe and threaten no one, leave me alone,
let me go and help an old friend and then let me go home.

Tomorrow he would be there, late tomorrow afternoon he
would ride into Lusaka. He had read the signs – no roadblocks

outside Gaborone, no hot pursuit by the Oryx, obviously they did not want to involve the Botswana government, they wanted to keep it in the family. Probably they were waiting for him in Lusaka – but that was good, he could handle that, he was trained in the art of urban warfare. Tomorrow it would all be over. He felt as if he were sinking into the bed, deeper and deeper, so weary, his whole body exhausted, but his brain was flashing images of the day that lay behind him. He was aware of the physiology of the bullet wounds, the feverishness, the effects of the painkillers and four cans of cola and the brandy he'd had after his room service meal. *We have a club sandwich and chips or a cheeseburger and chips, take your pick*. He could rationalize his emotions, but he could not suppress them, he felt so alone.

Not for the first time. Other cities, other hotel rooms, but that had been different, there had been no Miriam before.

There had never been a Miriam before he had found her. There had been other women; at Odessa there were the prostitutes, the official Stasi-approved whores to see to their needs, to keep the levels of testosterone under control so that they would pay attention to their training. Afterwards he was under instructions – don't get involved, don't get attached, don't stay with a woman. But his Eastern Bloc masters had not reckoned on the Scandinavians' obsession with black men. Lord, those Swedish women, shamelessly hot for him, on his first visit in '82 three of them had approached him in a coffee shop in Stockholm, one after another until he had fled, sure of a plot, some NATO counter-intelligence operation. Eventually, a year later Neta had explained it to him, it was just a thing they had, she couldn't say why. Agneta Nilsson, long fine blonde hair and two wild weeks of passion in Brussels until the KGB had sent a courier to say that was enough, you are trespassing, looking for trouble. He, Thobela Mpayipheli from the Kei had eaten white bread, the whitest to be had, sated himself to bursting point but not his heart, his heart had remained empty until he had seen Miriam. Not even in '94 had his heart been so empty, waiting for the call from a man who was now Minister, waiting for his reward, waiting to be included in the victory, to share the fruits, waiting. Days of wandering the streets, a stranger in his own land, among his own people. He had thought of his father in those weeks, played with the idea of taking the train to visit his parents, to stand in the doorway and say 'Here I am, this is what happened to me,' but there was too much baggage, the gulf was too wide to cross and in the evenings he went back to the room and waited for the call that never came, rejected, that was how he felt, a feeling that slowly progressed to one of betrayal. They had made him what he was and now they didn't want to know. Eventually he went to Cape Town so that he could hear the tongue of his ancestors again, until he decided to offer his services where they would be appreciated, where he would be included, where he could be part of something.

It had not worked out as he'd thought it would. The Flats had been good to him, but he had remained the outsider, still alone, alone among others.

But not so lonely as now, not like now. Fevered chills, strange dreams, a conversation with his father that never ended, explanation, justification, on and on, words flowing out of him and his father receding, shaking his head and praying and then he forced himself to wake sweating and the pain in his hip was a dull throbbing and he got up and drank of the cold sweet water from the tap in the bathroom.

Somewhere in the pre-dawn Allison Healy woke from sleep for a brief moment, just long enough to register one thought: the decision to withhold the information that he had given her had been the best decision of her life.

Had she known, in those moments when she'd had to decide? Had she known, despite her fears and insecurities?

It no longer mattered. She rolled over, pressing her voluptuousness against Van Heerden's back and thighs and sighed with joy before she softly sank away into sleep again.

38

When Lien and Lizette crept into the double bed beside her, Janina Mentz woke up and rubbed her eyes. 'What time is it?' she asked.

Lien said, 'It's early, ma, sleep a little longer.'

She checked the clock radio. 'It's half-past six.'

'Very early,' said Lizette.

'Time to get ready,' she said without enthusiasm. She could sleep for another hour or two.

'We're not going to school today,' said her youngest.

'Oh, really?'

'It's National Keep-your-mother-at-home-at-any-cost Day.'

'Hah!'

'Failure to obey is punishable with a fine of five hundred rands' worth of new clothes for every descendant.'

'That will be the day.'

'It is the Day. National Keep-your-mum—'

'Put on the TV.'

'Watching TV so early in the morning is harmful to the middle-aged brain, you know that, ma.'

'Middle-aged, my foot. I want to see the news.'

'Maaa . . . leave the work until we go to school.'

'It's not work, it's a healthy interest in my environment and my world. An attempt to demonstrate to my darling daughters that there are more things in life than Britney Spears and horny teenage boys.'

'Like what?' said Lien.

'Name one thing,' said Lizette.

'Put on the TV.'

'OK, OK.'

'Middle-aged. That's a new one.'

'People should be comfortable with their age.'

'I hope I see the same level of wisdom on your report cards.'

'There you go – the middle-aged brain's last resort. The school report.'

Lien pressed the button on the small colour television. A sports programme on M-net appeared slowly on the screen.

'The middle-aged brain wants to know who has been watching TV in my room.'

'I had no choice. Lien was busy entertaining horny teenage boys in the sitting room.'

'Put it on TV2 and stop talking rubbish.'

'Isn't there an educational programme . . .'

'Shhh . . .'

. . . details about the South African weapons scandal. The newspaper quotes a source saying the data Mpayipheli is carrying contains the Swiss bank account details of government officials involved in the weapons deals, as well as the amounts allegedly paid in bribes and kickbacks. A spokesperson for the office of the Minister of Defence strongly denied the allegations, saying it was, quote, another malicious attempt by the opposition press to damage the credibility of the government with deliberate lies and fabrications, unquote.

The spokesperson also denied any military involvement in the disappearance of Mrs Miriam Nzululwazi, the common-law wife of the fugitive Mpayipheli, and her six-year-old son. According to the Cape Times, *a man identifying himself as an employee of the Department of Defence took young Pakamile Nzululwazi into his custody last night, after his mother was arrested at her place of work, a commercial bank, earlier in the day.*

Meanwhile, rival motorcycle groups seemingly supporting Mr Mpayipheli clashed in Kimberley last night. Police were called in to break up several fights in the city. Nine motorcyclists were treated for injuries in hospital.

Moving on to other news . . .

The other fear embraced Allison Healy when she woke and found Van Heerden gone. No note, nothing, and she knew that the fear would be her constant companion until she heard from him again. Until she saw him again the impulse to dial his number, to seek reassurance and confirmation, would strengthen through the day, but she had to resist it at all costs.

She stood up, looking for salvation in routine, swung the gown over her shoulders, put on the kettle, opened the front door and retrieved the two newspapers. Went back to the kitchen, scanned the *Times*, everything was as she had written it, the main story, the boxes, the other two stories. She glanced quickly at pages two and three, did not see the small report hidden away, unimportant.

LUSAKA – Zambian Police are investigating the death of two American tourists after their bodies were found by pedestrians on the outskirts of the capital yesterday.

A law-enforcement spokesman says that the tourists died of gunshot wounds, and the apparent motive was robbery. The names of the two men are expected to be released today, after the American Embassy and relatives have been notified.

No arrests have been made.

She was in a hurry to get to the *Burger*. She opened the newspaper on the breakfast bar.

Weapons Scandal:
Motorcycle Man holds the key

CAPE TOWN – Full particulars of the South African weapons scandal, including names, relevant sums and Swiss bank account numbers of government officials are allegedly contained in the computer disk in the possession of the fugitive Mr Thobela Mpayipheli – the motorcyclist who still evades arrest by the authorities.

Sweet lord, she thought, *where did this come from?*

According to advocate Pieter Steenkamp, previously of the directorate for the investigation of serious economic crimes (Disec), there was frequent mention of the hard disk during the hearing of evidence relating to alleged irregularities in the weapons transaction of R43.8 billion last year.

'Come on,' murmured Allison.

'We conducted more than a hundred interviews and, according to my notes, at least seven times there was mention made of complete electronic data in the possession of an Intelligence agency,' said Advocate Steenkamp who joined the Democratic Alliance in November last year.

'My allegations will probably be dismissed as petty politicking. We will just see more cover-up. It is in the interest of the country and all its people that Mr Mpayipheli is not apprehended. His journey has more significance than that of Dick King who rode on horseback from Durban to Grahamstown in 1842 to warn the English of the Boer siege.'

The fugitive motorcyclist was still on the loose at the time of going to print after leaving Cape Town on a stolen BMW R 1150 GS (see article below) the day before yesterday. According to a SAPS source Mpayipheli evaded government authorities at Three Sisters during one of the worst thunderstorms in recent memory (article on p. 5, weather forecast on S8).

An extensive operation at Petrusburg in the Free State also failed to apprehend the Umkhonto veteran last night. Unconfirmed reports claim that he crossed the border into Botswana late last night.

Allison Healy considered the report, staring at the magnets on her fridge.

Not impossible.

And if they were right she had been scooped. Badly.

She looked down at the page again. There was another article, presented in box form beside the picture of a man standing next to a motorcycle

By Jannie Kritzinger, Motoring Editor

This is the motorcycle that created a sensation last year by beating the legendary sports models like the Kawaski ZX-6R, Suzuki SV 650 S, Triumph Sprint ST and even the Yamaha YZF-R1 in a notorious Alpine high-speed road test run by the leading German magazine, Motorrad.

But the BMW R 1150 GS is anything but a racing motor-cycle. In truth, it is the number-one seller in a class or niche that it has created – the so-called multipurpose motorcycle that is equally at home on a two-track ground road or the freeway.

While the GS stands for 'Gelände/Strasse' (literally 'veld and street'), the multipurpose idea has expanded to include models from Triumph, Honda and Suzuki, which all use drive-chain technology.

She scanned the rest, wanting to page to the promised article on page two (*Motorcyclist is Psychopath, says Brigadier* and *Mpayipheli Mutilated Me – Rehabilitated Criminal Tells All* and *The Battle of Kimberley: Biker Gangs Hand-to-hand*), but her cellphone rang in the bedroom and she ran, praying *Please let it be him.*

'Allison, I have a guy on the phone who says he rescued the boy last night. Can I give him your number?'

Thobela's plate was filled with sausage and eggs, fried tomato and bacon, beans in tomato sauce and fried mushrooms. Hot black bitter coffee stood steaming on the starched white tablecloth and he ate with a ravenous appetite.

He had overslept, waking only at twenty to seven, the pain from his wounds excruciating, wobbly on his feet, hands still trembling but controllable like an idling engine. He had bathed without haste, carefully inspected the bloody mass, covered it up again, taking only one pill this time, dressed and come down to eat.

In the upper corner of the dining room the television was fixed to a metal arm. CNN reported on share prices and on George Bush's latest faux pas with the Chinese and on the European Community that had turned down yet another corporate merger and then the newsreader murmured something about South Africa and he looked up to see the photo of his motorbike on the screen and froze. But he could not hear so he went forward till he was directly under the screen.

. . . The fugitive's common-law wife and her son have since

gone missing. Mpayipheli is yet to be apprehended. Other African news: Zimbabwean police arrested another foreign journalist under the country's new media legislation, this time The Guardian *correspondent Simon Eagleton . . .*

Gone missing?

What the fuck did they mean by 'gone missing'?

Captain Tiger Mazibuko ate in the Golf. He had pulled off the road two hundred metres south of the Zambezi bridge and he had the tasteless hamburger on his lap and was drinking out of the Fanta Orange can. He wished he could brush his teeth and close his eyes for an hour or two, but at least he was reasonably sure the Dog had not passed here yet.

He had stopped at every filling station – Mahalapye, Palapye, Francistown, Mosetse, Nata and Kasane – and no one had seen a motorbike. Every petrol attendant he had gently nudged awake or otherwise woken had shaken their heads. Last week, yes, there had been a few. Two, three English but they were going down to Johannesburg. Tonight? No, nothing.

So Mazibuko could wait, his furry mouth could wait for toothpaste, his red eyes for healing water, his sour body could wait for a hot, soapy shower.

When he had eaten, he unlocked the boot, lifted the cover of the spare wheel, loosened the butterfly nut, lifted the wheel and extracted the parts of his weapon.

It took two trips to transfer the parts of the R4 to the front seat without obviously looking as though he was holding a firearm in his hands. There were people walking and cars passing continuously between the border post a kilometre or so north and the town of Kasane behind him. He assembled the assault rifle, keeping his movements below the steering wheel away from curious eyes.

He would use it to stop the cunt. Because he had to come this way, he had to cross this bridge, even if he avoided the border post.

And once he had stopped him . . .

39

The battle raged in Mpayipheli as he stood in front of the hotel, booted and spurred, ready to ride. The urge to turn around, to go back was terrifically powerful. If they harmed Miriam and Pakamile . . . *Gone missing* – he had tried to convince himself that she could have taken her child and fled, if the media knew about them there would be continuous calls and visitors and he knew Miriam, he knew what her reaction would be. He had phoned from his hotel room, first her house, where the phone rang without ceasing. Eventually he gave up and thought desperately whom he could call, who would know at eight in the morning. Van Heerden, he could not remember the number, had to call International Enquiries, give the spelling and hold on for ages. When it came he had to write hurriedly on a piece of torn-off hotel stationery. He phoned but Van Heerden was not at home. In frustration he threw the phone down, took his stuff, paid the account and went and stood by the motorbike. Conflicting urges battled within him, he was on the point of going back, Lobatse, Mafeking, Kimberley, Cape Town. No, maybe Miriam had fled; it would take him two days, better finish one thing, what if . . .

Eventually he left and now he was on the road to Francistown, barely aware of the long straight road. Worry was one travelling companion, the other was the truth that he had uncovered through an African song under the Modder River bridge.

*　　*　　*

'I want to bring the boy to you,' said Vincent Radebe to Allison Healy over the phone.

'Where is he?'

'He's waiting in the car.'

'Why me?'

'I read your story in the paper.'

'But why do you want to bring him to me?'

'Because it is not safe. They will find me.'

'Who?'

'I'm in enough trouble already. I cannot tell you.'

'Do you know where his mother is?'

'Yes.'

'Where?'

Radebe answered so quietly that Allison could not hear what he said. 'What did you say?'

'His mother is dead.'

'Oh, God.'

'I haven't told him yet. I can't.'

'Oh, my God.'

'He has no family, I would have taken him to family, but he says there is no one. And he is not safe with me; I know they will find me. Please help.'

No, she wanted to say, no, she couldn't do this, what would she do, how would she manage?

'Please, Miss Healy.'

Say no, say no.

'The newspaper,' she said. 'Please take him to the office. I will meet you there.'

All the Directors were there – NIA, Secret Service, Presidential Intelligence, heads of Defence and Police – and the Minister, the attractive Tswana minister stood in the centre and her voice was sharp and cutting and her anger filled the room with shrill decibels because the President had called her to account, not phoned but called her in. Stood her on the red carpet and dressed her down. The President's anger was always controlled, they said, but it had not been so that morning. The Minister said the President's anger was terrible, because everything hung in the balance, Africa stood with a hand out for its African Renaissance plan and the USA and the EU and the Commonwealth and the World Bank had to decide. As if all the misunderstandings and undermining with the whole AIDS mess was not enough, now we are abducting women and children and chasing war veterans across the veld on a motorbike of all things, and everyone who has a nonsensical theory about what is on the hard disk is creeping out of the woodwork and the press are having a field day, even the *Sowetan*, that damned assistant editor's piece, he was with Mpayipheli at school, he talked to the man's mother. How does that make us look?

The Minister was the torch-bearer of the President's anger and she let it burn high, sparing no one, focusing on no one, she addressed them collectively and Janina Mentz sat there thinking it was all in vain because there were twenty agents in Lusaka and within the hour they would storm the Republican Hotel and make an end. And sometime today, Tiger Mazibuko would shoot the big bad biker from his celebrated fucking BMW and then it would no longer matter that the woman was dead and the child gone and it would be business as usual again in Africa. Tomorrow, the day after there would be other news, the Congo or Somalia or Zimbabwe, it was just another death in Africa; did the Minister think America cared? Did she think the European Union kept count?

The telephone rang on the Minister's desk and she glared at it, Janina was amazed that the phone neither shrank nor melted, the minister went to the door and yelled, 'Did I not tell you to hold all calls?' and a nervous male voice answered. The Minister said, 'What?' and an explanation followed. She slammed the door and the telephone continued to ring and the Minister went to her desk and in a tone lost between despair and madness said, 'The boy. They have the boy. The newspaper. And they want to know if the mother is dead.'

CIA

Eyes Only

For attention: Assistant Deputy Director (Middle East and Africa), CIA HQ, Langley, Virginia

Prepared by: Luke John Powell (Senior Agent in Charge – Southern Africa), Cape Town, South Africa

Subject: Operation Safeguard: The loss of four agents in the protection of South African Source Inkululeko

1. Background to Operation Safeguard

Inkululeko is the code name for a source the CIA acquired in 1996 in the South African government. The source was secured after tentative signals from subject during an embassy function were explored. Subject's motivation at the time was stated as disillusionment with SA government's continued support of rogue states, including Iraq, Iran, Cuba and Libya. This author recruited subject personally,

as it was the first acquisition inside the
ANC/Cosatu Alliance that was not previously
Nationalist Government-aligned. Subject's
motivation was suspicious at the time, but
they have since proven their value as a source.

Exact motivation still unknown.

It took the leader of the operation seven minutes and five thousand American dollars to buy over the manager of the Republican Hotel and to pinpoint the room where Johnny Kleintjes was being held.

He had a team of twenty agents, but he chose just five to accompany him to 227. The others were ordered to man the entrances, the fire escape and lifts, the rest watching windows and balconies from outside, or sitting in one of the vehicles with engines idling, ready for the unpredictable.

The leader had a key in his hand, but first he sprayed silicon in the keyhole, using a yellow can with a thin red tube on the cap. His colleagues stood ready at his back with firearms pointing at the roof. The leader fitted the key carefully and quietly turned it. The lubricated mechanism opened soundlessly. The leader gave the signal and opened the door in one smooth motion and the first two agents rolled into the room, but all they saw was the body of an old coloured man with gruesome wounds all over his body.

On Johnny Kleintjes's lap lay two disks and on his chest a word had been carved with a sharp instrument.

KAATHIEB.

'Leave him with me,' said the black male secretary of the Minister and Allison Healy bent down to Pakamile Nzululwazi who gripped her hand. She said, 'We have to go and talk in there, Pakamile. Will you stay with this nice man for a while?'

The child's body posture expressed anxiety and her heart contracted. He looked at the secretary and shook his head. 'I want to stay with you,' he said and she hugged him to her, not knowing what to do.

The secretary said something in Xhosa, in a quiet voice, and she said sharply, 'Talk so I can understand.'

'I only said that I will tell him a story.'

Pakamile shook his head. 'I want to stay with you,' he repeated. She had become his anchor when Radebe had handed him over to her, he was confused, afraid and alone. He had asked for his mother a hundred times and she didn't know how much more of this she could stand.

'He had better come along,' said her editor to the secretary.

They were a delegation of four, not counting the boy. The editor and herself and the managing director and the news editor, not one of whom had ever been here before. The door opened and the Minister stood there and looked at Pakamile and there was so much compassion in her eyes.

She held the door for them and Allison and the child walked ahead, the men behind them. Inside a white woman and a black man were already seated. The man stood up and Allison saw that he was small and there was the bulge of a hump at his neck.

Thobela Mpayipheli stopped at Mahalapye for petrol and crossed over to the small café in search of a newspaper, but the thin local paper had nothing and so he went on. The African heat reflected sharply from the black tar road and the sun was without mercy. He ought to have taken more pills as the pain of the wound was paralysing him. How badly was he damaged?

Huts, small farmers, children cavorting without a care beside the highway, two Boer goats sauntering to greener pastures across the road, oh Botswana, why couldn't his own country lie across the landscape as easily, so without fuss, why couldn't the faces of his people remain as carefree, as easily laughing, as at peace? What made the difference? Not the artificially drawn lines through the savannah that said this country ends here and that one begins there.

Less blood had flowed here, for sure; their history was less fraught. But why?

Perhaps they had fewer reasons to shed blood. Fewer gripping vistas, less succulent pastures, fewer hotheads, less valuable minerals. Perhaps that was the curse of South Africa, the land where God's hand had slipped, where He had spilled from the cup of plenty – green mountains and valleys, long waving grass as far as the eye could see, precious metals, priceless stones, minerals. And He looked over it and thought *I will leave it so, let it be a test, a temptation, I will put people with a great thirst here. I will let them come from other parts of Africa and from the white North and I will see what they do with this paradise.*

Or perhaps Botswana's salvation was merely that the gap between rich and poor was so much smaller. Less envy, less hatred. Less blood.

His thoughts were invaded again. *Gone missing*, the refrain ran in his mind, *gone missing*, it blended with the monotonous drone of the GS's engine, the wind that hissed past his helmet, the rhythms of his heart pushing blood painfully through his hip. He sweated, the heat increased with every kilometre and it came from inside him. He would have to be careful, keep his wits, he would need to rest, take in fluids, shake the dullness from his head. His body was very sick. He counted the kilometres, concentrated on calculations of average speed, so many kilometres per minute, so many hours left.

Mpayipheli eventually stopped at Francistown.

He dismounted with difficulty at the petrol station and put the bike on the stand. There was a slippery feel to the wound as if it was opening up.

The petrol jockey's voice was distant. 'Your friend was looking for you early today.'

'My friend?'

'He went through here early this morning in a Golf.' As if that explained everything.

'I don't have a friend with a Golf.'

'He asked if we'd seen you. A black man on a big orange BMW motorbike.'

'What did he look like?'

'He's a lion. Big and strong.'

'Which way did he go?'

'That way.' The man pointed his finger to the north.

40

Allison the onlooker.

She was always good at that, looking on from outside, being part of a group but in her head being apart. She had worried about it, thought it over for hours at a time, analysed it for years and the best conclusion she had come to was that that was how the gears and springs and levers of her brain were put together, a strange and accidental product, no one's fault. Yesterday afternoon she had known already that he was like that too. Two freaks who had sniffed each other out in a sea of normality, two islands that had improbably collided. But once again she found herself with that distance separating her from others, the itch of it was a gnawing voice of conscience that it was a form of fraud, to pretend that you were part of something when you did not fit. You knew that you did not belong here. The advantage was that it made her a good reporter because she saw what others were blind to.

There was an undercurrent to the negotiations.

The communication was stilted, in English, grown-ups speaking grown-up language so that the child would be protected and the painful truths delayed.

The conversation was not for the record, the Minister said. The nature of it was too sensitive and she wanted agreement on that from all the parties.

One after the other they nodded.

'Good,' the Minister said. 'We will proceed.' There was a child psychologist on the way. Also two women from the day-care centre, as the therapist said familiar figures would be an emotional cushion when the news was broken to Pakamile. Also a man and a woman from Child Welfare would be arriving soon. Senior people, very experienced.

Everything would be done, everything the State had access to, and the full machinery would be turned on, because what we had here was a tragedy.

Allison read the subtext. The Minister watched the other woman, not continuously, but as staccato punctuations in the discourse as if she were checking that she was on the right path.

This other woman. Not officially introduced. Sat there in her business suit like a finalist for Businesswoman of the Year, grey trousers, black shoes, white blouse, grey jacket, hands manicured but without colour on the nails, make-up soft and subtle, hair tied back, eyes without expression, a hint of beauty in a face with stern unapproachable lines, but it was the body language that spoke louder, of control, a figure of authority, driven, self-assured.

Who was she?

A tragedy, the Minister was saying, carefully choosing adult words and phrases, euphemisms and figurative speech to spare the child. Innocent people who were involved through chance. She wished she could tell the media everything, but that was impossible, and so she had to make an appeal. They would have to trust her that you couldn't make an omelette without breaking eggs and that made Allison shiver, we live in a dangerous world, a complicated world and to help this young democracy to survive was much more difficult than the press could ever imagine.

There was the operation, a sensitive, necessary, well-planned operation, fully within the stipulation of the National Strategic Intelligence Act of 1994 (Act 94-38, 2 December 1994 as amended) and in the national interest, she did not use the term lightly knowing how often that had been abused in the past, but they would have to take her word for it. National interest.

She wanted to make one thing clear: the operation as planned by the Intelligence Services did not require the involvement of innocent parties. To be frank, great efforts had been made to avoid that. But things had gone wrong. Things that nobody could have foreseen. The operation that had run so smoothly had been derailed. Civilians were drawn in by underhand methods, an innocent bystander was sucked into the vortex by an Evil Force, a third party, resulting in tragedy. If she could turn back the clock and change it she would, but they all knew that was beyond the realm of possibility. A tragedy, because a civilian had died possibly by her own hand, the motivation, the precise circumstances were not wholly clear, but for the Minister that was one civilian too many and she mourned, she could tell them she mourned for that life that had been blotted out. But (a) it had nothing to do with any weapons scandal, of that she was absolutely sure and (b) there would be a complete, official, and rigorous enquiry into the Great Loss and (c) if there was any responsibility or negligence on the part of any official they would proceed relentlessly with a disciplinary hearing according to Article 15 of the Intelligence Services Act of 1994 (as amended) and (d) the young dependant would receive the best care available, after ascertaining beyond doubt whether any relatives existed and if there were none the State would fulfil its responsibilities, that was her personal promise, she would stake her entire reputation, her career even on that.

The Minister looked at everyone and Allison knew that she was trying to gauge whether they accepted her explanation.

What would have happened if Pakamile had not been dropped off at the *Cape Times* offices? She knew the answer to that. It would have been hushed up. Wife and child?

What wife and child? We know nothing about that. But there was a righteousness in the Minister, a desperation to her honour.

'Madam Minister,' said the editor, the bespectacled, dignified coloured man whom Allison greatly respected. 'Let me just say that we are not the monsters politicians always make us out to be.'

'Of course,' said the Minister.

'We have sympathy for your role and your position.'

'Thank you.'

'But we do have one small problem. Having now gone on record that these two civilians have gone missing, and in the light of the Huge Tragedy that is, to some extent at least, public knowledge, especially if you are going to involve two ladies from the childcare centre, we cannot write absolutely nothing.'

Inkululeko is the Zulu word for 'freedom' and there's an interesting historical footnote to this code name: Apparently, there were constant rumours in the Seventies and Eighties that a mole of Zulu origin existed in the echelons of the ANC/SA Communist Party Alliance – a mole that allegedly leaked information to both the CIA and the SA Apartheid government. As you may know, there was no truth in this rumour. We had no reliable source within the movement at the time. Although several low-key attempts to acquire one were made, the CIA did not regard it as a high priority, due to the intelligence available through Eastern Bloc entities at the time, and the view that the ANC/SACP did not constitute a threat to the USA or NATO.

However, when a code name had to be assigned after

the 1996 recruitment, the subject suggested
'Inkululeko', and pointed out the potential
disinformation value thereof, as she had no Zulu
ties whatsoever, being of European extraction.

The importance of this source multiplied wonderfully
in 2000 when she was approached and recruited for
the position of Chief of Staff: Operations for a
newly created governmental agency, the PIA, or
Presidential Intelligence Agency.

We believe that the PIA was set up in an effort to
counter the never-ending infighting, the legacy
of jealousy and politics of the other three arms
of the SA Intelligence community, the National
Intelligence Agency, the Secret Service, and
Military Intelligence. All PIA staff were drawn
from non-intelligence sources, with the sole
exception of the Director, an ANC and Umkhonto
veteran.

2. Origin of Operation Safeguard

In March of this year, a known member of a Cape-based
militant Muslim splinter group with suspected
ties to al-Qaeda and Iranian strongman Ismail Khan
was arrested by the SAPS on charges of the illegal
possession of firearms

During interrogation, the suspect, one Ismail
Mohammed, indicated that he had information that
could be of use to the SA intelligence community,
and intended to use this information as plea-
bargain leverage.

As luck would have it, a member of the PIA conducted

`an interview with the suspect. The information`
`regarded the identity of Inkululeko.`

Allison Healy's heart was full when she walked out into the sun and the south-easter. Pakamile was inside being clucked over by two black ladies from the day-care centre who had taken him to their bosoms. The child psychologist, a short dapper white man in his thirties with put-on caring and an inflated idea of his own importance, was waiting for his five minutes of fame. The Welfare people with their forms and files knew their place in the hierarchy of bureaucracy and so sat outside on a wooden bench.

Allison walked with her male colleagues down the steps and over the street as Van Heerden once more invaded her thoughts. She said, 'You go ahead,' because she wanted to turn on her cellphone – maybe there was a message. She dawdled as the wind plucked at her dress, punching in her *pin* number and waiting for the phone to pick up a signal.

She saw the woman in the grey suit leave the building with the small hunchbacked man.

She looked down at the phone again. *You have two messages. Please dial* 121.

Thank goodness. Keyed in the numbers, waited, her brown-eyed gaze following the man and woman up Wale Street.

'Hello, Allison, it's Rassie. Good articles this morning – well done. Phone me, there are some interesting things. Bye.'

To save this message, press nine. To delete it, press seven. To return a call, press three. To save it—

She hurriedly pressed seven.

Next message:

'Allison, Nic here. I just want to . . . I want to see you, Allison. I don't want to wait till the weekend. Please. I . . .

miss you. Phone me, please. I know I'm a pain. I talk too much. I'm available tonight. Oh, good work in the paper today. Phone me.'

To save this message—

Irritated, she pressed seven.

End of new messages. To listen to your . . .

Why didn't Van Heerden call?

The white woman and the black man were disappearing up the street and on impulse she followed them. It was something to occupy her mind. She walked fast, the wind at her back. She pushed the cellphone into her handbag and tried to catch up, her eyes searching until she saw the woman turn in at a building. Someone called her name. It was the Somali at the cigarette stand. 'Hi, Allison, not buying today?'

'Not today,' she said.

'Don't work too hard.'

'I won't.'

She walked fast to the place where the woman had turned in, eventually looking up at the name above the big double doors.

Wale Street Chambers.

Just a simple call. *Hi, Allison, how's it going*? How much would that take? Was that too much to ask?

Some of the information from the interview with Ismail Mohammed was surprisingly accurate. He stated that:

(i) Inkululeko was a more recent source than generally believed.

ii) There was no evidence that Inkululeko had a direct Zulu connection, and that the contrary should be explored.

iii) Inkululeko was not a member of parliament,
nor the ANC leadership (which the constant
rumours had indicated over the years).

iv) Inkululeko was most definitely part of
the current SA Intelligence set-up, and held
a senior position within the Intelligence
community.

v) The Muslim structures (unspecified) were
getting closer to identifying Inkululeko,
and it was only a matter of time before full
identification would be made.

It is significant to note that Mohammed referred
to Inkululeko as 'he' and 'him' during several
interviews, indicating the level of true knowledge,
despite the accuracy of the above statements.

The major question, of course, is how the SA Muslim
structures acquired this knowledge.

According to Mohammed, they have been feeding
disinformation regarding international Muslim
activities, operations and networks into the SA
governmental and Intelligence systems through a
deliberate and well-planned process, with checks
and balances on the other side to try and determine
which chunks of disinformation got through to
the CIA. One such instance that we know of is the
warning this office passed on to Langley in July
of 2001 of a pending attack on the US embassy
in Lagos, Nigeria. The tip-off was received
from Inkululeko, and additional US Marines were
deployed in and around the Lagos embassy at the
time. As you know, the attack never materialized,

but the intensified security measures should
have been easy to monitor by Muslim extremists in
Nigeria.

Fortunately for us, Inkululeko received the
report on the Mohammed interview directly, and was
understandably disturbed by the contents. After
giving the matter some thought, she put a proposal
to this office.

41

On the road between Francistown and Nata a strange thing happened.

Mpayipheli seemed to withdraw into a cocoon, the pain melted away, the overpowering heat in him and around him dissipated, he seemed to leave the discomfort of his body behind and float above the motorbike, distanced from reality and though he could not understand how it had happened he was awed by the wonder of it.

He was still aware of Africa around him, the grass shoulder to shoulder in khaki-green and red-brown columns marching across the open plains beside the black ribbon of tarmac. Here and there acacias hunched in scrums and rucks and mauls. The sky was a dome of azure without limits and the birds accompanied him, hornbills would shoot across his field of vision, swallows diving and dodging, a bateleur tumbling out of the heavens, vultures riding the thermals far to the west in a spiral endlessly reaching upwards. For a moment he was with them, one of them, his wings spanned tight as wires registered every shuddering turbulence and then he was back down here and all the time the sun shone, hot and yellow and angry, as if it would sterilize the landscape, as if it could burn clean the evil sores of the continent with steadfast light and searing fire.

Why was the heat no longer in him, why did the shiver of intense cold run through his body like the frontal gusts of a storm?

It freed thoughts, like the chunks of a melting ice sheet,

mixed up, jumbled, floating in his heart, things he had forgotten, wanted to forget. And right at the back of his mind a monotonous refrain of whispers.

Gone missing.

His father in the pulpit with pearls of perspiration beading his forehead in the summer heat, one hand stretched out over the congregation, the other palm down, resting on the snow-white pages of the big Bible in front of him. A tall man in a sombre black toga, his voice thundering with disapproval and reproach. 'What ye sow shall ye reap. It is in the Book. God's Word. And what do we sow, my brothers and sisters, what do we sow? Envy. Jealousy. And hate. Violence. We sow, every day in the fields of our lives and then we cannot understand when it comes back to us, we say, *Lord, why?* As if it was He that poured the bitter cup for us, we are dismayed. So easily we forget. But it is what we have sown.'

In Amsterdam the air was as heavy and sombre as his mood. He wandered through the busy streets, with his thick grey coat wrapped around him, Christmas carols spilling out from the doors along with the heating and eddying over the pavement, children in bright colours with red cheeks laughing like bells. He cast a long shadow in all this light. The assassination in Munich lay a week behind him, but he could not shake off the shame of it, it clung to him, this was not war. A little shop on a corner opposite the canal, he spotted the ostrich eggs first, a heap in a grass basket, fake Bushman paintings on the oval, creamy white orbs, CURIOS FROM AFRICA, cried the display window. He saw wood carvings, the familiar mother-and-child figures and the tidy row of small carved ivory hippopotami and elephants, Africa in a nutshell for the Continental drawing room, sanitized and tamed, the Dark Wound bound up with a white capitalistic bandage, people's tongues and cultures packaged in a few wooden masks with horrible expressions and in tiny white ivory figurines.

Then he spotted the assegai and the oxhide shield, dusty and half forgotten, and he pushed open the door and went in. The bell tinkled. He picked up the weapon, turning it in his hands. The wooden shaft was smooth, the metal tip very long. He tested the shiny blade that was speckled with flecks of rust.

It was expensive, but he bought it and carried it off, an awkward parcel gift-wrapped in colourful ethnic paper.

He had sawn off the spear's shaft in the shower of his hotel room and the smell of the wood had crept up his nose and the sawdust powdered the white tiles like snow and he remembered. He and his Uncle Senzeni on the undulating Eastern Cape hill, the town down below in the hollow of the land as if God's hand was folded protectively over it. 'This is exactly where Nxele stood' – he laid out the history of his forefathers, broadly painted the battle of Grahamstown, this was where the soldiers had broken off the shafts of the long assegais, where the stabbing spear was born, not in Shaka's land, that was a European myth, just another way to rob the Xhosa. 'Even our history was plundered, Thobela.'

That was the day that Senzeni had said, 'You have the blood of Nqoma, Thobela, but you have the soul of Nxele. I see it in you. You must give it life.'

He had laid the sawn-off assegai at the feet of his Stasi masters and had said that from now on this would be how he would wage war, he would look his opponents in the eye, he would feel their breath on his face, they could take it or leave it.

'Very well,' they agreed with vague amusement behind the understanding frowns, but he did not care. He had made the scabbard himself so that the weapon could lie against his body, behind the great muscles and the spine, so that he could feel it where it lay ready for his hand.

Gone missing sang the male-voice choir in his head and a

road sign next to his path said Makgadikgadi and he found the rhythm in the name, the music of syllables.

'The sins of the fathers shall be visited upon the children even unto the third and fourth generation,' said his father in the pulpit.

Makgadikgadikgadikgadi, *gone missing, gone missing, gone missing.*

'We are our genes, we are the accidental sum of each our forefathers, we are the product of the fall of the dice and the double helix. We cannot change that,' said Van Heerden with joy, finding excitement in that.

In Chicago he was awed by the unbelievable architecture and the colour of the river, by the plenty and the streets that were impossibly clean. He walked self-consciously through the South Side and shook his head at Americans' definition of a slum and wondered how many people of the Transkei would give their lives to let their children grow up here. Once he called out a greeting in Xhosa instinctively as they were all black as he was, but their throats had ages since outgrown the feel of African sounds and he knew himself a stranger. He waited for the young Czech diplomat below the rumbling of the 'El', the elevated railway in the deep night shadows of the city. When the man came he stood in front of him and said his name and he saw only fear in the rodent eyes, a tiny scavenger and when his blade did the work there was no honour in the blood and Phalo and Rharhabe and all the other links in his genetic chain drooped their heads in shame.

Gone missing – one day his victims would return, one day the deeds of his past would visit him in the present, the dead would reach out long cold fingers and touch him, repayment for his cowardice, for the misuse of his heritage, for breaking the code of the warrior, because – with the exception of the last – they were all pale plump civil servants, not fighters at all.

He thought that the assegai blade, the direct confrontation, would make a difference. But to press the cold steel into the hearts of pen-pushers betrayed everything that he was, to hear the last breaths of grey, unworthy opponents in your ears was a portent, a self-made prophecy, a definition of your future – somewhere, one day, it will come back to you.

Gone missing.

Were the same words used for the people he had killed? Some were fathers, at least somebody's son, although they were men, although they were part of the Game, although they were every one a traitor to the Conflict. And where was that Conflict now, that useless chess game, where were the ghosts of the Cold War? All that remained were memories and consequences, his personal inheritance.

The emptiness in him had grown, merely the nuances had changed with each city where he found himself, with the nature of each hotel room. The moments of pleasure were on the journey to the next one when he could search for meaning anew at the next stop, search for something to fill the great hole, something to feed the monster growing inside.

The praise songs of his masters grew more hollow as time passed. At first it was salve to his soul. The appreciation that rolled so smoothly off their tongues had stroked the shame away. 'Look what your people say,' and they showed him letters from the ANC in London that praised his service in flowery language. *This is my role*, he told himself. *This is my contribution to the Freedom fight.* But he could not escape, not in the moments when he turned off the light and laid down his head and listened to the hiss of the hotel air-conditioning. Then he would hear his Uncle Senzeni's voice and he longed to be one of Nxele's warriors who stood shoulder to shoulder, who broke the spear with a crack over his knee.

Nata, said the road sign but he scarcely saw it. He and the machine were a tiny shadow on the plateau, they were one, grown together on a journey, every kilometre closer to completion, to fulfilment, engine and wind combining in a deep thrumming, a rhythmic swell like the breaking of waves. 'Your friend was looking for you early today,' the jockey in Francistown had said. He knew, he knew it was Mazibuko, the voice of hate. He had not only heard the hate, he had recognized it, felt the resonance and knew that here was another traveller, this was himself ten or fifteen years ago, empty and searching and hating and frustrated, before the insight had come, before the calm of Miriam and Pakamile.

He was in the hospital, he and Van Heerden, when it happened. When he saw himself for the first time. Afterwards, not a day would pass that he did not think of it, that he did not try to unpick the knot of destiny.

He was shuffling down the hospital passage late one evening, his body still broken from the thing that he and Van Heerden had been in. He stood in a doorway to catch his breath, that was all. No deliberate purpose, just a moment of rest and he glanced into the four-bed ward and there beside the bed of a young white boy a doctor was standing.

A black doctor. A Xhosa as tall as he was. Round about his fortieth year, a hint of grey at the temples.

'What are you going to become one day, Thobela?' His father, the same man who, Sunday after Sunday, hurled God's threats so terrifyingly from the pulpit with a condemning finger and a voice of reproach, was soft and gentle now to chase away the fear of an eight-year-old for the dark.

'A doctor,' he had said.

'Why, Thobela?'

'Because I want to make people better.'

'That is good, Thobela.' That year he had had the fever and the white doctor had driven through from Alice and come into the room with strange smells around him and compassion in his eyes. He had laid cool hairy hands on the little black body, pressed the stethoscope here and there, had shaken out the thermometer. 'You are a very sick boy, Thobela,' speaking Xhosa to him, 'but we will make you better.' The miracle had happened, that night he broke through the white-hot wall of fever into the cool clear pool on the other side where his world was still familiar and normal and that was when he knew what he wanted to be, a healer, a maker of miracles.

Where he stood watching the white boy and the black doctor from the doorway, he relived the scene, heard his own words to his father and felt his knees weaken at the years that had been lost in the quicksand. He saw his life from another angle; saw the possibilities of other choices. He sagged slowly down against the wall, the weight too much to bear, all the brokenness, all the hatred, the violence and death and the consuming deep craving to be free of it swallowed him up. Oh Lord, to be born again without it – he sank to his knees and stayed like that, head on his chest and deep dry sobs tearing through his chest opening up more memories until everything lay open before him, every thing.

He had felt the black doctor's hand on his shoulder and later was conscious that the man was holding him, that he was leaning on the shoulder of the white coat and slowly he calmed down. The man helped him up, supporting him, laid him down on his bed and pulled the sheets up to his chin, *you are a very sick boy but we will make you better.*

He had slept and woken and he had fought again, bare-fisted, honestly and honourably against the self-justification and rationalization. Out of the bloodied bodies of the dead rose a desire – he would be a farmer, a nurturer. He could not undo what had happened, he could not blot out who he had been but he could determine where and how he would go from here. It would not be easy, step by step, a lifetime task and that night he had eaten a full plate of food and thought through the night. The next morning before six he went to Van Heerden's room and woke him and said he was finished and Van Heerden had looked at him with great wisdom and so he had asked with astonishment at the way he was underestimated: 'You don't believe I can change?'

Van Heerden had known. Known what he had discovered last night under a bridge in the Free State.

He was Umzingeli.

Twenty kilometres south of Mpadamatenga, through the fever and hallucinations, he became aware of movement to the left of him. Between the trees and grass he saw three giraffes moving like wraiths against the sun, cantering stately as if to escort him on his journey, heads dipping to the rhythm in his head. And then he was floating alongside them, one of them and he felt a freedom, an exuberance and then he was rising higher and looking down on the three magnificent animals thundering on, he surged up higher and turned south and caught the wind in his wings and it sang. It swept him along and all was small and unimportant down there, a scrambling after nothing, he flew over borders, rolling koppies and bright rivers and deep valleys that cut the continent and far off he saw the ocean and the song of the wind became the crash of the breakers where he stood looking out from the rocky point. Sets of seven, always sets of seven, he folded his wings and waited for the oasis of calm between the thunder, the moment of perfect silence that waited for him.

42

By a quarter past two sleep began to overcome Tiger Mazibuko so he put the machine pistol under the rubber mat at his feet and climbed out of the car for the umpteenth time. Where was the fucker? Why wasn't he here yet?

He stretched and yawned and walked around the car, once, twice, three times and sat on the edge of the bonnet, wiping the sweat from his face with a sleeve, folded his arms and stared down the road. He did the calculations again. Maybe Mpayipheli had stopped for lunch or to have his wounds tended by a quack in Francistown. He looked again at his wristwatch – any minute now things should start happening. He wondered if the Dog was riding with his headlight on as bikers did. Probably not.

Sweat ran down his back.

He did not pay the Land Rover Discovery much heed as other luxury four-wheel-drive vehicles had passed. This was tourist country, Chobe and Okavango to the west, Makgadikgadi south, Hwange and Vic Falls to the east. The Germans and Americans and the Boers came to do their Livingstone thing here with air-conditioned four-by-fours and khaki outfits and safari hats and they thought the suspect drinking water and a few malaria mosquitoes were a hang of an adventure and went home to show their videos, look, we saw the big five, look how clever, look how brave.

It approached from the direction of Kazangula and he tried to stare past it to keep watch on the road. Only when it pulled off the road opposite him did he look, half angry because he did not want to be distracted. Two whites in the front of the green vehicle, the thick arm of the passenger hanging over the wound-down window. They looked at him.

'Fuck off,' he called across the road.

The small eyes of the passenger were focused on him, the face expressionless on top of the thick neck. He could not see the driver.

'What the fuck are you staring at?' he called again, but they did not answer.

Jissis, he thought, *what the fuck?* And he raised himself from the Golf's bonnet and looked left and right before he began to cross. He would quickly find out what was their story was, but then the vehicle began to move, the big fellow's stare still fixed on Mazibuko and they pulled away and he stood in the middle of the road watching them drive away. *What the fuck?*

3. The Nature of Operation Safeguard

The plan devised by Inkululeko was essentially a disinformation initiative, primarily aimed at directing suspicion away from her.

Although the transcript of the Mohammed interview was in her sole possession, Inkululeko knew suppression thereof would be potentially dangerous and incriminating, due to the fact that both the police (to a lesser extent) and interviewer had some degree of knowledge, which was bound to surface at some time or other.

She approached this office with suggestions that were developed into Safeguard in conjunction with us.

The core of the operation plan was to 'hunt down' Inkululeko, to 'flush him out'.

Our source recruited the services of a retired intelligence officer from the former military arm of the ANC, Umkhonto we Sizwe (MK), one Jonathan ('Johnny') Kleintjes. This was a particularly brilliant move, for the following reasons:

(i) Kleintjes was in charge of MK/ANC Intelligence computer systems during the so-called Struggle in the period before 1992.

(ii) He was the leader of the project to integrate those systems of the former Apartheid government's intelligence agencies almost a decade ago.

(iii) He was suspected of having secured sensitive and valuable information during the process. Like so many of these intelligence rumours, there were different versions. The most persistent was that Kleintjes had found evidence within the mass of electronic information that both the ANC/SACP alliance and the Apartheid government had been up to some dirty tricks in the Eighties. In addition, a very surprising list of double agents and traitors on both sides, some of them very prominent people, was contained in the data.

(iv) Kleintjes had apparently deleted these files, but only after making back-ups and securing them somewhere for possible future use and reference.

Inkululeko's aim was to use Kleintjes as a credible
operative (both from a South African and US
perspective) for the disinformation project to
protect her cover, and win his trust at the same
time, the latter pertinent to acquiring the missing
data at a later stage.

The Operation Plan was fairly simple: Under
her orders, Kleintjes would prepare a hard
disk with fabricated intelligence about the
'true identity of Inkululeko'. He would then
approach the US embassy directly and ask to
speak to someone from the CIA about 'valuable
information'.

We, in turn, would act predictably and tell
him never to come to the embassy again, but
leave his contact details, as we would be in
touch.

A meeting would be set up in Lusaka, Zambia, away
from prying eyes, during which the data could be
examined by the CIA, and if credible, be bought for
the price of $50,000 (about R575,000).

Obviously, our side of the bargain was to accept the
data as the real thing, thereby casting suspicion
on the persons mentioned therein, and drawing away
any possible attention to her as a candidate for the
identity of Inkululeko.

She would then write a full report on the operation
and present it to the Minister of Intelligence for
further action, bypassing her immediate superior,
a man of Zulu extraction whose name would be amongst

the strongest 'candidates' for the identity of Inkululeko.

Again, this was a shrewd move, as she was next in line for his position, and the Minister would have little choice but to suspend him from duties until the matter had been resolved. Which would have placed her in the top echelon: The National Intelligence Coordinating Committee, chaired by an Intelligence Coordinator, which brings together the heads of the different services and reports to the Cabinet or President.

Unfortunately, Operation Safeguard did not go as planned.

The Ops Room was almost empty.

Janina Mentz sat at the big table and watched one of Rajkumar's assistants disconnect the last computer and carry it off piece by piece. The television monitors were off, the radio and telephone equipment's red and white lights were out, the soul of the place was dead.

A fax lay in front of her, but she had not yet read it.

She thought back over the past two days, trying hard to see something positive in the whole mess, trying to identify the moment when it all went wrong.

KAATHIEB.

The team leader in Lusaka had sent digital photos via e-mail. The letters in Johnny Kleintjes's chest had been carved in deep red cuts as if by a raging devil.

LIAR.

'It's Arabic,' said Rajkumar once he had completed his search.

How?

How had the Muslims known about Kleintjes?

There were possibilities that she dared not even think of.

Had Johnny dropped a word to someone, somewhere? Deliberately? The Director had his suspicions that Kleintjes had Islamic connections. But why then would they kill him? It made no sense.

Had she been sold out by the Americans?

No.

Mpayipheli?

Had he made a call for help somewhere along the road? Did he have links with the extremists? Had he, like some of his KGB masters since the fall of the USSR, gone in search of Middle Eastern pastures? Had he built up contacts on the Cape Flats while he worked for Orlando Arendse?

But Kleintjes was supposed to be his friend. That didn't fit.

The treachery lay elsewhere.

The treachery lay here. In their midst.

Would it not be ironic to have two traitors in one intelligence unit? But that was the scenario that fitted best.

Luke Powell had said that he had lost his two agents yesterday, time of death not yet determined, but if the Muslims had left yesterday evening as the news broke here in the Ops Room, then the timetable fitted well.

Mentz dropped her head into her hands, massaging her temples with her fingertips.

Who?

Vincent? The reluctant Radebe?

Quinn, the coloured man with Cape Flats roots? Rajkumar? Or one of their assistants? The variable grew too many and she sighed and sank back into her chair.

The plan was so good. The operation was so clever, so demoniacally brilliant, her creation. So many flies swatted with one stroke of genius. She was so self-satisfied that she found secret pleasure in it, but it had been born of need and panic.

Lord, how that transcript of Ismail Mohammed had shaken her.

All she could think of were her children.

Williams had called her from the police cells and said he had a bomb; he had better meet her at the office. He had played the tape for her and she had had to keep cool because he was sitting opposite her and a part of her wondered if the shock was visible in her expression. Could he see the paleness that came over her face? The other part was with her children. How was she going to explain to her girls that their mother was a traitor? How would she ever make them understand? How do you explain to someone that there is no Big Reason, there was just a single moment, a dramatic happening that night in the American Embassy, but it had to be held in the light of a lifetime of disappointment, of disillusion, of fruitless struggle and frustration, decades of pointless aspiration that had prepared her for that moment.

Would anyone believe that she had not planned it? It had just happened like an impulse buy at the supermarket. She and Luke Powell had been in conversation among forty or fifty people. He had asked her opinion on weighty matters, politics and economics, he had fucking respected her, deferred to her as if she were more than an invisible gear in the great engine room of government.

In that moment all the flotsam and jetsam of her life pressed on her with unbearable weight and she had thrown it off.

Who would ever understand?

When Williams turned off the tape recorder she did not trust her voice but it came out right, soft and easy just as she wished.

'You had better transcribe that personally,' she said to him. Once he had left she remained sitting in her chair, crushed by the weight, her brain darting this way and that like a cornered rat.

Strange how quick the mind was when there was danger, how creative you could be when your existence was threatened. How to draw attention away from yourself? The cells in her brain had dreamed up the Johnny Kleintjes plan out of what had long lain stored away – the rumours that Kleintjes possessed forbidden data. That had not been a priority with her, just something to store in the files in the back of her head. When the need was greatest it had come springing out into her consciousness, a germinating seed that would grow diabolically.

So brilliant. Those had been Luke Powell's words. *You are brilliant.*

He had appreciated her from the beginning. Sincerely. With each piece of intelligence that she sent to him through the secret channels, the message came back. *You are priceless. You are wonderful. You are brilliant.*

And here she sat. Eight months later. Priceless and wonderful and brilliant, with a traitor's identity that was probably secured, but heads would roll and chances were good that one of them would be hers.

And that could not happen.

There must be a scapegoat; and there was one.

Ready to sacrifice.

She was not finished. She was not nearly finished.

She smoothed her hair down and pulled the fax nearer.

This was the story that the Minister was talking about. The one that had appeared in the *Sowetan*. She did not want to read it. She wanted to move on, in her mind this chapter was closed.

Mpayipheli – the prince from the past, said the title.

By Matthew Mtimkulu, assistant editor.

Isn't it strange how much power two words can have? Just two random words, seventeen simple letters, and when I heard them over the radio in my car, it opened the floodgates of the past, and the memories came rushing back like rippling white water.

Thobela Mpayipheli.

I did not think about the meaning of the words – that came later, as I sat down to write this piece: Thobela means 'mannered', or 'respectful'. Mpayipheli is Xhosa for 'one who does not stop fighting', a warrior, if you will.

My people like to give our children names with a positive meaning, a sort of head start to life, a potential self-fulfilling prophecy. (Our white fellow citizens attempt the same sort of thing – only opting not for meaning, but for sophistication, the exotic or cool to do the job. And my coloured brothers seem to choose names that sound as much uncoloured as possible.)

What really matters, I suppose, is the meaning the person gives to the name in the course of his life.

So, what I remembered as I negotiated early-morning rush hour was the man. Or the boy, as I knew him, for Thobela and I are children of the Ciskei, we briefly shared one of the most beautiful places on earth: the Kat River valley, described by historian Noël Mostert in his heartbreaking book Frontiers *as 'a narrow, beautiful stream that descended from the mountainous heights of the Great Escarpment and flowed through a broad, fertile valley towards the Fish river . . .'*

We were teenagers and it was the blackest decade of the century, the tumultuous Seventies, Soweto was burning and the heat of the flames could be felt in our little hidden hamlet, our forgotten valley. There was something in the air in the spring of 1976, an anticipation of change, of things to come.

Thobela Mpayipheli, like me, was fourteen. A natural athlete, the son of the Muruti of the Dutch Reformed Mission Church, and it was well known that his father was a descendant of Phalo along the Maqoma lineage. Xhosa royalty, if you will.

And there was something princely about him, perhaps in his bearing, most definitely in the fact that he was a bit of a loner, a brooding, handsome outsider of a boy.

One day in late September, I was witness to a rare event. I saw Mpayipheli beat Mtetwa, a huge, mean, scowling kid two years his senior. *It was a long time coming between the two of them, and when it happened, it was a thing of beauty. On a sliver of river sand in a bend of the Kat, Thobela was a matador, calm and cool and elegant and quick. He took some shuddering punches, because Mtetwa was no slouch, but Thobela absorbed it, and kept on coming. The thing that fascinated me most was not his awesome deftness, his speed or agility, but his detachment. As if he was measuring himself. As if he had to know if he was ready, confirmation of some inner belief.*

Just three years later, he was gone, and the whispers up and down the valley said he had joined the Struggle, he had left for the front, he was to be a soldier, a carrier of the Spear of the Nation.

And here his name was on the radio, a man on a motorcycle, a fugitive, a common labourer, and I wondered what had happened in the past twenty years. What had gone wrong? The prince should have been a king – of industry, or the military, perhaps a Member of Parliament, although, for all his presence, he lacked the gift of the gab, the oily slickness of a politician.

So I called his mother. It took some time to track them down, a retired couple in a town called Alice.

She didn't know. She had not seen her son in more than two decades. His journey was as much a mystery to her as it was to me. She cried, of course. For all that was lost – the expectations, the possibilities, the potential. The longing, the void in a mother's heart.

But she also cried for our country and our history that so cruelly conspired to reduce the prince to a pauper.

43

The late afternoon brought a turning point.

With every hour Tiger Mazibuko's frustration and impatience grew. He no longer wanted to wait here, he wanted to know where the Dog was, how far off, how long to wait. His eyes were tired from staring down the road, his body stiff from sitting and standing and leaning against the car. His head was dulled by continually running through his calculations, from speculating and guesswork.

But above all it was the anger that exhausted him, the stoking of the raging flames consumed his energy.

Eventually, when the shadows began to lengthen, Captain Tiger Mazibuko leapt from the Golf and picked up a rock and hurled it at the thorn trees where the finches were chittering irritably and he roared something unintelligible and turned and kicked the wheel of the car, threw another stone at the tree, another and another and another, until he was out of breath. He blew down with a hiss of air through his teeth and calm returned.

Mpayipheli was not coming.

He had taken another road. Or the wounds, perhaps . . . No, Mazibuko was not going to start speculating again, it was irrelevant, his plan had failed and he accepted it. Sometimes you took a chance and you won and sometimes you lost. He made a decision, he would wait till sunset, relax, watch the day fade to twilight and the twilight to dark and then he was done.

When he climbed back in the car they came for him.

Three police vehicles full of officials in uniform. He saw the three vehicles approaching, but only registered when they stopped. He only realized what was going on when they poured out of the doors. He sat tight, hands on the steering wheel until one of them shouted at him to get out with his hands behind his head.

He did that slowly and methodically, to prevent misunderstandings.

What the hell?

He stood by the Golf and a pair of them ducked into the car and one emerged triumphant with the Heckler & Koch. Another searched him with busy hands, pulled his hands behind his back and clamped the handcuffs around his wrists.

Sold out. He knew it. But how? And by whom?

4. The Execution of Operation Safeguard.

After Mr Johnny Kleintjes had visited the US Embassy, we set up contact with him, and agreed to meet him in Lusaka.

Inkululeko kept her side of the bargain by duly recording the embassy visit, as well as starting a surveillance program of Kleintjes.

The Operation went perfectly according to plan.

Due to the controlled nature of Safeguard, this office did not deem it necessary to allocate more than two people for the Zambia leg. And agents Len Fortenso and Peter Blum from the Nairobi office were drafted for the Lusaka 'sale' of the data. I acted as supervisor from Cape Town, and take full responsibility for subsequent events.

```
Fortenso and Blum confirmed arrival in Lusaka after
a chartered flight from Nairobi. That was the last
contact we had with them. Their bodies were found
on the outskirts of Lusaka two days later. The
cause of death was gunshot wounds to the back of
the head.
```

Allison Healy wrote the lead article with great difficulty. Her emotions were divided between anger at Van Heerden and sadness for the lot of Pakamile.

She had cried when she'd left him behind, she had hugged him tight and the ironic part that broke her heart was the way the child had comforted her.

'Don't be sad. Thobela is coming back tomorrow.'

For the sake of the child she had rung every contact and informant who might possibly know something.

'It depends who you believe,' Rassie had said from Laingsburg. 'One rumour says he's wounded. The other says they have shot him dead in Botswana. But I don't believe either of them.'

'Shot dead, you say?'

'It's a lie, Allison. If the Botswana police had shot him it would have been headline news.'

'And what about the wounding story?'

'Also a load of rubbish. They say a chopper pilot shot him, but not with the chopper's armament, you know what I mean. With this kind of thing rumours run wild. All I know is that the RU have gone home and the whole operation in the Northern Cape has been called off.'

'That is not good news.'

'How do you mean?'

'It could mean that it's all over. That he is dead.'

'Or that he is over the border.'

'That's true. Thanks, Rassie. Phone me if you hear something.'

And that was the sum total of information. The other sources knew or said even less so at last she began with the story, building it paragraph by paragraph, without enthusiasm and with Van Heerden's betrayal hanging over her like a shadow.

A member of the Presidential Intelligence Unit's operational staff is under house arrest and awaiting an internal disciplinary hearing after the tragic accidental death of Mrs Miriam Nzululwazi last night.

The rest was more of a review than anything else because they had laid down guidelines for the report, she and the news editor and the editor. The final agreement with the Minister was that they would break this news exclusively, but sympathetically, sensitive to the nuances of national interest and covert operations. When Allison was finished she went outside to smoke in the St George's Mall and watched the rest of the world on their way home. Streams of people so determined, so serious, so stern, going home just to journey back tomorrow morning, a never-ending cycle to keep body and soul together until the Reaper came. This useless, meaningless life went on with grey efficiency, pitiless, tomorrow there would be other news, the day after another scandal, another matter dished up in big black sans serif lettering to the people.

Damn Van Heerden. Damn him for being like all other men, damn him for a shoplifter, a swindler.

Damn Thobela Mpayipheli, for deserting a woman and child for a pointless chase across this bloody country. All it would leave was yellowing front pages in newspaper archives. Didn't he know that next month, next year no one would even remember except Pakamile Nzululwazi living somewhere in a bloody orphanage, staring out the window every evening hoping, until that too like other hopes faded irrevocably and left nothing but the vicious cycle of waking up and going to sleep.

She crushed the cigarette under her heel.

Fuck them all.

And she knew how to do it.

5. Muslim extremist involvement

Mr Johnny Kleintjes was found executed in a room in the Republican Hotel in Lusaka, the word 'KAATHIEB' slashed with a sharp pointed object into his chest – Arabic for 'liar'.

Muslim extremist involvement is assumed, but neither Inkululeko nor this office can explain how local or foreign groups gained knowledge of the operation. One possibility is a leak within the Presidential Intelligence Unit itself.

The suspected Muslim group, I believe, was not after the fabricated Kleintjes data but the information he had allegedly secreted during the 1994 integration process.

The reasons are twofold:

(i) After eliminating Fortenso and Blum, the unknown operatives blackmailed Kleintjes's daughter in Cape Town to bring a specific hard disk to Lusaka. (She asked one Thobela Mpayipheli, a former friend and colleague of Kleintjes Senior, to do this on her behalf, as she is physically challenged – see below.)

(ii) Furthermore, the PIU member arrested
by Botswana police was waiting in ambush to
intercept Mpayipheli and the hard disk, close to
the Zambian border. We believe they were tipped
off to stop the disk from falling into the hands
of the PIU.

If our theory is correct, it naturally follows
that the original data might shed some light on the
Muslim mole within the South African intelligence
community.

At this time, the hard disk is still missing.

6. The matter of Umzingeli

In 1984, a top CIA field agent and a decorated, much
valued veteran, Marion Dorffling, was eliminated
in Paris. The modus operandus of the assassin was
similar to at least eleven (11) similar executions
of US assets and operatives.

The CIA had enough intelligence from Russian and
Eastern European sources to conclude, or at least
strongly suspect, that one Thobela Mpayipheli, code
name 'Umzingeli' (a Xhosa word for 'Hunter') was
responsible for the murder. According to available
information, Mpayipheli was an MK soldier on loan
from the ANC/SACP alliance to the KGB and Stasi as a
wet-work specialist.

Coincidentally, I was a rookie member of the
CIA team in Paris at the time.

When Mpayipheli's involvement in Operation
Safeguard became public knowledge, I filed a
request to the field office in Berlin for possible

documentation from former Stasi files to confirm
the 1984 suspicions. Our colleagues in Germany
obliged within hours (for which I can only commend
them).

The Stasi records confirmed that Mpayipheli/
Umzingeli was Marion Dorffling's assassin.

I notified Langley, and the response from deputy
director's level was that the Firm was still
very much interested in leveling the score. Two
specialized field agents from the London office
were sent to deal with the matter.

Allison Healy's fingers danced lightly but intently across
the keyboard. Her passion appeared in the words on the
screen.

*Fugitive motorcyclist Thobela Mpayipheli was a ruthless
assassin for the KGB during the Cold War, responsible for the
deaths of at least fifteen people.*

*According to his long-time friend and former policeman, Dr
Zatopek van Heerden, Mpayipheli was recruited by the Sovi-
ets during MK training in what was then the USSR. Van
Heerden is currently a staff member of the UCT Department
of Psychology.*

She scanned it quickly before continuing, suppressing with
difficulty the impulse to write *his long-time friend, the world-
class asshole Dr Zatopek van Heerden.*

*In an exclusive and frank interview, Dr Van Heerden disclosed
that . . .*

The phone rang and she grabbed it up angrily and said,
'Allison Healy' and Van Heerden asked, 'Have you got a
passport?' and she said, 'What?'

'Have you got a passport?'

'You asshole,' she said.

'What?'

'You are a total, complete, utter asshole,' she said before realizing that her voice was so loud her colleagues could hear. She took the cellphone and walked towards the bathrooms, speaking in a whisper now. 'You think you can fuck me and run off like a . . . like a . . .'

'Are you cross because I didn't leave a message?'

'You could have phoned, you bastard. What would it have taken to make one call? What would it have cost to say thank you and goodbye, it was good, but it's over. You men are all the same, too fucking cowardly . . .'

'Allison . . .'

'But not last night, oh no, last night you couldn't talk enough, all the things that you said and today not a bloody word. Couldn't you lift a finger to press a telephone button?'

'Allison, are you interested in—'

'I am interested in nothing to do with you.'

'Would you like to meet Thobela Mpayipheli?'

The words were queuing up behind her tongue but she swallowed them down. He had taken the wind from her sails.

'Thobela?'

'If you have a passport, you can come along.'

'Where to?'

'Botswana. We are leaving in . . . er . . . seventy minutes.'

'We?'

'Do you want to come or not?'

44

Van Heerden had to give Allison the last directions over the cellphone as it was an obscure route at the Cape Town International Airport behind hangars and office buildings and between small single-propeller airplanes that looked like children's toys left around in loose rows. Eventually she found the Beechcraft King Air ambulance with its Pratt & Whitney engines already running.

Van Heerden was standing in the door of the plane waving to her and she grabbed the overnight bag from the back seat, locked the car and ran.

He stood aside so that she could climb the steps and then he pulled the door shut behind her, signalling to the pilot. The Beechcraft began to move.

He took her bag and showed her where to sit – on one of the three seats at the back. After making sure that her seat belt was fastened he sat down beside her with a sigh. He leaned over and kissed her full on the lips before she could pull away and then he grinned at her like a naughty schoolboy.

'I should—' she began seriously but he stopped her with a raised hand.

'May I explain first?' His voice was loud to make himself heard over the engine noise.

'It's not about us. It's about Miriam Nzululwazi.'

'Miriam,' he said with grim foreboding.

'She's dead, Zatopek. Last night.'

'How?'

'All they will say is that it was an accident. She fell. Five storeys down.'

'Good Lord,' he said and let his head drop back against the cushion of the seat. He sat like that for a long time, staring ahead, and Allison wondered what his thoughts were. Then, just before the Beechcraft sped down the runway, he said something she couldn't hear and shook his head.

'You have a terrible temper,' Van Heerden said as the roar of the engines quietened at cruising altitude and he loosened his safety belt. 'Do you want some coffee?'

'And you are a bastard,' Allison said without conviction.

'I was in conference all day.'

'Without tea or lunch breaks?'

'I meant to phone you in the afternoon, when it was more quiet.'

'And so?'

'Then I had a call from a Doctor Pillay of Kasane who said he had found my telephone number in the pocket of a badly injured black man who had fallen off his motorbike in northern Botswana.'

'Oh.'

'Coffee?'

She nodded, watching him as he made the same offer to the doctor and pilot in the cockpit. She thought how close she had come to putting the article into the system. She had been at the door of the editorial office when she turned and ran back to delete it. She had a temper. That was true.

'What is his condition?' Allison asked Van Heerden when he came back.

'Serious, but stable. The doctor said he has lost a lot of blood. They gave him transfusions but he is going to need more and blood is in short supply up there.'

'What happened to him?'

'Nobody knows. He has two bullet wounds in the hip and his left shoulder was badly bruised in the fall. Some locals found him beside the road near the Mpandamatenga turn-off. By the grace of God no one phoned the authorities, they just loaded him on a bakkie and took him to Kasane.'

She absorbed the news and another question arose. 'Why are you doing this?'

'He is my friend.' Before she could respond, he added, 'My only friend, to be honest,' and she wondered about him, who he was and what made him this way.

'And this?' She indicated the medical equipment. 'What is all this going to cost?'

'I don't know. Ten or twenty thousand.'

'Who is going to pay?'

He shrugged. 'I will. Or Thobela.'

'Just like that?'

He grinned but without humour.

'What?'

'Perception and reality,' he said. 'I find it very interesting.'

'Oh?'

'Your perception is that he is black – and a labourer, from Guguletu. Therefore he must be poor. That is the logical view, a reasonable conclusion. But things are not always what we expect.'

'So he has money? Is that from the drugs or the assassinations?'

'A valid question. But the answer is from neither of those.'

He saw her shake her head doubtfully and he said, 'I had better tell you the whole story. About me and Orlando and Thobela and more American dollars than most people see in a lifetime. It was two years ago. I was moonlighting as a private investigator, probing a murder case the cops couldn't crack. In a nutshell, it came out that the victim was involved in a clandestine army operation, weapons transactions for Unita in Angola, diamonds and dollars . . .'

Van Heerden finished the story by the time they landed in Johannesburg to refuel. When they took off again Allison pushed up the armrest between them and leaned against him.

'Am I still a bastard?' he asked.

'Yes. But you are my bastard.' And she pressed her face against his neck and inhaled his smell with her eyes shut.

This afternoon she had thought she had lost him.

Before they flew over the N1 somewhere east of Warmbad she was asleep.

Allison stayed in the plane, looking out the oval window of the Beechcraft. The air coming in the open door was hot and rich in exotic scents. Outside the night was lit up by car lights, the moving people casting long deep shadows, and then four men appeared from behind a vehicle with a stretcher between them and she wondered what he looked like, this assassin, drug soldier, the man for whom Miriam Nzululwazi had wept in her arms, the man who had dodged the entire country's law enforcers for two thousand kilometres to do a friend a favour. What did he look like? Were there marks, recognisable features on his face that would reveal his character?

They struggled up the steps with the weighty burden. Allison went and sat at the back, out of the way, her eyes searching but Mpayipheli was hidden by the bearers, Van Heerden, the doctor who had flown with them, Dr Pillay and one other. They shifted him carefully onto the bed in the aircraft. The white doctor connected a tube to the thick black arm, the Indian said something softly into the patient's ear, pressing the big hand that lay still and then they went out and someone pulled the door up and the pilot started the engines.

She stood up to see his face. The gaze caught hers, like a searchlight finding a buck, black-brown and frighteningly intense, so that she could see nothing else and she felt a thrill of fear and enormous relief. Fear for what he could do and relief that he would not do it to her.

The black man slept and Van Heerden sat with Allison again and she asked: 'Have you told him?'

'It was the first thing he wanted to know when he saw me.'

'You told him?'

He nodded.

She looked at the still figure, the dark brown skin of his chest and arms against the white bedding, the undulations of caged power.

William Blake, she thought.

> *What immortal hand or eye*
> *Could frame thy fearful symmetry?*

'What did he say?' she asked.

'He hasn't said a word since.'

Now she understood the intensity of those eyes.

> *In what distant deeps or skies*
> *Burnt the fire of thine eyes?*

'Do you think he will . . .'

Allison looked at Van Heerden and for the first time saw the worry.

'How else?' he said in frustration.

On what wing dare he aspire?
What the hand, dare seize the fire?

'But you can help him. There must be a legal—'

'It is not he who will need help.'

That was when she grasped what Van Heerden was afraid of and she looked at Mpayipheli and shivered.

When the stars threw down their spears
And water'd heaven with their tears
Did he smile his work to see?
Did he who made the lamb make thee?

On the last leg to Cape Town Allison woke with a heavy body and a stiff neck and she saw Van Heerden sitting next to Mpayipheli, his white hand holding the Xhosa's and she heard the deep bass voice, soft, the words were nearly inaudible to her above the noise of the engines and she closed her eyes again and listened.

'. . . Go away, Van Heerden? Is that part of our genetic make-up too? Is that what makes us men? Always off some-where?' He spoke in slow measured tones.

'Why was it that I could not say no? She knew, from the beginning. She said men go away. She said that is our nature and I argued with her, but she was right. We are like that. I am like that.'

'Thobela, you can't . . .'

'Do you know what life is? It is a process of disillusionment. It frees you of your illusions about people. You start out trusting everyone, you find your role models and strive to be like them and then you are disappointed by one after the other and it hurts, Van Heerden, it is a painful road to walk and I never understood why it must be so, but now I do. It is because every time the hope in you dies a little, with every disillusion, each disappointment in others becomes a disappointment in yourself. If others are weak, that weakness lies in you. It is like death, when you see others die you know it lies in wait for you. I am so tired of it, Van Heerden, I am so tired of being disillusioned, of seeing all these things in people and in myself, the weakness, the pain, the evil.'

'It's . . .'

'You were right. I am what I am. I can deny it, I can suppress it . . . and hide it, but not for ever. Life does as it will, it throws you around. Yesterday there was a moment when I realized I was living again. For the first time in . . . a long time. That I was doing something meaningful. With satisfaction. That I was vibrating inside and outside, in time, in rhythm. And do you know what was my first reaction? To feel guilty, as if that cancelled out the meaning of Miriam and Pakamile. But I have had time to think, Van Heerden. I understand it better. It is not what I am that is wrong. It is what I use it for. Or let it be used for. That was my mistake. I allowed other people to decide. But no more. No more.'

'You have to rest.'

'I will.'

'I left money with the doctor for the motorbike. They will send it down with a transport carrier in a week or so.'

'Thank you, Van Heerden.'

'We land in twenty minutes,' said the pilot.

November

45

In her lunch hour, Allison Healy drove out to Morningside with the long parcel and takeaways on the back seat. Mpayipheli sat on the veranda in the sun, his bare torso showing the bright white bandage around his waist.

She walked towards him with the parcel in her hand.

'I hope this is what you wanted.'

He pulled off the gaudy gift-wrapping with its multi-coloured African motif.

'They insisted on wrapping it,' she apologized.

He held the assegai in his hands, tested the strength of the steel, drew a finger down the edge of the blade.

'Thank you very much,' he said quietly.

'Is it . . . good enough?'

'It is perfect,' he said. He would have to shorten it, saw off more than half of the shaft, but he would not spoil her effort with details.

She put the bowls of curry and plastic cutlery on the table. 'Would you prefer a proper knife and fork?'

'No, thank you.' He leaned the assegai against the table and took his food.

'How are you feeling?' she asked.

'Much better.'

'I'm glad.'

'I want to start on Monday, Allison.'

'Monday? Are you sure?'

'I can't wait any longer.'

'You're right,' she said. 'I will show you.'

Quinn phoned Mentz from the airport.

'The name is false and they paid in cash, ma'am, but the pilot's flight plan was submitted according to regulations. There is not much we can do.'

'What does he say?'

'They landed in Chobe, ma'am. That's almost on the Zambian border. The patient was a big black man with two gunshot wounds in the hip. His condition was stable. They gave him about two litres of blood. The other two were white, a man and a woman. The woman had red hair, and was plump and light-skinned. The man was dark and lean, of average height. He and the black man spoke in Afrikaans, he and the woman spoke English. When they arrived they transferred the patient to a station wagon or a four-wheel drive, he's not sure. They did not take the registration number.'

'Thank you, Quinn.'

'What shall I do with the pilot?'

'Just thank him and come back.'

Transcript: Commission of Inquiry into
the death of Mrs Miriam Nzululwazi (38). 7
November.

Present: Chairman: Adv. B. O. Ndlovu. Assessors:
Adv. P. du T. Mostert, Mr K. J. Maponyane. For
the PIU: Ms J.M. Mentz. Witnesses: No witnesses
were called.

Chairman: Mr Radebe, according to Article 16 of
         the Intelligence Services Act 94-38 of
         1994, as amended, you have the right to
         representation during these proceedings.
         Have you waived this right?

_r Chairman.

_ understand the nature of the

_quiry and the charge of misconduct
against you?

_e: I understand it.

_airman: According to Article 16 (c) you are
entitled to representation by a person in
your department, and if no such person is
available or suitable, by someone outside
your department. Are you aware of this
right?

Radebe: I am, Mr Chairman.

Chairman: Do you waive your right to representation?

Radebe: Yes.

Chairman: According to Article 15 (1) you are
required to prepare a written admission or
rejection of the charge against you. Has
this document, as submitted by you, been
composed of your own free will?

Radebe: It has, Mr Chairman.

Chairman: Would you read it to this committee,
please?

Radebe: I, Vincent Radebe, admit that my conduct
and actions hindered and complicated an
official operation of the Presidential
Intelligence Unit.

I admit that through gross negligence
I was responsible for the death of Mrs
Miriam Nzululwazi on the 26 October this
year. I neglected to lock the door of the
interview room, which resulted directly
in Mrs Nzululwazi leaving the room
without escort and in a disturbed state of
mind. Her fatal fall from the fire escape
of the building was a direct result of my
conduct.

I admit, further, that on the same
day I unlawfully and without official
sanction abducted the six-year-old son
of Mrs Nzululwazi and kept him at my
abode overnight. I admit that on the 27
October I handed over the boy, Pakamile,
to personnel of the *Cape Times* and thereby
undermined an official operation of the
Presidential Intelligence Unit.

I declare that I acted alone in both
instances and wish to blame or involve no
other person.

I wish to plead the following mitigating
factors, Mr Chairman: when I made my
career choice on completion of my studies
at the University of the Witwatersrand, it
was my genuine desire to make a positive
contribution to this country. Like so
many of my compatriots, I was inspired by
the forgiving and positive vision of Mr
Nelson Mandela. I also wished to dedicate
my life to the building of the rainbow
nation. The Presidential Intelligence
Unit, in my opinion, presented me with
that opportunity.

But sometimes passion and dedication
are not enough. Sometimes zeal blinds us
to our own faults and shortcomings.

I understand that the protection of the
State and the democracy sometimes demands
difficult decisions and actions from its
office bearers, actions whereby ordinary
and innocent civilians are an occasion
directly and negatively affected.

I know now that I am not suited to this
career – and never was. The incidents

of 26, 27 and 28 October were extremely
traumatic for me. I was deeply disturbed
by the manner in which, in my opinion,
the basic human rights of, first, Mr
Thobela Mpayipheli and, later, Mrs Miriam
Nzululwazi were infringed upon. Even now,
as I read this document, I am unable to
grasp how the purpose of the operation,
however important or vital to national
security it might have been, justified the
means.

My mistake, Mr Chairman, was to allow
my dismay to affect my good judgement.
I was negligent when I should have been
diligent. I regret deeply my part in Mrs
Nzululwazi's death and particularly
that I did not make a stronger stand or
protest more vigorously through official
channels. My greatest weakness was to
doubt my own judgement of right and wrong.
This country and its people deserve
better than that, but I can assure you
that that will never happen again.
That is all, Mr Chairman.

Chairman: Thank you, Mr Radebe. Do you agree that
this document be recorded as written
admission of the charge against you?

Radebe: I agree.

Chairman: Have you any questions, Mrs Mentz?

Mentz: I have, Mr Chairman.

Chairman: Proceed.

Mentz: Vincent, do you believe that part of, as
you would call it, the building of the
rainbow nation is to supply classified
information to the intelligence services
of other nations?

Radebe: No, ma'am.

Mentz: Then why did you?

Radebe: I did no such thing.

Mentz: Do you deny that that during the operation
           you supplied information to Muslim
           extremist groups?

Radebe: I deny that emphatically.

Chairman: Mrs Mentz, do you have proof of these
           allegations?

Mentz: Mr Chairman, we have tangible evidence
           that key information was leaked to
           an international network of Muslim
           extremists. We cannot directly link
           Vincent with this process, but his
           undermining behaviour speaks for itself.

Chairman: I have two problems here, Mrs Mentz.
           Firstly, Mr Radebe has not been charged
           with high treason, but with negligence.
           Secondly, your allegations rest on
           circumstantial evidence, which I cannot
           allow.

Mentz: With respect, Mr Chairman, I do not
           believe that leaving the interview room
           door unlocked was negligence. I believe it
           was deliberate.

Chairman: Your allegations must be proven, Mrs
           Mentz.

Mentz: The truth will out.

Chairman: Do you wish to lead evidence, Mrs Mentz?

Mentz: No.

Chairman: Do you have any further questions?

Mentz: No.

Chairman: Do you wish to introduce evidence
           regarding further questions, Mr Radebe?

Radebe: No, Mr Chairman.

Chairman: Mr Radebe, this commission of inquiry

```
has no choice but to find you guilty
of misconduct as noted. We take note
of your presentation of mitigating
circumstances. This commission is
adjourned until 14:00, when we will
consider actions to be taken against you.
```

As the woman drove out of the parking garage at Wale Street Chambers, Allison Healy followed her with her heart in her throat. Mpayipheli lay flat on the rear seat. They drove through the city always four or five car lengths behind, down the Heerengracht onto the N1 and then east towards the northern suburbs.

'Please don't lose her,' came the deep voice from the back.

It was Williams, who had begun the thing, who nearly ended it.

Williams, who knew everyone – but no one knew him. Williams whom she had plucked out of the SAPS, an affirmative-action appointee wasting his time behind a desk somewhere in the Regional Commissioner's office. The rumours had spread over the Western Cape in fragments: twenty-eight years in the police and never took a bribe. If you want to know something, ask Williams. If you need someone you can trust, get Williams. A coloured man from the heart of the Flats, joined the Force with Standard Eight and climbed the ladder like a phantom, without powerful friends or powerful enemies, without fanfare, the invisible man. Just what Mentz wanted and it was so easy to get him. Merely the sincere promise that he would never again be chained to a desk did the trick.

'Janina,' he said. He had called her that from the beginning. 'Do you want his address?' His tone of voice was somewhere between irony and seriousness.

'Go for it,' she said and picked up a pen.

'I expect that you will find him at the house of a Dr Zatopek van Heerden, Plot 17, Morning Star.'

'A medical doctor?'

'That I cannot say?'

'How, Williams?'

'They brought the motorbike in through the Martin's Drift border post, ma'am. On a three-tonner, without papers, and the story that it belongs to a South African who had an accident somewhere in Northern Botswana.'

'And they let him in?'

'Money changed hands.'

'And?'

'The driver had an address with him that was copied down.'

'How did you—'

'Oh, I hear things.'

46

The Stasi records confirmed that Mpayipheli/
Umzingeli was Marion Dorffling's assassin.

I notified Langley, and requested two specialized
field agents from the London office to help with the
process of securing the hard drive.

After the tip-off from Inkululeko, the agents flew
to Northern Botswana, acquired a vehicle and made
visual contact with the PIU Reaction Unit member
who was waiting in ambush for Mpayipheli. They
witnessed the arrest of the Reaction Unit member by
Botswana authorities but, despite waiting at the
roadside through the night, could not intercept
Mpayipheli or the hard disk.

They returned to Cape Town and were about to leave
for London when the urgent contact signal was
received from Inkululeko (she leaves her car's
indicator on in her home's driveway). When contact
was established, Inkululeko supplied the address
where Mpayipheli was apparently recuperating from
wounds sustained during his cross-country flight.
She granted us three hours before the PIU Reaction
Unit would reach the same address.

The image that remained with Allison Healy afterwards was the one of blood – the carotid artery that kept pumping spouts of the liquid, first against the wall and later onto the floor, powerful jets in an impossibly high arc that gradually lessened until the fountain of life dried up with repulsive finality.

In long discussions afterwards with Van Heerden she would try to purge it from her mind by reconstructing the events over and over again. Try to analyse her emotions from how they had been as they ate their meal through to the end of it all one day later.

They sat at the table in Van Heerden's kitchen. At Mpayipheli's request, his psychologist friend had made *coq au vin* in the traditional Provençal manner. The serving dish stood in the middle of the table steaming a heavenly aroma, golden couscous in a dish alongside. Three people in a happy domestic scene, the Xhosa man's hunger practically visible on his face, the way he eyed the food, eager posture, hands ready, impatient for her to finish serving.

It was a pleasant occasion, a convivial gathering, a mental photograph frozen in time to be taken out and remembered with satisfaction later. *Don Giovanni* playing in the sitting room, a baritone aria that she was unfamiliar with but that fell with melodious machismo on her ear, the man she was beginning to love beside her, who continually surprised her with his cookery skills, his fanatical love of Mozart, his deep friendship with the black man, his ongoing teasing of the both of them. And Thobela who carried his grief for Miriam Nzululwazi with so much grace – how her perception of him had changed. A week ago on the plane he and his past had filled her with fear, but now tenderness grew in her out of the conversations on the veranda when he had related his life to her. There had been moments when he had described how he had met Miriam and how their love and companionship had blossomed when she had had to fight back the tears. Here they sat now on the eve of his attempt to claim Pakamile, the future full of promise for everyone and the world, a wonderful moment framed in the dark reflection of a glass of red wine.

Allison would never be sure if she had heard the sound. Perhaps, but even if she had, her untrained ear could never have distinguished it from others, nor could her consciousness have read danger in it.

Mpayipheli had moved with purpose, one moment in the chair beside her, the next a mass of kinetic energy moving in the direction of the sitting room. And then everything had happened at once. Chaos and noise that she could only sort chronologically with great difficulty after the fact. First the dull thud of human bodies colliding with great force, then the apologetic reports of a silenced firearm, a short staccato of four-five-six shots followed by the crack of the coffee table breaking, shouts of men like bellowing animals and she found herself in the doorway of the living room, the only light shining over her shoulder and all she could see were rolling shadows and half-light.

Mpayipheli and a man were on the ground, writhing and grunting for life or death, the silver flash of a steel blade in between and another man, tall and athletic on the other side of the room with a gun in his hand, the long snout of a silencer searching out a target on the floor, but calm and calculating, unhurried by the frenetic motion of the two figures.

And then Van Heerden. She had not seen him leave the kitchen, was unaware that he had gone out the other door into the passage. Only when the tall man placed his gun on the floor did she realize that Van Heerden was holding the double-barrelled shotgun to the man's head as he called to her, 'Allison, go into the kitchen, close the door.' But she was frozen, why could she not move, why could she not react, she would ask herself and Van Heerden over and over in the weeks afterwards.

Mpayipheli and the other one stood up against each other. His opponent, the one with the knife, had small eyes close together and a thick neck on massive shoulders.

'Tiny,' Van Heerden called and threw something across the room that the Xhosa deftly caught. *Tiny*. Everything regressed, everything rolled back to an ancient time and the one with the neck said, 'Amsingelly', his head lowered and his broad-bladed knife weaving in front of him.

'Umzingeli.' Thobela's voice was a deep growl and then softer, much softer, 'Mayibuye'.

'What fucking language is that, nigger?'

'Xhosa' – and she would never forget the look on Mpayipheli's face, the light from the kitchen slanting on to it and there was something indescribable there, a strange illumination and then she saw the object that he had plucked out of the air, it was the assegai, the one she had bought for him in the curio shop in Long Street.

```
This office has been unable to re-establish
contact with the two agents, and can only assume
that the mission was not a success. Inkululeko
has been unable to supply any information as to
what transpired at the house that belongs to a
member of a local university's department of
psychology.

We will continue to pursue the matter, but
regret to inform you that we have to presume the
worst.
```

'He's not here, ma'am,' screamed Captain Tiger Mazibuko

over the phone with a raging frustration that made Mentz shudder.

'Tiger . . .'

'The doctor is here and he says that if we don't leave within fifteen minutes, we will never see the hard disk again. And a redhead who says she is from the press. Something happened here, there's blood on the walls and the furniture is fucked, but the Dog is not here and these fucking people won't cooperate—'

'Tiger.' Her voice was stern and sharp, but he ignored her, he was out of his mind.

'No,' he said. 'I am finished. Totally fucking finished. I've already made a cunt of myself, I am finished. I didn't sit for two fucking days in a cell in Botswana for this. I didn't sign up for this. I will not expose my people to this, enough, it's fucking enough.'

She tried calm. 'Tiger, slow down . . .'

'Christ, Jissis,' he said and he sounded as if he would cry.

'Tiger, let me speak to the doctor.'

'I'm finished,' he said again.

'Tiger, please.'

High on the slopes of Tygerberg in the heart of a white neighbourhood Mpayipheli climbed out of Van Heerden's car. He was one block away from his destination, because there could be eyes, possibly two sets of them in a vehicle in front of the door and one or two bodyguards inside.

He moved purposefully to the dark patches on the pavement, because a black man here in the small hours was out of place. On the street corner he stopped. The Cape night opened up for him, a fairy tale of a thousand flickering lights as far as the eye could see, from Milnerton in the west the coastline swept down to the lighted carbuncle of the mountain. The city lay there like a slowly beating heart, the arteries curling away to Groote Schuur and Observatory and Rosebank and Newlands and from there the Flats made a curve east, through Khayalitsha and Guguletu to Kraaifontein and Stellenbosch and Somerset West. Rich and poor, shoulder to shoulder, sleeping now, a resting giant.

He stood, hands by his sides. He looked.

Because tomorrow would be his last day here.

Somewhere between three and four in the morning a part of Janina Mentz's consciousness dragged her from a deep sleep. A sense that all was not right, a panicky suffocating feeling and she opened her eyes with a jerk of her body and the big black hand was over her mouth and she smelt him, the sweat, saw the blood on the torn clothes, saw the short assegai in his hand and she made a sound of terror, her body instinctively shrinking away from him.

'My name,' he said, 'is Thobela Mpayipheli.'

He pressed the blade to her throat and said, 'We don't want to wake the children.'

She moved her head up and down, pulling the sheets instinctively up over her chest where her heart leapt around like a wild animal.

'I am going to take my hand off your mouth. I want only two things from you and then I will leave. Do you understand?'

Again she nodded.

He lifted his hand, shifting the blade away from her, but still he was too close to her, his eyes watchful.

'Where is Pakamile?'

Her voice would not function, it came hoarsely through her dry mouth that failed to form words. She had to start over. 'He is safe.'

'Where?'

'I don't know the exact place.'

'You lie.' And the blade came nearer.

'No . . . Welfare, they took him.'

'You will find out.'

'I will, I . . . There isn't . . . Tomorrow I'll have to . . .'

'You will find out tomorrow.' And her head worked frantically up and down in confirmation – her heart had slowed a fraction.

'Tomorrow morning at eleven you will have Pakamile at the underground parking lot of the Waterfront. If he is not there I will send a copy of the hard disk to every newspaper in the country, understand?'

'Yes.' Grateful that her voice flowed more easily now.

'Eleven o' clock. Do not be late.'

'I won't.'

'I know where you live,' Mpayipheli said and stood up. And then he was gone, the room empty and she took a deep breath before slowly getting out of bed and going to the bathroom to throw up.

47

Bodenstein saw the GS stop in the street just before opening Mother City Motorrad and he knew he knew the rider, but only recognized him when Mpayipheli removed the helmet.

'Fuck,' said Bodenstein and went out, amazed.

'Thobela,' he said.

'I came to pay you.'

'Look at the bloody bike.'

'A few scrapes. It's fine.'

'A few scrapes?'

'I've come to buy it, Bodenstein.'

'You what?'

'And I need another helmet. One of those System Fours that we only have in small sizes left. There are still a couple in the storeroom behind those boxes that the exhausts came in.'

It was just Van Heerden and Mpayipheli in the parking garage. He stood by the motorbike; Van Heerden sat in his car with the CIA agent's silenced machine pistol.

Allison had chosen not to come.

At one minute to eleven a black man came walking towards him from the shopping centre entrance with a long, confident stride and he knew instinctively that it was Mazibuko – he matched the voice and the rage to the physical form before him.

'I will get you, Dog,' said Mazibuko.

'Where is Pakamile?'

'I'm telling you I will get you, one day when this data is not important any more, I will find you and I will kill you, as God is my witness, I am going to kill you.'

They faced each other and Mpayipheli felt the hate radiating from the man and the temptation was strong – the fighting blood welled up in him.

'The question you must ask, Mazibuko, is whether there is more in you than just the anger you feel. What is left if that is gone?'

'Fuck you, Xhosa,' spittle sprayed.

'Are they using you? Are they using the rage that is eating you?'

'Shut up, you dog. Come, take me now, you fucking coward.' Tiger's body leaned forward, but an invisible thread held him back.

'Ask yourself: how long until it's no longer useful, before things change? A new administration or a new system or a new era. They are using you, Mazibuko. Like a piece of equipment.'

Captain Tiger Mazibuko cracked at that moment, his hand went to the bulky bulge under his jacket and it was only the sharp voice of Janina Mentz that made him waver a moment, an authoritarian cry of his nickname and he stood, torn between two alternatives, his eyes wild, his body a hair trigger, his fingers on the butt of the gun and then Mpayipheli said quietly: 'I am not alone, Tiger. You are dead before you can point that thing.'

'Tiger,' Janina called again.

Like a man on a high wire, he struggled to maintain balance.

'Don't let them use you,' said Mpayipheli again.

Tiger dropped his hand, speechless.

'Where is the hard disk?' He heard Mentz's voice from somewhere between the cars.

'Safe,' he said. 'Where is Pakamile?'

'In the car back here. If you want the child you will have to give the disk to Tiger.'

'You don't understand your alternatives.'

'That is what *you* don't understand. The child for the hard disk. Non-negotiable.'

'Watch me carefully. I am going to take a cellphone out of my pocket. And then I am going to phone a reporter from the *Cape Times* . . .'

Mazibuko stood in front of him, watching his every move, but his eyes had changed. The wildness had gone and there was something else growing.

He took out the cellphone, held it in front of him and keyed in the number.

'It's ringing,' he said.

'Wait,' screamed Mentz.

'I have waited long enough,' he said.

'I will get the boy.'

'Please hold on,' Mpayipheli said over the phone and then to Mentz: 'I am waiting.'

He saw Mazibuko turn away from him.

'You stay here,' he said, but Mazibuko did not hear. He was walking towards the exit and Thobela saw something in the set of the shoulders that he understood.

'You have two choices in life,' he said so only Mazibuko could hear it. 'You can be a victim. Or not.'

Then he saw Pakamile and the child saw him and the emotion of the moment threatened to overcome him completely.

The white Mercedes-Benz stopped at the traffic lights and one of the street hawkers with packs of white plastic clothes-hangers and sunshades for cars and little brown teddy bears knocked on the window and the driver let it slide down electronically.

'The hard disk is safe,' said the driver. 'Not in our possession, but I believe it is absolutely secure.'

'I will pass it on,' said the hawker.

'Allah Akhbar,' said the driver and then the light changed to green up ahead and he put the car in gear.

'Allah Akhbar,' said the hawker. 'God is great.' And he watched the car drive away.

The driver switched on the radio as the announcer said . . . *And here is the new one from David Kramer, singing with his new find, Koos Kok, 'The Ballad of the Lonely Motorbike Rider'* . . . He smiled and ran a finger under the snow-white shirt collar to relieve the pressure a fraction against the small hump.

Reverend Lawrence Mpayipheli was busy searching for the ripest tomatoes and snipping them loose with the pruning shears, the scent of the cut stems full in his nose, the plump firmness of the red fruit under his fingers, when he heard the engine before the door and stood up stiffly from behind the high green bushes.

There were two of them on the motorbike, a big man and a little boy, and he thought *It can't be* and he prayed, just a short 'Lord, please,' aloud, there in the middle of the vegetable garden. He waited for them to take off the hard hats so that he could be sure, so that he could call his wife in the clear voice that could reverberate across the back yards of Alice like the ringing of a church bell.

Acknowledgements

I am indebted to so many people and institutions who made this book possible. I can never thank you all enough:

The Afrikaanse Taa-en Kultuurvereniging for their grant, which made it possible to take the GS on most of the routes described in *Heart of the Hunter*, and take a motorcycle tour of the Kat river valley and do research in Grahamstown.

Lisa Ncetani and the never-ending list of Xhosa, Zulu, Tswana, Ndebele and Sotho shoeshine people, business-men, taxi drivers, porters and co-passengers on business flights between Cape Town and Johannesburg: thank you for answering my questions so patiently, and helping a white, middle-class Afrikaner understand a little better.

One of the most unsettling discoveries during my research was the sad lack of websites about the more recent Xhosa lifestyle, culture and history. But Timothy Stapleton's *Maqoma – Xhosa resistance to Colonial Advance* (Jonathan Ball, 1994) and Noël Mostert's incomparable *Frontiers* (Pimlico, 1992) were two wonderful sources I utilised.

Dr Julia C. Wells, historian at the University of Grahamstown, provided insightful information and comments on the history and development of the short stab spear or *assegaay*. Muneer Manie helped with the Arabic, and Ronnie Kasrils' book,

Armed & Dangerous (Mayibuye, 1993, 1998), was a similarly rich source of information on Umkhonto we Siswe and the role of the East Germans and Soviet Russia during the Struggle.

Francois Viljoen from BMW South Africa did not let my constant e-mails spoil our friendship and intriguing conversations with the late reverend Harwood Dixon, who was a missionary in the Eastern Cape for many years, and the enigmatic prof. Dap Louw from the University of the Free State's Department of Psychology had a great influence on the characters of *Heart of the Hunter*. Similarly, I am indebted to Stephen Pinker's *How the mind works* (W.W. Norton & Company, 1997), John L. Casti's *Paradigms Regained* (Abacus, 2000), Richard Dawkins's *River out of Eden* (Phoenix, 2001), Desmond Morris's *The Naked Eye* (Ebury Press, 2000), the brilliant *The evil that men do* by Brian Masters (Black Swan, 1996) and Geoffrey Miller's astounding *The Mating Mind* (Vintage, 2001)

The Internet archives of the newspapers *Die Burger, Beeld* and especially *Volksblad* were of great use. Other websites plundered were: Kalashnikov (*www.kalashnikov.guns.ru*), Valeri Shilin'se Gun Club (*www.club.guns.ru*), the U.S. Marines (*www.hqmc.usmc.mil*), Denel (*www.denel.co.za*), Heckler & Koch (*www.hecklerkoch.de*), Frikkie Potgieter's resource on the SA Defense Force (*http://members.tripod.com/samagte/index.html*), Frans Nel's Griqua Afrikaans (*www.ugie.co.za*), the Intelligence Resource Program (FAS) (*www.fas.org*) and the Central Intelligence Agency (*www.cia.gov*).

I would also like to profusely thank my colleagues, friends and family for their support during the writing process. My Afrikaans editor, Etienne Bloemhof, translator Laura Seegers, agent Isobel Dixon, and British Editor Wayne Brookes all contributed their amazing talents to hide the considerable gaps in mine. I can never repay you for your support, hard work, motivation and friendship.

Thanks to Lida, Johan, Liam and Kontanz, who never complained after hearing 'Dad has to write'. And to my beautiful wife Anita: Thank you for your love, faith and friendship.

Deon Meyer
Melkbosstrand
May 2003

La Reine de l'Oracle

Le Royaume de Tobin

******

Lynn Flewelling

La Reine de l'Oracle

Le Royaume de Tobin

******

ÉDITIONS FRANCE LOISIRS

Titre original : *The Oracle's Queen Tamìr Triad* – Livre III
(deuxième partie).
Publié par Bantam.

Traduit de l'américain par Jean Sola.

Édition du Club France Loisirs,
avec l'autorisation des Éditions Pygmalion.

Éditions France Loisirs,
123, boulevard de Grenelle, Paris.
www.franceloisirs.com

© Lynn Flewelling, 2006.
© Éditions Flammarion, département Pygmalion, 2008, pour l'édition en
langue française.
ISBN 978-2-298-01837-0

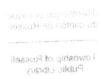

Pour Patricia York
14 août 1949-21 mai 2005.

En déplorant que tu ne sois pas là pour voir comment celui-ci s'achève.

Avec toute ma gratitude pour m'avoir constamment rappelé « que la question n'est pas de savoir combien de fois nous respirons mais combien d'instants nous coupent le souffle ».

En attendant nos retrouvailles, ma bonne, ma chère amie.

L'ANNÉE SKALIENNE

I. SOLSTICE D'HIVER – Nuit du Deuil et Fête de Sakor ; observance de la nuit la plus longue et célébration du rallongement des jours ultérieurs.

  1. Sarisin : mise bas.
  2. Dostin : entretien des haies et des fossés. Semailles des fèves et des pois destinés à nourrir le bétail.
  3. Klesin : semailles de l'avoine, du froment, de l'orge (destinée au maltage), du seigle. Début de la saison de pêche. Reprise de la navigation en pleine mer.

II. ÉQUINOXE DE PRINTEMPS – Fête des Fleurs à Mycena. Préparatifs en vue des plantations, célébration de la fertilité.

  4. Lithion : fabrication du beurre et du fromage (de préférence au lait de brebis). Semailles du chanvre et du lin.
  5. Nythin : labourage des terres en jachère.
  6. Gorathin : désherbage du maïs. Toilettage et tonte des moutons.

III. SOLSTICE D'ÉTÉ

7. Shemin : au début du mois, fauchage des foins ; à la fin, puis le mois suivant, pleine période des moissons.

8. Lenthin : moissons.

9. Rhythin : engrangement des récoltes. Labourage des champs et semailles du blé d'hiver ou du seigle.

IV. PLEINS GRENIERS – Fin des récoltes, temps des gratitudes.

10. Erasin : on expédie les cochons dans les bois se gorger de glands et de faines.

11. Kemmin : nouveaux labourages en vue du printemps. Abattage des bœufs et autres bêtes de boucherie, préparation des viandes. Fin de la saison de pêche. Les tempêtes rendent dangereuse la navigation hauturière.

12. Cinrin : travaux d'intérieur, battage inclus.

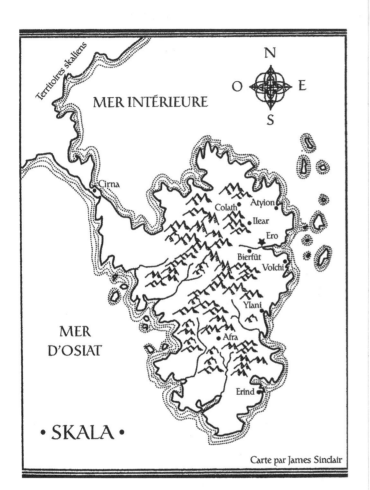

1

Les trois jours suivants s'écoulèrent trop v
de Ki, tout écartelé qu'il se retrouvait entre l'e
d'exercer le commandement pour la premiè
le sentiment de culpabilité que lui causait sa s
d'avec Tamìr. Il consacra ses journées à v
l'équipement de sa compagnie et à dresser (
avec Jorvaï en vue de la première confro
laquelle il serait associé. Quant à ses soiré
passait auprès de Tamìr, à guetter dans se
l'ombre d'un regret, mais il n'y perçut que d
tement pour lui-même et l'ardent désir de l'
se distinguer au cours des opérations.

Le soir qui devait précéder son départ, il
chez elle après que les autres se furent tou
Comme ils se tenaient assis près de la fenêtr
à siroter leur dernière coupe de vin tout e
l'oreille aux chants des grillons, il fut surp
vision qu'il avait d'elle. Elle était en
contempler d'un air pensif les constellatio
mament, et l'un de ses doigts délicats parco
tement le motif en relief de son hanap d'ar
portait en l'occurrence une robe brodée de

13

r et dont le rouge sombre lui seyait à merveille. La
·ière de la chandelle adoucissait ses traits et mettait
 reflets mouvants dans sa chevelure qui se répandait
·ement sur ses épaules et sa poitrine.

En ce moment précis, Ki perdit Tobin de vue
·me cela ne lui était encore jamais arrivé. Les
·es de Tamìr lui semblèrent aussi pulpeuses que
·les de toutes les filles qu'il avait jamais embrassées,
 joues aussi lisses que celles d'une jouvencelle et
·· plus d'un garçon imberbe. Sous ce jour-là, elle lui
·nait presque un sentiment de fragilité. Il avait
·nme l'impression qu'il la voyait pour la toute pre-
·re fois.

Et puis elle se tourna vers lui et haussa un sourcil
·une expression tellement coutumière qu'elle lui res-
·cita Tobin sur-le-champ, Tobin qui le dévisageait
· même œil que toujours.

« Qu'y a-t-il ? C'est ton dîner qui ne passe pas ? »
·l lui sourit d'un air penaud. « J'étais seulement en
·n de me dire... » Il s'arrêta pile, le cœur galopant.
·e regrette que tu ne viennes pas avec moi, demain.

— Moi aussi. » Son sourire triste était bien celui de
·in, lui aussi. « Promets-moi que tu... » Là-dessus,
· s'interrompit, manifestement embarrassée. « Enfin,
·va pas t'amuser jusqu'à te faire tuer.

— Je ferai de mon mieux pour éviter ça. Jorvaï
·se que la plupart de nos adversaires renonceront
·· battre, de toute façon, dès qu'ils te verront fer-
·ment résolue à marcher contre eux. Il se peut que
·'aie même pas l'occasion de défourailler mon épée.

— Je ne sais si je préfère te souhaiter qu'il ne

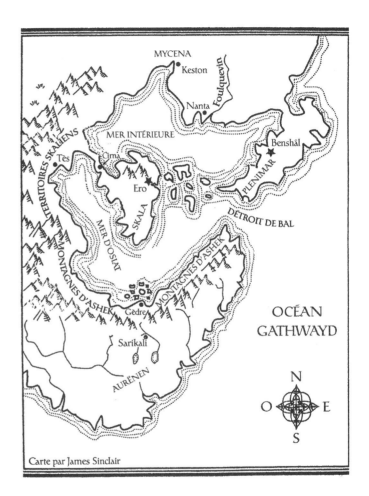

14

t'arrive rien ou que tu brilles au combat. À propos, s'il advenait que tu aies à te battre, hein ? Tiens, j'ai bricolé ça pour toi. » Elle farfouilla dans sa manche et en retira un disque d'or large environ d'un pouce de diamètre et le lui offrit. Dessus était ciselée en ronde bosse une chouette aux ailes déployées tenant entre ses serres un croissant de lune. « L'idée m'en est venue voilà quelques jours. Je l'ai modelée en cire et fait réaliser au village.

— Elle est magnifique ! Et quelle joie de voir que tu te remets à créer des objets ! » Ki dénoua la lanière de cuir qui enserrait son col et y enfila l'amulette en un pendentif jouxtant le cheval sculpté. « À présent, j'ai les deux dieux de mon côté.

— C'était ça, l'idée. »

Elle se leva et tendit la main. Se dressant à son tour, il la lui serra. « Pour te guider, Ki, déclara-t-elle, le feu de Sakor et la lumière d'Illior. »

Sa main était chaude dans la sienne, la paume rendue rugueuse par le maniement de l'épée, les doigts vigoureux et calleux par la pratique de l'arc. Il attira Tamìr dans ses bras et l'étreignit très fort, éperdu du désir de connaître son propre cœur. Elle lui retourna son étreinte et, lorsqu'ils se détachèrent, il eut l'impression d'entr'apercevoir dans ses yeux un éclair fugitif de son embarras personnel. Mais, avant qu'il n'ait eu le temps d'en acquérir la certitude, elle se détourna pour reprendre sa coupe en main. « Il est tard. Tu devrais t'accorder un peu de repos tant que tu en as la possibilité.

— Peut-être bien, ma foi. » Elle continuait à ne pas

le regarder. L'avait-il fâchée ? « Je... je pourrais rester un moment de plus. »

Elle lui répliqua par un sourire et secoua la tête. « Ne sois pas idiot. File te reposer. Je serai là pour assister à ton départ. Bonne nuit, Ki. »

Il ne trouva rien d'autre à dire dans sa cervelle, pas même ce qu'il avait envie de dire. « Merci pour ma mission, lâcha-t-il enfin. Je te donnerai lieu de t'enorgueillir.

— Je le sais déjà.

— Eh bien... bonne nuit. »

Une douzaine de pas seulement séparaient sa propre porte de celle de Tamìr, mais ils lui avaient fait l'effet d'être un mille quand il réintégra sa chambre. Il fut suffoqué d'y trouver Tharin, planté près du râtelier auquel était suspendue son armure.

« Ah, te voilà. Comme tu ne possèdes pas d'écuyer personnel, je me suis mis en tête de soumettre tes armes à une dernière inspection. » Tharin marqua une pause en le lorgnant d'un air bizarre. « Quelque chose cloche ?

— Rien ! » se récria vivement Ki.

Avec trop de vivacité, vu la façon dont les yeux de Tharin se plissèrent. « Tu viens tout juste de chez Tamìr ?

— Oui. Je tenais à... je tenais à la remercier. Elle s'inquiète pour moi, et... » Son bafouillage n'alla pas plus loin.

Après l'avoir considéré en silence pendant un moment, Tharin se contenta de branler du chef.

16

Tamìr passa une nuit sans sommeil. À chaque fois qu'elle fermait les yeux, elle revoyait l'expression angoissée qu'elle avait surprise sur les traits de Ki et revivait la sensation qu'elle avait éprouvée quand il la serrait dans ses bras. *Il ne sait toujours pas quoi faire de moi, et moi non plus !*

L'aube n'était pas encore levée quand Tamìr se débarbouilla à sa table de toilette avant d'enfiler une robe sombre et un corselet de plates destinés aux cérémonies. Il y avait une dernière chose qu'elle entendait faire. Tharin et les Compagnons attendaient dans le corridor et lui emboîtèrent le pas comme un seul homme. Pour la première fois, elle était douloureusement sensible à l'absence de Ki à ses côtés, de même qu'à celle de Lynx, qui allait lui aussi partir comme capitaine de l'état-major de Ki.

« Ce coup-ci, tu vas vraiment le faire, n'est-ce pas ? demanda Nikidès.

— Il sera fort en peine de refuser, cette fois », murmura-t-elle avec un sourire malin.

Les compagnies montées avaient déjà formé les rangs quand ils atteignirent la cour, et le spectacle du départ y avait attiré des centaines de courtisans qui s'alignaient le long des murs et des escaliers.

Entièrement revêtus de leur armure, Jorvaï et Ki avaient eux aussi devancé Tamìr sur les lieux pour la saluer. Elle leur souhaita bonne chance à tous deux et prononça quelques mots à l'adresse des capitaines. Enfin, tout en s'efforçant de conserver une mine austère, elle se tourna derechef vers Ki. « Il nous reste encore une broutille à régler. Veuillez vous agenouiller et me présenter votre épée. »

L'apostrophe lui fit ouvrir de grands yeux, mais sans qu'il ait d'autre solution que d'obtempérer.

Tamìr dégaina sa propre lame et lui en toucha la joue et les épaules. « En présence de ces témoins, et pour prix des années d'amitié probe et loyale durant lesquelles vous m'avez sauvé plus d'une fois la vie, je vous adoube Lord Kirothius de La Chesnaie-Mont et de Reine Merci, et je vous accorde le domaine de votre naissance, ainsi que les rentes, possessions et principaux droits afférents au village de Reine Merci. En outre, il vous est remis un présent fondateur de cinq mille sesters d'or. Puissiez-vous en user sagement, pour l'honneur de votre maison comme pour celui de Skala. Relevez-vous, Lord Kirothius, et recevez vos armoiries. »

Plusieurs jeunes femmes s'avancèrent alors. L'une lui apportait sa bannière montée sur une hampe d'étendard. Une paire d'autres déployait un tabard. Les deux objets arboraient son nouvel emblème, conçu et dessiné par Nikidès. L'écu était divisé en diagonale, de senestre à dextre, par la barre blanche symbolisant la naissance légitime. Au centre de celle-ci figurait une peau de lion qui, drapée sur un bâton, commémorait la première fois où Ki avait risqué ses jours pour défendre Tobin. Tamìr le vit sourire à ce rappel de leur lointaine enfance. Le champ de gauche était vert, avec un arbre blanc, pour La Chesnaie-Mont. Celui de droite était noir, avec une tour blanche, pour Reine Merci. Enfin, surmontant l'ensemble du motif, une flamme d'argent recueillie au creux d'un croissant de lune rendait un double hommage aux dieux réconciliés.

« Eh bien, vous vous en êtes donné, du mal, hein ? » grommela Ki d'un ton qui voulait paraître contrarié, mais que démentaient ses joues rouges et ses yeux brillants. Il endossa le tabard puis dressa son épée devant son visage. « La maison de La Chesnaie-Mont et de Reine Merci sera toujours la plus fidèle de vos servantes, Majesté. »

Tamìr lui saisit la main et le fit pivoter de manière à le placer face à l'assemblée. « Ô vous tous, faites bon accueil à Lord Kirothius, mon ami et ma main droite. Honorez-le comme vous m'honorez. »

Des ovations retentirent, et la rougeur de Ki s'accentua. Tamìr lui administra une tape sur l'épaule et mima, muette, du bout des lèvres : « Sois prudent. »

Il enfourcha son cheval et arrima son heaume. Dégainant son épée, Jorvaï clama : « Pour l'honneur de Skala et pour la reine ! » et ses cavaliers reprirent le cri.

Ki fit de même en vociférant à son tour : « Pour Tamìr et Skala ! » et son invocation fut répétée par un millier de gorges enthousiastes.

« J'espère que vous évaluez l'étendue de ma jalousie », commenta Tamìr, une fois que le silence fut retombé.

« C'est votre propre ouvrage. » Jorvaï se mit à rire en enfonçant sur son crâne son heaume cabossé par les batailles. « Ne vous inquiétez pas. Ki et moi ferons tout notre possible pour nous conserver mutuellement en vie et, si nous n'y parvenons pas, l'un rapportera les cendres de l'autre.

— Bon. Allez montrer à nos adversaires qu'il ne faut pas badiner avec ce "garçon dingue affublé d'une robe". »

Leur chevauchée les mena d'abord vers l'important fief du duc Zygas, un vieux dur à cuire de lord. Il possédait une grande forteresse de pierre munie de puissantes murailles d'enceinte, mais l'essentiel de sa fortune était constitué par des champs de céréales en pleine maturité. Il avait établi quelques escouades de combattants sur la route aux abords de ses domaines mais, après avoir marché toute la nuit, Jorvaï et Ki leur tombèrent dessus à l'improviste juste après le lever du soleil. Ki les attaqua avec un groupe d'avant-garde et eut tôt fait de liquider toute résistance. Abandonnant aux capitaines le soin de conduire l'infanterie, Jorvaï et les cavaliers foncèrent au galop jusqu'aux portes de la place forte, et il expédia en avant un héraut porteur de la bannière blanche.

Les murailles qui surplombaient le fossé de terre étaient hérissées d'archers, et la lumière y faisait étinceler le métal des heaumes et des armes, mais aucun trait ne pouvait être décoché de part ni d'autre tant que le héraut n'avait pas pris la parole et ne s'était pas retiré.

Frappée de ses trois chevaux, la bannière blanche et noire de Zygas fut brandie au-dessus de la barbacane. Un homme se pencha vers l'extérieur et lança d'une voix teigneuse : « Qui donc bafoue mes droits et mon hospitalité de cette manière indigne ? Je ne reconnais là qu'un seul pavillon. Jorvaï de Colath, il n'y a jamais eu de méchante querelle sanglante entre nous. Pour quelle raison vous trouvez-vous devant mes portes comme si j'étais un Plenimarien ?

— Le héraut parle en mon nom, riposta Jorvaï à pleine voix.

— Monseigneur, j'apporte une lettre de Tamìr Ariani Ghërilain, reine de Skala, annonça le héraut.

— J'ignore tout d'une reine pareille, mais je respecterai la bannière blanche. Débitez votre message.

— À vos portes flottent les bannières de Lord Jorvaï de Colath et de Lord Kirothius de La Chesnaie-Mont et de Reine Merci, hommes liges de Tamìr Ariani Ghërilain, reine de Skala par droit du sang et de la naissance.

« Soit dûment établi, Zygas, fils de Morten, duc d'Ellsgué et de la Rivière de Feu, que par votre opiniâtre et ignoble déloyauté vous avez encouru le déplaisir de la Couronne. Si vous ne renoncez pas dès aujourd'hui à vous livrer à ce genre de forfaiture et si, muni d'un sauf-conduit, vous ne vous rendez pas tout de suite à Atyion pour jurer votre foi à la reine légitime en abjurant toute autre espèce de fidélité, alors, vous serez d'emblée déclaré traître et dépouillé de tous vos titres, terres, rentes et propriétés. Si vous refusez l'accès de votre demeure aux gentilshommes ici présents, le choix exprès de Sa Majesté, vos champs seront incendiés, votre bétail sera saisi, vos portes seront enfoncées et votre château sera rasé. Vous-même et vos héritiers serez faits prisonniers puis emmenés toutes affaires cessantes à Atyion pour affronter la justice de la reine.

« La reine Tamìr, dans sa sagesse, vous conjure de saisir la main miséricordieuse qui vous est tendue en ce jour et de tourner le dos à toute autre alliance erronée. Délivré aujourd'hui de ma propre main. »

S'ensuivit un long silence. Ki se démancha le col pour essayer d'apercevoir la figure de l'antagoniste, mais Zygas s'était écarté des créneaux.

« Qu'en pensez-vous ? » demanda-t-il tout bas à Jorvaï pendant que, toujours en selle, ils patientaient.

« Erius a souvent été l'hôte de cette maison, et Zygas s'est battu pour lui de l'autre côté de la mer Intérieure. En revanche, ce que j'ignore, c'est s'il est beaucoup plus informé sur Korin qu'il ne l'est sur Tamìr. »

Ils restèrent campés là tandis que le soleil s'élevait dans le ciel et que l'atmosphère s'échauffait. En nage dans son armure et sous son tabard, Ki écoutait clabauder des chiens et bêler des moutons derrière les remparts de la place forte. Au-delà du fossé, le pont-levis était relevé pour abriter les portes. Il était façonné en planches massives et clouté de cabochons en cuivre grosses comme des boucliers. Il faudrait probablement recourir à des catapultes et au feu pour ouvrir la brèche, si l'on en venait à cette extrémité.

Les ombres projetées par les jambes de son cheval avaient quasiment marqué l'écoulement d'une heure quand s'entendit le bruit d'une cavalcade qui contournait la forteresse au galop. Zygas disposait d'une poterne quelque part derrière, et il s'en était servi pour se risquer dehors.

Il montait un grand destrier bai, mais ne portait aucune armure. En revanche, il était accompagné par son héraut personnel brandissant la bannière inviolable. Il se dirigea à bride abattue droit sur eux, la tête dressée, et s'immobilisa des quatre fers à leur hauteur. Il gratifia Jorvaï d'un hochement de tête avant d'appesantir sur Ki un regard froid. « Je ne vous connais pas, vous.

— Permettez-moi de vous présenter Lord Kirothius. Il est l'homme de la reine, tout comme moi-même, lui précisa Jorvaï. Eh bien, qu'avez-vous à nous dire ? Puisque vous n'êtes pas parti pour le nord, peut-être éprouvez-vous quelques doutes ?

— Vous croyez à cette absurdité d'un garçon qui se transforme en fille, n'est-ce pas ?

— J'ai assisté à sa métamorphose de mes propres yeux, et vous ne m'avez jamais considéré comme un menteur, n'est-ce pas ? Le phénomène s'est produit sur les marches mêmes du château d'Atyion. Lord Kirothius est l'ami et l'écuyer de notre jeune reine depuis leur petite enfance à tous deux.

— Sur mon honneur, Monseigneur, c'est la vérité pure », confirma Ki.

Zygas accueillit l'assertion par un reniflement. « Sur l'honneur d'un blanc-bec de lord élevé à cette dignité par cette soi-disant reine de fille, hein ?

— Vous n'avez qu'à venir à Atyion vous en rendre compte par vous-même. Jetteriez-vous cette accusation de mensonge à la figure du grand prêtre d'Afra ? »

répliqua tranquillement Ki. Il leva de nouveau les yeux vers les créneaux. « Je ne vois flotter là-haut que votre bannière personnelle et pas celle du prince Korin. Attendriez-vous l'issue de l'affrontement pour vous rallier par la suite au vainqueur ?

— Surveillez votre langue, espèce de petit parvenu !

— Il a raison, Zygas, le morigéna Jorvaï. Je ne vous ai jamais considéré comme un type particulièrement résolu, mais il semblerait qu'avec la vieillesse vous incliniez de plus en plus vers l'indécision. »

Le duc les considéra tous les deux pendant un moment, puis il secoua la tête. « J'attends depuis des mois que Korin fasse mouvement pour défendre son trône, mais tout ce qu'il me donne, ce sont des faux-fuyants. Alors que vous êtes ici, vous deux. Vous avez toujours été un gaillard honnête, Jorvaï. Quelle confiance puis-je avoir dans le discours que m'a fait tenir votre reine ?

— Vous pouvez tout autant vous fier à elle pour accepter votre féauté si vous vous mettez en route aujourd'hui même que vous pouvez vous fier à nous pour brûler chaque champ, chaque étable et chaque chaumière dès l'instant où vous déclarerez vouloir en agir autrement.

— Ouais, et vous avez amené des troupes pour le faire, en plus, n'est-ce pas ? » Zygas soupira. « Et si je dis que j'irai, pour voir les choses par moi-même ?

— Insuffisant. Dans le cas où vous rentreriez dans le droit chemin en offrant votre foi, j'ai ordre de vous enjoindre de vous mettre en route incessamment sous la protection de mes propres hommes et de vous faire accompagner par votre épouse et vos enfants. Vous avez bien un fils établi sur ses propres terres à cette heure, si ma mémoire ne m'abuse, et d'autres plus jeunes qui résident encore sous votre toit ?

— Elle exige donc des otages, hein ?

— C'est à elle qu'il appartiendra de trancher ce point lorsque vous serez arrivés là-bas. Vous n'auriez pas dû attendre aussi longtemps. Vos terres ne sont demeurées indemnes jusqu'à aujourd'hui que grâce à la bonté de son cœur, mais sa patience est désormais à bout. À vous de vous résoudre maintenant, et terminons-en avec cette affaire. »

Zygas promena un regard circulaire sur les champs et les fermes dont le séparait la ligne de cavaliers en armes. Dans le lointain avançaient à marche forcée les troupes d'infanterie, soulevant la poussière de la route et manifestement prêtes à se battre. « Ainsi, elle est véritablement la fille de la princesse, cachée depuis tant d'années ?

— Sans conteste. Vous verrez Ariani en elle. Clair comme le jour. Les seigneurs des contrées du sud sont en train d'affluer en masse vers elle. Nyanis se trouve à ses côtés, ainsi que Kyman. Vous ne les prenez pas pour des écervelés, si ? »

Zygas passa une main dans sa barbe grise et soupira. « Non, pas plus que vous-même. Si j'y vais, est-ce qu'elle me confisquera mes terres ?

— C'est à elle d'en décider après qu'elle vous aura vu, répondit Jorvaï. Mais abstenez-vous d'aller la rejoindre, et elle n'y manquera pas, aussi sûres et certaines que sont les pluies printanières du Créateur. »

Ki voyait nettement les débats intérieurs de leur interlocuteur. Lequel finit par demander : « Suis-je également tenu d'emmener mes fillettes ? Comment pourrai-je assurer leur protection pendant le trajet, si je n'ai pas d'escorte à moi ? Je ne veux pas qu'on abuse d'elles.

— Tamìr mettrait à mort quiconque porterait la main sur elles, et j'en ferais de même, lui assura Ki. J'ai des femmes parmi mes guerriers. Je chargerai certaines d'entre elles de vous tenir lieu d'escorte. Elles ne permettront à personne au monde de toucher vos filles. »

Zygas jeta un nouveau regard à la ronde sur les combattants massés à sa porte. « Très bien, mais ma malédiction s'abattra sur vous tous et sur votre reine si cela n'est que tricherie.

— Tamìr ne vous demande rien de plus que votre loyauté », lui garantit Ki.

Le duc s'inclina devant eux d'un air résigné. « Si cette reine qui est la vôtre est aussi miséricordieuse que vous la dépeignez, alors peut-être mérite-t-elle d'être soutenue, légitime ou non. »

Il repartit par où il était venu, et Ki exhala un souffle de décontraction. « Ça n'a pas été si dur que ça. »

Jorvaï gloussa sombrement et désigna d'un geste en arrière les forces qui les appuyaient. « Voilà un argument persuasif. Enfin, vous avez vu comment ça se goupille. J'espère que vous trouverez Lady Alna d'aussi bonne composition. »

Malheureusement, tel ne fut pas le cas. Ki et sa compagnie ne marchèrent pendant trois jours par une chaleur accablante que pour découvrir le village déserté, les champs moissonnés et la noble dame prête à les recevoir.

C'était une veuve d'âge mûr, dont les longs cheveux jaunes encadraient une physionomie dure et hautaine. Elle sortit à cheval de chez elle comme l'avait fait Zygas mais écouta le héraut délivrer son message avec une impatience à peine voilée.

« Mensonges ou nécromancie ? Duquel des deux s'agit-il, messire ? » ironisa-t-elle d'un ton méprisant, sans déguiser qu'elle était moins qu'impressionnée par Ki. « J'ai un millier d'hommes d'armes derrière mes murs, et mon grain s'y trouve en sécurité, lui aussi. Le roi Korin m'a fait parvenir des assurances que sous sa bannière mes terres seraient agrandies et mon titre protégé. Menaces à part, de quoi me régale votre reine ?

— Vous avez été convoquée à plus d'une reprise, et l'on vous a donné toute chance d'adopter la cause de la reine légitime », répliqua Ki, sans rien laisser percer de son irritation.

Elle émit un reniflement de dédain. « Reine légitime ! Ariani n'avait aucune fille.

— Elle en avait une, et vous avez entendu parler de sa métamorphose, j'en suis convaincu.

— Alors, c'est de la nécromancie. Nous faut-il nous aplatir devant un overlord appuyé par la magie noire, comme le font les Plenimariens ?

— Ce n'était pas de la magie noire... », débuta Ki, mais elle le coupa d'un ton coléreux.

« Ma parenté se composait pour moitié de magiciens, de magiciens libres de Skala, mon gars, et du genre puissant. Ils étaient incapables de réaliser le genre d'opération magique que tu me décris. »

Il n'était assurément pas près de lui révéler que cette dernière avait été l'ouvrage d'une sorcière des collines. « À vous de choisir, maintenant, déclara-t-il. Ou vous partez tout de suite pour Atyion avec vos enfants, ou bien je n'hésiterai pas à exécuter les ordres que j'ai reçus.

— Ah bon ? » Alna l'examina longuement. « Non, je pense que vous n'en ferez rien. Aux dieux vat. Je me suis montrée loyale envers le roi Erius, et je ne trahirai pas son fils. » Là-dessus, elle fit volter sa monture et repartit en direction de ses portes. Conformément aux principes en matière de pourparlers, Ki n'eut d'autre solution que de regarder celles-ci se refermer pesamment derrière elle.

En se détournant à son tour, il découvrit Lynx et Grannia qui le dévisageaient, dans l'expectative. « Grannia, vous brûlez le village. Lynx, amène les sapeurs et les incendiaires. Montrez-vous sans merci vis-à-vis de quiconque porterait une arme. Tels sont vos ordres. »

2

Le cœur de Tamìr bondissait à l'apparition de chaque héraut.

Le premier qui se montra finalement apportait les salutations et les excuses du duc Zygas, présentement en route pour jurer allégeance. Tout ayant semblé indiquer qu'il serait l'un des plus rétifs, elle vit un bon présage dans sa soumission. Il survint avec sa famille quelques jours plus tard à bord d'une voiture. Elle le reçut d'un air sévère, mais il fit preuve de tant d'inquiétude pour ses enfants et de tant de sincérité dans son serment qu'elle fut heureuse de le confirmer dans ses titres.

Quelques jours plus tard, un deuxième héraut de Jorvaï apporta la nouvelle d'une autre victoire obtenue sans effusion de sang. Lord Erian était sorti faire sa reddition au moment même où les troupes de Jorvaï se présentaient à l'horizon, ce sans savoir apparemment si c'était à Korin ou à Tamìr qu'il était sur le point de se rendre. La lettre de Jorvaï était pleine de mépris. « Gardez cet individu-ci soigneusement sous votre coupe. Les roquets couards sont ceux qui mordent le plus souvent. »

Mais elle n'avait toujours pas vent de Ki. Les nuits étaient longues, sachant que la chambre voisine était inoccupée, et Frère était au surplus revenu tourmenter ses rêves.

Finalement, le dernier jour de Shemin, un héraut se

présenta pour annoncer que Ki avait triomphé de ses adversaires et le suivait de près.

Il survint en effet juste après la tombée de la nuit avec sa cavalerie et se rendit droit à la grande salle, flanqué de Lynx et de Grannia. Tous les trois affichaient des mines sombres et fatiguées, et leurs tabards respectifs portaient encore les sinistres stigmates des combats.

« Bienvenue pour votre retour », dit Tamìr en s'efforçant de préserver sa dignité devant la cour, alors que tout ce qu'elle désirait vraiment était de sauter à bas de l'estrade pour étreindre Ki. « Qu'avez-vous à nous rapporter ?

— Majesté, Lord Ynis s'est rendu, et il s'achemine en ce moment vers vous. Lady Alna s'y est refusée. » Ki adressa un signe de tête à Lynx.

Ce dernier retira de sous son manteau un sac de cuir puis l'ouvrit. Ki y plongea la main et en extirpa une tête de femme qu'il tenait par ses cheveux blonds maculés de sang.

Tamìr ne broncha pas à la vue de ces lèvres flasques et de ces yeux ternes et laiteux, mais ce spectacle la contrista. « Fichez-la sur les remparts au-dessus de la porte à côté des restes de Solari, et signalez par une pancarte son nom et son crime. Est-ce vous qui l'avez tuée, Ki ?

— Non, Majesté. Elle a péri de sa propre main le quatrième jour du siège. Elle a également mis à mort ses deux filles et son fils, ou bien les a fait exécuter. Nous les avons trouvés gisant tous ensemble dans ses appartements. »

Tamìr ne doutait pas un instant qu'il s'en serait chargé lui-même en cas de nécessité, mais elle fut secrètement soulagée qu'il n'ait pas eu à le faire. En tout état de cause, Alna lui avait épargné à elle-même les affres d'une exécution.

« Dépêchez des hérauts diffuser la nouvelle dans chaque ville et chaque fief, ordonna-t-elle. Veillez à ce que les crieurs de toutes cités répandent le message. Je me suis montrée miséricordieuse envers ceux qui m'ont donné leur foi. La félonne n'a pas été épargnée. Lord Kirothius, agréez mes remerciements et l'expression de la gratitude du pays. Je vous accorde solennellement l'ensemble des domaines de Lady Alna, en l'honneur de votre première victoire sous votre propre bannière. »

Elle se sourit à elle-même lorsque Ki s'inclina derechef. Sa décision ne pouvait susciter aucune espèce de murmures. Il en allait ainsi des dépouilles de guerre.

En revanche, ce fut de Ki lui-même que vinrent les doléances, dès qu'ils eurent pris place côte à côte pour le festin de cette nuit-là.

« Tu n'avais pas à faire un truc pareil, ronchonna-t-il. Tu m'as déjà suffisamment fait ployer sous les terres et les rentes, et ce sans parler du titre.

— Et maintenant, tu possèdes en propre des hommes d'armes et des cavaliers dans lesquels puiser, la prochaine fois que j'aurai besoin de toi, lui riposta-t-elle allégrement. Terminé pour vous, messire, les brocards sur le "chevalier de merde" ! »

Ki se croisa les bras, reconnaissant par là sa

déconfiture. « Aussi longtemps du moins que tu me laisseras me battre de nouveau, je suppose que je pourrai tenir le coup sous la contrainte.

— Donnez-nous des détails sur votre premier commandement ! le pressa Una. Et vous aussi, Lynx. Ça vous fait quoi, d'être le capitaine de Ki ?

— Il appartient à Ki de raconter sa propre histoire », se récusa modestement Lynx, mais Tamìr aperçut son écuyer qui, debout près du seuil des cuisines, entretenait Lorin et Hylia d'un air emballé.

« Je le forcerai à vous parler de son propre rôle, rassurez-vous ! » Ki se mit à rire. « Lui et le capitaine Grannia m'ont comblé d'orgueil.

— Peut-être, mais c'était toi qui étais en première ligne, et à chaque pas », signala Lynx.

Tamìr scruta le visage de Ki pendant qu'il se livrait au récit minutieux des combats. La place s'était révélée de première force et bien préparée pour soutenir un siège. Ki décrivit les opérations en utilisant des morceaux de pain et des assiettes pour les illustrer. Il se gardait de toute fanfaronnade personnelle en évoquant les choses, et ne s'y attribuait que fort peu de mérite. Il se rembrunit, cependant, lorsqu'il aborda finalement l'épisode de la découverte des corps d'Alna et des siens.

« C'était tout aussi bien comme ça pour elle, commenta Grannia de sa place à la table basse. Il est plus honorable de finir ainsi que de se voir pendu comme traître.

— Je n'aurais pas fait de mal à ses enfants », déclara tristement Tamìr.

Lorsque Ki et les Compagnons la reconduisirent à sa chambre, ce même soir, elle eut le sentiment que les divers courtisans qu'ils croisèrent en chemin le considéraient d'un air plus respectueux qu'ils ne l'avaient fait jusqu'alors. Elle n'en remarqua pas moins les mines curieuses qu'elle suscitait en l'invitant à pénétrer dans ses appartements.

Ils se regardèrent l'un l'autre pendant un moment. Ces semaines de séparation ne semblaient avoir eu d'autre effet que de renforcer leur embarras mutuel. Avec un soupir, Tamìr le serra dans ses bras et il lui rendit son étreinte, mais cela fut bref, et ils s'empressèrent de gagner la table à jeu près de la fenêtre.

« Ainsi donc, tu as maintenant reçu le baptême du sang en qualité de commandant, dit-elle en jouant avec un pion sculpté. Quelle impression cela fait-il ? »

Ki sourit tout en faisant courir un doigt sur les lignes de l'échiquier. « Je n'ai pas pris de plaisir à me battre sans toi, là-bas, mais à part ça... » Il lui adressa un grand sourire, l'œil de nouveau chaleureux. « Merci.

— Je suis désolée pour Alna. »

Il acquiesça d'un hochement chagrin. « Ce n'était pas un bien joli spectacle. Les enfants avaient la gorge tranchée. Je me demande si la forteresse sera désormais hantée.

— C'est probable, avec ce genre de morts-là.

— Eh bien, je n'ai pas du tout l'intention d'y vivre. Tu ne vas pas m'y forcer, n'est-ce pas ?

— Non, je te veux ici », répondit-elle, avant de se maudire pour sa rougeur soudaine. « Mais à présent que tu es de retour, sans bataille à livrer, ne vas-tu pas en avoir par-dessus la tête ? »

Il produisit sa bourse à pierres de bakshi, la secoua pour la faire tinter en guise de défi et repartit : « Il y a d'autres sortes de batailles auxquelles nous pouvons nous livrer ici. Et maintenant, j'ai de l'or à moi pour miser. »

Ils disputèrent une demi-douzaine de parties sans vraiment se soucier de savoir qui gagnait ou perdait puis, celles-ci terminées, Ki se leva pour prendre congé. Tout en tripotant nerveusement sa bourse à pierres, il dit : « Je pensais sincèrement ce que je t'ai confié, à propos du malaise que j'éprouvais à me battre sans toi. » Il se pencha vers elle et lui déposa un baiser hâtif sur la joue.

Elle demeura quelque temps assise à sa place, les doigts pressés sur l'endroit de sa joue qu'il avait touché de ses lèvres, à s'interroger sur ce qu'il fallait penser de son geste et à s'efforcer de ne pas s'aban-donner à des espérances fallacieuses.

3

Nyrin avait surpris les coups d'œil furtifs jetés par Nalia du haut de son balcon le soir des flagellations, et il était enchanté de constater à quel point ce spec-tacle l'avait effarouchée. Elle s'était montrée depuis d'une extrême apathie. Même Korin en avait fait la remarque.

Elle n'avait pas encore perdu toute énergie la première fois où ce dernier était arrivé chez elle. Sa haine et sa colère avaient été palpables, tout autant que son désespoir. Nyrin s'en était alarmé au point de fourbir un sortilège sur le balcon et les fenêtres pour lui interdire de se précipiter dans le vide.

Le temps et les attentions de Korin l'avaient calmée, et la vision de la justice implacable de son époux semblait avoir abattu ses dernières résistances. Elle se montrait soumise à table et pendant ses promenades vespérales sur les remparts. Nyrin veillait méticuleusement à lui faire passer en revue les têtes des traîtres qui s'y trouvaient exposées. La seule manquante était celle de l'individu qui, quel qu'il fût, avait laissé s'échapper Caliel et ses acolytes.

Cependant, Korin devenait, lui, de plus en plus difficile à manipuler. La boisson prélevait son péage, et Alben et Urmanis se révélaient impuissants à l'arrêter de se soûler. Au pire de sa forme, Korin était tour à tour morose et fébrile. La trahison de ses Compagnons l'avait profondément affecté ; Nyrin s'était minutieusement employé à envenimer cette blessure à ses propres fins. Il avait fallu dresser plusieurs nouveaux gibets en dehors des murs de la forteresse. Les cadavres qui s'y boursouflaient servaient à rafraîchir efficacement la mémoire de tout un chacun.

Ce que Nyrin était en revanche incapable de maîtriser, c'était la soif de bataille qui tenaillait les alliés de Korin, soif qui ne fit que s'accroître lorsque des espions rapportèrent que Tobin avait envoyé son armée contre certains des nobles qui refusaient de reconnaître ses prétentions, et que ses généraux remportaient succès après succès.

Les chefs militaires de Korin ne furent pas en reste lorsqu'on leur lâcha la bride contre une poignée de lords secondaires qui s'opposaient à lui. Certains se battaient pour l'honneur du roi, mais un plus grand nombre ne le faisaient que dans la perspective de dépouilles éventuelles. Le partage des terres et de l'or saisis de la sorte n'allait pas sans grincements de dents, cependant Korin avait une armée à solder et des hommes à nourrir. Les impôts du nord affluaient à Cirna mais, faute de trésor royal où puiser, Korin se taillait la part du lion dans l'ensemble des prises de guerre.

Un soir qu'il feuilletait les dépêches du jour dans ses appartements, Nyrin y repéra un petit nombre de noms familiers. Lord Jorvaï se trouvait avec Tobin à Atyion, et les forces qu'il avait laissées sur ses terres ne faisaient pas le poids face au duc Wethring et à son armée. La forteresse et la ville avaient été passées à la torche et les champs incendiés.

Nevus assiégeait actuellement une place de moindre taille. Il s'agissait en fait d'un petit fort misérable dans les collines appelé Rilmar, mais Nyrin sourit en lisant le nom du vieux chevalier qui le défendait : sieur Larenth, Maréchal des Routes.

« Oh là là ! » s'exclama-t-il avec un sourire en coin, tout en exhibant le rapport sous le nez de Moriel.

« M'est avis qu'il s'agit là de la famille du jeune Ki, n'est-ce pas ? »

Le sourire triomphant du Crapaud valait son pesant de poison. « Oui, messire. Le roi Erius a précisément concédé ces terres à son père en guise de faveur au prince Tobin.

— Eh bien, dans ce cas, il n'est que justice que le fils du roi les récupère. »

Auparavant, Korin s'était laissé aller à une nostalgie momentanée sur ce chapitre. « Père avait expédié les Compagnons là-bas pour que nous y fassions nos premières armes contre des bandits. Sieur Larenth s'était brillamment illustré au combat dans son temps, et il fut dans son genre un hôte accueillant.

— On lui a offert des conditions, Sire, et il a refusé dans les termes les plus colorés, lui assura maître Porion.

— Vous ne sauriez vous permettre de faire grâce à ces gens-là, pas plus qu'il ne vous était possible de le faire à ces Compagnons rebelles. Les faux amis font les plus âpres ennemis », lui remémora Nyrin.

En dépit de cela, le magicien surprit un éclair de culpabilité dans les yeux de Korin et traqua celle-ci en se faufilant mine de rien dans la mémoire du jeune homme. Elle recelait de la honte, celle d'une défaillance concernant Rilmar. En cachette, les doigts crochus de Nyrin tramèrent un sortilège qui attisa la douleur des souvenirs enfouis.

« Vous avez raison, bien évidemment, chuchota Korin en se frottant les yeux. Il ne peut y avoir de miséricorde pour les rebelles, en aucun cas. » Il convoqua un héraut. « Allez trouver Lord Nevus. Dites-lui que je veux lui voir épargner les filles qui ne sont pas entraînées au maniement des armes et les petits enfants. Pour tous les autres, pendaison. »

« Regardez là-bas », dit Korin tandis qu'ils se promenaient plus tard, ce soir-là, sur le chemin de ronde, le doigt tendu vers la constellation qui planait à l'est juste au-dessus de l'horizon, « Voilà le Chasseur. L'été est en passe de s'achever, et je me planque encore ici, ligoté par des flux d'entrailles ! Par la Flamme, c'est comme si je ne servais à rien d'autre qu'à obtenir des mioches d'une bonne femme !

— Ce n'est pourtant pas faute d'essayer, hein ? » Alben se mit à glousser. « Tu es assez souvent là-haut. J'espère pour toi qu'elle n'est pas stérile...

— Messire ! » Nyrin conjura d'un signe la malchance. « Les femmes de sa famille ont la réputation de s'enflammer lentement, mais de porter des enfants sains, et elles ont tendance à faire des filles. »

Korin soupira. « Je dois absolument affronter Tobin sur le champ de bataille avant que ne survienne la neige et le vaincre une fois pour toutes ! »

Encore un peu de patience, mon roi, songea Nyrin. D'après la vieille Tamara, Nalia avait du mal à garder son petit déjeuner.

4

La nouvelle des agissements de Tamìr contre les nobles récalcitrants se propagea comme une traînée de poudre, et la noblesse du bas comme du haut de la côte commença à expédier des hérauts porteurs de missives conciliatoires. Les puissants seigneurs du nord et quelques-uns de l'ouest demeurèrent néanmoins iné-branlables dans leur soutien à Korin. Jorvaï avait été l'un des rares de cette région à prendre le parti de la reine. D'après ce que rapportaient les espions de Tamìr et les magiciens d'Arkoniel, Korin s'obstinait toujours à ne pas bouger de Cirna.

Elle ne savait trop que déduire du comportement de son cousin. À sa place, avec à sa disposition des forces supérieures, elle se serait depuis longtemps mise en marche, et pourtant on ne relevait toujours pas le moindre indice de mouvement. L'opinion de Ki était que Korin avait peur de se battre, mais Tamìr ne démordait pas de son sentiment qu'il devait y avoir quelque anguille sous roche.

Dans tous les cas, ils jouissaient à présent d'une période de paix relative, et Imonus saisit cette oppor-tunité pour presser Tamìr une fois de plus de se rendre à Afra.

« Il est temps, Majesté. À défaut d'autre chose, il faut que l'on vous voie honorer l'Illuminateur comme vos ancêtres l'ont toujours fait.

— Il a raison, vous savez, abonda Illardi. Chaque

nouvelle reine y est allée et en a rapporté une prophétie pour le peuple. »

Tamìr n'avait pas besoin de se laisser convaincre. Elle en avait jusque-là de la vie de cour, et puisqu'il ne lui était décidément pas possible de livrer une bataille, alors la perspective d'un voyage avait de quoi la séduire.

Sur les conseils d'Imonus, elle fixa la date de leur départ pour la première semaine de Lenthin. Cela les amènerait à Afra pendant le premier quartier de la lune – époque éminemment propice, à en croire les prêtres.

Il n'était pas question de se faire accompagner de troupes considérables. Le sanctuaire se trouvait à une grande altitude dans les montagnes à l'ouest d'Ylani, et l'on n'y accédait que par une seule route des plus tortueuse et qui, selon Imonus et Iya, était à peine assez large à certains endroits pour livrer passage à un seul cavalier de front.

« Les lieux sont un territoire sacré. Nyrin en personne n'oserait pas les profaner en vous y attaquant, lui assura Imonus. Et personne ne consentirait à suivre Korin s'il commettait semblable sacrilège.

— J'espère que vous ne vous trompez pas, dit Tharin. Néanmoins, elle doit emmener une garde suffisante pour assurer sa protection sur la route.

— Ma garde personnelle devrait suffire, surtout alors avec Iya et Arkoniel, déclara Tamìr. Avec un peu de chance, je serai de retour avant que les espions de Korin n'aient seulement pu l'informer que j'étais partie.

— Saruel a demandé à être des nôtres, intervint Iya. Les Aurënfaïes éprouvent le plus grand respect pour l'Oracle, et elle aimerait visiter le temple.

— Je me fais une joie de l'emmener, répondit Tamìr. Elle est l'une de vos collègues les plus puissantes, n'est-ce pas ? Je me sentirai d'autant plus en sécurité qu'elle se trouvera là. »

La nuit précédant leur départ, Tamìr fut trop agitée pour dormir. Elle s'attarda longuement à jouer avec Ki et Una puis, assise près de la fenêtre pendant qu'ils disputaient la finale, regarda se lever la dernière demi-lune en plein déclin tout en tiraillant machinalement l'une de ses nattes. Una finit par remporter la victoire et prit congé d'eux, brûlant déjà d'impatience de se retrouver en route le lendemain.

« Que se passe-t-il ? Je m'attendais à ce que tu meures d'envie de partir, observa Ki pendant qu'il raflait leurs pierres de bakshi pour les faire réintégrer leurs bourses respectives et rangeait l'échiquier de bois.

— C'est le cas.

— Eh bien ! pour quelqu'un qui fait montre avant la bataille d'un sang-froid plus glacial que les eaux printanières, voici qu'une balade de rien du tout a l'air de te mettre les nerfs épouvantablement à vif... Ce sont les illiorains qui te flanquent la frousse ? À moi oui, je le reconnais. »

Elle se retourna et s'aperçut qu'il lui souriait à belles dents. « Arrête de me taquiner. Ce n'est pas toi, le dieu-touché. C'était angoissant, la vision que j'ai eue ! Je vais avoir affaire à l'Oracle le plus prodigieux du pays...

— Et qui pourrait être plus en sécurité que toi, là-bas ? contra-t-il. Allons, il y a quelque chose d'autre, pas vrai ?

— Et si ce qu'elle me dit n'est pas à mon goût ? Si j'apprends que je suis vouée à l'échec ou à devenir folle comme le reste de ma famille ou encore... je ne sais quoi ?

— Et ?

— Et Frère. Il n'arrête pas de me harceler à propos de sa mort. Je veux connaître la vérité, mais j'en ai peur aussi. Je n'arrive pas à l'expliquer, Ki. C'est une impression viscérale, ni plus ni moins.

— Qu'est-ce qui t'effraie le plus des deux ? Qu'il ne s'en aille pas une fois que tu lui auras donné satisfaction, ou justement qu'il s'en aille ?

— Je veux qu'il s'en aille. Seulement, je ne sais pas si je serai capable de lui donner le prix de son départ. »

Ils partirent le lendemain à la première heure et traversèrent au trot la ville endormie. Tamìr éprouva une vive bouffée d'exaltation quand la grand-route du sud s'étira longuement devant eux. Ce sentiment ne tenait pas simplement à la perspective de rencontrer finalement l'Oracle qui avait joué un rôle aussi décisif dans son existence. Le fait de chevaucher au triple galop devant des cavaliers armés était l'une des sensations les plus merveilleuses qu'elle connût.

Laïn, le plus jeune des religieux d'Afra qui étaient venus la rejoindre au nord avec Imonus, chevauchait en tête avec elle en qualité de guide, encore que le trajet fût tout aussi familier à Iya et à Arkoniel. Comme il était un être du genre effacé, Tamìr ne lui avait guère prêté d'attention jusqu'alors, mais il rayonnait littéralement aujourd'hui.

« C'est un immense honneur, Majesté, que de conduire une nouvelle reine à Afra. Je prie pour que vous y receviez une réponse limpide et du réconfort.

— Moi aussi », répondit-elle.

Arkoniel avait emmené Wythnir avec lui, et le gamin, vêtu d'une belle tunique neuve et chaussé de bottes, montait fièrement un poney personnel. Sa tenue le faisait paraître plus âgé. Les magiciens ne se quittaient guère, et le petit avait beau parler peu, selon sa coutume, Tamìr voyait clairement qu'il s'imprégnait de chacun des mots que prononçait son maître. Il supportait les longues heures passées à cheval sans l'ombre d'une plainte, manifestement ravi de se trouver auprès d'Arkoniel plutôt que de s'être vu délaisser une fois de plus.

Ils couchèrent à Ero la seconde nuit, et le lendemain l'intendant d'Illardi fit avec orgueil à Tamìr les honneurs de la nouvelle ville qui poussait le long de la rive nord de la rade. Bien des gens vivaient encore sous des tentes et sous des abris de fortune, mais il y avait de toutes parts des hommes à l'ouvrage, qui charroyant des pierres, qui s'échinant à monter des charpentes de maisons neuves. L'atmosphère embaumait la chaux et la sciure de bois. Tamìr multiplia les haltes afin d'observer le travail des divers corps de métier.

Arkoniel sourit en la voyant s'attarder à regarder un sculpteur sur bois s'activer sur un linteau ornemental. « Vous arrive-t-il jamais de souhaiter être plutôt née dans une famille d'artisans ?

— Parfois. J'ai perdu tous mes outils de ciselure et n'ai pas eu le temps de trouver à les remplacer. »

Arkoniel fouilla dans son escarcelle et lui tendit une petite boule de cire d'abeille fraîche. » Ceci fera-t-il l'affaire, pour l'instant ? Vous aviez l'habitude d'en porter toujours avec vous. »

Elle s'épanouit, Arkoniel avait été l'un des tout premiers à reconnaître et à encourager ses dons.

Mais pas le premier.

Le parfum suave lui remit en mémoire quelques précieux moments de paix avec sa mère – l'un des rares sourires qu'avait eus sa mère pendant qu'elle réchauffait un brin de cire entre ses mains. *Elle sent les fleurs et le soleil, n'est-ce pas ? Les abeilles la stockent tout l'été pour nous dans leurs maisons de cire.*

Le picotement de larmes derrière ses paupières la stupéfia. Tamìr avait si peu de bons souvenirs d'elle... Son regard s'abaissa vers le profil serein gravé sur sa bague, et elle se demanda ce que penserait Ariani de la voir sous sa forme véritable. L'aimerait-elle enfin, l'aimerait-elle autant qu'elle avait aimé Frère ? Les aurait-elle aimés tous les deux, et la démence lui aurait-elle été épargnée si Frère avait vécu ?

Elle secoua ces pensées douces-amères et poursuivit sa course en espérant qu'Arkoniel et les autres ne s'étaient pas avisés de sa faiblesse.

Après avoir bientôt délaissé la route du bord de mer, ils piquèrent vers le sud et l'ouest au cours des quelques journées suivantes en direction des montagnes. C'était en l'occurrence le trajet qu'elle avait précisément emprunté pour se rendre à Ero la première fois. Elle échangea sans mot dire un regard nostalgique avec Ki lorsqu'ils traversèrent le carrefour qui leur aurait permis de gagner le fort de Bierfût. Qui savait quand ils auraient le loisir d'y aller de nouveau ? Sa vieille nourrice, Nari, lui écrivait souvent, elle ne manquait jamais de répondre, mais sans pouvoir promettre de visite.

Une fois dépassée la route de Bierfût, Laïn leur fit suivre des voies secondaires qui évitaient les plus grosses villes et menaient invariablement vers l'intérieur. De modestes auberges établies sur les bas-côtés les hébergèrent durant les premières nuits, et les gens l'y accueillirent avec respect, l'œil agrandi par la stupeur, surtout quand leur nouvelle reine se contenta de dîner en leur compagnie dans la salle commune. Au cours de la soirée, elle entonnait autour du feu des chansons avec les Compagnons, tandis qu'Iya et Arkoniel divertissaient l'assistance avec des tours de magie simples et colorés, non sans tramer quelques raccommodages en faveur de ceux qui osaient les en prier.

En retour, les villages entretinrent Tamìr des récoltes et du banditisme. L'impudence de canailles de toutes sortes n'avait fait que croître et fleurir depuis la chute d'Ero. Tamìr expédia une estafette enjoindre à Illardi de dépêcher certains de leurs guerriers désœuvrés pour se mettre en chasse et régler leur compte aux brigands.

L'immense chaîne montagneuse qui constituait l'épine dorsale de la péninsule skalienne se rapprochait, toujours plus impressionnante, de jour en jour, ses cimes déchiquetées encore encapuchonnées de neige.

L'après-midi du septième jour, Laïn leur fit prendre une route plus fréquentée qui conduisait à l'intérieur du massif. La forêt à verdure persistante céda graduellement la place à des boqueteaux plus clairsemés de trembles et de chênes.

Le chemin se fit plus abrupt et se mit à sinuer, les contraignant à brider leurs chevaux pour les mettre au pas. L'air fraîchit progressivement autour d'eux, chargé d'effluves de plantes que Tamïr ne reconnut pas. Des arbres rabougris, tordus par le vent, s'accrochaient aux versants rocheux, et des mousses coriaces ainsi que de menues plantes bordaient la chaussée. Alors que l'été régnait encore à Atyion, l'atmosphère, ici, laissait subodorer des prémices automnales, et le feuillage des trembles commençait à se lisérer d'or. À des hauteurs incommensurables, les pics couronnés de neige brillaient contre la clarté de l'azur d'un éclat à vous blesser les yeux.

« Cela me rappelle mon chez-moi. Beaucoup de ces plantes y sont identiques, observa Saruel qui chevauchait aux côtés de Tamïr.

— Vous êtes originaire des montagnes ?

— Oui. Dans mon enfance, je ne voyais de terrain

plat que lorsque nous faisions le voyage de Sarikali pour les assemblées de clans. » Elle aspira une grande goulée d'air, et le fin réseau noir qui entourait ses yeux se distendit et se plissa lorsqu'elle sourit. « Ces parfums m'ont manqué, de même que la fraîcheur. J'ai pris grand plaisir à mon séjour dans votre capitale, mais c'était très différent de ce à quoi je suis accoutumée. »

Tharin émit un gloussement. « Ero la puante. Pour parler franc, elle était loin d'usurper son qualificatif, voilà qui est sûr.

— Je comprends. J'ai grandi dans les montagnes, moi aussi, dit Tamìr.

— On jurerait l'une de nos parties de chasse, n'est-ce pas, Tharin ? » Au même instant, quelque chose attira le regard de Ki, et il se courba périlleusement sur sa selle pour cueillir une fleur dans une touffe de corolles mauves en forme de clochettes qui poussait sur la paroi de la falaise. Les genoux serrés sur les flancs de sa monture pour conserver un équilibre précaire, il parvint à ses fins et offrit en souriant sa conquête à Tamìr. « Regarde. Une pensée sauvage, pour te rappeler de meilleurs souvenirs. »

Tamìr la huma, savoura sa senteur capiteuse et familière, puis elle se la planta derrière l'oreille. Ki n'avait jamais rien fait de pareil jusque-là. Ce constat lui fit battre le cœur d'une ivresse inconnue, et elle poussa son cheval au trot pour empêcher les autres de surprendre sa rougeur subite.

Ils campèrent au bord d'un torrent dans une haute vallée battue par le vent, cette nuit-là. Sur le velours du firmament, les étoiles avaient l'air énorme, exactement comme à Bierfût jadis, et elles étincelaient si vivement qu'elles donnaient à la neige des pics l'aspect de l'argent.

Saruel et Laïn ramassèrent de conserve des poignées de petites baies bleues et leur en concoctèrent une agréable infusion résineuse.

« La plupart d'entre vous n'avez jamais voyagé dans des cols aussi élevés. L'air se raréfie au fur et à mesure que nous grimpons, expliqua le prêtre. Il y a des personnes à qui ce phénomène procure une sensation de malaise oppressante, mais ce breuvage les soulagera. »

Tamïr n'avait rien éprouvé jusque-là de ces effets indésirables, mais Nikidès, Una et les nouveaux écuyers reconnurent avoir souffert d'un vague vertige vers la fin de la journée.

Dans ces parages, les chouettes étaient nombreuses et plus grandes que celles des basses terres, leurs têtes rondes s'ornaient de touffes de plumes semblables à des oreilles de chat, et l'extrémité de leurs rectrices arborait des bandes d'une blancheur éblouissante. Ki découvrit quelques échantillons de leur plumage accrochés aux buissons d'ajoncs qui environnaient le camp, et il les donna à Tamïr. Elle en jeta une pincée dans le feu tout en murmurant une prière propitiatoire.

Ils couchèrent à même le sol, enveloppés dans leurs manteaux et leurs couvertures, et découvrirent à leur

réveil la vallée plongée dans une brume dense et glaciale qui tapissait leur chevelure et la robe de leurs
chevaux de gouttelettes scintillantes comme des
joyaux. Les bruits portaient de façon bizarre. Tamìr
pouvait à peine entendre la conversation de ceux qui
se tenaient à l'autre bout du campement, mais les
coups de bec répétés d'un pivert sonnaient à ses
oreilles aussi nettement que s'il était perché sur son
épaule.

Après un petit déjeuner froid et une nouvelle rasade
de l'infusion de Saruel, ils reprirent leur route en
menant leurs montures par la bride jusqu'à ce que la
brume se soit éclaircie.

Les crêtes se reployèrent tout autour d'eux, et le
chemin se resserra. Sur leur droite, la paroi rocheuse
les surplombait, à pic, et elle faisait même saillie par
intermittence au-dessus du maigre sentier, de sorte
qu'ils étaient souvent obligés de baisser la tête et
d'adopter en selle des postures de biais scabreuses
pendant qu'ils chevauchaient à la queue leu leu derrière le prêtre et les magiciens. Sur leur gauche
s'ouvrait un précipice dont la chute vertigineuse se
perdait au sein des nappes persistantes du brouillard.
Tamìr lança une pierre par-dessus le bord mais elle ne
l'entendit jamais frapper le fond du gouffre.

L'après-midi commençait à décliner quand Tamìr
remarqua les premiers croissants de lune et les bribes
d'inscriptions éraflant la nudité de la paroi rocheuse
qui commémoraient le passage de générations de
voyageurs et de pèlerins.

« Nous approchons, lui dit Iya pendant qu'ils

laissaient leurs montures se reposer et brouter l'herbe clairsemée qui poussait sur les bords du chemin. Quelques heures encore, et nous parviendrons à la porte peinte qui vous est apparue dans votre vision. Afra se trouve juste au-delà. »

Arkoniel se livra à un examen minutieux des inscriptions lorsqu'ils se remirent en route. Tout à coup, il tira sur les rênes pour immobiliser son cheval et pointa un doigt vers l'une d'entre elles. « Regardez, Iya, voici la prière que j'ai tracée la première fois que vous m'avez amené ici.

— Je me rappelle, fit-elle avec un sourire. Je dois avoir laissé quelque part dans le coin des marques de mes divers passages, moi aussi.

— Pourquoi faites-vous cela ? demanda Saruel.

— La coutume, je suppose. Et pour la bonne fortune, aussi, répondit Iya.

— N'est-ce pas là ce que les gens disent toujours à propos de ce genre de trucs ? » lança Lynx, qui demeurait un inflexible adepte de Sakor, en dépit de tout ce qu'il avait vu.

« Vous feriez bien de ne pas vous gausser des dévotions des illiorains, mon jeune sire, dit Laïn qui avait entendu par hasard. Ces prières durent infiniment plus longtemps qu'aucun charme livré aux flammes. Il ne faudrait pas plus les prendre à la légère que les faire à l'étourdie. » Il pivota sur sa selle. « Vous devriez écrire quelque chose, reine Tamìr. Toutes vos aïeules l'ont fait, quelque part, le long de cette route. »

C'était là une pensée réconfortante et qui lui donna,

une fois de plus, le sentiment d'être reliée à la lignée des femmes qui l'avaient précédée.

Tout le monde mit pied à terre et s'éparpilla en quête de cailloux pointus permettant de griffonner ses nom et message respectifs.

Saruel fit comme les autres mais, contrairement à eux, se borna à passer sa main sur la pierre. Y apparurent un petit croissant d'argent et des mots d'une belle graphie. « C'est une bonne chose que d'honorer l'Illuminateur sur le chemin qui mène à son sanctuaire sacré, murmura-t-elle en regardant d'un air approbateur le jeune écuyer de Lynx tracer sa propre marque. Vous avez du sang 'faïe en vous, Tyrien í Rothus, ajouta-t-elle. La couleur de vos yeux suffit à me le révéler.

— C'est ce que m'a dit ma grand-mère, mais comme cela remonte très loin, je ne peux pas en avoir beaucoup », répondit le garçon, ses prunelles grises tout illuminées par le plaisir qu'elle l'ait néanmoins remarqué. « Je n'ai rien d'un magicien, de toute manière.

— La quantité ne fait rien à l'affaire, c'est le lignage qui importe, et même cela n'est pas une garantie », l'informa Iya, qui avait surpris leur échange. « Une bonne chose aussi. Si chacun des Skaliens qui possède une goutte de sang 'faïe dans les veines était magicien-né, les guerriers n'auraient pas grand-chose à faire.

— Est-ce que tes parents étaient des mages ? » demanda Saruel à Wythnir, qui était en train de tracer sa marque à peu de distance plus loin.

« Je ne le sais pas, répondit doucement l'enfant. J'étais encore tout petit quand ils m'ont vendu. »

C'était plus que Tamìr ne l'avait jamais entendu dire d'une seule traite, et la plus grande confidence qu'il eût jamais faite. Elle sourit en voyant la manière dont la main d'Arkoniel se posait sur l'épaule de son disciple et le regard d'adoration que cela lui valut. Elle se surprit à déplorer de ne pas l'avoir mieux traité quand elle était enfant. Il s'était montré tout aussi attentionné vis-à-vis d'elle, à cette époque comme maintenant. Il était son ami.

Interroge Arkoniel ! Le malaise causé par le défi de Frère la glaçait encore.

Elle écarta cette idée en en repoussant l'examen à plus tard et attacha son regard sur la portion de paroi plate qu'elle avait choisie, on ne peut plus perplexe quant à ce qu'elle devrait y inscrire. Finalement, elle l'égratigna simplement d'un « Reine Tamìr II, fille d'Ariani, pour Skala, par la volonté d'Illior ». Dessous, elle ajouta un petit croissant de lune, puis elle transmit à Ki le caillou qu'elle venait d'utiliser en guise de burin.

Il se pencha près d'elle et grava son nom et un croissant de lune en dessous des siens puis entoura d'un cercle leurs deux signatures.

« Pourquoi as-tu fait cela ? » s'enquit-elle.

Ce fut au tour de Ki de rougir quand il répondit tout bas. « Pour demander à l'Illuminateur de nous garder ensemble. C'était ma prière. »

Sur ces entrefaites, il s'éloigna bien vite et s'affaira à contrôler la sous-ventrière de son cheval. Tamìr soupira intérieurement. D'abord la fleur, et maintenant ceci, mais sans cesser de conserver ses distances. Autrefois, elle s'était imaginé qu'elle connaissait son cœur jusqu'en son tréfonds. À présent, elle n'avait pas la moindre idée de ce qu'il recelait, et elle avait peur d'espérer.

Le soleil était en train de sombrer derrière les montagnes lorsque, au détour d'un virage, Tamìr fut frappée par un sentiment vertigineux de familiarité.

Le paysage qui se déroulait devant elle était la réplique exacte de celui que lui avait dévoilé sa vision d'Ero. Les méandres du petit sentier se perdaient d'abord de vue pour reparaître dans le lointain, là où se dressait de manière déconcertante la porte qui l'enjambait, peinte de couleurs vives et rutilantes dans les derniers feux du jour. Tamìr avait beau savoir que son existence était bel et bien réelle, celle-ci persistait à lui donner l'impression d'être quelque peu issue d'un rêve. Tandis qu'on s'en rapprochait, elle distingua des dragons stylisés qui, réalisés en tons presque criards de rouge, de bleu et d'or, se jumelaient autour de l'étroite ouverture comme s'ils étaient vivants et défendaient le passage sacré, tous crocs dehors et crachant le feu.

« La Serrure d'Illior.

— Magnifique, non ? dit Arkoniel. Est-ce que vous en reconnaissez le style ?

— J'ai vu des ornements de ce genre dans le Palais Vieux. Cela fait des siècles qu'ils ont été exécutés. Depuis combien de temps se trouve-t-elle ici ?

— Au moins aussi longtemps, mais elle n'est que

la plus récente, dit Iya. D'autres l'ont précédée, qui, tombées en ruine, ont été successivement remplacées. À en croire la légende, une porte se dressait déjà là quand, à la suite d'une vision, les premiers prêtres de Skala s'aventurèrent jusqu'au site sacré. Nul ne sait qui construisit la première porte ni pour quelle raison.

— On nous enseigne que ce fut un dragon qui édifia la porte originelle avec les pierres de la montagne, afin de garder la caverne inviolable d'Illior, les informa Laïn.

— Mon peuple raconte la même histoire au sujet de nos sanctuaires personnels, intervint Saruel. Bien entendu, des dragons continuent à réaliser des choses analogues à Aurënen.

— Il arrive quelquefois que l'on découvre des os de dragons dans les vallées supérieures. De temps à autre, nous tombons même au sanctuaire sur des spécimens minuscules. » Laïn se retourna pour s'adresser aux autres. « Autant que je vous en prévienne, s'il advenait que l'un d'entre vous aperçoive ce qui ressemble à un petit lézard ailé, respectez-le comme il se doit et gardez-vous de le toucher. Les dragons miniatures eux-mêmes font de bien vilaines morsures.

— Des dragons ? » Les yeux de Wythnir s'éclairèrent d'une exaltation puérile.

« Mais minuscules, et il est très rare de les voir », lui répondit le religieux.

Il leur fallut démonter devant la porte et se faire suivre de leurs chevaux le long d'une sente rocheuse des plus exiguë. Afra se trouvait en haut d'un défilé qui n'était guère qu'une faille, à moins d'un mille à peu près par-delà. Celle-ci finit par déboucher sur une espèce de combe profonde et stérile. Elle était déjà plongée dans l'ombre, mais plusieurs prêtres à robe rouge et une poignée de jeunes garçons et de jeunes filles portant des torches les y attendaient. Derrière eux, la piste en zigzag s'enfonçait dans les ténèbres.

Ki huma l'air, où flottaient des odeurs de cuisine. « J'espère qu'ils nous ont mis de côté de quoi dîner. Mon ventre a l'impression qu'on m'a tranché la gorge.

— Bienvenue à la reine Tamìr II ! s'égosilla le prêtre de tête en s'inclinant bien bas avec sa torche. Je suis Ralinus, grand prêtre d'Afra en l'absence d'Imonus. Au nom de l'Oracle, permettez-moi de vous accueillir. Voilà longtemps qu'elle est à l'affût de votre visite. Louée soyez-vous, élue de l'Illuminateur !

— Est-ce qu'Imonus vous avait envoyé un message ? demanda Tamìr.

— Il n'a pas eu à le faire, Majesté. Nous savions. » Il s'inclina ensuite devant Iya. « L'Oracle m'ordonne de vous souhaiter aussi la bienvenue, Maîtresse Iya. Vous avez été d'une fidélité exemplaire depuis toutes ces années pour accomplir la tâche ardue qui vous était impartie. »

S'avisant alors de la présence de Saruel, il étendit ses paumes tatouées en signe d'accueil. « Et bienvenue à vous, fille d'Aura. Puissiez-vous être de tout cœur avec nous, ici, dans la demeure de l'Illuminateur.

— Dans les ténèbres et dans la Lumière, répondit-elle avec un hochement de tête respectueux.

— Des logements ont été préparés pour vous, ainsi

qu'un repas. Et voici qui est on ne peut plus providentiel, Majesté : une délégation d'Aurënfaïes est arrivée voilà trois jours et attend votre venue à la maison des hôtes en face des quartiers qui sont réservés à vos propres gens.

— Des Aurënfaïes ? » Tamìr décocha un regard soupçonneux en direction d'Iya et de Saruel. « Est-ce de votre fait ?

— Non, je n'ai pas eu le moindre contact avec qui que ce soit de là-bas, lui assura Saruel.

— Moi non plus », affirma Iya, malgré le plaisir évident que lui causait la nouvelle. « Je pensais toutefois que certains d'entre eux pourraient effectivement se manifester, dans un endroit ou dans un autre. »

Les porteurs de torches les débarrassèrent de leurs chevaux et les guidèrent pour contourner le dernier virage du chemin.

Coincée dans une crevasse plus profonde entre deux pics impressionnants, Afra n'était rien d'autre au premier coup d'œil qu'une étrange configuration de fenêtres et de portes profondément taillées dans les falaises de part et d'autre d'une modeste place pavée. Celle-ci était entourée de hautes torches fichées dans des cavités de la roche. D'un style analogue aux ornementations de la Serrure d'Illior, des espèces de découpures et de pilastres sculptés selon des motifs fort anciens encadraient toutes les ouvertures, nota machinalement Tamìr.

Mais ce qui captiva toute son attention sur le moment, ce fut la stèle de pierre rouge sombre qui se dressait au centre de la place, brillamment illuminée par les deux braseros qui la flanquaient. À sa base, conformément aux descriptions des magiciens, glou-gloutait une source dont l'eau se déversait dans un bassin de pierre avant de s'écouler par une rigole pavée et de courir se perdre sur la gauche dans le noir. À la faveur du jour de plus en plus falot, les flammes bondissantes projetaient des ombres qui dansaient sur les inscriptions qu'arborait le monument.

Tamìr toucha la pierre lisse avec vénération. Les paroles de l'Oracle au roi Thelátimos y étaient gravées en skalien et en trois autres langues. Elle identifia l'une de ces dernières comme de l'aurënfaïe.

« "Tant qu'une fille issue de la lignée de Thelátimos la gouverne et défend, Skala ne court aucun risque de se voir jamais asservir" », proclama Ralinus, et tous les prêtres et acolytes s'inclinèrent bien bas devant elle. « Veuillez vous abreuver à la source de l'Illumi-nateur, Majesté, et vous rafraîchir du long voyage que vous venez d'effectuer. »

Tamìr éprouva de nouveau ce sentiment profond d'appartenir à une continuité qui la recevait à bras ouverts. Subitement, l'air s'agita tout autour d'elle, et elle discerna du coin de l'œil des silhouettes indécises et vaporeuses d'esprits. Elle n'aurait pas su dire de qui ceux-ci étaient la manifestation, mais leur présence était réconfortante, et il n'émanait d'eux rien de sem-blable à la fureur froide de Frère. Quelle que pût être leur identité, ils se réjouissaient de sa venue.

Elle s'agenouilla devant la source et se rinça les mains, puis, comme il n'y avait pas de coupe, emplit ses paumes d'eau glacée. L'eau était douce mais tellement froide qu'elle lui fit mal aux doigts et aux dents.

« Est-ce qu'il est permis à ma suite d'en avoir aussi ? » demanda-t-elle.

Sa question fit rire tous les prêtres. « Naturellement, lui répondit Ralinus. L'hospitalité de l'Illuminateur ne connaît ni rang ni limites. »

Tamìr recula tandis que ses amis et sa garde buvaient tous une gorgée rituelle.

« Elle est fameuse ! » s'exclama Hylia après s'être agenouillée pour siroter la sienne en compagnie de Lorin et Tyrien.

Iya fut la dernière à boire. La longueur de la chevauchée ayant rendu ses mouvements passablement raides, Arkoniel lui offrit son bras pour l'aider à se relever. La vieille femme pressa sa main contre la stèle, puis contre son cœur.

« La première Ghërilain fut appelée la Reine de l'Oracle », articula-t-elle, et Tamìr fut suffoquée de voir des larmes dans ses yeux. « Vous êtes la seconde reine prédite en ces lieux.

— Et pourtant vous avez pris le nom d'une reine différente, et de l'une des moins illustres, en plus, remarqua Ralinus. Les raisons de ce choix me laissent toujours perplexe, Majesté.

— C'est la première Tamìr qui, m'apparaissant à Ero, me fit don de la prestigieuse Épée. Elle avait été assassinée par son frère, tout comme nombre des membres de ma parenté féminine furent assassinés par mon oncle, et son nom était entièrement tombé dans l'oubli du temps de celui-ci. Je l'ai pris afin d'honorer sa mémoire. » Elle s'interrompit, le regard fixé sur les rides argentées courant sur le bassin. « Et afin de remémorer à moi-même et aux autres que semblable abomination ne devra jamais se renouveler au nom de Skala.

— Un sentiment méritoire, reine Tamìr », dit une voix d'homme à l'accent somptueux qui provenait des ombres accumulées de l'autre côté de la place.

Elle releva les yeux et vit s'approcher quatre hommes et une femme. Elle les reconnut sur-le-champ pour des Aurënfaïes grâce au sen'gaï qui les coiffait et aux magnifiques bijoux qui paraient leur gorge, leurs oreilles et leurs poignets. Ils avaient tous de longs cheveux sombres et des prunelles claires. Trois des hommes étaient vêtus de tuniques tissées en laine blanche d'aspect moelleux qui retombaient sur des culottes en peau de daim enfilées dans des bottes basses. La femme était habillée de façon similaire, à ce détail près que sa propre tunique lui descendait au-dessous des genoux et était fendue des deux côtés jusqu'à la ceinture. Le cinquième, plus âgé, portait une longue robe noire. Son sen'gaï rouge et noir à franges, ses marques faciales et les lourds anneaux d'argent qui pendillaient contre son cou le désignaient comme Khatmé. La femme et l'un des hommes plus jeunes arboraient le rouge et le jaune éclatants dans lesquels Tamìr reconnut les couleurs de Gèdre. Le vert sombre des deux derniers prouvait leur appartenance à quelque autre clan.

Lorsqu'ils pénétrèrent dans la lumière plus vive aux

abords de la stèle, Ki poussa un cri de joie et courut embrasser le jeune homme gèdre.

« Arengil ! s'exclama-t-il en soulevant de terre dans son enthousiasme leur ami perdu. Tu t'es débrouillé pour nous revenir !

— J'avais bien promis de le faire, non ? » s'esclaffa celui-ci en retrouvant ses pieds et en empoignant Ki par les épaules. Ki le dépassait à présent d'une demi-tête, alors qu'ils étaient de la même taille quand Arengil avait été renvoyé chez lui. « Tu as grandi, et il t'a poussé de la barbe. » Il branla du chef puis aperçut Una parmi les Compagnons. « Lumière divine ! Est-ce là qui je crois que c'est ? »

Elle sourit à belles dents. « Bonjour ! Navrée de t'avoir mis dans un tel pétrin, ce jour-là. J'espère que ton père n'était pas trop en rogne ? »

La femme gèdre – sa tante, ainsi qu'on l'apprendrait bientôt – haussa un sourcil. « Ça, pour l'être, il l'était, mais Arengil a survécu, comme vous voyez. »

Tamìr s'avança d'un pas, non sans hésiter, ne sachant trop de quelle manière il réagirait face aux modifications de son aspect physique. Le sourire d'Arengil ne fit que s'élargir lorsqu'il l'étreignit, après avoir comblé la distance qui les séparait.

« Par la Lumière ! Je n'ai pas douté des révélations du voyant, mais je ne savais pas à quoi m'attendre non plus. » Il la maintint à longueur de bras puis hocha la tête. « Ça te va drôlement bien d'être une fille ! »

Tant de familiarité scandalisa manifestement le Khatmé, mais les autres ne firent que se gondoler.

« Mon neveu s'est donné un mal de tous les diables

pour notre visite, et c'est à toute force qu'il a voulu être de la partie », confia la femme à Tamìr. Elle parlait un skalien parfait, avec juste une imperceptible pointe d'accent. « Salut à vous, Tamìr, fille d'Ariani. Je suis Sylmaï ä Arlana Mayniri, sœur du Khirnari de Gèdre.

— Je suis honorée, dame », répondit Tamìr, qui ne savait trop que penser de tout cela ni de quelle manière s'adresser à eux. Les Aurënfaïes ne se servaient pas de titres officiels, exception faite pour leurs chefs de clan, appelés khirnaris.

« Salut à vous aussi, mes amis », dit Sylmaï à Iya et Arkoniel. Cela fait un bon bout de temps que je ne vous ai vus dans notre pays.

— Vous vous connaissez ? » questionna Tamìr.

Iya serra la main de la Gèdre et l'embrassa sur la joue. « Comme elle vient de le dire, il s'est écoulé bien des années depuis, et lors d'une seule et unique visite. Je suis honorée que vous vous souveniez de nous. Arkoniel était encore un petit garçon. »

Sylmaï se mit à rire. « Oui, vous êtes beaucoup plus grand, maintenant. Et ça ? » Elle se toucha le menton comme pour caresser une barbe et grimaça d'un air espiègle. « Même ainsi, je vous aurais reconnu à vos yeux. Le sang de notre peuple s'y révèle. Et vous avez aussi un certain nombre de nos cousins, à ce que je vois », ajouta-t-elle en souriant à Wythnir et Tyrien.

Tamìr tendit sa main à l'austère Khatmé. « Et vous, sieur ? Bienvenue dans mon pays.

— Je suis honoré, Tamìr de Skala. Je suis Khaïr í Malin Sekiron Mygil, l'époux de notre propre Khirnari. » Il avait une voix de basse et un accent beaucoup plus marqué. « Un membre de mon clan soutient votre cause, à ce que je vois. »

Saruel s'inclina. « Je suis honorée de vous rencontrer, Khaïr í Malin. Voilà bien des années que je ne suis allée chez moi. »

Les deux hommes au sen'gaï vert sombre s'avancèrent en dernier. Le plus âgé n'avait pas l'air d'avoir dépassé la trentaine, et le plus jeune n'était guère plus qu'un adolescent, mais, avec les 'faïes, les critères ordinaires ne signifiaient rien. Ils pouvaient avoir deux cents ans, pour autant qu'elle sache. Ils étaient également deux des plus beaux hommes qu'elle eût jamais vus, et son cœur trébucha d'un battement quand le plus grand des deux sourit et s'inclina devant elle à la mode skalienne.

« Je suis Solun í Meringil Seringil Methari, deuxième fils du Khirnari de Bôkthersa. Et voici mon cousin, Corruth í Glamien. »

Corruth saisit la main de Tamìr et s'inclina en la gratifiant d'un sourire timide. « Je suis honoré de rencontrer une reine de Skala. Mon clan a soutenu votre ancêtre contre Plenimar durant la Grande Guerre.

— Je suis honorée de vous rencontrer », répondit-elle, un peu intimidée aussi. La beauté de ces hommes et même leurs voix semblaient tramer un sortilège et faisaient galoper son cœur. « Je... c'est-à-dire, me faut-il présumer que vous n'êtes pas ici par hasard ?

— Nos voyants ont affirmé que Skala possédait de nouveau une reine, une reine qui porte la marque d'Illior, expliqua Solun.

— Je constate de mes propres yeux que vous êtes

sans conteste une femme, intervint Khaïr de Khatmé. Est-ce que vous portez encore la marque ?

— Ta marque de naissance, expliqua Arengil. C'est l'un des signes grâce auxquels nous devons te reconnaître. Cela, et la cicatrice en croissant de lune que tu as au menton. »

Tamìr remonta sa manche gauche et leur montra la marque de naissance rose sur son avant-bras.

« Ah, oui ! Est-elle identique à celle de tes souvenirs, Arengil ? questionna le Khatmé.

— Oui. Cela étant, j'aurais reconnu sans elle celle qui la porte rien qu'à ses yeux bleus.

— Mais vous venez tout juste d'arriver et vous avez des affaires personnelles à régler ici, s'interposa Solun. Vous devriez vous restaurer et vous reposer avant que nous causions.

— De grâce, ne vous joindrez-vous pas à nous ? » proposa Tamìr un peu trop précipitamment, au vu du regard horripilé que lui décochait Ki.

Solun lui répondit par un sourire qui accéléra d'autant plus ses chamades. « Nous en serions ravis. »

5

Ralinus emmena Tamìr de l'autre côté de la place vers l'une des hostelleries. Une porte de chêne massive et noircie par les siècles ouvrait sur une espèce de vestibule spacieux creusé dans la falaise. D'autres permettaient d'accéder à des chambres d'hôtes encore plus profondément taillées à même la roche. De jeunes acolytes conduisirent les visiteurs le long d'un corridor à celles qu'ils allaient occuper.

Elles étaient toutes petites, à peine plus grandes que des cellules, et meublées de manière rudimentaire : un lit, une table de toilette, quelques tabourets. Mais leurs murs étaient blanchis à la chaux et ornés comme la Serrure d'Illior de peintures de couleurs vives. Celle de Tamìr possédait une minuscule fenêtre obstruée par une jalousie de pierre. Tandis que Ki s'adjugeait d'autorité la chambre contiguë, le reste de ses gens furent répartis dans les suivantes, donnant toutes sur la même coursive. Il se révéla que la roche était truffée d'un labyrinthe de petites pièces dont la succession faisait l'effet d'une véritable garenne.

Tamìr se débarbouilla rapidement et laissa Una lui servir de cameriste pour se défaire de sa tunique souillée par le voyage et l'aider à enfiler l'une de ses robes. Ki se présenta lorsqu'elles en eurent terminé.

« C'est quand même quelque chose, ces 'faïes qui se pointent comme ça, là, observa Una tout en pliant la tunique de Tamìr avant de la déposer sur un coffre.

— Après toutes les histoires que j'ai entendues sur eux, je n'en suis pas vraiment étonnée », répondit Tamìr qui, armée d'un peigne, se battait pour démêler ses cheveux. « Que penses-tu d'eux jusqu'ici, Ki ? »

Il s'appuya contre le chambranle de la porte, se rongeant une cuticule. « Ces gens ne manquent pas de gueule, je dirais. »

Una se mit à rire. « Beaux leur va mieux ! Et j'ai bien aimé la manière dont le jeune Bôkthersan a rougi quand vous l'avez salué, Tamìr. »

Celle-ci s'épanouit. « Je n'ai pas encore rencontré d'Aurënfaïe laid. Croyez-vous qu'il y en ait ? » demanda-t-elle en continuant de malmener le peigne.

Ki s'avança pour lui retirer celui-ci des mains puis, tout en s'employant à désenchevêtrer le fouillis de sa crinière, grommela : « Peut-être que les laids, ils se gardent soigneusement de les envoyer à l'étranger. »

Una le regardait d'un drôle d'air, et Tamìr se rendit brusquement compte que jamais personne n'avait vu Ki faire cela pour elle. Soudain gênée, elle récupéra le peigne et déclara d'un ton léger : « Peut-être que ceux qu'ils trouvent laids sont quand même plaisants à nos yeux. »

Ki lâcha un grognement évasif puis se dirigea vers la porte à longues enjambées. « Venez çà, Votre Majesté, je meurs de faim, moi. »

Comme Tamìr se levait pour lui emboîter le pas, Una la retint par le bras et chuchota : « Il est jaloux ! Vous devriez fleureter avec le beau 'faïe. »

Tamìr la regarda d'un air incrédule et secoua la tête. Elle ne s'était jamais livrée à ces jeux de séduction et n'était pas près de s'y mettre à présent. Escortée par Una, elle suivit Ki pour regagner la grande salle, sur le devant de l'hostellerie, où le reste de leur compagnie se mêlait déjà aux Aurënfaïes et aux desservants du temple. Una devait forcément se tromper sur le comportement bizarre de Ki, se dit-elle ; il ne s'était auparavant jamais rien passé de semblable entre eux. Il ne s'intéressait même pas à elle, pas de cette façon !

Quoi qu'il en fût, elle éprouva un nouvel accès d'embarras quand Solun la salua en s'inclinant de l'autre bout de la pièce. Elle jeta un coup d'œil vers Ki, et, malgré son expression égale, elle eut l'impression que son regard n'arrêtait pas de revenir vagabonder dans la direction de l'éblouissant étranger.

« S'il vous plaît, Majesté », dit Ralinus en lui désignant le siège qu'on lui avait réservé au centre d'une des tables. Il s'assit avec elle et ses magiciens, Tharin, Ki et les Aurënfaïes. De jeunes garçons en robes blanches apportèrent des cuvettes pour qu'ils s'y rincent les doigts, pendant que d'autres leur servaient du vin. On procéda à de nouvelles présentations parmi les gens de la reine pendant qu'ils venaient occuper leurs places respectives aux différentes tables. Tamìr ne fut pas fâchée de se trouver installée juste en face des beaux Bôkthersans.

Après qu'elle eut versé une libation en l'honneur d'Illior et des Quatre, le repas débuta. Tout en mangeant, les convives échangèrent des plaisanteries. Tamìr questionna les 'faïes sur leur patrie et les observa pendant qu'ils s'entretenaient avec les autres. Una et Hylia faisaient toutes les deux les yeux doux à Solun, et les tentatives auxquelles il se livrait pour avoir un brin de conversation avec Corruth, son voisin de table, paraissaient passablement émoustiller Lynx.

Les deux hommes étaient indubitablement superbes, mais Tamìr ne comptait pas s'en laisser aveugler pour autant. Ils ne seraient pas venus de si loin s'ils n'avaient voulu obtenir quelque chose en contrepartie. À côté d'elle, Ki était en train de satisfaire à la curiosité d'Arengil par une évocation sommaire des combats auxquels ils avaient participé jusque-là.

« Si le roi ne nous avait pas attrapés en flagrant délit sur les toits, j'aurais été des vôtres, ronchonna leur ami. À Gèdre, nous nous entraînons bien pour la guerre, nous aussi, mais tout ce que nous avons à nous mettre sous la dent, ce sont de vulgaires pirates zengatis.

— Mon neveu s'était éperdument amouraché de l'existence tírfaïe, intervint Sylmaï en le regardant d'un air plein d'affection. Peut-être a-t-il besoin d'assister à une véritable bataille pour ne plus montrer autant d'empressement à aller chercher l'occasion d'en voir une. »

Après avoir débarrassé les tables, on déposa devant eux des tartes et du fromage servis avec un vin doux.

« Ralinus a dit que vous étiez venus expressément pour me rencontrer », reprit Tamìr à l'adresse de Sylmaï qui, selon toute apparence, occupait le rang le plus élevé du groupe. « Est-ce simplement la curiosité qui vous a fait entreprendre un aussi long voyage ? »

L'interpellée sourit d'un air entendu tout en grignotant une lichette de fromage, mais ce fut Khaïr qui répondit.

« Il a été prédit que vous redresseriez les torts dont l'Usurpateur s'est rendu coupable envers les fidèles. Cela nous incite à espérer que Skala pourrait dorénavant renoncer à ses agissements blasphématoires...

— Comme notre clan et celui de Bôkthersa ont à

certains égards les liens les plus étroits avec Skala, le coupa Sylmaï de façon plutôt abrupte, les khirnaris ont décidé de dépêcher des représentants pour faire votre connaissance et apprendre la vérité tout entière.

— Je n'en suis nullement offusquée, leur assura Tamìr. Les persécutions perpétrées par mon oncle à l'encontre des adeptes d'Illior sont impardonnables. Souhaitez-vous renouer des liens avec mon pays ?

— Peut-être, répliqua le Khatmé. Notre première tâche consistait à établir la validité de vos prétentions et à découvrir si vous entendiez dûment honorer l'Illuminateur, ainsi que l'ont toujours fait vos ancêtres.

— J'ai été le témoin direct des horreurs commises par mon oncle. Pour rien au monde je ne voudrais poursuivre pareille politique. Si les Quatre sont tous honorés à Skala, Illior est notre patron particulier.

— Veuillez pardonner sa rudesse à Khaïr », intervint Solun, les yeux plissés vers celui-ci. Les autres avaient l'air aussi choqués que Tamìr par l'agressivité de leur compagnon.

À la surprise de la jeune femme, le Khatmé se toucha le front. « Je n'avais pas du tout l'intention de vous manquer de respect. Votre seule présence en ces lieux témoigne de vos intentions.

— Mon clan verrait d'un bon œil le rétablissement de liens avec Skala, reprit Solun. Il y a encore parmi nous des gens qui se souviennent de votre Grande Guerre ; ce sont les enfants des magiciens qui se joignirent à la prestigieuse reine Ghërilain pour affronter les nécromanciens de Plenimar. Nous possédons des portraits d'elle à Bôkthersa. Arengil a raison. Vous avez ses yeux, Tamìr ä Ariani.

— Je vous remercie. » Elle se sentit rougir de nouveau, mortifiée de l'effet qu'il produisait sur elle. « Êtes-vous en train de m'offrir votre alliance contre mon cousin, le prince Korin ?

— Vos prétentions au trône sont les seules légitimes, énonça Khaïr.

— Est-ce qu'on en viendra vraiment à se battre ? s'enquit Arengil. Korin et son père faisaient deux. Nous étions bons amis.

— Il a changé depuis que tu nous as quittés, et pas pour le mieux, l'avisa Ki. Il s'est entiché de Lord Nyrin. Tu te rappelles Vieille Barbe de Goupil, hein ?

— Ce Nyrin est bien le magicien qui a constitué la clique des Busards, n'est-ce pas ?

— En effet, lui confirma Tamìr. D'après toutes les informations dont nous disposons, il s'est attaché aux basques de Korin. J'ai essayé d'entrer en contact avec mon cousin, mais il refuse toute espèce de pourparlers. Il proclame à cor et à cri que je suis soit démente, soit une menteuse.

— Vous n'êtes à l'évidence ni l'une ni l'autre, dit Solun, Nous en protesterons auprès de l'Iia'sidra. »

Au même instant, quelque chose émergea de l'ombre et se mit à papillonner juste en deçà de la clarté que diffusait le feu de la large cheminée de pierre.

« Maître, regardez ! » s'écria Wythnir.

Una eut un mouvement de recul. « Des chauves-souris ?

— Je ne pense pas. » Ralinus brandit sa main, comme s'il rappelait un faucon. Une minuscule créature ailée descendit en voletant se poser sur l'un de ses doigts tendus, s'y agrippant délicatement avec ses pattes griffues et y enroulant sa longue queue fine. « Regardez, Majesté. Un des dragons de l'Illuminateur vient vous présenter ses hommages, en définitive. »

Tamìr se pencha pour mieux voir, non sans se rappeler l'avertissement de ne pas toucher. L'animal était magnifique, une miniature parfaite des monstres colossaux qu'elle avait vus représentés dans des manuscrits, sur des tapisseries ou sur les murs de temples des environs d'Ero. Ses ailes étaient d'une forme assez semblable à celles d'une chauve-souris, hormis qu'elles étaient presque translucides et vaguement iridescentes, à l'instar de l'intérieur d'une coquille de moule.

« Je me figurais qu'il ne restait plus de dragons à Skala, dit Arengil.

— Ils sont rares, mais ces petits-là sont devenus plus communs dans les parages d'Afra depuis ces dernières années. L'Illuminateur a dû les envoyer pour accueillir leur nouvelle reine. » Ralinus tendit la petite créature à Tamìr. « Vous plairait-il de le tenir ? Je suis persuadé qu'il ira vers vous si vous restez calme. »

Tamìr dressa un doigt. Le dragon s'aplatit sur celui du prêtre pendant un moment, dénudant ses minuscules crocs et rejetant en arrière son col de serpent comme pour se disposer à mordre. Ses yeux étaient d'infimes perles d'or, et une crête acérée de piquants se hérissa sur son museau et sa tête, aussi délicate qu'un chef-d'œuvre de joaillerie. Tamìr nota chaque détail, songeant déjà à la façon dont elle s'y prendrait pour recréer l'original avec de la cire et de l'argent.

Elle avait suffisamment travaillé avec des faucons pour savoir qu'elle devait autant s'abstenir du moindre mouvement brusque que manifester quelque appréhension. Forte de cette expérience, elle amena lentement son doigt au contact de celui du prêtre. Un frémissement nerveux parcourut les ailes du dragon, puis il changea pas à pas de perchoir avant de lover sa queue autour du bout de l'index de Tamìr. Ses griffes étaient aussi pointues que des piquants de chardon. Alors qu'elle s'était attendue à ce qu'il ait le corps lisse et froid comme celui d'un lézard, elle sentit qu'il dégageait une chaleur ahurissante à l'endroit où son ventre reposait sur sa propre peau.

Elle déplaça doucement sa main pour permettre à Wythnir de mieux le contempler. Elle n'avait jamais vu l'enfant aussi rayonnant de bonheur.

« Est-ce qu'il peut cracher du feu ? demanda-t-il.

— Non, pas avant d'être beaucoup plus gros, si tant est qu'il survive, ce qui n'est pas le cas de la plupart des petits, même à Aurënen, dit Solun.

— Ces bouts de chou sont à peine plus que des lézards, ajouta Corruth. Ils changent en grandissant et deviennent tout à fait dangereux au fur et à mesure de leur croissance. L'un de nos cousins s'est fait tuer par un *efir*, l'année dernière.

— C'est quoi, un effer ? demanda Ki, que la petite créature plongeait également dans le ravissement.

— *Efir*. Un jeune dragon, de la taille à peu près

d'un poney. Leurs esprits ne sont pas encore formés, mais ils sont extrêmement féroces.

— Celui-ci n'a pas l'air dangereux du tout », gloussa Ki en se penchant pour l'examiner de plus près. Peut-être bougea-t-il trop vite, car la bestiole se détendit soudain et le mordit à la joue, juste en dessous de l'œil gauche.

Ki fit un bond en arrière en piaulant, la main plaquée contre sa joue. « Enfer et damnation, ça cuit comme une morsure de serpent ! »

Tamìr demeura d'un calme imperturbable, mais le dragon se raidit, la mordit à son tour et prit son essor pour retourner dans l'ombre d'où il était venu. « Aïe ! cria-t-elle en secouant son doigt, tu as raison, ça fait vraiment mal.

— Tenez bon, vous deux ! » s'esclaffa Corruth. Le jeune Bôkthersan extirpa de sa bourse une fiole de grès puis tamponna rapidement les deux morsures avec quelques gouttes d'un liquide sombre.

La douleur s'amenuisa d'emblée, mais lorsqu'il épongea le surplus, Tamìr s'aperçut que la drogue avait maculé les imperceptibles empreintes laissées par les crocs. Elle avait quatre taches indigo sur le flanc de son doigt, juste en dessous de la première phalange. Ki portait sur la joue une marque identique et qui était en train d'enfler.

« Nous sommes assortis », observa-t-elle d'un ton narquois.

Arengil morigéna Corruth dans leur langue, et celui-ci s'empourpra. « Pardonnez-moi, je n'ai pas réfléchi, dit-il, abasourdi. C'est ce que nous faisons toujours.

— Corruth était bien intentionné, mais j'ai peur que les traces ne soient indélébiles maintenant, expliqua Solun. Le lissik sert à teinter les morsures afin qu'elles restent toujours visibles. » Il montra à Tamìr une tache beaucoup plus large qui s'étalait entre son pouce et son index. « Elles sont considérées comme des porte-bonheur éminents, des signes de la faveur de l'Illumi-nateur. Mais peut-être préféreriez-vous ne pas les avoir ?

— Non, cela m'est égal, lui assura Tamìr.

— Toi, tu tiens là pour de bon ta marque de beauté, Ki ! » s'esbaudit Nikidès.

Ki polit sur sa cuisse la lame de son poignard et la brandit comme un miroir pour voir la marque. « Elle n'est pas si mal. Garantit une bonne histoire à conter si quiconque m'interroge à son propos.

— Les dragons sont peu fréquents ici, et les mor-sures le sont aussi, dit Ralinus en inspectant plus minu-tieusement la marque sur la joue de Ki. Consentiriez-vous à m'enseigner la recette de cet onguent, Solun í Meringil ?

— Les plantes que nous utilisons ne poussent pas dans vos parages, mais je pourrais toujours, le cas échéant, vous expédier certaines de nos mixtures. »

Khaïr prit gentiment la main de Tamìr dans les siennes pour examiner attentivement la marque. « Une croyance de notre peuple veut qu'après avoir atteint ses pleines dimensions d'intelligence, un dragon se rappelle le nom de toutes les personnes qu'il a mordues et se trouve lié à elles.

— Combien de temps cela prend-il ? demanda Ki.

— Plusieurs siècles.

— Ça nous fait une belle jambe, alors.

— Peut-être pas, mais vous aurez tous les deux une place dans les légendes dragoniennes.

— S'il vous arrivait jamais de venir à Aurënen, une marque comme celle-ci vous mériterait un respect unanime. Les Tírfaïes qui en portent ne sont pas foule », avança Corruth, qui déplorait toujours d'être intervenu aussi précipitamment.

« Cela vaut bien la peine d'être mordu, alors. Votre médicament a déjà supprimé le plus pénible de la souffrance. Merci. » Ki lui adressa un grand sourire, et ils échangèrent une vigoureuse poignée de main. « Ainsi, les tout-petits ne sont pas en mesure de parler non plus ?

— Non, cela ne leur vient qu'à un âge très avancé.

— Les Aurënfaïes sont les seuls à posséder dans leur pays des dragons dotés d'une telle longévité, spécifia le prêtre. Personne ne sait pour quelle raison. Il y en avait de semblables à Skala dans des temps très anciens.

— Cela vient peut-être de ce que nous sommes les plus fidèles, répondit Khaïr, repris par sa rudesse antérieure. Vous autres adorez les Quatre, tandis que nous reconnaissons exclusivement Aura, que vous appelez Illior. »

Ralinus demeura muet, mais Tamìr surprit dans ses yeux un éclair d'aversion.

« C'est une vieille discussion, et qu'il vaut mieux reporter à de tout autres temps, s'empressa d'intervenir

Iya. Mais je suis sûre que même les Khatmés ne sau-
raient mettre en doute l'amour que l'Illuminateur porte
maintenant à Skala, manifesté qu'il est en la personne
de Tamìr.

— Elle a déjà été gratifiée d'une vision véridique,
sous la forme d'une mise en garde avant la seconde
offensive plenimarienne, dit Saruel au malotru. Sauf
votre respect, Khaïr í Malin, vous n'avez pas vécu
chez les Tírs comme je l'ai fait. Ils font preuve d'une
dévotion fervente, et la bénédiction d'Aura leur est
acquise.

— Pardonnez-moi, Tamìr ä Ariani, déclara Khaïr.
Une fois de plus, je me suis montré offensant, mais
c'était sans male intention.

— J'ai grandi parmi des soldats. Ce sont des gens
qui ne mâchent pas leurs mots non plus. J'aime cent
fois mieux vous entendre exprimer sans ambages votre
pensée que de vous voir vous soucier d'étiquette et de
façons de cour. Et vous pouvez compter sur la réci-
proque de ma part. »

Solun poussa un gloussement chaleureux et amical,
et Tamìr se retrouva rougissante à nouveau sans
motif valable.

Solun échangea un regard amusé avec ses compagnons gèdres, puis il retira de son poignet un lourd
bracelet d'or serti d'une pierre rouge polie et se leva
pour le lui présenter. « Bôkthersa serait volontiers
l'ami de Skala, Tamìr ä Ariani. »

Elle reçut le bracelet et vit du coin de l'œil qu'Iya
lui faisait signe de le mettre. Elle l'enfila sur son
poignet gauche en essayant de se rappeler la kyrielle

de noms que portait Solun, mais sans y parvenir. L'or était tiède sur sa peau, ce qui n'était pas fait pour l'aider à recouvrer son calme. Encore réussit-elle à ne pas bafouiller quand elle remercia. « C'est un honneur pour moi que d'accepter ce don, et j'espère que vous me considérerez toujours comme votre amie dévouée. »

Sylmaï lui fit présent d'un collier constitué de minuscules feuilles d'or montées avec des pierres blanches scintillantes. « Puissent les vaisseaux de Gèdre et de Skala mouiller dans les mêmes ports comme par le passé. »

Le Khatmé fut le dernier à s'avancer, et son offrande fut d'une autre espèce. Il lui donna une petite bourse de cuir dans laquelle elle découvrit un pendentif taillé dans une pierre cireuse vert sombre et enchâssée dans de l'argent massif. Elle était couverte de menus symboles, à moins qu'il ne s'agît de lettres, qui entouraient l'œil nébuleux d'Illior.

« Un talisman en pierre de Sarikali, expliqua-t-il. C'est le plus sacré de nos sanctuaires, et ces talismans-là confèrent des rêves et des visions authentiques à ceux qui vénèrent Aura. Puisse-t-il vous servir à votre entière satisfaction, Tamìr ä Ariani. »

À l'expression de stupeur que prirent les physionomies des autres, Tamìr devina que c'était là faire un cadeau peu banal à un étranger. « Merci à vous, Khaïr í Malin. Il me sera aussi précieux que le souvenir de votre honnêteté. Puissent tous mes alliés faire preuve d'autant de franc-parler.

— Un noble espoir, quoique bien mince »,

commenta-t-il avec un sourire. Là-dessus, il se leva et lui souhaita une bonne nuit. Les autres ne le suivirent pas tout de suite.

Solun prit à son tour la main de Tamìr dans la sienne pour se livrer à un nouvel examen de l'empreinte bleue de la morsure du dragon. Elle sentit à son contact un picotement agréable lui parcourir le bras. « Grâce à cette marque, nous vous reconnaîtrons toujours dorénavant, ô Élue d'Aura. Je pense que mon père sera dans les meilleures dispositions pour vous soutenir. Faites appel à nous si vous vous trouvez dans le besoin.

— Il en va de même pour Gèdre, affirma Sylmaï. Le commerce avec votre pays nous a manqué. » Elle se tourna vers Iya et Arkoniel, qui étaient restés non loin de là, et se mit à bavarder tout bas avec eux.

« Je viendrai me battre pour toi, moi aussi, dit Arengil d'un air plein d'espoir.

— Et moi donc ! s'écria Corruth.

— Vous serez toujours les bienvenus, guerre ou pas. Si vos khirnaris y consentent, vous occuperez tous deux une place d'honneur parmi mes Compagnons », répondit Tamìr.

Un jeune acolyte arriva de l'extérieur sur ces entrefaites et chuchota quelque chose à l'oreille du supérieur.

Ralinus acquiesça d'un hochement de tête et se tourna vers Tamìr. « La lune est maintenant bien audessus des pics. Il n'y a pas de meilleure heure pour consulter l'Oracle, Majesté. »

Tamìr refoula le flottement nerveux que ces mots

suscitaient dans sa poitrine et glissa le talisman du Khatmé dans son escarcelle. « Très bien, alors. Je suis prête. »

<h1 style="text-align:center">6</h1>

Dans l'intervalle des falaises qui les surplombaient, le firmament formait une mince bande toute piquetée d'étoiles brillantes, et la blancheur argentée de la lune planait au-dessus. En levant les yeux pour la contempler, Tamìr se sentit envahie par un frémissement d'impatience prémonitoire.

« N'y a-t-il pas quelque espèce de cérémonie ? » s'enquit Nikidès, pendant que les autres Compagnons et les magiciens se rassemblaient auprès de la source. Wythnir se cramponnait de nouveau à la main d'Arkoniel, comme s'il redoutait qu'on l'abandonne en arrière.

Ralinus sourit. « Non, messire. Ce n'est nullement nécessaire, comme vous le constaterez par vous-même si vous décidez de descendre. »

Un jeune porte-lanterne brandit sa hampe et, prenant la tête, leur fit quitter la place par un chemin montant, battu et rebattu, qui plongeait dans les ténèbres encore plus denses de l'étroite faille au-delà.

La pente se fit plus raide presque tout de suite, et le chemin ne tarda pas à se réduire en une vague sente qui sinuait entre les rochers. Devant, la lanterne oscillait et se balançait, faisant danser des ombres au dessin fantastique.

Le sol était étonnamment uni sous le pied, voire glissant par endroits, tant l'avait usé le passage de milliers de pèlerins depuis des siècles et des siècles.

Les falaises se reployaient de plus en plus autour d'eux, et ils finirent par déboucher sur le cul-de-sac exigu qu'occupait le sanctuaire. La margelle de pierre d'un puits se trouvait là, presque à ras de terre, auprès d'un modeste appentis sans mur de façade, tout cela tel que l'avait décrit Arkoniel.

« Venez, Majesté, et je vous guiderai, souffla Ralinus. Vous n'avez rien à craindre.

— Je n'ai pas peur. » S'approchant du puits, elle en sonda d'un coup d'œil la noirceur abyssale puis opina du chef à l'adresse des porteurs de cordes. « Je suis prête. »

Ceux-ci lui en passèrent l'extrémité en boucle par-dessus la tête et la laissèrent filer jusque derrière ses genoux. Avec des jupes, c'était plutôt encombrant. Tamìr regretta de ne pas s'en être tenue au port de hauts-de-chausses. Après avoir resserré le nœud coulant autour de ses cuisses, les prêtres lui montrèrent comment s'asseoir sur le rebord du trou, tout en assurant sa prise avec les mains sur le mou de la corde contre sa poitrine.

En voyant ses jambes baller dans le vide, Ki ne parvint guère à dissimuler son angoisse. « Accroche-toi bien ! »

Elle lui adressa un clin d'œil, empoigna la corde à deux mains et se jeta d'un coup de reins dans le noir.

La dernière chose qu'elle aperçut fut la petite bouille solennelle de Wythnir.

Elle ne put s'empêcher d'avoir le souffle coupé quand la corde accusa le poids de son corps. Elle s'y agrippa d'autant plus étroitement qu'elle se mit à tournoyer lentement lorsque les religieux la laissèrent descendre.

Des ténèbres impénétrables se refermèrent sur elle comme de l'eau. Il lui était impossible de rien voir, maintenant, sauf, tout en haut, un cercle d'étoiles de plus en plus floues. À en croire les dires d'Iya, la caverne était extrêmement vaste, et Tamìr se mit à comprendre ce qu'elle avait entendu par là.

Il y régnait un silence extraordinaire ; aucun bruissement de brise, aucun ruissellement d'eau, pas même de volettements de chauves-souris... ni de dragons, d'ailleurs. Il n'y avait pas le moindre indice de murs ni de sol, rien d'autre que la sensation vertigineuse d'un vide infini. Cela vous donnait l'impression d'être comme en suspens dans le ciel nocturne.

Plus elle s'engouffrait là-dedans, plus l'atmosphère se refroidissait. Elle déroba un nouveau coup d'œil vers le haut, utilisant comme ancre visuelle le cercle d'étoiles en train de se rétrécir au-dessus de la gueule du puits. Après ce qui lui fit l'effet d'une durée presque interminable, ses pieds touchèrent la terre ferme. Elle reprit son équilibre avec quelque difficulté puis se délivra de la corde avant de l'enjamber. En levant les yeux, elle chercha vainement l'ouverture du puits. Elle se trouvait dans un noir total.

Elle pivota lentement, encore incertaine de son équilibre, et eut la joie de discerner une faible lueur au loin, sur sa gauche. Plus elle la regardait, plus celle-ci prenait d'éclat, tant et si bien qu'elle finit par réussir à voir juste assez du sol de la caverne pour être certaine de son chemin. Rassemblant son courage, elle se dirigea vers la lumière.

Celle-ci provenait d'un globe de cristal posé sur un trépied. Ce fut d'abord tout ce que Tamìr parvint à distinguer mais, quand elle s'en rapprocha, elle vit qu'une jeune femme à chevelure sombre était assise près de lui sur un tabouret bas. La froideur de la lumière affectait sa peau d'une pâleur mortelle, et ses cheveux lui cascadaient sur les épaules et se déversaient jusqu'au sol de part et d'autre de sa personne. En dépit de l'atmosphère glaciale, elle ne portait rien d'autre qu'une simple camisole de lin qui laissait à découvert ses bras et ses pieds. Elle tenait les paumes ouvertes sur ses genoux, son regard fixé à terre devant elle. Tous les oracles étaient déments, d'après ce que l'on avait enseigné à Tamìr, mais la femme semblait seulement pensive... du moins jusqu'au moment où elle leva lentement les yeux.

Tamìr se pétrifia sur place. Elle n'avait jamais vu d'yeux aussi vides. Ils lui donnaient le sentiment de contempler un cadavre vivant. Les ombres resserrèrent leur proximité, malgré la constance lumineuse du globe.

La voix de l'Oracle était tout autant dénuée d'émotion quand elle chuchota : « Bienvenue, deuxième Tamìr. Tes ancêtres m'ont prévenue de ta venue. »

Un nimbe argenté auréola brillamment sa tête et ses épaules, et ses yeux rencontrèrent à nouveau ceux de Tamìr. Ils n'étaient plus vides mais irradiaient, lumineux et d'une intensité terrifiante.

« Salut, reine Tamìr ! » Sa voix était profonde et sonore, à présent. Elle emplissait les ténèbres. « Le noir fait le blanc. Le putride fait le pur. Le mal crée la grandeur. Tu es une graine arrosée de sang, Tamìr de Skala. Souviens-toi de la promesse que tu as faite à mes élus. T'es-tu occupée de l'esprit de ton frère ? »

C'étaient trop de choses à comprendre d'emblée. Tamìr eut l'impression que ses jambes s'étaient liquéfiées. Elle s'effondra sur ses genoux devant la présence redoutable de l'Illuminateur. « Je... J'ai essayé.

— Il se tient maintenant derrière toi, pleurant des larmes de sang. Le sang t'environne. Le sang et la mort. Où se trouve ta mère, Tamìr, Reine des Fantômes et des Spectres ?

— Dans la tour où elle est morte, répondit-elle dans un souffle. Je veux l'aider, ainsi que mon frère. Dans une vision, il m'a dit de venir ici. De grâce, dites-moi ce que je dois faire ! »

Le silence tomba autour d'elles, si absolu qu'il faisait tinter les oreilles de Tamìr. Elle n'arrivait pas à déterminer si l'Oracle respirait ou non. Elle attendit, les genoux endoloris par la pierre froide. Elle n'avait quand même pas fait tout ce long voyage rien que pour ce résultat-là ?

« Du sang, chuchota de nouveau l'Oracle avec une

tristesse audible. Devant toi et derrière toi, un fleuve de sang t'emporte vers l'ouest. »

Tout à coup, Tamìr sentit une espèce de chatouillement sur la partie de sa poitrine où se trouvait cachée sa vieille balafre. Elle abaissa le col de sa robe, et ce qu'elle découvrit là lui coupa le souffle.

La blessure qu'elle s'était infligée à Atyion, le fameux jour où elle avait dû se charcuter pour découdre les points méticuleux de Lhel et extraire de sa chair l'esquille de Frère s'était spontanément cicatrisée pendant la métamorphose, sans laisser d'autre trace à son emplacement qu'un imperceptible trait pâle. Or, elle s'était rouverte maintenant, et si profondément qu'elle lui permettait de distinguer l'os de son sternum. Le sang ruisselait à flots entre ses seins. Il lui barbouillait les mains et, dégoulinant le long de la robe, lui éclaboussait les genoux. Chose pour le moins bizarre, c'était indolore, et c'est avec un étrange détachement que Tamìr regarda le sang se répandre à terre et former devant elle une flaque circulaire.

Lorsque celle-ci eut la taille d'un bouclier, sa sombre surface se rida, et des silhouettes commencèrent à s'y esquisser. L'hémorragie devait l'avoir débilitée pour lors, car elle ressentit une faiblesse croissante, et les images se mirent à flotter dans le sang, brouillées en un vertigineux halo de couleurs.

« Je... je vais... » Elle était à deux doigts de s'évanouir.

Le contact d'une main glacée sur la sienne la fit revenir à elle. Rouvrant les yeux, elle se découvrit debout avec Frère sur une falaise battue par les vents qui dominait la mer. C'étaient là les lieux qu'elle avait si fréquemment visités en rêve, à ceci près qu'elle s'y était toujours trouvée avec Ki, et que le ciel était bleu. Or, en l'occurrence, le ciel promettait la pluie, et la mer avait un gris de plomb.

Là-dessus, elle entendit des armes s'entrechoquer bruyamment, tout comme ç'avait été le cas dans le temple d'Atyion. Sous ses yeux s'affrontaient au loin deux armées, mais elle n'avait aucun moyen de les rejoindre. Un ravin rocheux la séparait du champ de bataille. Fort au-delà des combattants, elle parvenait tout juste à discerner ce qui semblait être les tours d'une ville immense.

La bannière de Korin émergea des ombres à ses pieds, flottant en suspens dans l'air comme si des mains invisibles la brandissaient.

Tu dois te battre pour ce qui t'appartient en toute légitimité, Tamìr, reine de Skala, lui chuchota à l'oreille une voix confidentielle. *Par le sang et l'épreuve, tu dois tenir ton trône. De la main de l'Usurpateur tu arracheras l'Épée.*

Encore du sang ! songea-t-elle avec désespoir. *Pourquoi faut-il qu'il en soit ainsi ? Il doit y avoir un autre moyen, un moyen pacifique ! Je ne veux pas verser le sang d'un de mes parents !*

Tu es née du sang répandu.

« De quoi parlez-vous ? » s'écria-t-elle tout haut. Le vent s'engouffra dans la bannière et lui en cingla le visage au point de l'aveugler. Ce n'était rien de plus

qu'une aune de soie et de broderie, mais qui lui enveloppa la gorge comme une chose vivante, lui coupant
la respiration.

« Frère, aide-moi ! » chuinta-t-elle en griffant la
bannière mais sans trouver de prise sur l'insaisissable
tissu que le vent mettait en lambeaux.

Un éclat de rire à vous glacer d'épouvante lui
répondit. *Venge-moi, Sœur. Venge-moi, avant de
demander la moindre faveur nouvelle à la victime de
tous les torts !*

« Illior ! Illuminateur, j'en appelle à toi ! cria-t-elle
en se débattant avec désespoir. Comment puis-je
l'aider ? Je t'en conjure, accorde-moi un signe ! »

La bannière argentée s'évapora autour d'elle comme
une brume matinale, la laissant de nouveau plongée
dans les ténèbres.

Non, pas dans les ténèbres, car elle aperçut dans le
lointain une froide lueur blanche, et elle comprit tout à
coup qu'elle était revenue dans la caverne de l'Oracle.
D'une manière ou d'une autre, captive de la vision,
elle s'était éloignée de la lumière. Elle se sentit les
mains poisseuses. Elle les leva pour loucher sur elles
dans le clair-obscur douteux, et elle finit par constater
qu'elle avait les bras ensanglantés jusqu'au coude.

« Non ! » murmura-t-elle en les essuyant en toute
hâte sur ses jupes.

Lentement, les jambes cotonneuses, elle retourna
vers le siège de l'Oracle, mais, au fur et à mesure
qu'elle s'en rapprochait, elle se rendit compte que
quelqu'un d'autre avait pris sa place, quelqu'un qui,
vêtu de robes, se distinguait par une longue tresse grise

familière, et qui se tenait à genoux, la tête baissée, devant un Oracle beaucoup plus jeune. Tamìr reconnut Iya dès avant que la magicienne n'ait relevé la tête. À quel moment était-elle descendue, et pourquoi ? Le prêtre avait pourtant bien dit qu'il n'était permis de s'aventurer en bas qu'à une seule personne à la fois.

Iya tenait quelque chose dans ses bras. Une fois plus près, Tamìr vit que c'était un nouveau-né. Celui-ci était tout flasque et silencieux, et ses yeux sombres étaient vacants.

« Frère ? chuchota Tamìr.

— Deux enfants, une seule reine, souffla l'Oracle puéril d'une voix trop ancienne et profonde pour sa petite taille. Dans cette génération vient l'enfant qui incarne les fondements de ce qui doit arriver. Deux enfants, une seule reine marquée par le sang du passage. »

La fillette se tourna vers Tamìr, les yeux illuminés d'une blancheur incandescente qui semblait sonder jusqu'en son tréfonds l'âme même de la jeune reine. « Interroge Arkoniel. Seul Arkoniel peut te renseigner. »

Terrifiée sans savoir pourquoi, Tamìr tomba sur ses genoux et exhala tout bas : « L'interroger sur quoi ? Sur ma mère ? Sur Frère ? »

Des mains glacées se refermèrent par-derrière sur son cou, l'étranglant comme l'avait fait la bannière. « Interroge Arkoniel, lui souffla Frère à l'oreille. Interroge-le sur ce qui s'est passé. »

Les mains de Tamìr volèrent vers sa gorge ; elle s'attendait d'autant moins à toucher réellement Frère ou à l'arrêter qu'elle n'était jamais parvenue à le faire. Mais, cette fois, ses doigts rencontrèrent de la chair froide et des poignets durs et tendineux. Elle s'y agrippa tandis qu'une puanteur abominable déferlait sur elle et lui soulevait l'estomac.

« Donne-moi la paix ! » gémit une voix pâteuse et haletante près de son visage. Ce n'était plus le fantôme de Frère qu'elle avait derrière elle, mais son cadavre. « Donne-moi le repos, Sœur. »

Il la relâcha, et elle tomba face en avant sur ses mains puis se retourna vivement pour affronter l'horrible chose dressée dans son dos.

Au lieu de cela, elle se retrouva en train de dévisager à nouveau l'Oracle, redevenue entre-temps la femme avec qui elle avait conversé. Celle-ci était toujours assise comme auparavant, les paumes ouvertes sur ses genoux, les yeux écarquillés et de nouveau vides.

Tamìr leva ses mains et les découvrit sèches et propres. Son corsage n'était nullement délacé. Il n'y avait aucune trace de sang nulle part.

« Vous ne m'avez rien dit », hoqueta-t-elle.

Le regard de l'Oracle était stupidement fixé par-delà sa personne, comme si Tamìr n'avait même pas été là.

Une rage telle qu'elle n'en avait jamais éprouvé jusque-là la submergea. Elle empoigna l'Oracle par les épaules et se mit à la secouer, dans l'espoir de voir reparaître l'intelligence du dieu dans ses prunelles éteintes. Cela lui fit l'effet de secouer une poupée.

C'était une poupée, grande comme une femme, mais faite d'une mousseline bourrée de coton, avec une figure grossièrement peinte et des membres asymétriques. Elle ne pesait rien et s'affala mollement entre ses mains.

De stupeur, Tamìr la laissa tomber, puis l'examina avec une horreur redoublée. La poupée était en tous points semblable à celle de jadis, celle à l'intérieur de laquelle Mère avait cousu les os de Frère. Elle portait même, étroitement noué autour de son cou flasque, un cordon noir de cheveux torsadés. Il n'y avait aucun indice de l'Oracle. Tamìr se trouvait seule dans la salle sombre, et la lumière émise par le globe baissait insensiblement.

« Mais qu'essaies-tu de me montrer ? s'écria-t-elle, les poings crispés de désespoir. Je ne comprends pas ! Quel rapport cela a-t-il avec Skala ?

— Tu es Skala, chuchota la voix du dieu. Telle est l'unique vérité de ton existence, jumelle du mort. Tu es Skala, et Skala est toi, tout comme tu es ton frère et lui toi. »

La lumière s'était presque éteinte quand Tamìr sentit quelque chose se resserrer autour de son torse. Prise de panique, elle baissa les yeux, se demandant si l'effroyable poupée était revenue à la vie ou si c'était encore un tour que lui jouait le cadavre répugnant de Frère. Au lieu de quoi elle s'aperçut que c'était la corde des prêtres dont la boucle, allez savoir comment, lui emprisonnait de nouveau le corps. Quelqu'un s'était mis à tirer sur le mou, et elle eut tout juste le temps de l'agripper pendant qu'empoignée comme à bras-le-corps on la hissait, la soulevait de terre, et qu'elle se mettait à tournoyer dans le noir compact.

Elle regarda frénétiquement vers le haut, y découvrit le cercle d'étoiles et n'en détacha plus le regard tandis qu'il s'élargissait au fur et à mesure qu'elle s'en rapprochait. Elle arrivait même à présent à distinguer le sombre contour de têtes qui s'y découpaient, et des mains se tendaient déjà pour l'aider à enjamber le rebord du puits. C'étaient celles de Ki, et ses bras forts et sûrs la ceignirent par la taille lorsque ses genoux se dérobèrent sous elle.

« Tu es blessée ? » demanda-t-il d'une voix anxieuse, tout en la soutenant pour l'aider à s'asseoir sur la margelle de pierre. « Nous avons attendu, attendu, attendu... mais sans recevoir le moindre signal de ta part.

— Frère, hoqueta-t-elle en se cramponnant au col de sa robe.

— Quoi ? Où ça ? » cria-t-il, affolé, sans cesser de l'étreindre.

Elle s'abandonna, pleine de gratitude, à cet embrassement. « Non... C'était seulement... seulement une vision. » Mais elle n'arrivait pas à réprimer ses tremblements.

« Le dieu vous a parlé », dit Ralinus.

Elle laissa échapper un rire corrosif. « Si l'on peut appeler ça parler ! Des énigmes et des cauchemars. »

Subitement, elle entendit comme un bruit de griffures derrière elle. En se retournant, elle fut horrifiée de voir Frère qui, plus bas dans le puits de la caverne, la dévisageait, les traits déformés en un masque de haine. Sa peau blême se ratatina peu à peu sur son crâne, et des mains semblables à des serres émergèrent en grattant le sol lorsqu'il entreprit de s'extirper du trou.

Tu es lui, et il est toi, chuchota l'Oracle d'en bas.

Ces mots suivirent Tamìr dans les ténèbres lorsqu'elle perdit connaissance.

7

Tamìr était aussi froide qu'un cadavre quand on la remonta de la salle de l'Oracle. Ki l'arracha aux autres et s'assit pour lui bercer la tête contre sa poitrine.

« Maître, est-ce que l'Oracle lui a fait du mal ? interrogea Wythnir tout bas.

— Chut ! Ce n'est qu'un évanouissement. » Prenant les choses en main, Iya écarta Arkoniel et les prêtres, s'agenouilla et pressa sa paume sur le front moite de la jeune fille.

« C'est un bon présage, déclara Ralinus au reste des assistants pour essayer de les tranquilliser. Elle a dû avoir une vision d'importance, pour être épuisée à ce point. »

Les yeux de Tamìr se rouvrirent en papillotant puis se levèrent vers Iya. Celle-ci en eut froid dans le dos ; dans le clair de lune, ces yeux-là étaient aussi noirs que ceux du démon, et tout aussi accusateurs. Tamìr repoussa la main de la magicienne et se dégagea des bras de Ki pour se rétablir sur son séant.

« Que... que s'est-il passé ? » questionna-t-elle en

un chuchotement fébrile. Puis son regard se reporta vers le puits, et elle se mit à trembler d'une manière incoercible. « Frère ! J'ai vu...

— Compagnons, ramenez votre reine à son logement, ordonna Iya.

— Je n'ai pas besoin qu'on me porte ! » Tamìr lui décocha un nouveau regard noir avant de se lever vaille que vaille en titubant. « Il me faut redescendre là. Quelque chose est allé de travers. Je n'ai pas compris ce que l'Illuminateur m'a montré.

— Soyez patiente, Majesté, répliqua le prêtre. Si obscure que puisse paraître la vision au premier abord, je vous le garantis, quels qu'ils soient, tous ces éléments sont véridiques. Vous devez méditer sur ce qui vous a été révélé, et, le moment venu, vous en percevrez la signification.

— *Le moment venu ?* Iya, saviez-vous que cela se produirait ? Pourquoi ne m'avez-vous pas prévenue ? » Elle darda sur Arkoniel un regard vindicatif « Ou vous ?

— Chacun vit sa consultation de l'Oracle en fonction de sa propre personnalité. Nous ne pouvions courir le risque d'influer sur vos propres attentes.

— Laissez vos amis vous aider à rentrer, dit Iya d'un ton sévère. Nous ne tenons pas à vous voir faire une chute ou vous fracasser le crâne dans le noir. »

Tamìr ouvrit la bouche pour protester, mais Ki se précipita et lui entoura la taille d'un bras ferme. « Calme-toi et cesse de te montrer si foutrement têtue ! »

Elle prit en frissonnant une profonde inspiration

puis à contrecœur le laissa la soutenir pour la reconduire à la maison d'hôtes.

Il est le seul à pouvoir la dissuader comme cela de n'en faire qu'à sa fantaisie, songea Iya. *Le seul en qui elle ait une confiance aussi profonde.* Le regard dont Tamìr l'avait elle-même gratifiée chantait une tout autre chanson.

Une fois de retour à la maison d'hôtes, cependant, Ki lui-même ne réussit pas à la convaincre d'aller se coucher. « Ralinus, il me faut avoir un entretien tout de suite avec vous, tant que la vision m'est encore parfaitement présente à l'esprit.

— Très bien, Majesté. La porte du temple se trouve juste à côté...

— Iya et Arkoniel, vous m'attendez, commanda-t-elle. Je veux causer avec vous par la suite. »

L'âpreté de son ton surprit Iya comme l'avait fait précédemment l'agressivité de son regard. Elle pressa sa main sur son cœur et s'inclina. « Vos désirs sont des ordres, Majesté.

— Ki, viens avec moi. » Tamìr s'éloigna vivement là-dessus, et Ralinus et Ki la suivirent à toutes jambes.

Arkoniel la regarda partir, puis tourna vers la magicienne un visage anxieux. « Elle sait, n'est-ce pas ?

— Si telle est la volonté d'Illior. » Iya pénétra lentement dans la maison d'hôtes en affectant de ne pas remarquer les mines perplexes des jeunes prêtres et des Compagnons qui avaient assisté à l'échange.

J'ai tenu ma parole, Illuminateur. Je continuerai à la tenir.

Le temple d'Illior était une minuscule pièce, basse de plafond, taillée dans la face de la falaise. À l'intérieur régnait une atmosphère froide et humide, et l'éclairage y était chichement dispensé par un seul brasero qui brûlait devant un bas-relief peint représentant l'œil d'Illior. Les murs, ou ce que Ki parvenait à en distinguer, étaient maculés de fumée.

« Es-tu certaine de vouloir que j'assiste à ce qui va se passer ? » demanda-t-il à voix basse tout en regardant Ralinus se couvrir le visage d'un masque d'argent poli.

Tamìr hocha posément la tête, les yeux fixés sur le religieux.

« Mais ne vaudrait-il pas mieux y associer aussi les magiciens ? Je veux dire, ils sont experts en ce genre de choses. »

Leur seule mention fit se durcir à nouveau le regard de Tamìr. « Non. Pas maintenant. »

Après s'être agenouillé devant le brasero, Ralinus invita d'un geste Tamìr à venir le rejoindre. « Qu'avez-vous vu, fille de Thelátimos ? »

Ki demeura debout, gauchement immobile, pendant que Tamìr rapportait par à-coups ce que l'Oracle lui avait fait voir.

« Elle a dit que je devais arracher l'Épée des mains de l'Usurpateur », déclara-t-elle, les yeux emplis de chagrin. « Cela signifie la guerre avec Korin, n'est-ce pas ? Elle me montrait qu'il n'existait pas de moyen pacifique susceptible de régler la situation.

— Je crains qu'il n'en soit ainsi, répliqua le prêtre.

— C'est ce que nous n'avons pas arrêté de lui

répéter nous-mêmes, intervint Ki. Et c'est maintenant d'un dieu que tu viens d'en obtenir la confirmation.

— Il semble en effet que je n'aie pas d'autre solution, murmura Tamìr.

— À cela ne se réduit pas ce que l'Oracle vous a montré, repartit le prêtre. Quelque chose d'autre vous a bouleversée. »

Elle frissonna de nouveau, comme elle l'avait fait dans la caverne. Ki se rapprocha et lui prit la main. Elle serra si fort la sienne qu'elle lui fit mal. « Mon frère... Je l'ai vu, en bas, mais pas... Pas comme cela m'arrive d'habitude. Il m'a toujours ressemblé, ou du moins son aspect ressemblait au mien quand j'étais un garçon. Il est désormais un jeune homme, comme j'aurais dû en être un moi-même. » Elle laissa échapper un petit rire sans joie. « Il a même un soupçon de barbe naissante. Mais, cette fois-ci... » Elle tremblait si fort de tous ses membres que Ki fut violemment tenté de l'enserrer dans ses bras, mais il n'osa pas l'interrompre.

« C'était comme si... comme si son corps d'adulte était un cadavre. On aurait dit... qu'il était réel. »

Ki perçut un brusque refroidissement de l'atmosphère et jeta un regard circulaire, les nerfs à fleur de peau, tout en s'interrogeant s'il était loisible à Frère d'apparaître à l'intérieur d'un temple.

« Et je l'ai vu aussi remonter à ma suite du fond du puits. C'est alors que je me suis évanouie », chuchota-t-elle, affreusement gênée. « De grâce, vénéré, il me faut comprendre. Tout ce qu'elle m'a montré m'a paru inextricablement embrouillé avec Frère et avec la façon dont nous sommes Skala, lui et moi, quoi que cela puisse signifier.

— Je l'ignore, Majesté, sauf que le lien qui vous attache l'un à l'autre n'a pas encore été tranché. Mettez de côté cet aspect des choses si vous le pouvez, et tournez vos pensées vers le trône. La reine est le pays, comme vous l'a déclaré l'Illuminateur. Votre existence même est vouée à la protection de votre peuple et à sa préservation, et vous devez de votre plein gré tout sacrifier pour accomplir cette mission sacrée, dût-ce être au prix de votre propre vie. »

Tamír fronça les sourcils tout en tiraillant l'une de ses nattes. « Je suis censée combattre Korin. Mais si la bannière de ma vision le représentait, alors, je n'ai pas su de quelle manière m'y prendre ! Elle m'étranglait. J'étais en train de perdre.

— Mais vous n'avez pas vu de défaite.

— Je n'ai pas vu quoi que ce soit. Ça s'est seulement terminé. » Elle marqua une pause. « Bref, elle m'étranglait, et j'ai appelé Illior à mon aide. Frère s'y refusait ; il continuait simplement à me répéter que je devais le venger.

— La vision a pris fin dès l'instant où vous avez invoqué l'Illuminateur ? »

Elle acquiesça d'un hochement.

Le prêtre réfléchit sur ce phénomène. « Il vous faut conserver cela dans votre cœur, Majesté. Illior guide vos pas et garde sa main étendue sur votre personne.

— L'Oracle m'a qualifiée de "graine arrosée de sang". Elle a dit qu'elle voyait du sang m'entraîner comme un fleuve. Suis-je obligée de me comporter comme mon oncle, pour le salut de Skala ? Comment le moindre bien peut-il sortir du mal ?

— Vous devrez découvrir cela par vous-même, quand le moment sera venu.

— Que dirai-je au peuple, lorsque je rentrerai à Atyion ? Ils s'attendent tous à quelque verdict décisif d'Illior, analogue à celui dont jouit la reine Ghërilain. Or, je n'ai rien que je puisse souhaiter faire graver en lettres d'or. » Elle secoua la tête. « Un fleuve de sang. »

Après être resté silencieux pendant un bon moment, Ralinus se pencha et lui posa une main sur l'épaule. « Le sang n'est pas exclusivement ce qui se répand, c'est également ce qui coule dans vos veines, Majesté. Ce même sang se perpétuera vivant dans vos enfants, de même qu'il vit en vous, reliant le passé à l'avenir. N'est-ce pas un fleuve, cela aussi ?

« Daignez me permettre de vous expliquer quelque chose de très important pour vous. En votre qualité d'ami indéfectible de Tamìr, Lord Kirothius, il est nécessaire que vous l'appreniez vous-même, puisqu'elle vous associe à sa confidence. Ce que je vais vous dire maintenant, chaque prêtre d'Illior le sait. Vous, en tant que reine, vous bénéficiez des révélations des dieux parce que vous êtes forte et en raison de votre élection toute particulière. Mais ce que vous révélerez à votre peuple ne devrait être pas plus, et pas moins non plus, que ce dont vos auditeurs seraient susceptibles de tirer le plus grand profit. »

Tamìr échangea avec Ki un regard abasourdi. « Êtes-vous en train de me conseiller de leur mentir ?

— Non, Majesté. Vous leur annoncerez qu'Illior a confirmé vos droits à la couronne "par le sang et l'épreuve". Vous les préviendrez du conflit qui les attend, mais vous ferez en outre appel à eux pour vous prêter sans réserve leur énergie afin d'accomplir la volonté de l'Illuminateur.

— Et ils n'ont que faire de savoir que je suis hantée par mon défunt frère ?

— Cela n'a rien d'un secret, Majesté. Il est en train de se forger à toute vitesse une légende parmi le peuple que vous avez un esprit gardien.

— Un démon », rectifia Ki.

Le prêtre haussa un sourcil réprobateur à son adresse. « Et en quoi profiterait-il au peuple de se figurer que vous êtes maudite ? Abandonnez-lui le soin de broder votre histoire à votre place, Tamìr. »

Tamìr dégagea sa main de celle de Ki et se leva. « Je vous remercie, vénéré. Vous m'avez aidée à y voir plus clair.

— La coutume veut que le grand prêtre se charge en votre faveur de consigner par écrit ce genre de vision sur un parchemin que vous emporterez. Le rouleau sera à votre disposition dans la matinée. »

Pendant qu'il sortait sur la place avec elle, Ki se rendit parfaitement compte que Tamìr était toujours aussi profondément troublée. Perdue dans ses pensées, elle demeura longuement debout près de la source. Il attendit en silence, les bras croisés pour se préserver tant bien que mal du froid. Les étoiles étaient si brillantes, ici, qu'elles projetaient des ombres sur le sol.

« Que t'inspire tout cela ? demanda-t-elle finalement.

— Un guerrier digne de ce nom sait faire la différence entre le bien et le mal, l'honneur et le déshonneur. » Il se rapprocha et lui posa délicatement les mains sur les épaules. Elle ne releva pas les yeux mais ne s'écarta pas non plus. « Tu es la meilleure et la plus honorable personne que je connaisse. Si Korin est décidément trop aveugle pour s'apercevoir de cette évidence, alors c'est de sa propre faiblesse qu'il administre encore une fois la démonstration. Et si tu es Skala, c'est une bonne chose pour tout un chacun. »

Elle soupira puis recouvrit l'une des mains de Ki avec la sienne. Ses doigts étaient glacés.

Ki dégrafa la broche qui fermait son col puis drapa les épaules de Tamìr dans son manteau, par-dessus celui qu'elle portait elle-même.

Elle lui adressa un sourire moqueur. « Tu es aussi collant que Nari !

— Comme elle n'est pas ici, libre à moi de te tenir à l'œil. » Il lui frictionna les bras pour la réchauffer. « Là, c'est mieux. »

Elle finit par se dérober puis se contenta de rester là, les yeux baissés. « Tu... c'est-à-dire... j'apprécie ta... » Elle mit un terme à ses bredouillements, et il soupçonna qu'elle rougissait.

Ces moments de timidité soudaine entre eux n'avaient été que trop fréquents ces tout derniers mois. Elle avait besoin de lui. Sans s'inquiéter du fait que quelqu'un risquait de les voir, Ki l'attira contre lui et l'étreignit farouchement.

La joue de Tamìr était froide et lisse contre la sienne. Il resserra l'étau de ses bras, désireux de parvenir à lui communiquer sa propre chaleur. Il éprouvait un plaisir merveilleux à tenir de nouveau son amie de cette façon. Elle avait les cheveux encore plus soyeux, sous ses doigts, que dans ses souvenirs.

En soupirant, Tamìr l'enlaça par la taille à pleins bras. Le cœur de Ki se gonfla, et des larmes lui piquèrent les yeux. Après avoir dégluti violemment, il chuchota : « Je serai toujours là pour toi, Tob. »

À peine s'était-il avisé de sa gaffe qu'elle fit un bond en arrière et retourna à grands pas vers la maison des hôtes.

« Tamìr ! Tamìr, je suis désolé. J'ai oublié ! Cela ne veut rien dire. Reviens ! »

La porte claqua comme une gifle derrière elle, et Ki se retrouva seul, là, dans la clarté glaciale des étoiles, empêtré dans des sentiments qu'il n'était toujours pas prêt à revendiquer clair et net et se traitant de crétin, d'imbécile et de tous les noms d'idiot possibles et imaginables.

Un pressentiment de mauvais augure pesait sur le cœur d'Arkoniel pendant qu'Iya et lui-même attendaient, assis dans la petite chambre de Tamìr. Iya demeurait obstinément muette, et il en était réduit à subir les assauts délirants de son imagination la plus noire.

Lorsque Tamìr finit par entrer, l'expression de sa physionomie ne fit qu'empirer la détresse du magicien. Elle ne jeta qu'un coup d'œil vers Iya puis, se croisant les bras, le fixa, lui, d'un regard dur. « Je veux que vous me disiez ce qui est véritablement arrivé à mon frère. Qu'est-ce qui l'a rendu tel qu'il est ? »

Et voilà qu'elle était posée, la question qu'il redoutait depuis si longtemps. Avant même d'ouvrir la bouche, Arkoniel sentit que la fragile confiance qui s'était tout récemment restaurée entre eux deux se déchirait comme une soierie usée. Comment serait-il à même de justifier aux yeux de Tamír ce qui avait été perpétré au nom de l'Illuminateur, alors qu'au fond de lui-même il ne s'était jamais pardonné la part qu'il avait prise à la misère de leur protégée ?

Il cherchait encore éperdument ses mots quand un froid glacial et humide comme le brouillard d'un marécage les environna. Frère apparut aux côtés de sa sœur, attachant sur Iya un regard furibond. Le démon présentait un aspect très similaire à celui qu'Arkoniel lui avait connu les rares fois où il l'avait vu ; celui d'une caricature grêle, méchante et spectrale d'un Tobin qui aurait accédé à la virilité d'un jouvenceau. Toutefois, les jumeaux se ressemblaient beaucoup moins maintenant, et Arkoniel puisa là une espèce de réconfort étrange, en dépit de la colère qui flambait conjointement dans leurs prunelles et qui ressuscitait la gémellité.

« Eh bien ? questionna Tamír d'un ton sec. Si vous me considérez véritablement comme votre reine et pas uniquement comme une marionnette manipulable à merci, dans ce cas, révélez-moi la vérité. »

Iya persista dans son mutisme.

Arkoniel eut l'impression qu'une part de son être

était en train de mourir quand il se contraignit à pro-férer : « Votre frère nouveau-né fut sacrifié pour vous protéger.

— Sacrifié ? Assassiné, vous voulez dire ! Et c'est à cause de cela qu'il est devenu un démon ?

— Oui, reconnut Iya. Que vous a-t-il appris ?

— Rien, sauf que c'est *vous* qui me le diriez, Arkoniel. Et l'Oracle m'a montré... » Elle se retourna lentement du côté d'Iya. « Vous. "Deux enfants, une seule reine", vous avait déclaré l'Oracle, et je vous ai vue tenir le nouveau-né mort. C'est vous-même qui l'avez tué !

— Ce n'est pas moi qui lui ai ôté la vie, mais il est indiscutable que j'ai été personnellement l'instrument de sa mort. Ce que vous avez vu est cela même qui m'avait été montré. Vous et votre frère, vous vous trouviez encore alors en sécurité dans le sein de votre mère. Mais vous étiez déjà, vous, désignée pour sauver Skala. Il fallait vous protéger coûte que coûte, en parti-culier contre la magie de Nyrin. Je n'ai pu concevoir qu'un seul moyen sûr pour y parvenir. »

Frère se rapprocha d'elle sournoisement, et Arkoniel fut frappé d'horreur par la jubilation noire qui se lisait sur ce visage contre nature.

D'un simple regard, Tamìr immobilisa le démon. « Qu'avez-vous *fait*, Iya ? »

La magicienne affronta son regard sans ciller. « J'ai découvert Lhel. Je sais quel genre de magie pratique son acabit. Seule une sorcière des collines était capable de réaliser ce qui devait l'être. Aussi l'ai-je ramenée à

101

Ero et introduite dans la maison de votre mère la nuit de votre naissance. Vous êtes née la première, Tamìr, et vous étiez une beauté. Parfaite. En grandissant, vous seriez devenue une fille vigoureuse à longs cheveux noirs, et vos traits auraient beaucoup trop rappelé ceux de votre mère pour que l'on réussisse jamais à dérober cette ressemblance aux regards à l'affût. Tandis que vous reposiez dans les bras de votre nourrice, Lhel a retiré votre frère du sein maternel. Elle comptait l'étouffer avant qu'il n'ait eu le temps de respirer. C'est là le secret, voyez-vous, la chose pour laquelle elle savait comment procéder. Si ce corps chétif était demeuré privé de souffle, il n'y aurait pas eu de meurtre, et cette abomination que vous appelez Frère n'aurait jamais existé. Mais il se produisit une interruption, et vous connaissez la suite. » Elle branla tristement du chef. « Ainsi, c'était nécessaire. »

Tamìr tremblait de tous ses membres. « Par les Quatre ! Cette chambre, alors, en haut de l'escalier... Il a tenté de me faire voir... »

Frère se mit tout près d'elle et chuchota : « Sœur, notre père se tenait là, passif, à regarder. »

Elle s'écarta de lui si vivement qu'elle heurta de plein fouet le mur derrière elle. « Non ! Père n'aurait jamais fait cela ! Tu mens !

— À mon grand regret, non », dit Arkoniel. Après toutes ces années de silence, les mots se déversaient finalement de sa bouche avec l'impétuosité des flots d'un barrage rompu. « Votre père éprouvait une répugnance invincible pour recourir à de telles extrémités, mais il n'avait pas le choix. Ce devait être une opération rapide et miséricordieuse. Nous le lui avions promis mais avons échoué. »

Tamìr se couvrit le visage avec des mains tremblantes. « Que s'est-il donc passé ?

— Votre oncle est arrivé, escorté de Nyrin et d'une meute de spadassins, juste après la naissance de votre frère », dit Arkoniel dans un souffle. Les braises du souvenir n'avaient jamais cessé de couver dans son esprit, chaque détail, effilé comme la pointe d'un poignard, s'acharnait à le déchirer, et l'horreur de cette nuit-là le tenaillait toujours. « Le vacarme a pétrifié Lhel, dont l'attention s'est détournée au moment critique. Le nouveau-né s'est gorgé d'air, et son esprit fut scellé dans sa chair. »

La face du démon se tordit sur un grondement glacial. Arkoniel s'arc-bouta, s'attendant à une agression mais, à sa stupéfaction, Tamìr se tourna vers son frère et lui dit quelque chose à voix basse. Celui-ci n'en demeura pas moins auprès d'elle, et sa physionomie reprit immédiatement son apparence de masque inexpressif, exception faite de ses prunelles. Elles brûlaient toujours de haine et de désir.

« Votre mère était censée ne jamais rien savoir de tout cela, reprit Iya. Je la droguai de manière à lui en épargner le choc, mais elle comprit d'une manière ou d'une autre. C'est cela qui l'a détruite. »

Tamìr enserra dans ses bras sa maigre poitrine, avec l'air d'éprouver une violente douleur physique. « Mon frère. Mère... L'Oracle avait raison. C'est bien moi, la "graine arrosée de sang". »

Iya hocha tristement la tête. « Oui, mais pas par malveillance ou malignité. Il vous fallait coûte que coûte survivre et gouverner. Pour y parvenir, il vous fallait vivre et revendiquer votre véritable forme. Et c'est ce que vous avez fait. »

Tamìr essuya une larme égarée sur sa joue puis se mit debout. « Ainsi, c'est par votre volonté que mon frère est mort ?

— Oui.

— Lhel a tué Frère et pratiqué l'opération magique, mais c'est à votre instigation que cela s'est fait ?

— La responsabilité n'en incombe qu'à moi. C'est pour cette raison qu'il m'a toujours voué une haine aussi farouche. Je vois encore en lui qu'il désire ma mort. Quelque chose le retient. Vous, peut-être ? » Elle s'inclina bien bas, la main sur son cœur. « Ma tâche sera achevée, Majesté, lorsque l'Épée de Ghërilain se trouvera dans votre poing. Cela fait, je ne demanderai pas grâce.

— Et vous, Arkoniel ? » Les yeux de Tamìr étaient à présent presque suppliants. « Vous avez déclaré que vous étiez présent, cette nuit-là.

— Il n'était à l'époque que mon élève. Il n'avait pas son mot à dire..., commença Iya.

— Je ne réclame pas d'absolution, la coupa Arkoniel. Je connaissais la prophétie et j'y croyais. Je n'ai pas bougé pendant que Lhel mettait en œuvre sa magie.

— Et cependant Frère ne vous attaque pas. Il vous déteste, mais pas plus qu'il ne déteste la plupart des gens. Et pas comme il déteste Iya.

— Il a pleuré pour moi, chuchota Frère. Ses larmes ont coulé sur ma tombe, et je les ai goûtées.

— Il est incapable d'aimer, dit tristement Iya. Il est seulement capable de ne pas exécrer. Il ne vous exècre pas, Tamìr, et Arkoniel non plus. Il n'exécrait pas davantage votre mère, pas plus que Nari, d'ailleurs.

— Nari aussi... ? » murmura Tamìr, sombrant dans un chagrin de plus en plus profond.

« Je détestais Père ! gronda Frère. Détestais Oncle ! Mère le détestait et avait peur de lui ! J'ai connu sa peur dans son ventre, tout comme la nuit même de ma naissance. Elle continue de le détester et d'en avoir peur. Tu as oublié de haïr, Sœur, mais nous pas. Jamais.

— Vous avez pleuré sur sa tombe ? » Tamìr aspira une goulée d'air tremblante. « Iya, c'est donc vous et Lhel qui avez versé le sang de mon frère ?

— Oui. »

Tamìr hocha lentement la tête puis, les joues humectées de larmes qui dégoulinaient peu à peu, proféra d'une voix nette : « Vous êtes bannis.

— C'est impossible, vous ne parlez pas sérieusement ! s'étrangla Arkoniel.

— Si. » Les pleurs de Tamìr redoublèrent, mais ses yeux flambaient d'une colère telle qu'il ne lui en avait jamais vu jusque-là. « J'ai juré devant le peuple que je considérerais comme un ennemi personnel quiconque verserait le sang de ma parentèle. Vous saviez cela, et néanmoins vous n'avez rien dit. Vous, qui avez assassiné mon frère ! Détruit ma mère. Ma... vie ! » Elle reprit son souffle en un sanglot. « Mon existence tout entière... un mensonge ! Un fleuve de sang. Toutes ces filles de notre lignée que mon oncle a fait périr ? Leur sang me tache les mains, lui aussi, parce que c'était moi qu'il cherchait. Nyrin... c'est moi qu'il cherchait !

— Oui. » Iya n'avait toujours pas bougé.

« Sortez ! » siffla Tamìr d'une voix qui, dans sa fureur, ressemblait à celle du démon. « Vous êtes bannis de Skala à jamais. Je ne veux plus jamais revoir aucun de vous deux ! »

Mais Iya demeura immobile. « Je partirai, Tamìr, mais vous devez garder Arkoniel avec vous.

— Ne vous avisez plus jamais de me donner des ordres, magicienne ! »

Iya ne bougea toujours pas, mais l'air s'épaissit autour d'elle, et la pièce s'enténébra. Les poils qui tapissaient les bras d'Arkoniel se hérissèrent désagréablement pendant que la puissance de sa vieille amie saturait l'atmosphère de la minuscule pièce.

« Je vous ai donné ma vie, ingrate et stupide enfant que vous êtes ! jappa-t-elle. N'avez-vous rien appris ? Rien *vu* ces derniers mois ? Peut-être que je ne mérite pas votre gratitude, mais tout ce à quoi j'ai travaillé pour vous, je ne vous laisserai *pas* le défaire pour la seule et unique raison que vous n'aimez pas beaucoup la manière dont marche le monde. Vous figurez-vous que j'aie beaucoup aimé ce que j'ai dû faire ? Eh bien, non ! Je l'ai détesté ; mais nous ne choisissons pas nos destins, nous autres tels que vous ou moi, à moins de nous muer en pleutres et de nous enfuir. Oui, je suis responsable de tout ce qui vous est arrivé, mais je n'en éprouve pas une once de regret !

« Est-ce que le sacrifice d'une vie, de cent vies, ne vaut pas le coût, quand il s'agit de soulager le pays de la malédiction qui l'accable ? Pour quoi d'autre vous imaginez-vous que vous êtes née ? Continuez, alors. Tapez du pied et hurlez contre moi les mots de meurtre et de justice, mais qu'adviendrait-il de Skala si la lignée de fils engendreurs de monstres issue d'Erius gouvernait encore ? Croyez-vous que Korin se trouve en train de mijoter là-haut, à Cirna, votre couronnement ? Croyez-vous qu'il vous accueillera à bras ouverts si vous allez le rejoindre ? Il est temps que vous arrêtiez de faire l'enfant, Tamìr d'Ero, et que vous vous comportiez en reine !

« Je partirai, conformément à votre décret, mais je ne vous permettrai pas d'écarter Arkoniel. Il porte la touche d'Illior, exactement comme vous-même. Mais plus que cela, il n'a pas cessé de vous aimer et de vous servir depuis votre naissance, et il aurait retenu la main de Lhel s'il l'avait pu. Il doit demeurer à vos côtés pour accomplir la volonté de l'Illuminateur !

— Et elle consiste en quoi ? » demanda Tamìr, sur la défensive. « J'ai survécu. Vous m'avez faite reine. Que lui reste-t-il donc à réaliser ? »

Iya joignit ses mains, et la tension qui régnait dans la chambre s'amenuisa juste un petit peu. « Vous avez besoin de lui, et vous avez besoin des magiciens que lui et moi avons rassemblés pour vous. L'éblouissant palais de magiciens dont nous vous avons parlé n'est pas quelque oiseuse chimère. Il était une vision véridique, et il fait tout autant partie de la future force de Skala que vous-même. Vous imaginez-vous que les autres magiciens resteront avec vous si vous vous comportez maintenant de cette façon ? Je vous le garantis, la plupart d'entre eux n'en feront rien. C'est uniquement à cause de vous qu'ils se sont associés, mais ils sont des magiciens libres, ils ne doivent rien à personne, pas même à vous, et ils ne vous serviront pas s'ils croient que vous êtes une réincarnation de votre oncle. C'est Arkoniel et moi qui les avons convaincus d'aller contre leur nature et de devenir la Troisième Orëska. C'est une confédération plus fragile que vous ne le soupçonnez, et le destin d'Arkoniel est de la consolider. J'ai vu cela par moi-même le jour où votre avenir me fut révélé. Les deux sont indissociablement liés. »

Tamìr les dévisagea pendant un bon moment, les poings crispés contre ses flancs. Finalement, elle opina du chef. « Il reste. Et je reconnais ce que vous avez fait pour ce pays, Iya, vous et toute votre espèce. C'est pour cela que j'épargne vos jours. Mais je vous préviens : si mes yeux se posent à nouveau sur vous après l'aube, je vous ferai exécuter. Pour le bien du pays. Ne vous figurez pas qu'il s'agisse là d'une menace en l'air.

— À votre guise. » Iya s'inclina et sortit en trombe de la chambre sans jeter ne serait-ce qu'un coup d'œil d'adieu en direction d'Arkoniel.

Médusé, ce dernier regarda avec horreur Frère sourire d'un air diabolique et s'évaporer peu à peu.

« Tamìr, par pitié, rappelez-le. Il va la tuer !

— Je lui ai déjà commandé de s'en abstenir, mais c'est tout ce que je puis faire. Vous et Lhel y avez veillé. » Elle s'essuya la figure sur sa manche en évitant de le regarder. « Frère a parlé en votre faveur. C'est pourquoi je vous laisserai demeurer à ma cour. Mais pour l'heure, je... je... » Sa voix se brisa. « Fichez-moi le camp ! »

Comme il ne pouvait rien faire en l'occurrence pour la réconforter, il s'inclina vaille que vaille et se dépêcha de sortir. Lynx et Nikidès étaient de garde à la porte et en avaient suffisamment entendu pour lui décocher un regard soupçonneux.

« Où est Ki ? demanda-t-il.

— Dehors, je crois, l'avisa Lynx. Que diable vient-il de se passer ? »

Arkoniel ne prit même pas le temps de répondre. La chambre d'Iya était vide, découvrit-il, et il n'y avait que Wythnir dans la sienne.

« Maître ?

— Va te coucher, mon garçon, dit-il aussi gentiment qu'il lui fut possible. Je vais revenir. »

Se précipitant à l'extérieur, il y repéra Ki appuyé contre la stèle. « Tamìr a besoin de toi. »

À sa stupéfaction, Ki répliqua d'abord par un simple haussement d'épaules. « Je suis la dernière personne qu'elle ait envie de voir en ce moment même. »

Avec un grognement exaspéré, Arkoniel l'empoigna par son col et le propulsa sans ménagement vers la maison d'hôtes. « Certainement *pas* ! Va ! »

Sans attendre pour voir si Ki lui obéissait, il descendit en courant aux écuries.

Ça ne peut pas se terminer de cette manière-là ! Pas après tout ce qu'elle a fait !

Iya était là, sellant son cheval.

« Attendez ! cria-t-il en trébuchant dans le fumier. C'était le choc. Elle est bouleversée. Elle ne saurait avoir véritablement l'intention de vous bannir. »

La magicienne administra une claque sur le flanc de sa monture et resserra la sous-ventrière. « Bien sûr que si. Et c'est son devoir de le faire. Non pas par ingratitude, mais parce qu'elle est la reine et que cela l'oblige à tenir sa parole.

— Mais...

— J'ai toujours su que ce jour viendrait. J'ignorais simplement quand et sous quelle forme. Pour être honnête, je suis soulagée. J'avais présumé que je mourrais lorsque Tamìr apprendrait la vérité. Au lieu de quoi, je recouvre en définitive ma liberté. » Sa main gantée lui effleura la joue. « Eh là, Arkoniel, vraiment ? Des larmes à ton âge ? »

Il s'épongea vivement les yeux sur sa manche, mais cela ne servit à rien. Elles continuaient à ruisseler. Il se cramponna à la main d'Iya, ne pouvant pas croire que c'était la dernière fois qu'ils se verraient tous les deux. « Il y a maldonne, Iya. Que vais-je devenir sans vous ?

— Tu t'es parfaitement débrouillé sans moi ces dernières années. En plus, c'est le cours naturel des choses. Tu n'es plus mon apprenti, Arkoniel. Tu es un magicien puissant, tu jouis de l'autorité que confère un mandat de l'Illuminateur, et tu as plus d'idées en matière de magie que je n'en ai jamais vu à quiconque. Tu pèches par excès de modestie, mon cher, et cela t'empêche de te rendre pleinement compte de tout ce que tu as déjà mené à bien grâce à la combinaison de la magie de Lhel avec la tienne. Rares sont ceux qui se risqueraient dans une aventure pareille, alors que toi tu t'y es engouffré en fonceur. Je suis plus fière de toi que je ne saurais dire. »

Elle battit des paupières et se remit à ajuster sa selle. « Ainsi suis-je sûre que, pris entre les soins que va réclamer notre nouvelle Orëska et celui de veiller sur notre petite reine, tu seras trop occupé pour que je te manque tant que ça. Sans compter qu'en outre nous sommes tous les deux Gardiens, et cela n'est pas non plus sans nous réserver des quantités d'embûches.

— Gardiens ? » Il accordait à peine au bol plus de considération qu'à un simple élément de son paquetage habituel. L'usage qu'Iya venait de faire du titre officiel lui donna des sueurs froides, en lui rappelant la prophétie que lui avait transmise la vieille Ranaï avant de mourir, le songe visionnaire du Gardien Hyradin : *Et finalement sera de nouveau le Gardien, dont le lot est amer, aussi amer que fiel quand se produira la rencontre sous le Pilier du Ciel.* Le sentiment que ces mots s'appliquaient à tous égards à Iya le fit frissonner de nouveau. « Qu'est-ce que cela a à voir avec quoi que ce soit de ce qui nous arrive ?

— Peut-être rien, peut-être tout. C'est par la volonté d'Illior que t'échoit simultanément le double fardeau du bol et de la reine. Tu es à la hauteur de la tâche, tu sais. Jamais je n'aurais remis aucun des deux à ta garde si je ne l'avais pas cru.

— Vous reverrai-je jamais ? »

Elle lui tapota le bras. « Je ne suis que bannie, mon cher, pas morte. Je t'enverrai de mes nouvelles.

— Frère va se lancer à vos trousses. Je pense qu'il vous a suivie. » Arkoniel scruta nerveusement les ténèbres.

« Je suis capable de m'en occuper. Je l'ai toujours fait. »

Il la regarda, navré, emmener son cheval au-dehors près du montoir puis grimper lentement en selle. « Votre bagage ! Attendez, je vais vous le chercher. Tamìr a dit que vous aviez jusqu'à l'aube.

— Pas besoin, Arkoniel. Je n'avais rien apporté d'important. » Elle lui ressaisit la main. « Promets-moi que tu resteras. Il était temps qu'elle sache la vérité, mais il lui faut désormais l'accepter et continuer à s'occuper des affaires. Aide-la dans sa tâche, Arkoniel. Cette nuit, tu risques de ne pas le croire, et peut-être se refuserait-elle à le croire aussi, mais elle a véritablement confiance en toi. Toi, Tharin et Ki, vous êtes tout ce qui lui reste de ce qui peut passer pour une famille. Aime-la comme tu l'as toujours fait et ne lui tiens pas rigueur de son attitude envers moi. »

Il se cramponna à sa main un moment de plus, avec le sentiment qu'il se comportait un peu comme le faisait Wythnir. « Accordez-moi le temps d'aller au moins récupérer votre manteau. Il fait froid.

— Très bien, alors, mais dépêche-toi ! »

Il prit ses jambes à son cou pour regagner la maison

des hôtes et décrocha le vieux manteau de voyage d'Iya d'une patère proche de sa porte. Il ne s'était absenté que quelques instants mais, lorsqu'il revint, la cour était vide. Il n'y avait plus trace d'Iya, et l'on n'entendait même pas les sabots de sa monture. Arkoniel dévala le sentier qui menait à la Serrure d'Illior, dans l'espoir de la rattraper. Les étoiles illuminaient toute la vallée, mais la route était déserte en aval comme en amont.

Il ne douta pas que la magicienne fût là, quelque part, mais elle s'était toujours montrée experte en l'art de se rendre invisible. Elle s'était servie du même sortilège, la nuit où ils avaient amené Lhel au Palatin, mais elle n'y avait jamais recouru pour se cacher de lui.

« Bonne chance ! » cria-t-il à la route déserte, debout, là, les mains chargées du manteau roulé en boule. Son cri se répercuta dans la passe en échos creux. « Je ferai tout ce que vous m'avez commandé ! Je le ferai ! Et... et merci ! » La voix lui manqua, tandis qu'une nouvelle crise de larmes brouillait les étoiles du firmament en les faisant virevolter. « Je ne vous oublierai pas », chuchota-t-il.

L'unique réponse qu'il obtint fut le hululement d'une chouette en chasse.

Sans se soucier du fait que des sentinelles risquaient de se trouver dans les parages à faire le guet, il enfouit son visage dans le manteau abandonné par son bien-aimé professeur et se mit à sangloter éperdument.

8

Aiguillonné par la peur et par la colère qu'il avait perçues dans la voix d'Arkoniel, Ki oublia ses appréhensions personnelles et se précipita vers la chambre de Tamìr. Postés devant la porte, Lynx et Nikidès tendaient l'oreille avec des mines manifestement anxieuses.

« Que s'est-il donc passé ? souffla-t-il.

— Elle a banni maîtresse Iya, je crois, et peut-être même Arkoniel, répondit Lynx. Il y a eu pas mal de gueulantes et, je te jure, la terre a tremblé. Puis nous avons entendu Tamìr leur aboyer de ficher le camp.

— En effet, je viens tout juste de croiser Arkoniel. C'est lui qui m'envoie.

— Elle ne veut voir personne. Ses ordres ont été formels, lui dit Nikidès d'un air contrit.

— Moi, elle me verra. »

Lynx se recula en invitant d'un geste Nikidès à faire de même. Ki les remercia d'un signe de tête et souleva le loquet.

Tamìr était assise devant le feu sur un tabouret bas, les genoux enserrés dans ses bras. Frère se trouvait accroupi près d'elle, les traits défigurés en un masque furibond, et il lui sifflait des choses rageuses, mais trop bas pour que Ki l'entende. L'atmosphère était lourde de menaces. En voyant Frère tendre la main lentement vers elle, Ki tira sa lame et se rua vers le démon. « Ne la touche pas ! »

Frère virevolta et vola à sa rencontre.

« Non ! » hurla Tamìr.

Avec un regard sournois, Frère poursuivit sa course, et Ki sentit un froid mortel l'environner. Le démon disparut. L'épée s'échappa des doigts engourdis de Ki, et lui-même se démena pour rester sur ses pieds, tandis qu'une vague de faiblesse le submergeait.

Tamìr bondit à ses côtés et l'empoigna par un bras pour le stabiliser. « Est-ce qu'il t'a blessé ?

— Non, juste flanqué la trouille.

— Bon. » Elle le relâcha puis se rassit, la tête détournée. « Va-t'en, Ki. Je n'ai pas envie de voir quiconque en ce moment. »

Il attira un tabouret près de celui qu'elle occupait et s'assit. « Tant pis, parce que je reste.

— Dehors. C'est un ordre. »

Il croisa résolument ses bras.

Elle le foudroya d'un regard furieux puis, renonçant à le voir obéir, enfouit son visage dans ses mains. « Iya et Lhel ont tué mon frère. »

Dans un certain sens, cette annonce ne le surprit pas. Sans piper mot, il attendit qu'elle continue.

« C'est à cause de moi qu'il est comme il est maintenant.

— Ce n'est pas ta faute. Par les couilles de Bilairy, tu n'étais toi-même qu'un nouveau-né ! Je suis sûr qu'elles l'ont fait uniquement parce qu'elles y étaient obligées.

— Pour Skala, précisa-t-elle d'une voix lourde de désolation.

— Je ne vais pas te dire que c'était juste, se servir

ainsi d'un bébé, mais si ton oncle t'avait trouvée, *toi*, et tuée ? Que serait-il alors advenu de Skala ?

— Tu parles exactement comme eux ! J'aurais dû tuer Iya pour le crime qu'elle a commis. Mon frère était un prince du sang. Mais... je n'ai pas pu ! » Ses épaules se secouèrent. « Je me suis bornée à la bannir, et maintenant Frère est plus haineux que jamais, et je ne sais pas comment j'arriverai jamais à poser de nouveau les yeux sur Arkoniel... J'étais juste en train de commencer à avoir de nouveau confiance en lui, et... » Elle se recroquevilla, pliée en deux comme un nœud de misère.

Oubliant leur brouille de tout à l'heure, Ki l'attira de nouveau dans ses bras. Elle ne pleurait pas, mais son corps était tout rigide et agité de tremblements. Il lui caressa de nouveau les cheveux, et elle finit au bout d'un moment par se détendre un petit peu. Un moment plus tard, elle lui ceignit la taille et se cacha la figure au creux de son cou.

« Est-ce que je suis un monstre, Ki ? Une chose contre nature ? »

Il tirailla l'une de ses mèches. « Ne sois pas stupide. »

Elle exhala un rire étranglé puis se redressa sur son siège. « Mais c'est Tobin que tu vois encore, n'est-ce pas ? »

Elle avait retrouvé sa fragilité, comme ce fameux soir avant qu'il ne parte se battre. « Je vois l'être qui est mon ami, l'être que j'ai aimé le jour de notre rencontre.

— Aimer. Comme un frère, dit-elle avec amertume. Et ça fait quoi de moi, maintenant ? Ta sœur ? »

Le chagrin qu'il voyait dans ses yeux lui tordit le cœur. *Si ce n'est une sœur, alors quoi ?* La crainte et la gêne retenaient encore sa langue, mais il n'avait pas oublié l'expression qu'avait prise tout à l'heure sa physionomie quand il l'avait appelée par son nom de garçon, pas plus que ce qu'il avait lui-même ressenti au cours du souper chaque fois qu'elle souriait à ce bellâtre d'Aurënfaïe. *Est-ce que je... ? Se pourrait-il que je... ?*

Les prunelles sombres de Tamìr s'agrandirent lorsqu'il se pencha pour effleurer timidement sa bouche avec la sienne et essayer de lui donner ce dont elle avait besoin.

Le contact fit trembler ses lèvres pendant un instant, puis elle détourna le visage. « Qu'est-ce que tu fais là ? Je n'ai que faire de ta pitié, Ki.

— Ce n'en est pas. » *N'en est-ce pas ?* Il baissa la tête. « Excuse-moi. »

Non sans soupirer, elle enfouit de nouveau son visage entre ses mains. « Je ne saurais exiger de toi des sentiments différents de ceux que tu éprouves. »

C'était là le problème. Il ne connaissait pas ses propres sentiments. *Elle est une fille, que diable ! Tu sais comment faire plaisir à une fille !* Il l'attira sur ses pieds, l'enlaça d'un bras par la taille et l'embrassa cette fois de manière plus décidée.

Elle ne le repoussa pas, mais ses bras demeurèrent ballants le long de ses flancs et ses poings serrés. Ce n'était pas comme embrasser un garçon, pas exactement, mais ce n'était pas non plus un bon vrai baiser. Il y avait des larmes et de la défiance dans les yeux de Tamìr quand il la relâcha.

« Qu'est-ce que tu vas faire maintenant, me balancer sur le plumard ? »

Accablé, il secoua la tête d'un air misérable. « Excuse-moi.

— Arrête de dire ça !

— Enfin, merde, Tamìr, je fais de mon mieux !

— Navrée que ce soit une telle corvée ! »

Ils se dévisagèrent pendant un instant, puis Ki tourna les talons et sortit en claquant la porte, non sans se dire qu'il s'agissait là d'une retraite stratégique.

Il n'eut pas le loisir de s'échapper que Lynx le rattrapa par le bras et le propulsa de nouveau carrément dans la chambre. « Retournes-y, espèce de lâche ! »

Déséquilibré par l'élan forcené de son irruption, Ki donna de plein fouet dans Tamìr, et leur culbute simultanée les fit s'effondrer sur le lit. Les sangles du sommier gémirent sous eux pendant qu'ils se débattaient pour se désenchevêtrer. Haletants et rouges de confusion, ils finirent par se réfugier aux extrémités opposées de la pièce.

« Lynx m'a poussé, marmonna Ki.

— Je sais. » Elle rabattit ses jupes en désordre sur ses genoux.

Un silence pénible déferla sur eux, sans rien pour le rompre que les craquements du feu. L'imagination de Ki lui fournissait en tout et pour tout le spectacle des autres, dehors, l'oreille collée à la porte. Il s'apprêtait à faire amende honorable, une fois de plus, mais un regard de Tamìr lui imposa de la fermer.

Au bout d'un nouveau moment de silence insoutenable, elle soupira et tendit la main. « Tu seras toujours mon meilleur ami, Ki. »

Ki la lui serra puis lâcha étourdiment : « Je t'aime, moi, *vraiment* ! Je t'aimerai toujours.

— Mais pas en tant que... ? »

Il baissa les yeux vers leurs mains jointes, fouillant dans son cœur à la recherche d'une étincelle de désir. Mais il lui était toujours impossible de s'imaginer en train de coucher avec elle comme il l'avait fait avec toutes ces servantes, toutes ces filles de cuisine. Tout se passait comme si quelque magicien lui avait jeté un sort et glacé les reins. « Je donnerais volontiers tout ce que je possède pour le faire de cette manière-là. »

Le sanglot qu'étouffa Tamìr et la vue des nouvelles larmes qui glissaient sur ses joues tordirent à nouveau le cœur de Ki. Ravalant durement sa salive, il se rapprocha d'elle et l'attira contre lui. Cette fois, elle pleura tout son soûl.

« Je suis maudite, Ki. Frère le dit, d'ailleurs.

— Enfin, tu n'es pas obligée de croire tout ce qu'il raconte... ! Tu sais quel menteur il est.

— Tu ne trouves pas que j'ai eu tort de laisser partir Iya, n'est-ce pas ?

— Non. Je trouve que tu aurais eu tort de la tuer. »

Elle se redressa et torcha son nez sur sa manche en lui adressant un sourire tremblant et penaud. « Je me suis vraiment changée en femme, hein ? Il n'a jamais été dans mes habitudes de chialer comme ça.

— Ne laisse pas Una t'attraper en train de parler de cette manière ! »

Elle s'arracha un semblant de sourire. « Ton amitié m'est plus précieuse que tout au monde. Si c'est tout ce que nous possédons jamais...

— Ne dis pas cela. » Il plongea franchement son regard dans les yeux si tristes de Tamìr, bien tenté de pleurer lui-même. « Mon cœur t'appartient. Il t'a toujours appartenu, et il t'appartiendra toujours. »

Tamìr poussa un soupir saccadé. « Et le mien t'appartient.

— Je le sais. Aussi, ne va pas... Eh bien, ne me laisse pas encore tomber, d'accord ? »

Elle fut sur le point de dire quelque chose, puis se ravisa. En revanche, elle se rassit et s'essuya la figure une fois encore. « Je présume que nous ferions mieux de dormir un brin.

— Veux-tu que je reste ? »

Elle secoua la tête, et Ki comprit lorsqu'elle évita son regard qu'ils ne pouvaient revenir ni l'un ni l'autre sur la tournure différente qu'avait prise cette nuit l'état de leurs relations.

Il ignora les regards interrogateurs de ses amis lorsqu'il ressortit. Il n'avait que quelques pas à faire dans le corridor de pierre bas de plafond pour rallier la chambre qu'on lui avait attribuée, mais la perspective de coucher tout seul dans le noir lui fit prendre la direction opposée.

Tharin se trouvait encore dans la grande salle, en train de jouer au bakshi avec Aladar et Maniès. Ki le salua d'un hochement de tête au passage avant de s'aventurer au-dehors. Il avait traversé la moitié de la place quand il entendit dans son dos la porte s'ouvrir et se refermer. Il se retourna, les bras croisés sur la poitrine, et attendit que Tharin l'ait rejoint.

Sans s'arrêter, celui-ci se contenta de frôler le bras du jeune homme en disant : « Allons faire un tour », puis se dirigea comme en flânant vers le sentier qui menait à la salle de l'Oracle.

Ils le remontèrent de conserve en s'avançant à pas précautionneux parmi les éboulis rocheux et dans les endroits glissants. Tharin avait l'air de chercher quelque chose. Qui se révéla être finalement l'espèce d'abri que formait une saillie de la falaise en surplomb du chemin. Il s'y installa, le dos contre la paroi du roc et fit signe à Ki de s'asseoir à ses côtés.

Ki remonta ses genoux et les enlaça dans ses bras, le cœur battant trop vite, dans l'attente de ce que Tharin avait à lui dire, quoi que ce fût. « Qu'est-ce que vous avez ouï dire, au juste ?

— Des pièces et des morceaux. Iya a été congédiée, et il se peut qu'Arkoniel soit parti avec elle. Je ne l'ai pas revu depuis qu'il t'a fait rentrer dare-dare. Qu'est-ce qu'il t'est possible de me raconter ? »

Ki lui déballa tout son sac à propos de la magicienne et de Frère et de ses propres échecs de balourd pour réconforter Tamìr. « J'ai même essayé de l'embrasser, confessa-t-il d'un ton lamentable. Elle a envie que je sois plus que juste son ami, Tharin.

— Je sais. »

Ki le regarda d'un air suffoqué.

Tharin sourit. « Elle me l'a confié, voilà des mois de ça. »

Ki sentit ses joues devenir brûlantes, en dépit de la froideur nocturne. « Pourquoi ne m'en avez-vous pas parlé ?

— Dans quel but ? J'ai des yeux, Ki.

— Vous voulez me flanquer des gifles ? Je le mérite. »

Au lieu de cela, Tharin se borna à lui administrer une tape sur le genou. « Tu ne peux pas changer ton cœur, Ki, pas plus que lui donner des ordres comme à un guerrier sur le champ de bataille.

— Les gens vont encore jaser.

— Ça, pas moyen d'y échapper. Les gens se plaisent à jaser.

— Ils ont toujours cancané à notre propos. Même quand Tamìr était un garçon, ils croyaient que nous couchions ensemble.

— Si vous l'aviez fait alors, cela vous faciliterait peut-être les choses aujourd'hui. Mais j'ai compris depuis longtemps que ce n'était pas votre genre.

— Dans ce cas, pourquoi suis-je incapable de répondre à son attente, maintenant qu'elle est une fille ? Par les couilles de Bilairy, Tharin, je l'aime, je l'aime vraiment, mais coucher avec elle, non, ça me paraît impensable, inimaginable.

— Tu l'as fait avec d'autres filles. Est-ce que tu les maltraitais ?

— Quoi ? Bien sûr que non !

— Est-ce que tu as aimé l'une d'elles ?

— Non, on s'envoyait en l'air, c'est tout.

— Et tu ne peux donc pas te faire à l'idée de t'envoyer en l'air avec notre Tamìr ? »

Ki se cabra, horrifié. « Évidemment pas ! »

Il s'attendait à ce que Tharin le tabasse ou du moins lui donne un conseil, mais celui-ci branla simplement son pouce en direction de la caverne de l'Oracle. « As-tu envisagé de descendre là-bas toi-même ?

— Non, je ne vais pas me saloper avec toute cette magie lunatique et fumeuse. Il est foutrement plus propre de suivre les voies de Sakor. Tu te bats, et tu vis ou crèves. Pas question de me colleter avec ces fantômes et ce sang ! »

Tharin se mit debout et s'étira. « Bah, les choses changent », dit-il d'un ton paisible, avant de se tourner et d'adresser à Ki un regard que celui-ci ne sut pas du tout comment interpréter. « Il suffit d'être patient, des fois. Rentrons. Il fait froid. »

Étant obligé de passer devant la porte de Tamìr pour regagner sa propre chambre, Ki dut essuyer le regard accusateur de Lynx. Plus tard, comme il reposait sur sa couche étroite, sachant pertinemment que le sommeil lui demeurerait étranger, il déplora de n'avoir pas davantage foi dans les assertions de Tharin. Il y avait tout bonnement des choses immuables, si fort que vous désiriez les voir se modifier.

9

Arkoniel passa le restant de la nuit assis sur une pierre au bord de la route. Enveloppé dans le manteau d'Iya, il contempla les étoiles parcourir le ciel et s'y effacer peu à peu.

La première lueur du jour posait une touche de rose sur les pics encapuchonnés de neige quand il entendit survenir derrière lui des cavaliers.

C'étaient les Aurënfaïes, emmitouflés dans des manteaux et coiffés du sobre sen'gaï blanc qu'ils avaient l'habitude de porter en voyage.

« Vous vous êtes levé bien tôt, magicien, lui dit Solun en guise de salutations.

— Vous aussi, répondit-il tout en se dressant sur ses jambes engourdies. Vous partez si vite ?

— Je serais volontiers resté », fit Arengil du tac au tac, d'un air un peu maussade. « Tamìr m'a offert une place au sein des Compagnons.

— Et moi donc ! » enchaîna Corruth, pas plus enchanté, manifestement.

Sylmaï les foudroya tous deux d'un regard réprobateur. « C'est à vos parents de trancher.

— Vous n'avez pas beaucoup vu Tamìr », observa Arkoniel, non sans inquiétude.

« Assez pour notre gouverne, lui assura Solun.

— Est-ce qu'Aurënen reconnaîtra ses prétentions ?

— Il appartient à chacun des clans d'en décider, mais je presserai Bôkthersa pour ma part de le faire.

— J'agirai de même à Gèdre, déclara Sylmaï.

— Elle entend déclarer la guerre, vous savez.

— Nous prendrons la chose en considération. Nos vaisseaux sont prompts, dût le besoin s'en faire sentir, répliqua-t-elle. Comment vous y prendrez-vous pour nous avertir ? »

Arkoniel lui fit une démonstration du charme de fenêtre. « Si je parviens à vous trouver, je puis vous parler à travers l'orifice, mais vous ne devez surtout pas le toucher.

— Cherchez-moi à Gèdre, alors. Adieu, et bonne chance. »

Les autres lui adressèrent un hochement de tête avant de se remettre en route, et l'ensemble de la troupe eut bientôt disparu dans les brumes du petit matin. Le Khatmé, nota-t-il, n'avait pas pipé mot d'éventuel soutien.

Il remonta lentement, troublé, vers la maison des hôtes.

Tamìr et les Compagnons prenaient leur petit déjeuner, assis en rond devant la grande cheminée. Ni elle ni Ki n'avaient de mine reposée, mais du moins étaient-ils assis côte à côte. Elle leva bien les yeux quand lui-même entra, mais elle s'abstint de l'inviter à la rejoindre. Il se demanda tristement si elle s'était ravisée sur la question de son bannissement. Avec un soupir intérieur, il se dirigea vers le buffet, s'y servit de pain et de fromage et les emporta dans sa chambre.

Le feu s'était éteint, et il régnait un froid sépulcral dans la cellule minuscule. Wythnir dormait encore à poings fermés, recroquevillé en boule sous les couvertures. Après avoir déposé quelques bûches dans l'âtre,

Arkoniel recourut à un sortilège. Il gaspillait rarement la magie sur des broutilles aussi triviales qu'un feu matinal, mais il était trop démoralisé pour faire l'effort de battre le briquet. Le bois prit instantanément, et une éclatante flambée l'embrasa.

« Maître ? » Wythnir se dressa sur son séant, l'air soucieux. « Est-ce que la reine a vraiment renvoyé Iya ? »

Arkoniel s'assit sur le bord du lit et lui tendit une bouchée de son propre repas. « Oui, mais tout va bien.

— Pourquoi est-ce qu'elle a fait ça ?

— Je te le dirai une autre fois. Mange. Nous ne tarderons pas à partir. »

Le petit grignota consciencieusement le fromage.

Arkoniel portait encore le manteau d'Iya. L'odeur de celle-ci imprégnait le lainage. Cela, et le vieux sac râpé qui traînait à côté du lit, voilà tout ce qu'il lui restait de toute une vie passée avec elle, à ce qu'il semblait.

Iya avait dit vrai, bien sûr. Dans des circonstances normales, il l'aurait quittée à la fin de son apprentissage pour suivre sa propre voie ; mais les événements les avaient gardés ensemble et, d'une manière ou d'une autre, il s'était toujours imaginé qu'ils le resteraient, surtout à partir du moment où ils avaient entrepris de rallier à eux d'autres magiciens.

Une petite main se referma sur la sienne. « Je suis désolé que vous ayez tant de chagrin, Maître. »

Arkoniel le prit contre lui et posa son visage dans ses cheveux. « Merci. Elle va me manquer. »

Malgré tous ses efforts, il ne se découvrit pas

beaucoup d'appétit. Comme il jetait au feu le pain qu'il n'avait pu manger, Tamìr se faufila dans la pièce sans avoir frappé.

« Bonjour. » Il tâcha de prendre un air jovial, mais il eut du mal à sourire, tant il en avait encore gros sur le cœur du châtiment qu'elle avait infligé à Iya. « Wythnir, la reine et moi devons nous parler seule à seul. Va finir de déjeuner dans la grande salle. » L'enfant se glissa tout de suite hors du lit, encore vêtu de sa longue chemise de nuit. Arkoniel l'enveloppa dans le manteau de la magicienne avant de le laisser filer.

Après quoi Tamìr referma la porte et s'y adossa, les bras sévèrement croisés sur le plastron de sa tunique. « J'ai expédié Una et des cavaliers enrôler du monde dans les domaines du sud. Je compte entreprendre mes préparatifs de guerre aussitôt que nous atteindrons Atyion.

— Tant mieux. »

Elle resta là un moment, muette, puis soupira. « Je ne regrette pas, vous savez, en ce qui concerne Iya. Frère voulait que je la tue. La renvoyer... c'était le mieux que je puisse faire.

— Je sais. Elle l'a compris.

— Mais je devine... enfin, je suis contente que vous soyez toujours ici, même s'il ne nous est plus possible d'être amis. »

Il avait envie, *quelque part*, de la rassurer, mais les mots se refusèrent à sortir. « Est-ce pour me dire cela que vous êtes venue me voir ?

— Non. Elle a prétendu qu'il me fallait vous garder

à cause de la vision que vous avez eue ici. J'aimerais en apprendre davantage sur ce sujet.

— Ah. C'est à Iya que fut accordée la vision du palais blanc. Mais elle m'y distingua. J'étais un grand vieillard, et j'avais un jeune apprenti à mes côtés. L'immense demeure fourmillait de magiciens et de gosses magiciens-nés, tous réunis là pour apprendre et partager leurs pouvoirs en sécurité, pour le bien du pays.

— Votre Troisième Orëska.

— Oui.

— Où doit-elle se trouver ? À Atyion ?

— Non. Selon ses dires, Iya vit une belle ville neuve au sommet d'une haute falaise qui dominait la mer et surplombait une baie profonde. »

À cette description, Tamìr releva les yeux. « Vous pensez donc que cette ville n'existe pas encore ?

— Non. Dans sa vision, comme je vous l'ai dit, j'étais un homme très âgé. »

Elle parut désappointée.

« Qu'y a-t-il, Tamìr ? »

Elle frotta d'un air absent la menue cicatrice de son menton. « Je continue à rêver que je me trouve sur des falaises à contempler une baie profonde en contrebas. C'est quelque part sur la côte ouest, mais il n'y a pas de ville. J'ai vu cet endroit si souvent que cela me donne l'impression d'y être allée, mais j'ignore ce que cela signifie. Parfois, il y a un homme dans le lointain qui agite la main vers moi. Je n'ai jamais été capable de distinguer qui c'était, mais maintenant je pense que c'est peut-être vous. Ki figure dans mon rêve, lui aussi.

Je... » Elle s'interrompit et se détourna, ses lèvres pincées en une fine ligne. « À votre avis, c'est le même endroit que nous avons vu, Iya et moi ?

— C'est possible. Avez-vous questionné l'Oracle à ce propos ?

— J'ai essayé de le faire, mais j'ai seulement obtenu la réponse dont je vous ai déjà parlé. Qui n'était pas d'un grand secours, n'est-ce pas ?

— Peut-être plus que vous ne le croyez. À l'époque, Iya n'avait aucune idée non plus de ce que pouvait signifier sa vision. C'est seulement maintenant que celle-ci commence à avoir un semblant de sens. Mais il est encourageant que les lieux que vous avez vus toutes deux soient éventuellement les mêmes. Et je soupçonne que c'est bien le cas.

— Est-ce que vous me détestez de l'avoir renvoyée ?

— Bien sûr que non. Elle me manquera, mais je comprends. Et vous, me détestez-vous ? »

Elle rit tristement. « Non. Je ne suis même pas certaine de détester Iya. En fait, c'est Lhel qui a tué Frère, mais je n'arrive pas à la détester du tout ! Elle a été si bonne pour moi en m'aidant quand j'étais toute seule...

— Elle vous aime énormément.

— J'aimerais bien savoir quand je la reverrai. Peut-être que nous devrions faire un détour par le fort en rentrant chez nous pour essayer de la retrouver. Elle y est toujours, d'après vous ?

— Je l'ai cherchée, le soir où je suis allé récupérer votre poupée, mais sans réussir à lui mettre la main dessus. Vous savez comment elle est...

— À propos, en quoi consistait votre propre vision, lors de votre première visite ici ?

— Je me suis vu moi-même, tenant dans mes bras un mioche à cheveux noirs. Maintenant, je sais qu'il s'agissait de vous. »

Il remarqua à quel point ses lèvres tremblaient quand elle chuchota : « C'est tout ?

— Il arrive à l'Illuminateur de se montrer parfois extrêmement lapidaire, Tamìr. » Elle avait l'air si jeune et si désemparée qu'il lui tendit la main. Elle hésita, les sourcils froncés, puis vint s'asseoir avec raideur auprès de lui sur le bord du lit.

« Je me fais encore l'effet d'être un imposteur dans ce corps-ci, même après l'avoir trimbalé pendant des mois et des mois.

— Ça ne fait pas si longtemps que ça, comparé à la durée de votre existence antérieure. Et vous avez eu tant de motifs d'inquiétude, en plus... Je suis désolé que les choses aient dû se passer de la sorte. »

Elle se mit à fixer le feu, battant violemment des paupières pour éviter de pleurer. En fin de compte, elle exhala dans un souffle : « Je n'arrive pas à croire que Père n'ait pas seulement ébauché un geste pour s'interposer. Comment a-t-il pu se conduire ainsi vis-à-vis de son propre enfant ?

— Il n'a eu connaissance du plan dans toute son étendue que cette nuit-là. Si ceci peut vous apporter quelque réconfort, il était ravagé. Je pense qu'il ne s'en est jamais remis. Illior sait quelle punition ce fut pour lui que de regarder les conséquences qui en résultèrent pour votre mère et pour vous.

— Vous le connaissiez bien, vous et Iya ?

— Nous avons eu cet honneur. C'était un homme éminent, un homme de cœur, et un guerrier incomparable. Vous lui ressemblez beaucoup. Vous avez toute sa hardiesse et sa bonté sans bornes. Toute jeune que vous êtes, je distingue déjà sa sagesse en vous. Mais vous possédez aussi les meilleures qualités de votre mère, telle qu'elle était avant votre naissance. » Il toucha la bague portant l'effigie du couple. « Je suis heureux que vous ayez trouvé ce bijou. Chacun de vos parents vous a transmis ses dons supérieurs, et l'Illuminateur ne vous a pas choisie par hasard. Vous êtes l'élue d'Illior. N'oubliez jamais cela, quelque autre événement qui puisse survenir. Vous serez la reine la plus prestigieuse qu'ait connue Skala depuis Ghërilain.

— J'espère que vous ne vous abusez pas », dit-elle avec tristesse avant de prendre congé.

Arkoniel demeura quelque temps immobile à contempler fixement le feu. Tout soulagé qu'il était que leur bonne intelligence eût résisté à l'épreuve, la douleur de la perte d'Iya persistait d'autant plus à lui serrer le cœur que Tamìr était encore très fragile, en dépit de sa remarquable énergie. Mais aussi, quel fardeau pesait sur ses frêles épaules... ! Il résolut finalement de mieux s'appliquer à l'aider à le porter.

C'est obsédé par cette intention qu'il sortit en catimini pour retourner à la caverne de l'Oracle. Pour la première fois de sa vie, il s'y rendait seul, et avec ses propres questions fermement ancrées dans l'esprit.

Les prêtres masqués le firent descendre, et il se retrouva plongé dans les ténèbres familières. Loin d'éprouver la moindre peur, ce coup-ci, il n'était que détermination.

Lorsque ses pieds touchèrent la terre ferme, il se dirigea sur-le-champ vers la douce lueur voisine.

Il se pouvait que la femme assise sur le tabouret de l'Oracle soit en fait la jeune fille avec laquelle il avait déjà parlé. C'était difficile à dire, et personne d'autre que le grand prêtre d'Afra ne savait comment on procédait pour choisir les Oracles ni combien ils étaient à un moment donné. Car ce n'étaient pas toujours des filles ou des femmes. Il connaissait des magiciens qui s'étaient entretenus dans ce même lieu avec de jeunes hommes. Le seul facteur commun de la corporation semblait être un grain de démence ou de débilité.

Elle secoua sa crinière hirsute et le dévisagea pendant qu'il prenait place sur le tabouret qui lui faisait face. Le pouvoir du dieu faisait déjà flamboyer ses yeux, et sa voix, lorsqu'elle prit la parole, avait ce timbre étrange qui sonnait plus qu'humain.

« Sois à nouveau le bienvenu, Arkoniel, dit-elle comme si elle lisait dans ses pensées. Tu te tiens aux côtés de la reine. Félicitations.

— Ma tâche n'en est qu'à ses débuts, n'est-ce pas ?

— Tu n'avais pas besoin de venir ici pour le savoir.

— Non, mais je veux vous demander conseil, sublime Illior. Que dois-je faire pour aider Tamìr ? »

Elle agita une main, et les ténèbres s'ouvrirent auprès d'eux comme une fenêtre immense. La ville s'y encadrait, perchée sur les falaises, avec une foule d'immenses maisons, de parcs boisés et de larges rues. Elle était infiniment plus vaste qu'Ero, d'aspect plus propre et plus régulier. En son cœur se dressaient deux palais. L'un était bas et avait l'allure rébarbative d'une forteresse, construite à l'intérieur d'un rempart de courtine. Le second était une tour colossale, carrée, svelte et gracieuse, dont chacun des quatre angles était équipé d'une tourelle surmontée d'un dôme. Lui n'était gardé que par un simple mur, et sur son terrain s'étendaient des jardins diversement plantés. Arkoniel vit des gens s'y promener, des hommes, des femmes et des enfants, des Skaliens, des 'faïes et même des centaures.

« Tu dois lui offrir cela.

— C'est la nouvelle capitale qu'elle doit fonder ?

— Oui, et les membres de la Troisième Orëska en seront les gardiens secrets.

— Les gardiens ? C'est un titre qui m'a déjà été imparti.

— Tu conserves le bol ?

— Oui !

— Enfouis-le profondément dans le cœur du cœur. Il n'est rien pour toi ni pour elle.

— Mais, dans ce cas, pourquoi me faut-il le conserver ? demanda-t-il, déçu.

« Parce que tu es le Gardien. En le gardant, tu gardes Tamìr et Skala tout entière et le monde entier.

— Ne pouvez-vous me dire ce qu'il est au juste ?

— Il n'est rien par lui-même, mais il fait partie d'un gigantesque maléfice.

— Et c'est cela que vous voudriez me voir enfouir au cœur de la ville de Tamìr ? Quelque chose de maléfique ?

— Peut-il exister du bien sans la connaissance du mal, magicien ? Peut-il exister une existence sans équilibre ? »

La vision de la ville se dissipa, supplantée par une grande balance d'or. Sur l'un de ses plateaux reposaient la couronne et l'épée de Skala. Sur l'autre gisait, nu, un nouveau-né mort : Frère. Arkoniel frissonna et réprima sa folle envie de regarder ailleurs. « Le mal va donc toujours se trouver au cœur de tout ce que Tamìr accomplira ?

— Le mal est en permanence avec nous. L'équilibre est tout.

— Alors, je crois qu'il me faudra faire infiniment de bien, pour préserver votre équilibre. Parce que j'ai indiscutablement le sang de ce nouveau-né-là sur les mains, en dépit des allégations spécieuses de tout le monde. »

Autour d'eux, la salle devint extrêmement sombre. Arkoniel sentit l'atmosphère s'alourdir, et les poils follets de sa nuque se hérissèrent. Néanmoins, l'Oracle se mit simplement à sourire et s'inclina en courbant la tête. « Tu es incapable d'agir d'une autre manière, enfant d'Illior. Tes mains et ton cœur sont forts, et tes yeux voient clair. Tu ne saurais ni t'empêcher de voir ce que les autres ne peuvent pas se permettre d'admettre, ni de proférer la stricte vérité. »

Dans l'intervalle qui les séparait apparut à même le sol un couple d'amants nus qui s'en donnaient éperdument. C'était lui-même, se démenant entre les cuisses de Lhel qui l'agrippait à bras-le-corps. Elle avait la tête rejetée en arrière, et sa noire chevelure en friche se déployait autour de sa face extasiée. Or, alors que, confronté à ce spectacle, Arkoniel s'empourprait de façon cuisante, Lhel ouvrit les yeux et darda son regard droit sur lui.. « Tu possèdes toujours mon amour, Arkoniel. Garde-toi de me pleurer jamais. »

La vision se dissipa rapidement. « Pleurer ?

— Tu as fouillé dans sa chair, et elle t'a laissé gravide de magie. Fais-en bon usage et avec sagesse.

— Elle est morte, n'est-ce pas ? » Semblable à un poing, le chagrin se reploya autour de son cœur et le lui broya. « Comment ? Vous est-il possible de me le montrer ? »

L'Oracle se borna à le regarder de ses yeux brillants. « Ce fut une mort consentante. »

Cette réponse n'atténua nullement sa peine. Depuis leur séparation, il n'avait pas un instant cessé d'envisager avec impatience l'occasion de repartir à sa recherche et de la trouver en train de l'attendre.

Il pressa ses paumes contre son visage, les paupières brûlées de larmes contenues. « D'abord Iya, et maintenant Lhel ?

— Toutes deux consentantes, chuchota l'Oracle.

— Le beau réconfort que voilà ! Que vais-je raconter à Tamìr ?

— Ne lui dis rien. Cela n'est pas indispensable, pour le moment.

— Peut-être pas. » Il s'était depuis longtemps accoutumé à porter secrets et douleurs. Pourquoi devrait-ce différer si peu que ce soit, maintenant ?

10

Au retour de sa flânerie coutumière de l'après-midi parmi les divers campements, Nyrin trouva Moriel et maîtresse Tomara qui l'attendaient dans ses appartements privés. Cette dernière serrait un petit baluchon blanc contre son ventre, et elle rayonnait littéralement.

« Elle est finalement enceinte, messire ! » Elle ouvrit son ballot pour exhiber tout un assortiment des sous-vêtements de lin de Nalia.

Nyrin les examina minutieusement. « En êtes-vous tout à fait certaine, femme ?

— Pas la moindre trace de sang depuis les deux dernières pleines lunes, messire, et elle n'a pas gardé son petit déjeuner depuis le soir des flagellations. J'ai d'abord cru que c'était simplement à cause de sa tendance à la compassion, mais les troubles ont persisté. Elle est verte comme une courgette jusqu'à midi, et la chaleur la fait s'évanouir. J'ai été sage-femme, aussi bien que camériste d'une grande dame, pendant quarante ans, et je me flatte de connaître les symptômes.

— Eh bien, voilà une heureuse nouvelle. Le roi Korin va en être enchanté, je suis sûr. Il vous faudra venir demain l'annoncer devant la cour.

— Vous ne souhaitez pas vous charger d'en faire part vous-même, messire ?

— Non, ne la gâchons pas à Sa Majesté. Laissons-lui croire qu'il est le premier à l'apprendre. » D'un geste assez cabotin de conjurateur, il fit surgir de l'air deux sesters d'or et les lui offrit. « Dans l'intérêt du roi ? »

Tomara empocha les pièces et lui adressa un clin d'œil. « Naturellement, messire. »

Tomara valait autant que sa parole, et c'est sans jeter ne serait-ce qu'un coup d'œil en direction des magiciens qu'elle se présenta le lendemain matin devant Korin pendant qu'il tenait sa cour.

Il avait beau se trouver plongé jusqu'au cou dans les rapports de ses généraux, cela ne l'empêcha pas de relever des yeux stupéfaits quand il l'aperçut en ces lieux à cette heure-là. « Oui, qu'y a-t-il ? Est-ce que vous venez m'apporter un message de la part de votre maîtresse ? »

Tomara fit une révérence. « Oui, Sire. Son Altesse m'enjoint de vous annoncer qu'elle porte un enfant. »

Il la dévisagea pendant un moment puis poussa une exclamation joyeuse et administra des claques dans le dos d'Alben et d'Urmanis. « Ça y est ! Voilà le signal que nous escomptions. Maître Porion, faites prévenir tous mes généraux. Nous marchons enfin contre Atyion ! »

La salle bondée se mit à rugir et à l'ovationner. Nyrin s'avança pour se porter aux côtés de Korin.

« Êtes-vous sûr que le moment soit bien choisi ? » lui murmura-t-il, trop bas pour que quiconque d'autre puisse surprendre ses paroles. « Après tout, sa grossesse ne peut dater que d'une lune ou deux. Ne serait-il pas plus sage de patienter un tout petit peu plus, par simple mesure de sécurité ?

— Le diable vous emporte, Nyrin ! Vous êtes pire qu'une vieille femme ! » s'écria Korin en prenant ses distances. « Entendez-vous ça, messeigneurs ? Mon magicien pense que nous devrions attendre un ou deux mois de plus ! Pourquoi pas jusqu'au printemps prochain ? Non, les neiges vont survenir et les mers se durcir. Si nous faisons mouvement dès à présent, nous risquons même de les surprendre avant qu'ils n'aient moissonné leurs champs. Qu'en dites-vous, messeigneurs ? Avons-nous lanterné suffisamment longtemps ? »

De nouvelles acclamations tonitruantes saluèrent son discours, et Nyrin se dépêcha de s'incliner devant Korin d'un air chagriné. « Vous êtes le mieux avisé, Sire, j'en suis persuadé. Je m'inquiète uniquement pour votre sécurité personnelle et pour votre trône.

— Mon trône se trouve à Ero ! » cria Korin en tirant son épée et en la brandissant. « Et l'on n'aura pas engrangé la totalité des récoltes que je me tiendrai sur le Palatin pour y faire dûment valoir mes droits. Sus à Ero ! »

L'assistance reprit en chœur le cri de ralliement, et, transmis de gorge en gorge, il ne tarda pas à retentir à l'extérieur dans les cours de la forteresse et à se propager au-delà des remparts jusqu'aux camps.

Nyrin échangea un coup d'œil ravi avec Moriel. Son petit numéro avait marché à merveille et obtenu les résultats escomptés. Personne ne pourrait contester que le processus avait été déclenché par la volonté du roi plutôt que par celle de ses magiciens.

En entendant ce concert de hurlements, Nalia sortit précipitamment sur son balcon pour voir si c'était la nouvelle qui la concernait qu'on était en train de célébrer là.

Éparpillée sur les deux côtés de la forteresse, l'armée de Korin formait une immense mer de tentes et d'enclos pour les bêtes. Elle apercevait des estafettes qui se dispersaient en tous sens et, dans leur sillage, des hommes qui sortaient des tentes. Elle tendit l'oreille un bon moment pour essayer de distinguer les mots que scandait tout ce monde. Lorsqu'elle y parvint, ce fut pour éprouver un accès de dépit.

« À Ero ? Voilà tout ce que lui inspire mon état ? » Elle retourna à ses travaux d'aiguille.

Peu de temps après, cependant, elle perçut le pas familier de Korin dans l'escalier de la tour.

Il entra en trombe et, pour la première fois depuis qu'elle avait fait sa connaissance, ses yeux sombres étaient illuminés par une joie sincère. Tomara pénétra à sa suite et, par-dessus l'épaule de Korin, adressa à Nalia un clin d'œil radieux.

« Est-ce vrai ? » lui demanda-t-il, tout en la contemplant d'un air ahuri comme s'il ne l'avait jamais vue auparavant. « Vous portez mon enfant ? »

Notre enfant ! songea-t-elle, mais elle sourit d'un air modeste en pressant une main sur son ventre encore plat. « Oui, messire. Tout indique que j'en suis à près de deux mois. La naissance aura lieu au printemps.

— Oh, quelle nouvelle merveilleuse ! » Il se laissa tomber à genoux aux pieds de la jeune femme et posa sa main sur la sienne. « Les drysiens vont veiller sur vous. Vous ne manquerez de rien. Exprimez seulement un désir, et il est d'avance exaucé ! »

Elle abaissa sur lui un regard suffoqué. Il ne lui avait jamais parlé jusqu'alors de cette manière-là... – comme si elle était véritablement son épouse. « Soyez-en remercié, messire. J'aimerais plus que tout au monde jouir de davantage de liberté. Je vis tellement confinée, ici... Me serait-il possible d'avoir une chambre digne de ce nom, en bas, dans la forteresse ? »

Il fut sur le point de rebuter sa requête, mais elle avait bien choisi son moment. « Bien entendu. On vous donnera la chambre la plus somptueuse et la plus accueillante possible de cette demeure arriérée. J'engagerai des peintres pour la décorer à votre goût avec des tapisseries neuves... Oh, et puis je vous ai apporté ceci. »

Il tira de sa manche une bourse de soie qu'il déposa dans son giron. Nalia dénoua le cordon de soie coulissant qui la fermait, et un long sautoir de perles de mer éblouissantes se déversa sur ses genoux. « Merci, messire. Elles sont très jolies ! »

— Elles passent pour porter bonheur aux femmes enceintes et pour assurer la sécurité de l'enfant dans les eaux du sein maternel. Portez-les en ma faveur, voulez-vous ? »

Une ombre s'abattit sur le cœur de Nalia tandis qu'elle mettait docilement le collier. Les perles étaient belles, et elles avaient une nuance rose adorable, mais il s'agissait là d'un talisman, pas d'une parure. « Je les porterai, conformément à votre souhait, messire. Merci. »

Korin lui sourit à nouveau. « Ma première épouse raffolait de prunes et de poisson salé quand elle était grosse. Avez-vous éprouvé le moindre désir impérieux ? Puis-je envoyer quérir quelque chose de spécial que vous n'ayez pas ?

— Il ne me manque qu'un peu plus d'espace pour me promener », répondit-elle, poussant plus loin son avantage.

« Vous l'aurez, sitôt qu'on aura préparé une pièce. » Il lui prit la main dans les siennes. « Vous ne serez pas toujours claquemurée dans cette place morne, je vous le promets. Je vais bientôt marcher contre le prince Tobin, afin de reconquérir ma ville et mon pays. Nos enfants joueront dans les jardins du Palatin. »

Ero ! Elle avait toujours eu envie d'y aller, mais Nyrin n'avait jamais voulu en entendre parler. Voir finalement une grande ville, y être consort... « Cela sera très agréable, messire.

— Avez-vous déjà consulté la bague ?

— Non, nous avons pensé qu'il vous plairait d'y assister, Sire », mentit Tomara, non sans adresser un nouveau clin d'œil à Nalia. Bien sûr qu'elles l'avaient fait, dès l'instant où la vieille avait présumé que la grossesse était en cours.

Affectant l'ignorance, Nalia se laissa aller contre le dossier de son fauteuil et tendit à Tomara la bague que Korin lui avait donnée le jour de leur mariage. Tomara puisa dans la poche de son tablier une longueur de fil rouge au bout duquel elle accrocha la bague, puis

141

laissa pendre l'ensemble au-dessus du ventre de sa maîtresse. Au bout d'un moment, la bague se mit à bouger et à décrire de tout petits cercles. Ces premiers mouvements n'avaient aucune espèce de signification. Si la sage-femme possédait authentiquement des dons de sourcier, la bague commencerait à se balancer d'avant en arrière si l'enfant était un garçon, à décrire de plus larges cercles s'il était une fille.

Or les cercles finirent par s'élargir, exactement comme lors de la première expérience.

« Une fille, à coup sûr, Sire, annonça Tomara d'un ton péremptoire.

— Une fille. Une petite reine. Tant mieux. » Le sourire de Korin perdit un peu de son assurance quand il renfila la bague sur le doigt de Nalia.

Il s'inquiète qu'elle me ressemble. Nalia refoula cette idée blessante et pressa la main de Korin. Elle ne pouvait pas l'en blâmer, supposa-t-elle. Peut-être qu'au contraire l'enfant lui ferait la faveur de tenir de lui. Si elle avait son teint, elle serait une jolie fille.

Korin la surprit une nouvelle fois en portant sa main à ses lèvres et en la baisant. « Peut-être vous sera-t-il possible de me pardonner nos débuts difficiles ? Avec un enfant et le trône assuré, je m'efforcerai de me comporter envers vous en meilleur époux. J'en fais le serment par Dalna. »

Faute de mots pour lui exprimer à quel point sa gentillesse la touchait, elle lui baisa la main à son tour. « Je serai une bonne mère pour nos enfants, messire. »

Peut-être, songea-t-elle, *que je pourrai en venir à l'aimer, en définitive.*

11

Ki n'avait pas été fâché de quitter Afra. Loin de rasséréner Tamìr, sa visite à l'Oracle paraissait l'avoir perturbée plus que jamais. Elle ne desserra guère les dents lorsqu'ils s'en allèrent, et les embûches vicieuses de la marche réclamèrent ensuite trop d'attention pour autoriser de longues conversations. Il n'en perçut pas moins la profonde tristesse où elle était plongée.

Il savait qu'il ne pouvait l'imputer tout entière à l'Oracle. Il lui avait salement manqué par sa propre maladresse, et tous deux en demeuraient blessés. Enroulé tout seul dans ses couvertures, chaque nuit, il rêvait de leurs baisers désastreux et se réveillait lourd de fatigue et de remords.

Dans les rares occasions où son rêve se débrouillait de son propre chef pour savourer ces maudits baisers, lui se réveillait encore plus déboussolé. Ces matins-là, quand il la regardait se débarbouiller la figure dans un ruisseau puis peigner ses cheveux, il déplorait plus que jamais que leurs relations ne soient pas restées telles qu'elles étaient pendant leur enfance commune. Il n'y avait eu aucune espèce d'ombre entre eux, aucune espèce d'équivoque. Dans ce temps-là, il pouvait regarder Tobin ou le toucher sans éprouver tous ces remous intimes. Il ne doutait pas de l'amour qu'ils se vouaient réciproquement, mais ce n'était pas là du tout le genre d'amour que Tamìr souhaitait, qu'elle méritait.

Il gardait tout cela renfermé au fond de son cœur ;

elle avait besoin qu'il se montre énergique et lucide, au lieu de se morfondre comme l'un de ces soupirants gavés de poèmes à l'eau de rose. En dépit de tous ses efforts, et il avait fait de son mieux, les autres en avaient suffisamment entendu, cette nuit-là, dans la maison des hôtes, pour se tracasser. Aucun d'eux ne lui posait la moindre question directe, mais il surprenait souvent leurs regards posés sur Tamìr et sur lui.

Le comportement d'Arkoniel était un mystère presque aussi indéchiffrable que celui de Tamìr. Il devait être encore indubitablement très malheureux du bannissement d'Iya. Et cependant, lui et Tamìr semblaient en termes plus intimes qu'ils ne l'avaient été depuis des mois. Il chevauchait chaque jour à ses côtés, l'entretenant de ses magiciens et de leurs compétences respectives, ainsi que de la nouvelle capitale qu'elle projetait d'édifier. Elle avait déjà évoqué avec Ki ses rêves d'un lieu situé sur la côte ouest mais, dans ses visions d'Afra, quelque chose avait captivé son imagination, et le magicien paraissait ardemment désireux de l'encourager à concrétiser de tels plans, malgré ce qui s'y opposait de toute évidence.

Ces obstacles, Ki s'en souciait comme d'une guigne. Il savait seulement que la tristesse disparaissait des yeux de Tamìr quand elle parlait de cette chimère, en échafaudant les moyens d'en faire une ville beaucoup plus grandiose qu'Ero. Elle retrouvait alors son regard coutumier d'autrefois, pendant qu'elle était en train de travailler sur quelque motif inédit destiné à

144

orner une bague ou un corselet de plates. Elle n'était jamais si heureuse que lorsqu'elle mijotait une nouvelle création.

Arkoniel avait énormément voyagé, et il dissertait avec autant de facilité de drainage et d'égouts qu'il parlait de son art personnel. Saruel renseigna Tamìr sur les villes aurënfaïes et sur les innovations dont elles se dotaient en matière de chauffage et de ventilation. Les 'faïes semblaient particulièrement experts pour tout ce qui touchait aux bains. Ils leur consacraient des salles entières, équipées de conduites pour l'eau chaude et de sols spéciaux qui pouvaient se chauffer par en dessous grâce à un double niveau de briques. Certaines des plus grandes demeures possédaient des espèces de piscines suffisamment vastes pour permettre à des quantités de gens d'y faire simultanément trempette à loisir. Il s'y négociait même des contrats d'affaires, apparemment.

« À vous entendre, on jurerait que votre peuple passe plus de temps à se baigner qu'à faire quoi que ce soit d'autre », fit observer Una, non sans un grand sourire.

« Certainement plus que les Skaliens ! » lui rétorqua Saruel, narquoise. « Les bains ne sont pas uniquement hygiéniques mais bons pour l'esprit. Et, conjugués avec des massages et les herbes appropriées, ils constituent en plus une excellente médication. Si j'en crois ma propre expérience, les 'faïes sentent non seulement meilleur que vos compatriotes, mais ils sont un peuple plus sain. »

Cette déclaration fit glousser Nikidès. « Êtes-vous en train de nous accuser de puer ?

— Je constate simplement un fait. Quand vous vous mettrez à bâtir votre fameuse ville neuve, Tamìr, vous pourriez trouver bénéfique de fonder des établissements de bains dignes de ce nom et accessibles à tous, pas exclusivement à vos classes privilégiées. Envoyez vos bâtisseurs à Bôkthersa apprendre nos méthodes. On y est particulièrement compétent pour ce genre de choses.

— Je ne répugnerais pas trop à me rendre là-bas moi-même, si tous les habitants ressemblent à ce Solun et à son cousin ! » murmura Una, et plus d'un des Compagnons acquiesça d'un hochement de tête.

« Ah, oui, sourit Saruel. Même chez les 'faïes, ils sont considérés comme singulièrement beaux.

— Il me faudra tâcher d'aller y faire un tour, déclara Tamìr avec un petit sourire en coin. Pour m'initier à la science des bains, naturellement. »

Sa réflexion lui valut un succès franc et massif d'hilarité unanime. Unanime, à l'exception de Ki. Il s'était aperçu de l'immense intérêt qu'elle avait porté au superbe Aurënfaïe. Sur le moment, il avait tout fait pour affecter de l'ignorer, mais à l'entendre en plaisanter, comme ça, devant tout le monde, un nouvel accès lancinant de jalousie le tenailla. Il le refoula mais, pour la première fois, il lui fallut affronter le fait qu'elle devrait bien épouser quelqu'un, et ce sans tarder. Il essaya de se figurer la chose, mais ce fut en pure perte. Seule lui trottait en tête la façon qu'elle avait eue de regarder Solun, et à quel point ça l'avait démangé de flanquer le type dehors, avec sa jolie gueule.

Et pourtant, je n'arrive même pas à l'embrasser, songea-t-il, écœuré. *De quel droit puis-je me targuer pour être jaloux ?*

Le chapitre de l'architecture et des hypocaustes ne lui fournissait guère l'occasion de briller, mais il se rendit compte que sa propre imagination était captivée par l'idée de voir prendre forme une nouvelle ville, surtout une ville édifiée sous la houlette de Tamìr et de son esprit créatif. Elle était déjà en train de penser à des jardins et des fontaines, ainsi qu'à des fortifications. Les avantages présentés par une capitale sise à l'ouest se concevaient fort bien, militairement parlant, à condition qu'on puisse surmonter le problème posé par les voies commerciales intérieures.

« Il doit exister un moyen de tracer une bonne route à travers les montagnes », musa-t-il à voix haute pendant qu'ils dressaient le camp près d'une rivière dans le piémont, le troisième jour de leur voyage. « Je présume que tout dépend en fait du site exact destiné à la ville, mais il y a déjà des chemins praticables. J'ai entendu Corruth parler de celui qu'ils avaient emprunté pour se rendre à Afra. C'est par bateau qu'ils sont venus de Gèdre, mais à cheval qu'ils ont effectué le reste du trajet.

— Il n'en manque pas, en effet, mais pas un seul ne se prête au trafic, répondit Saruel. Et les cols ne sont ouverts que quelques mois par an. Les Retha'noïs contrôlent encore certains des meilleurs, en plus, et ils sont hostiles aux étrangers, tant 'faïes que Tirs. Quiconque a des marchandises à vendre est obligé d'aller par bateau. Des pirates écument les deux mers : les Zengatis la mer d'Osiat, et des bandits de toutes sortes les archipels de la mer Intérieure. Et, bien entendu, les clans de la côte méridionale sont forcés de franchir le détroit de Riga, qui est passablement périlleux même par très beau temps. Mais c'est tout de même plus sûr que la voie de terre.

— Cette solution n'est pas plus favorable aux échanges de Skala, repartit Tamìr. Je vois mal quel bien cela nous ferait d'avoir une capitale entièrement isolée du reste du pays. »

Alors même qu'elle soulevait cette objection, néanmoins, Ki n'eut qu'à repérer son regard perdu au loin pour se rendre compte qu'elle voyait tout de même sa ville, du fin fond du réseau complexe des canalisations d'égouts jusqu'aux tours altières de la maison des magiciens d'Arkoniel.

« Il serait plus court et plus sûr de contourner le nord de la péninsule, si l'isthme ne se trouvait pas juste en travers, fit-il observer.

— Eh bien, jusqu'à ce que quelqu'un découvre un moyen de le déménager de là, j'ai bien peur qu'il faille nous taper de mauvaises routes ou une interminable navigation. » En riant, Tamìr se tourna vers Arkoniel. « Qu'en dites-vous ? Est-ce qu'en recourant à ses prodigieux sortilèges, votre Troisième Orëska peut me résoudre ce casse-tête ? »

À la stupeur de Ki comme du reste des auditeurs,

Arkoniel eut plutôt l'air de réfléchir pendant un moment avant de répondre : « Cela mérite assurément d'être envisagé. »

Tamìr avait beau être pleinement consciente des cruelles souffrances de Ki, il n'était pas plus en son pouvoir de lui apporter le moindre réconfort que de se consoler elle-même. Au fur et à mesure que les jours passaient et que les montagnes s'abaissaient progressivement derrière le cortège, elle fit tout son possible pour appliquer son esprit à d'autres sujets, mais ses nuits étaient hantées.

Où se trouve ta mère, Tamìr ?

La question de l'Oracle l'avait glacée, dans les ténèbres de cette caverne, et ces mots la poursuivaient, maculés de taches encore plus noires par la confession d'Iya. L'Oracle ne lui avait rien offert d'autre que du silence, mais elle avait perçu dans ce silence-là comme une exigence.

Du coup, comme elle approchait avec sa modeste escorte du carrefour d'où partait la route de Bierfût, elle finit par se décider. Il lui fallut rassembler tout son courage en se rappelant que personne d'autre qu'Arkoniel et Ki ne savait rien sur l'ignominieux secret de la mort de Frère, pas plus que sur la présence du spectre enragé dans la tour.

« Je veux m'arrêter au fort pour la nuit », annonça-t-elle quand ils parvinrent en vue du virage de la route de la rivière.

Sa déclaration fit hausser un sourcil à Tharin, et Ki

lui adressa un coup d'œil interrogatif, mais personne d'autre ne manifesta plus qu'une vague surprise. « Ce détour ne rallonge pas beaucoup le trajet, et nous serons mieux installés pour dormir là-bas que dans une auberge ou en plein air, poursuivit-elle en affectant un ton léger.

— Un jour ou deux de différence, cela ne devrait guère importer, commenta Arkoniel. Cela fait près d'un an que vous n'y êtes pas allée.

— Il me tarde de voir la tête que fera Nari quand nous franchirons le pont ! s'exclama Ki. Et tu sais que Cuistote fera tout un foin de n'avoir pas préparé suffisamment à manger. »

L'idée de quelque chose d'aussi familier que de se faire gronder par sa vieille cuisinière réchauffa Tamìr en la soulageant un brin du malaise que lui faisait éprouver la véritable tâche qui l'attendait là-bas. Avec un grand sourire, elle répliqua : « Probablement, mais la surprise nous vaudra un souper froid. Viens, allons les faire sursauter ! »

Ils poussèrent tous deux leur monture au galop, riant par-dessus l'épaule de voir les autres à la traîne derrière eux. Tharin les eut bientôt rattrapés, et il n'y avait pas à s'y méprendre, son sourire était un défi. Chevauchant tous trois en tête du peloton, ils rivalisèrent de vitesse sur la chaussée, dépassant des carrioles chargées dans un vacarme assourdissant qui ne manqua pas d'abasourdir aussi les villageois lorsqu'ils atteignirent les prairies environnant Bierfût.

Tamìr regarda par-dessus les champs le hameau

blotti dans ses murs sur une courbe de la rivière. Elle l'avait pris pour une vraie ville, la première fois que son père l'avait emmenée le visiter. Ce n'était pas là un souvenir particulièrement heureux ; elle avait bêtement voulu choisir une poupée pour cadeau d'anniversaire, plutôt qu'un jouet de garçon typique, et Père en avait été humilié devant toute la foule du marché. Elle comprenait mieux maintenant pourquoi il avait réagi comme il l'avait fait, mais y repenser la hérissait encore aujourd'hui.

Elle secoua la tête, laissant le vent lui fouetter le visage et la débarrasser de ses ressentiments. Ce jour-là, Père lui avait aussi offert Gosi, son premier cheval, et Tharin donné sa première épée d'exercice en bois. Tous ses souvenirs de prime jeunesse étaient comme ça, un mélange inextricable de ténèbres et de lumière, mais les ténèbres lui semblaient avoir toujours, et largement, prédominé. *Le noir fait le blanc. Le putride fait le pur. Le mal crée la grandeur*, lui avait déclaré l'Oracle. De fait, ces formules-là résumaient son existence entière...

Après avoir traversé la forêt comme des flèches, ils débouchèrent finalement au bas de la vaste prairie en pente. Sur la crête qui la dominait, l'antique castel se découpait sur l'arrière-plan des montagnes, sa tour carrée pointée comme un index menaçant vers le ciel. Au bout de son mât, la bannière royale de Tamìr flottait sur le toit, mais ce ne fut pas ce détail qui attira son œil.

La fenêtre de la tour qui faisait face à la route avait

perdu l'un de ses volets à rayures rouges et blanches. La peinture du second, vermoulu, s'écaillait, et il pendait de travers, retenu par un seul de ses gonds. Il fut trop facile à Tamìr de s'imaginer qu'une figure blême s'y encadrait.

Elle se détourna, tout en refrénant Minuit pour le mettre au pas lorsqu'elle remarqua des signes de vie dans le paysage des alentours.

La prairie avait été fauchée, et de petites meules de foin parsemaient le versant. Des chèvres et des moutons broutaient autour d'eux, grappillant le regain de l'herbe. Il y avait des oies sauvages et des cygnes sur la rivière, et un tout jeune serviteur pêchait sur la berge, juste au-dessous du pont de planches. Il bondit sur ses pieds et les dévisagea pendant qu'ils se rappro- chaient puis détala vers la porte du fort.

Un toit tout neuf couvrait les baraquements, et l'on avait à côté d'eux soigneusement entretenu et même agrandi les parterres de plantes et de fleurs qu'elle et Ki avaient aidé Arkoniel à semer. Des bordures aux couleurs éclatantes s'y épanouissaient, et il y avait aussi des rangées de légumes. Une corbeille posée sur la hanche, deux jeunes filles contournèrent l'angle des bâtiments puis, rebroussant chemin, disparurent aussi vite que l'avait fait le petit garçon.

Qui sont tous ces gens-là ? demanda Ki.

— De nouveaux serviteurs originaires du village », lui répondit Arkoniel, qui les avait rejoints juste à temps pour surprendre sa question. « Quand je me trouvais ici avec les enfants, Cuistote a eu besoin d'auxiliaires supplémentaires. Tout semble indiquer qu'elle en a engagé davantage depuis mon départ.

— Et Frère n'était pas ici pour les faire fuir, terrifiés », murmura Tamìr. Avant de chuchoter au magicien : « Est-ce que ma mère les a tourmentés ?

— Non, lui assura-t-il. Je suis le seul à l'avoir jamais vue.

— Ah. » Tamìr regarda de nouveau vers le haut, et quelque chose d'autre attira son attention : un large pan de mur aveugle, alors que, normalement, cette partie de la maçonnerie aurait dû se trouver percée d'un certain nombre de fenêtres. « Qu'est-ce qui s'est passé là ?

— Oh, ça ? dit Arkoniel. C'est moi qui me suis livré à quelques modifications, il y a un certain temps de ça, pour dissimuler ma présence. Ne vous inquiétez pas, c'est seulement de la magie. Rien de définitif. »

Ils immobilisèrent leurs montures devant la porte d'entrée principale juste au moment où celle-ci s'ouvrit brusquement. Plantées comme des souches sur le seuil, Nari et Cuistote dévisagèrent Tamìr d'un œil rond, la main plaquée sur la bouche. La nourrice fut la première à se remettre du choc.

Ouvrant largement les bras, elle fondit en larmes de bonheur et s'écria : « Oh, mes chéris, mettez pied à terre, que je vous embrasse ! »

Tamìr et Ki sautèrent à bas de leur selle, et elle les enferma tous deux dans une même étreinte. Tamìr fut suffoquée de la trouver d'aussi petite taille. Elle dépassait maintenant Nari d'une bonne tête.

Celle-ci se dressa sur la pointe des orteils pour leur planter sur les joues un baiser sonore. « Comme vous avez grandi depuis l'année dernière, l'un et l'autre ! Et Ki qui a un soupçon de barbe ! Et toi, mon enfant ! » Elle abandonna Ki entre les bras déjà prêts de Cuistote et saisit le visage de Tamìr entre ses mains, pour y chercher sans aucun doute quelque chose du garçon qu'elle avait connu. Tamìr ne discerna rien d'autre dans ses yeux que de l'amour et de la stupéfaction. « Créateur miséricordieux, mais regarde-toi, ma fille bien-aimée ! Mince comme un jonc, et l'image même de ta chère mère. Tout juste comme je me l'étais toujours imaginé.

— Tu me reconnais ? lâcha Tamìr avec soulagement. Je ne suis pas si changée que ça ?

— Oh, mon chou ! » Elle l'étreignit de nouveau. « Garçon ou fille, tu es tout de même l'enfant que j'ai nourri de mon sein et tenu dans mes bras. Comment ne te reconnaîtrais-je pas ? »

Cuistote l'embrassa à son tour puis la maintint à longueur de bras pour la regarder. « Tu as poussé comme une mauvaise herbe, n'est-ce pas ? » Elle se mit à lui pétrir le biceps et l'épaule. « Pas une once de viande, aucun de vous deux, sur les os ! Tharin, cette tante que vous avez ne leur donne rien à manger ? Et ce pauvre Maître Arkoniel ! Vous avez de nouveau l'air d'un épouvantail, après que moi je vous ai tous gavés comme il faut, avant... Entrez, vous autres, allez. On a tenu la maison prête, et le garde-manger est plein comme un œuf. Pas un de vous n'ira au lit le ventre creux, ce soir, promis, juré ! »

Tamìr gravit les marches de pierre usée qui menaient à la grande salle. Elle la trouva tout à fait semblable aux souvenirs qu'elle en conservait depuis sa visite d'anniversaire, en bon état, mais avec un aspect poussiéreux et terni. Malgré le soleil de l'après-midi qui brillait à travers les portes ouvertes et les fenêtres, des ombres étaient néanmoins tapies dans les coins et dans la poutraison sculptée. De bonnes odeurs flottaient dans l'air toutefois : épices, tourte aux pommes et pain chaud.

« Mais tu as fait de la cuisine... Est-ce que tu savais que nous allions venir ?

— Non, Majesté, mais vous auriez quand même pu envoyer quelqu'un me prévenir ! la réprimanda Cuistote. Non, je me suis mise à commercer avec la ville, et j'en tire un bout de profit pour vous. J'ai mis des bons vins à la cave, et la souillarde est bourrée. Quand vos gens seront installés, j'aurai mis en route de quoi vous régaler comme il faut. Miko, va vite m'allumer le feu, ah, le bon garçon que voilà ! Les filles, vous vous occupez du linge. »

Les servantes qu'ils avaient aperçues près du pont sortirent de l'ombre près de la porte et coururent accomplir les tâches qu'on leur assignait.

Pendant qu'elle se dirigeait vers les escaliers, Tamìr entendit Tyrien chuchoter à Lynx : « C'est ici que la reine a grandi ? »

Se souriant à elle-même, elle grimpa les marches quatre à quatre, talonnée par Ki. Elle se demanda quand il lui serait possible de s'esquiver pour dénicher

Lhel, ou si celle-ci se manifesterait même spontanément. Mais si tel était le cas, que dirait-elle à la sorcière, maintenant ?

Leur ancienne chambre commune était aussi propre et bien aérée que s'ils habitaient encore le fort. Toujours la meublaient l'armoire avec laquelle Frère avait essayé d'écraser Iya et le coffre à vêtements sculpté qui avait autrefois servi de cachette pour la poupée. Tamìr ressentit un serrement de cœur familier quand ses yeux se posèrent sur l'immense lit, ses tentures fanées et sa courtepointe matelassée. Elle surprit un reflet de la même peine sur la physionomie de Ki lorsqu'il franchit le seuil de la pièce aux joujoux contiguë.

« La literie d'appoint s'y trouve encore, lui cria-t-il. Les Compagnons et moi pourrons coucher là. »

Tamìr passa la tête par l'embrasure et parcourut d'un coup d'œil la cité miniature et les autres vestiges hétéroclites de leur enfance éparpillés de-ci de-là. Les seules choses manquantes étaient la vieille poupée de chiffon et la présence revêche de Frère. Avant que Ki ne vienne vivre avec elle, le démon avait été son unique compagnon de jeux. Elle ne l'avait pas senti rôder autour d'elle ni revu depuis Afra.

Elle traversa le corridor et se tint un moment dans la chambre de Père, à tâcher de s'imaginer qu'elle pouvait encore y percevoir son esprit ou retrouver son odeur. Mais ce n'était qu'une pièce quelconque, abandonnée depuis des lustres.

Arkoniel fit halte sur le seuil, les bras chargés de son baluchon de voyage. « Je vais m'installer dans ma chambre d'autrefois, là-haut, si vous n'y voyez pas d'inconvénient.

— Aucun, bien entendu », répondit-elle machinalement, pensant à une tout autre chambre qu'à celle-là. Elle s'y rendrait plus tard, et seule.

Elle s'attarda un moment de plus, et Tharin entra sans mot dire la rejoindre. Il portait ses fontes de selle sur une épaule et paraissait vaguement perplexe.

« Les gardes vont occuper les baraquements. J'y ai toujours mon ancienne chambre, mais... Bref, peut-être préférerais-tu me voir prendre l'une des chambres d'hôtes à l'étage supérieur ?

— Ce serait un honneur pour moi si tu couchais dans celle de Père. » Sans lui laisser le loisir d'élever la moindre objection, elle ajouta : « Cela me réconforterait de savoir que tu te trouves aussi près.

— Comme tu voudras. » Il se déchargea de ses fontes et jeta un regard circulaire. « C'est bon d'être de retour. Tu devrais venir plus souvent, quand les choses se seront tassées. La chasse d'ici me manque. »

Elle hocha la tête, comprenant à demi-mot tout ce qu'il ne pouvait pas dire. « À moi aussi. »

12

Cuistote tint à merveille sa parole : le souper fut aussi copieux que bien accueilli. Tout le monde se groupa autour d'une longue table, et les écuyers aidèrent les filles de service à apporter les plats des cuisines et à les y remporter.

Assise à la gauche de Tamìr, Nari l'assaillit sans trêve de questions sur ses batailles et sur Ero, comme sur tout ce qui se passait à Atyion, en prévision de la confrontation avec Korin, mais elle ne l'interrogea pas une seconde sur la métamorphose. Elle la traitait exactement comme elle avait traité Tobin, sans se montrer le moins du monde embarrassée par son changement de sexe. Elle ne s'oublia même pas à l'appeler Tobin. Pas une seule fois.

Après le repas, les convives, munis de leur coupe de vin, prirent place autour du feu, et ils racontèrent de nouvelles histoires à propos des combats auxquels ils avaient participé. Puis Tharin et les deux bonnes femmes se mirent à évoquer les souvenirs qu'ils conservaient de Tamìr et de Ki, lorsque ceux-ci n'étaient encore que des mioches et vivaient en ces mêmes lieux, récits qui amusèrent fort les autres Compagnons. Arkoniel entra dans le jeu, non sans enjoliver avec un plaisir manifeste le terrible tintouin que lui avait donné Ki par son chétif appétit pour l'étude. Sans qu'il ait été fait la plus petite allusion à la mort et à la tragédie dont la demeure avait été le témoin, Tamìr surprit les regards nerveux que jetaient à la ronde les plus jeunes des écuyers pendant que la nuit tombait.

« J'ai entendu dire que ce fort était hanté », finit par hasarder Lorin. Mis en garde par un coup d'œil foudroyant de Nikidès, il se ratatina sur le banc et murmura : « C'est seulement ce que j'ai entendu dire. »

Faute de divertissement adéquat, contraindre l'assistance à se coucher tard ne s'imposait guère. Tamìr souhaita bonne nuit à Nari et à Cuistote en les embrassant puis congédia les gardes.

« Il est temps d'aller dormir un peu, hein ? » dit Nikidès pour rallier les autres.

Tout le monde se souhaita bonne nuit avant de s'engouffrer dans ses chambres respectives, mais Ki s'attarda devant la porte de Tamìr. « Je resterai, si tu le souhaites. Personne n'en a cure, ici. »

La tentation de dire oui fut si forte qu'elle en eut le souffle coupé, mais elle secoua la tête. « Non, mieux vaut pas.

— Bonne nuit, alors. » Il pivota pour obtempérer, mais pas assez vite pour qu'elle n'ait eu le temps de surprendre l'expression douloureuse de son regard.

C'est mieux pour nous tous. Cette tâche-ci n'incombe qu'à moi. Il ne peut pas m'aider, et il n'arriverait qu'à se mettre en danger sans nécessité. C'est mieux pour nous tous...

Elle continua de se le ressasser tandis qu'elle attendait, assise en tailleur sur son lit, que les autres aient achevé de s'installer dans la pièce voisine.

Quelqu'un éclata de rire. Un vague brouhaha de voix s'ensuivit, puis les grommellements d'une querelle amicale lorsque les malheureux écuyers se virent relégués sur les paillasses étendues par terre. Elle entendit des traînements de pieds, le grincement des sangles du sommier, puis l'extinction progressive des chuchotements.

Elle patienta quelque temps encore et se dirigea vers la fenêtre. Le clair de lune illuminait la prairie et faisait miroiter la rivière. Le menton appuyé dans ses mains, elle revécut en pensée les fois innombrables où elle avait joué là avec Ki, les soldats de neige qu'ils avaient combattus, leurs parties de pêche et leurs séances de natation, et le jour où, tout simplement couchés dans l'herbe haute, ils s'amusaient à contempler les nuages et à leur trouver des silhouettes fantastiques.

Une fois satisfaite par le silence total qui régnait à côté, elle saisit sa lampe de chevet et se faufila dans le corridor. Aucun bruit n'émanait de la chambre de Tharin non plus, et il n'y avait pas de rai de lumière sous sa porte.

À l'étage supérieur, une seule lampe brûlait dans sa niche à proximité des appartements d'Arkoniel. Elle les dépassa sur la pointe des pieds, sans cesser de fixer la porte de la tour. Ce fut seulement après avoir posé la main sur le loquet terni qu'elle se rappela que l'on avait fermé à triple tour depuis la mort de Mère et jeté la clef voilà bien longtemps. C'était Frère qui lui avait ouvert, la dernière fois.

« Frère ? chuchota-t-elle. S'il te plaît ? »

Elle appliqua son oreille contre le vantail, attentive au moindre indice de réponse éventuelle. Le bois était froid, beaucoup plus froid qu'il n'aurait dû l'être en cette nuit d'été, même ici.

Un autre souvenir se réveilla. Elle s'était déjà tenue là auparavant, à s'imaginer que le fantôme en colère et sanglant de sa mère se trouvait juste de l'autre côté, dans une marée montante de sang. Elle baissa les yeux, mais il ne sortit rien d'autre de dessous la porte qu'une grosse araignée grise. Elle tressaillit lorsque la bestiole passa à toutes pattes sur son pied nu.

« Tamìr ? »

Elle faillit laisser tomber sa lampe en pirouettant comme une folle. Arkoniel la lui retira des mains et la déposa en sécurité dans une niche près de la porte.

« Par les *couilles* de Bilairy ! Vous m'avez foutu une trouille à pisser aux culottes ! s'étrangla-t-elle.

— Désolé. Je savais que vous viendriez, et j'ai pensé que vous pourriez avoir besoin d'aide pour cette serrure. Et vous aurez également besoin de ceci. »

Il ouvrit la main gauche, et un petit caillou qui rougeoyait dedans fit fuser de la lumière entre ses doigts.

Tamìr s'en empara. Il était aussi frais au contact que le clair de lune. « Moins de risque avec ça que je flanque le feu à la baraque, je suppose.

— Il serait préférable que je vous accompagne.

— Non. L'Oracle a dit que c'était mon fardeau. Ne bougez pas d'ici. Je vous appellerai si j'ai besoin de vous. »

Il plaqua sa paume contre le vantail auprès de la serrure, et Tamìr entendit les mécanismes grincer puis jouer. Elle souleva le loquet et poussa la porte qui s'ouvrit en couinant sur ses gonds rouillés. Une rafale d'air glacé se rua au-dehors, qui sentait la poussière et les souris et la forêt par-delà la rivière.

Ils pénétrèrent de conserve dans l'étroit intervalle libre qui séparait le seuil de la tour du bas de l'escalier, puis le magicien repoussa la porte contre son chambranle, la laissant entrebâillée d'à peine un cheveu.

Tamìr gravit lentement les marches, levant à bout de bras la pierre lumineuse et s'appuyant de l'autre main contre le mur pour assurer son équilibre. La sensation poisseuse de lichens et de fientes d'oiseaux fit ressurgir d'autres souvenirs. Elle eut l'impression d'être de nouveau le moutard qui grimpait à la suite de sa mère ce même escalier pour la première fois.

Je suis comme ces hirondelles, avec mon nid perché là-haut, par-dessus le fort.

La porte du palier supérieur béait, grande ouverte, telle une gueule noire. Dans la pièce au-delà, Tamìr entendit distinctement soupirer la brise et des souris trottiner. Il lui fallut tout son courage pour monter les quelques dernières marches qui l'en séparaient encore.

Elle s'immobilisa sur le seuil et, se cramponnant au chambranle, scruta les ténèbres abyssales qui régnaient à l'intérieur. « Mère, vous êtes ici ? Je suis revenue à la maison. »

Ki s'était douté de ce que Tamìr se proposait de faire dès l'instant où ils s'étaient détournés de leur route pour se diriger vers le fort. Au cours du souper, il n'avait pas manqué de remarquer avec quelle fréquence son regard s'égarait vers les escaliers. Et lorsqu'elle déclina son offre de rester avec elle cette nuit-là, il eut enfin la certitude qu'elle comptait se rendre toute seule dans la tour.

Allongé dans le lit aux côtés de Lynx, il écouta,

l'oreille tendue à en avoir des bourdonnements, jusqu'au moment où il entendit la porte voisine s'ouvrir en catimini et des pas feutrés de pieds nus passer devant la leur.

Elle m'aurait demandé de venir si elle avait souhaité que je l'accompagne. Elle s'était toujours montrée des plus taciturne à propos des fantômes qui hantaient les lieux, même avec lui. Aussi lutta-t-il contre lui-même pour tâcher de dormir, mais tout son instinct lui disait de la suivre.

Il s'était couché sans ôter sa chemise et ses chausses. Il n'eut aucun mal à s'esquiver du lit et à contourner précautionneusement les paillasses des écuyers. Il croyait tous les autres endormis, mais, lorsqu'il ouvrit la porte pour se glisser dehors, il jeta un coup d'œil en arrière et vit Lynx qui le regardait.

Il posa un doigt sur ses lèvres puis referma tout doucement la porte derrière lui, non sans se demander quel but son ami attribuerait à cette escapade. Mais il était tout à fait vain de s'en inquiéter maintenant.

N'apercevant pas trace de Tamìr, il grimpa l'escalier en tapinois puis fit halte pour embrasser d'un coup d'œil furtif le corridor du second étage, et ce juste à temps pour voir Arkoniel se glisser dans la tour.

Il en demeura pétrifié. Tamìr l'avait planté là, lui, mais elle avait prié le magicien de la seconder ? Tout blessé qu'il était, Ki ravala sa rancœur et scruta de nouveau les lieux à la dérobée avant de s'y aventurer. La porte de la tour était légèrement entrebâillée, et il la poussa.

Assis sur la première marche, Arkoniel tripotait nerveusement sa baguette magique. Une pierre lumineuse éclaboussait de son éclat la marche suivante.

Arkoniel sursauta lorsqu'il aperçut Ki, puis il secoua la tête. « J'aurais dû m'attendre à ton apparition, chuchota-t-il. Elle a exigé de monter seule, mais je n'aime pas beaucoup ça. Reste avec moi. Elle doit m'appeler, en cas de besoin. »

Ki prit place à ses côtés. « Sa mère se trouve réellement là-haut ?

— Oh oui. Qu'elle décide ou non de se manifester... »

Il n'acheva pas sa phrase, et tous deux regardèrent en l'air lorsque leur parvint le son presque imperceptible de la voix de Tamìr. Ki en eut la chair de poule, comprenant ce que cela signifiait. Tamìr était en train de parler avec la morte.

« Mère ? »

Pas de réponse.

L'état de la pièce était exactement tel que Tamìr se le rappelait. Meubles fracassés, rouleaux de tissu en décomposition, balles de bourre de laine rongées par les souris, tout gisait encore à l'endroit où Frère l'avait lancé. Une table avait été redressée sous la fenêtre est, et les dernières des poupées sans bouche de Mère y étaient alignées, avachies les unes contre les autres pour se soutenir comme des ivrognes. C'était dans leur fouillis qu'Arkoniel avait retrouvé sa poupée à elle ; une brèche lui révéla la place qu'elle y occupait alors.

Tamìr s'approcha de la table et y rafla l'un des

tristes fantoches. Il était tout moisi et décoloré, mais les petits points minutieux de Mère se voyaient encore sur les coutures. Tamìr l'éleva vers sa pierre lumineuse pour en examiner la face inexpressive. Encore rembourré de toute sa laine, il était rondouillard, et il avait des membres flasques et inégaux. À sa grande surprise, elle fut violemment tentée de l'emporter. Dans un sens, la poupée informe qu'elle avait cachée pendant si longtemps lui manquait, tout accablant pour elle que ç'avait été de la détenir, à l'époque. Mais elle avait aussi été un lien avec Mère, ainsi qu'avec son propre passé. Une impulsion subite lui fit serrer celle-ci contre son cœur. En avait-elle eu envie, que Mère en fasse une pour elle ! Des larmes lui piquèrent les yeux, et elle les laissa déborder, pleurant l'enfance qui lui avait été refusée.

Un soupir léger fit se hérisser les petits cheveux de sa nuque. Elle se retourna d'un bloc et, brandissant la pierre lumineuse, fouilla la chambre du regard, sans cesser d'étreindre la poupée.

Le soupir se fit de nouveau entendre, plus fort cette fois. Tamìr scruta les ténèbres amassées près de la fenêtre ouest – la fenêtre par où Mère s'était précipitée dans le vide, cette épouvantable journée d'hiver. Celle par où elle avait essayé de la précipiter elle aussi.

Frère n'est pas là pour me sauver, ce coup-ci.

« Mère ? » chuchota-t-elle derechef.

Après des froufroutements de jupes qui frôlaient le sol lui parvint à l'oreille un nouveau soupir éperdument douloureux. Puis une voix fantomatique exhala, en un souffle à peine audible : *Mon enfant..*

L'espoir étrangla la respiration de Tamìr. Elle se rapprocha d'un pas. « Oui, c'est moi ! »

Où est mon enfant ? Où ? Où...

Le bref et poignant accès d'espoir de sa fille s'évanouit, ainsi qu'il l'avait fait invariablement jusque-là. « Mère ? »

Où est mon fils ?

Tout se passait exactement de la même manière qu'aux pires jours de l'existence de Mère. Elle n'avait même pas conscience de la présence de Tamìr, obsédée qu'elle était par la douleur de l'enfant qu'elle avait perdu.

Tamìr allait se remettre à parler quand un craquement suraigu la fit tressaillir d'une manière si brutale qu'elle faillit presque en lâcher la pierre lumineuse. Les volets de la fenêtre ouest vibraient comme si l'on venait de les heurter de plein fouet, puis ils grincèrent en pivotant lentement sur leurs gonds, poussés par des mains invisibles.

Tamìr serra convulsivement la poupée mais sans céder un pouce de terrain, malgré son horreur grandissante lorsqu'elle discerna une silhouette noire se détacher des ténèbres et se diriger vers l'embrasure de la fenêtre à pas lents, saccadés. Son visage était détourné, et il s'inclinait comme pour contempler le cours de la rivière en contrebas.

La femme spectrale portait une robe sombre, et elle étreignait quelque chose contre sa poitrine. Elle était de la même taille que Tamìr, et sa longue chevelure noire et brillante pendait librement en désordre jusqu'à sa ceinture. Des mèches folles batifolaient autour d'elle, mollement bouclées par le courant d'air. Découpée là, sur le ciel nocturne, elle paraissait tout aussi tangible qu'un être vivant.

« M... Mère ? Regardez-moi, Mère. Je suis ici. Je suis venue pour vous voir. »

Où est mon enfant ? Cette fois, le murmure s'apparentait plutôt à un chuintement rageur.

Où est ta mère ? La voix de l'Oracle aiguillonna Tamìr. « Je suis votre fille. Je m'appelle Tamìr. J'étais Tobin, mais je suis maintenant Tamìr. Mère, regardez-moi. Écoutez-moi ! »

Fille ? Le fantôme se tourna lentement, toujours affecté de cette allure artificielle et saccadée, d'hésitation, comme s'il avait oublié de quelle manière se meut un corps. Ce qu'il tenait, c'était la vieille poupée informe de naguère, ou du moins son fantôme. Tamìr retint son souffle en apercevant une joue livide, un profil familier. Puis, sa mère ayant fini par lui faire face, sa vue lui fit l'effet qu'elle se trouvait devant un miroir fantasmagorique.

Les autres avaient raison, somme toute, songea-t-elle, hébétée, au-delà de la peur quand ces yeux-là vinrent se poser sur elle avec quelque chose comme un air de la reconnaître. Au fil des mois écoulés depuis la métamorphose, les traits de Tamìr s'étaient modifiés d'une façon subtile, non pas tant en s'adoucissant qu'en dérivant vers davantage de ressemblance avec ceux de cette femme morte. Elle fit un pas vers elle, vaguement consciente du fait qu'elles étreignaient chacune sa poupée de la même manière, au creux de leur bras gauche.

« Mère, c'est moi, votre fille », s'évertua-t-elle de nouveau, guettant une lueur de compréhension sur cette physionomie vide.

Fille ?

« Oui ! Je suis venue vous dire qu'il faut poursuivre votre route jusqu'à la porte. »

Le fantôme la vit désormais. *Fille ?*

Tamìr transféra la lumière dans sa main gauche et tendit le bras vers elle. Sa mère la refléta en agissant de même. Le bout de leurs doigts se frôlèrent, et Tamìr sentit nettement le contact de ceux du fantôme, aussi palpables que les siens, mais d'un froid mortel, comme ceux de Frère.

Sans se démonter, elle serra très fort cette main glacée. « Mère, vous devez vous reposer. Vous ne pouvez plus rester ici. »

La femme se rapprocha, dévisageant fixement Tamìr comme si elle essayait de comprendre qui elle était.

Une larme chatouilla la joue de Tamìr. « Oui, c'est moi. »

Tout à coup, la pièce s'illumina autour d'elles. Les rayons du soleil s'y déversaient à flots par toutes les fenêtres, et la chambre était douillette, pleine de couleurs et de bonnes odeurs de bois, de linge séché en plein air et de bougies. L'âtre était bourré de fleurs sèches, et les fauteuils se tenaient bien droits devant lui, leurs coussins de tapisserie intacts et impeccables. Des poupées jonchaient la table, toutes propres et vêtues de petits atours en velours.

Maman était bien vivante, ses prunelles bleues

chaleureusement animées par l'un de ses rares sourires. « As-tu appris ton alphabet, Tobin ?

— Oui, Maman. » Tamìr pleurait maintenant carrément. Elle laissa tomber la poupée et la pierre lumineuse pour la serrer dans ses bras. Cela faisait un effet bizarre d'être assez grande pour enfouir son visage dans cette chevelure noire et soyeuse, mais elle n'ergota pas là-dessus, désarçonnée par le léger parfum de fleurs qu'elle connaissait si bien. « Oh, Mère, je suis revenue à la maison pour vous aider. Je regrette d'avoir été absente si longtemps. Je me suis efforcée d'aider Frère. Je l'ai vraiment fait ! »

Des mains chaudes lui caressèrent les cheveux et le dos. « Là, là, ne pleure pas, mon chéri. Ne voilà-t-il pas un gentil petit garçon... »

Tamìr se figea. « Non, Mère, je ne suis plus un petit garçon... » Elle tenta de prendre du recul, mais sa mère la serrait trop étroitement.

« Mon doux, mon cher petit garçon. Oh, comme je t'aime ! J'avais tellement peur de ne pas arriver à te revoir. »

Tamìr commença à se débattre, et puis elles s'immobilisèrent toutes les deux en entendant sur la route, dehors, des cavaliers qui venaient vers elles.

Ariani la relâcha et courut vers la fenêtre est. « Il nous a retrouvés !

— Qui ? Qui nous a retrouvés ? chuchota Tamìr.

« Mon frère ! » Les yeux d'Ariani étaient agrandis de terreur et noirs comme ceux de Frère quand elle se rua sur Tamìr et lui empoigna le bras avec une

violence atroce. « Il arrive ! Mais il ne nous aura pas !
Non, il ne nous aura pas ! »

Et elle traîna Tamìr vers la fenêtre ouest.

Arkoniel et Ki s'étaient déplacés jusqu'à mi-hauteur
de l'escalier pour s'efforcer de saisir ce que Tamìr était
en train de dire. Brusquement, ils l'entendirent appeler
sa mère et l'implorer à propos de quelque chose.

Et puis la porte du palier supérieur fut si
bruyamment claquée à la volée que Ki perdit pied et
dégringola à la renverse en culbutant le magicien.

Tamìr comprit sans l'ombre d'un doute qu'elle se
battait pour sauver sa vie, exactement comme elle
l'avait fait jadis. À l'époque, sa mère était beaucoup
trop forte pour qu'elle lui oppose une résistance
efficace, et voilà que son fantôme n'avait aucun mal à
la dominer maintenant non plus. Prisonnière de cette
étreinte inexorable, Tamìr se vit traîner par terre vers la
fenêtre comme si elle ne pesait pas plus qu'un mioche.

« Non, Mère, non ! » l'implora-t-elle en se
démenant pour tenter de lui faire lâcher prise.

Mais ce fut peine perdue. Sur une dernière traction
saccadée du spectre, Tamìr se retrouva à moitié pro-
pulsée en dehors de la fenêtre, oscillant sur son ventre
dans l'embrasure, et préservée seulement de la chute
par le reploiement de ses genoux. Il faisait de nouveau
nuit. La rivière coulait, toute noire, argentant les
rochers qu'elle ourlait de ses flots tumultueux, et
Tamìr basculait de plus en plus vers le vide en s'égo-
sillant, dépassée par quelque chose de sombre qui

l'entraînait invinciblement, une vision blême à jupes virevoltantes et chevelure de jais hirsute...

Arkoniel et Ki dévalèrent l'un par-dessus l'autre jusqu'au pied de l'escalier. Ki fut le premier à se relever, et il regrimpa comme une fusée, sans se soucier de ses ecchymoses et du goût de sang qui lui emplissait la bouche ni des marches usées qu'il enjambait quatre à quatre. Il essaya de défoncer la porte à coups d'épaule, secoua le loquet, mais quelque chose ou quelqu'un la maintenait fermée de l'intérieur. Il entendait des bruits de lutte et les cris de terreur inarticulés que poussait Tamìr.

« Au secours, Arkoniel ! hurla-t-il désespérément. Tu m'entends, Tamìr ?

— Tire-toi de là ! » tonitrua le magicien.

À peine Ki eut-il le temps de se baisser qu'une vague d'une puissance inouïe déferla par-dessus sa tête et arracha la porte de ses gonds. Ki se redressa et bondit dans la pièce. L'atmosphère y était glaciale, et une odeur pestilentielle de marécage flottait dans l'air. Une pierre lumineuse traînait par terre parmi des monceaux d'épaves, et elle éclairait suffisamment les lieux pour qu'il aperçoive l'horrible figure sanglante qui s'acharnait à vouloir précipiter Tamìr par la fenêtre ouest. Tout ce qu'il pouvait voir de la seconde était l'agitation convulsive de ses jambes et de ses pieds nus. Et il eut beau se précipiter à la rescousse, l'immonde chose n'en persista que davantage à la tirer vers l'extérieur par-dessus le bord auquel Tamìr s'agrippait de son mieux.

Il s'agissait d'une femme, à cela seul se réduisait sa certitude pendant qu'il se ruait à corps perdu vers l'ouverture. La forme était pâle et instable comme un feu follet. Ki crut deviner des cheveux noirs qui se contorsionnaient, des yeux noirs et vides, un visage d'une blancheur d'os. Des mains semblables à des serres s'agrippaient à la chevelure et à la tunique de Tamìr pour contraindre son buste à basculer de plus en plus avant.

« Non ! » Ki atteignit Tamìr à l'instant même où elle commençait à vaciller par-dessus bord. Il se jeta à travers le spectre et ressentit un froid encore plus intense, mais ses mains étaient vigoureuses et sûres quand il rattrapa Tamìr par l'un de ses pieds nus et, tirant dessus de toutes ses forces, la hissa rudement pour la remettre en sécurité.

Elle s'affaissa par terre comme une chiffe, évanouie. Ki s'accroupit sur elle, prêt à repousser l'esprit vindicatif de sa mère à mains nues si la nécessité le lui imposait, mais il n'y avait plus trace d'elle maintenant.

Il tira Tamìr loin de la fenêtre puis, doucement, la retourna sur le dos. Elle avait les yeux fermés, et elle était d'une pâleur épouvantable. Du sang coulait d'une profonde entaille qui barrait son menton, mais elle respirait.

Arkoniel trébucha sur l'amas de décombres qui jonchaient le sol et s'effondra sur ses genoux aux côtés de ses protégés. « Comment va-t-elle ?

— Je ne sais pas. »

Des mains s'échinèrent à l'agripper par le dos, puis voilà qu'elle se retrouva projetée vers l'arrière. Quelque chose lui heurta le menton assez violemment pour l'assommer. Le monde se mit à tourbillonner... étoiles et rivière et murailles de pierre grossièrement taillée et ténèbres.

Ensuite, elle était allongée dans la pièce sombre et de nouveau saccagée, et quelqu'un la serrait fort, si fort dans ses bras qu'elle n'arrivait pas à respirer.

« Mère, non ! cria-t-elle en se débattant avec le peu de forces qu'il lui restait.

« Non, Tamìr, c'est moi ! Ouvre les yeux. Pour l'amour de l'enfer, Arkoniel, *faites* quelque chose ! »

Elle entendit un craquement aigu, et voilà qu'elle papillotait au sein d'une pâle lumière douce. C'était dans les bras de Ki qu'elle se trouvait, et son visage était ravagé de chagrin. Arkoniel se tenait juste derrière lui, sa baguette à la main, le front ensanglanté par une estafilade. Une odeur bizarre flottait dans l'air, âcre comme celle de cheveux brûlés.

« Ki ? » Elle essaya vainement de saisir ce qui venait tout juste de se passer. Elle se sentait glacée jusqu'à la moelle, et son cœur cognait si durement que c'était douloureux.

« Je te tiens, Tamìr. Je vais t'emmener hors d'ici. » Il lui rebroussa les cheveux en les caressant d'une main tremblante.

« Ma mère...

— Je l'ai vue. Je ne la laisserai plus te faire de mal. Viens ! » Il l'attira sur son séant puis lui passa un bras autour de la taille pour la soutenir.

Elle parvint de la sorte à se relever et à se diriger avec lui d'un pas chancelant vers la porte. Malgré la vigueur et la sûreté du bras qui l'enlaçait, elle continuait à sentir l'étreinte glacée des mains de sa mère.

« Conduis-la dans ma chambre à l'étage en dessous. Moi, je vais condamner cette porte », dit Arkoniel derrière eux.

Ki se débrouilla va savoir comment pour lui faire descendre l'escalier sans qu'ils se cassent la figure et se hâta de la faire entrer dans la chambre du magicien. Des chandelles et des lampes y brûlaient à qui mieux mieux, éclairant les lieux d'une lumière vive et réconfortante.

Après avoir précautionneusement installé Tamìr dans un fauteuil près de l'âtre vide, Ki arracha une couverture du lit pour l'y envelopper, puis, s'agenouillant, lui frictionna les mains et les poignets. « Dis quelque chose, par pitié ! »

Elle battit lentement des paupières. « Je vais bien. Elle... elle n'est pas là. Je ne perçois plus sa présence. »

Ki jeta un coup d'œil circulaire avant d'émettre un rire tremblotant. « Une bonne nouvelle, ça ! Je n'ai aucune envie de *jamais* rien revoir de semblable. » Il se servit d'un coin de la couverture pour lui tamponner le menton. Cela lui fit mal, car elle ne put réprimer un mouvement de recul.

« Ne bouge pas, commanda Ki. Tu saignes. »

Elle se toucha le menton et le sentit poisseux d'un liquide chaud. « Le rebord. Je me suis cognée contre le rebord. Exactement comme autrefois. »

Ki lui repoussa gentiment les doigts. « Oui, exactement comme autrefois, sauf que, ce coup-ci, tu vas avoir une belle cicatrice. »

Tamìr enserra son front dans ses mains, prête à défaillir. « Il... Frère ? C'est lui qui m'a retenue ?

— Non, c'est moi. Je t'ai entendue crier, et je suis arrivé là juste... » Ils étaient si proches l'un de l'autre qu'il avait les genoux de Tamìr pressés contre son ventre. Il tremblait de tout son être.

« Par la Flamme ! poursuivit-il d'une voix désormais moins ferme. Il s'en est fallu de rien qu'elle te largue à l'extérieur, cette horreur-là. Elle était pire que Frère... » Il s'interrompit de nouveau pour l'enlacer à pleins bras comme si elle risquait encore de tomber.

« Et c'est toi qui m'as retenue ? lui souffla-t-elle au creux de l'épaule.

— Oui, mais j'ai bien failli te perdre. Enfer et damnation ! Mais qu'est-ce qui t'est passé par la tête, de monter là-haut toute seule ? »

Il sanglotait ! Tamìr le serra contre elle et enfouit une main dans ses cheveux. « Ne pleure pas. Tu étais là, Ki. Tu m'as sauvée. Tout va bien. »

S'inquiéter pour lui balaya les derniers vestiges de sa terreur. Elle ne l'avait jamais entendu pleurer aussi fort jusque-là. Il en avait le corps tout secoué, et il l'étreignait de nouveau si fort qu'il lui faisait mal, mais c'était une sensation délicieuse.

Finalement, il s'assit sur ses talons et s'épongea le visage d'un revers de manche. « Je suis confus ! Je... simplement j'ai... j'ai cru... » Tamìr lut une peur indiscutable dans ses yeux. « J'ai cru que je n'arriverais pas à te rejoindre à temps. Pas avant qu'elle... » Il la saisit par les bras tandis que sa peur cédait la place à la colère. « Pourquoi, Tamìr ? Qu'est-ce qui t'a poussée à monter là-haut toute seule ?

— L'Oracle a dit... »

Il la secoua rageusement. « Que tu devais te faire assassiner ?

— Que vous a-t-elle dit au juste ? demanda Arkoniel, qui entrait les rejoindre au même moment.

— Elle m'a dit que ma mère... l'état dans lequel elle se trouve maintenant... c'était mon fardeau. J'ai pensé que cela signifiait que j'étais censée la délivrer. J'ai pensé que si elle me voyait sous ma véritable forme, cela pourrait... je ne sais pas, que ça lui donnerait la paix. Mais ça pas été le cas, acheva-t-elle misérablement. Tout s'est passé exactement de la même manière que le terrible jour où mon oncle est arrivé ici.

— Alors, Nari avait raison. » Arkoniel caressa les cheveux de Tamìr. « Pourquoi ne m'en avoir jamais parlé ?

— Je ne sais pas. Je suppose que j'avais honte.

— De quoi ? » demanda Ki.

Elle baissa la tête. Il leur était impossible de se douter de l'effet que ça lui avait fait, de n'être pas assez, de n'être pas *visible*.

« Pardonnez-moi, Tamìr. Je n'aurais jamais dû vous laisser y aller seule. » Arkoniel soupira. « On ne saurait raisonner un esprit comme celui-là, pas plus que vous ne pouviez arriver à raisonner Frère.

— Dans ce cas, pourquoi l'Oracle lui a-t-elle enjoint de le faire ? s'insurgea Ki.

— Je ne parviens pas à imaginer de motif ! Peut-être Tamìr s'est-elle méprise.

— Je ne le pense pas, souffla-t-elle.

— Maudits illiorains !

— Il ne faut pas blasphémer, Ki », le réprimanda le magicien.

Ki se leva et s'essuya la figure. « Je reste avec toi, au cas où elle reviendrait. N'essaie même pas de m'en dissuader. Tu peux marcher ? »

Elle était trop épuisée pour affecter de ne pas désirer sa présence auprès d'elle.

« Restez ici, dit Arkoniel. J'ai de quoi assurer votre protection dans cette pièce, et je monterai la garde à l'extérieur. Reposez-vous bien. »

Tamìr laissa Ki la fourrer dans le lit d'Arkoniel et lui prit la main quand il en eut terminé. « Dors avec moi. Je... j'ai besoin de toi. »

Ki grimpa se glisser sous les couvertures auprès d'elle et l'attira entre ses bras. Elle l'enlaça par la taille avec un des siens et se détendit contre son épaule. Il lui caressa les cheveux pendant quelques minutes, puis elle sentit la chaude pression de ses lèvres sur son front. Elle lui prit la main, la porta aux siennes pour lui retourner son baiser.

« Merci. Je sais que ceci n'est pas... »

Une bouche appliquée sur la sienne coupa court aux excuses. Ki l'embrassait, l'embrassait *pour de vrai*. Cela dura plus longtemps qu'aucun des bécots fraternels qu'ils avaient jamais échangés, et c'était infiniment plus doux, quoique plus résolu, que sa maladroite tentative d'Afra.

Même à présent que Tamìr se trouvait dans ses bras, saine et sauve, Ki continuait à revivre l'horrible moment où il était tellement certain de ne pas réussir à la rejoindre à temps. À force d'y penser et d'y repenser encore et encore, il n'imaginait que trop bien ce qu'il aurait éprouvé si elle était morte. Il avait été humilié par ses larmes de tout à l'heure, mais son baiser subit, impulsif ne l'humiliait pas. Il en mourait d'envie, et elle répondait. Tout comme était en train de le faire son propre corps.

Tamìr, c'est Tamìr, pas Tobin, se dit-il, mais il n'arrivait toujours pas à croire tout à fait qu'il faisait là ce qu'il faisait.

Lorsque cela prit fin, ils se dévisagèrent l'un l'autre, les yeux agrandis par le scepticisme, et elle lui adressa un sourire hésitant.

Cela lui fit un effet qu'il fut incapable de s'expliquer, et il l'embrassa de nouveau, mais en s'y attardant un peu plus longuement cette fois. Son menton heurta la blessure de celui de Tamìr, et il essaya de se reculer, mais le bras qui lui entourait le torse resserra son étau, et il la sentit comme s'insérer en lui. Il enfouit ses doigts dans sa chevelure pour y attraper une natte. Tamìr tressaillit quand ça tirailla puis se mit à glousser.

En entendant cela, il eut l'impression que quelque

chose qui avait été sévèrement endigué dans son cœur débordait enfin. Il écarta ses doigts et les plongea avec plus d'assurance dans les cheveux de Tamìr puis se fraya une voie caressante jusqu'à sa taille. Elle était encore habillée de pied en cap et portait la robe qu'elle avait enfilée en l'honneur de Nari pour le souper. La jupe en était un peu remontée. Il percevait la chaleur de ses jambes nues contre les siennes à travers ses propres chausses. Non, ce qu'il avait entre les bras n'avait décidément rien d'un garçon. C'était Tamìr, aussi chaude et aussi différente de son corps à lui que n'importe laquelle des filles avec lesquelles il avait jamais couché. Son cœur se mit à battre plus vite quand il approfondit son baiser et qu'elle y répondit avec une ardeur évidente.

Tamìr ne se méprit pas plus sur la différence des attouchements de Ki que sur l'indéniable érection qu'elle sentait se développer contre sa cuisse. Sans trop savoir ce qu'elle désirait au juste ni à quoi cela aboutirait mais résolue de toute manière, elle lui saisit la main et l'appliqua sur son sein gauche. Il le cueillit tendrement à travers le tissu puis, délaçant le corsage, écarta la chemise et faufila le bout de ses doigts dans l'ouverture pour caresser Tamìr à même la peau. Tièdes et rugueux, ceux-ci rencontrèrent la cicatrice entre les seins et la suivirent avec délicatesse, avant d'effleurer la pointe d'un mamelon. Jamais il n'avait rien fait de semblable avec Tobin. Son geste déclencha des ondes successives de chaleur en elle qui finirent par s'épanouir entre ses jambes en une sensation jusqu'alors inconnue.

Voilà donc l'impression que cela procure ? songeat-elle, alors qu'il l'embrassait en descendant jusqu'à sa gorge et lui mordillait doucement le côté du cou.

Elle retint son souffle, et ses yeux s'agrandirent en sentant que son entrejambe s'embrasait de plus en plus. Tout comme par le passé, elle conservait nettement la conscience de sa virilité fantomatique d'autrefois, mais assortie dorénavant de quelque chose de bien plus profond, dans les organes qui sont l'apanage exclusif de la féminité. Si elle possédait véritablement les deux sexes à la fois, alors tous deux étaient mis en émoi par les lèvres et les mains de Ki sur sa peau.

C'était trop, trop déconcertant, cette impression de dédoublement. Elle s'écarta d'un rien, le cœur battant la chamade, sa chair traîtresse simultanément écartelée entre le désir et la peur. « Ki, je ne sais pas si je peux... »

Il retira sa main et lui caressa la joue. Il était lui aussi hors d'haleine, mais il souriait. « Tu n'as pas de bile à te faire. Je n'exige pas ça tout de suite. »

Ça ? Par les couilles de Bilairy, il a cru que je voulais dire baiser ! s'avisa-t-elle du coup, consternée. *Évidemment, tiens. C'est ce qu'il fait avec les autres filles.*

« Tamìr ? » Il la contraignit d'une main douce et ferme à reposer sa tête contre sa poitrine et l'enserra passionnément. « Tout va bien. Je ne veux penser à rien d'autre qu'à ta présence ici, juste maintenant, vivante et en pleine forme. Si tu avais..., si tu étais morte cette nuit, là, comme ça... » Sa voix s'enroua de nouveau. « Je n'aurais pas pu le supporter ! » Il retomba dans le silence pendant un moment, et ses bras resserrèrent davantage encore leur étreinte. « Je n'avais jamais eu aussi peur pour toi sur le champ de bataille. Qu'est-ce que ça signifie, à ton avis ? »

Elle lui prit une main et la serra dans la sienne. « Que, quoi qu'il en soit, nous sommes toujours des guerriers l'un et l'autre, avant toute autre chose ? » Dans un certain sens, c'était réconfortant. Au moins à cet égard, elle savait encore qui elle était.

Elle continuait à le sentir bander dur contre sa cuisse, mais Ki paraissait comblé de se trouver tout simplement allongé auprès d'elle, selon leur habitude d'autrefois. Sans y réfléchir, elle déplaça légèrement sa jambe pour s'assurer un meilleur contact avec son intimité.

C'est plus gros que ce que j'avais, songea-t-elle, avant de se pétrifier lorsque Ki exhala un léger soupir puis se plaqua un peu plus contre elle.

Assis sur le seuil de sa salle de travail, le regard obstinément attaché sur la porte de la tour, Arkoniel se demandait s'il pouvait se permettre d'abandonner sa garde le temps d'aller chercher Tharin. Il se ressentait douloureusement çà et là de sa dégringolade dans les escaliers, et ses oreilles sonnaient encore du sortilège qu'il avait tramé pour condamner la porte.

Non, décida-t-il finalement. Il resterait là jusqu'à

l'aube, puis il descendrait s'assurer que les autres ne s'inquiétaient pas de découvrir vide le lit de Tamìr.

Et que ferai-je, si Ariani vient tout de même chercher de nouveau son enfant ?

C'était Ki, pas lui, qui avait sauvé Tamìr. Lui-même n'avait rien fait d'autre que de repousser le fantôme, une fois le sauvetage dûment opéré.

Saint Illuminateur, quel dessein te proposais-tu donc en lui inspirant pareille démarche ? Comme tu ne pouvais vouloir qu'elle meure, que souhaitais-tu lui montrer, alors ? Pourquoi rouvrir maintenant ces vieilles blessures ?

Ses membres meurtris commençaient à s'ankyloser. Il se leva pour arpenter le corridor, non sans s'arrêter un moment devant la porte de la chambre à coucher. De l'intérieur ne lui parvint aucun bruit. Il tendit la main vers le loquet, histoire de vérifier que tout allait bien pour ses protégés, puis la retira. Il s'attarda toutefois un instant de plus, ne sachant à quoi se résoudre, et finit par opter de préférence pour le recours à son œil magique.

Tamìr et Ki dormaient comme des souches, enlacés dans les bras l'un de l'autre comme des amants.

Amants ?

Arkoniel examina plus attentivement. Ils étaient encore habillés l'un et l'autre comme auparavant, mais il parvint à distinguer le léger sourire qui flottait en plein sommeil sur leurs deux physionomies. Sur le menton de Ki se voyait une tache de sang séché dont la forme coïncidait à merveille avec celle de la plaie qui affectait le menton de Tamìr.

Arkoniel dissipa le charme et se détourna en souriant. *Pas encore, mais il est intervenu une modification. Peut-être qu'en définitive il résultera quelque bien de cette maudite nuit.*

13

Alors qu'il avait eu l'intention de ramener Tamìr en bas dans sa propre chambre avant que quiconque ne se soit rendu compte de leur équipée, Ki s'était assoupi et à son réveil, juste après l'aube, elle reposait toujours dans ses bras. Elle ne remua pas quand il se démancha le col pour voir si elle dormait encore.

Elle avait le visage à demi dissimulé derrière une cascade de cheveux noirs. La plaie de son menton était complètement encroûtée, ses entours tout bleus et vaguement enflés. Cela lui vaudrait une nouvelle cicatrice et ne manquerait pas de trahir l'aventure de la nuit précédente.

Même à la lumière du jour, il éprouva des sueurs froides en repensant à l'esprit qui hantait la chambre de la tour. Il n'avait pas connu Ariani du temps où elle vivait encore. La nuit dernière, il n'avait pas vu trace de la femme qu'Arkoniel décrivait, rien d'autre qu'un spectre vindicatif. Il resserra inconsciemment son bras autour des épaules de Tamìr.

« Ki ? » Elle le considéra d'un air endormi pendant

un bon moment puis se dressa sur son séant, suffoquée, en prenant conscience du fait qu'ils se trouvaient toujours au lit ensemble. Les lacets de son corsage étaient encore dénoués, révélant le galbe d'un sein.

Ki détourna précipitamment les yeux. « Je suis confus. Je ne comptais pas rester toute la nuit. »

Il entreprit de se désenchevêtrer des draps, mais la façon qu'elle eut de rougir et de regarder ailleurs le fit s'interrompre. Il refoula d'une caresse les cheveux qui balayaient la joue de Tamìr puis se pencha pour l'embrasser de nouveau sur la bouche comme il l'avait fait quelques heures plus tôt. Il le fit autant pour se rassurer lui-même que pour la rassurer, elle, et il eut la joie de ressentir que le jour n'entamait en rien la véracité de ses impressions. Tamìr leva la main pour lui cueillir une joue, et il la sentit se détendre contre lui. Prunelles bleues et prunelles brunes se rencontrèrent et s'évasèrent en un aveu tacite.

« Désolé pour Afra », dit-il.

Elle referma la main sur la sienne sur l'édredon. « Désolée pour la nuit dernière. J'espérais simplement... Enfin, je suppose qu'il me faudra faire une nouvelle tentative. Mais je ne suis pas désolée pour... » Elle désigna d'un geste le désordre du lit.

« Moi non plus. Le premier bon sommeil nocturne dont j'aie joui depuis des mois. »

Avec un grand sourire, elle rejeta les couvertures et se leva. Ki eut un nouvel entr'aperçu de ses longues jambes nues avant que la retombée des jupes ne les lui dissimule. Elle avait beau demeurer très grêle encore comme une pouliche, ces jambes-là n'en étaient pas moins désormais celles d'une fille, avec des muscles imperceptiblement plus ronds, quoique toujours aussi nerveux, sur les os dégingandés. Comment avait-il pu ne pas s'en aviser jusqu'à présent ?

À son tour, il dévala du lit pour la rejoindre, tout en la détaillant à nouveau comme s'il la voyait correctement pour la toute première fois. Il ne la dominait guère que d'un empan.

Elle haussa un sourcil. « Eh bien ?

— Nari a raison. Tu es devenue plus jolie.

— Toi aussi. » Elle se lécha le pouce et frotta le sang séché qu'il avait au menton. Après quoi elle fit courir un index sur sa moustache clairsemée. « Ce hérisson-là me picote la lèvre lorsque tu m'embrasses.

— Tu es la reine. Tu peux bannir les barbes si cela te chante. »

Elle soupesa l'offre avant de l'embrasser de nouveau. « Non, je pense que j'arriverai à m'y accoutumer. Il ferait beau voir qu'on dise que tous les hommes de ma cour se sont métamorphosés en filles en même temps que moi, non ? »

Il acquiesça d'un hochement de tête puis formula la question qui restait pendante entre eux. « Et maintenant, dis, quoi ? »

Elle haussa les épaules. « Je ne puis pas prendre de consort avant d'avoir seize ans, mais c'est à peine dans deux mois. »

Elle s'arrêta net, rouge comme une cerise, en s'apercevant de ce qu'elle venait de lâcher. « Oh, Ki ! Je ne prétends pas... C'est-à-dire... »

Il haussa les épaules et se gratta nerveusement la nuque. Le mariage était une affaire trop importante pour s'envisager tout de suite, là.

Les yeux de Tamìr recelaient encore une question. Il lui prit le visage entre ses mains et l'embrassa derechef. C'était chaste, s'il se référait à son expérience personnelle des baisers, mais sa chair ne manqua pas de s'en échauffer, et il sut, rien qu'à la manière dont elle papillotait des paupières et les fermait, qu'elle éprouvait la même chose, elle aussi.

Il n'eut pas le loisir de trouver quelque chose à dire qu'Arkoniel frappa et entra. Ils se détachèrent l'un de l'autre en sursaut comme des coupables.

Le magicien s'épanouit. « Ah, bon, vous êtes éveillée ! En découvrant votre lit désert, Nari a failli avoir un coup de sang... »

Nari le bouscula pour passer et darda sur le jeune couple un regard filtrant. « Qu'est-ce que vous m'avez encore fabriqué, vous deux ?

— Rien dont tu doives te mettre martel en tête », lui assura Arkoniel.

Mais Nari continua de froncer les sourcils. « Ça fera du joli, qu'elle ait le gros ventre si jeune ! Ses hanches ne sont pas encore assez développées. Tu devrais avoir plus de jugeote, Ki, même si elle en est dépourvue !

— Je suppose que tu n'as pas tort », dit Arkoniel, avec la mine de quelqu'un qui réprime une envie de rire.

« Je n'ai rien commis de pareil ! s'insurgea Ki.

— Nous n'avons rien fait ! » se récria Tamìr en s'empourprant.

Nari la tança du doigt. « Eh bien, veille à t'abstenir tant que tu ignores comment t'y prendre pour éviter de concevoir. Je ne pense pas que qui que ce soit t'ait encore jamais appris à faire un *pessaire*, hein ?

— La nécessité ne s'imposait pas, lui rétorqua le magicien.

— Fous que vous êtes, tous les trois ! Toute fille qui a ses périodes lunaires devrait savoir ça sur-le-champ. Ouste, les hommes, allez, vous deux, que je puisse avoir un bout d'entretien convenable avec ma chère fillette là-dessus. »

C'est tout juste si elle ne les flanqua pas dehors avant de refermer la porte sur leurs talons.

« Les pessaires, je sais ce que c'est ! » grommela Ki. Il avait vu ses sœurs et les servantes, assises en rond autour du feu, préparer les petits écheveaux de laine et de charpie qu'elles imbibaient d'huile douce. Et, avec la maisonnée tout entière qui dormait, les uns empilés sur les autres, on n'avait pas fait de mystère non plus chez lui quant à leur usage. Si une fille ne voulait pas avoir de gosse, elle s'en fourrait un dans le minou avant de baiser avec son bonhomme. Mais il n'en revenait pas d'imaginer Tamìr sous cet éclairage-là, ça lui faisait un trop sale effet. « Je l'ai simplement embrassée. Je ne voudrais pour rien au monde la toucher de cette façon-là ! »

Arkoniel gloussa mais ne pipa mot.

D'un air renfrogné, Ki se croisa les bras et, campé dans le corridor, attendit Tamìr.

Quand elle finit par sortir, elle était un peu pâle.

187

Nari braqua un doigt accusateur vers Ki. « Toi, garde-moi tes culottes lacées, voilà tout !

— Je le ferai, zut ! » lui décocha-t-il dans le dos pendant qu'elle descendait pesamment l'escalier. « Tamìr, tu vas bien ? »

Elle avait toujours l'air un peu assommée. « Oui. Mais je crois que j'aimerais mieux foncer dans la bataille toute nue que d'avoir un enfant, si tout ce que Nari raconte est vrai. » Elle frissonna puis, se redressant, jeta un coup d'œil vers la porte de la tour. « Elle est verrouillée ? »

Arkoniel hocha la tête. « Je la rouvrirai, si tel est votre bon plaisir.

— Il me faut faire une autre tentative. Vous pouvez tous les deux m'accompagner là-haut.

— Essaie seulement de nous en empêcher », lui répondit Ki, d'un ton qui excluait la plaisanterie.

Arkoniel toucha le vantail, et celui-ci s'ouvrit à la volée. « Laissez-moi monter le premier, que je lève le sortilège qui bloque la porte du dernier étage. »

Ki serra de près Tamìr pendant qu'elle gravissait les marches, et il fut époustouflé de voir à quel point les lieux présentaient un aspect des plus banal à la lumière diurne. Des particules de poussière chatoyaient dans les rayons du petit matin, et la brise qui filtrait à travers les archères portait à ses narines le suave parfum des baumiers.

Un jour plus éclatant les accueillit dans la chambre d'Ariani, après qu'Arkoniel en eut descellé la porte, mais Ki ne lâcha pas Tamìr d'une semelle et scruta chaque coin de la pièce d'un air soupçonneux. Les

188

volets de la fenêtre ouest étaient demeurés béants et laissaient affluer les chants des oiseaux dans la forêt, mêlés au cours tumultueux de la rivière en contrebas.

Tamìr se campa au milieu du capharnaüm et pivota lentement sur elle-même. « Elle n'est pas ici », déclara-t-elle finalement, d'un air plus chagriné que soulagé.

« Non, convint Arkoniel. J'ai fréquemment perçu sa présence la nuit, mais jamais lorsqu'il faisait jour.

— Moi, je vois Frère à toute heure, qu'il fasse jour ou nuit.

— Il est un esprit d'une tout autre espèce. »

Elle se rendit vers la fenêtre. Ki lui emboîta le pas, peu disposé à prêter foi aux assertions d'Arkoniel en matière de fantômes. De son point de vue personnel, ce cauchemar sanguinolent risquait de surgir en trombe de nulle part à n'importe quel moment. Les fantômes étaient des créatures maléfiques, lui avait-on ressassé du moins, et ceux qui persécutaient Tamìr ne confirmaient que trop la véracité du propos.

« Qu'est-ce que je fais ? s'interrogea-t-elle tout haut.

— Peut-être rien, répondit le magicien.

— Pourquoi l'Oracle m'a-t-elle enjointe à revenir, alors ?

— Il y a des choses que l'on ne peut pas raccommoder, Tamìr.

— Qu'en est-il de Lhel ? questionna Ki. Nous ne l'avons pas même cherchée jusqu'ici. Elle savait toujours remettre Frère à sa place. Viens, Tamìr, partons

189

à cheval remonter la route, comme nous le faisions autrefois. »

Elle s'illumina sur-le-champ et retourna vers la porte. « Mais bien sûr ! Je parie qu'elle est en train d'attendre notre visite, comme toujours.

— Un instant ! » les rappela Arkoniel.

Ki se retourna et découvrit que le magicien les regardait d'un air affligé.

« Elle ne se trouve plus ici.

— Comment le savez-vous ? l'apostropha Tamìr. Vous connaissez son caractère. Si elle n'a pas envie de se laisser découvrir, on n'y peut rien, mais si elle y consent, elle est là tout bonnement à vous attendre, chaque fois.

— Je pensais la même chose, jusqu'à ce que... » Arkoniel n'acheva pas sa phrase, et Ki lut la vérité sur sa physionomie dès avant qu'il n'ajoute : « Elle est morte, Tamìr. L'Oracle me l'a révélé.

— Morte ? » Tamìr s'affaissa lentement sur ses genoux parmi les éparpillements de bribes de laine jaunie. « Mais comment ?

— Si je devais en croire mon intuition, c'est à Frère que j'imputerais sa disparition. Excusez-moi. J'aurais dû vous en avertir, mais vous aviez déjà tant de problèmes à affronter...

— Morte. » Tamìr frissonna et enfouit sa face entre ses mains. « Une de plus. Encore du sang ! »

Ki s'agenouilla auprès d'elle et l'enlaça d'un bras tout en battant des paupières pour refouler ses propres pleurs. « Je croyais... Je croyais qu'elle serait toujours à nous attendre, là-bas, dans son arbre creux.

— Moi de même », reconnut tristement le magicien.

Tamìr porta une main vers la cicatrice invisible de sa poitrine. « Je veux aller à sa recherche. Je veux l'enterrer. Ce n'est que justice.

— Mangez un morceau d'abord et changez de vêtements », conseilla Arkoniel.

Elle acquiesça d'un signe de tête et s'apprêta à quitter la pièce.

« De la tenue », dit Ki. Il passa ses doigts dans les cheveux emmêlés de Tamìr. « Vaut mieux, hein ? » reprit-il en rajustant sa propre tunique chiffonnée. « Inutile de leur fournir trop de motifs de commérages. »

C'était plus facile à dire qu'à faire. En regagnant sa chambre pour se changer, Tamìr s'aperçut que Lynx et Nikidès la lorgnaient par leur porte ouverte. Elle avait beau se dire que ni son attitude ni celle de Ki ne trahissaient rien, un simple coup d'œil leur suffit pour se détourner avec des sourires entendus.

« Enfer et damnation ! » ronchonna-t-elle, mortifiée.

« Je vais leur parler. » Ki lui adressa un regard navré puis la quitta pour régler l'affaire avec leurs amis.

En refermant sa propre porte, Tamìr secoua la tête. Qu'allait-il leur dire ? Elle n'était pas tout à fait sûre elle-même de ce qui s'était passé entre eux deux, mais elle se sentait va savoir comment plus légère et plus encline à l'espoir, en dépit même de la peine que lui faisait éprouver la perte de Lhel.

Quoi que leur eût raconté Ki, personne ne posa la moindre question.

Dès qu'il leur fut possible de s'éclipser, tous deux

partirent avec Arkoniel remonter la vieille route de la montagne.

Ç'aurait été une agréable chevauchée, n'eût été la triste certitude qui les accablait. Le soleil brillait de tous ses feux, et la forêt se parait de précoces éclaboussures d'écarlate et de jaune.

Ki repéra le vague indice d'une sente à un demimille du fort. Après avoir entravé leurs montures, ils l'empruntèrent à pied.

« Il pourrait bien ne s'agir là que d'une sente à gibier, fit-il observer.

— Non, voici la marque de Lhel », dit Arkoniel en désignant une espèce de signe délavé, couleur de rouille sur la blancheur d'un tronc de bouleau. En l'examinant de plus près, Ki se rendit compte que c'était l'empreinte d'une main beaucoup plus menue que la sienne.

« Elle provient de son charme dissimulateur, expliqua le magicien en la touchant avec chagrin. La puissance en est morte avec elle. »

Les traces déteintes d'autres empreintes similaires les guidèrent le long d'une piste presque invisible qui sinuait à travers les arbres et qui, après avoir escaladé une pente raide, débouchait finalement dans la clairière.

À première vue, rien n'avait changé. La portière de peau de daim recouvrait toujours l'embrasure basse qui s'ouvrait au pied du gigantesque chêne creux. À quelques pas de là, la source coulait en silence dans son bassin rond.

Comme ils approchaient de l'arbre, toutefois, Ki s'aperçut que les cendres tapissant le fond de la fosse à feu ne dataient pas d'hier, loin de là, et que les séchoirs à bois étaient vides et menaçaient de s'écrouler. Tamìr écarta la portière en peau de daim et disparut à l'intérieur du tronc. Ses deux compagnons la suivirent.

Des bêtes les y avaient précédés. Les corbeilles de Lhel étaient éparpillées, rongées, les fruits et la viande secs disparus depuis belle lurette. Ses quelques ustensiles reposaient encore sur des étagères basses, et sa literie de fourrures demeurait inviolée.

Ce qui subsistait de sa personne gisait dessus, comme si elle s'était allongée pour dormir et ne s'était jamais réveillée. Les animaux et les insectes avaient accompli leur œuvre. Les déchirures de la robe informe et son collier de dents de daim tiré de travers laissaient apercevoir dessous la nudité des os. La chevelure subsistait seule, sombre fouillis de boucles noires encadrant le crâne aux orbites vides.

Arkoniel s'effondra en gémissant et se mit à pleurer sans bruit. Tamìr demeura muette, sans verser de larmes. L'expression vide de son regard lorsqu'elle fit demi-tour en silence pour ressortir bouleversa Ki.

Il la retrouva debout près de la fontaine.

« C'est ici qu'elle m'a montré mon véritable visage », chuchota-t-elle, les yeux fixés sur son reflet mouvant dans l'eau. Ki fut tenté de lui enlacer la taille, mais elle se recula, toujours aussi vacante et perdue. « La terre est dure, et nous n'avons rien pour creuser. Nous aurions dû apporter une pelle. »

Il ne se trouvait rien non plus, parmi les maigres possessions de Lhel, pour les seconder dans leur tâche. Arkoniel découvrit son canif et son aiguille d'argent et les fourra dans sa ceinture. Ils abandonnèrent le reste tel quel et amassèrent des pierres devant l'entrée de l'arbre, transformant ainsi sa demeure en tombe. Le magicien trama un sortilège sur les pierres pour leur interdire de s'ébouler.

Durant toutes ces opérations, Tamír ne versa pas une seule larme. Une fois qu'ils eurent fini d'obstruer la brèche, elle plaqua l'une de ses mains contre le tronc noueux du chêne, comme afin de communier avec l'esprit de la femme qui s'y trouvait désormais emmurée.

« Il n'y a plus rien d'autre à faire ici, dit-elle finalement. Nous ferions mieux de repartir pour Atyion. »

Arkoniel et Ki échangèrent un regard navré puis se retirèrent à sa suite, la laissant seule à son deuil muet.

La mort, elle n'en a déjà vu que par trop, songea Ki. *Et nous avons encore une guerre à conduire...*

14

Le chagrin de la mort de Lhel, combiné avec la connaissance du rôle qu'elle avait joué dans la mort de Frère, était trop noir et trop profond pour se formuler. Tamír laissa ces sentiments derrière elle avec les os de la sorcière, ne remportant qu'une impression comme engourdie de choc et de perte.

Il n'y avait aucune raison de rester davantage, et le fort était une fois de plus devenu un lieu chargé de trop de mauvais souvenirs. Aussi repartirent-ils le jour même.

Nari et Cuistote les embrassèrent, elle et Ki, mille et mille fois tour à tour tous deux, puis enfouirent leurs larmes chacune dans son tablier lorsqu'ils finirent par prendre définitivement congé. Pendant qu'elle chevauchait le long de la rivière, Tamìr se retourna pour lever les yeux une dernière fois vers la fenêtre de la tour. Le volet brisé de la fenêtre est pendait toujours de biais sur un seul gond tordu. Elle ne discerna pas de visage dans l'ouverture mais, elle en eût juré, des yeux ne cessèrent de s'appesantir sur son dos jusqu'à ce qu'elle et sa suite eurent pénétré sous le couvert des bois.

Je regrette, Mère. Peut-être une autre fois.

Ki s'inclina vers elle et lui toucha le bras. « Laisse tomber. Tu as fait ce que tu pouvais. Arkoniel a raison. Il y a des choses que l'on ne peut pas raccommoder. »

Il se pouvait qu'il eût en effet raison, mais elle persistait encore à se sentir coupable d'un manquement.

Ils chevauchèrent dur cette journée-là et, la nuit suivante, dormirent à la belle étoile, emmitouflés dans leurs manteaux. Allongée là, parmi les autres, à même le sol, Tamìr palpa l'ecchymose de son menton tout en laissant ses pensées dériver vers Ki, s'attarder sur les sensations qu'elle avait éprouvées à l'embrasser puis à s'assoupir dans ses bras.

Il était étendu à portée de main, mais elle fut

incapable de le toucher. Elle allait tout juste se coucher à plat ventre quand il ouvrit les yeux et lui sourit.

C'était presque aussi délicieux qu'un baiser.

Elle se demanda ce qu'ils allaient bien pouvoir faire lorsque le retour au château les livrerait à l'affût du foisonnement des vigilances et des curiosités.

Quand ils ne se trouvèrent plus qu'à une demi-journée de marche de la ville, Tamìr dépêcha Lynx et Tyrien y annoncer la nouvelle de son incessante arrivée. En parvenant en vue d'Atyion tôt dans la soirée, de brillantes illuminations de torches et de lanternes l'accueillirent, et une foule immense s'était massée le long de la rue principale, attendant impatiemment de savoir ce que l'Oracle avait dit à sa reine. Revêtu de la robe et de la chaîne de son office, Illardi vint à cheval au-devant d'elle à la porte de la ville. Kaliya, la grande prêtresse du temple illiorain, d'Atyion, et Imonus se trouvaient avec lui.

« Majesté, l'Oracle vous a-t-elle parlé ? s'enquit ce dernier.

— Oui, elle l'a fait », répondit-elle, et d'une voix suffisamment forte pour être entendue de tous les gens qui s'étaient rassemblés sur le pourtour de la placette où la rencontre avait lieu.

« Si ce n'est abuser de sa bienveillance, Votre Majesté consentira-t-elle à nous faire part de la teneur de cet entretien sur l'esplanade des temples ? » demanda Kaliya.

Tamìr opina du chef et conduisit son entourage vers la place des Quatre. Illardi s'inclina sur sa selle pour lui glisser en confidence : « J'ai des nouvelles pour vous, Majesté. Ce jeune gaillard dont dispose Arkoniel – Eyoli – nous a fait parvenir de Cirna voilà quelques jours un pigeon porteur d'un message. Le prince Korin s'apprête à marcher contre vous. Il semble qu'il ait finalement réussi à engrosser son épouse.

— Il a déjà fait mouvement ? questionna Tharin.

— Pas encore, d'après le rapport d'aujourd'hui, mais à en croire ce que vos magiciens ont réussi à nous en montrer, les préparatifs de ses campements sont presque terminés.

— J'entrerai en communication avec Eyoli sitôt que nous en aurons terminé ici », murmura Arkoniel.

Le cœur de Tamìr chavira, bien qu'elle fût à peine étonnée. « Transmettez-lui mes remerciements. Et expédiez un mot à Gèdre et à Bôkthersa. Leurs émissaires devraient être rentrés chez eux, à présent. Lord Chancelier, je tiendrai conférence avec vous et mes généraux...

— Il sera toujours assez tôt demain, Majesté. Vous êtes épuisée, je le vois. Reposez-vous cette nuit. J'ai déjà commencé des préparatifs. »

Des badauds bondaient les perrons à degrés des quatre temples, et il y en avait des quantités d'autres perchés sur les toits, tous plus avides les uns que les autres d'entendre la première prophétie officielle du règne de Tamìr.

Toujours en selle, elle exhiba le rouleau que Ralinus lui avait confié. « Voici les paroles d'Illior, telles que me les a transmises l'Oracle d'Afra. »

La lecture qu'elle en avait déjà faite sur place l'avait

suffoquée. Alors qu'elle n'avait pas rapporté à Ralinus ce que l'Oracle avait effectivement dit, en tout cas pas mot pour mot, ce qu'il avait écrit n'en était pas moins la reproduction quasiment textuelle.

« Écoutez les paroles de l'Oracle, gens de Skala. » En plein air, sa voix sonnait grêle et perchée, et c'était une rude épreuve que de parler si fort, mais elle poursuivit tout de même. « "Salut à toi, reine Tamìr, fille d'Ariani, fille d'Agnalain, enfant légitime de la lignée royale de Skala. Par le sang tu fus protégée, et par le sang tu régneras. Tu es une graine arrosée de sang, Tamìr de Skala. C'est par le sang et l'épreuve que tu tiendras ton trône. De la main de l'Usurpateur tu arracheras l'Épée. Devant toi et derrière toi se trouve un fleuve de sang qui porte Skala vers l'ouest. Là, tu bâtiras une nouvelle ville en mon honneur." »

Un silence médusé accueillit ces mots.

« Le prince Korin se qualifie lui-même de roi à Cirna, et il est en train d'y masser une armée contre moi, continua-t-elle. Je lui ai envoyé des messages pour le prier de renoncer à ses prétentions et de se voir honorer comme mon parent. Sa seule réponse fut le silence. J'apprends maintenant qu'il entend marcher sur Atyion avec une armée dans son sillage. Quelque douleur que j'en éprouve, je m'en tiendrai aux paroles de l'Oracle et aux visions dont je me suis vu gratifier. Je suis votre reine, et j'écraserai cette rébellion contre le Trône. Me suivrez-vous ? »

Le peuple l'ovationna et agita en l'air des épées et des bannières multicolores. Cet enthousiasme lui fit chaud au cœur en l'allégeant un peu des ténèbres qui l'accablaient. Korin avait pris sa décision. C'était à elle désormais d'agir conformément à la sienne, si pénible qu'en soit l'issue.

Son devoir achevé, Tamìr remit à Kaliya le rouleau pour qu'il soit affiché dans le temple et copié et lu par des hérauts dans tout le pays.

« Ça s'est bien passé, commenta Ki pendant qu'ils se dirigeaient vers le château.

— Les gens t'aiment, et ils se battront pour toi », ajouta Tharin.

Tamìr resta muette, la tête occupée par tout le sang que lui avait montré l'Oracle. Elle le sentait déjà lui souiller les mains.

Après avoir franchi la barbacane, ils trouvèrent Lytia et presque toute la maisonnée qui attendaient Tamìr dans la cour du château. « Soyez la bienvenue pour votre retour, Majesté, la salua Lytia pendant qu'elle mettait pied à terre et se dégourdissait les jambes en les étirant.

— Merci. J'espère que vous ne vous êtes pas donné le tracas d'apprêter un banquet. Je n'ai envie que de deux choses, un bain et mon lit. »

Il y avait également dans l'assistance quelques-uns des magiciens et des enfants.

« Où est maîtresse Iya ? » s'enquit Rala.

Tamìr entendit et se demanda ce qu'Arkoniel dirait à ses collègues et s'ils resteraient. Mais, pour l'heure, il esquiva leurs questions tout en les entraînant à l'écart et en s'empressant de les interroger sur ce qu'ils savaient de Korin.

L'abandonnant à ce soin, Tamìr gravit promptement

le perron, désireuse de se détendre en privé avant que les obligations de cour ne fondent à nouveau sur elle. Celles-ci ne lui avaient certes pas manqué le moins du monde...

Lytia les accompagna à l'étage, elle et les Compagnons. Une fois arrivée devant la porte des appartements de Tamìr, elle lui toucha la manche et chuchota : « Un mot en tête à tête, Majesté ? Pour une affaire des plus conséquente. »

Tamìr l'invita à la suivre d'un signe de tête, laissant les autres à l'extérieur.

Baldus était pelotonné dans un fauteuil, Queue-tigrée lové au creux de ses genoux. Il repoussa le matou pour bondir sur ses pieds et s'incliner. « Bienvenue à vous, reine Tamìr ! Souhaitez-vous que j'allume le feu ?

— Non, va dire aux servantes de me monter une baignoire. Et fais en sorte que l'eau soit bouillante ! »

Le page se rua dehors, tout heureux que sa maîtresse soit de retour. Elle se demanda fugitivement à quoi il pouvait bien s'occuper lorsqu'il se trouvait dispensé de service quand elle n'était pas là. Elle déboucla son baudrier d'épée, le jeta sur le siège délaissé puis entreprit de dégrafer vaille que vaille son corselet de plates. Le chat s'enroula autour de ses chevilles en ronronnant à pleine gorge, au risque de la faire presque trébucher.

« Majesté, certains des autres Compagnons sont arrivés pendant votre absence. Et comme ils ont fait un voyage terriblement éprouvant...

— Una ? Elle est blessée ? » L'anxiété la contraignit

à s'asseoir brusquement. Avec un crachement de fureur, Queue-tigrée fusa se planquer.

« Non, Majesté. Il s'agit de Lord Caliel, de Lord Lutha et de son écuyer. Je les ai installés dans l'une des chambres d'hôtes de cette même tour. »

Tamìr se remit debout d'un bond, plus enchantée de la nouvelle qu'elle n'aurait pu l'exprimer. « Loués soient les Quatre ! Mais pourquoi diable n'étaient-ils pas en bas pour m'accueillir ? Nos amis seront transportés de les retrouver.

— Je me suis dit que peut-être vous-même et Lord Ki souhaiteriez les voir d'abord seuls. Il y a quelqu'un d'autre avec eux.

— Qui ça ? » demanda-t-elle, déjà sur le seuil de la porte.

Les Compagnons campaient dans le corridor. Lytia leur décocha un coup d'œil furtif, puis reprit tout bas : « Je vous le dirai pendant que nous monterons. »

Malgré sa perplexité, Tamìr acquiesça d'un hochement. « Ki, tu m'accompagnes. Attendez ici, vous autres. »

Lytia leur fit emprunter un second corridor à l'autre extrémité de la tour puis, faisant halte un instant, souffla : « L'étranger qui est avec eux ? Eh bien, tout semble indiquer qu'il appartient au peuple des collines, Majesté. Lord Lutha affirme qu'il s'agit en fait d'un sorcier.

— Un sorcier ? » Tamìr et Ki échangèrent un regard de stupéfaction.

« C'est ce qui m'a incitée à penser que vous devriez monter sans trop de témoins, se hâta d'expliquer Lytia.

Daignez me pardonner si j'ai commis une faute en laissant entrer une créature pareille, mais les trois autres ont refusé de se voir séparés de lui. Il m'a donc fallu les placer tous sous bonne garde. Ils sont heureusement arrivés de nuit, de sorte que seuls une poignée de gardes et de serviteurs les ont aperçus. Aucun d'entre eux ne bavardera. Je leur ai fait jurer de se taire jusqu'à ce que vous vous soyez prononcée sur le cas.

— Est-ce que cet individu reconnaît qu'il est un sorcier ? demanda Tamìr.

— Oh, ça oui. Il n'en fait aucunement mystère. Il était abominablement crasseux au moment de leur arrivée... – enfin, ils l'étaient tous, ces pauvres garçons –, et il me fait l'effet d'être un simple d'esprit, mais les autres se sont portés garants pour lui et affirment qu'il les a aidés. Ils ont subi de cruels sévices.

— De la part de qui ?

— Ils ont refusé de le dire. »

Quatre hommes armés se trouvaient en faction devant la porte de la chambre d'hôtes, et le vieux Vornus et Lyan étaient installés sur un banc juste en face de celle-ci, leurs baguettes magiques en travers des genoux, comme s'ils s'attendaient à devoir à tout moment repousser quelque agression. Ils se levèrent et s'inclinèrent lorsqu'ils virent Tamìr s'approcher.

« Pouvez-vous me dire ce qui se passe ? les interrogea-t-elle.

— Nous avons constamment tenu à l'œil votre visiteur incongru, répondit Vornus. Il s'est parfaitement comporté jusqu'ici.

— Nous n'avons pas perçu ne serait-ce qu'une once de magie émaner de sa personne, ajouta Lyan en refourrant sa baguette dans sa manche. Il fait une peur horrible à vos gens, mais je n'ai pour ma part senti en lui aucune espèce de malignité.

— Merci de votre vigilance. Veuillez continuer à monter la garde pour l'instant. »

Les gardes s'écartèrent, et Tamìr frappa à la porte.

Celle-ci s'ouvrit à la volée, et Lutha s'encadra là, pieds nus et vêtu d'une longue chemise et de braies. Il était maigre et blême, et ses nattes avaient été tranchées, mais l'expression que prit sa physionomie lorsqu'il reconnut Tamìr frôlait le comique. À l'autre bout de la chambre, Caliel était couché à plat ventre sur un grand lit, et Barieüs se tenait à son chevet, recroquevillé dans un fauteuil. Tous deux la fixèrent, écarquillés comme s'ils se trouvaient en présence d'un fantôme.

Lutha s'étrangla. « Par les Quatre ! Tobin ?

— C'est Tamìr, maintenant », l'informa Ki.

Un silence tendu s'ensuivit, puis Lutha s'illumina d'un grand sourire mouillé de larmes. « C'est donc vrai ! Par les couilles de Bilairy, des rumeurs nous en ont rebattu les oreilles depuis notre départ d'Ero, mais Korin ne voulait pas le croire. » Il s'épongea les yeux. « Je ne sais que dire, sauf que je suis foutrement heureux de voir que vous êtes tous les deux vivants !

— Qu'est-ce qui vous est arrivé ?

— Entrez d'abord, que les autres vous voient comme il faut. »

Il les conduisit vers le lit, et Tamìr fut frappée par

l'extrême raideur qui affectait ses mouvements, comme si bouger le faisait souffrir.

Caliel se redressa en grimaçant pendant qu'elle et Ki s'approchaient. Barieüs se leva lentement et lui adressa un sourire mal assuré, l'émerveillement et la perplexité s'affrontant dans ses yeux.

« Oui, c'est bien Tobin, lui assura Ki. Mais elle est désormais la reine Tamìr. »

Le regard de Barieüs alla de Tamìr à Ki. « Vous vous êtes battus tous les deux ? Tamìr..., ton menton ? Et toi, Ki, qu'est-ce qui est arrivé à ta joue ?

— J'ai fait une chute, et Ki a été mordu par un dragon. Nous l'avons été tous les deux, en fait.

— Un dragon ?

— Juste un tout petit », lui dit Ki.

Lutha se mit à rire. « On a manqué des tas de choses, apparemment. »

C'était un plaisir de le voir sourire, mais leur maintien à tous, joint aux révélations de Lytia, lui perça le cœur d'un pressentiment. Aucun d'entre eux n'avait plus de nattes.

« Comment ? » demanda Caliel en la considérant d'un air consterné. Son beau visage était bariolé d'ecchymoses en voie d'effacement, et il avait un regard hanté.

Avec un soupir, Tamìr esquissa promptement les divers détails de sa métamorphose et regarda leurs yeux s'agrandir de stupéfaction.

« Je sais que cela ressemble à un épisode d'un conte de barde, leur confirma Ki, mais j'ai vu de mes propres yeux s'opérer son changement, ici même, à Atyion, et en présence de mille autres témoins.

— Maintenant, racontez-moi ce qui vous est arrivé à tous les trois », les pressa Tamìr.

Lutha et Barieüs se retournèrent et retroussèrent leurs chemises. Après avoir hésité, Caliel fit lentement de même.

« Par les couilles de Bilairy ! » hoqueta Ki.

Sur les dos de Barieüs et de Lutha s'entrecroisaient des marques de fouet à moitié guéries, mais on avait dû flageller Caliel encore plus vilainement. De la nuque à la taille, sa peau formait un magma de croûtes et de chair couturée de tissu cicatriciel d'un rouge agressif.

La gorge de Tamìr se dessécha. « Korin ? »

Lutha rabattit sa chemise et aida Caliel à baisser la sienne. Puis ils prirent tous des mines humiliées lorsqu'il se mit à raconter par à-coups leur séjour à Cirna et la manière dont la lettre de Tamìr à Korin avait été reçue.

« En ce qui te concernait, nous n'avions rien su que par l'intermédiaire des espions de Nyrin, et nous ne leur faisions pas confiance, expliqua Caliel. Je souhaitais venir me rendre compte ici par moi-même, mais Korin m'a opposé un non ferme et définitif.

— Et tu es parti tout de même », commenta Tamìr.

Caliel acquiesça d'un hochement de tête.

« Nyrin nous faisait surveiller par ses mouchards, reprit amèrement Lutha. Tu te rappelles Moriel, qui voulait si salement supplanter Ki pour te tenir lieu d'écuyer ?

— Le Crapaud ? Tu parles ! grommela Ki. Ne me dis pas qu'il est encore avec Korin ?

— Il est le roquet de Nyrin, maintenant, et il était à l'affût de nos moindres faits et gestes pour les rapporter à son maître, spécifia Caliel.

— Oh, mes amis ! » chuchota Tamìr, profondément émue par leur foi en elle. « Alors, qu'en dites-vous, à présent que vous m'avez vue ? »

Caliel la considéra pendant un moment, et son regard hanté reparut. « Eh bien, tu n'as pas l'air dément. Quant à tout le reste, je suis encore en train d'essayer de m'y retrouver. » Il se tourna vers Ki. « Je suppose que tu ne marcherais pas dans une combine qui mettrait en jeu la nécromancie ?

— Pas nécromancie. Liaison retha'noï », intervint une voix basse et amusée.

L'état pitoyable de ses amis avait tellement alarmé Tamìr qu'elle en avait complètement oublié le sorcier des collines. Quand il se leva de la paillasse étendue dans un coin et s'avança, elle constata qu'il était plutôt habillé comme un paysan skalien, mais on ne pouvait cependant se méprendre sur sa nature.

« Je te présente Mahti, dit Lutha. Avant que tu te mettes en colère, autant que tu saches que sans lui nous ne serions jamais arrivés ici.

— Je ne suis pas en colère », murmura-t-elle, en examinant au contraire l'homme avec intérêt. Il était petit et noiraud comme Lhel, avec la même carnation olivâtre et le même fouillis de longues boucles noires hirsutes autour des épaules, les mêmes pieds nus cornés et malpropres. Il portait un collier et des bracelets faits de dents de bêtes enfilées, et il tenait une longue et bizarre espèce de cor décoré de motifs complexes.

Il se rapprocha d'elle et lui adressa un large sourire. « Lhel me commander venir à toi, fille qui étais garçon. Tu connaître Lhel, oui ?

— Oui. Quand l'as-tu vue pour la dernière fois ?

— La nuit avant aujourd'hui. Elle dit que toi venir. »

Ki fronça les sourcils et vint se planter plus près de Tamìr. « Ce n'est pas possible. »

Mahti lorgna Tamìr d'un air entendu. « Toi savoir que les morts n'arrêtent pas de venir s'ils veulent. Elle me dire aussi de ton *noro'shesh*. Tu as des yeux qui voient.

— Il est en train de parler de fantômes ? marmonna Barieüs. Il ne nous a jamais rien dit là-dessus, à nous. Il se contentait d'affirmer qu'il nous avait vus dans une vision ou un truc de ce genre et qu'il était censé venir avec nous.

« Toi être effrayé. » Mahti gloussa puis tendit le doigt vers Tamìr. « Elle pas être effrayée.

— Comment as-tu rencontré Lhel la première fois ? demanda-t-elle.

— Elle venir en vision. Déjà morte quand je la connais.

— Il n'a jamais dit non plus quoi que ce soit sur qui que ce soit nommé Lhel. De qui s'agit-il ? s'enquit Lutha.

— Aucun problème. Je pense que je comprends. »

207

Le sorcier opina tristement du chef. « Lhel t'aime toujours. Elle me dire tout le temps que moi falloir venir à toi.

— C'est son fantôme qui te l'a commandé, tu veux dire ? » interrogea Ki.

Mahti hocha la tête. « Son *mari* venir à moi quand je fais rêve avec oo'lu.

— C'est comme ça qu'il appelle son instrument, dit Barieüs. Il s'en sert pour ses opérations magiques, comme un magicien.

— Korin avait lancé des traqueurs à nos trousses, avec un magicien, mais Mahti joua de ce cor, et aucun d'entre eux ne nous aperçut, bien que nous fussions sur la route en pleine vue, expliqua Lutha.

— Il est aussi un bon guérisseur avec ce truc et avec ses herbes, ajouta Barieüs. Aussi bon qu'un drysien. Et il connaissait un raccourci à travers les montagnes, en plus.

— Sans lui, je n'aurais pas survécu pour arriver ici, conclut Caliel. Quoi qu'on puisse dire de lui par ailleurs, il a pris le plus grand soin de nous.

— Merci d'avoir secouru mes amis, Mahti, dit Tamìr en lui tendant la main. Je sais à quel point il est dangereux pour les tiens de pénétrer aussi loin dans nos terres. »

Le sorcier lui effleura la main et se remit à glousser. « Pas danger pour moi. Mère Shek'met protéger, et Lhel être guide.

— Il n'empêche, je veillerai à ce qu'on te laisse passer sain et sauf lorsque tu regagneras tes collines.

— Je venir à toi, fille qui étais garçon. Je venir pour aider.

— M'aider à quoi faire ?

— Moi aider comme Lhel aider. Peut-être avec ton *noro'shesh* ? Celui-là pas dormir encore.

— Non, en effet.

— De quoi parle-t-il ? » demanda Lutha.

Tamìr secoua la tête avec lassitude. « Je suppose que je ferais mieux de tout vous raconter. »

Elle attira un fauteuil près du lit, sur le bord duquel Ki et Lutha s'assirent précautionneusement aux côtés de Caliel. Lorsqu'elle se mit à leur confier ce qu'elle savait, Mahti s'accroupit par terre et écouta attentivement, le front plissé par l'effort de la suivre dans son récit.

« On a donc tué ton frère pour te permettre d'emprunter ses dehors ? lâcha Caliel quand elle eut fini. N'est-ce pas là de la nécromancie ? »

Mahti secoua la tête avec véhémence. « Lhel faire une faute en faisant mourir le bébé. Pas aurait dû... » Il s'arrêta, cherchant le terme, puis prit une profonde inspiration, l'index pointé vers sa propre poitrine. « Lhel te dit ça ?

— Lhel ne m'a jamais dit comment il était mort. Je n'ai appris la vérité qu'il y a quelques jours, par des magiciens qui se trouvaient présents.

— Iya ? demanda Caliel.

— Oui.

— Pas souffle. *Premier* souffle. Porte *mari* dans... » Après avoir marqué une nouvelle hésitation, Mahti pinça la peau du dos de sa main.

« Dans le corps ? » suggéra Ki, se touchant la poitrine à son tour.

« Corps ? Oui. Pas souffle dans corps, pas vie. Pas *mari* pour être comme lui. Mauvaise chose. Pas souffle pour corps, *mari* pas avoir maison.

— *Mari* doit signifier esprit, musa Ki.

— Sans vouloir t'offenser, Tob... – Tamìr, peut-être qu'il ne comprend pas ce qu'est la nécromancie, avertit Caliel. Qui d'autre est capable de maîtriser fantômes et démons, hormis les nécromanciens ?

— Pas nécromancie ! s'insurgea Mahti mordicus. Vous autres, Skaliens, vous pas comprendre Retha'noïs ! » Il brandit de nouveau son cor. « Pas nécromancie. Bonne magie. Aider vous, oui ?

— Oui, admit Caliel.

— Pourquoi voudrait-il nous aider, s'il est malicieux, Cal ? » insista Lutha, et son intervention fit à Tamìr l'effet qu'ils reprenaient là une discussion antérieure. « Tamìr, cette amie à toi, maîtresse Iya, ne serait-elle pas en mesure de nous préciser s'il appartient à cette engeance ou non ?

— Iya ne se trouve plus avec moi, mais je dispose d'autres conseillers. Ki, va faire chercher Arkoniel. Il est plus au fait du peuple de Mahti que n'importe qui d'autre. »

Caliel attendit que Ki soit sorti pour déclarer : « Je dois te prévenir, Tamìr, que je ne suis pas ici de mon propre gré. Quand j'ai voulu venir te voir auparavant, c'était pour parlementer en faveur de Korin. Il est mon ami et mon suzerain. Le serment que je lui ai juré en tant que Compagnon, je ne le romprai pas. Je ne te veux aucun mal, mais je ne saurais me déshonorer en acceptant ton hospitalité par des subterfuges. Je ne suis pas un espion, mais je ne suis pas un renégat non plus.

— Non, mais tu es un bougre d'imbécile ! gronda Lutha. C'est Korin qui est fou à lier. Tu l'as vu aussi clairement que moi, même avant qu'il ne te fasse fouetter presque à mort. » Il se tourna vers Tamìr, l'œil flamboyant d'indignation. « Il s'apprêtait à nous pendre tous ! Libre à toi de me qualifier de traître si ça te chante, Cal, mais je suis ici parce que je suis convaincu que Korin a tort. Je l'aimais, moi aussi, mais c'est lui qui a rompu son serment envers nous et envers Skala quand il s'est abaissé jusqu'à devenir la marionnette d'une créature telle que Nyrin. Il m'est impossible de déshonorer plus longtemps le nom de mon père en servant dans une cour pareille.

— Il est ensorcelé », marmonna Caliel en se prenant la face entre les mains.

Ki revint et s'installa de nouveau sur le lit, tout en considérant Caliel avec inquiétude.

« Cette ordure a conduit Korin à voir des traîtres dans la moindre ombre, poursuivit Lutha. Quand l'unique devoir d'un chacun est de le désapprouver, on a toute chance de finir au bout d'une corde.

— Comment êtes-vous parvenus à vous tirer de ce guêpier ? demanda Ki.

— Grâce à ton espion, Tamìr. Un gars qui s'appelle Eyoli, c'est ça ? Je ne sais pas comment il s'est débrouillé, mais toujours est-il qu'il nous a délivrés.

— C'est un magicien, lui révéla Ki.

— Je me doutais bien qu'il risquait d'être quelque chose de ce genre-là.

— Comment se passent actuellement les choses à Cirna ? demanda Tamìr.

— Ça grommelle pas mal dans les rangs. Il y en a certains qui ne sont pas d'accord avec les manigances de Nyrin. D'autres commencent à s'impatienter de voir Korin se borner à bouder là, dans la forteresse. Il a bien envoyé quelques troupes mater des gentils-hommes qui s'étaient déclarés pour toi, mais ses généraux souhaitent qu'il te coure sus.

— Il s'y est finalement résolu, l'avisa-t-elle. Je viens tout juste de l'apprendre. »

Cela fit relever les yeux à Caliel. « Sauf ton respect, je ne veux pas être ici pour entendre ça. Je regrette, Tamìr. Il m'est impossible de participer à quelque conversation que ce soit dirigée contre Korin. Je... je devrais retourner près de lui. Sakor m'est témoin que je n'ai pas la moindre envie de te combattre, mais ma place est là-bas.

— Il te pendra, aussi sûr que je suis assis sur ce lit ! s'exclama Lutha. Pour l'amour de l'enfer, nous ne t'avons pas traîné tout du long jusqu'ici pour que tu fasses juste demi-tour et te jettes dans la gueule du loup ! » Il prit Tamìr et Ki à témoin. « Voilà comment il a été sans arrêt. Il refuse d'entendre raison !

— Vous auriez dû m'abandonner, alors ! jappa Caliel.

— Peut-être bien que nous aurions dû !

— S'il vous plaît, ne vous disputez pas ! » Tamìr tendit la main et saisit celle de Caliel. Il tremblait d'émotion. « Tu n'es pas en état d'aller où que ce soit. Repose-toi ici jusqu'à ce que tu aies recouvré quelque force. Honore les lois de l'hospitalité, et je continuerai de te traiter en ami.

— Bien sûr. Je te donne ma parole. »

Elle se tourna vers le sorcier, qui avait assisté à toute la scène avec un intérêt manifeste. « À toi, maintenant. Consens-tu à jurer par ta grande et vénérable Mère de ne faire de mal dans ma demeure à aucun de mes gens ? »

Mahti empoigna son cor à deux mains. « Par la pleine lune de Mère Shek'met et par le *mari* de Lhel, je venir seulement pour aider. Je faire pas de mal.

— J'accepte ta foi. Tu es sous ma protection. Vous l'êtes tous. » Elle regarda tristement ses amis. « Je ne retiendrai aucun d'entre vous ici contre sa volonté ni n'escompterai non plus que vous me serviez comme vous serviez Korin. Aussitôt que vous serez à même de monter à cheval, je vous accorderai un sauf-conduit pour vous rendre où vous voulez.

— M'est avis que tu n'as vraiment pas changé du tout, indépendamment de la manière dont tu t'appelles, répondit Lutha en souriant. Si vous voulez bien de ma personne, reine Tamír, je suis prêt à vous servir d'ores et déjà.

— Et toi, Barieüs ?

— Moi aussi. » Ses doigts se portèrent furtivement vers les cheveux cisaillés de ses tempes pendant qu'il ajoutait : « Si tant est que vous daigniez me prendre.

— Évidemment que je le veux.

— Et toi, Cal ? » demanda Ki.

Caliel haussa simplement les épaules et se détourna.

Arkoniel entra sur ces entrefaites et se pétrifia net en apercevant Mahti.

Le sorcier le lorgna avec tout autant d'intérêt. « Orëskiri ?

— Retha'noï ? »

Mahti hocha la tête et toucha son cœur puis répliqua longuement dans son idiome personnel.

Tous deux conversèrent pendant plusieurs minutes. Tamìr reconnut au passage le terme « enfant » et le nom de Lhel mais sans comprendre un traître mot de plus. Arkoniel hocha tristement la tête à la mention de la sorcière défunte puis poursuivit son interrogatoire. Il s'empara de la main de son interlocuteur, mais celui-ci la dégagea vivement tout en branlant un index accusateur vers lui.

« Que dit-il ? » questionna Tamìr.

Arkoniel lui adressa un hochement de tête penaud. « Mille excuses. Il s'agissait simplement d'un truc que Lhel m'a enseigné, mais c'était offensant. »

Mahti hocha la tête puis tendit au magicien son cor oo'lu pour lui permettre de l'examiner.

Une fois sa curiosité satisfaite, ce dernier se retourna vers Tamìr et le reste de l'assistance. « Il affirme que l'esprit de Lhel s'est manifesté à lui dans une vision pour lui enjoindre de venir vous protéger. Elle lui a servi de guide et l'a conduit à vos amis pendant qu'ils venaient ici.

— C'est ce qu'il a déjà prétendu. Qu'en pensez-vous ?

— Je ne saurais imaginer qu'un sorcier des collines

ait accompli un aussi long voyage sans raison valable. Ses pareils n'ont jamais été gens à envoyer des assassins. Mais je dois vous prévenir cependant qu'il est capable de tuer avec sa magie et qu'il l'a déjà fait, mais uniquement pour assurer sa sauvegarde, à ce qu'il prétend du moins. À vous de le prendre au mot ou de le congédier. Pour ma part, je le conserverais volontiers actuellement parmi nos collègues, si tant est que vous n'y voyiez pas d'objections ?

— Parfait. Je descendrai lorsque j'en aurai terminé ici. »

Arkoniel tendit sa main à Mahti. « Viens, mon ami. Nous avons à parler, toi et moi, de quantité de choses.

— Lutha, toi et Barieüs avez toute liberté de rejoindre les autres Compagnons », déclara Tamìr, une fois que les deux autres se furent retirés.

« Qui reste-t-il ? demanda Lutha.

— Nikidès...

— Nik est vivant ? s'écria-t-il. Loué soit Sakor ! Je pensais l'avoir condamné à mort par mon abandon. Qui d'autre ?

— Uniquement Lynx et Tanil. Mais nous avons quelques nouveaux membres.

— Tanil ? s'étrangla Caliel.

— Nous est-il possible de les voir dès à présent ? s'enquit Barieüs, que la seule mention de Lynx avait fait rayonner de façon notable.

— Bien entendu. Ki, va les chercher, veux-tu ?

— Et Tanil ? demanda Ki.

— Lui aussi. Je m'expliquerai sur son cas pendant ton absence. »

Ki acquiesça d'un signe de tête et se dépêcha de sortir.

« Qu'est-il arrivé à Tanil ? s'inquiéta Caliel.

— Les Plenimariens se sont conduits avec lui de manière ignoble. » Elle leur raconta toute l'histoire, malgré son désir de leur épargner les détails, mais l'évidence leur sauterait aux yeux lorsqu'ils le verraient.

Caliel poussa un gémissement et ferma les paupières.

« Enfer et damnation ! » grommela Lutha.

Ki ne tarda pas à revenir accompagné du reste de la bande. Nikidès s'immobilisa juste au-delà du seuil, le regard fixé sur Lutha et Barieüs.

« Je... Peux-tu me pardonner ? » lâcha finalement Lutha d'une voix tremblante d'émotion.

Nikidès éclata en larmes et les embrassa tous les deux.

Enlaçant d'un bras la taille de Tanil, Lynx lui parlait tout bas. Mais lorsque l'écuyer aperçut Caliel, il se dégagea pour se précipiter vers lui.

« J'ai perdu Korin ! » exhala-t-il dans un souffle en s'agenouillant près du lit, les yeux pleins de larmes. « Je n'arrive pas à le retrouver ! »

Caliel lui saisit la main et palpa les bourrelets de cicatrices pourpres de son poignet. « Tu ne l'as pas perdu. C'est nous qui t'avons perdu. Korin en a été très affligé, il croyait que tu étais mort.

— Vraiment ? » Il se releva sur-le-champ et parcourut la chambre d'un regard circulaire. « Où est-il ?

— À Cirna.

— Je vais tout de suite seller nos chevaux !

— Non, pas encore. » Caliel l'attira de nouveau vers lui.

« Ne te tracasse plus. Je suis sûr que Korin n'y verra pas d'inconvénient, dit Lynx. Il souhaitera que tu prennes soin de Cal, n'est-ce pas ?

— Mais... Mylirin ?

— Il est mort, l'informa Caliel.

— Mort ? » Tanil le dévisagea d'un air absent pendant un moment, puis il enfouit sa face entre ses mains et se mit à pleurer sans bruit.

« Il est tombé avec honneur. » Caliel le fit s'asseoir sur le lit et l'y maintint. « Veux-tu me tenir lieu d'écuyer à sa place jusqu'à ce que nous partions retrouver Korin ?

— Je... je ne suis plus digne d'être un Compagnon.

— Bien sûr que si. Et tu regagneras tes nattes aussitôt que nous serons de nouveau en bonne forme tous les deux. N'est-ce pas, Tamìr ?

— Oui. Les guérisseurs ont fait du bon travail. Pour l'instant, c'est à Caliel que tu te dois. »

Tanil s'essuya les yeux. « Je suis désolé pour Mylirin, mais je suis heureux de te revoir, Caliel. Korin sera si content de ne pas t'avoir perdu non plus ! »

Caliel échangea avec Tamìr un regard navré. Pour l'instant, ils laisseraient Tanil se cramponner à ses espoirs.

Après avoir bavardé un moment pour rattraper le temps perdu de part et d'autre, ils laissèrent Tanil

217

avec Caliel pour aller se réfugier dans la chambre de Nikidès.

« Cal ne va pas changer d'avis, tu sais, confia Lutha à Tamìr pendant qu'ils s'acheminaient vers l'appartement de cette dernière. S'il n'avait pas été si grièvement blessé, il n'aurait pas manqué de rebrousser chemin.

— Il fera ce qu'il estime être son devoir. Je ne l'en empêcherai pas. »

Tharin se trouvait là avec les jeunes écuyers, et il serra joyeusement les mains de Lutha et de Barieüs. Tamìr s'attarda encore un petit peu en leur compagnie puis se leva pour se retirer. Ki fit de même dans l'intention de la suivre, mais elle sourit et lui fit signe de rester là.

Elle marqua une pause sur le seuil de la porte, heureuse au-delà de toute expression de voir ses amis à nouveau réunis. Et même si Caliel ne pouvait se résoudre à se joindre à eux, du moins était-il vivant.

15

Arkoniel fit descendre le sorcier des collines par des escaliers de service et des coursives dérobées sur les arrières pour l'emmener dans son appartement. Les rares personnes qu'ils croisèrent ce faisant ne prêtèrent à l'étranger que peu d'attention, tant elles s'étaient accoutumées à voir le magicien introduire dans le château des vagabonds de tout acabit.

Avec ses tentures éclatantes et ses meubles anciens délicatement sculptés, sa chambre était de loin la plus luxueuse dont il eût jamais disposé. Le reste de ses collègues était logé dans des pièces similaires donnant sur la petite cour. Fidèle à sa promesse, Tamìr leur avait alloué des fonds généreux sur son trésor personnel et procuré tout l'espace nécessaire pour s'exercer à loisir et prodiguer leur enseignement.

Wythnir se trouvait là où son maître l'avait laissé, pelotonné dans l'embrasure profonde d'une fenêtre d'où il regardait les autres gosses s'amuser dehors dans le crépuscule. Il bondit sur ses pieds dès que les deux hommes entrèrent et dévisagea Mahti avec un intérêt non déguisé, sans une once de sa timidité coutumière, à l'intense surprise du magicien.

« Vous êtes un sorcier, n'est-ce pas, tout à fait comme maîtresse Lhel ? J'ai su par elle qu'il pouvait y avoir aussi des hommes pratiquant la sorcellerie. »

Mahti sourit au gamin. « Oui, *keesa*.

— Elle s'est montrée très gentille avec nous. Elle nous a appris à trouver de la nourriture dans la forêt et empêché les gens de découvrir notre refuge.

— Toi être orëskiri, petit ? Je sentir magie dans toi. » Il plissa légèrement les yeux. « Ah oui. Et aussi petit bout de magie retha'noï ici.

— Lhel a enseigné aux enfants et à quelques-uns des magiciens plus âgés une pincée de menus sortilèges. Grâce à elle, je pense que la plupart de mes collègues se montreront plus accueillants à ton endroit.

— Je faire magie avec ça. » Il tendit l'oo'lu à Wythnir pour l'encourager à le prendre en main. Après avoir consulté Arkoniel d'un coup d'œil pour se rassurer, l'enfant s'empara de l'instrument dont le poids le fit quelque peu se voûter.

« Ce moutard-là n'a pas peur de moi », remarqua Mahti dans sa propre langue, tout en le regardant ajuster sa menotte dans l'empreinte de paume brûlée dans le voisinage de l'extrémité de l'oo'lu. « Peut-être que toi et lui réussirez à apprendre aux autres à ne pas redouter mon peuple et à partager leur magie avec nous, comme l'a fait Lhel.

— Ce serait une bonne chose pour tout le monde. Dis-moi, d'où viens-tu ?

— Des montagnes de l'ouest. Je n'aurais pas trouvé ma route sans l'aide de Lhel et de mes visions.

— Voilà qui est très étrange, à la vérité.

— Tu parles très bien ma langue, Orëska. Cela me facilite les choses, et ça me permet de m'exprimer de façon claire.

— À ton aise. » Changeant d'idiome, il ajouta : « Wythnir, sors jouer avec tes copains pendant qu'il reste encore un peu de jour. Je suis convaincu que tu leur as manqué pendant notre voyage. »

Le gosse hésita puis baissa les yeux et se dirigea vers la porte.

« Il redoute d'être séparé de toi, fit observer Mahti. Pourquoi ne pas lui permettre de rester ? Il ne comprend pas ma langue, n'est-ce pas ? Et même s'il le faisait, je n'ai rien à dire qu'un enfant ne puisse entendre.

— Tu peux rester, Wythnir, si ça te fait plaisir. » Arkoniel prit un siège auprès de l'âtre, et le garçonnet s'assit tout de suite à ses pieds, les mains croisées sur ses genoux.

« Il est docile et intelligent, cet enfant, reprit Mahti d'un ton approbateur. Il sera un puissant orëskiri, si tu arrives à le guérir de la peur qui le tenaille. Il a été profondément meurtri.

— C'est ce qui arrive souvent aux enfants nés dans la misère ou l'ignorance et doués du pouvoir. Mais il ne veut pas parler de son passé, et le magicien qui l'avait avant n'a pas l'air de savoir grand-chose de lui.

— Tu es bon pour lui. Il t'aime comme un père. »

Arkoniel sourit. « C'est là l'idéal entre maître et apprenti. Il est un excellent garçon. »

Mahti s'accroupit en tailleur sur le sol en face d'eux, son oo'lu en travers des genoux. « Je t'ai vu dans ma vision, Arkoniel. Lhel t'a aimé lorsqu'elle était vivante, et elle t'aime toujours. Et comme elle a partagé beaucoup de sa science magique avec toi, elle devait également te faire confiance.

— J'aurais plaisir à le croire.

— Ce n'est pas contraire aux usages de votre peuple de recourir à notre magie ?

— Bien des gens le prétendent, mais mon professeur et moi n'étions pas d'accord avec ce point de vue. Iya s'est tout spécialement mise en quête de Lhel parce que celle-ci connaissait le sortilège susceptible d'assurer le genre de liaison qui protégerait Tamìr. Je me rappelle que, lorsque nous l'avons découverte, elle ne fut nullement étonnée de notre visite. Elle aussi nous affirma nous avoir vus dans une vision.

— Oui. Mais la méthode qu'elle a utilisée pour cacher la fille était des plus violente. Ta maîtresse, elle comprenait que cela impliquerait fatalement la mort du nouveau-né mâle ?

— C'étaient des temps désespérés que ceux-là, et elle n'a pas vu d'autre solution. Lhel a été bonne pour Tamìr, et c'est à notre insu qu'elle a veillé sur elle pendant un certain temps.

— Elle a vécu dans une solitude affreuse, jusqu'à ce que tu entres dans son lit. Mais tu n'as pas pu lui remplir le ventre.

— Si ç'avait été possible, je l'aurais fait pour elle de gaieté de cœur. Les choses sont différentes avec votre peuple, n'est-ce pas ? »

Mahti se mit à glousser. « J'ai des quantités d'enfants, et ils seront tous des sorciers. C'est grâce à cela que nous préservons la force des nôtres dans leurs montagnes. Il nous faut être extrêmement forts, pour être encore en vie depuis que les Sudiens nous ont expulsés de nos terres.

— Ils redoutent votre race et votre magie. Ni nos magiciens ni nos prêtres ne sont capables de tuer aussi facilement que vous.

— Ou de guérir aussi bien, signala Mahti.

— Or donc, pourquoi te trouves-tu ici ? Pour achever le travail de Lhel ?

— La Mère m'a marqué pour de longs voyages. » Il passa une main caressante sur toute la surface de l'oo'lu jusqu'à l'empreinte en forme de main voisine du bout. « La première vision que j'ai eue de mon époque voyageuse fut celle de Lhel, debout avec cette fille et avec toi. C'était à la saison de la fonte des neiges, et je n'ai pas arrêté de marcher depuis pour venir vous rejoindre.

— Je vois. Mais pourquoi ta déesse veut-elle que ses sorciers nous secondent ? »

Mahti lui décocha un sourire goguenard. « Voilà bien des années que les gens de ton peuple traitent les gens du mien comme des bêtes, nous traquent et nous chassent de nos lieux sacrés près de la mer. Moi aussi, j'ai souvent demandé à la Mère : "Pourquoi aider nos oppresseurs ?" Sa réponse est cette fille, et peut-être toi-même. Vous avez honoré Lhel tous les deux, vous avez été ses amis. Tamìr-qui-était-un-garçon m'a accueilli la main ouverte, et elle m'a déclaré bienvenu, lors même que j'en voyais d'autres dans cette immense maison faire des signes de conjuration et cracher par terre sur mon passage. Cette reine que vous avez pourrait bien obliger son peuple à mieux traiter les Retha'noïs.

— Je crois qu'elle le fera, si elle le peut. Son cœur déborde de bonté, et elle n'aspire qu'à la paix.

— Et toi ? Tu as pris notre magie et tu ne la qualifies pas de nécromancie. Le garçon de là-haut se trompait. Je sais ce qu'est la nécromancie : une magie impure. Les Retha'noïs ne sont pas un peuple impur.

— Lhel m'a enseigné cela. » La manière dont Iya et lui-même l'avaient d'abord prodigieusement sous-estimée le remplissait encore de honte. « Mais la plupart des Skaliens ont un mal fou à percevoir la différence, parce que vous recourez vous aussi au sang et maîtrisez les morts.

— Tu peux apprendre aux autres la vérité. Je t'aiderai si tu les empêches de me tuer d'abord.

— J'essaierai. Maintenant, venons-en à ce que tu as dit à Tamìr ; es-tu en mesure de contraindre son démon de jumeau à prendre le large ? »

Mahti haussa les épaules. « Ce n'est pas ma magie personnelle qui l'a suscité, et il est plus qu'un simple fantôme. Les âmes démoniaques comme la sienne sont particulièrement rebelles aux opérations magiques. Il vaut parfois mieux se contenter de leur ficher tout simplement la paix.

— Un autre fantôme hante Tamìr, celui de sa mère, qui s'est jadis donné la mort. Elle est très puissante et dans un état de fureur invincible. Elle a le pouvoir de toucher les vivants, et elle cherche à leur faire du mal.

— C'est à la magie féminine de s'occuper des esprits de cette espèce-là. Et voilà pourquoi ta maîtresse a préféré chercher une sorcière plutôt qu'un sorcier. Nous autres, les hommes, nous avons essentiellement affaire aux vivants. Est-ce que le fantôme se tient dans cette maison-ci ?

— Non. Elle hante les lieux témoins de sa mort. »

Mahti haussa les épaules. « Le choix dépend d'elle. Moi, je suis ici pour la fille. »

On frappa à la porte, et Tamìr entra. « Pardonnez mon intrusion, Arkoniel, mais Melissandra m'a dit que je vous trouverais tous les deux dans cette pièce.

— Je vous en prie, entrez donc », dit Arkoniel.

Elle s'assit auprès de lui et considéra le sorcier en

silence pendant un moment. « Lhel est venue à toi sous les espèces d'un fantôme.

— Oui.

— Elle t'a envoyé spécialement me trouver ? »

Arkoniel traduisit sa question, et Mahti hocha la tête.

« Pourquoi ? »

Il jeta un coup d'œil furtif en direction du magicien puis haussa les épaules. « Pour t'aider, manière que toi pas faire mal aux Retha'noïs.

— Je n'ai nullement l'intention de faire du mal à ton peuple, dans la mesure où il reste pacifique vis-à-vis du mien. » Elle s'interrompit, et ses yeux s'affligèrent. « Est-ce que tu sais comment Lhel est morte ?

— Elle pas me dire. Mais elle n'est pas un esprit en colère. Paisible. »

Tamìr eut un vague sourire en apprenant cet aspect des choses. « Je m'en réjouis.

— Nous étions tout juste en train de discuter sur ce qui a conduit Mahti ici, dit Arkoniel. Il vient de quelque part dans les montagnes de l'ouest.

— De l'ouest ? De quelle distance dans l'ouest ?

— Presque de l'Osiat, apparemment. »

Elle se dirigea vers le sorcier et s'agenouilla devant lui. « Je jouis de visions, moi aussi, et de rêves de l'ouest. Peux-tu m'aider à les démêler ?

— Je tenter. Que vois-tu ?

— Arkoniel, vous avez de quoi faire un croquis ? »

Le magicien s'approcha d'une table qui croulait sous des monceaux de son attirail et farfouilla dans ce fatras jusqu'à ce qu'il y pêche un morceau de craie. Il devina ce qu'elle avait en tête, mais le résultat lui paraissait plutôt improbable.

Après avoir déblayé le sol d'une portion de la jonchée qui le tapissait, Tamìr entreprit néanmoins de dessiner sur le dallage de pierre ainsi mis au jour. « Je vois un endroit dont je sais qu'il se trouve sur la côte ouest au-dessous de Cirna. Il comporte une rade profonde gardée par deux îles. Comme ceci. » Elle les dessina. « Et une falaise très haute domine le tout. C'est là que je me tiens dans le rêve. Et si je regarde en arrière, je vois une campagne ouverte et des montagnes dans le lointain.

— Combien distantes, les montagnes ? demanda Mahti.

— Je ne suis pas sûre. Peut-être une journée de chevauchée ?

— Et ça ? » Il indiqua du doigt les dalles laissées vierges au-delà des petits ovales censés représenter les îles. « C'est la mer de l'ouest ? » Il fixa la carte en se rongeant la peau d'un ongle. « Je connais cet endroit.

— Tu peux l'affirmer, rien qu'à partir de ça ? l'interrogea le magicien.

— Moi pas mentir. J'ai été à cet endroit. Je montrer. »

Il dressa son poing devant son visage, ferma les yeux, et commença à marmonner à part lui. Arkoniel perçut le chatouillement de la magie en voie de concentration dès avant que le motif de lignes noires enchevêtrées n'ait apparu sur la figure et les mains du sorcier. Il reconnut le sortilège.

Mahti souffla dans son poing puis joignit son pouce

et son index en anneau. Un disque lumineux prit forme et puis s'agrandit pendant qu'il l'encadrait avec son autre main et l'étirait pour l'élargir jusqu'aux dimensions d'un plateau. Ils entendaient au travers des appels d'oiseaux de mer et le flux et le reflux des vagues sur une grève.

« Maître, il connaît votre charme de fenêtre ! » s'exclama Wythnir à voix basse.

Dans l'ouverture se découvrit, du haut d'une falaise dominant la mer, un panorama tout à fait identique à celui qu'avait décrit Tamìr. Alors qu'il faisait déjà sombre à Atyion, là, le soleil couchant traçait encore un sillage cuivré sur les flots sous un ciel nuageux. Le sol, au sommet de la falaise, était accidenté et envahi de longues herbes. Des bandes de mouettes innombrables voguaient dans les nues orangées. Leurs cris emplissaient la chambre d'Arkoniel. Il s'attendait presque à sentir le parfum de la brise marine qui lui caressait le visage.

Mahti bougea vaguement, et la vue se modifia avec une vitesse vertigineuse, de sorte qu'ils se retrouvèrent à contempler par-dessus le rebord de l'à-pic une rade profonde très loin en contrebas.

« C'est bien ça ! » s'exclama tout bas Tamìr, et Arkoniel dut la retenir par le bras pour l'empêcher de se pencher trop près de l'embrasure. « Peut-être est-ce dans le but de me montrer le site que Lhel t'a conduit jusqu'à moi, de préférence à quelque autre émissaire que ce soit.

— *Remoni*, nous l'appelons, lui dit le sorcier. Signifie "bonne eau". Bonne à boire, au sortir de terre.

— Des sources ? »

Arkoniel traduisit, et Maliti opina du chef. « Beaucoup sources. Beaucoup bonne eau.

— Regardez, vous voyez qu'il y a largement assez d'espace au pied de la falaise pour une ville, hein ? reprit Tamìr. Une citadelle établie sur les falaises au-dessus la rendrait inattaquable, contrairement à ce qui s'est passé à Ero. Où se trouve cet endroit, Mahti ? À proximité de Cirna ?

— Je ne connais pas ton *sir-na*. »

Le magicien trama un charme de fenêtre de sa façon pour lui faire voir la forteresse sur son étroite bande de terre.

« Je connais ce coin-là ! Je m'en suis approché lorsque j'étais à la recherche de Caliel et de ses amis », expliqua-t-il dans sa propre langue, abandonnant à Arkoniel le soin de servir de truchement pour Tamìr. « Mais j'ai vu aussi cette énorme bâtisse dans une vision. C'est de là que provenaient Caliel et les autres. Il y a de la méchanceté qui séjourne dans cette demeure, et une immense tristesse, en plus.

— À quelle distance se trouve Remoni d'ici ?

— Trois, peut-être quatre jours de longue marche à pied. Vous autres, gens du sud, Remoni, vous n'y allez pas. Nous avons encore des lieux sacrés, près de cette mer. Il arrive parfois que des bateaux pénètrent dans les eaux abritées par les îles, quand les gens viennent pour pêcher, mais personne n'habite les parages. Pourquoi veut-elle aller là-bas ?

— Que dit-il ? » demanda Tamìr.

Arkoniel le lui expliqua.

« Il suffirait peut-être de deux jours, en chevauchant dur, musa-t-elle. Dites-lui que je vais y construire une ville nouvelle. Voudra-t-il me guider ? »

Arkoniel traduisit, mais Mahti se frottait maintenant les yeux, comme s'ils lui faisaient mal. « Besoin sommeil. Je vais là. » Il désigna le jardin sur lequel donnait la fenêtre. « Trop de temps dans cette maison. Besoin ciel et besoin terre.

— Mais il y a tant de choses que j'ai envie de savoir !

— Laissez-le se reposer quelque temps », lui conseilla Arkoniel, devinant que le sorcier avait quelque raison pour ne pas lui répondre. « Vous devriez vous reposer aussi, et vous préparer en vue de votre conférence avec vos généraux. »

Comme elle se détournait pour se retirer, Mahti releva les yeux et se tapota la poitrine. « Tu as douleur. Ici.

— Douleur ? Non.

— Où Lhel faire liaison magique à toi, il y a douleur », insista-t-il en la fixant très attentivement, pendant que sa main se portait à la dérobée sur son long cor une fois de plus. « Je faire chanson de rêve pour toi. Enlever un peu de douleur. »

Tamìr secoua précipitamment la tête. « Non ! C'est guéri. Je ne ressens aucune douleur. »

Mahti fronça les sourcils et se remit à parler dans sa langue. « Orëskiri, dis-lui que la magie de Lhel n'est toujours pas brisée. La seule magie qu'elle ait connue enfant était cruelle ou terrifiante. Cette peur la hante encore, malgré tout ce qu'elle a vu d'autre. Elle répugne à la laisser pratiquer sur sa personne, même pour son bien. »

Il la regarda d'un air pensif, tandis qu'elle le considérait avec davantage de circonspection. « Elle ne saurait être complètement elle-même tant qu'elle n'aura pas été libérée de ces derniers fils, mais je ne ferai rien sans son consentement.

— Donne-lui du temps.

— Que dit-il ? » demanda-t-elle en les dévisageant tour à tour successivement.

Arkoniel l'entraîna dans le corridor. « Vous êtes encore liée à Frère d'une certaine façon.

— Je m'en suis bien assez rendu compte par moi-même.

— Mahti s'en inquiète sérieusement. »

Elle s'immobilisa et croisa ses bras. « Vous avez déjà confiance en lui.

— Je crois que oui. »

Pendant un instant, elle parut balancer, comme s'il y avait quelque chose qu'elle avait envie de dire, mais au lieu de le faire, elle secoua simplement la tête. « Cette magie-là, j'en ai eu ma dose. Je suis une fille, à présent. Cela suffit. Je suis capable de me débrouiller avec Frère. »

Arkoniel soupira en son for intérieur. Même s'il avait pu la contraindre, il s'y refusait.

En retournant dans sa chambre, il trouva Wythnir et Mahti assis par terre côte à côte. Une main du gosse était tendue, et un globe argenté oscillait sur sa paume.

« Regardez ce que maître Mahti m'a appris à faire », dit-il, sans détacher son regard du globe.

Arkoniel s'agenouilla près d'eux, écartelé entre la curiosité et l'instinct protecteur. « Qu'est-ce que c'est ?

— Uniquement de l'eau, lui assura le sorcier. C'est l'un des premiers sortilèges qu'apprennent les enfants sorciers, en guise de jeu, pour rire. »

Wythnir perdit sa prise sur le charme, et le globe d'eau tomba, éclaboussant sa main et ses genoux.

Mahti lui ébouriffa les cheveux. « Bonne magie, petit *keesa*. Un truc à apprendre à tes copains.

— Je peux, Maître ?

— Demain. Il est l'heure d'aller leur souhaiter bonne nuit. Moi, je dois veiller au confort de notre hôte. »

La lune était presque pleine. Mahti s'assit dans l'herbe humide auprès d'un rosier, savourant la suavité de ses fleurs et les odeurs saines de grand air et d'humus. Arkoniel avait renvoyé du jardin tous les gens du Sud pour lui permettre de s'y trouver seul sous le firmament. Le sorcier rendait grâces à sa solitude. S'être vu confiner dans une pièce si loin au-dessus du sol pendant tant de jours l'avait soumis à rude épreuve. La détresse et l'appréhension des trois jeunes étrangers dont il avait pris soin en saturaient l'atmosphère comme du brouillard.

Lutha et Barieüs étaient heureux, maintenant qu'ils avaient parlé à Tamìr. Il s'en réjouissait pour eux ; ils l'avaient bien traité depuis le début. Le plus âgé, Caliel, remâchait des idées plus noires, et pas seulement à cause de la crainte que lui inspirait Mahti. Il portait dans son âme une plaie profonde. La trahison d'un ami était une vilaine blessure, très difficile à guérir. Mahti avait eu beau lui réparer les os et le débarrasser par le jeu de son oo'lu des poisons lorsqu'ils s'efforçaient de faire front commun, les ténèbres occupaient toujours le cœur de Caliel. Il en allait de même avec le dénommé Tanil. Il avait suffi d'un coup d'œil au sorcier pour deviner les sévices qu'il avait subis. Celui-là, il n'était même pas sûr de pouvoir le secourir.

Et puis il y avait Tamìr. Ses blessures étaient insondables, mais elle ne les sentait pas. En l'observant du coin de l'œil, il avait nettement distingué les vrilles noires qui émergeaient encore de l'endroit où Lhel avait pratiqué la suture magique. L'esprit de Tamìr demeurait toujours lié avec le *noro'shesh*, et ces nœuds interdisaient sa guérison complète à l'intérieur de sa nouvelle forme. Elle était une jeune femme, sans conteste, mais des vestiges de son vieux moi persistaient en elle. En témoignaient suffisamment, aux yeux de Mahti, ses joues creuses et les lignes anguleuses de son corps.

Il rejeta la tête en arrière et gorgea ses prunelles de blancheur lunaire. « Je l'ai vue, maintenant, Mère Shek'met. Ai-je fait cet interminable voyage uniquement pour parachever la magie de Lhel en guérissant sa protégée ? Elle s'y refuse. Que dois-je faire pour pouvoir rentrer chez moi ? »

Tout en conservant ces questions dans son esprit, il éleva l'oo'lu vers ses lèvres et entama le chant de prières. La lune enceinte le remplit et lui prêta ses pouvoirs.

Des images commencèrent à se former derrière ses paupières et, au bout d'un certain temps, la surprise fit s'affaler ses sourcils. Il joua le chant jusqu'à la dernière note et, lorsqu'il en eut terminé, il releva les yeux vers le pâle visage de la lune et branla du chef. « Ta volonté, Mère, est bizarre, mais je vais faire du mieux que je pourrai. »

Que penses-tu d'eux ? De ma jouvencelle et de mon orëskiri ? lui chuchota Lhel du sein des ombres.

« Tu leur manques », chuchota-t-il en retour, et il la sentit toute triste. « Ils te retiennent ici ? »

Je reste pour eux. Quand tout sera fini, je me reposerai. Tu feras comme la Mère t'a montré ?

« Si cela m'est possible, mais notre peuple ne fera pas bon accueil à ta protégée.

— Tu dois la lui faire voir comme je la vois.

— Est-ce que je te reverrai jamais, maintenant que je l'ai trouvée ? »

Il sentit une caresse invisible, et puis elle ne fut plus là.

Un homme remua dans le noir, près de la porte de la cour. Arkoniel était entré dans le jardin pendant que Mahti rêvait. Sans un mot, l'orëskiri disparut de nouveau à l'intérieur.

Il y avait là aussi une prodigieuse douleur.

Mahti mit son cor de côté et s'allongea dans l'herbe pour dormir. Il agirait conformément aux exigences de la Mère, et puis il rentrerait chez lui. C'était fatigant de se trouver parmi ces opiniâtres de Sudiens qui se refusaient à demander de l'aide quand ils en avaient besoin.

Assis près de sa fenêtre, Arkoniel regardait dormir Mahti. Celui-ci paraissait très paisible, là, sur la terre nue, la tête posée sur son bras.

Le cœur du magicien était en plein désarroi. Il avait entendu la voix de Lhel, senti son parfum dans l'air. Il comprenait pourquoi elle était allée chercher Mahti, mais pourquoi n'était-elle jamais venue le trouver, lui ?

« Maître ? demanda Wythnir d'une voix ensommeillée du fond de son lit.

— Tout va bien, enfant. Rendors-toi. »

Au lieu d'en rien faire, le petit le rejoignit, grimpa sur ses genoux puis, se pelotonnant dans son giron, nicha sa tête sous son menton.

« Ne soyez pas triste, Maître », murmura-t-il, déjà à demi assoupi. Quand Arkoniel revint de sa stupéfaction, le gamin dormait à poings fermés.

Touché par cette innocente affection, Arkoniel demeura là quelque temps immobile, à se contenter de le tenir, la confiance du petit dormeur lui rappelant le travail qui l'attendait.

Tamìr trouva les Compagnons réunis dans l'appartement de Nikidès. Lutha et Barieüs étaient allongés à plat ventre en travers du grand lit. Tharin et Ki étaient assis à leurs côtés, sur le bord de celui-ci, et ils lui firent une place entre eux. Les autres étaient vautrés dans des fauteuils ou à même le sol. Ki était en train de parler aux convalescents du dragon qu'ils avaient tous vu à Afra. « Montre-leur ta marque », dit-il quand Tamìr entra.

Elle exhiba son doigt.

« Ce que j'aurais aimé y être avec vous ! s'exclama Barieüs avec envie.

— Tu y seras la prochaine fois, promit-elle. Dis-m'en davantage sur Korin. Y a-t-il une quelconque chance de pouvoir l'amener à la raison ? »

Lutha secoua la tête. « Je ne pense pas qu'il arrive jamais à te pardonner, Tamìr.

— Et maintenant, il va avoir un héritier, dit Ki. Raison de plus pour qu'il se batte.

— Lady Nalia est enceinte ? Eh bien, ça ne m'étonne pas », maugréa Lutha, non sans rougir un brin. « Il se donnait assez de mal pour ça. Je suppose que ça a fini par prendre.

— Que savez-vous d'elle ? demanda Tamìr.

— Presque rien, en dehors de ce que nous en a dit Korin. Il la garde claquemurée dans sa tour la plupart du temps. Mais elle s'est toujours montrée gracieuse envers nous quand il nous est arrivé de la voir.

— C'est vrai qu'elle est laide ? interrogea Ki.

— Quelconque, plutôt. Avec une grosse marque de naissance rose sur la figure et sur le cou. » Barieüs en dessina les contours sur sa propre joue. « Du genre de celle que tu as toi-même sur le bras, Tamìr.

— Quelle autre information pouvez-vous me fournir, maintenant que nous ne risquons plus d'embarrasser Caliel ? » questionna-t-elle.

Lutha soupira. « Voilà que je me fais l'effet d'être

un mouchard. Korin a rassemblé des forces considérables – cavaliers, hommes d'armes, quelques bateaux, pour la plupart originaires des domaines du nord et des territoires du continent. Il a fait lancer quelques raids contre tes partisans.

— J'ai agi de même.

— Je le sais, répliqua Lutha. Ça l'a formidablement exaspéré, de même que les rapports sur ta seconde victoire contre les Plenimariens. Je ne sais pas s'il faut l'imputer à l'influence de Nyrin sur lui ou simplement à sa jalousie personnelle, mais maintenant qu'il est prêt à faire mouvement, je ne crois pas qu'il se satisfasse de quoi que ce soit de moins que d'une lutte à outrance.

— Dans ce cas, c'est ce qu'il va avoir. Il ne nous reste plus que quelques bons mois avant que l'hiver ne survienne. Tharin, prie Lytia de faire préparer un inventaire exhaustif des réserves pour mon audience de demain matin. J'ai besoin de savoir combien de temps nous serions en mesure de soutenir un siège ici, au cas où les choses en viendraient là. Dépêche des estafettes à tous les camps et des hérauts à tous les seigneurs qui sont repartis pour leurs terres au nord d'Atyion. J'entends marcher aussitôt que possible.

— Avec tes Compagnons à tes côtés, spécifia Ki. Au moins avec ceux d'entre nous qui sont en pleine forme, ajouta-t-il en adressant à Lutha un regard contrit.

— Nous sommes en assez bonne forme pour cela ! » lui protesta celui-ci.

En jetant à la ronde un regard sur les physionomies

farouchement souriantes de ses amis, Tamìr se demanda combien cette guerre-là ferait de victimes supplémentaires dans leur groupe avant la fin des hostilités.

Les pensées belliqueuses se dissipèrent toutefois pendant un moment lorsqu'elle et Ki retournèrent vers leurs chambres respectives. En atteignant sa propre porte, Ki s'arrêta d'un air incertain. Tamìr comprit qu'il attendait qu'elle se prononce sur l'endroit où il dormirait.

Elle balança, elle aussi, trop pleinement consciente de la présence des gardes apostés dans les parages immédiats.

Ki loucha lui-même de leur côté puis soupira. « Eh bien, bonne nuit. »

Plus tard, couchée toute seule dans son immense lit, Queue-tigrée lové contre elle et ronronnant sous son menton, elle se passa un doigt sur les lèvres, obsédée par le souvenir des baisers échangés quelques nuits seulement plus tôt.

Je suis reine. Si j'ai envie de coucher avec lui, rien ne me l'interdit ! songea-t-elle, mais cette idée la fit rougir. Ç'avait été facile quand ils étaient tous deux si terrifiés, si loin de la cour. Peut-être même qu'il le déplorait ?

Elle repoussa cette pensée, mais non sans que persiste en elle une once de doute. À présent qu'ils se trouvaient de retour parmi leur entourage ordinaire, il se comportait à nouveau comme il l'avait toujours fait...

Et je fais la même chose. Et ce n'est pas le moment de songer à faire l'amour ! Les propos sévères de Nari l'avaient également conduite à envisager d'autres sujets de réflexion. Ce genre d'amour-là risquait évidemment d'entraîner des grossesses indésirables si l'on ne prenait pas de précautions. La nourrice lui avait donné un pot de pessaires, juste au cas où.

Au cas où...

Si brûlante que fût sa nostalgie de Ki, le fait était là que la perspective de leur accouplement l'effrayait plus qu'elle n'avait envie d'en convenir. Si elle utilisait son corps de cette façon, cela reviendrait en définitive à admettre qu'elle était une fille – non, une femme –, dans la pleine acception du terme.

Néanmoins, sa couche lui faisait l'effet d'être excessivement vaste pour sa solitude, surtout en sachant que Ki se trouvait aussi près. Elle tripota la blessure en voie de guérison de son menton. Il lui était totalement indifférent qu'elle laisse une cicatrice. Chaque fois qu'elle la voyait dans son miroir, c'était Ki qu'elle lui rappelait, Ki et les sensations qu'elle avait éprouvées, quand elle était allongée près de lui dans le lit du fort. Elle effleura sa gorge jusqu'à sa poitrine d'une lente caresse en pensant aux doigts qu'il avait aventurés sur le même trajet.

Quand elle frôla la cicatrice de son torse, le souvenir lui revint brusquement de ce qu'avait dit le sorcier. Qu'avaient donc signifié ses propos ? La plaie s'était complètement refermée. Elle ne lui faisait pas mal du tout.

Elle resserra ses bras sur le chat, toute au regret que sa fourrure soyeuse ne soit pas plutôt les cheveux et la peau de Ki. Pour la première fois de son existence, elle se demanda à quoi ressembleraient leurs relations si elle était une fille ordinaire, sans secrets ténébreux ni destin grandiose, et s'ils n'avaient ni l'un ni l'autre jamais mis les pieds à Ero.

« Si les vœux étaient de la viande, les mendiants auraient alors de quoi manger », chuchota-t-elle dans le noir. Elle était ce qu'elle était, et il était impossible d'y rien changer.

Lorsqu'elle finit par s'endormir, toutefois, ce ne fut pas de Ki qu'elle rêva, mais de bataille. Elle revit ce site rocheux, dont la bannière rouge de Korin se rapprochait de plus en plus.

16

Tamìr se leva de bonne heure le lendemain matin, plus fraîche et dispose qu'elle ne l'avait escompté. Ayant finalement accepté la voie qu'elle devait emprunter, elle brûlait de se mettre en mouvement. Si c'était là le seul moyen qui lui permit de rencontrer Korin, eh bien, soit.

Una n'étant toujours pas revenue, elle s'offrit le luxe de s'habiller elle-même, sans autre aide, et minime, que celle de Baldus. Elle se para du collier et du bracelet que les Aurënfaïes lui avaient offerts, et elle était en train de se coiffer quand Ki frappa à sa porte. Le page le laissa entrer. En se retournant, son peigne à la main, elle s'aperçut qu'il la regardait fixement. « Qu'est-ce qu'il y a qui cloche ?

— Hmmm... rien », répondit-il en se dirigeant vers le râtelier d'armures. « Tu veux ta cuirasse ?

— Oui », répliqua-t-elle, déconcertée par la bizarrerie de son comportement.

Il l'aida à endosser son corselet de plates brunies puis le lui boucla sur le flanc.

« Là. Est-ce que j'ai la dégaine d'une reine-guerrière ? » les interrogea-t-elle tout en ajustant son baudrier d'épée autour de ses hanches.

« Tout à fait. »

Là-dessus reparut sur la physionomie de Ki cette étrange mine embarrassée.

« Baldus, va me chercher Lord Tharin et le reste des Compagnons. Avertis-les que je suis prête pour l'audience. »

Le page prit ses jambes à son cou pour aller transmettre l'ordre de Tamìr.

« Lutha et Barieüs ont bien dormi ? demanda-t-elle.

— Oui.

— Je présume que Caliel n'a pas changé d'avis ?

— Non. Mais Tanil se porte mieux qu'avant. Il a dormi la nuit dernière avec Cal et ne veut pas être séparé de lui. Caliel lui-même semble aller un peu mieux.

— Leur cas n'est peut-être pas si désespéré que ça.

— J'emmènerai plus tard Lutha et Barieüs à la recherche d'un forgeron capable de leur fournir une épée. Ils sont irrévocablement décidés à chevaucher avec toi. » Il tendit la main derrière elle pour dégager une mèche coincée sous la cuirasse, puis effleura du pouce la blessure de son menton. « Tu n'es pas bellotte, mais c'est en train de se cicatriser. »

Ils se tenaient très près l'un de l'autre, presque à se toucher. Cédant à une impulsion subite, elle palpa la morsure du dragon sur sa joue. « Toi non plus.

— Ça ne me fait plus mal du tout. » Il garda les yeux attachés sur son menton, ses doigts se bornant à lui frôler la joue. Ce contact fit courir un petit frisson le long des bras de Tamìr, et elle retint son souffle, tandis que les sensations qu'avait éveillées en elle la nuit du fort déferlaient à nouveau dans son être... un plaisir auquel s'enchevêtrait l'impression confuse et déroutante de posséder deux corps à la fois.

Cela ne l'empêcha pas de s'incliner vers lui pour l'embrasser légèrement sur les lèvres. Il lui retourna son baiser avec infiniment de délicatesse tout en cueillant sa joue au creux de sa paume. Elle glissa ses doigts dans les cheveux tièdes et soyeux de sa nuque, et sa chair s'embrasa et se glaça simultanément. Enhardie, elle l'enlaça à pleins bras, mais elle lui coupa si bien le souffle avec sa cuirasse qu'il se mit à rire.

« Tout doux, Majesté ! Votre humble écuyer a besoin de ces côtes-là.

— Mon homme lige, Lord Kirothius », rectifiat-elle en gloussant et en l'embrassant avec davantage de ménagements, non sans repérer son propre émerveillement reflété dans le tréfonds de ses sombres prunelles brunes. Entre ses jambes, la torture s'aggrava, et la gêne commença à se laisser supplanter par quelque chose d'autre.

Elle s'apprêtait à l'embrasser de nouveau lorsque le bruit de la porte qui s'ouvrait les fit se disjoindre en sursaut, tout rougissants d'un air coupable.

Nikidès se tenait sur le seuil, avec une mine amusée. « Tharin, maître Arkoniel et le sorcier sont là. Puis-je me permettre de les introduire ?

— Naturellement. » Tamìr rebroussa ses cheveux en arrière, tout en se tâtant pour atténuer la brûlure de ses joues.

Ki battit en retraite vers le râtelier d'armures pour tâcher de dissimuler son propre embarras en affectant d'y contrôler le bon entretien de la cotte de mailles.

Le sourire de Nikidès s'élargit tandis qu'il prenait congé. Arkoniel ne se rendit nullement compte de leur état lorsqu'il pénétra en coup de vent, un gros rouleau coincé sous son bras, talonné de près par les autres.

Mahti était habillé comme un hobereau. Ses cheveux, peignés, se trouvaient rejetés en arrière en une queue broussailleuse, et il ne portait plus ses bijoux barbares. Il s'était également défait de son cor, remarqua Tamìr, qui devina que c'était l'ouvrage du magicien. Le sorcier n'en paraissait pas spécialement enchanté. Il ne souriait pas.

« Mahti a quelque chose à vous raconter », dit Arkoniel, d'un air passablement excité.

« J'ai vision pour toi, déclara le Retha'noï. Je montrer toi un chemin vers l'ouest.

— Vers cette rade, tu veux dire ? Remoni ? demanda-t-elle.

— Tu aller être partir à l'ouest. Ma déesse dit ainsi.

— Et tu as vu cette route dans une vision ? »

Il secoua la tête. « Je connaître route. Mais la Mère ordonner je t'amener là. » Il semblait désormais encore moins content. « Être chemin caché, interdit à ceux pas de mon peuple. Ça, mon aide pour toi. »

Abasourdie, Tamìr jeta un coup d'œil interrogatif à Tharin et Arkoniel. « C'est tout à fait intéressant, mais dans l'immédiat, je suis plus soucieuse de...

— Ah, mais je pense que cela risque d'être utile. » Tharin s'empara du rouleau d'Arkoniel et le déploya sur le lit. Il s'agissait d'une carte du nord de Skala et de l'isthme. « Selon toute probabilité, Korin foncera directement t'attaquer ici par la route côtière. Il ne dispose pas d'une flotte assez conséquente, d'après ce qu'a dit Lutha, pour amener par mer toute son armée. Le chemin dont parle Mahti semble passer par ici, à travers les montagnes. » Le trajet que traça son doigt contournait Colath par le sud et l'ouest. « Cela t'amènerait là-bas, non loin de ton fameux port. De là, tu bénéficies d'une distance de frappe commode, soit pour couper Korin sur l'isthme, soit pour lui tomber dessus par-derrière pendant qu'il se dirige vers l'est.

— Il s'agit d'un sentier que les Retha'noïs maintiennent occulte en recourant à la même magie que celle dont se servait Lhel pour cacher son camp, expliqua Arkoniel. De nombreux villages le bordent,

243

et ils ne seront pas hospitaliers pour des étrangers, mais Mahti se flatte de te le faire emprunter en toute sécurité. »

Tamìr se plongea dans l'étude de la carte, le cœur battant un peu plus vite. Était-ce cela que l'Oracle s'était efforcée de lui montrer ? Était-ce à cela que conduisaient tous ses rêves du havre au bas des falaises ?

« Oui, je vois », prononça-t-elle d'une voix défaillante. Cela lui donnait l'impression qu'elle inhalait de nouveau la fumée des illiorains.

« Tu ne te sens pas bien ? s'inquiéta Ki.

— Si. » Elle prit une profonde inspiration, en se demandant ce qui clochait en elle. « J'attaque de l'ouest, peut-être même que je le surprends s'il se figure que je me trouve encore ici, m'apprêtant à subir un siège. »

Elle leva les yeux vers Mahti. « Pourquoi ferais-tu cela ?

— Tu donneras parole de faire paix aux Retha'noïs. Vous ne nous tuerez plus. Nous être libres de quitter les montagnes.

— Je m'y efforcerai de bon cœur, mais je ne saurais promettre de changer les choses du jour au lendemain. Arkoniel, faites-le-lui comprendre. Je veux accomplir ce qu'il me demande, mais il ne sera pas aisé de modifier les mentalités.

— Je le lui ai dit, mais il est convaincu que vous êtes capable d'y contribuer. Une meilleure compréhension entre nos deux peuples travaillera aussi en votre faveur.

— Il sera difficile d'acheminer le ravitaillement à travers les montagnes, observa Tharin. Il ne s'agit pas là d'une route à proprement parler.

— Les Gèdres pourraient assurer nos fournitures sur place, souligna Arkoniel. Leurs vaisseaux sont rapides. Ils seraient probablement à même d'atteindre la rade de Remoni en même temps que nous.

— Contactez-les tout de suite, ordonna Tamìr. Et les Bôkthersans aussi. Solun avait l'air très désireux de nous seconder.

— Pas rien que l'air, des fois ? » grommela Ki.

La nouvelle de ses projets se répandit promptement. La salle d'audience était archicomble lorsqu'elle y pénétra. Ses généraux et capitaines se pressaient au pied de l'estrade, mais une foule d'autres assistants – courtisans, simples soldats, citadins – bondait l'espace entre les piliers, tous bavardant avec excitation.

Elle monta sur l'estrade, et les Compagnons prirent leurs places derrière elle. Lutha et Barieüs se tenaient parmi eux, pâles mais fiers dans leurs vêtements d'emprunt.

Tamìr tira son épée, consciente de l'importance capitale de ce qu'elle allait faire. « Messires, généraux et vous, mes bonnes gens, je me présente devant vous pour déclarer formellement que, par la volonté d'Illior, je vais marcher contre le prince Korin afin d'assurer mon trône et de mettre fin par l'union aux divisions de notre pays.

— Trois bans pour notre bonne reine ! » cria Lord Jorvaï en brandissant son épée vers le ciel.

L'appel fut repris à la ronde, et les ovations se poursuivirent jusqu'à ce qu'Illardi martèle le sol avec le bâton de son office et rétablisse l'attention de l'assistance.

« Merci. Que les hérauts portent aux quatre coins de Skala le message suivant : tous ceux qui combattent avec moi sont mes amis et de véritables Skaliens. » Après un instant de silence, elle ajouta : « Et tous ceux qui s'opposent à moi seront qualifiés de traîtres et dépouillés de leurs terres. Puisse Illior nous donner la force de remporter une prompte victoire et la sagesse de nous montrer justes. Lord Chancelier Illardi, je vous charge à présent de superviser les levées de guerriers et les réquisitions de fournitures. À vous, intendante Lytia, de vous occuper des vivandiers et des fourgons de bagages. J'entends me mettre en marche avant la fin de la semaine. Tous les capitaines doivent rejoindre leur compagnie et commencer les préparatifs sur-le-champ. »

Abandonnant la cour à sa frénésie, Tamìr se retira vers la salle des cartes avec ses généraux et Compagnons. Arkoniel l'y attendait avec Mahti et ses principaux magiciens, Saruel, Malkanus, Vornus et Lyan.

Les Compagnons s'installèrent à leur place autour de la table, mais Jorvaï et une poignée d'autres nobles se pétrifièrent, tourneboulés par la vue du sorcier des collines.

« Que signifie ceci, Majesté ? demanda le premier.

— C'est grâce à cet homme que mes amis nous

sont revenus sains et saufs, et il se trouve sous ma protection. J'ai déjà bénéficié des secours de ses semblables, et j'en suis venue à respecter leur magie. Je vous invite tous à faire de même.

— Sans manquer au respect qui vous est dû, Majesté, comment pouvez-vous savoir s'il ne mijote pas quelque vilain tour ? s'inquiéta Nyanis.

— J'ai lu dans son cœur, répondit Arkoniel. Certains des autres magiciens de la reine l'ont également fait. Il dit la vérité, et il est venu à l'aide de Sa Majesté Tamìr guidé par des visions, exactement comme nous-mêmes jadis.

— Il est un ami de la Couronne, reprit Tamìr d'un ton ferme. Je vous demande d'accepter mon jugement sur ce point. Je déclare d'ores et déjà solennellement la paix entre Skala et le peuple des collines, les Retha'noïs. À dater d'aujourd'hui, pas un Skalien ne leur fera subir la moindre violence, à moins d'être attaqué par eux. Telle est ma volonté. »

Il y eut bien quelques grommellements et des mines méfiantes, mais tout le monde s'inclina en signe d'obéissance.

« Voilà une affaire réglée, alors. » Tamìr exposa son plan pour déborder Korin, utilisant pour sa démonstration la carte d'Arkoniel et plusieurs autres étalées sur l'immense table.

« J'ai parlé avec le Khirnari de Gèdre, les avisa Arkoniel. Il connaît la rade et y enverra des bateaux de ravitaillement et des archers. Il a également transmis mon message à Bôkthersa. Avec un peu de chance, ils seront là-bas pour nous recevoir.

— Ce sera là un beau stratagème, si toutefois Korin ne se trouve pas déjà à mi-chemin d'Atyion lorsque nous aurons fini par traverser, objecta Jorvaï. S'il apprend que vous êtes partie d'ici, il n'y accourra que d'autant plus vite. Les greniers et le trésor d'Atyion seraient pour lui des prunes pulpeuses s'il parvenait à les cueillir, sans parler du château lui-même. M'est avis qu'il a dû fameusement maigrir, terré à Cirna pendant tous ces mois.

— Il est vrai qu'il a besoin d'or, intervint Lutha.

— C'est pourquoi je ne prendrai pas le risque de laisser Atyion sans défense, répliqua Tamìr. Je vais y maintenir deux bataillons de la garnison en tant que troupes de couverture. Si Korin arrive vraiment aussi loin, il lui faudra se frayer passage de vive force. Cela le ralentira suffisamment pour me permettre de le rattraper. » Son doigt remonta le long de la côte est. « L'armée d'Atyion peut se porter contre lui à partir du sud. Au lieu de cela, j'espère attirer Korin à l'ouest, mais il pourrait se scinder pour nous attaquer sur les deux côtes. » Elle marqua une pause puis, se tournant vers Tharin : « Lord Tharin, je vous nomme maréchal des défenses orientales. Arkoniel, choisissez parmi vos magiciens ceux qui peuvent le mieux l'appuyer dans ce rôle. »

Les yeux de Tharin s'agrandirent, et elle comprit qu'il était à deux doigts de lui chercher querelle. Seule la présence des autres l'en empêcha, et c'est pour cette raison qu'elle s'était résolue à aborder le sujet ici plutôt qu'en privé. Elle lui posa une main sur l'épaule.

« Vous êtes un homme d'Atyion. Les guerriers vous connaissent et vous respectent.

— Après Sa Majesté Tamìr elle-même, il n'est absolument personne d'autre qu'on respecte mieux dans les rangs, approuva Jorvaï.

— En plus, vous connaissez mieux que n'importe quel autre de mes généraux les nobles détenteurs de fiefs entre ici et Cirna, ajouta Tamìr. Si jamais vous marchez effectivement vers le nord, vous pourriez bien être capable de recruter des combattants supplémentaires en route.

— Qu'il en soit selon votre bon plaisir, Majesté », fit Tharin, bien que sa contrariété fût manifeste.

« Ce n'est pas là manquer à la foi jurée à mon père, lui dit-elle avec gentillesse. Il comptait sur vous pour assurer ma protection. Vous ne sauriez mieux exaucer son vœu en pareilles circonstances.

— Il est aventureux de diviser vos forces, signala Nyanis. Tous nos rapports concordent sur le fait que Korin bénéficie vis-à-vis de nous de l'avantage du nombre à près de trois contre un.

— Mon infériorité numérique me permet de me déplacer plus rapidement. L'itinéraire de Mahti va nous faire économiser bien des jours. » Elle se tourna vers le sorcier. « Nous sera-t-il possible d'y faire passer des chevaux ?

— La voie étroite par endroits. À d'autres, dure à grimper à pied.

— Les Retha'noïs n'utilisent pas de chevaux. Ils transportent tout à dos d'homme, l'informa Arkoniel.

— Dans ce cas, nous devrons faire la même chose

et espérer que les 'faïes arrivent au moment voulu. »
Elle se pencha de nouveau sur la carte, les sourcils
froncés, puis releva les yeux vers ses lords. « Que
conseillez-vous ?

— Je serais d'avis de constituer la plus grande
partie de vos forces avec des hommes d'armes et des
archers, Majesté, répondit Kyman. Il vous faudra des
chevaux pour opérer des reconnaissances, mais moins
nous en aurons à fournir en fourrage, mieux cela vaudra.

— Vous pourriez aussi mettre à profit ce que vous
possédez de navires à Ero, suggéra Illardi.

— Ils ne nous rallieraient pas à temps pour nous
être d'un grand secours. Conservez-les là et utilisez-
les pour défendre Ero et Atyion. Illardi, vous aurez la
haute main sur eux. Jorvaï, Kyman, Nyanis, vous êtes
mes maréchaux. »

Ils consacrèrent le reste de la journée à mettre au
point leurs plans. Les inventaires de Lytia étaient
encourageants ; même en tenant compte de l'approvi-
sionnement de l'armée de Tamìr, il faudrait à Korin
des mois pour réduire la place par la famine avec ce
qui lui resterait encore de réserves. La garnison
conserverait deux compagnies ; Tharin emmènerait
une infanterie de deux mille hommes et cinq cents
cavaliers. Le restant, soit près de dix mille fantassins
et archers d'élite, ainsi qu'un cent de cavalerie, traver-
serait la montagne avec la reine à sa tête et Mahti
pour guide.

Tamìr et les Compagnons venaient tout juste
d'entrer dans la grande salle pour le repas du soir

quand Baldus se fraya précipitamment passage vers elle à travers la cohue en esquivant de justesse les serviteurs et les courtisans médusés.

« Majesté ! » cria-t-il, tout en agitant dans sa main un bout de parchemin plié.

Il s'arrêta pile hors d'haleine devant elle et prit à peine le temps de s'incliner. « J'ai trouvé ça... sous votre porte. Lady Lytia m'a ordonné de vous l'apporter tout de suite. Il lui a demandé des vêtements... Lord Caliel...

— Chut. » Elle s'empara du message et n'eut qu'à le déployer pour reconnaître instantanément l'élégante écriture de Caliel.

« Il est parti, n'est-ce pas ? » demanda Ki.

Après avoir parcouru les quelques lignes du billet, elle le lui tendit avec un soupir résigné. « Il remmène Tanil à Korin. Il a préféré s'en aller avant de risquer d'apprendre nos plans.

— Le diable l'emporte ! » s'écria Lutha, les poings crispés de contrariété. « Je n'aurais jamais dû le laisser seul. Il faut nous lancer à sa poursuite.

— Non.

— Quoi ? Mais il est fou d'y retourner !

— Je lui ai donné ma parole, Lutha, lui rappela-t-elle avec tristesse. Il est seul maître de son choix. Je n'y mettrai pas d'entraves. »

Lutha resta immobile un moment, une supplication muette dans ses yeux, puis se retira, tête basse.

« Tamìr ? » dit Barieüs, manifestement écartelé entre ses devoirs et le souci de son ami.

« Vas-y, répondit-elle. Ne le laisse pas commettre quelque bêtise que ce soit. »

Une fois le conseil de guerre achevé, Arkoniel remmena Mahti aux quartiers de l'Orëska et réunit les autres dans la cour pour mettre au point leurs propres plans.

« Haïn, Lord Malkanus et Cerana, je vous prie de m'accompagner. Melissandra, Saruel, Vornus, Lyan et Kaulin, je vous confie le soin du château et le reste des magiciens. » Il jeta un coup d'œil sur les enfants assis côte à côte dans l'herbe près de lui. Wythnir lui adressa un regard déchirant qui le bouleversa, mais les circonstances imposaient leur séparation.

« Moi, je dois rester là, mais *ça* part ? » demanda Kaulin, branlant un pouce pour désigner le sorcier qui se trouvait avec les gamins. « Il est des nôtres, maintenant ? »

Arkoniel soupira intérieurement. Kaulin était celui de ses collègues qu'il aimait le moins. « Il a été guidé vers Sa Majesté Tamìr par des visions, exactement comme nous autres. Que cela ait été le fait de sa déesse ou de nos dieux, il n'en est pas moins membre de notre confrérie tant qu'il sert la reine. Vous étiez avec nous dans les montagnes ; vous savez quelle est notre dette vis-à-vis de Lhel. Honorez-la en l'honorant, lui. Nous ne pouvons pas laisser plus longtemps l'ignorance nous diviser. Néanmoins, si vous souhaitez venir avec moi, Kaulin, vous êtes le bienvenu. » Il promena sur les autres un regard circulaire. « Vous êtes tous ici de votre propre chef. Vous êtes libres comme toujours de préférer suivre vos voies personnelles. Je ne suis le maître d'aucun magicien indépendant. »

Kaulin céda. « J'irai avec vous. Je ne suis pas tout à fait ignare en matière de guérison.

— Je préférerais vous accompagner, moi aussi, déclara Saruel.

— Je la suppléerai ici, proposa Cerana.

— Très bien. Quelqu'un d'autre ?

— Vous nous avez sagement répartis, Arkoniel, répondit Lyan. Nous sommes suffisamment nombreux dans les deux endroits pour malmener l'ennemi et protéger les nôtres.

— J'en suis d'accord, dit Malkanus. Vous nous avez judicieusement conduits, et vous étiez le plus intime avec maîtresse Iya dont vous avez partagé la vision. Je ne vois aucun motif de changer les choses à présent.

— J'apprécie que vous soyez encore ici et souhaitiez soutenir la reine.

— Je suppose qu'Iya avait ses raisons de partir, mais sa puissance va sûrement nous manquer, soupira Cerana.

— Oui, elle nous manquera », répliqua tristement Arkoniel. Il leur avait simplement déclaré qu'ayant achevé son rôle la magicienne les avait quittés de son propre gré. Tamìr avait besoin de leur loyauté, et ces liens étaient encore trop ténus pour qu'il prenne le risque de révéler tout de suite la vérité pleine et entière, là, carrément.

« Tu as oublié ton épée, Cal », remarqua tout à coup Tanil pendant qu'ils chevauchaient vers le nord sur la grand-route dans le déclin du crépuscule. Il baissa la tête d'un air contrit. « Moi, j'ai perdu la mienne.

— Aucun problème. Nous n'en avons pas besoin », lui assura Caliel.

Tanil n'avait nullement rechigné à quitter Atyion, tant il lui tardait de revoir Korin. Grâce à la générosité de Tamìr, ils disposaient tous les deux de tenues convenables et d'un peu d'or, suffisamment pour une paire de chevaux et pour se nourrir à leur faim pendant le voyage.

« Mais si nous tombions de nouveau sur les Pleni-mariens ?

— Ils ont décampé. Tamìr les a repoussés.

— Qui ça ?

— Tobin, rectifia Caliel.

— Ah... oui. Ma mémoire continue de flancher. Je suis désolé. » Il était de nouveau en train de tripoter cette fichue natte tranchée.

Caliel se pencha pour lui repousser la main. « Aucun problème, Tanil. »

Physiquement, Tanil s'était remis, mais il était brisé intérieurement, son esprit tendait à battre la campagne et se fixait difficilement. Caliel avait envisagé de l'emmener tout simplement puis de disparaître, mais il savait que, s'il agissait de la sorte, Tanil ne cesserait jamais de languir après Korin.

Et où irais-je pour arriver à l'oublier ?

Caliel s'interdisait pour sa part de s'appesantir sur l'accueil probable qu'on lui réserverait à Cirna. Il ramènerait Tanil à Korin, voilà tout, comme un dernier acte de devoir et d'amitié.

Non, rectifia-t-il en silence. *Que mon dernier acte soit de tuer Nyrin afin de délivrer Korin.*

Après quoi, sans l'ombre d'un regret, libre à Bilairy de le prendre.

17

Nalia avait très peu vu Korin depuis qu'il avait appris sa grossesse. Il s'abstenait désormais totalement de fréquenter la couche conjugale – un répit bienvenu – et passait toutes ses journées à organiser sa guerre et à échafauder des plans.

Du haut de son balcon, elle observait l'activité des campements et les allées et venues permanentes dans les cours de la forteresse en contrebas. L'air retentissait sans relâche du vacarme que faisaient les armuriers, les maréchaux-ferrants et le roulement des fourgons.

Elle n'était pas oubliée pour autant. Korin lui faisait parvenir chaque jour ses petits présents, et Tomara allait le voir chaque matin pour l'informer de la santé de sa maîtresse. Dans les rares moments où il venait lui rendre visite, il se montrait gentil et attentionné. Pour la première fois, elle guettait en fait avec impatience le bruit de ses pas dans les escaliers.

Korin ne songeait pas à elle tandis qu'escorté de ses hommes il descendait à cheval la route sinueuse qui menait au port. Avant son arrivée à Cirna, celui-ci n'était rien d'autre qu'un minuscule village de pêcheurs, mais il s'était singulièrement transformé durant l'été. Des rangées de maisons bâties de bric et de broc, de tavernes rudimentaires et de longs baraquements avaient poussé sur la pente abrupte qui s'étendait entre les falaises et la ligne des côtes.

Une vive brise marine agitait les boucles noires de Korin et séchait la sueur sur son front. L'été courait vers son terme jour après jour, mais les ciels étaient encore limpides. Les navires du duc Morus mouillaient en eau profonde, et plus d'une douzaine d'autres les avaient désormais rejoints. Il y en avait trente-trois en tout. Le tonnage de certains était inférieur à celui des gros caboteurs, mais il disposait de vingt belles caraques solides, chacune capable de transporter une centaine d'hommes.

Lorsqu'il atteignit la jetée de pierre, l'odeur pestilentielle de poiscaille et de goudron bouillant se mêlait à la vivifiante salinité de l'air. « Que ne pouvons-nous faire voile à leur bord, lança-t-il par-dessus l'épaule à l'adresse d'Alben et d'Urmanis. Quelques jours de navigation leur suffiront pour gagner Ero, pendant que nous serons encore en train de nous farcir péniblement la route.

— Certes, mais tu commanderas la majeure partie des forces », répliqua Alben.

Urmanis et lui étaient les derniers de ses Compagnons d'origine et ses derniers amis. Il avait également élevé Moriel à la dignité de Compagnon. Comme Nyrin ne s'était pas fait faute de le souligner, le Crapaud avait prouvé ce qu'il valait tout au long des mois précédents, et si le magicien ne s'était pas privé sans répugnance de ses services, il avait dû convenir qu'il restait assez peu de jeunes gens convenablement entraînés pour combler les vides des rangs. Alben en avait toujours parlé avec faveur, et Korin en personne se demandait pourquoi il ne l'avait pas engagé plus tôt.

Morus l'accueillit chaleureusement. « Bonjour, Majesté. Comment se porte aujourd'hui dame votre épouse ?

— Elle va très bien, messire, répondit Korin en lui serrant la main. Où en est ma flotte ?

— Nous allons entreprendre son chargement et appareillerons aussitôt que vous aurez accompli la libation. Avec un bon vent arrière, nous devrions jeter l'ancre d'ici à trois jours au-dessus d'Ero et nous tenir prêts à refermer l'étau sur Atyion dès votre propre arrivée. »

Cette perspective fit sourire Moriel. « Vous coincerez Tobin comme une noisette entre deux cailloux.

— Oui. » Chaque fois que l'on mentionnait son cousin, Korin avait l'impression que son cœur se pétrifiait dans sa poitrine comme un gros glaçon. Il n'avait jamais détesté personne comme il haïssait Tobin. Celui-ci hantait ses rêves sous les espèces d'une silhouette blême et railleuse, qui se contorsionnait comme un spectre aux yeux noirs. Rien que la nuit dernière, il avait rêvé qu'il s'empoignait avec lui, chacun s'efforçant de dépouiller l'autre de la couronne qu'il portait.

Tobin avait dupé la moitié du pays avec ses prétentions démentielles, et les quelques victoires qu'il avait remportées impressionnaient les gens. Celles-ci horripilaient Korin, et la jalousie dévorait son cœur. Et voilà que le petit parvenu lui avait même subtilisé Caliel. Jamais il ne pardonnerait à aucun d'entre eux.

Nyrin parlait sombrement des magiciens qui étaient en train de se rassembler à la cour de Tobin. Rares étaient ceux qui s'étaient présentés à Cirna, et la poignée de Busards qui étaient arrivés au nord formait une bande de bons à rien, tout juste capables, aux yeux de Korin, de brûler leur propre espèce et de terrifier les soldats. S'il fallait en croire les rumeurs, ceux de Tobin possédaient en revanche des pouvoirs prodigieux. Oh, par la Flamme, ce qu'il l'exécrait, ce marmot !

« Korin, tu ne te sens pas bien ? » lui chuchota Urmanis à l'oreille.

Korin papillota et s'aperçut que Morus et les autres le dévisageaient. Alben le tenait par le coude, et Urmanis le flanquait tout près de l'autre côté, l'air alarmé.

« Qu'est-ce que vous avez tous à me fixer de cette façon ? » les foudroya Korin avec un regard furieux pour couvrir sa défaillance passagère. À la vérité, il éprouvait un rien de tournis, et ses poings crispés brûlaient d'écraser quelque chose. « Allez, convoquez vos hommes, Morus. »

Ce dernier donna le signal à l'un de ses capitaines. L'homme porta un cor à ses lèvres et sonna le rassemblement. En peu de temps, l'appel fut répercuté par les timoniers des bateaux comme du sommet des collines. Korin s'assit pour attendre sur une bitte d'amarrage et regarda des files successives d'hommes se déverser en bon ordre des baraquements et descendre vers les appontements. Des chaloupes nagèrent sur la surface lisse de la baie pour se porter au-devant d'eux.

« Tu vas mieux ? » murmura Alben, planté tout près de Korin, tout en s'arrangeant pour le dérober à la vue du reste de l'assistance.

« Oui, bien entendu ! » jappa le prince, puis, avec un soupir : « Mon absence a duré longtemps, cette fois-ci ?

— Rien qu'un moment, mais tu avais l'air prêt à zigouiller quelqu'un. »

Korin se frotta les yeux pour essayer de refouler la migraine qui s'accumulait peu à peu derrière eux. « Je serai en pleine forme aussitôt que nous nous mettrons en marche. »

Cette fois, il ne manifesterait pas de faiblesse et ne commettrait pas d'erreurs. Cette fois, il serait le digne fils de son père.

18

Korin monta rendre visite à Nalia la nuit précédant son départ, revêtu de son armure et d'un beau tabard de soie frappé des armoiries royales de Skala. Elle ne l'avait pas vu habillé de la sorte depuis leur première rencontre nocturne. Il était alors un inconnu terrifiant, exténué, sale et couvert de sang. Maintenant, chaque pouce de son allure était royal, et il portait sous son bras un heaume étincelant cerclé d'or.

« Je suis venu vous faire mes adieux, dit-il en s'installant dans son fauteuil habituel en face d'elle. Nous partons aux premières lueurs de l'aube, et j'ai fort à faire d'ici là. »

Elle aurait souhaité qu'il s'assoie plus près d'elle et lui prenne à nouveau la main mais, au lieu de cela, il s'installa avec raideur sur son siège. Il ne l'avait jamais embrassée non plus, se bornant à lui baiser la main. L'esprit de la jeune femme s'égara juste un instant vers les souvenirs de la passion fallacieuse qu'elle avait partagée avec Nyrin. Elle refoula bien vite de telles pensées, comme si elles étaient susceptibles de faire d'une manière ou d'une autre du mal à son enfant.

Elle avait eu beau redouter comme la peste de se retrouver enceinte, la petite existence qui se développait en elle lui inspirait des sentiments protecteurs invincibles. Elle garderait l'enfant dans ses entrailles, et celle-ci naîtrait saine et belle. Sa rivale morte depuis longtemps n'avait mis au monde que des garçons, à ce que prétendait du moins Tomara. Illior consentirait assurément à laisser vivre une fille.

« Il se peut que mon absence se prolonge durant tout l'hiver, si les circonstances nous obligent à dresser un siège, reprit-il. Je déplore que l'aménagement de vos nouveaux appartements ne soit pas encore terminé, mais il le sera très bientôt. Et je m'assurerai que ceux qui vous attendront à Ero soient encore plus confortables. M'écrirez-vous ?

— Je n'y manquerai pas, messire, promit-elle. Je vous tiendrai informé de la croissance de votre enfant. »

Korin se leva et lui saisit la main. « Je ferai quant à moi des offrandes à Dalna et à Astellus en faveur de votre santé et de celle de notre enfant. »

Notre enfant. Nalia sourit et toucha son collier de perles pour lui porter bonheur. « J'agirai moi aussi de même, messire, et pour votre personne.

— Eh bien, voilà une bonne chose alors. » Il marqua une pause, puis se pencha et l'embrassa gauchement sur le front. « Au revoir, ma dame.

— Adieu, messire. » Elle le suivit du regard pendant qu'il se retirait. Oui, peut-être y avait-il de l'espoir.

Elle sortit sur le balcon quand il fut parti, sachant qu'elle ne trouverait pas le sommeil. Elle y monta sa veille solitaire, enveloppée dans un châle pour se préserver de l'humidité. Tomara roupillait dans un fauteuil, le menton sur la poitrine, en ronflant tout bas.

Nalia s'établit près de la balustrade, le menton appuyé sur les mains. Dans la plaine, au sud, des colonnes étaient en train de se former dans le noir, projetant des carrés et des rectangles mouvants sur l'herbe éclairée par la lune. Des feux de guet brûlaient partout, et elle distinguait des silhouettes qui passaient devant eux, faisant clignoter et scintiller leurs flammes dans le lointain comme des étoiles jaunes.

Lorsque la première lueur de la fausse aurore perça le brouillard en fusant à l'est, la garde de Korin se mit en formation dans la cour en contrebas. En voyant Korin enfourcher son grand cheval gris, Nalia ne put réprimer un soupir. Il était si beau d'aspect, si fringant...

Peut-être ne s'est-il adouci qu'à cause de l'enfant, mais ça m'est égal. Je lui en donnerai beaucoup d'autres, et je m'attacherai son cœur. Il n'a pas à m'aimer ou à me trouver belle, sa gentillesse me suffit. À son corps défendant, elle avait commencé à espérer.

Pendant qu'elle s'abandonnait à ces pensées, elle fut étonnée d'entendre un bruit de pas dans l'escalier. Elle se leva et se tint sur le seuil du balcon, l'oreille tendue avec une terreur croissante. Elle connaissait la légèreté de cette démarche.

Nyrin entra et s'inclina devant elle. « Bonjour, ma chère. Je pensais bien que je vous trouverais déjà réveillée. Je voulais vous faire mes adieux. »

Il était en tenue de voyage et avait presque son air d'autrefois quand il venait la voir à Ilear. Les avait-elle désirées, ses visites, à l'époque, et l'avait-elle mise en transe, son apparition ! Ce souvenir lui soulevait maintenant le cœur. Il avait l'air tellement ordinaire...

Et cette barbe rouge et fourchue, comment avait-elle jamais pu la trouver attrayante ? Elle ressemblait à une langue de serpent.

Tomara s'agita puis se leva pour plonger dans une révérence. « Messire. Vous ferai-je une infusion ?

— Laissez-nous. Je souhaite passer un moment avec votre maîtresse.

— Restez », commanda Nalia, mais la vieille sortit néanmoins comme si elle n'avait pas entendu.

Le magicien ferma la porte derrière elle et poussa le loquet. Lorsqu'il retourna vers Nalia, son regard la jaugeait, et l'ombre d'un sourire flottait sur ses lèvres minces.

« Ça, alors ! La grossesse te va comme un gant. Il irradie maintenant de ta personne un certain éclat, comme ces perles que t'a données ton époux bien-aimé. Sur mes conseils, d'ailleurs. Ce pauvre Korin a des antécédents plutôt tragiques en ce qui concerne la procréation d'héritiers. Il ne faut négliger aucune pré-caution.

— Est-il vrai que toutes ses autres femmes ont avorté de monstres ?

— Oui, c'est vrai.

— Qu'adviendra-t-il de ma propre enfant, alors ? Comment la protégerai-je ? Tomara prétend que c'est la colère d'Illior qui a flétri ces autres fœtus.

— Une version éminemment commode, et que j'ai été plus qu'heureux de soutenir. La véritable expli-cation se trouve un peu plus près de chez nous, j'ai peur. » Il s'approcha d'elle et lui effleura la joue d'un doigt ganté, tandis que la répulsion figeait Nalia sur place. « Tu n'as pas de crainte à avoir pour ton enfant, Nalia. Elle sera parfaite. » Il marqua une pause et puis suivit de l'index le tracé de la marque de naissance qui massacrait sa joue et son menton fuyant. « Enfin, peut-être pas parfaite, mais pas monstrueuse du tout. »

Nalia eut un mouvement de recul. « C'était donc vous ! C'est vous qui avez flétri ces autres petits.

— Ceux qu'il était nécessaire de supprimer. Les jouvencelles perdent souvent leur premier d'elles-mêmes, sans qu'on ait le moins du monde à intervenir. Quant à régler leur compte à ces autres-là, c'était une bagatelle, réellement.

— C'est vous, le monstre ! Korin vous ferait brûler vif s'il l'apprenait.

— Peut-être, mais il ne l'apprendra jamais. » Son petit sourire s'élargit malicieusement. « Qui le lui révélerait ? Toi ? De grâce, fais-le appeler tout de suite et essaie.

— Ce sortilège dont vous m'avez frappée...

— ... est toujours en vigueur. Je t'ai très joliment environnée de charmes, tous destinés à te maintenir saine et sauve, ma chère. Il ne faut pas que tu le tracasses avec des broutilles, quand il a tant de motifs d'inquiétude plus importants. La perspective de la bataille le terrifie littéralement, tu sais ?

— Menteur !

— Je t'assure, c'est vrai. Là, je n'y suis pour rien ; c'est sa nature, tout bonnement. Avec toi, il est admirablement parvenu à ses fins toutefois. Il a toujours excellé en matière de rut.

— Et voilà donc dans quel dessein vous m'avez dénichée puis condamnée à la clandestinité pendant toutes ces années..., murmura-t-elle.

— Naturellement. » Il sortit sur le balcon et l'invita d'un signe à l'y suivre. « Regarde là-bas dehors, dit-il en désignant d'un geste théâtral les troupes massées devant la forteresse. Cela aussi, c'est mon ouvrage. Une armée, prête à valider les prétentions de ton époux une fois pour toutes. Et elle le fera. Au mieux, son dément de cousin a deux fois moins d'hommes. »

Nalia s'immobilisa sur le seuil de la baie pendant que Nyrin s'appuyait sur la balustrade.

« Korin *va* gagner ? Vous avez vu ça ?

— Cela importe à peine, désormais, non ?

— Que voulez-vous dire ? Comment cela pourrait-il ne pas importer ?

— Ce n'est pas Korin que je vois dans mes visions, ma chère petite, mais l'enfant que tu portes en ton sein. Je les ai mal déchiffrées pendant longtemps, et cela m'a coûté des efforts considérables, mais à présent tout est devenu clair. Le rejeton de sexe féminin que j'avais prévu n'est autre que ta fille. Les choses étant ce qu'elles sont, le peuple doit actuellement choisir entre un roi usurpateur, voué à la malédiction d'Illior, ou une donzelle démente suscitée par nécromancie.

— Une donzelle ? Vous voulez dire le prince Tobin ?

— Je ne suis pas absolument sûr de ce qu'est Tobin, et n'en ai cure. Lorsque ta fille naîtra, nul ne saurait

265

en revanche contester l'authenticité ni de son sexe ni de son sang. Elle est de la plus pure lignée royale.

— Et qu'en est-il de mon époux ? insista Nalia, pendant qu'une peur glaciale l'envahissait. Comment pouvez-vous, en dépit de tous, le traiter d'usurpateur ?

— Parce que c'est ce qu'il est. Tu connais la prophétie aussi bien que moi. Korin, et son père avant lui, n'étaient que des fonctionnaires utiles, rien de plus. Skala doit avoir sa reine. Nous lui en donnerons une.

— Nous ? » chuchota Nalia, la bouche soudain sèche.

Nyrin se pencha par-dessus bord et contempla d'un air manifestement amusé ceux qui se démenaient en contrebas. « Vise-moi un peu dans quelle effervescence les mettent leurs lubies de victoire. Korin se figure qu'il va reconstruire Ero. Il se voit déjà en train d'y jouer avec ses gosses. »

Nalia se cramponna au chambranle de la porte-fenêtre, ses genoux menaçant de céder sous elle. « Vous... Vous pensez qu'il ne reviendra pas. »

Le ciel était désormais beaucoup plus lumineux. Elle surprit le regard oblique et sournois que le magicien faisait peser sur sa personne.

« Tu m'as manqué, Nalia. Oh, je ne te blâme pas de m'en avoir tellement voulu, mais il fallait sauver les apparences. Allons, tu ne vas quand même pas me dire que tu t'es amourachée de lui ? Je connais son cœur, ma chère. Tu n'es rien d'autre à ses yeux qu'une paire de cuisses entre lesquelles fourgonner, qu'un ventre à remplir.

— Non ! » Elle se couvrit les oreilles.

266

« Oh, il se flatte d'avoir un cœur chaleureux. Regarde comme il a garni de plumes ton petit nid d'ici. C'était bien plus pour se donner bonne conscience que pour te le rendre douillet, je te le garantis. Nous étions d'accord, lui et moi, sur le fait que tu avais juste assez d'esprit pour essayer de t'évader, si l'occasion s'en présentait, aussi valait-il mieux te tenir prudemment en cage, comme tes jolis oiseaux, au sommet de cette tour. À ce détail près qu'il ne t'a jamais qualifiée de jolie, toi.

— Assez ! » cria-t-elle. Des larmes lui emplirent les yeux, brouillant Nyrin jusqu'à le réduire à une sombre silhouette menaçante qui se découpait sur le ciel. « Pourquoi me montrer tant de cruauté ? Il éprouve *véritablement* de l'affection pour moi. Il en est venu à m'en témoigner.

— C'est toi qui en es venue à t'énamourer de lui, tu veux dire. Somme toute, je ne devrais pas en être autrement étonné. Tu es jeune et romanesque, et Korin n'est pas foncièrement méchant, dans son genre et à sa manière. Mais je déplore néanmoins que tu te sois attachée à lui. Cela ne fera qu'empirer les choses, en fin de compte. »

Nalia se glaça encore davantage. « Que dites-vous là ? »

Elle entendait distinctement Korin saluer ses hommes et lancer des ordres. Sa voix respirait un tel bonheur !

« Tu devrais le regarder un bon coup, maintenant, tant que cela t'est possible, ma chère.

— Il ne reviendra *pas*. » Les ténèbres menaçaient de se reployer sur elle.

« Il a joué son rôle, quoique à contrecœur, musa Nyrin. Songe à quel point cela va être du velours ; toi, mère de la souveraine au berceau, et moi, son Lord Protecteur. »

Nalia le fixa d'un air incrédule. Nyrin était en train d'agiter la main pour saluer quelqu'un en bas. Peut-être que Korin l'avait aperçu en levant les yeux.

Elle l'imagina se fiant en Nyrin tout comme elle l'avait fait elle-même.

Elle imagina l'existence qui se déroulait devant elle, celle d'un pion muet sur l'échiquier de Nyrin, d'un pion condamné au silence par sa magie. Et son enfant, sa petite fille encore à naître, levant les yeux vers cette figure de faux jeton. N'allait-il pas un jour ou l'autre la séduire, elle aussi ?

Nyrin s'appuyait toujours à la balustrade, une hanche remontée sur le bord tandis qu'il agitait la main tout en souriant de son sourire hypocrite et vide.

Une rage trop longtemps accumulée flamba dans le cœur meurtri de la jeune femme et embrasa comme du feu grégeois les fagots de sa peine et de son amour bafoué. Réduisant à néant sa terreur et son hébétude, elle la propulsa en avant. Ses mains semblèrent se mouvoir d'elles-mêmes quand elle se rua vers Nyrin et le poussa de toutes ses forces.

Pendant une seconde, ils se trouvèrent face à face, presque assez près pour s'embrasser. Le sourire fallacieux du magicien s'était évanoui, supplanté par un regard écarquillé d'incrédulité. Nyrin griffa l'air, la saisit par sa manche tout en essayant vainement de se soustraire au point de bascule. Mais il était trop lourd pour elle et, au lieu d'arriver à se rétablir, l'entraîna avec lui par-dessus le rebord.

Ou peu s'en fallut. Pendant un instant interminable, elle demeura en suspens dans le vide, à peine retenue par l'accoudoir, et elle vit Korin et ses cavaliers dont, tout en bas, les visages se réduisaient à des ovales blêmes et des bouches béantes. Elle allait s'écraser aux pieds de Korin. Elle et son enfant périraient là, juste devant lui.

Au lieu de cela, quelque chose l'empoigna et la retira de l'appui. Le temps d'entr'apercevoir une dernière fois la physionomie incrédule de Nyrin pendant qu'il tombait, et elle s'écroula comme une chiffe sur le balcon, où elle demeura vautrée en un amas tremblant, non sans percevoir le hurlement bref et soudain tronqué du magicien tout autant que les cris épouvantés des témoins de sa chute.

Je t'ai très joliment environnée de charmes, tous destinés à te maintenir saine et sauve, ma chère.

Préservée par ses maudits sortilèges... !

Elle éclata d'un rire nerveux. Toute tremblante, elle se leva vaille que vaille et, d'une démarche mal assurée, s'approcha de la balustrade pour jeter un coup d'œil dans la cour.

Nyrin gisait recroquevillé comme une poupée de chiffon puérile sur les pavés de pierre. Il avait atterri à plat ventre, de sorte qu'elle ne put voir s'il affichait toujours son air décontenancé.

Korin leva les yeux et aperçut Nalia puis se précipita à l'intérieur de la tour.

Nalia rentra d'un pas chancelant dans sa chambre et s'effondra sur son lit. Elle lui révélerait la vérité, sans lui celer le moindre détail de la traîtrise du magicien à leur encontre. Il comprendrait. Elle reverrait ce sourire affectueux.

Quelques instants plus tard, Korin entra en trombe et la trouva couchée là. « Par les Quatre, Nalia, qu'avez-vous fait ? »

Elle essaya de lui répondre, mais les mots lui restèrent collés au fond du gosier, exactement comme ils l'avaient déjà fait auparavant. Elle s'étreignit la gorge tandis que les larmes lui montaient aux yeux. Tomara survint dans la pièce et courut la prendre dans ses bras, Lord Alben était là, lui aussi, la main crispée sur le bras de Korin, ainsi que maître Porion et d'autres que Nalia ne connaissait pas. Dans la cour, en bas, quelqu'un gémissait plaintivement. Le timbre de la voix semblait être celui d'un jeune homme.

Nalia tenta de nouveau de dévoiler la vérité à Korin, mais l'horreur qu'elle lut dans ses yeux la réduisit au silence aussi implacablement que le sortilège qui paralysait encore sa langue. Finalement, elle réussit à chuchoter : « Il est tombé.

— Je... j'ai vu..., bégaya Korin en secouant lentement la tête. Je vous ai vue !

— Fermez cette porte, ordonna Porion en désignant par-delà Nalia celle du balcon. Fermez-la, et fermez-la bien. Barrez les fenêtres aussi ! » Puis il entraîna

Korin de vive force pour l'éloigner d'elle avant qu'elle n'ait pu trouver les termes propres à s'en faire comprendre.

Il était pervers. Il allait se débarrasser de vous comme il s'est débarrassé de moi ! Il allait prendre votre place !

Les mots refusaient de sortir.

« Je vous ai vue », hoqueta Korin de nouveau, avant de tourner les talons et de quitter la pièce à grandes enjambées. Les autres lui emboîtèrent le pas, et elle l'entendit crier d'une voix furieuse : « C'est la démence ! C'est dans le sang ! Gardez-la ! Veillez à ce qu'elle ne fasse pas de mal à mon enfant ! »

Nalia s'effondra en sanglots dans les bras de Tomara, et elle continua de pleurer toutes les larmes de son corps bien après que le tapage des trompettes et des chevaux se fut progressivement éteint dans le lointain, en dehors de la forteresse. Korin était parti faire sa guerre. Il ne lui sourirait plus jamais de nouveau, même s'il revenait.

Je suis enfin délivrée de Nyrin, en tout cas, songea-t-elle pour se consoler avec cette certitude. *Mon enfant ne sera jamais souillée par son contact ni par ce sourire faux !*

19

Le ciel de l'arrière-été avait le bleu d'un lapis zengati le jour où Tamìr partit d'Atyion à la tête de son armée. Dans les vignobles qui bordaient la route, des femmes équipées de corbeilles profondes coupaient de lourdes grappes de raisin. Parmi des multitudes de chevaux cabriolaient dans les prairies lointaines une centaine de magnifiques jeunes poulains, et les champs de céréales brillaient dans la lumière comme de l'or.

Tharin chevauchait auprès d'elle, pas encore prêt à lui faire ses adieux.

Derrière eux, des rangs d'hommes d'armes, d'archers et de combattants montés marchaient sous sa bannière personnelle et sous celles de plus d'une douzaine de nobles maisons originaires de la zone allant d'Ilear à Erind.

D'autres recrues, qu'on avait levées dans les villes et les campagnes, étaient seulement armées de coutelas, de faucilles ou de gourdins, mais leur attitude était aussi fière que celle des lords qui les conduisaient.

Les Compagnons portaient tous de longs tabards bleus, blasonnés sur la poitrine par leur cotte d'armes, ainsi que par le baudrier de leur maisonnée.

Lutha et Barieüs chevauchaient d'un air altier malgré leur état, non sans quelque incommodité, et bavardaient joyeusement avec Una, revenue la veille avec plusieurs régiments d'Ylani.

Mahti chevauchait pour l'heure avec les magiciens,

son oo'lu lui barrant le dos comme l'aurait fait une épée. Les commérages des soldats étant ce qu'ils étaient, la nouvelle qu'on aurait pour guide cet étrange individu avait eu tôt fait de se propager. Quant à celle de la subite affection de leur reine pour le peuple des collines, elle s'était répandue à la vitesse du feu grégeois. Cela n'allait pas sans murmures, mais les lords et les capitaines tenaient tout leur monde en main.

Au milieu de l'après-midi, Mahti pointa le doigt vers les montagnes de l'intérieur. « Nous aller ce côté. »

Tamìr mit sa main en visière pour s'abriter les yeux. Il n'y avait pas de route, rien d'autre que des moutonnements de champs, de prairies et des contreforts boisés au-delà.

« Je ne vois aucun passage, dit Ki.

— Je connais chemin, insista Mahti.

— Très bien, alors. Nous irons vers l'ouest. » Tamìr immobilisa sa monture pour se séparer de Tharin.

Il lui adressa un sourire attristé quand ils échangèrent une poignée de main. « Cette fois, c'est toi qui t'en vas, pas moi.

— Je me rappelle l'effet que cela me faisait de vous regarder partir, Père et toi. Nous aurons quelques bonnes histoires à nous raconter lorsque nous nous retrouverons.

— Puisses-tu tenir l'Épée de Ghërilain avant que les flocons ne se mettent à voler ! » Brandissant la sienne, il rugit : « Pour Skala et Tamìr ! »

L'armée lui fit écho, et le cri roula vers l'arrière de

proche en proche tout le long de l'immense file comme la houle d'une marée.

Sur un dernier geste de la main, Tharin et son escorte firent volter leurs chevaux et retournèrent au galop vers Atyion.

Après l'avoir regardé s'éloigner, Tamìr concentra son attention sur les montagnes.

Le jour suivant les amena jusqu'aux contreforts, et celui d'après jusqu'aux forêts qui tapissaient le pied de la chaîne.

Tard dans l'après-midi, Mahti tendit l'index vers une sente à gibier qui se faufilait au travers d'un épais fourré de groseilliers sauvages.

« C'est là que débute ton chemin secret ? questionna Tamìr.

— Y arriver bientôt », répondit Mahti. Suivit un exposé rapide à destination d'Arkoniel.

« Nous suivons ce sentier pendant une journée, puis nous remontons un cours d'eau jusqu'à une chute, résuma le magicien. La route occultée démarre juste au-delà. Il dit que la marche est plus facile ensuite. Nous atteindrons le premier village des gens des collines d'ici deux jours.

— Je ne me doutais pas qu'il en vivait aussi près.

— Je pas connaître ces Retha'noïs, mais ils voir mon oo'lu et savoir je être sorcier. » Il s'adressa de nouveau à Arkoniel, dans l'intention manifeste de s'assurer que Tamìr comprendrait ensuite clairement ce qu'il exprimait.

Tout en écoutant, la physionomie du magicien prit

une expression des plus grave. « Dès l'instant où vous apercevrez des gens des collines, il vous faudra immédiatement ordonner une halte et observer un mutisme absolu. Il prendra les devants pour leur parler en votre faveur. Faute de quoi, ils risquent fort de nous attaquer. »

Là-dessus, Mahti disparut dans les taillis pendant un moment. À son retour, il portait ses propres vêtements et son collier et ses bracelets de dents d'animaux. Une fois remonté à cheval, il adressa à Tamìr un hochement de tête. « Nous aller maintenant. »

La forêt se referma tout autour d'eux, peuplée de grands sapins qui embaumaient l'atmosphère et dont la densité étouffait la végétation des fourrés. Ils ne virent âme qui vive ni ce jour-là ni le lendemain. Le terrain devint plus abrupt, et les versants boisés des collines étaient jonchés de gros rochers. Mahti les conduisit au torrent dont il avait parlé, et l'on atteignit la modeste cascade au cours de l'après-midi. La vague sente à gibier que l'on avait empruntée jusque-là paraissait s'achever au bord du bassin que formait la chute.

« Bonne eau », les avisa le sorcier.

Tamìr ordonna un arrêt puis mit pied à terre, imitée par son escorte, afin de remplir sa gourde.

Après s'être lui-même désaltéré, Mahti dégagea son oo'lu de sa bandoulière et se mit à jouer. Ce fut une mélodie brève et stridulante, mais lorsqu'il en eut terminé, Tamìr découvrit un sentier battu et rebattu qui partait du bord de la mare et dont rien n'avait indiqué jusque-là l'existence. Sur les troncs des arbres qui le bordaient de part et d'autre se discernaient des empreintes de main décolorées analogues à celles qu'elle avait aperçues autour du camp abandonné de Lhel.

« Venir ! » Mahti remonta à vive allure le nouveau chemin. « Tu être endroit retha'noï. Tenir promesse. »

Pendant qu'ils établissaient leur camp, ce soir-là, Arkoniel rejoignit Tamìr et les autres autour du feu.

« Je viens juste de m'entretenir avec Lyan. La flotte de Korin a essayé de prendre terre à Ero. Les magiciens et les guetteurs ont averti Tharin qu'elle cinglait vers le port, et Illardi l'y attendait de pied ferme avec nos collègues. Il a utilisé les quelques navires que vous aviez sur place comme des brûlots pour prendre ceux de l'adversaire dans la nasse. Les flammes se sont propagées, et nos magiciens se sont servis de leurs propres sortilèges. Tous les bâtiments ennemis ont été détruits ou capturés.

— Voilà d'excellentes nouvelles ! s'exclama Tamìr. Aucune, en revanche, d'une attaque par voie de terre ?

— Nevus descend vers le sud à la tête d'une armée considérable. Tharin est déjà en train de se porter à sa rencontre.

— Puisse Sakor lui porter chance ! » dit Ki, tout en jetant un bout de bois sur le feu.

Couchée sous ses couvertures cette nuit-là, les yeux attachés sur les frondaisons qui se balançaient en voilant et dévoilant tour à tour les étoiles, Tamìr elle-même adressa au ciel une prière silencieuse en faveur de Tharin, dans l'espoir qu'il ne lui serait pas enlevé, lui aussi.

Le lendemain, le chemin se mit à grimper plus raide, et il n'y avait toujours pas trace de village. Juste avant midi, toutefois, Mahti leva la main pour enjoindre aux autres de s'arrêter.

« Là. » Il dressa son doigt pour signaler un fouillis de pierres éboulées sur la droite.

Tamìr donna le signal de la halte. Il lui fallut un moment pour discerner l'homme accroupi sur le rocher le plus élevé. Il lui retournait son regard droit dans les yeux et avait un oo'lu pressé contre ses lèvres.

Mahti brandit son propre cor par-dessus sa tête et attendit. Au bout d'un moment, l'autre abaissa le sien et cria quelque chose au sorcier.

« Toi pas bouger de là », enjoignit ce dernier à Tamìr, avant d'escalader avec agilité le chaos rocheux pour rejoindre l'inconnu sur son perchoir.

« Nous ne sommes pas seuls, chuchota Ki.

— Je les vois. » On distinguait au moins une douzaine d'autres Retha'noïs qui les surveillaient de part et d'autre du défilé. Certains portaient des arcs, d'autres de longs cors analogues à celui de Mahti.

Personne ne bougea. Tamìr se cramponna aux rênes, l'oreille tendue vers l'imperceptible murmure de la conversation des deux sorciers. De temps à autre, la voix de l'inconnu s'élevait à un diapason coléreux, mais lui et Mahti dévalaient à présent l'éboulis pour se planter sur le chemin.

« Il parler à toi et l'orëskiri, lança Mahti à Tamìr. Autres pas bouger.

— Je n'aime pas beaucoup ça, maugréa Ki.

— Ne t'inquiète pas, je resterai avec elle », lui dit Arkoniel. Tamìr démonta et tendit la bride à Ki puis déboucla son ceinturon d'épée et le lui confia également.

Elle et Arkoniel s'avancèrent de conserve vers les sorciers, paumes tendues afin de montrer qu'ils étaient désarmés.

L'homme était plus vieux que Mahti, et il lui manquait la plupart des dents. Ses marques de sorcier se voyaient nettement sur sa peau, avertissant qu'il s'était par avance muni de quelque espèce de charme.

« Lui Sheksu, la renseigna Mahti. Je dire lui toi venir apporter paix. Il demander comment.

— Arkoniel, dites-lui qui je suis et que je commanderai à mon peuple d'arrêter de persécuter les Retha'noïs, dans la mesure où ceux-ci se montreront pacifiques envers nous. Dites-lui que notre unique désir est d'emprunter cette vallée en toute sécurité. Nous ne venons pas plus en conquérants qu'en espions. »

Après qu'Arkoniel eut transmis ses propos, Sheksu posa une question d'un ton acerbe.

« Il demande pourquoi il devrait croire une jeune fille sudienne qui n'a même pas encore connu d'homme.

— Comment l'a-t-il su ? » souffla-t-elle, tout en s'efforçant de dissimuler sa surprise. « Dites-lui que je le jurerai par chacun de mes dieux.

— Je ne pense pas que cela le convaincra. Piquez-vous le doigt et offrez-lui une goutte de sang. Cela lui prouvera que vous n'essayez pas de lui cacher quoi que ce soit. Utilisez ceci. » Il tira de sa bourse l'aiguille de Lhel.

Tamìr se piqua l'index et le tendit à Sheksu. Celui-ci prit la gouttelette et la frotta entre son pouce et son propre index. Il décocha un regard surpris à Mahti puis lui dit quelque chose.

« Il vient de déclarer que vous avez deux ombres, murmura Arkoniel.

— Frère ?

— Oui. »

Les deux sorciers se remirent à causer.

« Mahti est en train de lui expliquer le rôle de Lhel, chuchota le magicien.

— Il vouloir voir marque, reprit finalement Mahti.

— La cicatrice ? Cela va m'obliger à ôter mon armure. Dis-lui qu'il me faut sa parole que ce n'est pas une ruse.

— Il dire pas ruse, par la Mère.

— Très bien, dans ce cas. Arkoniel, pouvez-vous m'aider ? »

Celui-ci se débrouilla pour défaire un des côtés de sa cuirasse et le maintint soulevé pendant qu'elle retirait son tabard.

« Que diable êtes-vous en train de faire ? » les apostropha Ki en faisant mine de s'avancer.

Sheksu leva une main dans sa direction.

« Ki, arrête-toi ! Reste où tu es, commanda Arkoniel.

— Fais ce qu'il te dit », lui enjoignit calmement Tamìr.

Il obtempéra d'un air renfrogné. Derrière lui, les autres Compagnons demeurèrent tendus, en alerte.

Tamìr retira son haubert et rabattit le col de sa chemise matelassée et du justaucorps qu'elle portait dessous pour montrer à Sheksu la cicatrice entre ses seins. Il effleura d'un doigt la trace blanchâtre des points puis plongea son regard au fond de ses yeux. Il sentait la graisse et les dents gâtées, mais ses prunelles noires étaient perçantes comme celles d'un faucon et tout aussi chargées de circonspection.

« Dis-lui que Lhel m'a aidée pour que nos peuples puissent faire la paix », reprit Tamìr.

Sheksu recula, sans cesser de la scruter attentivement.

« Il serait peut-être utile que Frère fasse une apparition, chuchota Arkoniel.

— Vous savez bien que je ne puis pas le faire venir et partir à ma guise... »

Or, subitement, Frère se trouva là. Cela ne dura qu'un instant, mais assez long pour lui permettre d'émettre tout bas un sifflement moqueur qui hérissa les cheveux de la nuque et le duvet des bras de sa sœur ; mais, pendant cet instant, elle perçut une autre présence avec lui, et un parfum de feuilles fraîchement pilées flotta dans l'atmosphère. Elle jeta prestement un regard circulaire, dans l'espoir d'apercevoir Lhel, mais il n'y avait rien d'autre que la sensation d'elle et le parfum.

La physionomie de Sheksu trahissait sa satisfaction pendant qu'il s'entretenait avec Mahti et Arkoniel.

« Il vous croit, parce qu'aucun magicien de l'Orëska ne serait capable de réaliser cette opération magique, commenta Arkoniel. Frère vient de vous rendre un immense service.

— Pas Frère. Lhel, répliqua-t-elle à voix basse. Je me demande s'il l'a vue.

— Lui voir, l'avisa Mahti. Elle parler pour toi. »

Sheksu se remit à causer avec Mahti, tout en indiquant d'un geste ses compatriotes toujours debout là-haut, puis le chemin dans la direction que comptaient prendre Tamìr et les siens.

« Il dire toi pouvoir passer avec ton peuple mais toi devoir aller vite, expliqua Mahti. Il enverra chanson sur toi au prochain village, et eux envoyer au suivant. Il dire lui pas... » Il fronça les sourcils et regarda Arkoniel pour l'inviter à clarifier les choses.

« On vous a accordé de passer sans encombre, et Sheksu fera transmettre votre histoire de proche en proche. Il ne peut vous promettre que vous serez la bienvenue, seulement qu'il aura plaidé votre cause. »

Sheksu ajouta quelque chose d'autre, et Arkoniel s'inclina devant lui. « Vous l'avez impressionné en lui offrant votre sang et par ce qu'il y a lu. Il dit que vous bénéficiez de la faveur de sa déesse. Si vous tenez votre parole, vous devriez être en sécurité.

— Sa confiance est un honneur pour moi. » Elle préleva un sester d'or dans son aumônière et le lui offrit. La pièce était frappée du croissant de lune d'Illior et de la flamme de Sakor. « Dites-lui que ce sont les symboles de mon peuple. Dites-lui que je le considère comme un ami. »

Sheksu accepta la pièce et la frotta entre ses doigts, puis dit quelque chose d'un ton amical.

« Il est impressionné, murmura Arkoniel. L'or est très rare dans ces parages, et il est hautement prisé. »

En retour, Sheksu lui offrit l'un de ses bracelets, fait de dents et de griffes d'ours.

« Il vous conférera de la force contre vos ennemis et vous désignera comme une amie du peuple des collines, interpréta le magicien.

— Dites-lui que je m'honore de le porter. »

Après lui avoir fait ses adieux, Sheksu disparut parmi les rochers.

« Partir vite maintenant », la pressa Mahti.

Elle endossa de nouveau son armure et retourna vers les Compagnons.

« Ç'a eu l'air de bien se passer », murmura Ki, tout en lui rendant son épée.

« Nous n'avons pas encore franchi les montagnes. »

20

La mort de Nyrin et la façon dont elle avait eu lieu jetèrent un linceul sur le cœur de Korin. Tandis qu'il conduisait son armée vers l'est, il ne parvenait pas à secouer le sentiment d'appréhension superstitieuse qui l'obsédait.

Nalia avait assassiné le magicien ; là-dessus, il n'avait aucun doute, en dépit de son assertion bégayante qu'il était simplement tombé. « Est-ce qu'une malédiction vouerait à la démence toutes les femmes de la lignée royale ? » avait-il divagué à l'adresse d'Alben pendant qu'on emportait la dépouille désarticulée de Nyrin et que Moriel suivait le brancard en chialant comme une femme sur son ancien maître.

« Démente ou pas, elle porte ton enfant. Que vas-tu faire d'elle ? questionna Alben.

— Pas rien qu'un enfant. Une fille. Une nouvelle reine. J'ai juré devant l'autel de l'Illuminateur qu'elle serait mon héritière. Pourquoi suis-je encore maudit ? »

Il avait interrogé les prêtres sur ce chapitre avant de se mettre en marche, mais il ne restait plus d'illiorains à Cirna, et les autres avaient trop peur de lui pour lui offrir quoi que ce soit d'autre que des garanties creuses. Le prêtre dalnien lui avait assuré que certaines femmes devenaient folles pendant leur grossesse, mais qu'elles recouvraient leur équilibre mental après l'accouchement, et il lui avait donné des charmes censés guérir l'esprit de Nalia. Korin avait chargé Tomara de les apporter en haut de la tour.

La pensée d'Aliya et de la chose monstrueuse qu'elle avait mise au monde en mourant revint aussi hanter ses rêves. Parfois, il se retrouvait avec elle dans la chambre de ces couches-là ; d'autres nuits, c'était Nalia qui occupait le lit, et des souffrances atroces tordaient son visage amoché pendant qu'elle poussait pour évacuer une nouvelle abomination.

Autrefois, Tanil et Caliel savaient l'apaiser d'habitude au sortir de pareils cauchemars.

Alben et Urmanis faisaient désormais de leur mieux en lui apportant du vin lorsqu'ils l'entendaient se réveiller.

Et puis il y avait Moriel. Plus Korin s'éloignait de Cirna, plus il se surprenait à se redemander avec stupeur pourquoi il avait fini par consentir à doter le Crapaud d'un brevet de Compagnon, tout en sachant pertinemment qu'il avait été la créature d'Orun et le larbin de Nyrin.

En dépit de tous ces soucis, il se sentit de plus en plus léger au fur et à mesure que les jours passaient. Il s'était traité avec la dernière des lâchetés depuis son départ d'Ero, se rendit-il compte non sans quelque dépit. Il avait laissé le chagrin et le doute l'émasculer, et s'en était trop remis à Nyrin. Son corps était encore vigoureux, sa main d'épée solide, mais son esprit s'était affaibli par défaut d'usage. Les derniers mois écoulés lui semblaient très sombres, à la réflexion, comme si le soleil n'avait jamais brillé sur la forteresse.

Il pivota sur sa selle pour contempler les milliers d'hommes qui le suivaient.

« C'est un formidable spectacle, n'est-ce pas ? » dit-il à maître Porion et aux autres, les yeux fièrement attachés sur les rangées de cavaliers et de fantassins.

Grâce au duc Wethring et à Lord Nevus, presque tous les nobles de la région qui s'étendait de là jusqu'à Ilear se trouvaient soit avec lui, soit morts, soit décrétés d'exécution. Il réglerait leur compte à ces derniers dès qu'il se serait occupé de Tobin et emparé d'Atyion.

Tobin. Les mains de Korin se crispèrent sur les rênes. Il n'était que temps d'en finir avec lui, une fois pour toutes.

Korin était trop homme d'honneur à ses propres yeux pour reconnaître la jalousie qui couvait derrière sa colère – une jalousie sous-jacente, amère et corrosive, alimentée par le souvenir de ses propres déficiences de jadis, propulsées au grand jour par leur contraste saisissant avec la valeur naturelle de son jeune cousin. Non, il n'allait pas se permettre de penser à cela. Il avait rejeté dans l'oubli cette époque-là, comme des erreurs de jeunesse. Il ne cafouillerait pas, ce coup-ci.

Ils quittèrent l'isthme et piquèrent vers le nord et l'est en direction de Colath. Les pluies survinrent, mais le moral demeurait excellent dans les rangs comme au sein des Compagnons. Dans quelques jours, on serait en vue du territoire d'Atyion, non loin des opulentes ressources qu'il recelait – chevaux et greniers, sans compter les fabuleux trésors du château. Korin n'avait guère eu plus que des promesses en poche jusque-là pour tenir ses lords ; de prodigieuses dépouilles se trouvaient désormais presque à portée de leurs mains. Il raserait Atyion et se servirait de ses richesses inépuisables pour reconstruire une Ero plus prestigieuse que jamais.

Cet après-midi-là, cependant, l'un des éclaireurs

avancés revint au triple galop sur une monture couverte d'écume, suivi de près par un autre cavalier.

« Boraeüs, n'est-ce pas ? » dit Korin, reconnaissant en ce dernier l'un des principaux espions de Nyrin.

« Sire, je vous apporte des nouvelles du prince Tobin. Il s'est mis en marche !

— Combien d'hommes avec lui ?

— Cinq mille peut-être. Je ne suis pas sûr. Mais il ne remonte pas la route côtière. Il envoie à votre rencontre une autre force commandée par Lord Tharin...

— Tharin ? » murmura Porion en fronçant les sourcils.

Alben émit un gloussement. « Ainsi, c'est sa nourrice sèche que Tobin nous dépêche au train ? Il a donc finalement dû apprendre à se torcher le nez !

— Tharin a servi au sein des Compagnons de votre père, Sire, lui rappela Porion en décochant à Alben un coup d'œil lourd de mise en garde. Il était le plus vaillant capitaine du duc Rhius. Il n'y aura ni rime ni raison à le sous-estimer.

— Il ne s'agit là que d'une feinte, Sire, expliqua l'espion. Le prince est en train d'emprunter une route secrète à travers les montagnes pour vous déborder à partir de l'ouest.

— Nous y veillerons », gronda Korin.

Il ordonna de faire halte et convoqua ses autres généraux, puis fit répéter les nouvelles en leur présence par le messager.

« Voilà d'excellentes nouvelles ! Nous allons submerger comme une marée de tempête le contre-feu de cette force dérisoire et nous emparer de la ville en votre nom, Sire ! » s'exclama Nevus, dans son ardeur à venger la mort de son père.

Un coup d'œil à la ronde permit à Korin de lire dans les yeux de tous les assistants la même lueur affamée de convoitise et de vengeance. Ils étaient déjà en train de dresser l'état du butin.

Un grand calme intérieur se fit en lui pendant qu'il prêtait l'oreille à tous leurs débats, et ses idées n'en devinrent que d'autant plus nettes. « Lord Nevus, vous prendrez cinq compagnies de cavalerie pour affronter la force de l'est. Prenez-la en tenaille de conserve avec les troupes du duc Morus et écrasez-la. Capturez-moi Lord Tharin ou apportez-moi sa tête.

— Sire ?

— Atyion n'est rien. » Korin dégaina l'Épée de Ghërilain et la brandit. « Il ne peut y avoir qu'un seul et unique souverain de Skala, et c'est celui qui tient cette lame-ci ! Transmettez l'ordre : nous marchons vers l'ouest afin d'aller y écraser le prince Tobin et son armée.

— Vous scindez la vôtre ? demanda posément Porion. Vous risquez de condamner les navires de Morus. Il n'y a plus moyen de les avertir, maintenant. »

Korin haussa les épaules. « Il n'aura qu'à se débrouiller tout seul. La chute de Tobin entraînera la chute d'Atyion. Telle est ma volonté, et tels sont les ordres que je vous donne. Expédiez sur-le-champ des escouades d'éclaireurs au nord et au sud. Je ne veux pas que nos ennemis s'emparent de Cirna sous notre nez. La princesse consort doit être protégée coûte que coûte. C'est nous qui prendrons le prince à l'improviste, messires, et quand nous le ferons, nous l'écraserons et mettrons un terme à ses prétentions une fois pour toutes. »

Les généraux s'inclinèrent bien bas devant lui et se retirèrent pour diffuser ses ordres.

« Voilà qui est bien joué, Sire, dit Moriel en lui offrant sa propre gourde de vin. Lord Nyrin s'enorgueillirait de vous voir en ce moment. »

Korin se retourna et poussa la pointe de son épée sous le menton du flagorneur. Le Crapaud blêmit et se figea, le dévisageant d'un air effaré. La gourde de vin lui tomba des mains et éclaboussa de son contenu l'herbe foulée.

« Si tu souhaites rester parmi les Compagnons, tu ne t'aviseras plus de me mentionner à nouveau cette créature.

— Vous serez obéi, Sire », souffla Moriel.

Après avoir rengainé son épée, Korin s'éloigna à grands pas, sans se soucier du regard rancunier qui le talonnait.

Porion remarqua celui-ci, cependant, et en récompensa Moriel d'une sévère calotte sur l'oreille. « Sois reconnaissant au roi de sa patience, l'avertit-il. Ton maître est mort, et je t'aurais noyé depuis des années s'il n'avait dépendu que de moi. »

Caliel avait espéré rencontrer Korin sur la route, mais il n'y trouva pas l'ombre d'une armée ni d'indice de son passage. Ils chevauchèrent tout du long jusqu'à la route de l'isthme sans repérer la moindre trace de lui, et Caliel apprit dans les villages qu'ils traversaient qu'il avait rebroussé chemin et pris la direction du sud pour aller affronter Tamìr sur la côte ouest.

Après avoir parcouru quelques milles supplémentaires, les champs piétinés, les chemins défoncés et les ornières creusées par de lourds fourgons révélèrent à Caliel que des troupes étaient passées par là.

« Pourquoi sont-ils partis pour l'ouest ? demanda Tanil. Il n'y a rien là-bas.

— Je l'ignore. » Il s'interrompit et examina furtivement l'écuyer. Celui-ci avait encore quelques absences mais, plus ils se rapprochaient de Korin, plus il avait l'air heureux.

Il n'est pas du tout en état de se battre. Je devrais l'emmener à Cirna et l'y laisser d'une façon ou d'une autre, pour qu'il y soit en sécurité. Mais la nostalgie qu'il lisait dans ses yeux quand ils se perdaient vers l'ouest lui faisait l'effet de refléter les sentiments de son propre cœur. Ils étaient tous deux des hommes de Korin. Leur place était à ses côtés, quelle qu'elle fût.

Il se força à sourire et mit son cheval au pas. « Eh bien, allons. Rattrapons-le.

— Il sera suffoqué de nous voir ! » s'esclaffa Tanil.

Caliel acquiesça d'un hochement de tête, non sans se demander une fois de plus quel genre de réception lui serait personnellement réservé.

21

La fin du franchissement des montagnes mit leurs nerfs à rude épreuve pendant quatre interminables journées supplémentaires. Le chemin courait le long des berges de rivières torrentueuses avant d'escalader des défilés rocheux qui aboutissaient dans de petites vallées verdoyantes où broutaient des troupeaux de chèvres et de moutons. On relevait çà et là des empreintes de couguars et d'ours et, la nuit, des lynx poussaient des feulements perçants de femmes à l'agonie.

Il n'y avait que dans les vallées que Tamìr pouvait regrouper l'ensemble de ses troupes au lieu de les laisser s'échelonner comme les éléments d'un collier brisé. Nikidès revint un jour rapporter qu'il leur faudrait deux heures pour passer par un certain endroit.

La nouvelle de l'approche de Tamìr la précédait, conformément aux promesses de Sheksu. Plusieurs fois par jour, Mahti prenait les devants et disparaissait en empruntant un sentier latéral qui grimpait vers quelques villages cachés. Ceux qu'on voyait de la route étaient constitués de quelques huttes en pierres sèches auxquelles des peaux tendues tenaient lieu de toiture. Leurs habitants se planquaient ou prenaient la fuite, mais de la fumée montait des feux de cuisine, et des bandes de chèvres ou de poulets vagabondaient parmi les demeures silencieuses.

Sur les conseils de Mahti, Tamìr laissait des présents sur le bord du chemin pour chacun des villages : de l'argent, de la nourriture, de la corde, de petits couteaux et autres choses semblables. Parfois, ils trouvaient eux-mêmes des paniers de vivres déposés à leur intention – viande de chèvre fumée graisseuse, fromages à l'odeur fétide, baies et champignons, parfois des pièces de bijouterie primitive.

« Ils entendre bien de toi, l'informa le sorcier. Toi prendre cadeau ou faire insulte.

— On se passerait volontiers de tout ça », fit Nikidès, le nez plissé de dégoût, pendant que Lorin et lui inspectaient le contenu d'une corbeille.

« Ne fais pas le délicat », s'esclaffa Ki en croquant dans une tranche de viande coriace comme du cuir. Tamìr en tâta elle-même. Cela lui remémora ce que Lhel leur avait jadis donné à manger.

De temps à autre, le sorcier local, qu'il fût homme ou femme, se risquait dehors pour satisfaire sa curiosité, mais il se montrait circonspect même à l'endroit de Mahti, et il n'observait les intrus que de loin.

Le temps se boucha pendant qu'ils franchissaient un col vertigineux et commençaient à descendre vers la côte ouest. De lourds nuages et du brouillard flottaient presque à ras de l'étroit défilé. Des filets d'eau qui suintaient à travers les rochers transformaient par moments la route en ruisseau, rendant la marche périlleuse sur les pierres instables. Ici, les arbres étaient différents, les trembles encore verts et les fourrés beaucoup plus denses dans les sous-bois.

La pluie survint sous la forme d'averses patientes

et continuelles, et bientôt chacun fut trempé jusqu'à l'épiderme. Tamìr dormit mal sous l'abri malingre d'un arbre, pelotonnée pour avoir chaud avec Ki et Una, et elle découvrit à son réveil un couple de salamandres qui s'ébattait perché sur la pointe boueuse d'une de ses bottes.

Le lendemain, alors qu'ils passaient à proximité d'un gros village, ils aperçurent trois sorciers juchés sur un talus juste en surplomb du chemin : une femme et deux hommes, avec leur oo'lu prêt à sonner.

Tamìr refréna son cheval à l'écart, accompagnée par Mahti, Arkoniel et Ki.

« Je connaître ceux-là, dit Mahti. J'aller.

— J'aimerais m'entretenir avec eux. »

Mahti les héla, mais ils conservèrent leurs distances et lui adressèrent des signes de main.

« Non, ils dire ils parlent à moi. » Il s'avança seul.

« C'est fichtrement angoissant, marmonna Ki. J'ai l'impression qu'il y a des tas d'yeux qui nous guettent à notre insu.

— Ils ne nous ont pas agressés, pourtant. »

Mahti les rejoignit quelques instants plus tard. « Ils pas entendre parler de toi. Peur de si nombreux et être en colère que j'être avec vous. Je leur dire tu... » Il marqua une pause puis demanda quelque chose au magicien.

« Ils ne savent que penser d'une armée qui traverse leur territoire sans les attaquer », expliqua celui-ci.

Mahti hocha la tête pendant qu'ils redémarraient. « Je dire eux. Lhel dire, elle aussi. Toi aller, et ils envoyer chanson. »

L'un des sorciers se mit à jouer un vrombissement grave pendant qu'ils le dépassaient.

« Je croirais volontiers que des gens réfugiés si loin dans les montagnes n'ont jamais vu aucun Skalien jusqu'ici », observa Lynx, tout en continuant à surveiller les Retha'noïs d'un œil inquiet.

« Pas voir, mais entendre parler, comme vous entendre parler des Retha'noïs, fit Mahti. Si *keesa* être... » Il s'arrêta net de nouveau, branlant du chef avec dépit, puis il se tourna vers Arkoniel et lui dit quelque chose.

Le magicien se mit à rire. « Si un enfant n'est pas sage, sa mère lui dit : "Sois gentil, sans quoi le peuple pâle viendra te prendre durant la nuit." Je lui ai raconté que les Skaliens tenaient le même discours à leur progéniture à propos des siens.

— Ils voir tu avoir plein de monde, mais tu pas faire mal ou brûler. Ils se rappeler toi.

— Pourraient-ils nous faire du mal s'ils le voulaient ? » demanda Ki, sans cesser lui non plus de lorgner avec méfiance les trois sorciers.

Mahti trancha simplement la question par un hochement de tête catégorique.

Enfin, le sentier les ramena par une pente régulière dans des forêts de chênes et de sapins surmontées de brume. Dans l'après-midi du cinquième jour, ils émergèrent des nuages qui plafonnaient presque au ras du sol, et leurs regards plongèrent sur un immense versant boisé et des prairies vallonnées. Dans le lointain, Tamìr discerna la sombre courbe de la mer d'Osiat.

« Nous avons réussi ! cria Nikidès.

— Où se trouve Remoni ? » demanda Tamìr.

Mahti pointa le doigt droit devant, et elle sentit son cœur battre un peu plus vite. Une journée de marche tout au plus, et elle verrait sa fameuse baie. Dans ses rêves, elle et Ki s'étaient tenus juste au-dessus, côte à côte et à un souffle d'un baiser. Cela faisait quelque temps maintenant qu'elle n'avait pas fait ce rêve, pas depuis Afra.

Et nous nous sommes embrassés, songea-t-elle avec un sourire intérieur, malgré le fait que le loisir leur avait manqué pour de telles choses depuis bien des jours. Elle se demanda si le rêve serait différent, maintenant.

« Tu avoir bonne pensée ? »

Planté près de son cheval, Mahti lui adressait un large sourire.

« Oui, admit-elle.

— Regarder là. » Il indiqua derrière la voie qu'ils avaient empruntée pour venir, et Tamìr tressaillit en voyant que le front de la crête était bordé de silhouettes sombres, des centaines peut-être, qui regardaient défiler l'interminable ligne de fantassins.

« Ton peuple en sécurité, si tu n'essaies pas passer de nouveau par là, expliqua-t-il. Tu faire ta bataille et aller à ton propre pays par un autre sentier. Sentier du sud.

— Je comprends. Mais tu nous quittes déjà ? Je ne sais pas comment trouver Remoni.

— Je te mener, puis aller chez moi.

— Je n'en demande pas davantage. »

La vue de la ligne de côtes lointaine avait aussi fait bondir le cœur d'Arkoniel. Si les visions étaient véridiques – et si la campagne en cours s'achevait par une victoire –, il atteindrait bientôt les lieux où son existence devait se terminer. Quitte à lui faire une impression bizarre, cette perspective n'en était pas moins exaltante.

Une fois au-delà des limites étriquées du sentier de montagne, la marche devint plus facile. Le chemin était dûment battu et suffisamment large à certains endroits pour deux chevaux de front.

Malgré les allées et venues intermittentes de la pluie, le bois à brûler ne manqua pas cette nuit-là, ce qui permit aux Skaliens de bénéficier d'un confort bien supérieur à celui des jours précédents. Pendant que les autres allumaient un feu et préparaient le repas du soir, Arkoniel entraîna Tamìr à l'écart sous un chêne. Ki les suivit et s'assit près d'elle.

Le magicien s'efforça de ne pas sourire. Les deux jeunes gens tâchaient comme d'un accord tacite de n'en rien laisser transparaître, mais leurs relations s'étaient quelque peu modifiées depuis la nuit du fort. Ils ne se regardaient plus l'un l'autre d'un air purement amical, et ils se figuraient que personne d'autre ne pouvait s'en apercevoir.

« Arkoniel, vous avez retrouvé Korin ? demanda-t-elle.

— C'est ce que je m'apprête à vérifier. Consentez-vous à me laisser pratiquer sur vous deux l'œil du magicien ?

« — Oui », répondit Ki, manifestement désireux de tenter l'expérience.

Tamìr se montra moins enthousiaste, comme toujours. Arkoniel n'avait jamais cessé de déplorer de l'avoir effrayée par sa balourdise, la première fois où il s'était avisé de l'associer à l'utilisation de ce sortilège. Elle finit néanmoins par lui adresser un hochement succinct.

Arkoniel trama le charme et concentra son esprit sur les trajets probables. « Ah ! Voilà. » Il leur tendit une main à chacun.

Tamìr saisit celle qu'il lui destinait, crispée d'avance par la prévision de l'inévitable accès de vertige qui la prenait invariablement chaque fois qu'il cherchait à lui montrer quelque chose de cette manière. Ce ne fut pas différent cette fois. Elle ferma violemment les yeux lorsqu'elle sentit le charme engloutir tout son être.

Elle dominait de très haut une immense étendue de campagne vallonnée, et elle distingua une armée campée sur le bord d'une vaste baie. Une multitude de feux de veille ponctuait la plaine plongée dans le noir. « Tant de monde ! chuchota-t-elle. Et regardez tous ces chevaux ! Des milliers. Pouvez-vous me dire à quelle distance il se trouve de nous ?

— Selon toute apparence, la baie doit être celle des Baleines. Peut-être à deux jours de marche de notre propre destination ? Peut-être moins.

— Il lui aurait été possible d'être déjà à Atyion. Croyez-vous qu'il ait eu vent de mes mouvements ?

— Oui, je dirais. Laissons ça un moment. Je vais élargir la recherche. »

Tamìr rouvrit les yeux et découvrit que Ki lui souriait d'un air épanoui.

« C'était fantastique ! » chuchota-t-il, l'œil étincelant.

« Ça rend des services », admit-elle.

Arkoniel se frotta les paupières. « Ce sortilège exige pas mal d'efforts. »

« Korin aura dépêché des éclaireurs à notre recherche, dit Ki. Vous avez repéré le moindre indice de leur présence ? »

Le magicien lui décocha un regard pince-sans-rire. « Rien qu'une armée.

— Nous n'avons pas besoin de magie pour nous renseigner à cet égard-là, dit Tamìr. Nous ferions mieux de poursuivre notre route à vive allure, avant qu'il ne se décide à venir me trouver lui-même. »

Loin de là, à l'est, Tharin, du haut de sa selle, comptait les bannières de la force déployée dans la plaine devant lui. Il était à la tête de deux mille hommes, mais Nevus en avait au moins deux fois plus. Il les avait surpris à moins d'une journée de chevauchée d'Atyion, deux jours plus tôt, et il n'avait pas été étonné de voir Nevus refuser toute espèce d'accommodement visant à éviter la bataille.

Tirant son épée, Tharin la brandit en l'air, et il entendit un millier de lames lui répondre en chantant au sortir du fourreau, ainsi que le ferraillement de centaines de carquois. De l'autre côté du champ, Nevus fit de même.

« Je verrai ton corps pendu près de celui de ton père », murmura Tharin, en notant sa position. Se haussant sur ses étriers, il vociféra : « Pour Tamìr et Skala ! »

Ses soldats répercutèrent le cri, et leurs clameurs déferlèrent à travers la plaine en la submergeant comme un raz-de-marée pendant qu'ils chargeaient sus à l'ennemi.

Tamìr passa la journée du lendemain à remonter le long de la ligne avec quelques-uns de ses Compagnons pour faire le point sur ses guerriers. Certains étaient tombés malades pendant les nuits froides et humides, et quelques-uns avaient péri sous des éboulements au cours de la traversée des cols supérieurs. Il y avait eu un certain nombre de règlements de comptes sanglants, et une poignée d'hommes avaient tout bonnement disparu. D'aucuns murmuraient qu'ils avaient été capturés par le peuple des collines, mais leur désertion était beaucoup plus probable, ainsi que des accidents. Il n'y avait plus une goutte de vin dans les gourdes, et les rations s'amenuisaient.

Tamìr s'arrêtait fréquemment pour bavarder avec les capitaines et les simples soldats, attentive à leurs doléances, et leur promettait des dépouilles sur le champ de bataille, tout en vantant leur endurance. Leur loyauté et leur détermination à remettre les choses d'aplomb lui réchauffaient le cœur. Certains faisaient un peu trop de zèle en lui offrant de lui apporter la tête de Korin au bout d'une pique.

« Amenez-le-moi vivant, et je paierai sa rançon en

or, leur dit-elle. Versez délibérément le sang de mon parent, et vous n'obtiendrez aucune récompense de moi.

— Je gage que Korin n'est pas en train de faire ce genre de distinguo », fit observer Ki.

À quoi Tamìr répliqua d'un ton las : « Je ne suis pas Korin. »

L'atmosphère se réchauffa au fur et à mesure que l'on s'éloignait des montagnes. Il y avait du gibier à foison, et l'on expédia des archers pallier la diminution des réserves de vivres avec de la venaison, des lièvres et des grouses. Les escouades d'éclaireurs ne découvrirent pour leur part aucune trace d'habitations.

On atteignit la côte à la fin l'après-midi, et Tamìr savoura la vivifiante salinité de l'air après tant de jours passés à l'intérieur des terres. La ligne de côtes rocheuse était profondément entaillée de baies aux parois abruptes et de criques. Constellée d'îles éparpillées, la sombre Osiat se déployait de toutes parts jusqu'à l'horizon brumeux.

Mahti vira vers le nord. Des prairies ouvertes entre la mer et la forêt qui les bordait à l'est s'étendaient sans fin devant eux. Des daims y paissaient, et l'approche des chevaux faisait subitement détaler des lapins de l'herbe où ils étaient tapis.

Le terrain s'élevait progressivement, et ils finirent par se trouver bien au-dessus des flots sur un promontoire herbeux. Parvenue au sommet d'une crête, Tamìr eut le souffle coupé en reconnaissant les lieux avant même que Mahti ne tende le doigt vers le bas et n'annonce : « Remoni.

— Oui ! » Sous ses yeux s'étalait bel et bien la longue et profonde rade abritée par les deux îles sur lesquelles il était impossible de se méprendre.

Elle mit pied à terre pour se rendre au bord de la falaise. L'eau se trouvait à des centaines de pieds en contrebas. Dans ses rêves, elle y avait vu son reflet, mais ce n'avait été qu'une illusion. En réalité, il y avait au pied des falaises une assez vaste superficie de terrain plat, tout à fait idéale pour héberger une ville portuaire et des jetées. L'astuce consisterait à établir une voie d'accès praticable jusqu'à la citadelle établie sur les hauts.

Ki la rejoignit. « Tu as réellement rêvé ceci ?

— Tant et tant de fois que j'en ai perdu le compte répondit-elle. N'eût été la multitude d'yeux posés sur eux, elle l'aurait embrassé, rien que pour s'assurer qu'il n'allait pas disparaître, et elle, se réveiller.

« Bienvenue dans votre nouvelle ville, Majesté, dit Arkoniel. Mais elle exige quelques travaux. Je n'ai vu de taverne convenable nulle part. »

Lynx ne bougeait ni pied ni patte, la main en visière pour abriter ses yeux de la lumière oblique, pendant qu'elle contemplait son havre. « Hum... Tamìr ? Où sont donc les navires 'faïes ? »

Toute à son exaltation d'avoir découvert son fameux endroit, elle avait négligé ce détail capital. La rade était déserte, en bas.

Ils dressèrent leur camp sur place, après avoir disposé des piquets de sentinelles au nord et à l'est. Comme Mahti l'avait garanti, il y avait là quantité de sources excellentes et largement assez de bois pour un bon bout de temps.

Il fallut plusieurs heures pour que l'intégralité de la colonne ait achevé de les rattraper, sauf quelques traînards qui continuèrent encore d'affluer des heures durant.

« Mes gens sont épuisés, Majesté », rapporta Kyman.

Lorsqu'ils arrivèrent à leur tour, Jorvaï et Nyanis rapportèrent la même chose.

« Dites-leur qu'ils ont bien gagné le droit de se reposer », répondit Tamìr.

Après avoir chichement soupé de pain rassis, de fromage coriace et d'une poignée de baies ratatinées reçues du peuple des collines, elle alla baguenauder avec Ki parmi les feux de camp, l'oreille attentive aux fanfaronnades des soldats sur les batailles à venir. Ceux qui avaient de la viande fraîche la partagèrent avec eux, et en retour elle leur demanda comment ils s'appelaient et d'où ils venaient. Leur humeur était au beau fixe et, la rumeur de sa vision de Remoni ayant fait le tour des troupes pendant la marche, ils considéraient comme un heureux présage qu'un tel endroit existât réellement et que leur reine les y eût conduits.

La lune décroissante brillait haut dans le ciel chargé de nuages tourmentés quand ils regagnèrent la tente de Tamìr. Devant eux flamboyait un feu magnifique, autour duquel étaient assis ses amis. Encore dissimulée dans le noir, elle s'arrêta pour bien enregistrer dans sa mémoire une fois de plus leurs visages souriants, rieurs. Elle avait pu évaluer la dimension des forces de Korin ; d'ici peu de jours, ils risquaient de n'avoir plus guère lieu de rire ni de sourire.

« Allons, viens », murmura Ki, tout en lui glissant un bras autour des épaules. « M'est avis que Nik pourrait bien avoir encore un reste de vin. »

C'était le cas, et la chaleur qu'il diffusa en elle lui remonta le moral. Ils pouvaient bien avoir faim, mal aux pieds, les vêtements trempés... n'empêche, ils étaient ici.

Elle était sur le point de rentrer dormir sous sa tente quand elle entendit retentir quelque part dans les parages le vrombissement bas et lancinant du cor de Mahti.

« Qu'est-ce qu'il fabrique maintenant ? » s'étonna Lutha à voix haute.

S'orientant sur le son, ils découvrirent le sorcier assis sur un rocher qui dominait la mer, les yeux clos tandis qu'il faisait résonner son étrange musique. Tamìr s'approcha en silence. La mélodie foisonnait d'aigus et de graves singuliers, de croassements et de vibrations qui lui évoquèrent des cris d'animaux, le tout enfilé pêle-mêle sur un courant sans fin de souffle continu. Elle se mariait aux appels des oiseaux nocturnes, au glapissement lointain d'un renard et aux voix de l'armée, à ses chansons, ses rires et, de temps à autre, à un coup de gueule, un juron rageur, mais Tamìr n'y percevait pas de magie. Se détendant pour la première fois depuis des jours et des jours, elle appuya son épaule contre celle de Ki et contempla la mer baignée par le clair de lune. Elle avait presque l'impression d'y flotter elle-même, dansant sur les vagues comme une feuille. Elle était presque assoupie quand s'interrompit le chant.

« Qu'est-ce que c'était ? » demanda Ki tout bas.

Mahti se leva. « Chanson d'adieu. Je vous amener à Remoni. Je rentrer chez moi maintenant. » Il fit une pause, les yeux attachés sur Tamìr. « Je faire guérison pour toi, avant de partir.

— Je te l'ai déjà dit, je n'ai nullement besoin de guérison. Mais je souhaiterais que tu restes avec nous. Nous aurons bientôt besoin de tes connaissances.

— Je pas faire pour combat comme toi. » Ses sombres prunelles la dévisagèrent pensivement. « Je rêver de nouveau de Lhel. Elle dire pas oublier ton *noro'shesh*. »

Tamìr savait que ce terme désignait Frère. « Je ne l'oublierai pas. Elle non plus, je ne l'oublierai jamais. Dis-le-lui.

— Elle savoir. » Il ramassa son modeste paquetage et les raccompagna jusqu'au feu de camp pour faire ses adieux à Arkoniel et aux autres.

Lutha et Barieüs lui serrèrent la main.

« Nous te devons la vie, dit Lutha. J'espère que nous nous reverrons.

— Vous être bons guides. Amener moi à la fille qui était garçon, juste comme je dire. Amener elle à mon peuple. Vous être amis des Retha'noïs. » Il se tourna vers Arkoniel et lui parla dans sa propre langue. Le magicien s'inclina puis lui répondit quelque chose.

Mahti chargea son cor sur son épaule et puis renifla la brise. « Encore pluie venir. » Lorsqu'il s'éloigna, ses pas ne firent aucun bruit sur l'herbe sèche, et les intervalles de ténèbres entre les feux de camp ne tardèrent pas à l'engloutir comme s'il n'avait jamais été là du tout.

22

Korin rêvait de Tobin presque chaque nuit, et ses rêves étaient plus ou moins identiques. Il lui arrivait d'être en train de déambuler soit dans la grande salle de Cirna, soit dans les jardins du palais d'Ero, lorsqu'il remarquait devant lui une silhouette familière. Chaque fois, Tobin se retournait pour lui adresser un sourire grinçant puis prenait la fuite. Fou de rage, Korin tirait son épée et se précipitait à sa poursuite, mais il n'arrivait jamais à le rattraper. Parfois, le rêve semblait se prolonger durant des heures, et il se réveillait en nage et les nerfs à vif, le poing serré autour d'une poignée imaginaire.

Or, cette fois, le rêve fut totalement différent. Il chevauchait au bord d'une haute falaise, et Tobin l'attendait au loin. Mais celui-ci ne détalait pas lorsqu'il éperonnait sa monture pour la lancer au galop, il demeurait juste planté là, rieur.

Se riant de lui.

« Korin ? »

Korin se réveilla en sursaut et découvrit Urmanis penché au-dessus de lui. Il faisait encore noir. Le feu de veille du dehors projetait de longues ombres sur les parois de sa tente. « Qu'y a-t-il ? » marmonna-t-il d'une voix râpeuse.

« L'une de nos escouades d'éclaireurs du sud a fini par retrouver Tobin. »

Korin le fixa pendant un moment, se demandant s'il était encore en train de rêver.

« Tu es réveillé, Kor ? Je t'annonçais que nous venions de retrouver Tobin ! Il est à peu près à une journée de marche plus au sud.

— Sur la côte ? murmura Korin.

— Oui. » Son interlocuteur le regarda d'un air bizarre en lui tendant une coupe de vin coupé d'eau.

C'était une vision, songea-t-il en avalant sa boisson du matin. Il rejeta les couvertures et rafla ses bottes.

« Il est passé par les montagnes, exactement comme on nous en avait avertis, poursuivit Urmanis en lui tendant une tunique. S'il tente de marcher sur Cirna, nous n'aurons aucun mal à l'intercepter ici. »

En jetant un coup d'œil par la portière ouverte, Korin s'aperçut que l'aube était près de poindre. Porion et les Compagnons étaient plantés là, dans l'expectative.

Il les rejoignit. « Nous n'allons pas rester sur nos culs à l'attendre un instant de plus. Garol, fais sonner la levée du camp. Et qu'on se prépare à marcher. »

L'écuyer prit ses jambes à son cou.

« Moriel, convoque mes nobles.

305

— Tout de suite, Sire ! » Le Crapaud s'empressa de filer.

Après avoir sifflé sa dernière gorgée de vin clairet, Korin rendit la coupe à Urmanis. « Où sont les éclaireurs qui lui ont mis la main dessus ?

— Ici, Sire. » Porion lui présenta un individu blond et barbu : « Le capitaine Esmen, Sire, qui appartient à la maisonnée du duc Wethring. »

L'homme salua Korin. « Mes cavaliers et moi, nous avons localisé sur la côte des forces considérables, hier, juste avant le coucher du soleil. Je m'en suis personnellement approché pour épier les piquets dès la nuit tombée. C'est sans discussion possible le prince Tobin. Ou la reine Tamìr, comme nous l'avons entendu appeler », ajouta-t-il avec un petit sourire en coin.

Une fois que Wethring et les autres grands seigneurs les eurent rejoints, Korin leur fit répéter la nouvelle par l'éclaireur. « Quelle est l'importance des troupes dont il dispose ?

— Je ne saurais l'évaluer avec certitude, Sire, mais je la dirais largement inférieure à la vôtre. Composée pour l'essentiel d'hommes d'armes, et assez peu fournie en cavalerie. Peut-être deux cents chevaux.

— Avez-vous vu des étendards ?

— Uniquement celui du prince Tobin, Sire, mais les hommes que j'ai entendus bavarder mentionnaient Lord Jorvaï. Je les ai aussi entendus se plaindre d'être affamés. Je n'ai pas vu la moindre trace d'un train de bagages.

— Cela expliquerait comment il a pu franchir si rapidement les montagnes, commenta Porion. Mais c'était folie de sa part que de venir avec des moyens aussi limités.

— Nous sommes quant à nous bien approvisionnés et reposés, musa Korin. Nous allons pousser notre avantage. Rassemblez ma cavalerie et donnez le signal en vue d'une progression des plus rapide. »

Le capitaine Esmen s'inclina de nouveau. « Daignez me pardonner, Sire, mais j'ai encore autre chose à dire. Il a été fait également mention de la présence de magiciens.

— Je vois. Rien de plus ?

— Non, Sire, mais certains de mes hommes sont restés en arrière sur mon ordre afin de venir annoncer s'il démarre en direction du nord.

— Bien joué. Lord Alben, veillez à ce que cet homme soit récompensé.

— Est-ce que vous ferez devancer vos troupes par un héraut, roi Korin ? » interrogea Wethring.

Korin lui répondit avec un sourire sinistre : « La vue de mon étendard sera l'unique avertissement que mon cousin recevra de moi. »

Mahti ne s'était pas trompé quant au temps. Une pluie chargée de brume arriva par la mer au cours de la nuit, mouillant les feux de veille et trempant jusqu'aux os les soldats déjà éreintés. Quoiqu'il fît de son mieux pour le cacher, Barieüs n'avait pas arrêté de tousser de toute la soirée.

« Dors sous ma tente cette nuit, lui dit Tamìr. C'est un ordre. J'ai besoin que tu sois en forme demain.

« — Merci », répondit-il d'une voix rauque, tout en étouffant une nouvelle quinte derrière sa main.

Lutha le regarda d'un air inquiet. « Prends mes couvertures. Je n'en aurai pas besoin pour monter la garde.

— Tu devrais te reposer autant que tu le pourras, conseilla Ki à Tamìr.

— Je le ferai. Mais pas tout de suite. Il me faut parler avec Arkoniel.

— Je sais où il est. »

Il embrasa une torche et la reconduisit vers les falaises. Arkoniel s'y trouvait en compagnie de Saruel, agenouillé auprès de son maigre feu personnel. À force de tramer des charmes de recherche, ils avaient tous deux les orbites creuses, et pendant qu'elle se rapprochait, Tamìr s'aperçut que le magicien toussait par accès déchirants dans sa manche.

— Vous êtes malade, vous aussi ? s'alarma-t-elle.

— Non, c'est simplement l'humidité, répliqua-t-il, mais elle soupçonna qu'il mentait.

— Un quelconque indice de la présence des 'faïes jusqu'ici ? demanda Ki.

— Je crains que non.

— C'est le début de la saison des tempêtes sur cette mer, fit Saruel. Ils pourraient avoir été déroutés par le vent.

— Et en ce qui concerne Tharin ? »

Arkoniel soupira en branlant du chef. « Atyion n'est pas assiégé. Voilà tout ce que je puis vous dire. Lyan n'a pas envoyé de message.. »

N'ayant plus rien d'autre à faire que d'attendre

dorénavant, Tamìr laissa Ki la reconduire à sa tente et s'efforça de prendre quelques heures de repos. Ses vêtements humides et la toux intermittente de Barieüs l'empêchèrent de dormir comme une souche. Après avoir somnolé par à-coups, elle se leva avant le point du jour et découvrit le monde enveloppé dans la purée de pois. La pluie tombait toujours, froide et persistante. Lorin et Tyrien montaient la garde à l'extérieur, recroquevillés sous leurs manteaux lorsqu'ils mettaient du bois pour alimenter le feu qui fumait d'abondance.

Elle s'éloigna pour soulager sa vessie. Le simple fait de n'avoir qu'à dénouer les aiguillettes de ses culottes continuait à lui manquer. En tout état de cause, au moins le brouillard la dispensait-il de devoir aller au diable pour pisser.

Le monde qui l'environnait n'était que grisaille et noirceur. Elle arrivait à discerner le bord de la falaise et les sombres silhouettes des hommes et des chevaux, mais ce de manière aussi indistincte que le paysage d'un rêve. Elle entendait des grommellements, des papotages et des crises de toux dans les parages des feux autour desquels remuaient des ombres. Trois formes emmitouflées se dressaient sur le bord de la falaise.

« Faites attention où vous posez les pieds », la prévint l'une d'elles pendant qu'elle allait les rejoindre.

Perdus dans quelque sortilège, Arkoniel et Lord Malkanus avaient tous deux les yeux fermés. Kaulin se trouvait avec eux, les tenant chacun par un coude.

« Il a passé toute la nuit à la tâche ? » s'enquit-elle à voix basse.

Kaulin répliqua par un signe de tête affirmatif.

« Repéré quoi que ce soit ? » Elle devinait déjà la réponse.

Lord Malkanus rouvrit les yeux. « Je regrette, Majesté, mais je n'ai toujours pas vu la moindre trace de bateaux. Mais le brouillard est très dense, et l'immensité de la mer ne nous facilite pas les choses.

— Cela ne signifie pas qu'ils ne se trouvent pas au large quelque part ici ou là, soupira Arkoniel en rouvrant les yeux à son tour. Non que cela importe actuellement. Korin est en train de lever le camp. J'ai recouru au charme de fenêtre tout à l'heure. Je n'ai toujours pas réussi à le focaliser sur Korin, mais je suis quand même arrivé à découvrir ses généraux. Il était question dans leur conférence de faire mouvement vers le sud. Je le soupçonne de savoir que vous vous trouvez à proximité, vu sa décision de se mettre en marche aussi subitement. »

Tamìr se frictionna le visage avec une main qu'elle enfouit ensuite dans ses cheveux sales pour les rebrousser, tout en essayant d'ignorer les gargouillements de son estomac. « Dans ce cas, nous n'avons pas beaucoup de temps. »

Elle retourna à sa tente, où l'attendaient ses maréchaux et les autres. Ki lui tendit une grouse rôtie, toute brûlante encore sur la brochette qui avait servi à la faire cuire. « Un cadeau de l'un des hommes de Colath. »

Tamìr détacha du bréchet un morceau de blanc puis la lui rendit. « Partagez-vous le reste à la ronde. Messires, Korin est en chemin, et il n'est qu'à une journée plus ou moins de distance. Mon avis est de choisir le terrain et de nous tenir prêts à l'accueillir à son arrivée ici plutôt que de nous porter à sa rencontre. Nyanis, Arkoniel et les Compagnons chevaucheront avec moi. Au restant d'entre vous d'alerter vos compagnies respectives et de faire passer le mot. Et avertissez-les de rester à l'écart des falaises jusqu'à ce que se lève ce foutu brouillard ! On ne peut se permettre le moindre accident. »

La pluie se réduisit lentement à une espèce de bruine tandis qu'ils chevauchaient vers le nord, et le vent qui se mit à souffler déchiqueta des lambeaux de brouillard autour d'eux.

« Le nombre joue en faveur de Korin, ainsi que la puissante cavalerie dont il bénéficie. Il nous faut trouver un moyen pour amenuiser son avantage », songea Tamìr à voix haute, tout en examinant la campagne qu'ils traversaient.

« Vos archers constituent votre puissance de frappe la plus importante, fit observer Nyanis.

— Et si maître Arkoniel tramait un charme de fenêtre au travers duquel vous tireriez sur Korin, comme vous l'avez fait avec les Plenimariens ? » suggéra Hylia.

Tamìr fronça les sourcils à l'adresse de la jeune fille écuyer. « Ce serait déshonorant. Lui et moi sommes parents et guerriers, et c'est en tant que guerriers que nous nous affronterons sur le champ de bataille.

— Pardonnez-moi, Majesté, répondit Hylia. J'ai parlé sans réfléchir. »

Au-delà de leur camp, le terrain s'abaissait, et la forêt se reployait vers les falaises, non sans ménager un espace découvert de moins d'un demi-mille de large entre sa lisière et la mer. Plus loin, le terrain se redressait en pente raide au-delà d'un petit ruisseau.

Tamìr démonta là pour laisser son cheval s'abreuver. La terre cédait mollement sous ses bottes. Elle franchit le ruisseau d'un bond et parcourut la rive opposée en tapant du pied. « C'est marécageux de ce côté-ci. Si la cavalerie de Korin dévale au galop, elle risque fort d'y trouver piètre appui. »

Après avoir retraversé, elle se remit en selle puis gravit au galop la colline avec Nyanis et Ki pour scruter du sommet le panorama. Au-delà de la crête, le sol était ferme et sec pour autant que la portée de son regard lui permettait d'en juger. La forêt n'était plus aussi proche de ce côté-là et, à partir de cette direction, l'espace ne cessait de se rétrécir au fur et à mesure que l'on s'enfonçait plus avant sur l'autre versant.

« S'il charge d'ici, ce sera comme des pois dans un entonnoir, fit Tamìr. Une large ligne de front finirait fatalement par se contracter et par s'entasser sur elle-même, à moins que Korin ne resserre ses rangs.

— Si vous marchiez depuis le nord, ces lieux sembleraient excellents pour prendre position, dit Nyanis. Vous auriez les hauteurs.

— C'est ce qu'il y a de mieux pour la défense, toutefois. Or, il nous faut les amener à fondre sur nous.

— Korin tiendra une charge d'infanterie pour nulle et non avenue, dit Ki. Il y a fort à parier qu'il réussirait à rompre nos lignes, au demeurant, s'il dispose d'autant de monde que vous l'affirmez, Arkoniel.

— C'est précisément ce qu'il va penser », déclara Tamìr, qui voyait déjà les choses dans son esprit. « Ce qu'il nous faut, c'est un héraut et un hérisson. »

23

Après avoir coupé plein ouest jusqu'à la côte de l'Osiat, Korin se tourna ensuite vers le sud avec sa cavalerie, laissant à l'infanterie l'ordre de rattraper rapidement son retard sur eux.

Sans jamais perdre la mer de vue, il chevaucha dur toute la journée, traversant des herbages découverts et contournant la forêt profonde.

« Campagne d'aspect opulent », remarqua Porion lorsqu'ils firent halte pour abreuver leurs montures au gué d'une rivière.

Mais Korin n'avait pas plus d'yeux pour les basses terres que pour les boqueteaux d'arbres. Son regard ne cessait de fixer les lointains, où il voyait déjà mentalement l'apparition de son cousin. Après tous ces mois d'incertitude et d'atermoiements, c'était tout juste s'il arrivait à croire qu'il allait finalement affronter Tobin et décider du sort de Skala une fois pour toutes.

Il fallut attendre le milieu de l'après-midi avant que ne surgisse un éclaireur apportant des nouvelles de l'armée de Tobin.

« Ils se sont avancés de quelques milles vers le nord, Sire, et ils semblent s'attendre à votre arrivée, l'informa le cavalier.

— Ce sera l'ouvrage de ses magiciens », dit Alben.

Korin opina sombrement du chef. Comment se faisait-il que Nyrin et sa clique ne lui aient jamais été d'une telle utilité ?

Ils étaient sur le point de se remettre en route quand il entendit un cavalier survenir de l'arrière à un galop impitoyable. L'homme le salua tout en immobilisant sa monture.

« Sire, on a capturé deux cavaliers à la queue de la colonne. L'un d'entre eux prétend être votre ami, Lord Caliel.

— Caliel ! » Pendant un moment, Korin eut du mal à retrouver sa respiration. Caliel, ici ? Il vit sa propre stupéfaction reflétée sur les visages des Compagnons restants, Moriel mis à part, qui paraissait décontenancé.

« Il réclame de votre indulgence que vous le voyiez, lui et l'homme qu'il vous a amené, reprit le messager.

— Amenez-les-moi tout de suite ! » ordonna Korin, tout en se demandant ce qui avait bien pu inciter Caliel à revenir. Il se mit à déambuler sans trêve ni cesse pendant qu'il attendait, les poings bloqués derrière son dos, sous le regard d'Alben et des autres qui demeuraient cois. S'agissait-il d'une ruse de Tobin, lui renvoyant ce traître pour l'espionner ? Que pouvait espérer gagner Caliel en intervenant si tard dans la partie ? Korin n'arrivait pas à imaginer pour quel autre motif il aurait risqué sa tête en refaisant surface. Pour se venger, peut-être ? Mais c'était tout bonnement suicidaire, étant donné les circonstances.

Sur ces entrefaites apparut une escorte armée au milieu de laquelle Korin distingua Caliel à cheval, les mains attachées devant lui. Quelqu'un d'autre chevauchait à ses côtés. Comme l'intervalle s'amenuisait, Korin ne put réprimer un hoquet de stupeur, tandis que son cœur chavirait dans sa poitrine. « Tanil ? »

L'escorte s'immobilisa, et quatre hommes arrachèrent les prisonniers de leur selle et les propulsèrent vers l'endroit où se tenaient en observation Korin et les autres. Caliel soutint son regard sans ciller puis planta un genou en terre devant lui.

Tanil était blême et maigre. Il avait l'air terriblement hébété, mais il s'épanouit en un beau sourire lorsqu'il aperçut Korin et tenta de s'avancer vers lui, mais on le retint de force.

« Je vous ai retrouvé, messire ! cria-t-il en se débattant faiblement. Prince Korin, c'est moi ! Pardonnez-moi... Je me suis perdu, mais Cal m'a ramené !

— Relâchez-le ! » ordonna Korin. Tanil se précipita vers lui et tomba sur ses genoux, tout en se cramponnant à la botte de Korin avec ses mains liées. Korin dénoua la corde et entoura gauchement de ses bras les épaules tremblantes de l'adolescent. Tanil riait et sanglotait en même temps, tout en balbutiant des flopées d'excuses cent fois répétées.

En se portant au-delà de lui, le regard de Korin découvrit Caliel qui les considérait avec un sourire navré. Il était crasseux et blême, lui aussi, et il semblait sur le point de s'évanouir, mais il *souriait* tout de même.

« Que faites-vous ici ? » questionna Korin, pas encore tout à fait maître de sa voix.

« Je l'ai trouvé à Atyion. Comme il n'aurait pas connu de repos avant d'être retourné auprès de vous, je l'ai emmené. »

Korin se libéra de l'étreinte de Tanil et marcha droit sur Caliel, tout en tirant son épée pendant qu'il s'avançait.

« Est-ce Tobin qui vous a envoyés ?

— Non, mais elle s'est fait honneur de nous laisser partir, même en sachant que c'était pour retourner vers vous. »

Korin pointa la lame sous le menton de Caliel. « Vous ne me parlerez pas de lui de cette façon-là, compris ?

— Si tel est votre souhait, messire. »

Korin abaissa la lame de quelques pouces. « Pourquoi es-tu revenu, Cal ? Tu te trouves encore sous le coup d'une condamnation à mort.

— Alors, tue-moi. J'ai accompli la tâche que je m'étais assignée en venant. Seulement..., de grâce, montre-toi gentil envers Tanil. Il a suffisamment souffert, pour l'amour de toi. » Sa voix était rauque et creuse quand il eut fini, et il tanguait sur son genou. Korin resongea à la flagellation qu'il avait subie et se demanda par quel miracle il avait seulement réussi à y survivre. Il ne s'en était guère soucié, à l'époque. À présent, il éprouvait les premiers tiraillements de la honte.

316

« Détachez-le, commanda-t-il.

— Mais, Sire...

— J'ai dit de le détacher ! aboya Korin. Apportez-leur de la nourriture et du vin, ainsi que des vêtements convenables. »

Une fois délié, Caliel se frictionna les poignets, mais il demeura agenouillé. « Je n'escompte absolument rien, Korin. Je voulais juste ramener Tanil.

— Tout en sachant que je te ferais pendre ? »

Caliel haussa les épaules.

« À qui va ton allégeance, Cal ?

— Tu doutes encore de moi ?

— Où sont les autres ?

— Ils sont restés à Atyion.

— Mais pas toi ? »

Caliel le fixa de nouveau droit dans les yeux. « Comment le pourrais-je ? »

Korin demeura immobile un moment, aux prises avec son propre cœur. Les accusations portées par Nyrin contre Caliel lui semblaient si creuses maintenant. Comment avait-il pu croire son ami coupable de telles infamies ?

« M'engages-tu solennellement ta foi ? Me suivras-tu, accepteras-tu de seconder mon entreprise ?

— Je l'ai toujours fait, Sire. Je le ferai toujours. »

Comment peux-tu me pardonner ? se demanda Korin, abasourdi. Il tendit la main pour attirer Caliel sur ses pieds, puis le maintint à bras-le-corps en constatant que ses genoux flageolaient sous lui. Il le sentit maigre et frêle sous sa tunique et l'entendit exhaler un gémissement étouffé quand ses mains se refermèrent sur son dos. Les touffes trahissant l'emplacement des nattes tranchées de Caliel le narguaient comme une dérision.

« Je suis désolé, lui chuchota-t-il de manière à n'être entendu que de lui. Terriblement désolé.

— Garde-t'en bien ! » Les mains de Caliel se resserrèrent sur les épaules de Korin. « Pardonne-moi de t'avoir fourni l'occasion de douter de moi.

— C'est oublié. » Puis, à l'assistance sous les yeux de laquelle il se donnait personnellement en spectacle, il déclara d'un ton bourru : « Lord Caliel s'est racheté lui-même. Lui et Tanil font à nouveau partie des Compagnons. Alben, Urmanis, prenez soin de vos frères. Assurez leur confort et trouvez-leur des armes. »

Les autres aidèrent délicatement Caliel à s'asseoir au bord de la rivière. Tanil demeura aux côtés de Korin, mais son attention n'arrêtait pas de s'égarer en direction de son sauveur. Moriel papillonnait à leurs côtés, mais Korin surprit le regard ouvertement haineux dont Caliel foudroya le Crapaud et celui qu'il en obtint en retour. « Moriel ! jappa-t-il. Va donc t'occuper des chevaux, toi. »

24

Entre-temps, Tamìr avait infatigablement attelé tout son monde à la tâche des préparatifs en vue de l'arrivée de Korin, et Ki ne la lâchait pas d'une semelle. Le brouillard acheva de se dissiper vers midi, mais sans que les nuages cessent de planer bas, et la pluie soufflant de la mer s'acharna toute la journée, maintenant l'humidité des vêtements, faisant fumer les feux quand elle ne les éteignait pas. Les archers contrôlaient leurs arcs, retendaient les cordes un peu lâches et les enduisaient consciencieusement de cire.

La totalité des troupes se déplaça vers le nord pour se masser sur la bordure du terrain découvert qu'avait choisi Tamìr. Ki et plusieurs des meilleurs archers de Nyanis emportèrent leurs arcs sur la crête de la colline afin de décocher des flèches en direction de leur propre côté du champ de bataille, tantôt pour leur faire décrire une parabole en l'air, tantôt pour les tirer droit au but, de manière à en tester la portée. Les autres Compagnons marquaient soigneusement l'endroit où elles touchaient terre, ce qui permettait à Tamìr d'établir la position de ses futures lignes.

« Korin a bénéficié des mêmes leçons que nous, s'inquiéta Ki en la rejoignant. Ne crois-tu pas qu'il se demandera pourquoi tu lui concèdes l'avantage ? »

Elle haussa les épaules. « Nous occuperons nos positions et n'en bougerons pas jusqu'à ce qu'il vienne au-devant de nous. »

Après avoir rassemblé ses commandants près du

ruisseau, elle ramassa un long bâton dont elle se servit pour tracer son plan dans la terre meuble. « Nous devons l'attirer. »

Elle envoya des sapeurs munis de leurs pioches s'activer à creuser des tranchées et des fosses destinées à engloutir les chevaux en train de charger, tandis que d'autres ouvraient tout le long de la berge de petits canaux de dérivation pour permettre à l'eau de se répandre et de rendre la terre encore plus molle. Les archers pénétrèrent dans la forêt pour y tailler des pieux.

Au fur et à mesure que s'écoulait la matinée puis que survenait l'après-midi, Ki remarqua la fréquence avec laquelle Tamìr scrutait le sud, dans l'espoir d'en voir surgir l'un des guetteurs qu'elle avait laissés postés à Remoni. On n'avait toujours pas de nouvelles des 'faïes.

Ils étaient en train de bavarder avec les sapeurs quand quelques-uns des hommes qui se trouvaient derrière eux se mirent à pousser des cris, l'index tendu vers le sommet de la colline. Ki eut à peine le temps d'entrevoir un homme à cheval que l'intrus faisait déjà demi-tour et disparaissait au galop.

« Ce doit être l'un des éclaireurs de Korin, dit Ki.

— Nous lancerons-nous à ses trousses, Majesté ? » demanda Nyanis.

Tamìr se fendit d'un large sourire. « Non, laissez-le filer. Il vient de m'épargner l'ennui d'expédier un messager. Nikidès, va chercher ta plume et fais appeler un héraut. Toi, Lutha, retourne avec Barieüs vers les guetteurs. Et dis à Arkoniel que je veux lui parler.

— Ils se sont sacrément bien comportés »,
murmura Ki en les regardant sauter en selle et partir
au galop. Lutha lui avait laissé voir le matin même les
zébrures de son dos. Elles étaient en assez bonne voie
de guérison, mais certaines des entailles les plus profondes s'étaient rouvertes et avaient saigné durant la
rude et longue traversée des montagnes. L'état de
Barieüs n'était guère plus satisfaisant. Mais tous deux
étaient aussi secs et nerveux qu'opiniâtres, et ils
auraient mieux aimé subir une seconde flagellation que
d'exhaler la moindre plainte.

Tamìr les suivit des yeux, elle aussi. « Korin est un
crétin. »

Le soleil sombrait derrière les nuages quand Korin
s'approcha des lignes de Tamìr. Caliel était encore
faible, mais il avait insisté pour chevaucher à ses côtés.
Malgré les séquelles mentales des sévices que lui
avaient infligés les Plenimariens, Tanil s'était montré
tout aussi têtu.

Après avoir commandé à sa cavalerie de faire halte,
Korin prit les devants avec Wethring et sa garde pour
reconnaître le terrain.

Du haut d'une crête, il distingua l'armée de Tobin
qui campait entre la falaise et la forêt à un mille
environ de là.

« Tant de monde », grommela-t-il tout en s'efforçant
d'évaluer le rapport des forces en présence. C'était difficile, eu égard au déclin de la lumière, à la manière
dont l'adversaire s'était massé en un bloc compact,

mais il ne s'était pas attendu à trouver devant lui des troupes aussi considérables.

« Pas beaucoup de chevaux, toutefois, constata Porion. Si vous occupez les hauteurs, vous avez l'avantage. »

« Tamìr, regardez là-bas », dit Arkoniel en désignant de nouveau la colline.

Même au travers du rideau de pluie, Tamìr reconnut Korin à son assise en selle, ainsi qu'à l'étendard que faisait claquer le vent derrière lui. Elle reconnut aussi Caliel à ses côtés. Sans réfléchir, elle leva la main et l'agita pour les saluer. Elle savait que Korin ne la verrait pas, à pied parmi les autres, mais elle éprouva tout de même un choc quand il fit volter sa monture et disparut derrière le faîte de la colline. Elle ferma les yeux, tandis qu'un tumulte de sentiments contradictoires menaçait de la submerger. Le remords et le chagrin la frappèrent en profondeur tandis qu'affluaient à la surface de sa conscience les souvenirs de toutes les années heureuses qu'ils avaient passées ensemble. Était-il nécessaire d'en arriver là !

Une main chaude s'empara de la sienne, et elle découvrit en rouvrant les paupières Arkoniel qui, tout près, la préservait des regards de l'assistance.

« Remettez-vous, Majesté », chuchota-t-il en lui adressant un sourire compréhensif. Elle sentit aussitôt l'énergie lui revenir, mais sans pouvoir jurer que le phénomène résultait d'une quelconque opération magique de sa part ou de la pure et simple manifestation de son amitié.

« Oui. Merci. » Elle carra ses épaules et fit signe au héraut de venir la trouver. « Mon cousin le prince est arrivé. Va lui délivrer ton message et reviens avec sa réponse. »

Juchés sur leurs montures à la lisière de la forêt, Korin et ses généraux regardaient se déployer leurs cavaliers à travers la plaine tout en prairies qui dominait la mer. Derrière ces derniers, un éclair zébra les nuages en surplomb des flots. Un moment plus tard retentit un lointain roulement de tonnerre.

« Ce n'est pas le genre de temps propice pour se battre, avec la nuit qui tombe, conseilla Porion.

— Vous avez raison. Donnez l'ordre de dresser le camp. »

Du sein de l'opacité croissante surgit un cavalier seul, que son manteau bleu et blanc et le bâton blanc qu'il brandissait désignaient comme héraut. Alben et Moriel se portèrent à sa rencontre et l'escortèrent jusqu'à Korin.

L'homme mit pied à terre et s'inclina bien bas devant celui-ci. « Je suis porteur d'une lettre adressée par la reine Tamìr de Skala à son bien-aimé cousin, Korin d'Ero. »

Korin le toisa d'un air renfrogné. « Qu'a donc à me dire la fausse reine ? »

Le héraut tira une lettre de sous son manteau. « "À mon cousin Korin, de la part de Tamìr, fille d'Ariani, de la véritable lignée de Skala. Cousin, je me tiens prête à livrer bataille contre toi, mais sache que c'est l'ultime offre d'amnistie que je te fais là. Oublie ta colère et dépose les armes. Renonce à tes prétentions au trône, et soyons amis de nouveau. Je te donne ma parole la plus sacrée en jurant par Sakor, Illior et l'ensemble des Quatre que toi, dame ton épouse et l'enfant qu'elle porte serez comme il sied tenus en honneur au sein de ma cour, en qualité de Parents Royaux. Les nobles qui te suivent se verront traités avec clémence et conserveront tout à la fois leurs terres et leurs titres. J'en appelle à toi, cousin, pour renier tes prétentions illégitimes et faire en sorte que la paix règne entre nous." »

Le héraut lui tendit la lettre. Korin la lui arracha des mains et l'abrita de la pluie en la couvrant d'un pan de son manteau. C'était bien là l'écriture de Tobin, ainsi que son sceau. Il jeta un coup d'œil pour consulter Caliel, dans l'espoir de quelque commentaire, mais son ami se borna à se détourner sans proférer le moindre mot.

Korin secoua la tête et laissa choir le parchemin. « Remporte à mon cousin la réponse suivante, héraut. Je le rencontrerai demain au point du jour au bout de mon épée. Tous ceux qui combattent en son nom seront marqués au fer rouge en tant que traîtres et perdront toutes leurs terres, leurs titres et la vie. Il ne sera fait aucun quartier. Dis-lui également que j'arrive sans magiciens. S'il est homme d'honneur, il n'emploiera pas les siens contre moi. Enfin, remercie-le d'avoir permis à Lord Caliel et à mon écuyer de me revenir. Ils combattent à mes côtés. N'omets pas de lui spécifier que ce message lui est adressé par le roi Korin de Skala, fils d'Erius, petit-fils d'Agnalain. »

Le héraut répéta le message et prit congé.

Korin s'enveloppa plus étroitement dans son manteau et se tourna vers Porion... « Transmettez l'ordre de monter les tentes et de servir des repas chauds. Nous nous reposerons au sec, cette nuit. »

Tamìr rassembla ses maréchaux et capitaines devant sa tente pour entendre la réponse de Korin. Après que le héraut eut achevé de la transmettre, tout l'auditoire demeura muet pendant un moment.

« Cal n'est pas physiquement en état de se battre ! s'alarma Lutha. Et Tanil ? Korin rêve ou quoi ?

— Nous n'y pouvons rien », soupira Tamìr, tout aussi consternée par la perspective de les rencontrer sur le champ de bataille. « J'en viens à déplorer de ne pas les avoir retenus captifs à Atyion jusqu'à ce que cette affaire soit définitivement réglée.

— Ce n'aurait été faire une faveur à aucun des deux, répliqua Lynx. Ils sont là où ils désirent être. Le reste dépend de Sakor.

— Le croyez-vous, quand il prétend n'avoir pas de magiciens avec lui ? demanda-t-elle à Arkoniel. Il m'est impossible de me figurer qu'il n'ait pas emmené Nyrin.

— Nous n'avons pas vu trace de celui-ci ni relevé le moindre indice de magie autour de Korin, exception faite des amulettes dont Nyrin l'avait affublé pendant tous ces mois, répondit Arkoniel. Mais, une minute ! Vous ne comptez sûrement pas vous incliner devant ses conditions ?

— Bien sûr que si.

— Tamìr, non ! Vous avez déjà le désavantage du nombre...

— De quoi seriez-vous réellement capables ? demanda-t-elle en jetant un regard circulaire sur les magiciens. Je n'ai pas oublié ce que vous avez fait pour moi aux portes d'Ero, mais vous m'avez confié vous-mêmes qu'une seule attaque d'envergure exigeait la combinaison de toutes vos énergies réunies. Et j'ai vu moi-même à quel point cela vous mettait à bout de forces.

— Mais une attaque focalisée, comme celle que nous avons effectuée durant le second raid pleni-marien ?

— Êtes-vous en train de me proposer d'assassiner Korin sur le champ de bataille ? » Elle secoua la tête devant leur mutisme. « Non. Je ne conquerrai pas la couronne de cette façon-là. Vous autres, magiciens, m'avez déjà beaucoup aidée. Sans vous, je ne serais pas ici. Mais Illior m'a choisie telle que je suis, un guerrier. J'affronterai Korin de manière honorable et vaincrai ou perdrai de manière honorable. Je dois aux dieux comme à Skala d'effacer les péchés de mon oncle.

— Et s'il ment quand il nie posséder des magiciens ? demanda Arkoniel.

— Alors, le déshonneur en retombe sur sa tête, et libre à vous d'agir à votre guise. » Elle lui saisit la main. « Dans tous les rêves et les visions que j'ai eus, mon ami, je n'ai pas vu de magie me donner la victoire. "Par le sang et l'épreuve", a déclaré l'Oracle. Korin et moi avons reçu ensemble une éducation de guerriers. Il n'est que justice que nous réglions notre différend conformément à nos propres voies. »

Elle tira son épée et la brandit en présence des autres. « J'ai l'intention de troquer demain cette lame contre l'Épée de Ghërilain. Héraut, va dire au prince Korin que je l'affronterai à l'aube et prouverai ma légitimité. »

L'homme s'inclina et partit rejoindre sa monture.

Tamìr jeta un nouveau regard circulaire sur l'assistance. « Dites à mes gens de se reposer s'ils le peuvent et de faire des offrandes à Sakor et Illior. »

Comme ils saluaient et s'éloignaient chacun de son côté, elle se pencha vers Ki et marmonna : « Et prie Astellus de nous convoyer ces maudits vaisseaux gèdres ! »

Saruel et Malkanus entraînèrent Arkoniel à l'écart du feu de veille en vue d'un entretien privé.

« Vous n'avez pas véritablement l'intention de nous voir demeurer tranquillement planqués dans notre coin comme des fainéants, n'est-ce pas ?

— Vous avez entendu ce qu'a déclaré la reine. Nous servons en fonction de son bon plaisir. Je ne saurais en l'occurrence la contrarier, quelque sentiment que cela m'inspire. La Troisième Orëska doit jouir de sa confiance. Nous ne pouvons pas utiliser de magie contre Korin.

— À moins qu'il n'y recoure lui-même contre elle. C'est du moins ainsi que j'ai compris la déclaration de Tamìr, objecta Lord Malkanus.

— Peut-être, convint Arkoniel. Mais, même en

admettant cette hypothèse, il n'est pas en notre pouvoir, ainsi qu'elle l'a judicieusement souligné, de faire plus que de susciter une perturbation momentanée.

— Parlez pour vous », grommela sombrement Saruel.

L'infanterie et le train de bagages arrivèrent à la tombée de la nuit, et Korin ordonna de distribuer du vin aux hommes.

Il festoya ce soir-là autour d'un bon feu avec ses généraux et ses Compagnons, et ils mirent au point leur stratégie tout en partageant du pain rapporté du nord, de la grouse et de la venaison rôties.

« C'est bien ce que nous pensions, lui dit Porion. Il manque à Tobin une cavalerie convenable. Vu la supériorité de vos propres forces, vous devriez être en mesure de rompre leurs lignes et de les écraser.

— Nous les disperserons comme une volée de poulets », se promit Alben en levant son hanap pour saluer Korin.

Celui-ci s'envoya une longue lampée du sien pour s'efforcer d'engourdir la peur tapie tout au fond de son cœur. Ç'avait été pareil à Ero, mais il s'était figuré que d'une façon ou d'une autre les choses seraient différentes cette fois-ci. Mais pas du tout. Ses tripes se liquéfiaient à la seule pensée de charger du haut de cette colline, et il gardait les deux mains soigneusement serrées autour de son hanap quand il n'était pas en train de boire afin d'en réprimer le tremblement. Maintenant que l'heure décisive était imminente, des souvenirs de ses défaillances honteuses le rongeaient, menaçant de l'émasculer une fois de plus. L'impudente assurance du message de Tobin avait échaudé son orgueil.

Pour la première fois depuis une éternité, il n'arrivait pas à chasser de sa mémoire cette nuit d'Ero où Père, contraint à s'aliter par ses blessures alors que la bataille tournait de plus en plus au désastre, avait fait appel à Tobin et pas à son propre fils... plaçant sa confiance en ce novice de gamin plutôt qu'en lui-même. Ç'avait été la preuve d'un mépris que Korin avait toujours subodoré, et le refus glacial par lequel Père avait exclu de lui confier le commandement suprême après le départ de Tobin avait apposé d'une manière évidente pour tous le sceau d'un opprobre humiliant sur sa propre personne.

Père était mort, ses meilleurs généraux avaient succombé, et il n'avait plus eu d'autre solution que de se fier aveuglément à Nyrin et de prendre la fuite, abandonnant à Tobin la gloire de triompher une fois de plus.

Autrefois, il aurait pu confier ses doutes à Caliel, mais son ami était livide et muet, et Korin avait vu dans ses yeux une douleur sincère alors que le héraut leur délivrait le message de Tobin.

Lorsqu'on se retira pour la nuit, il marqua une pause avant d'attirer Caliel à l'écart des autres. « Nyrin ne se trompait pas complètement sur ton compte, n'est-ce pas ? Tu persistes à aimer Tobin. »

Caliel hocha lentement la tête. « Mais toi, je t'aime bien davantage.

— Et si tu le rencontres sur le champ de bataille ?

329

— Pour toi, je me battrai contre n'importe qui »,
répondit Caliel, et Korin perçut dans sa voix qu'il
disait la vérité. En se ressouvenant de son dos ensanglanté, cette réponse lui fit l'effet d'un coup de poignard.

Il se retira avec Tanil pour seule compagnie, et
celui-ci sombra presque tout de suite dans un sommeil
harassé. Korin se demanda comment il parviendrait à
le convaincre de rester à l'arrière le lendemain. Le malheureux n'était absolument pas en état de combattre.

Le vin était l'unique réconfort auquel le prince pût
désormais recourir. Il n'y avait plus que lui pour
chasser la honte et la peur, ou du moins pour les noyer
dans une chaleur engourdissante. Korin ne s'autori-
serait pas néanmoins à aller jusqu'à se soûler. Il était
un buveur assez expérimenté pour ne pas ignorer
quelle quantité d'alcool suffisait pour maintenir la
trouille à distance respectueuse.

25

Tamìr et son armée passèrent dans la plaine une nuit
pénible. Le brouillard affluait à nouveau de la mer, si
dense qu'il masquait entièrement la lune et que l'on
avait grand-peine à voir d'un feu de veille à tel ou tel
autre. Eyoli, que son existence au sein de l'armée
n'avait pas empêché de rester assez longtemps
indemne pour effectuer le voyage dans ses rangs,

quitta furtivement le camp de Korin en passant par la forêt. Il apportait non seulement la terrible confirmation des effectifs dont disposait le prince, mais la nouvelle que Caliel et Tanil projetaient bel et bien tous les deux de combattre.

« Il est impossible que Tanil soit encore assez vigoureux », ronchonna Ki.

Mais Lutha échangea avec Tamìr un coup d'œil triste et entendu. Seule la mort empêcherait dorénavant l'écuyer de se trouver aux côtés de Korin.

Enroulée dans ses couvertures humides, Tamìr n'arrêtait guère de s'agiter, tourmentée par de vagues rêves du site rocheux de sa vision. Là aussi, le brouillard sévissait, et elle distinguait de sombres silhouettes qui bougeaient autour d'elle, mais sans pouvoir les identifier. Elle se réveilla en sursaut et tâcha de se redresser sur son séant, mais ce ne fut que pour découvrir Frère qui, installé à califourchon sur elle, la plaquait au sol d'une main glaciale serrée autour de sa gorge.

Sœur, siffla-t-il, penché sur elle pour la dévisager d'un air sournois en pleine figure. *Ma sœur sous ton véritable nom.* Il accentua la pression sur sa gorge. *Toi qui t'es refusée à me venger.*

« Je l'ai bannie ! » suffoqua-t-elle.

Au travers d'un halo flou d'étoiles multicolores dansantes, elle s'aperçut qu'il était nu, décharné, d'une saleté repoussante, et que ses cheveux formaient une masse hirsute autour de sa face. La plaie de son torse était encore béante. Tamìr en sentait le sang froid dégoutter sur son ventre, détremper sa chemise et lui geler la peau.

Il fit courir un doigt glacé sur la cicatrice de la poitrine de sa sœur. *Je serai avec toi, aujourd'hui. Je ne tolérerai pas d'être mis à l'écart.*

Il disparut, et elle se débattit pour se relever, hors d'haleine et tout son être secoué de tremblements. « Non ! croassa-t-elle tout en se frictionnant la gorge. C'est moi qui livrerai mes propres batailles, maudit sois-tu ! »

Une ombre se dessina sur la portière de la tente, et Ki risqua sa tête à l'intérieur. « Tu as appelé ?

— Non, juste... juste un cauchemar », chuchota-t-elle.

Il s'agenouilla près d'elle et repoussa d'une main caressante les cheveux qui lui couvraient le front. « Est-ce que tu vas tomber malade ? La fièvre rôde dans le camp.

— Non, c'est seulement ce foutu brouillard. J'espère qu'il se dissipera demain. » Elle hésita puis avoua. « Frère était ici.

— Qu'est-ce qu'il voulait ?

— Toujours pareil. Et il m'a annoncé qu'il serait tout à l'heure avec moi.

— Il t'a déjà aidée. »

Elle lui adressa un regard aigrelet. « Quand ça lui convenait. Je n'ai que faire de son aide. Cette bataille est une affaire personnelle.

— Tu penses qu'il pourrait s'en prendre à Korin, comme il l'a fait avec Lord Orun ? »

Elle scruta les ténèbres environnantes à la recherche

du démon. Le souvenir de la mort d'Orun lui donnait encore des nausées.

« Korin est le fils d'Erius, après tout, et il occupe la place qui te revient.

— Il n'a rien eu à voir avec ce qui nous est arrivé, à Frère et à moi. » Elle rejeta ses couvertures et palpa sa tunique maculée de sueur. « Je pourrais aussi bien me lever. Tu as envie de dormir un peu ?

— Je n'y arriverais pas. Mais je me suis débrouillé pour dénicher ceci. » Il retira de sa ceinture une gourde de vin plutôt flasque, et la secoua pour en faire clapoter le maigre contenu. « C'est une piquette infecte, mais elle te réchauffera. »

Elle en ingurgita une bonne lampée et grimaça. Un trop long séjour dans la gourde avait gâté le liquide aigre, mais il atténua un peu les crampes de la faim.

Tamìr s'approcha de la portière ouverte et jeta un regard au-dehors sur la mer de feux de veille au-delà. « Il nous faut absolument gagner, Ki. J'ai éreinté mes hommes avec notre randonnée par-dessus les montagnes, et voilà qu'ils ont tous maintenant le ventre vide. Par la Flamme, j'espère que je n'ai pas fait une erreur en les entraînant ici. »

Ki se tenait juste derrière elle, à regarder par-dessus son épaule. « Korin peut bien avoir davantage d'hommes, mais nous avons, nous, plus à perdre. Chacun des hommes et des femmes qui sont là dehors cette nuit sait pertinemment qu'il nous faut vaincre ou mourir en essayant. » Son sourire s'évasa de nouveau. « Et, pour ma part, je sais lequel des deux j'aimerais le mieux. »

Elle se retourna, le repoussa d'un pas à l'intérieur de la tente et l'embrassa gauchement sur sa joue hérissée de picots. Il avait la peau rugueuse, et elle lui laissa sur les lèvres une saveur de sel. « Ne meurs pas. Voilà l'ordre exprès que je te donne, à toi. »

Elle l'enlaça étroitement par la taille pendant que leurs lèvres se joignaient à nouveau, en proie à une chaleur délectable qui ne devait rien à l'absorption de l'affreux picrate. Elle trouvait maintenant presque naturel de l'embrasser.

« J'écoute et j'obéis, Majesté, répliqua-t-il tout bas, sous réserve que vous me promettiez la pareille. » Il se recula et la repoussa doucement vers la portière. « Viens t'asseoir au coin du feu. Là-dedans, tu ne feras rien d'autre que ruminer. »

La plupart des Compagnons partageaient leurs manteaux avec leurs écuyers pour se tenir chaud. Tamìr aspirait à prendre modèle sur eux, et elle n'y aurait pas réfléchi à deux fois, dans le temps. Encore tout échauffée par le baiser de Ki, elle se sentit trop embarrassée de scrupules en présence des autres.

Haïn, Lord Malkanus et Eyoli se trouvaient avec ces derniers.

« Où sont vos collègues ? leur demanda-t-elle.

— Kaulin est en train de seconder les guérisseurs, répondit Eyoli. Arkoniel et Saruel cherchent encore à relever quelque indice des navires 'faïes. »

Barieüs dodelinait sur l'épaule de Lutha. Il s'agita, puis éructa une toux rauque en papillotant comme une chouette.

« Tu as de la fièvre ? s'alarma Tamìr.

— Non », répliqua-t-il un peu trop vite, avant de se remettre à tousser.

« Il y a une grippe qui se propage dans les rangs, expliqua Nikidès. Les quelques drysiens que nous avons sous la main sont débordés.

— J'ai entendu grommeler que c'est une espèce de maladie qui nous a été infligée par le peuple des collines, dit Una.

— Typique ! » se gaussa Ki.

Tamìr reporta de nouveau son regard sur les feux de camp des alentours. *Trop de nuits sous la pluie, et trop peu de nourriture. Si nous perdons demain, nous risquons de n'être pas assez vigoureux pour nous battre de nouveau.*

Une brise fraîche signala l'approche de l'aube, mais le soleil demeura caché derrière des bancs de nuages sombres.

Tamìr rassembla ses magiciens, ses maréchaux et leurs capitaines et procéda à un ultime sacrifice. Arkoniel vint les rejoindre. Il n'y avait toujours pas trace des 'faïes.

Chacune des personnes présentes répandit sur le sol ce qu'il restait encore de vin au fond de sa gourde et jeta dans le feu des chevaux de cire et d'autres offrandes. Tamìr y ajouta une poignée de plumes de chouette puis un grand sachet d'encens qu'Imonus lui avait procuré.

« Illior, si ta volonté est que je gouverne, donne-nous la victoire aujourd'hui », pria-t-elle, pendant que s'élevaient des tourbillons de fumée à l'odeur suave.

Une fois achevées les prières, elle jeta un regard circulaire sur les visages exténués de ses partisans. Certains d'entre eux, tels le duc Nyanis et les gens de Bierfût, la connaissaient depuis sa plus tendre enfance. D'autres, à l'instar de Grannia, ne la suivaient que depuis quelques mois, mais elle lut sur les traits de tous la même détermination.

« Ne vous inquiétez pas, Majesté », déclara Jorvaï, se méprenant sur sa sollicitude. « Nous connaissons le terrain, et vous avez les dieux de votre côté.

— Avec votre permission, Majesté, mes collègues et moi avons préparé quelques charmes pour contribuer à vous protéger en ce jour, dit Arkoniel. C'est-à-dire, enfin, si vous ne considérez pas que ce serait là manquer à la parole que vous avez donnée à Korin.

— Je me suis engagée à ne pas utiliser de magie directement contre lui. Je ne pense pas que ceci compte, n'est-ce pas ? Allez-y. »

Les magiciens s'approchèrent tour à tour de chacun des maréchaux et des Compagnons pour tramer des sortilèges destinés à sécuriser leurs armures et à les délivrer de la faim qui leur tenaillait les tripes. Ensuite, ils soumirent les capitaines aux mêmes opérations.

Arkoniel en vint à Tamìr et brandit sa baguette, mais elle secoua la tête. « Je jouis de toute la protection dont j'ai besoin. Économisez votre énergie pour les autres.

— Comme il vous plaira. »

Tamìr se tourna vers ses maréchaux. « C'est l'heure.

— Commandez, Majesté, répondit Nyanis.

— N'accordez de quartier à personne, à moins que

nos ennemis ne se rendent explicitement. La victoire ou la mort, messires ! »

Maniès déroula sa bannière et la secoua pour lui faire prendre le vent pendant que l'on répercutait le cri. Le trompette personnel de Tamìr sonna un bref appel feutré, et le signal fut répandu de proche en proche par tous ses collègues.

Arkoniel étreignit Tamìr puis la maintint à longueur de bras comme s'il voulait s'imprégner de ses traits. « Voici venu le moment pour lequel vous êtes venue au monde. Que la chance d'Illior soit avec vous, ainsi que le feu de Sakor.

— Ne faites donc pas cette gueule lugubre ! le morigéna-t-elle. Si les dieux veulent véritablement une reine, qu'y a-t-il dès lors à redouter ?

— Quoi, effectivement ? » dit-il, s'efforçant de sourire.

Ki le serra ensuite dans ses bras et chuchota : « Si les choses tournent mal, je n'ai rien à branler de Korin et de sa conception de l'honneur. Vous *faites* quelque chose ! »

La conscience déchirée, Arkoniel ne parvint qu'à lui retourner son embrassement.

Telle une énorme bête en train de se réveiller, l'armée de Tamìr se massa pêle-mêle pour remonter vers ses positions initiales, ses rangs hérissés de piques et d'angons. Personne ne soufflait mot, mais le tintement et le cliquetis des diverses armures, le ferraillement des traits dans des centaines de carquois et le pas de milliers de pieds foulant l'herbe humide remplissaient l'air d'un vacarme assourdissant.

Tamìr et les Compagnons chargèrent sur leurs épaules arcs et boucliers avant d'aller se placer au centre de la ligne de front. Ils avaient laissé leurs montures à l'arrière avec les jeunes garçons du camp ; ils se battraient d'abord à pied.

Le brouillard se déroba autour de leurs chevilles en loques effilochées tandis que les deux ailes principales entreprenaient de se former. Il restait en suspens comme de la fumée dans la membrure des arbres voisins pendant qu'on déployait les étendards au bout de leurs longues hampes.

Tamìr et sa garde rapprochée occupaient le centre du dispositif, flanqués de part et d'autre par une compagnie d'archers d'Atyion et appuyés juste derrière eux par trois compagnies d'hommes d'armes. À Kyman était échu le flanc gauche, sur la gauche duquel se trouvait la falaise. Le flanc placé sous les ordres de Nyanis, à droite, s'étendait jusqu'à la forêt. Les deux ailes se composaient de groupes d'archers postés à l'extérieur et d'hommes d'armes vers le centre qui encadraient les archers de Tamìr. Les guerriers de Jorvaï constituaient l'aile de réserve, à l'arrière, mais ses archers personnels décocheraient leurs flèches par-dessus les têtes des troupes qui se tenaient devant eux.

Chaque maréchal avait sa bannière, et chaque capitaine aussi. Une fois au contact de l'adversaire, chaque compagnie se rallierait à son propre étendard, de manière à se mouvoir comme un seul homme, en dépit du vacarme et de l'inévitable embrouillamini de la mêlée.

La ligne de front de Tamìr était établie juste en retrait de la portée de tir de la colline. De là, on entendait distinctement le tintamarre de l'approche de l'armée de Korin.

« Archers. Installez les pieux », commanda Tamìr, et les capitaines firent circuler l'ordre tout le long des deux flancs de la première ligne.

La moitié des archers de chaque compagnie plantèrent dans le sol leurs pieux pointus selon un angle aigu qui les orientait face à l'ennemi, formant ainsi le « hérisson », une haie largement espacée de pals acérés dissimulés au sein des rangs comme des piquants dans de la fourrure.

Ils s'affairaient encore à donner les dernières touches mortelles à l'agencement de ce piège quand une clameur s'éleva de l'arrière-garde.

« On est en train de nous prendre en tenaille ! Prévenez la reine, on est en train de nous tourner ! »

« Tenez vos positions ! cria-t-elle avant de partir se rendre compte par elle-même.

— Sacrebleu, il doit avoir dépêché du monde à travers la forêt ! » gronda Ki en la suivant tandis qu'elle se frayait passage à coups d'épaules à travers les troupes.

La brume s'était éclaircie, leur permettant de voir la sombre masse d'une armée qui s'approchait, précédée par quatre cavaliers lancés au galop.

« Pourrait bien être des hérauts », fit Ki. Lutha et lui vinrent néanmoins se placer devant Tamìr afin de la couvrir avec leurs boucliers.

Or, à la faveur de l'intervalle qui se réduisait, elle reconnut le cavalier qui menait le train. C'était Arkoniel, et il agitait la main en s'époumonant. Elle n'identifia pas les autres, mais elle vit qu'ils étaient armés.

« Laissez-les venir », ordonna-t-elle, en voyant certains des archers encocher des traits sur leurs cordes.

« Ils sont arrivés ! hurla Arkoniel en freinant des quatre fers. Les Aurënfaïes ! Ils sont ici ! »

Les cavaliers qui se trouvaient avec lui se débarrassèrent vivement de leur heaume. C'étaient Solun de Bôkthersa et Arengil, accompagnés par un homme plus âgé.

L'inconnu s'inclina du haut de sa selle. « Salut à vous, reine Tamìr. Je suis Hiril í Saris, de Gèdre. C'est moi qui commande les archers de Gèdre.

— J'ai moi-même une compagnie de Bôkthersa. Pardonnez-nous d'arriver si tard, dit Solun. Les vaisseaux de Gèdre se sont arrêtés pour nous, et puis nous avons eu un temps épouvantable pendant la traversée.

— Il nous a détournés de notre itinéraire. Nous avons accosté hier plus bas que votre port, expliqua Hiril.

— Nous vous avons apporté des vivres et du vin et amené deux cents archers de chacun des clans », dit Arengil. Il retira de l'intérieur de son tabard un petit rouleau et le lui tendit avec un grand sourire fier. « Et j'ai la permission de mon père et de ma mère de devenir l'un de vos Compagnons, reine Tamìr... si vous voulez encore de ma personne ?

— Avec joie, mais, pour aujourd'hui, je pense qu'il vaudrait mieux que tu restes avec les gens de ton propre peuple. »

Il en parut un peu désappointé, mais il pressa sa main sur son cœur, selon le mode skalien.

Tamìr expliqua rapidement son plan à Solun et Hiril et leur fit poster leurs archers au centre du troisième rang.

Pendant qu'elle et les Compagnons regagnaient leurs positions sur la ligne de front, un fracas formidable en provenance de la colline éclata brusquement. Les hommes de Korin étaient en train de marteler leurs boucliers et hurlaient des cris de guerre tout en s'avançant vers leurs places. Ce tapage avait quelque chose de déprimant, et il devint encore plus tonitruant quand leurs premiers rangs émergèrent de la brume matinale.

« Ripostez-leur ! » vociféra Tamìr. Ki et les autres dégainèrent leurs épées et en martelèrent leurs boucliers, tout en clamant à pleine gorge : « Pour Skala et la reine Tamìr ! »

Le cri de bataille se répandit à travers les rangs en une clameur assourdissante qui ne fit que croître pendant que l'armée de Korin se massait au-dessus de ses adversaires.

Quand se fut éteint le tollé général, les deux armées s'immobilisèrent enfin face à face. La bannière de

Korin flottait au premier plan, et Tamìr distingua le tabard rouge qu'il portait.

« N'est-ce pas la bannière du duc Ursaris, là-bas ? fit Ki. Celui que tu as envoyé balader ?

— Si, répondit Lutha. Et sur la gauche, voici celle de Lord Wethring. À droite, c'est le duc Syrus avec ses archers. Mais Korin compte assurément par-dessus tout sur sa cavalerie et sur ses hommes d'armes, puisque c'est ce qu'il possède en plus grand nombre.

— Où se trouve le général Rheynaris ? demanda Ki.

— Il est mort à Ero. Caliel disait qu'aucun de ces autres-là ne lui arrivait à la cheville comme tacticien.

— Alors, c'est une bonne nouvelle pour nous.

— Korin a encore maître Porion, signala Barieüs.

— Par les couilles de Bilairy, j'espère qu'aucun de nous n'aura à l'affronter ! » murmura Ki, exprimant là un sentiment partagé de tous.

« Merde ! » maugréa Lutha, les yeux toujours fixés sur le sommet de la colline.

« Qu'y a-t-il ? questionna Tamìr.

— À la droite de Korin. Tu ne les vois pas ? »

Elle mit sa main en visière pour abriter ses yeux et regarda plus attentivement. « Merde ! »

Même à cette distance, elle reconnaissait la blondeur dorée du cavalier.

C'était Caliel. Et là, entre lui et Korin, il y avait également Tanil.

« Lutha, toi et Barieüs avez ma permission de ne pas le combattre, et Tanil non plus, leur dit-elle. Je ne vais pas exiger ça de vous. »

Lutha branla sombrement du chef. « Nous ferons ce que nous devons, le moment venu. »

Le héraut attitré de Korin descendit au petit galop vers le pied de la colline, et Tamìr quitta son poste pour se porter à sa rencontre. Ils s'entretinrent brièvement, échangèrent des intentions, puis retournèrent vers leurs camps respectifs.

« Le roi Korin exige que vous vous rendiez ou que vous vous battiez, Majesté. Conformément à vos instructions, je lui avais déjà transmis le même message de votre part. »

Tamìr ne s'était attendue à rien de moins. « Tu peux te retirer.

— Plaise à Illior de vous accorder la victoire, Majesté. » Après l'avoir saluée, l'homme s'éloigna le long de la ligne. En pleine bataille également, ses pareils étaient sacrés, ils observaient le déroulement des combats et véhiculaient ensuite partout la nouvelle de leur issue.

Monté sur son cheval d'emprunt et revêtu d'une armure qui lui allait aussi mal que possible, Caliel avait son dos lacéré tout endolori sous la chemise grossière dont on l'avait doté. Autant de désagréments dont il n'avait cure, toutefois, tandis qu'il contemplait d'un cœur lourd les lignes adverses, en bas. Il découvrit Tamìr au centre, exactement comme il s'y était attendu, et à pied. Ki était là, lui aussi, ainsi que Lynx. Espérant contre tout espoir, il scruta les visages de ses autres proches, et son cœur chavira lorsqu'il repéra celui de Lutha.

Fermant les paupières, il adressa une prière silencieuse à Sakor. *Préserve-moi de les croiser sur le champ de bataille.*

S'il devait sa loyauté à Korin, c'est à Lutha et Barieüs qu'il devait la vie, et Tanil devait la sienne à Tamìr, même s'il ne saisissait toujours pas que c'était face à cette dernière qu'ils se trouvaient actuellement. Korin avait bien essayé de le reléguer à l'arrière avec le train de bagages, il avait même envisagé de le faire ligoter, mais il s'était heurté aux larmes et aux supplications de son écuyer, persuadé qu'on prétendait le traiter de la sorte parce qu'il était en disgrâce.

« Laisse-le venir, avait finalement dit Caliel. Il est assez vigoureux pour se battre. Et s'il succombe ? C'est lui témoigner plus de sollicitude que de le condamner à demeurer ce qu'il est à présent. Au moins périra-t-il en homme rétabli dans sa virilité. »

En observant Tanil maintenant, il trouva justifié que Korin ait fini par donner son accord. Depuis leurs retrouvailles d'Atyion, il ne lui avait jamais vu l'air si alerte et vivant.

À la vue de la bannière de Tamìr qui flottait là-bas, cependant, la lutte de ses doutes personnels et de ce qu'il considérait comme son devoir lui donnait de vagues haut-le-cœur. Korin se refusait à entendre la vérité sur le chapitre de Tamìr, et lui, son serment l'obligeait à garder le silence. *Mais si elle était une reine authentique ?* Sa conscience parlait avec la voix

344

de Lutha. *À quoi rime notre attitude, si c'est contre la reine authentique que nous marchons ?*

Il reporta son regard sur Korin et soupira. Non, il avait fait son choix. Et il allait s'y tenir, advienne que pourra.

Campé à la droite de Tamír, c'est le cœur gros que Ki promena son regard à la ronde. Lynx, Una, Nikidès et leurs écuyers formaient un carré autour d'eux, tous intrépides et prêts à la lutte. Il lut la même résolution sur le visage des soldats. Grannia et les femmes de sa garde fixaient d'un air farouche l'autre armée, là-haut... Une armée au sein de laquelle elles auraient été tout sauf bienvenues. Il se demanda où diable se trouvait Tharin, et s'il avait été victorieux. La seule idée de la présence de Caliel et de Porion dans la ligne opposée le révulsait, mais il balaya ses regrets. Ils avaient tous choisi leur camp.

À la faveur du silence impressionnant qui s'abattit sur le terrain, il entendit bavarder des hommes dans les rangs de Korin et retentir des quintes de toux dans les leurs. Derrière les nuages, le soleil levant n'était guère plus qu'un vague disque blanchâtre. Dans la forêt, des oiseaux étaient en train de se réveiller, mêlant leurs chants aux soupirs mesurés de la mer au bas des falaises. L'atmosphère était étrangement paisible.

Une heure s'écoula, puis une deuxième, Tamír et Korin attendant chacun de l'autre qu'il fasse le premier mouvement. Dans ses cours sur l'art de la guerre, leur vieux Corbeau de professeur avait déclaré que le plus dur dans une bataille, c'était l'attente. Ki se vit forcé d'en convenir. Le temps devenait lourd et le faisait transpirer dans ses vêtements humides. Son ventre vide gargouillait sous son ceinturon, et il avait mal à la gorge.

Une nouvelle heure passa, et les deux adversaires commencèrent à échanger des quolibets. Mais Tamìr demeura immobile et muette, le regard attaché sur Korin qui avait finalement mis pied à terre afin de s'entretenir avec quelques-uns de ses généraux.

Nyanis remonta la ligne pour rejoindre la reine et son entourage. « Il ne va pas bouger. »

— Alors, nous aurons à l'y forcer, tout simplement, rétorqua-t-elle. Préparez vos archers. Grannia, faites passer le mot le long de l'aile de Kyman. »

Le message parcourut la ligne, et le ferraillement des carquois que l'on était en train d'apprêter y répondit bientôt. Ki déchargea son épaule du sien et encocha une flèche sur la corde de son arc.

Tamìr tira son épée et la brandit. « Archers, en avant ! »

Toute la ligne de front se gondola quand les archers coururent combler la marge de tir qui les séparait de la ligne ennemie. Les rangs de derrière étaient eux-mêmes remontés d'autant par la même occasion, de manière à préserver le savant camouflage du hérisson.

Les archers lâchèrent leurs traits, visant haut et faisant s'abattre une grêle de flèches meurtrières sur les têtes et les boucliers dressés des troupes de Korin. Les railleries de l'ennemi se transformèrent en jurons

et en cris de douleur auxquels se mêlaient les hennissements stridents des chevaux blessés.

Tamìr n'avait pas quitté son porte-étendard pendant
que Compagnons et archers décochaient trait sur trait.
Les flèches se déversèrent comme une pluie noire et
continuelle pendant plusieurs minutes, car les archers
tiraient à volonté, jusqu'au moment où ils retraitèrent
vers leurs positions initiales.

Sur la colline, des chevaux se cabraient et prenaient
le mors aux dents. La bannière de Korin vacilla mais
ne tomba pas. La ligne demeurait solide et, comme
l'avait espéré Tamìr, la première attaque débuta.

Korin vit Tobin s'avancer à pied. Cette bannière
bleue le narguait pendant qu'il se blottissait sous son
bouclier et celui de Caliel afin de se garantir contre
l'averse de flèches sifflantes. Trois d'entre elles frappèrent son bouclier, lui ébranlant le bras, et une autre
ricocha sur sa cuisse tapissée de mailles.

Les montures de Garol et de Porion furent atteintes
et les désarçonnèrent. Urmanis tendit son bras de bouclier pour protéger son écuyer affalé par terre, puis
dégringola de sa selle à rebours, la gorge empennée
d'une flèche. Garol rampa vers lui et le maintint
pendant qu'il tentait de se cramponner au bout de
hampe qui dépassait de la plaie.

« Emportez-le à l'arrière », ordonna Korin, en se
demandant si ce n'était pas également là un mauvais
présage. *Un de plus qui m'est enlevé !*

« Regardez, Sire, ils se sont repliés, dit Ursaris.

Vous devez riposter avec une charge avant qu'ils ne se remettent à tirer. Voilà venue votre heure, Sire ! »

Korin tira son épée et la brandit, donnant par là le signal à la cavalerie de Syrus et de Wethring de charger à partir des ailes.

Avec des cris de guerre à vous glacer le sang, ils bottèrent les flancs de leurs chevaux pour leur faire dévaler la colline au vol et déferler comme une vague gigantesque sur les combattants de Tobin. Les hommes d'armes de la ligne de front se précipitèrent à leur suite.

« Regardez-moi ça, ils sont déjà en train de se débander ! » s'exclama Alben, tandis qu'une force plus limitée de Tobin reculait immédiatement.

Or, loin de s'enfuir et de se débander, les rangs se bornèrent à se replier pour démasquer une haie hérissée de pieux obliques que les cavaliers en train de charger aperçurent trop tard. Pendant ce temps, une nouvelle volée drue de flèches partie de l'arrière s'abattit avec une efficacité mortelle sur les agresseurs montés. Certains furent projetés à bas de leur selle ou s'effondrèrent avec leurs chevaux. D'autres, dans les rangs de tête, incapables de s'arrêter à temps, mordirent la poussière lorsque leurs bêtes vinrent s'empaler d'elles-mêmes sur les pieux ou se cabrèrent et s'emballèrent. D'autres encore s'embourbèrent inexplicablement ou tombèrent par-dessus ceux qui gisaient à terre et furent piétinés par ceux qui continuaient de charger.

La charge tint néanmoins et se heurta violemment à la ligne de front de Tobin. Le centre plia, et Korin se berça d'un espoir momentané quand l'étendard de son cousin pivota sauvagement. Mais, au lieu de céder, la ligne de Tamìr rebondit de nouveau vers l'avant, emprisonnant la cavalerie de Korin entre la cohue de ses propres hommes d'armes qui survenaient tout juste pour l'appuyer. Coincés entre la forêt, les falaises et la ligne solide de Tobin, ses guerriers se trouvaient aussi sévèrement tassés qu'un bouchon dans le goulot d'une bouteille. Une autre volée de flèches s'éleva derechef des arrières et, décrivant une parabole par-dessus les rangs de Tobin, fit pleuvoir la mort au sein des forces bloquées de Korin.

Exactement comme l'avait espéré Tamìr, l'avant-garde de Korin s'était gravement resserrée pendant qu'elle chargeait, et sa ruée tête baissée rendait impossible à ceux qui menaient le train d'éviter les pieux, la boue, les fosses et les tranchées qu'on avait préparés pour les prendre au piège. Lorsque les archers aurënfaïes lâchèrent leur deuxième volée, le carnage empira, et l'atmosphère fut saturée par les hennissements stridents des chevaux blessés et les cris de leurs cavaliers. Cela n'interrompit pas la charge, la ralentit seulement un peu et suscita la confusion.

« Défendez la reine ! » aboya Ki, et les Compagnons se refermèrent autour d'elle pendant que survenaient de nouveaux cavaliers ennemis.

Ses archers lâchèrent leurs arcs et se battirent à l'épée, quand ce ne fut pas avec les maillets dont ils s'étaient servis pour planter les pieux. Les compagnies d'hommes d'armes s'élancèrent à leur tour, désarçonnant les cavaliers à l'aide de leurs angons ou bien les arrachant de selle avant de les achever à coups d'épée et de gourdin. Déjà en posture désavantageuse, la charge qu'ordonna Korin à sa ligne de fantassins ne contribua qu'à resserrer l'étau sur sa cavalerie.

« Pour Skala ! » cria Tamìr en se jetant dans la mêlée.

Comme il ne pouvait être question de barguigner, Ki s'était précipité pour rester à la hauteur de Tamìr quand, l'épée au poing, il rencontra l'ennemi.

Cela faisait l'effet de tailler dans un mur de chair et, pendant quelque temps, ils eurent l'impression qu'ils allaient être repoussés. Le boucan de la bataille était assourdissant.

Sans céder un pouce de terrain ni cesser de frapper d'estoc et de taille à tout va, Tamìr beuglait des encouragements et les pressait tous d'avancer. Son épée reflétait la lumière avec des flamboiements rouges. Pris dans la trappe de la cohue, son porte-étendard tomba, mais Hylia empoigna la hampe qui vacillait et la redressa fièrement.

Alors que les combats semblaient partis pour s'éterniser, l'ennemi finit par lâcher pied et par battre en retraite dans le plus grand désordre de l'autre côté du ruisseau, abandonnant sur le terrain piétiné des centaines des siens morts ou presque. Des flèches aurënfaïes le talonnèrent, massacrant les retardataires qui s'échinaient à regrimper en haut de la colline.

Korin lâcha un juron retentissant quand son avant-garde se démantela en s'éparpillant confusément pour un sauve-qui-peut généralisé. La bannière de Tobin persistait à tenir ferme, et il eut la certitude d'apercevoir celui-ci toujours aussi hardiment campé sur le front des troupes.

« Maudit soit-il ! » gronda-t-il, furieux. « Porion, faites à nouveau sonner la charge. Et, cette fois, c'est moi qui la conduirai ! Nous les frapperons avant qu'ils ne puissent se regrouper. Wethring, je veux qu'on dépêche une force latérale à travers la forêt se battre sur leurs arrières.

— Sire, attendez au moins que les autres soient de retour, préconisa tout bas Porion. Autrement, c'est sur le corps de vos propres hommes que vous passerez ! »

Non sans grincer des dents, Korin abaissa son épée, conscient des nombreux regards qui pesaient sur lui. Pendant qu'il attendait, tout en contemplant les cadavres qui jonchaient le champ de bataille, la peur revint le ronger.

Non, je ne faillirai pas, cette fois, se jura-t-il en silence dur comme fer. *Par l'Épée de Ghërilain et le nom de mon père, je me comporterai aujourd'hui en roi !*

Il jeta un coup d'œil oblique vers Caliel qui, d'un tel calme en selle à ses côtés, contemplait le champ de bataille d'un air impassible.

Il puisa de l'énergie dans la présence de son ami. *Je ne me couvrirai pas de honte devant toi.*

Aussitôt que la première vague de Korin eut évacué le terrain, Tamìr envoya ses gens recueillir les blessés pour les emporter à l'arrière. Sur son ordre, les ennemis blessés devaient se voir traités avec la même courtoisie plutôt que d'être achevés sur place, à moins qu'il soient mortellement atteints.

Elle-même demeura en position, tout à bout de souffle et ensanglantée qu'elle était. Les Compagnons n'étaient pas moins couverts de sang qu'elle, mais exclusivement jusque-là de celui de l'adversaire et non du leur.

Nikidès lui adressa un sourire goguenard lorsque, s'épongeant la figure sur la manche de son tabard, il ne réussit qu'à les rendre encore plus sanglantes toutes les deux. Disparu, le garçon lymphatique et timide qu'il avait été. Après des jours et des jours de rude marche et de vie dure, il était aussi crasseux et barbu que n'importe lequel des autres, et il paraissait fier de lui.

« Tu n'as pas encore besoin de te dénicher un nouveau chroniqueur, lui fit-il observer en gloussant.

— Veille à m'épargner cette corvée-là. » Lutha et Barieüs la tracassaient bien davantage. Ils étaient tous les deux livides sous leur heaume.

« Ne t'inquiète pas pour nous, lui dit Lutha. Nous avons fermement l'intention de rendre à Korin la monnaie de sa pièce aujourd'hui. »

La brume s'était complètement dissipée, et la pluie se clairsemait. Le soleil indiquait midi. Ki tendit à Tamìr une gourde d'eau, et elle but goulûment, debout, tout en regardant Korin s'entretenir avec ses nobles.

Juste au même instant se produisit derrière elle une espèce de bousculade parmi les soldats. Arengil se fraya passage dans leurs rangs, les bras chargés de fromage et de saucisses.

« Notre train de bagages a quand même fini par nous rattraper, lui dit-il en lui offrant une saucisse. Hiril a pris la liberté de faire distribuer de la nourriture quand il a appris à quel point vous aviez eu faim. »

Elle mordit dans la saucisse avec un grognement de gratitude. C'était coriace et sacrément épicé. Elle en saliva si fort que sa bouche lui faisait mal.

« Me voilà maintenant encore plus content de votre arrivée ! » s'exclama Ki, les joues rebondies de fromage. « Je craignais que nous n'en soyons réduits à bouffer de la viande de cheval, ce soir. Je suppose que vous n'avez pas apporté de vin ?

— Il y a ça aussi. » Arengil tira de sa ceinture une fiasque de terre cuite et la lui tendit. Après en avoir tiré une lampée, Ki la passa à Tamìr.

Elle y sirota une gorgée puis la transmit à Lynx. « Par les couilles de Bilairy, ce que ça peut être bon ! »

Tout autour d'eux, ses gens riaient, et ils accueillaient par des ovations enthousiastes les provisions qu'on faisait circuler à travers les rangs.

Leur répit fut de courte durée. Des sonneries de trompettes retentirent, du côté du camp de Korin, et Tamìr s'aperçut qu'il était en train de masser ses troupes en vue d'une seconde charge.

Elle et les Compagnons envoyèrent chercher des montures, et elle convoqua ce qu'elle possédait de cavalerie, la disposant au centre et la faisant flanquer de part et d'autre par de profondes rangées d'archers.

Korin n'était pas idiot. S'étant déjà fait épingler une fois sur les piquants de son hérisson, il orienta sa nouvelle attaque contre son flanc droit, contournant la forêt pour fondre sur eux de biais. En franchissant le ruisseau, certains des chevaux s'embourbèrent dans la terre molle et culbutèrent dans les fosses, conformément à ce qu'avait escompté Tamìr, mais en trop petit nombre pour que cela modifie la donne.

« Kyman n'est pas en train de pivoter ! » hurla Ki, à qui un regard en arrière venait de permettre d'apercevoir les troupes du vieux général progresser parallèlement aux falaises.

La ligne de Korin était en train de s'incurver. Ceux de ses cavaliers qui bordaient de plus près la lisière de la forêt foulaient un sol plus accidenté qui leur interdisait d'adopter un train aussi rapide que celui de l'extrémité opposée du front. Kyman se dirigeait vers les traînards, prenant par là le risque de se voir repoussé jusqu'à la falaise.

Tamìr distingua l'étendard de Korin pendant qu'il descendait de la colline, et elle mena sa cavalerie droit sur lui pour l'affronter. Lorsque l'intervalle entre les deux forces se fut suffisamment amenuisé, elle repéra son cousin sur sa monture dans le cercle étroit de sa garde personnelle. Avec lui se trouvaient encore Caliel et Alben, ainsi que quelqu'un d'autre qui arborait l'emblème de Compagnon royal.

« Ça, c'est Moriel ! gueula Lutha.

— Ainsi donc, en définitive, il a dégotté ce qu'il

convoitait, commenta Ki. Voyons un peu de quelle manière il chérit ses obligations.

— De grâce, Tamìr, laisse-le-moi si nous parvenons à nous rapprocher assez, la pria Lutha. J'ai une ardoise à lui régler.

— Si telle est la volonté de Sakor, le Crapaud est à toi. »

Ki dut talonner son cheval comme un forcené pour se maintenir à la hauteur de Tamìr lorsqu'elle chargea. À pied, ç'avait été un jeu d'enfant de rester auprès d'elle. Cette fois, c'était Korin qui menait l'assaut, et Tamìr voulait l'atteindre coûte que coûte. Comme d'habitude, il appartenait à Ki et aux Compagnons de ne pas la lâcher d'une semelle lorsque la soif de se battre s'emparait d'elle. Lynx et Una galopaient à sa gauche. Nikidès et Lutha se trouvaient du côté de Ki, souriant d'un air farouche sous leur heaume d'acier.

Les deux lignes entrèrent en collision comme des vagues, chacune d'elles contrant l'élan de l'autre. Pendant un moment, elles conservèrent leur formidable compacité, mais juste après ce fut le chaos.

Les fantassins aussi ne tardèrent guère à survenir à gros bouillons derrière les chevaux, frappant les cavaliers avec leurs piques et leurs lances. Ki vit un homme qui, prenant Tamìr pour cible, inclinait sa pique dans l'intention de l'en transpercer par-dessous sa garde. Il poussa son cheval de l'avant et lui passa sur le corps, puis il en abattit deux autres qui se ruaient sur lui pour l'arracher de sa selle. Quand il releva les yeux, des flèches pleuvaient à verse sur les rangs massés de

Korin. À en juger d'après la parabole qu'elles décrivaient, c'étaient les Aurënfaïes qui les décochaient par-dessus leurs têtes à eux. Tout en priant qu'elles sachent distinguer l'ami de l'ennemi, il éperonna de nouveau son cheval.

Korin avait présumé que le front de Tamìr évaserait son angle pour se porter à sa rencontre, mais l'aile gauche, au loin, restait à l'écart, sans se laisser attirer dans la mêlée. Au lieu de quoi elle attendit pour venir menacer son propre centre comme un poing serré, contraignant par là une partie de sa cavalerie à pivoter pour aller l'affronter.

Korin força l'allure, sans perdre de vue la bannière de Tobin. Son cousin était monté, cette fois, et il semblait lui aussi s'efforcer de l'atteindre.

Toujours en tête, hein ?

Les deux armées attaquaient et refluaient tour à tour, barattant la terre molle et détrempée en un bourbier aussi mortellement glissant pour les hommes que pour les bêtes. Korin chevauchait l'épée au clair mais, cerné comme il l'était par sa garde, il ne pouvait rien faire d'autre pour l'instant que beugler des ordres.

Dans le lointain, il entendit retentir de nouvelles clameurs lorsque la force de débordement de Wethring surgit brusquement de la forêt pour prendre à revers les lignes arrière de Tobin. Exactement comme il s'en était flatté, ces lignes-là ne pouvaient rien faire d'autre que se retourner pour faire face à leurs agresseurs, divisant de ce fait les forces de Tobin de la même façon que les siennes l'avaient été.

Cela n'empêcha pourtant pas la ligne de front de Tobin de tenir ferme, et Korin se retrouva lui-même en train de se faire refouler vers la forêt.

Arkoniel et ses collègues s'étaient postés juste derrière les Aurënfaïes, déjà en selle et prêts à intervenir si les choses prenaient une tournure funeste. Saruel avait été la première à remarquer les cavaliers dans les bois.

« Regardez par là ! s'égosilla-t-elle dans sa propre langue. Solun, Hiril, retournez-vous ! Il faut vous retourner pour les affronter ! »

Les rangs des Bôkthersans se trouvaient les plus proches de la forêt, et ils décochèrent une volée de flèches assassines dans le tas des cavaliers lorsque ceux-ci émergèrent en trombe du couvert des arbres. Ils continuèrent à tirer pendant que leurs assaillants se ruaient sur eux.

Hiril et les Gèdres étaient plus loin derrière, et ils eurent davantage de temps pour se préparer, tandis que les hommes de Solun encaissaient le plus dur de la charge.

« Allons-nous vraiment jouer là les spectateurs passifs ? » s'écria Malkanus, au comble de la frustration.

« Nous avons donné notre parole à Tamìr », répondit Arkoniel, bien que l'inaction ne fût pas plus à son goût qu'à celui de ses deux collègues.

« Uniquement de ne pas recourir à la magie contre l'armée de Korin », affirma Saruel. Elle ferma les yeux, marmonna une formule de sortilège et frappa dans ses mains. De l'autre côté du terrain, les arbres à la lisière de la forêt d'où continuaient de surgir de nouveaux cavaliers s'embrasèrent subitement. Des flammes de feu grégeois léchèrent des troncs séculaires, se propagèrent le long de leurs branches et bondirent de là vers les membrures environnantes.

De l'endroit où Arkoniel se tenait en observation, rien n'indiquait que les hommes ou les chevaux prissent aussi feu, mais les bêtes, affolées par la fournaise et la fumée, jetaient à bas leurs cavaliers ou les emportaient au milieu des Aurënfaïes en essayant de s'enfuir. Arkoniel expédia un œil magique au-delà des flammes et distingua des cavaliers beaucoup plus nombreux qui s'efforçaient de maîtriser leurs montures et de découvrir un chemin qui leur permette de contourner la progression foudroyante de l'incendie.

« Si Tamìr me réprimande à propos de ça, lui dirai-je que vous avez attaqué les arbres ?

— Nous n'avions pas conclu de pacte avec la forêt », répliqua Saruel en toute sérénité.

Tout semblant d'ordre avait disparu quand la bataille dégénéra en un indescriptible corps-à-corps. Encore monté, Korin voyait nettement l'étendard de Tobin à une distance tentante de quelques centaines de pas, par-delà un magma compact d'hommes et de chevaux.

À force de se démener pour avancer, il finit par entr'apercevoir le heaume de Tobin dans le chaos puis, quelques moments plus tard, son visage. Maintenant à pied, celui-ci se dirigeait droit vers lui, les traits gondolés par ce même sourire railleur que Korin avait vu dans ses rêves.

« Là ! aboya Korin à Caliel et aux autres. Le prince Tobin ! Nous devons l'atteindre !

— Où ça, messire ? » lui retourna Caliel.

Korin jeta un coup d'œil en arrière, mais il n'y avait pas trace de son cousin. L'étendard de Tobin était non loin de là, oscillant par-dessus la cohue près de l'étendard de Lord Nyanis. Derrière, dans le lointain, des tourbillons de fumée blanche se détachaient contre le ciel, parsemés d'étincelles rouges.

« Ils ont mis le feu aux bois ! hurla Porion.

— Attention, Korin ! » cria Caliel.

Korin se tourna à temps pour voir sur sa gauche une femme armée d'une pique qui, se faufilant à travers sa garde, fonçait sur lui. Il essaya d'obliger son cheval à pivoter pour lui faire face, mais la maudite bête choisit juste ce moment pour trébucher dans un trou. Elle se déroba sous lui d'une embardée et s'effondra, le projetant aux pieds de la femme. Celle-ci darda vivement sa pique pour le transpercer, mais l'épée de Caliel s'abattit sur sa nuque et la tua d'un coup qui la décapita à demi. Le sang qui jaillit de la plaie aspergea la figure de Korin.

Caliel mit pied à terre et, d'une traction, le replanta debout, puis se retourna pour repousser l'afflux des ennemis. Tu es blessé, Kor ?

— Non ! » Korin essuya promptement le sang qui l'aveuglait. Au loin, il discerna Ursaris qui, toujours en selle, faisait de son mieux pour le rallier mais l'enchevêtrement des combats contrecarrait son dessein. Tandis qu'il observait son manège, il vit un homme équipé d'une pique le frapper en pleine poitrine et l'effacer de son champ de vision.

Par un phénomène étrange, maintenant qu'il se trouvait immergé au plus épais de la bataille, sa peur l'avait complètement abandonné. Il l'avait tenue à distance pendant la charge mais, une fois confronté à l'acharnement de la lutte, ses longues années d'entraînement reprirent le dessus, et le fait d'abattre adversaire sur adversaire lui parut soudain d'une étonnante facilité.

Une autre femme aux couleurs d'Atyion se précipita sur lui, glapissant un cri de guerre sans pour autant cesser de faire aller et venir son épée. Il se fendit pour lui porter une pointe sous le menton. Tandis qu'elle s'écroulait, il distingua un mouvement derrière elle et revit Tobin, à quelques pas de lui tout au plus cette fois. Celui-ci le dévisagea puis disparut.

« Là ! » cria Korin, tout en essayant de nouveau de se jeter à sa poursuite.

« De quoi parles-tu ? » lui gueula Caliel.

Subitement, une nouvelle nuée de flèches s'abattit sur eux en sifflant. Mago poussa un cri et tomba, les mains crispées sur le bois empenné d'un trait qui dépassait de sa poitrine. Alben l'empoigna par le bras tout en essayant de les abriter tous deux sous son bouclier brandi. Une flèche lui traversa la cuisse avant de percer le devant de son haubert, et il chancela. Korin se pencha pour casser net la longue extrémité du trait.

Elle n'était emplumée que de trois ailettes au lieu de quatre.

« Aurënfaïe. Ce doit être ça, les renforts que nous avons vus arriver. Alben, tu peux tenir debout ?

— Oui. Ce n'est pas profond. » Mais il resta agenouillé auprès de Mago, lui serrant la main, pendant que le jeune écuyer se tordait de douleur et que la bataille déferlait maintenant autour d'eux. Une écume sanglante se mit à moucheter les lèvres de Mago, et sa respiration était laborieuse et désespérée. De la blessure de sa poitrine qui émettait un bruit de succion cloquaient des bulles d'air et de sang.

Il n'était pas question de l'évacuer du champ de bataille et, s'ils l'y abandonnaient comme ça, il se ferait sûrement piétiner. Avec un sanglot, Alben se releva et l'acheva miséricordieusement d'un coup d'épée. Korin se détourna en se demandant s'il lui faudrait faire la même chose avant la fin de la journée. Tanil se trouvait encore à ses côtés, couvert de sang, l'œil égaré. Il pouvait bien avoir la cervelle faible, son bras ne l'était pas, lui. Il s'était vaillamment battu.

La bataille continua de faire rage pendant que l'après-midi tirait en longueur. Il était impossible à Korin de dire où se trouvaient ses autres généraux, sauf lorsqu'il lui arrivait d'entrevoir l'un d'eux ou leurs couleurs respectives.

L'étendard de Tobin apparaissait et disparaissait comme une vision torturante, et le jeune prince faisait de même. Il suffisait que Korin se dirige vers lui pour qu'un simple coup d'œil par-dessus l'épaule lui révèle qu'il s'était débrouillé pour s'esquiver dans la cohue. Sa vitesse de mouvement avait de quoi vous rendre dingue.

« Je veux sa tête ! aboya Korin en l'entr'apercevant à nouveau, cette fois à proximité de la lointaine lisière des arbres. « Rattrapez-le ! Il est en train de gagner la forêt ! »

Tamìr tâcha d'atteindre Korin, mais, en dépit de tous ses efforts, elle ne parvint pas à se frayer passage à travers la foule jusqu'à son étendard. Chaque fois qu'elle s'en rapprochait, il semblait se dissoudre.

« Korin nous a débordés ! lui hurla Lynx. Et il a mis le feu aux bois ! »

Elle jeta un regard en arrière et vit que sa dernière ligne était en train de se fissurer et qu'au loin, là-bas, s'élevaient des nuages de fumée. « Il n'y a pas moyen d'y remédier. Continuez de faire porter la pression sur Korin.

— Bon sang, mais attends-nous donc ! » rugit Ki, tout en tailladant un bretteur qui s'était insinué dans une brèche des Compagnons sur la droite de Tamìr.

Comme les Aurënfaïes s'étaient retournés pour affronter les cavaliers venus les prendre à revers, Tamìr n'avait plus à sa disposition que sa garde personnelle et l'aile de Nyanis, pendant que Kyman repoussait un autre régiment à peu près au milieu du champ de bataille.

À pied de nouveau, elle trébuchait sur des corps, certains morts, d'autres exhalant des cris de douleur pendant que les flux et reflux de la bataille leur passaient dessus. Ceux qui n'avaient pas la force de se traîner plus loin finissaient écrasés dans le bourbier.

Tamìr et le reste de sa garde rapprochée étaient tellement couverts de sang et de boue qu'il aurait fallu être bien fin pour dire s'ils étaient blessés ou non. Nik semblait privilégier son bras gauche, Lynx avait le nez barré par une entaille, et Barieüs titubait pas mal, mais ils demeuraient groupés autour d'elle et se battaient farouchement. Elle-même avait le bras de plus en plus lourd, et la soif lui brûlait le gosier.

Les combats étaient d'une telle densité qu'il était souvent difficile de savoir à quel endroit du champ de bataille on se trouvait. Au fur et à mesure que l'après-midi se prolongeait indéfiniment et que le ciel commençait à prendre une teinte dorée, Tamìr finit par se rendre compte qu'elle avait un pied dans les eaux bourbeuses et rougies de sang du ruisseau. Elle faisait face à la haute lisière sombre de la forêt, et elle aperçut tout à coup de nouveau la bannière de Korin, à moins de vingt pas cette fois.

« Ki, regarde ! Il va pénétrer sous les arbres, là !

— Se figure pouvoir s'y planquer, n'est-ce pas ? gronda Ki.

— À moi ! cria-t-elle en brandissant son épée pour montrer le chemin. En le capturant dans les bois, nous mettrons un point final à cette tuerie. »

26

Korin atteignit la lisière de la forêt et s'arrêta juste après l'avoir franchie, tympanisé par les battements de son cœur. L'odeur de la fumée lui chatouillait les narines, mais les flammes étaient encore loin de là.

« Korin, qu'est-ce que tu fiches ? haleta Caliel qui épongeait sa figure trempée de sueur et de sang quand il le rattrapa sous le couvert des arbres.

— Vous ne pouvez pas abandonner le champ de bataille maintenant ! » s'exclama Porion pendant que le reste de la garde de Korin et une vingtaine d'hommes d'armes se regroupaient autour de lui pour le protéger.

« Je ne fais rien de tel. J'ai vu Tobin entrer par ici.

— En êtes-vous certain, Sire ? » lui demanda Porion d'un air sceptique.

Korin surprit un éclair furtif bleu et blanc dans le sous-bois. « Là ! Voyez ? Venez ! »

La forêt vénérable se composait d'immenses sapins sous lesquels ne poussaient guère de fourrés. Le sol était couvert d'aiguilles sèches et de plaques vertes de mousse veloutée parsemées de champignons. Des arbres tombés gisaient de toutes parts, certains conservant des aiguilles ou des feuilles accrochées à leurs branches, d'autres argentés par la patine du temps qui les faisait luire dans la pénombre verte comme les ossements blanchis de géants défunts.

La lutte s'était déjà propagée dans la futaie, mais de manière éparse, sous la forme de groupuscules qui s'affrontaient parmi les arbres. Leurs cris et leurs jurons retentissants provenaient de toutes les directions.

Escorté de Caliel et de Tanil, Korin se précipita aux trousses de la bannière et, laissant aux autres le soin de le suivre, se mit à sauter par-dessus les troncs et les rochers, non sans trébucher sur le sol inégal. Sans cesser de courir, il fronça le nez ; l'air puait la mort et la putréfaction. Une odeur écœurante semblait constamment l'envelopper tandis qu'il pourchassait la silhouette floue qui filait juste devant lui.

Il était impossible de dire de combien d'hommes était accompagné Tobin, mais tout semblait indiquer qu'il ne disposait pas de forces considérables.

Il est en train de foutre le camp ! songea Korin avec une sinistre satisfaction. L'opprobre de Tobin lui permettrait de racheter son propre honneur.

Ki s'imaginait des archers ennemis planqués derrière chaque arbre pendant qu'il courait avec Tamìr. Il faisait beaucoup plus sombre sous les arbres. L'aprèsmidi touchait à son terme, et la pluie recommença à percer les frondaisons et à éclabousser le sol.

« Je ne suis pas sûr que ce que nous faisons soit bien judicieux, pantela Nikidès.

— Il lui est impossible de conduire toute une armée à travers cet embrouillamini, répliqua Tamìr en faisant halte afin de se repérer.

— Peut-être est-il en train de s'enfuir de nouveau, suggéra Ki.

— Je ne le crois pas. » Elle démarra derechef.

« Au moins, permettez-moi d'aller chercher du renfort, Majesté », suffoqua Una, tout en se maintenant à ses côtés.

« Peut-être avez-vous... » Tamìr se figea, les yeux attachés sur quelque chose de plus profondément enfoncé dans les bois.

« Quoi ? » Ki s'efforça de discerner ce qui avait captivé son attention.

« Je le vois, chuchota-t-elle.

— Korin ?

— Non. Frère. »

Le démon se distinguait à peine à travers les arbres, et il agitait la main à l'adresse de Tamìr. Dans la chaleur de la bataille, elle l'avait complètement oublié, mais il n'en était pas moins là, et il ne pouvait y avoir la moindre méprise sur ses intentions. Il voulait qu'elle le suive.

Ki lui saisit le bras lorsqu'elle se remit en marche. « Je ne vois rien du tout.

— Il est là, répondit-elle.

— Il pourrait s'agir d'un de ses coups fourrés !

— Je sais. » Mais elle le suivit tout de même. *Tu es Skala, et Skala est toi. Tu es ton frère, et il est toi.*

L'épée au poing, elle se mit à courir. Ki poussa un juron retentissant, mais cela ne l'empêcha pas plus que les autres de prendre ses jambes à son cou pour se lancer dans son sillage.

Korin fit brutalement irruption dans la clairière et s'arrêta court. Tobin s'y trouvait à l'attendre, assis sur une grosse pierre, le visage partiellement dissimulé par les protège-joues de son heaume. C'était insensé. Il était tout seul, sans le moindre garde en vue. Ses gens avaient dû se laisser distancer d'une manière ou d'une autre. Korin percevait des craquements de brindilles et des voix feutrées qui provenaient d'au-delà des arbres à proximité.

Il recula pour se camoufler derrière le tronc d'un grand arbre, au cas où il y aurait eu des archers à l'affût. « Cousin, tu es venu te rendre ? » lança-t-il.

Tobin leva les mains pour montrer qu'elles étaient vides. Trop facile.

« Il n'a pas plus l'air d'une fille que toi ! se gaussa dédaigneusement Alben.

— Korin, il y a là-dedans quelque chose qui n'est pas normal », le prévint Caliel, les sourcils froncés pour examiner le personnage silencieux.

Tobin se leva lentement puis fit un pas vers Korin. « Salut, cousin. »

La méchanceté pure inhérente à cette voix frappa Korin de plein fouet. Ce n'était pas le timbre de Tobin ; il était plus grave et rauque. Il entendit distinctement grincer et crisser les pièces de l'armure quand Tobin défit la jugulaire de son heaume et s'en décoiffa.

Jamais il n'avait vu d'expression aussi ouvertement haineuse sur le visage de son cousin, jamais il ne lui avait trouvé la mine aussi défaite ni le teint si blafard ; ses yeux étaient caves et tellement sombres qu'ils en paraissaient presque noirs. C'était le Tobin qu'il avait vu dans ses rêves.

Caliel l'agrippa par le bras. « Kor, ce n'est pas... »

Il n'eut pas le loisir d'en dire davantage que les embusqués surgirent du sous-bois à l'extrémité opposée de la clairière, et Korin entendit une voix familière qui criait : « Tamìr, reviens ! »

Ki et Lutha émergèrent tout à coup du couvert, talonnant de près quelqu'un qui portait le tabard et le heaume de Tobin.

« Au nom de Bilairy, qu'est-ce que c'est que ça ? » s'étrangla Porion, suffoqué par la vision fugitive du visage protégé par le heaume.

Ce fut Caliel qui répondit : « *Ça*, c'est Tamìr.

— Regarde, c'est Tobin. Et voilà Ki ! » Tanil entreprit de s'avancer au-devant d'eux en leur adressant un geste joyeux de la main. « Où étiez-vous passés ? »

Korin le rattrapa par le bras. « Non, ils sont maintenant nos ennemis. »

Les yeux du garçon se voilèrent d'égarement. « Non, ceux-là sont tes Compagnons.

— Oh, dieux ! grogna Korin tout bas. Cal, comment puis-je... ?

— Regarde-moi, Tanil », dit ce dernier en laissant tomber son épée. À peine l'écuyer se fut-il retourné que le poing de Caliel l'atteignit violemment au menton, et qu'il s'effondrait à ses pieds sans émettre l'ombre d'un son.

« Malédiction ! » s'exclama Ki en courant se poster devant Tamìr. Lutha et Lynx agirent de même afin de la protéger contre une attaque éventuelle. Korin était planté en pleine vue à l'opposé de la clairière avec Cal et Porion, parfaitement à portée de tir. Ki discerna de façon fugace de ce côté-là des mouvements à travers les arbres.

Au lieu de leur accorder la moindre attention, Tamìr regardait fixement Frère, accoutré de sa propre armure et de ses propres vêtements. « Toi ! »

Le démon se détourna légèrement pour la lorgner. Comme c'était toujours le cas, la lumière le frappait de manière incongrue, sans le toucher, comme elle touchait les vivants. Elle ne suscitait aucun reflet dans ses cheveux de jais. Ki ravala durement sa glotte en se rappelant ce que l'Oracle d'Afra avait dit à Tamìr. Quelque chose à propos d'elle qui était lui et de lui qui était elle. Ils n'avaient jamais présenté moins de ressemblance qu'à l'heure actuelle.

« De quel genre de tricherie s'agit-il ici ? l'apostropha Korin. As-tu en définitive amené tes nécromanciens ? »

Frère commença à s'avancer lentement sur lui, tout en sifflant : « Fils d'Erius, je ne suis pas Tobin et je ne suis pas Tamìr.

— Il va se jeter sur lui ! » chuchota Ki. Si Frère tuait Korin, c'en serait fini de tout ça.

« Frère, arrête ! cria Tamìr. Ne le touche pas. Je te l'interdis ! »

À la stupéfaction de Ki, Frère s'immobilisa et tourna la tête pour décocher à Tamìr un regard furibond.

« Ce combat est le mien ! Va-t'en ! » lui ordonnat-elle, comme elle avait l'habitude de le faire quand ils n'étaient tous encore que des enfants.

Frère lui répliqua en retroussant ses babines mais s'évanouit tout de même.

« De quel genre de tricherie s'agit-il ici ? demanda de nouveau Korin.

— C'est moi, Kor, lui répondit-elle. Lui, c'était mon frère, ou plutôt ce qu'il aurait dû être. Il a été tué pour me préserver de ton père.

— Non !

— C'était une tricherie, juste comme le disait Lord Nyrin, lâcha Moriel d'un ton méprisant.

— Tu te trompes, Crapaud ! lui rétorqua Lutha.

— Toi ! » L'air choqué de Moriel était presque comique.

« Tu devrais être un meilleur expert en matière de nécromancie que quiconque, après avoir été le toutou de Nyrin. Où donc se trouve ton maître, d'ailleurs ? Je suis surpris qu'il ait lâché ta laisse, espèce de lèche-cul ! »

La physionomie de Moriel prit une expression venimeuse. « Lui ne s'était jamais trompé sur ton compte, n'est-ce pas, traître ? »

Ki détourna son regard pour l'attacher sans ciller sur celui de Caliel, qui lui adressa un imperceptible hochement de reconnaissance. « Enfer et damnation ! » grommela Ki en le saluant d'un geste de la main.

« Qui es-tu réellement ? demanda Korin. Montre ton visage si tu l'oses ! »

Tamìr ôta son heaume et retira sa coiffe de mailles. « C'est moi, Kor, telle que j'étais censée être. Caliel peut se porter garant de moi. Interroge-le seulement.

Nous n'avons plus à combattre. Causons ensemble. Laisse-moi te montrer la preuve...

— Menteur ! » lui cracha Korin, mais Ki trouva que son ton trahissait quelque incertitude.

« Je dois être reine, Korin, mais tu demeures toujours mon parent. Te combattre, c'est comme combattre mon propre frère. Je t'en conjure, il nous est possible de faire ici la paix une fois pour toutes. Je te jure sur mon honneur que tu jouiras de ta place légitime à mes côtés. J'accorderai l'amnistie à tous ceux qui t'ont soutenu.

— Honneur ? » ricana Alben, railleur. « Que vaut la parole d'un parjure ? »

La main de Ki se crispa sur la poignée de son épée quand de nouveaux bretteurs sortirent des bois derrière Korin. « À quoi diable penses-tu, Tamìr, de rester comme ça, là, sans bouger ? Voilà qu'ils ont maintenant l'avantage du nombre, au moins à trois contre un !

— Il m'écoutera, à présent qu'il a vu la vérité, répondit-elle tout bas. Il est obligé de le faire ! »

Encore ébranlé par la vue du démon, Korin considéra fixement cette fille qui prétendait être son cousin. « Tobin ? » chuchota-t-il, luttant contre l'évidence qui lui crevait les yeux.

Le sourire, aussi soudain qu'inattendu, dont elle le gratifia – le sourire de Tobin – faillit le déconfire. « Je suis bel et bien Tamìr, exactement comme je te l'ai écrit. Lutha m'a dit que tu avais reçu ma lettre.

« — Mensonges !

— Non, Kor. Le mensonge, c'était Tobin. Je suis la fille d'Ariani. Je le jure par la Flamme et les Quatre. »

Korin pouvait à peine respirer.

Rien d'autre qu'un garçon affublé d'une robe, souffla dans son esprit la voix de Nyrin. Korin voulut à toute force s'accrocher maintenant à cette créance, alors qu'une impression nauséeuse de certitude le submergeait. Si Tobin – si *elle* – disait la vérité, alors Caliel avait toujours vu juste. Cal avait été prêt à se laisser pendre pour l'amener à entendre raison, et lui l'avait presque tué pour le châtier de son attitude.

« Nous pouvons être amis de nouveau, dit Tobin.

— Une tricherie ! » insista Moriel.

Une tricherie ! Une tricherie ! Une tricherie ! chuchota dans la mémoire de Korin la voix glaciale de Nyrin.

« Où êtes-vous, Majesté ? »

Tamìr entendit au loin derrière eux gueuler Nyanis, d'une voix si forte qu'elle dominait les bruits de lutte qui continuaient à leur parvenir du champ de bataille.

« Ici ! » rugit Una en retour.

Il y avait également des voix qui appelaient Korin, avertissant Tamìr qu'il allait bénéficier de nouveaux renforts. Sanglants seraient ici les combats si elle ne réussissait finalement pas à se faire croire de lui.

Elle continua à planter ses yeux dans les siens comme dans ceux d'un faucon qu'elle était en train de chercher à dompter. Elle le connaissait si bien ; elle perçait à jour les débats intérieurs dont il était la proie. L'espoir lui fit retenir son souffle.

Par le sang et l'épreuve, tu dois occuper ton trône. De la main de l'Usurpateur tu arracheras l'Épée de Ghërilain.

Non ! songea-t-elle. *Il ne faut pas que ça se passe de cette façon ! Je saurai me faire écouter de lui ! Frère s'est débrouillé pour nous réunir ici de manière à ce que nous parvenions à régler notre différend.* Avec un nouveau sourire, elle lui tendit la main.

« Korin, frappez ! Vous avez l'avantage du nombre, le pressa Porion. Frappez tout de suite !

— Oui ! Nous pouvons écraser Tobin une fois pour toutes », susurra Alben.

Caliel toucha le bras de Korin sans mot dire, mais ses yeux étaient suppliants.

Tamìr laissa tomber son heaume et dépassa Ki et Lynx. « Cela peut s'achever dès maintenant, Korin, dit-elle sans cesser de tendre la main vers lui. Donne-moi l'Épée de Ghërilain, et... »

Donne-moi l'Épée...

Korin en eut froid dans tout son être. À Ero, il avait parlé dans les mêmes termes à son père, cette nuit funeste, et il cuisait encore de honte en se rappelant de quelle manière les mains de celui-ci s'étaient resserrées sur la poignée de l'arme sacrée pendant que son regard se durcissait. *Une seule main manie l'Épée de Ghërilain. Tant qu'il me reste un souffle de vie dans le corps, le roi, c'est moi. Contente-toi de prouver d'ici là que tu es digne de la tenir.*

Sa propre main se cramponna sur la poignée cependant que le submergeaient à nouveau toute son ancienne rage, tout son sentiment de culpabilité et tout son chagrin, noyant le doute, noyant l'amour. « Non, *je* suis le roi ! »

Tamìr vit le mouvement fatal. Elle eut juste le temps de ramasser son heaume qui gisait à terre et de s'en recoiffer avant que les hommes de Korin ne se ruent contre son propre groupe. Seul Korin demeura en arrière, et Caliel avec lui.

Tamìr ne fut nullement étonnée de se retrouver en face d'Alben au milieu de la mêlée. Ils n'avaient jamais éprouvé beaucoup de sympathie l'un pour l'autre, et elle n'en vit aucune dans ses yeux lorsqu'il entama la lutte avec elle. Il avait toujours été un adversaire formidable, et c'était une rude épreuve pour elle que de lui tenir tête toute seule. Elle le pressa avec acharnement, sans discerner dans son regard l'ombre d'un remords pendant qu'ils se rendaient coup pour coup.

La clairière était désormais bondée de combattants, ce qui ne laissait guère d'espace pour des manœuvres sophistiquées. Ils se frappaient mutuellement de taille comme des coupeurs de bûches. À un certain moment, un poignard surgit dans la main gauche d'Alben, et il essaya de le lui enfoncer entre les côtes, alors que leurs gardes s'étaient bloquées l'une contre l'autre. Sa maille empêcha la pointe de pénétrer, et elle lui administra en pleine figure un coup de coude qui lui brisa le nez. Comme il reculait en titubant, elle lui balança son genou dans l'entrejambe, et il s'effondra par terre.

« Tamìr, derrière toi ! » aboya Ki, tout en repoussant un type qui maniait un gourdin.

Elle baissa la tête en se retournant et évita par là d'extrême justesse le coup que lui assenait Moriel.

« Chienne démoniaque ! » Il lui décocha un violent coup de pied au genou pour lui faire perdre l'équilibre et brandit son épée pour l'abattre à nouveau sur elle.

Avec un grognement de douleur, Tamìr chancela et releva sa lame pour la lui planter dans la gorge quand il revint à la charge, mais Moriel esquiva d'un pas de côté sa tentative maladroite.

Lutha sortit alors du chaos pour se jeter sur lui, et éloigna ainsi le Crapaud de Tamìr.

Elle lui abandonna la besogne et jeta un regard circulaire en quête d'Alben, mais au lieu de cela, découvrit Caliel qui lui faisait face. Il avait l'épée déjà levée, prêt pour un assaut, mais il demeura immobile.

« Je ne veux pas de ton sang, Cal.

— Je ne veux pas du tien », répliqua-t-il, et elle perçut la douleur derrière les mots, tandis qu'il brandissait son épée pour frapper, cette fois.

Elle leva la sienne pour parer le coup, mais avant même que leurs lames n'aient pu se rencontrer, elle aperçut un mouvement flou qui venait de la gauche et un éclair d'acier. Le heaume de Caliel s'envola et, l'œil vide, il s'écroula par terre. Nikidès le dominait de toute sa hauteur, étreignant à deux mains sa lame ensanglantée, la poitrine haletante. « Tamìr, derrière toi ! »

Sans savoir si Caliel était mort ou vivant, elle tourbillonna et bloqua l'épée d'un guerrier de haute taille. Pendant qu'elle le maintenait dans cette posture, Ki se fendit sous la garde de l'homme et lui perça la gorge.

Ki plaqua son dos contre celui de Tamìr, pantelant et le souffle en loques, ses deux mains cramponnées sur la poignée de son épée. « Tu es blessée ?

— Pas encore. » Elle fit peser tout son poids sur le genou meurtri par le Crapaud pour s'assurer qu'il ne lui faillirait pas. « Où est Korin ?

— Je ne le vois pas. »

De ce côté-ci, Sœur, lui siffla Frère dans le tuyau de l'oreille. Elle se retourna et entrevit la bannière de Korin près de la lisière de la forêt.

Un porteur de pique se présenta tout à coup, menaçant, sous le nez de Tamìr, mais ce ne fut que pour s'effondrer sur place, à la jubilation manifeste de Frère.

« Ce combat est le mien ! » lui cria-t-elle, quitte à se précipiter pour profiter de l'avantage de la brèche qu'il avait ouverte en sa faveur.

Épaule contre épaule, elle et Ki se frayèrent passage vers la bannière.

Korin vit Caliel tomber sous la lame de Nikidès.

« Traître ! Je vais te tuer ! » Avant qu'il n'ait pu l'atteindre, toutefois, un jeune écuyer portant le baudrier de Tobin surgit de la presse et lui barra le passage. Il fit sauter l'épée des mains du garçon d'un simple revers avant de lui passer sa lame au travers du

376

corps. Nikidès poussa un cri strident et vola vers lui, mais Porion s'avança et le refoula.

Korin était sur le point d'aller seconder le maître d'armes quand il aperçut au-dessus de la cohue un heaume couronné, juste à quelques pas de lui.

« Tobin est à moi ! » hurla-t-il. Ki essaya de s'interposer, mais Porion se jeta entre eux pour croiser le fer avec lui.

Korin se précipita contre Tobin de toute sa puissance, exacerbée par le sentiment ravivé d'avoir été trahi. Une fois face à face avec elle enfin, il discerna dans son regard quelque chose qui ressemblait à une douleur sincère, mais sans que Tamìr hésitât une seconde pour autant.

Ki tâcha de ne pas perdre de vue Tamìr du coin de l'œil pendant qu'il affrontait maître Porion. « Je ne veux pas me battre avec vous », lâcha-t-il, sans cesser de maintenir sa garde haute.

« Ni moi avec toi, mon garçon, mais c'est quand même ce qu'on va faire, riposta Porion. Allons-y, et voyons voir si tu as bien appris mes leçons. »

Tamìr n'avait affronté Korin qu'une seule fois jusque-là, le fameux jour où il l'avait laissée épuiser contre lui sa rage d'avoir à fouetter Ki. Beaucoup plus âgé et costaud, il s'était alors montré pour elle bien plus qu'un adversaire à sa mesure. Elle avait forci depuis, mais il demeurait toujours un dangereux antagoniste. La férocité de ses assauts était stupéfiante.

Il faisait pleuvoir coup sur coup, la forçant à parer tout en reculant. Ils tourbillonnèrent l'un autour de l'autre, frappant et se colletant, jusqu'au moment où ils se retrouvèrent presque dans les bois. Il la repoussa de nouveau vers l'arrière dans un massif de hautes fougères. L'odeur verte qu'elles exhalaient sous leurs piétinements montait les environner, et Tamìr perçut juste dans son dos un bruit d'eau courante.

« Tamìr ! hurla Ki, de beaucoup plus loin.

— Ici... », débuta-t-elle, mais Korin la repoussa de nouveau à reculons, et elle perdit pied en heurtant son talon contre quelque chose et en tombant à la renverse.

Le sol ne se trouvait pas là où elle s'était attendue à ce qu'il se trouve. Elle bascula par-dessus le bord d'un petit ravin camouflé par les fougères et dégringola en roulant une pente rocheuse, se meurtrissant douloureusement le coude gauche contre une pierre au cours de sa chute et perdant son épée quelque part le long du trajet. Elle s'immobilisa finalement dans la boue au bord d'un ruisseau. Le même, probablement, saisit-elle en prenant ses repères, que celui qui traversait le champ de bataille.

Elle se releva en titubant, soutenant délicatement son bras contusionné et promenant un regard alentour pour récupérer son épée. Elle découvrit celle-ci retenue par la racine déchaussée d'un arbre, à mi-hauteur de la berge abrupte. Elle entreprit de grimper l'y chercher, puis se figea lorsqu'elle prit conscience de son environnement. Il ressemblait presque trait pour trait aux lieux de sa vision.

La bannière ? Où est la bannière ?

Au lieu de cela, Korin survint à sa poursuite en bondissant par-dessus le bord du ravin, le meurtre dans les yeux. L'épée se trouvait trop loin pour qu'elle puisse l'atteindre avant qu'il ne soit sur elle.

« Illior ! » cria-t-elle en tirant sa dague et en se ramassant sur elle-même pour l'affronter.

« Tamìr ! » Ki surgit en trombe, le visage blême et couvert de sang. Il dévala la pente et déboula sur Korin avant que celui-ci n'ait pu parvenir à elle. Ils firent la culbute ensemble et atterrirent dans la boue à quelques pas de là, Ki dessous.

« Prends ton épée ! » aboya Ki, tout en luttant avec Korin.

Tamìr escalada à quatre pattes le ravin et empoigna son arme. Quand elle se retourna, elle fut horrifiée de voir Korin se redresser subitement et frapper Ki pendant que celui-ci se débattait par terre. C'était un acte ignominieux.

« Espèce de lâche ! » cria-t-elle d'une voix stridente. Il lui fallait rejoindre Ki, l'aider, mais c'était comme être pris au piège dans un cauchemar. Elle dérapait et glissait sur des pierres, allant droit sur eux, mais il lui semblait simplement qu'elle ne pouvait pas se mouvoir assez vite.

Korin abattit son épée sur le bras de Ki quand il essaya de lever sa lame pour le repousser. Elle entendit l'écœurant craquement de l'os et le grognement douloureux de Ki. Il tenta de se dérober de dessous Korin en roulant, mais le prince se fendit à sa suite et lui assena son épée sur le côté du heaume. Ki s'écroula sur le flanc dans la boue, et Korin, empoignant son épée à deux mains, l'abattit sur lui latéralement, juste au défaut de sa cuirasse.

« Salaud ! » hurla Tamìr. La peine et la fureur lui firent en un éclair franchir les quelques derniers pas qui la séparaient de Korin. Elle le frappa violemment en travers des épaules et le repoussa du corps de Ki. Il se déroba d'un bond et pivota pour lui faire face. Il y avait du sang frais sur sa lame, du sang qui se mêlait avec la pluie.

Le sang de Ki.

Avec un cri de rage, elle vola sur lui, le refoulant à force de taillades sauvages loin du corps inerte de Ki.

Ils traversèrent le ruisseau dans des gerbes d'éclaboussures avant de se porter sur un terrain plus haut. Korin se battait dur, la maudissant à chaque coup qu'elle parait. Leurs lames s'entrechoquaient avec un fracas que répercutait bruyamment le ravin. Tamìr l'atteignit au flanc, dentelant sa cuirasse d'acier. Il lui riposta par un coup oblique à la tête qui envoya valser son heaume. Elle n'avait pas eu le temps d'en ajuster la jugulaire.

Elle recula, dans l'espoir de le ramasser. Korin se mit à rire et pressa l'avantage, la repoussant vers le ruisseau, là où Ki gisait, griffant faiblement la terre.

Elle le contourna et regagna d'un bond sa place initiale afin, si possible, d'éloigner Korin à nouveau de lui. « Debout, Ki ! Prends ton épée ! »

Avec un sourire goguenard, Korin suspendit son

attaque et se tourna vers Ki, levant à nouveau sa lame pour assener le coup fatal.

Elle se jeta sur lui avec un cri de désespoir et sentit le froid mortel de Frère l'envelopper.

Cela lui donna l'impression que le démon s'insinuait à l'intérieur de sa propre peau, la remplissant de toute l'énergie qu'il tirait de sa haine inextinguible. Il lui retroussa les babines et découvrit les dents sur un grondement et lui arracha de la gorge un cri surnaturel. Grâce à la lucidité de la rage du démon, elle repéra le défaut du haubert sous le bras levé de Korin et se fendit en une longue botte infaillible.

La pointe de sa lame atteignit sa cible. Le sang de Korin détrempa la chemise et la maille et s'épanouit au travers comme la corolle d'une fleur rouge.

Korin se tortilla pour se délivrer avant que Tamír n'ait pu pousser sa pointe assez profondément, puis tournoya pour l'assaillir derechef, ce qui les fit tous deux trébucher sur Ki. Korin toussait du sang tout en l'accablant d'invectives, et ses coups redoublèrent de sauvagerie quand il reprit un combat titubant.

De la main de l'Usurpateur, tu arracheras l'Épée.

« Rends-toi ! » cria-t-elle en bloquant sa lame avec la sienne et en le maintenant dans cette posture, garde contre garde.

« Jamais ! » hoqueta-t-il en crachant du sang.

Comme ils se dégageaient l'un de l'autre, elle eut de nouveau l'occasion d'apercevoir Ki, et cela lui suffit pour sentir un nouvel accès de la haine froide de Frère s'emparer d'elle et se ruer dans chaque fibre de son être. Ki gisait à présent sans bouger du tout, et la boue qui l'entourait était maculée de rouge.

Cette fois-ci, elle accueillit favorablement l'énergie de Frère. Celle-ci se joignait à sa propre fureur trop longtemps contenue pour tout ce qu'elle avait perdu, tout ce qui lui avait été refusé : Ki, l'amour de sa mère, un frère vivant, la gentillesse de son père, sa véritable identité... tout cela sacrifié pour lui faire finalement vivre ce moment-là.

« Maudis sois-tu ! » rugit-elle en volant à nouveau vers Korin, en le martelant comme une forcenée, en le repoussant encore et encore. Un flamboiement rouge lui emplissait les yeux. « Maudits soyez-vous tous, pour nous avoir volé nos *vies* ! »

Korin l'atteignit à l'épaule gauche, mais comme la lame porta sur l'attache de cuir de sa cuirasse, Tamìr s'en ressentit à peine. Elle mit même à profit la violence du coup pour se baisser, tournoyer et décocher un formidable coup de pied derrière les genoux de son adversaire.

Il chancela, laissant tomber malgré lui sa garde en se démenant pour conserver son équilibre. Encore à demi accroupie, Tamìr tailla vers le haut de toute sa puissance et sentit la main de Frère posée sur la sienne accentuer sa prise sur la poignée de l'épée quand elle frappa Korin en travers de la gorge, juste en dessous du menton, et y enfouit le tranchant de sa lame.

Korin poussa un cri étrangle, et le sang chaud qui jaillit de la plaie faillit presque aveugler Tamìr. Elle libéra sa lame d'une simple traction et s'essuya vivement les yeux d'un revers de main.

Korin demeura debout, presque pétrifié, les yeux attachés sur elle d'un air incrédule. Il essaya de dire quelque chose, mais ses lèvres ne réussirent à émettre que de l'écume sanglante. Sa respiration faisait un bruit abominable, poisseux et sifflant, en passant par la plaie béante de sa gorge. Sa poitrine se souleva de nouveau, et il s'effondra vers l'arrière parmi les rochers. Du sang continuait à gicler de la plaie par petits jets spasmodiques au rythme des pulsations de son cœur et ruisselait entre les pierres.

Un fleuve de sang.

Tamìr l'enjamba, sa lame en suspens, prête à porter le coup final.

Korin leva les yeux vers elle. La rage en avait disparu, supplantée par une expression de chagrin terrible. La main toujours crispée sur la poignée de son épée, sa bouche n'articula qu'un seul mot muet : *Cousin.*

À son insu, l'épée de Tamìr lui glissa des doigts pendant qu'elle contemplait ces prunelles sombres d'où s'effaçait peu à peu la vie. Un dernier souffle, étranglé, et c'en fut terminé, Korin était parti, la main toujours aussi crispée sur la poignée de la prestigieuse Épée.

Frère avait déserté Tamìr, et l'horreur de la bataille déferla sur elle. « Oh ! Enfer ! Korin. » Dans la mort, étendu là, sanglant, comme un pantin désarticulé, il ressemblait de nouveau au jouvenceau avec lequel elle avait joué, s'était bagarrée pour rire, s'était enivrée.

Elle entendait les bruits de la bataille qui faisait

encore rage au-delà du ravin, et elle entendait aussi ses amis les appeler, elle et Ki, d'une voix frénétique.

Ki !

« Ici ! » essaya-t-elle de leur répondre, mais elle ne parvint à exhaler qu'un chuchotement étouffé. En pleurant, elle se dirigea d'un pas chancelant vers l'endroit où gisait Ki et tomba à genoux près de lui. Son tabard était trempé de sang, et son bras fracassé se trouvait coincé sous lui, tordu dans une position aberrante. Elle découvrit la boucle de son heaume cabossé et le lui retira, puis elle le palpa vainement en quête d'indices que son cœur battait encore. Ses cheveux bruns soyeux étaient trempés de sang du côté où le coup de Korin l'avait atteint.

Elle souleva délicatement son torse flasque pour l'enlacer dans ses bras, serrant sa main valide et berçant sa tête contre sa poitrine. « Oh, non. Non, par pitié, pas lui aussi ! »

Le sang de Ki s'infiltrait à travers son propre tabard et collait ses doigts aux siens. Tant de sang.

« C'est cela que tu voulais ? cria-t-elle à Illior. Est-ce là le prix à payer pour donner une reine à Skala ? »

Quelque chose lui heurta l'épaule puis fit un gros plouf dans l'eau non loin d'elle. Elle baissa les yeux pour se rendre compte et poussa un cri étranglé.

C'était la tête de Korin.

Frère se dressait au-dessus de Tamìr, plus fort et plus tangible d'aspect qu'il ne l'avait jamais été. Il tenait l'Épée sanglante de Ghërilain dans sa main droite et, tandis qu'elle le considérait, leva la gauche et lécha le sang qui lui couvrait les doigts comme s'il s'agissait de miel.

Il jeta l'Épée près d'elle puis, avec un sourire à vous glacer les moelles, lui caressa les joues, les barbouillant encore davantage avec le sang de Korin. *Merci, Sœur.*

Elle eut un mouvement de recul pour se soustraire au contact glacé, tout en étreignant Ki plus étroitement que jamais. « C'est terminé. Tu as eu ta vengeance. Je ne veux plus jamais te revoir. Jamais ! »

Sans cesser de sourire, Frère étendit la main en direction du jeune homme.

« Ne le touche pas ! » s'écria-t-elle en faisant un rempart de son propre corps à celui-ci contre le démon.

Épargne tes larmes, Sœur. Il est toujours en vie.

« Quoi ? » Elle appuya un doigt sur le côté du cou de Ki, en quête désespérée d'y percevoir de nouveau une pulsation. Elle découvrit le plus imperceptible des battements juste en dessous de sa mâchoire.

« Tamìr, où es-tu ? » C'était Lynx, fou d'angoisse, de manière audible.

« Ici ! » hurla-t-elle en retour, recouvrant la voix.

« Tamìr ! » Arkoniel apparut au sommet de la berge. Il embrassa d'un seul coup d'œil l'ensemble du tableau et dégringola la rejoindre.

« Il est vivant ! cria Tamìr. Trouvez un guérisseur ! »

Arkoniel toucha le front de Ki et se rembrunit. « Je m'en charge, mais vous, il vous faut partir mettre un terme à cette bataille. »

C'était un véritable arrache-cœur que d'abandonner Ki dans les bras du magicien, mais elle réussit tout de même à s'y résoudre vaille que vaille.

Non sans chanceler sur ses pieds, elle ramassa l'Épée de Ghërilain. Toute gluante de sang qu'était la poignée, elle s'adaptait aussi parfaitement à sa main que si elle avait été façonnée tout exprès pour elle.

Elle l'avait déjà tenue une fois, la nuit du premier festin pris en compagnie de son oncle. Les dragons d'or usé ciselés en haut relief sur les deux quillons incurvés de la garde étaient maintenant incrustés de sang, tout comme la poignée d'ivoire filetée d'or et le sceau de rubis en intaille serti sur le pommeau. Le Sceau Royal. Son propre sceau, dorénavant... Un dragon portant sur son dos la Flamme de Sakor inscrite dans un croissant de lune. Sakor et Illior réunis.

Tu es Skala.

Elle s'inclina sur le ruisseau pour y repêcher la tête de Korin par les cheveux et l'emporta, elle aussi, le dos de ses doigts sensible à la chaleur qui s'attardait encore dans la crinière noire.

« Prenez soin de Ki, Arkoniel. Ne le laissez pas mourir. »

Chargée de ses trophées macabres, elle jeta sur Ki un dernier regard angoissé, puis elle escalada la berge pour aller accomplir la volonté d'Illior.

27

Il faisait presque nuit et il pleuvait à verse quand Tamìr émergea du ravin. Ici, les combats étaient à peu près terminés. Porion, mort, gisait parmi les fougères piétinées. Un peu plus loin, Moriel baignait, recroquevillé, dans une mare de sang, le poignard de Lutha planté dans la nuque.

Elle retrouva Cal grâce à l'or blond de ses cheveux. Il était couché, face contre terre, à l'endroit même où il était tombé, et Nikidès était assis auprès de lui, pleurant à chaudes larmes et le poing crispé sur une épaule blessée. Una tenait Hylia, qui se révéla souffrir d'une fracture au bras.

Compagnon contre Compagnon, Skalien contre Skalien.

Comme à l'accoutumée, Lynx était encore sur ses pieds, et Tyrien aussi. Ils furent les premiers à voir Tamìr et ce qu'elle transportait.

« Korin est mort ! » hurla Lynx.

Tout sembla s'arrêter complètement pendant un moment. Les derniers des gens de Korin se replièrent, les yeux fixés sur Tamìr, puis prirent la fuite dans la forêt, abandonnant leurs camarades tombés.

Nikidès s'avança à sa rencontre d'un pas chancelant. Ses yeux s'agrandirent à la vue de ce qu'elle portait.

« Je l'ai tué. Le sang est sur mes mains. » Elle entendait sa propre voix sonner à ses oreilles comme provenant de très loin, comme si c'était celle de quel-qu'un d'autre. Elle se sentait engourdie de partout, trop épuisée pour s'endeuiller ou se percevoir victorieuse. Elle partit en direction du champ de bataille, assez vaguement consciente que d'autres leur emboîtaient le pas.

« Es-tu blessée ? » demanda Nikidès d'un ton inquiet.

« Non, mais Ki si... » *Non, je ne vais pas y penser maintenant.* « Arkoniel est avec lui. Comment vont les autres ?

— Lorin est mort. » Nikidès déglutit durement, his-toire de se ressaisir. « Hylia a un bras cassé. Le reste d'entre nous n'a que des blessures mineures.

— Et de leur côté ? Caliel ?

— Il est vivant. Je... j'ai fait dévier ma lame au dernier moment. Je regrette, mais je n'ai pas pu, voilà tout...

— Ne regrette rien, Nik. Tu as bien fait. Assure-toi que lui et tous les autres soient rapportés au camp. »

Il n'en persista pas moins à demeurer près d'elle, la dévisageant d'un air bizarre. « Tu es certaine que tu n'es pas blessée ?

— Fais ce que je te dis ! » Elle avait besoin de toute sa concentration pour continuer à poser un pied devant l'autre. Nikidès se retira, sans doute afin d'exécuter son ordre ; mais Lynx, Tyrien et Una se reployèrent autour d'elle quand elle atteignit la lisière opposée des bois.

Le champ de bataille offrait un spectacle de carnage. Des guerriers et des chevaux morts gisaient de toutes parts, les corps, à certains endroits, s'empilaient les uns sur les autres par couches épaisses de trois. Tant d'hommes étaient tombés dans la chausse-trape du ruisseau que, retenue derrière le barrage de leurs cadavres, l'eau s'accumulait en un étang rouge.

Il y avait encore des groupes épars qui poursuivaient la lutte. Une partie des forces de Korin s'était retirée en haut de la colline. D'autres allaient à l'aventure au milieu des morts.

Les doigts toujours crispés dans la chevelure de son cousin, Tamìr jeta un regard circulaire accablé.

Malkanus surgit subitement à ses côtés, quoiqu'elle n'eût pas remarqué son approche. « Permettez-moi, Majesté. » Il s'écarta quelque peu des autres et leva sa baguette. Un grondement terrifiant, semblable à un coup de tonnerre, roula à travers le champ de bataille, si brusque et violent que les hommes tombèrent à genoux et se couvrirent la tête.

D'une voix qui semblait aussi puissante que la foudre, Malkanus cria : « Écoutez la reine Tamìr ! »

Et cela eut l'effet escompté. Subitement, des centaines de visages se tournèrent vers elle. Tamìr s'éloigna davantage de la forêt puis brandit simultanément la tête de Korin et l'Épée. « Le prince Korin est mort ! » s'époumona-t-elle, sa voix bien ténue par comparaison. « Que le combat cesse ! »

On se passa le cri de proche en proche à travers le champ de bataille. Les derniers des guerriers de Korin opérèrent une retraite confuse pour se réfugier sur la rive opposée du ruisseau, au pied de la colline.

L'unique bannière encore visible au sein de leur débandade était celle de Wethring.

« Lynx, prends quelques hommes et rapportez la dépouille de Korin », ordonna-t-elle. Je veux qu'on la traite avec respect. Fabriquez un brancard et couvrez le corps, puis transportez-le jusqu'à notre camp. Avertissez les drysiens qu'il faut le préparer pour la crémation. Nik, tu t'occupes des restes de Lorin. Nous devrons les rendre à son père. Et que quelqu'un me trouve un héraut !

— Ici, Majesté. »

Elle lui tendit la tête de Korin. « Montrez ceci à Lord Wethring, et déclarez que la journée nous est acquise, puis rapportez le trophée à mon camp. J'exige que tous les nobles viennent se présenter devant moi toutes affaires cessantes, sous peine d'être déclarés traîtres. »

L'homme enveloppa la tête dans un pan de son manteau puis se dépêcha d'aller accomplir sa mission.

Une fois délivrée de ce fardeau, Tamìr essuya l'Épée de Ghërilain sur l'ourlet de son tabard crasseux puis la glissa dans son fourreau avant de retourner à pied vers la clairière.

On avait remonté Ki du fond du ravin. Arkoniel était assis par terre sous un grand arbre, tenant la tête du jeune homme dans son giron, pendant que Caliel s'efforçait d'étancher la plaie de son propre crâne.

Elle fut abasourdie de voir ce dernier conscient. Le pansement qu'il tenait tremblait dans ses mains, et des larmes ruisselaient le long de ses joues.

Elle s'agenouilla près d'eux et tendit une main hésitante pour toucher la face boueuse de Ki. « Est-ce qu'il vivra ?

— Je l'ignore », lui répondit le magicien.

Ces mots paisibles la frappèrent plus durement qu'aucun des coups que lui avait administrés Korin.

S'il meurt...

Elle se mordit la lèvre, incapable de formuler jusqu'au bout une idée pareille. Elle s'inclina pour embrasser Ki sur le front et chuchota : « Tu m'as donné ta parole.

— Majesté ? » demanda Caliel dans un souffle.

Faute de pouvoir encore arriver à le regarder en face, elle questionna : « Où est Tanil ?

— Dans les bois, juste en face, là. Vivant, je pense.

— Tu devrais aller le voir. Donne-lui les nouvelles.

— Merci. » Il se leva pour partir.

Relevant les yeux, elle examina sa figure mais n'y découvrit encore que du chagrin. « Vous êtes tous les deux bienvenus dans mon camp. »

Des larmes plus abondantes glissèrent lentement sur les joues de Caliel, creusant des traînées pâles à travers la crasse et le sang, quand il lui fit une révérence mal assurée.

« Prends-le pour ce que ça vaut, Cal, je regrette. Je n'ai jamais voulu me battre avec lui.

— Je le sais. » Il s'éloigna vers les arbres d'un pas chancelant.

Lorsqu'elle se retourna, elle surprit Arkoniel qui l'observait, le regard plus triste qu'elle ne l'avait jamais vu.

Des brancards pour les morts et pour les blessés furent bricolés à la hâte avec des petits sapins et des manteaux. Le corps de Korin fut emporté le premier, le transport de Ki suivit immédiatement. Tamìr marchait aux côtés de celui-ci, jetant sur lui tout du long jusqu'au retour au camp des regards furtifs pour contrôler que sa poitrine continuait de s'élever et de s'abaisser laborieusement. Alors qu'elle brûlait de sangloter, de crier, de le serrer très fort pour l'empêcher de la quitter, il lui fallait tenir la tête haute et rendre leurs salutations aux hommes et aux femmes qu'ils rencontraient sur leur passage.

Des guerriers originaires des deux partis vagabondaient parmi les morts, à la recherche qui d'amis tombés, qui d'ennemis à dépouiller. Les corbeaux étaient déjà arrivés, attirés par l'odeur de mort. Il y en avait des nuées qui, massés dans les arbres, emplissaient l'air de leurs cris rauques et affamés pendant qu'ils attendaient leur tour.

Au camp, c'est sous la tente de Tamìr que l'on déposa Ki pour le livrer aux soins des drysiens. Elle glissait un œil anxieux par la portière ouverte sur leurs manœuvres en attendant que les lords de Korin viennent à reddition.

Recouvert d'un manteau, le corps de Korin, flanqué de ceux de Porion et des Compagnons morts au combat, reposait non loin sur un catafalque improvisé. Tous les Compagnons de Tamìr montaient une veillée silencieuse en leur honneur, tous excepté Nikidès et Tanil.

En dépit de son propre chagrin et de sa blessure, Nik était entré sous la tente et s'employait à y régler consciencieusement les détails nécessaires, tels que ceux d'envoyer des hérauts répandre la nouvelle de la victoire et du décès de Korin ou de s'assurer qu'on lâche des oiseaux messagers pour en informer au plus vite Atyion. Tamìr lui savait gré, comme toujours, de sa compétence et de sa prévoyance.

Recroquevillé par terre auprès de son maître défunt, Tanil, lui, refusait de se laisser emmener ailleurs et poussait des sanglots inconsolables sous son manteau. Il était totalement incapable de comprendre ce qui s'était passé, et peut-être cela valait-il mieux. Caliel, à genoux, son épée plantée devant lui, demeurait avec le malheureux pour lui relater les événements de la journée. Il avait déjà rapporté avoir vu tomber Urmanis, Garol et Mago plus tôt dans la journée. On n'avait pas trouvé trace d'Alben, ni parmi les vivants ni parmi les morts.

Du côté de Tamìr, des émissaires vinrent annoncer que Jorvaï avait été blessé par une flèche à la poitrine ; mais Kyman et Nyanis survinrent indemnes, peu après. Le train de bagages de Korin avait été capturé, ce qui permit de disposer de vivres et de tentes supplémentaires – ce qui n'était pas un luxe. Cela, joint au ravitaillement apporté par les Aurënfaïes, serait suffisant pour camper sur place jusqu'à ce que le transport des blessés puisse s'effectuer sans risque.

Arengil apporta la nouvelle que ses compatriotes avaient exterminé les cavaliers dépêchés par Korin pour les prendre à revers, et ce sans perdre un seul des leurs. Solun et Hiril ne tardèrent pas à le suivre, porteurs des étendards pris à l'ennemi. Tamìr n'écouta que d'une moitié d'oreille. À l'intérieur de la tente, Ki demeurait inerte, et les drysiens paraissaient inquiets.

Wethring et quelques-uns des nobles restants se présentèrent sous une bannière de trêve. Tamìr les reçut debout, tira l'Épée et la brandit devant elle. Le héraut avait rapporté la tête de Korin et la plaça soigneusement sous le manteau qui recouvrait le corps.

S'agenouillant, Wethring inclina humblement la tête. « La journée vous est acquise, Majesté.

— Par la volonté d'Illior », répondit-elle.

Il leva les yeux pour examiner son visage.

« Croyez-vous ce que vos yeux vous montrent ? demanda-t-elle.

— Oui, Majesté.

— Me jurerez-vous votre foi ? »

Il papillota de stupéfaction. « Je le ferai si vous voulez bien l'accepter.

— Vous avez été loyal envers Korin. Faites preuve envers moi de la même loyauté, et je vous confirmerai dans vos titres et terres, en contrepartie du service du sang.

— Vous aurez les cieux, Majesté. Je le jure par les Quatre et me porte garant pour tous ceux qui avaient suivi ma bannière.

— Où se trouve Nevus, fils de Solari ?

— Il est parti vers l'est, à destination d'Atyion.

— Avez-vous reçu des nouvelles de lui ?

— Non, Majesté.

— Je vois. Et Lord Alben ? Est-ce qu'il a péri aujourd'hui ?

— Nul ne l'a vu, Majesté.

— Et pour ce qui est de Lord Nyrin ?

— Mort, Majesté, à Cirna.

— Korin l'a tué ? » demanda Lutha, ahuri

« Non, il est tombé de la tour de Lady Nalia.

— Tombé ? » Tamìr laissa échapper un rire bref et sans joie. C'était une mort ridicule pour quelqu'un d'aussi redouté. « Eh bien, voilà une pelletée de bonnes nouvelles, alors.

— Ai-je votre permission pour brûler nos morts ?

— Naturellement. »

Wethring jeta un coup d'œil navré vers la forme drapée toute proche d'eux. « Et Korin ?

— Il est mon parent. Je veillerai à ce qu'il soit brûlé comme il sied et à ce que ses cendres soient recueillies pour son épouse. Renvoyez votre armée dans ses foyers et soyez à mon service à Atyion dans un mois. »

Wethring se releva et lui fit de nouveau une profonde révérence. « J'entends et j'obéis, reine miséricordieuse.

— Je n'en ai pas encore tout à fait terminé avec vous. En quoi consistent les défenses de Cirna ? Quelles dispositions Korin a-t-il prises en faveur de Lady Nalia ?

— On a laissé là-bas la garnison de la forteresse. Il s'agit essentiellement de Busards de Nyrin, à l'heure actuelle, et de quelques magiciens.

— Va-t-elle se dresser contre moi ?

— Lady Nalia ? » Wethring sourit et secoua la tête. « Elle n'aurait pas l'ombre d'une idée sur la manière de s'y prendre, Majesté. »

Lutha, qui avait prêté une oreille des plus attentive à cet échange, s'avança sur ces entrefaites. « Il a raison, Tamìr. Elle a été mise à l'abri par le biais d'une pure et simple séquestration. Les nobles qui connaissent la cour de Korin ne sont pas sans le savoir. Elle ne peut compter sur les secours de personne, là-bas. Avec ta permission, j'aimerais emmener immédiatement une force au nord pour assurer sa protection.

— Vous devriez la ramener ici et la maintenir à proximité, conseilla Arkoniel. Vous ne sauriez courir le risque qu'elle et son enfant deviennent tôt ou tard des instruments manipulables contre votre personne. »

Lutha planta un genou devant elle. « De grâce, Tamìr. Elle n'a jamais fait le moindre mal à qui que ce soit. »

Elle devina que l'intérêt qu'il manifestait pour Lady Nalia n'était pas exclusivement dicté par la courtoisie. « Bien entendu. Elle te connaît. Tu serais mon meilleur émissaire auprès d'elle. Fais-lui comprendre qu'elle se trouve sous ma protection personnelle et pas en état d'arrestation. Mais il va te falloir des guerriers pour prendre la forteresse.

— J'irai, avec votre consentement », offrit Nyanis.

Tamìr hocha la tête avec gratitude. Elle avait confiance dans tous ses nobles, mais Nyanis lui en inspirait plus que quiconque. « Emparez-vous de la place et laissez-y une garnison. Lutha, ramène ici Lady Nalia.

— Je la préserverai au péril de mes jours, s'engagea solennellement Lutha.

— Arkoniel, vous et vos collègues y allez aussi, pour régler leur affaire aux magiciens de Nyrin.

— Je m'assurerai personnellement de notre succès, Majesté.

— Ne leur accordez pas plus de merci qu'ils n'en ont accordé eux-mêmes à ceux qu'ils ont brûlés vifs.

— Nous partirons, nous aussi, dit Solun, et anéantirons les blasphémateurs.

— Mes gens de même, ajouta Hiril.

— Je vous remercie. Allez, maintenant. Emportez ce qui vous est nécessaire de fournitures et chevauchez dur. »

Lutha et les autres saluèrent et s'empressèrent d'aller procéder à leurs préparatifs. Arengil esquissa le geste de les suivre comme ils s'éloignaient, mais Tamìr le rappela. « Souhaites-tu toujours faire partie des Compagnons ?

— Évidemment ! s'exclama le jeune Gèdre.

— Alors, reste. » Elle se leva pour aller retrouver Ki mais s'aperçut qu'Arkoniel s'était attardé.

« Mes collègues sont capables de s'occuper tout seuls des gens de Nyrin, si vous préfériez que je ne vous quitte pas.

— Il n'est personne en qui je me fie plus qu'en vous », lui dit-elle, et elle vit le rouge lui monter aux joues. « Je sais que vous ferez le mieux possible en ma faveur pour protéger Lady Nalia, de quelque manière que ce soit. Vous concevez mieux que quiconque au monde pourquoi je ne veux pas qu'on répande en mon nom du sang innocent.

— Cela m'importe plus que je ne saurais dire, répliqua-t-il d'une voix enrouée par l'émotion. Je garderai un œil sur vous ici et reviendrai sur-le-champ si vous avez besoin de moi.

— Je m'en sortirai. Allez, maintenant. » Là-dessus, elle se baissa pour franchir la portière basse de la tente puis la rabattit derrière elle.

L'odeur dégagée par les herbes des drysiens rendait l'atmosphère pesante à l'intérieur. Kaulin était assis près de Ki.

La fracture de ce dernier avait été réduite et son bras solidement enveloppé de bandages de fortune puis, en guise d'attelle, emprisonné dans la tige d'une botte découpée. Sa poitrine et sa tête étaient ceintes vaille que vaille de tissu lacéré. Sa figure était blanche et paisible sous les traînées de boue et de sang.

« S'est-il finalement réveillé ?

— Non, répondit Kaulin. L'épée n'a pas atteint le poumon. C'est le coup reçu à la tête qui est mauvais.

— J'aimerais rester seule avec lui.

— Comme il vous plaira, Majesté. »

S'asseyant auprès de Ki, elle saisit sa main gauche dans la sienne. Il respirait de façon presque imperceptible. Elle se pencha sur lui et chuchota : « Tout est terminé, Ki. Nous avons gagné. Mais je ne sais pas ce que je ferai si tu meurs ! » Le tonnerre gronda au loin quand elle pressa les doigts froids du mourant contre sa joue. « Même si tu ne veux jamais consentir à être mon consort... » L'engourdissement béni auquel elle s'était cramponnée jusqu'alors était en train de se dissiper, et les larmes vinrent.

« Je t'en conjure, Ki ! Ne t'en va pas ! »

28

Ki était perdu, et glacé jusqu'aux os.

Des images incohérentes fusaient derrière ses yeux. *Elle est en danger ! Je ne vais pas la rejoindre à temps !*

Une fenêtre étoilée, des jambes qui se démenaient.

Tamìr désarmée, sous l'épée flamboyante de Korin...

Trop loin ! Peux pas atteindre...

Non !

Les ténèbres l'engloutirent avant qu'il n'ait pu arriver jusqu'à elle, et la douleur. Tant de douleur.

Tout en dérivant, seul dans le noir, il crut entendre des voix lointaines qui l'appelaient. Tamìr ?

Non, elle est morte... j'ai échoué, et elle est morte...

Alors, laissez-moi mourir aussi.

Une telle douleur.

Suis-je mort ?

Non, pas encore, enfant.

Lhel ? Où êtes-vous ? Je ne peux pas voir !

Tu dois être fort. Elle a besoin de toi.

Lhel ? Comme vous m'avez manqué !

Tu m'as manqué toi aussi, enfant. Mais c'est à Tamìr que tu dois penser, maintenant.

La panique le lancina. *Je suis désolé. Je l'ai laissée mourir !*

Une petite main raboteuse se referma durement sur la sienne. *Ouvre les yeux, enfant.*

Subitement, Ki recouvra la vue. Il se tenait aux côtés de Lhel dans la tente. La pluie qui était en train de tambouriner sur la toile dégouttait au travers tout autour d'eux. Et Tamìr se trouvait là, endormie par terre, auprès d'une paillasse sur laquelle était allongé quelqu'un d'autre.

Elle est vivante ! Mais ce qu'elle a l'air triste... Nous avons perdu la bataille ?

Non, vous l'avez gagnée. Regarde plus attentivement.

Tamìr, nous avons gagné ! cria-t-il en essayant de lui toucher l'épaule. Mais il en fut incapable. Il ne pouvait plus du tout sentir sa main. En se penchant davantage sur elle, il aperçut des larmes séchées sur ses joues, ainsi que le visage de la personne auprès de laquelle dormait Tamìr.

C'est moi. Il pouvait voir son propre visage, blême, et les minces croissants blancs qui soulignaient ses cils écartés. *Je suis mort !*

Non, mais tu n'es pas vivant non plus, rétorqua Lhel.

Tu patientes. Frère apparut aux côtés de Tamìr, les yeux levés vers Ki d'un air moins hostile qu'à l'ordinaire. *Tu patientes quelque part entre vie et mort, comme moi-même. Nous sommes encore liés, tous les deux.*

Regarde plus attentivement, chuchota Lhel. *Regarde le cœur de Tamìr et les vôtres.*

À force de loucher, Ki parvint tout juste à discerner quelque chose qui, ressemblant à une fine racine noire et tordue, s'étirait de la poitrine de Frère à celle de Tamìr. Non, pas une racine, mais un cordon ombilical ratatiné.

En baissant les yeux, il vit un autre cordon entre lui-même et son propre corps, et encore un autre qui s'étirait de son corps à celui de Tamìr, mais ces deux-là étaient argentés et brillants. D'autres filaments, d'un éclat moins vif, rayonnaient à partir de là et disparaissaient dans toutes les directions. Il y en avait un sombre qui, à partir de la poitrine de Tamìr, traversait la tente jusqu'à la portière ouverte. Korin se tenait là, dehors, regardant à l'intérieur avec une expression perdue.

Qu'est-ce qu'il fiche ici, lui ?

Elle m'a tué, chuchota Korin, et la peur envahit Ki quand le sombre regard vide se tourna vers lui. *Faux ami !*

Ne te tracasse pas pour lui, enfant. Il n'a rien à réclamer de toi. Lhel toucha le cordon argenté qui joignait Ki à Tamìr. *Celui-ci est très solide, beaucoup plus solide que le cordon de ta propre vie.*

Je ne peux pas mourir ! Je ne peux pas l'abandonner ! Elle a besoin de moi.

Tu lui as sauvé la vie, aujourd'hui. Je l'avais prévu dès notre première rencontre, et bien d'autres choses encore. Elle sera très triste si tu meurs. Son ventre risque de ne jamais s'arrondir. Votre peuple a besoin des enfants qu'elle et toi vous lui donnerez. Si je t'aide à vivre, l'aimeras-tu ?

Jetant un regard sur sa propre face inerte, Ki vit des larmes rouler de dessous ses cils et ruisseler lentement le long de ses joues. *Mais je l'aime ! Je l'aime vraiment ! Aidez-moi, par pitié !*

Or, à l'instant même où il le disait, il sentit le cordon qui rattachait son esprit à son corps tirailler douloureusement sa poitrine et s'amenuiser. Il flottait au-dessus de lui-même, les yeux attachés sur Tamìr. Même dans son sommeil, elle lui tenait fermement la main, comme si elle pouvait ainsi le retenir et le soustraire à la mort.

Par pitié, chuchota-t-il, *je veux rester !*

Tiens bon, chuchota Lhel.

« Réveille-toi, *keesa*.

— Lhel ? » Tamìr se dressa sur son séant, suffoquée.

Il faisait encore noir, sous la tente, et la pluie persistait à marteler la toile. Un éclair fulgurant fit virer au gris les ténèbres. C'était Mahti qui se penchait sur elle, et non Lhel. Un coup de tonnerre ébranla le sol. Quelque chose lui cogna la joue ; de l'eau dégouttait de la tignasse du sorcier. Il venait tout juste d'entrer, trempé par l'orage.

« Mahti ? Tu es revenu !

— Chut, *keesa*. » Il pointa le doigt vers Ki. « Il très faible. Tu devoir me laisser jouer guérison pour lui. Son *mari* essayer de partir. »

Tamìr resserra son étreinte sur la main froide de Ki et hocha la tête. « Fais tout ce que tu peux. »

Un nouvel éclair illumina la tente, et le tonnerre ébranla si violemment le sol que le monde leur donna l'impression de s'écrouler autour d'eux.

Mahti s'assit aussi loin de Ki que le permettait l'exiguïté des lieux, le dos appuyé contre la toile détrempée. Il porta l'oo'lu à ses lèvres, laissant reposer l'autre extrémité de l'instrument près du flanc du patient, puis son souffle exhala le sortilège chanté.

L'esprit du garçon s'était déjà échappé de son corps. Mahti pouvait le sentir voleter dans les parages. Il pouvait voir Lhel et Frère, ainsi que l'esprit désolé qui rôdait dehors sous l'averse, mais comme Ki se trouvait, lui, pris entre la vie et la mort, il n'arrivait pas à le voir nettement. La mélopée destinée à soulager l'esprit de la pesanteur de la chair n'était pas nécessaire, mais le sorcier savait qu'il devait agir vite pour guérir suffisamment le corps pour empêcher l'esprit de s'évader avant qu'il ne soit perdu pour toujours.

La voix profonde de Séjour emplit la tête et la poitrine de Mahti tandis qu'il jouait, rassemblant la puissance indispensable. Lorsqu'elle fut assez conséquente, il orienta le chant vers l'esprit papillonnant pour l'envelopper dans un filet de sonorités qui lui interdisent de s'envoler. Ensuite, il entremêla les voix des grenouilles et des hérons nocturnes pour évacuer le sang noir accumulé dans le crâne du jeune homme. C'était une sale blessure que celle-là, mais d'un genre auquel il s'était déjà attaqué par le passé. Cela prit du temps, mais il finit par sentir qu'une partie de la douleur refluait.

Il joua là-dessus à l'intérieur du corps, abandonnant aux os du bras le soin de se ressouder d'eux-mêmes pour se concentrer sur la plaie profonde du flanc. Il recourut à la chanson des ours pour en retirer la chaleur ; à en croire les autres guérisseurs, il s'agissait là d'une bonne magie qui avait déjà fait ses preuves. Mahti l'appliqua et en reconnut les vertus. La guérison ne poserait pas de problème à cet endroit, si Ki survivait.

Il joua sur toutes les autres parties du corps, sans y découvrir grand-chose qui requît d'attention spéciale. Ki était jeune et vigoureux, et il avait envie de vivre.

Mais comme la blessure à la tête continuait à le combattre, Mahti accentua la puissance du chant pour en chasser la noire menace. Il lui fallut s'acharner longtemps, mais lorsqu'il eut achevé la troisième chanson du héron, la douleur était presque partie, et une expression plus paisible se lisait sur la physionomie de Ki. Mahti battit des paupières pour se débarrasser de la sueur qui l'aveuglait puis, gentiment, persuada l'esprit de réintégrer la chair. Celui-ci s'y prêta volontiers, à la manière d'un plongeon piquant sous l'eau à la poursuite d'un poisson.

Quand Mahti en eut terminé, seuls le bruit de la pluie et le vacarme du tonnerre emplissaient la tente, ainsi que la respiration oppressée de la fille et de son orëskiri qui attendaient, les yeux anxieusement fixés sur le garçon.

« Ki ? » Tamìr repoussa d'une main caressante les cheveux sales et encroûtés de sang qui retombaient sur son front bandé ; elle retint son souffle quand il battit faiblement des paupières.

« Ki, ouvre les yeux ! chuchota-t-elle.

— Tob ? » marmonna-t-il. Il ouvrit les yeux très lentement, sans les focaliser sur quoi que ce soit. Sa pupille droite était plus grande que la gauche.

« Louée soit la Lumière ! » Des larmes spontanées dévalèrent le long de ses joues quand elle s'inclina plus avant. « Comment te sens-tu. ?

— Fait mal. Mon bras... tête. » Son regard vaseux n'accommodait pas. « Parti ?

— Qui est parti ? »

Ses yeux finirent par la trouver, mais ils étaient encore très vagues. « Je... Je croyais... Je ne sais pas. » Il referma les yeux, et des larmes perlèrent sous ses cils. « J'ai tué maître Porion.

— Ne pense pas à ça maintenant.

— Tenir lui éveillé, lui dit Mahti. Il va... » Il mima le fait de vomir. « Pas dormir jusque le soleil descend de nouveau. »

Avec l'aide du sorcier, Tamìr redressa Ki en lui glissant un paquetage sous la tête. Il se mit à vomir presque tout de suite. Elle attrapa un heaume qui traînait par terre et le lui tint sous le menton pendant qu'il rejetait le peu qu'il avait avalé.

« Reposer, dit Mahti à Ki quand celui-ci retomba mollement en arrière dans les bras de Tamìr. Toi guérir maintenant.

— Comment puis-je te remercier ? demanda-t-elle.

— Tenir promesse, répondit Mahti. Et laisser moi jouer guérison pour toi. Lhel dire.

— Je n'arrête pas de te le répéter, je n'en ai pas besoin. »

Mahti l'empoigna par le genou, ses yeux sombres subitement intimidants. « Tu ne sais pas. Je sais ! Lhel savoir. » Il baissa la main et lui cueillit brutalement l'entrejambe. « Toi encore attachée au démon *ici*. »

Tamìr lui rembarra la main avec colère, mais au moment même où elle le faisait, elle éprouva de nouveau la sensation puissante et déconcertante de posséder deux corps à la fois, le sien et celui de Tobin.

« Ça finir magie, promit Mahti comme s'il comprenait. Faire toi propre. »

Propre. Oui, elle voulait cela. Non sans réprimer un tremblement d'appréhension, elle hocha la tête. « Qu'exiges-tu que je fasse ? »

Mahti se déplaça, de manière à laisser reposer la bouche de l'oo'lu près de la jambe de Tamìr. « Juste rester assise. »

Fermant les yeux, il commença à émettre un vrombissement grave et lancinant. Tamìr se crispa, dans l'expectative du brasier qui avait déjà réduit en cendres son corps précédent.

Mais ce ne fut pas du tout semblable, cette fois.

Lhel était assise tout près de Mahti, lui chuchotant à l'oreille ce qu'il devait chercher. C'était un sortilège féminin qu'il était en train de défaire, et il lui fallait se montrer prudent pour ne rien endommager de ce qui devrait subsister.

Frère s'accroupit à côté de Tamìr, les yeux attachés non pas sur elle mais sur Lhel.

Mahti commença à jouer une chanson d'eau, mais sur une tonalité différente. Il connaissait cette chanson-là ; c'était la première qu'il avait jouée sur Séjour. Désormais, elle lui faisait voir le gros cordon ombilical ratatiné qui joignait le frère et la sœur. Elle lui faisait voir la silhouette fantomatique du corps de garçon qui restait accrochée à la fille comme les lambeaux d'une peau de serpent à l'époque de la mue. La forme d'un pénis atrophié se discernait encore entre les cuisses. La chanson de Mahti détacha les derniers vestiges du corps spectral, laissant intacte uniquement la chair vivante.

La chanson de la peau de serpent, voilà comment il appellerait celle-ci, s'il lui arrivait jamais d'avoir à s'en resservir. Il en rendit grâces à Lhel en silence.

Le cordon ombilical qui joignait Tamìr à son frère était coriace comme une vieille racine, mais la chanson le calcina de part en part, lui aussi. Il tomba entre eux comme réduit en cendres.

Tu t'en vas, maintenant, chuchota-t-il mentalement à Frère.

Du coin de l'œil, il vit Lhel se lever et prendre par la main le démon tremblant. *Enfant, quitte cette vie qui ne fut jamais tienne. Va, et repose-toi pour la prochaine.*

La sorcière serra dans ses bras la pâle créature. Il se cramponna à elle pendant un moment, comme un garçon vivant, puis disparut en soupirant.

De la belle ouvrage, chuchota Lhel. *Les voici libres tous les deux.*

Mais Mahti vit qu'un autre cordon sombre joignait Tamìr à un autre fantôme, là, dehors. Il joua la chanson du canif et délivra l'homme mort aux yeux sombres pour lui permettre, à lui aussi, de poursuivre sa route jusqu'à la paix.

Il y avait un autre très vieux cordon qui partait du cœur de Tamìr et s'étirait loin, loin... Mahti le toucha mentalement. Tout au bout de celui-ci était tapi un esprit colérique et confus. Mère.

Tranche celui-là aussi, chuchota Lhel.

Mahti s'exécuta, et il entendit retentir un cri plaintif, bref et lointain.

Il y avait autour de Tamìr beaucoup d'autres cordons, comme il y en avait autour de tout un chacun. Certains étaient bienfaisants. Certains étaient nuisibles. Celui qui existait entre elle et le garçon qu'elle tenait dans ses bras était le plus solide, aussi lumineux qu'un éclair.

Lhel le toucha et sourit. Celui-là n'avait besoin d'aucun des sortilèges de Mahti.

Satisfait du cœur de la fille, il joua pour extirper la souffrance de ses blessures puis tourna son attention vers la fleur rouge de son sein. La liaison magique opérée par Lhel n'avait pas plongé jusqu'à ces profondeurs-là. En dépit de sa menue poitrine et de ses hanches étroites, le sein de Tamìr, bien bâti, était un berceau fertile qui n'attendait que d'être occupé. En revanche, Mahti joua son sortilège sur la ceinture

408

osseuse du pelvis, afin de faciliter la venue au monde des enfants pendant les années à venir.

Ce fut seulement quand il en eut fini qu'il s'avisa du départ de Lhel.

Tamìr fut étonnée de constater à quel point l'étrange musique de Mahti pouvait avoir d'agrément. Au lieu de la sensation froide et rampante dont Nyrin lui avait infligé l'expérience ou de l'effet vertigineux procuré par les sortilèges visuels d'Arkoniel, elle n'éprouvait rien d'autre qu'une douce chaleur. Quand il en eut terminé, elle poussa un soupir et rouvrit les yeux, se sentant plus reposée, fraîche et dispose qu'elle ne l'avait été depuis des jours et des jours.

« C'est tout ?

— Oui. Maintenant toi seulement toi, répondit-il en lui tapotant le genou.

— Comment te sens-tu ? » questionna Ki d'une voix râpeuse, en louchant vers elle comme s'il s'attendait à ce que son aspect se soit plus ou moins transformé.

Elle observa une immobilité frappante pendant un moment, son regard tourné vers l'intérieur. Elle percevait une différence, mais les mots lui manquaient encore pour la définir. « Merci, chuchota-t-elle finalement. Je te dois tant...

— Tenir promesse et souvenir Lhel et moi. » Non sans lui adresser un dernier sourire affectueux, Mahti se leva et quitta la tente.

Une fois seule à seul avec Ki de nouveau, elle porta les doigts de sa main valide à ses lèvres et les embrassa, tandis que de nouvelles larmes lui piquaient les paupières. « Il s'en est fallu de rien que tu ne me tiennes pas ta promesse, espèce de salopard, réussit-elle enfin à proférer.

— Moi ? Non ! » s'esclaffa-t-il tout bas. Il resta coi pendant un certain laps de temps, l'œil vaguement perdu quelque part dans les ombres qui le surplombaient. Elle craignit qu'il ne fût en train de dériver pour sombrer de nouveau dans le sommeil, mais tout à coup, sa main se reploya sur la sienne et la broya dans une étreinte douloureuse. « Korin ! Je ne suis pas arrivé à te rejoindre !

— Si, Ki, et il t'a presque tué.

— Non... J'ai vu... » Il ferma les yeux et fit une grimace. « Par les couilles de Bilairy !

— Quoi ?

— Je t'ai fait défaillance... quand cela comptait le plus !

— Non. » Elle le serra plus fort. « Il m'aurait eue, sans ton intervention.

— Pouvais pas le laisser... » Il frissonna contre elle. « Pouvais pas. Mais qu'est-ce qui... ? » Ses yeux tendirent à se refermer puis s'ouvrirent très largement. « C'est toi qui l'as tué ?

— Oui. »

Ki demeura muet pendant un moment, et elle vit que son regard s'égarait de nouveau vers la portière ouverte de la tente. « Je voulais t'épargner ça.

— C'est mieux ainsi. Je le vois maintenant. Ce combat était notre affaire. »

Ki soupira, et ses idées s'embrouillèrent à nouveau.

« Ki ? Ne te rendors pas. Il faut que tu restes éveillé. »

Il avait les yeux ouverts, mais elle voyait nettement que son esprit battait la campagne. De peur de le laisser s'assoupir, elle continua de jacasser pendant des heures à propos de rien – de ce qu'ils feraient lors de leur prochaine visite au fort, de chevaux, de n'importe quel sujet qui lui traversait la cervelle, afin de l'empêcher de fermer les yeux.

Il ne répondit pas du tout entre-temps, mais elle voyait scintiller des larmes dans ses yeux et, lorsqu'il les fixa de nouveau sur elle, ils avaient une expression douloureuse. « Je ne peux pas... arrêter de le voir se jeter sur toi. T'ai vue tomber. Je n'arrivais pas à te rejoindre...

— Mais tu l'as fait ! » S'inclinant précautionneusement sur lui, elle pressa ses lèvres contre les siennes et les sentit trembler. « Tu l'as fait, Ki. Tu es presque mort pour moi. Il... » Elle déglutit durement, car sa voix défaillait. « De bout en bout, c'est toi qui avais vu juste sur Korin.

— Désolé, marmonna-t-il. Tu l'aimais.

— C'est *toi* que j'aime, Ki ! S'il t'avait tué, je n'aurais pas toléré de te survivre. »

Il resserra de nouveau ses doigts sur les siens. « Je connais ce sentiment-là. »

Elle recouvra difficilement son souffle et sourit. « Tu m'as appelée "Tob" quand tu t'es réveillé. »

Il lâcha un rire faiblard. « Coup sur le crâne. Emberlificoté ma cervelle. »

Elle hésita puis demanda tout bas : « Suis-je Tamìr pour toi, maintenant ? »

Ki scruta son visage dans la pénombre puis lui adressa un sourire somnolent. « Tu seras toujours les deux, tout au fond de moi. Mais c'est Tamìr que je vois et Tamìr que j'embrasse. »

Les mots de Ki, mais aussi la chaleur de sa voix et de son regard, soulagèrent le cœur de Tamìr d'un poids. « Je ne supporterai plus jamais de me passer de ta présence ! » Les mots déferlèrent comme un torrent, sans qu'elle puisse les retenir. « Je *déteste* te laisser coucher dans d'autres chambres et je déteste me sentir mal dans ma peau chaque fois que je te touche. Je déteste ne plus savoir ce que nous sommes l'un pour l'autre. Je... »

Ki lui pressa la main une fois de plus. « Je présume que je ferais mieux de t'épouser pour clarifier la situation, hein ? »

Tamìr le dévisagea fixement. « Tu délires ! »

Le sourire de Ki s'évasa. « Peut-être, mais je sais parfaitement ce que je suis en train de dire. Veux-tu de moi ? »

Un mélange enivrant de joie et de peur lui donna l'impression qu'elle allait défaillir. « Mais pour ce qui est de... » Elle ne put se résoudre à exprimer cela. « Avec moi ?

— Nous nous débrouillerons. Qu'en dis-tu ? La reine de Skala daignera-t-elle consentir à prendre pour consort un chevalier de merde, fils d'un voleur de chevaux ? »

Elle exhala un rire tremblant. « Toi, et personne d'autre. Jamais.

— Bien. Affaire entendue, dans ce cas. »

Tamìr se déplaça pour caler son dos plus commodément contre le paquetage, la tête de Ki posée sur sa poitrine. C'était tout aussi agréable qu'auparavant, et pourtant différent aussi.

« Oui, chuchota-t-elle. Affaire entendue. »

Mahti s'arrêta près de la lisière de la forêt pour jeter un regard en arrière vers les feux épars et le rougeoiement lointain qui émanait de l'intérieur de la tente. Par-delà s'étendait le champ de bataille, où les esprits des morts récents se tortillaient en volutes semblables à des bouchons de brouillard que la pluie se révélait impuissante à dissiper.

« Or çà, Grande Mère, devrions-nous aider un tel peuple ? » chuchota-t-il en branlant du chef. Mais il n'y avait pas de réponse pour lui, et pas de compagnie non plus. Lhel était partie aussi sûrement que l'esprit du démon. Il se demanda s'il la rencontrerait de nouveau, dans les yeux d'un enfant ?

Comme il gagnait le couvert des arbres, une pensée le frappa, et il s'immobilisa de nouveau pour faire courir soigneusement ses mains sur toute la longueur de son oo'lu. L'instrument était encore en parfait état, sans aucun indice de la moindre craquelure.

Avec un sourire railleur, il se le jeta sur l'épaule et reprit sa route vers les montagnes. Ses pérégrinations n'étaient pas encore achevées. Il n'y voyait aucun inconvénient, en réalité. C'était un bon cor puissant qu'il possédait là. Il se demanda seulement qui serait son nouveau guide.

29

Tamìr maintint Ki éveillé toute la nuit en lui parlant de la bataille et de ses plans pour fonder une nouvelle ville. Ils évitèrent timidement tous deux le thème de l'accord auquel ils étaient arrivés. Il était trop frais, trop fragile pour qu'ils s'y appesantissent, alors que tant de tâches les attendaient encore. Regarder Ki vomir dans un heaume ne se prêtait guère à de telles idées non plus. Il avait la joue droite et l'œil vilainement contusionnés, et l'œdème l'éborgnait.

Aux abords de l'aube, il était à bout de forces et toujours mal en point mais plus alerte d'esprit. La pluie s'était calmée, et ils entendaient des gens bouger à l'extérieur et des blessés geindre. Le vent apportait jusqu'à eux l'odeur fétide de la fumée qui s'élevait du premier des bûchers.

Lynx leur apporta de quoi déjeuner – du pain et un peu de bon ragoût d'agneau envoyé par le capitaine de l'un des navires gèdres. Il avait aussi une potion tonique destinée à Ki. Il l'aida à la boire puis sourit à belles dents. « Tu as une gueule d'enfer ! »

Ki essaya de se renfrogner, grimaça de douleur à la

place, et brandit insolemment le majeur de sa main valide.

Lynx gloussa. « Tu te sens *vraiment* mieux !

— Comment vont nos amis ? » questionna Tamìr, tout en échangeant avec Ki des cuillerées de ragoût.

« Assez bien. Nous avons préparé des bûchers pour Korin et les autres. Ils sont impatients de vous voir tous les deux, si votre état vous le permet. »

La tente n'étant pas assez vaste pour contenir tout le monde, Tamìr sortit pour faire de la place. Lynx l'imita et resta planté là sans mot dire pendant qu'elle étirait son dos. Des tentes avaient poussé pendant la nuit, et on était en train d'en dresser d'autres. Les drysiens s'affairaient parmi les centaines de blessés encore en plein air et, dans le lointain, des colonnes de fumée noire se détachaient sur le ciel du matin. Plusieurs grands bûchers se dressaient non loin du bord de la falaise. La bannière de Korin et son bouclier décoraient l'un d'entre eux.

Les nuages étaient en train de se déchirer en longues effilochures prometteuses d'un temps meilleur, et la mer bleu sombre était mouchetée de blanc.

« Il semble qu'on va finalement arriver à se sécher, murmura-t-elle.

— Une bonne chose, ça aussi. J'ai attrapé de la mousse au cul. » Lynx lui décocha un coup d'œil oblique, et elle surprit sur ses lèvres un léger sourire. « Vous allez nous faire une annonce, vous deux, tout de suite, ou bien attendre que nous soyons rentrés à Atyion ?

— Tu as entendu ? » Elle sentit ses joues s'échauffer.

« Non, mais j'ai des yeux. Nik et moi avons fait des paris là-dessus depuis le départ de Bierfût. Ainsi, c'est vrai ? Ki est finalement revenu à lui ?

— On pourrait le dire de cette façon.

— Il était temps. »

Le regard de Tamìr s'égara vers les corps enveloppés qui gisaient encore non loin de là. Tanil et Caliel étaient toujours là, montant la garde. « Ne dis rien encore. Korin doit jouir d'un deuil séant. Il était un prince, après tout.

— Et un ami. » La voix de Lynx se réduisit à un filet rauque, et il se détourna. « Si je n'étais pas parti avec toi, cette nuit-là...

— Je suis heureuse que tu aies fini par te ranger de mon côté. L'es-tu, toi ?

— Je suppose que oui. » Il soupira et reporta son regard sur Caliel et Tanil. « Ça va être plus dur pour eux. »

On brûla Korin et les autres cet après-midi-là, l'ensemble des Compagnons tenant lieu de garde d'honneur. Ki insista pour qu'on le transporte à l'extérieur et, de son brancard, il demeura avec eux jusqu'à ce que ses forces l'abandonnent. Caliel se tenait debout, l'œil sec. Tanil était calme mais assommé.

Tamìr et son entourage tranchèrent la crinière de leurs chevaux et les jetèrent sur les bûchers. Elle-même y jeta aussi une mèche de ses propres cheveux pour Korin, Porion et Lorin.

Les feux brûlèrent tout le reste de la journée et

pendant la plus grande partie de la nuit, et on recueillit les cendres, une fois refroidies, dans des urnes de terre cuite pour les faire rapporter aux familles de chaque défunt. Tamìr emporta celles de Korin dans sa tente.

En réponse à la question qui était demeurée en suspens entre elle et Ki, et que se posait peut-être à présent le camp tout entier, elle étendit son sac de couchage auprès du sien cette nuit-là, et dormit à ses côtés en lui tenant la main.

30

Nalia fut réveillée en sursaut dans le noir par des cris et des piaffements de chevaux qui montaient de la cour. Pendant un instant, le saisissement lui fit croire qu'elle devait être en train de rêver de la nuit où Korin était arrivé pour la première fois.

Tremblante, elle envoya Tomara se renseigner sur ce qui se passait, puis elle enfila une robe de chambre et se précipita vers le balcon. Il n'y avait en bas qu'une poignée de cavaliers. Elle ne parvint pas à discerner ce qui se disait, mais le ton était tout sauf triomphal. Comme Tomara ne remontait toujours pas, elle s'habilla en un tournemain et s'assit au coin du feu, jouant nerveusement avec le sautoir de perles qui lui battait la poitrine.

Ses appréhensions furent confirmées. La porte

s'ouvrit à la volée, et Lord Alben entra d'un pas chancelant, pesamment appuyé sur Tomara. Sa figure et ses vêtements étaient ensanglantés, et ses cheveux enchevêtrés ne faisaient que souligner son teint livide.

« Tomara, va chercher de l'eau pour Lord Alben, et du vin ! Asseyez-vous, messire. »

Alben s'évanouit dans un fauteuil, et elles restèrent un bon moment sans pouvoir lui faire reprendre conscience si peu que ce soit. La vieille lui bassina le visage avec de l'eau de rose pour le ranimer, pendant que Nalia tournicotait anxieusement en se tordant les mains.

Finalement, Alben se remit suffisamment pour parler. « Majesté ! » hoqueta-t-il, et ses larmes soudaines corroborèrent leurs pires craintes. « Le roi est mort !

— Nous sommes perdus ! gémit Tomara. Oh, ma dame, que va-t-il advenir de vous ? »

Nalia s'effondra sur un tabouret près de son visiteur bouleversé, se sentant faible et engourdie tout à la fois. « Quand cela, messire ? Comment est-il mort ?

— Deux... non, voilà maintenant trois jours, de la main du traître Tobin. Je suis parti sur-le-champ pour vous mettre en garde. » Il lui serra la main encore plus fort. « Vous êtes en danger ici. Il faut vous enfuir !

— Mort. » Elle pouvait à peine respirer. *Je n'ai plus de mari désormais, mon enfant plus de père...*

« Vous devez venir avec moi, insista Alben. J'assurerai votre protection.

— Le feriez-vous ? » D'abord Nyrin, qui l'avait

trahie, puis Korin, qui ne pouvait pas l'aimer, et maintenant cet homme, qui n'avait jamais eu un mot gentil pour elle jusque-là ? Qui s'était ouvertement gaussé de ses traits disgraciés ? Il lui tiendrait lieu de Protecteur ? Tomara volait déjà autour de la chambre, relevant à grand fracas le couvercle des coffres pour en arracher des vêtements à emballer.

« Altesse ? » Alben attendait sa réponse.

Elle leva les yeux vers lui et les plongea dans ses sombres prunelles emplies de panique et de quelque chose d'autre. De quelque chose qu'elle reconnut bien, ne reconnut que trop. « Merci de votre offre obligeante, Lord Alben, mais je me sens tenue de la décliner.

— Êtes-vous folle ? Tobin et l'armée qu'elle a sont déjà sur mes talons !

— Elle ? Alors, c'était vrai, tout du long ?

— Je l'ai vue de mes propres yeux. »

Un mensonge de plus, Nyrin ?

« Dame, écoutez-le ! Il faut que vous preniez la fuite, et vous ne pouvez pas courir les routes toute seule ! intervint Tomara d'un ton suppliant.

— Non, répondit fermement Nalia. Je vous sais gré de votre proposition, messire, mais je n'y vois aucun avantage. Je resterai ici et y assumerai mes risques avec cette reine, quoi qu'elle soit. Si vous voulez m'aider, prenez le commandement de la garnison et veillez aux défenses de la forteresse. Allez, et faites ce que vous estimerez être le mieux comme préparatifs.

— C'est le choc, messire, dit Tomara. Laissez-la se reposer pour y réfléchir. Revenez demain matin.

419

— Libre à lui d'en agir à sa guise, mais ma réponse sera la même, repartit Nalia.

— Votre serviteur, Altesse. » Alben s'inclina et prit congé.

« Oh, ma pauvre dame ! Veuve avant d'être mère ! » sanglota la vieille en la prenant dans ses bras.

Nalia se mit alors à pleurer pour de bon, tandis que la conscience de sa véritable situation cheminait en elle. Elle pleura sur le sort de Korin, mais son chagrin se mêlait de remords. L'espoir d'être aimée de lui avait eu la vie courte, et elle l'avait anéanti de ses propres mains quand elle avait tué Nyrin. Elle souhaitait déplorer la perte de son époux et, au lieu de cela, ne parvenait qu'à imaginer ce qu'aurait été une existence entière vouée à sa froideur et à ses devoirs.

Quoi qu'il advienne, cela au moins me sera épargné.

Elle sécha ses larmes et retourna se coucher. Elle fouillait encore son cœur en quête de la peine adéquate sans parvenir à la découvrir quand elle s'assoupit.

Lorsqu'elle se réveilla, le soleil était déjà haut, et pas un bruit ne provenait de l'extérieur. Elle expédia Tomara chercher leur petit déjeuner. Comme elle ne possédait pas de vêtements appropriés à son nouveau statut de veuve, elle endossa sa plus belle robe – celle qu'elle avait eu l'intention de porter pour faire honneur à Korin lorsqu'il reviendrait.

Tomara reparut les mains vides et la mine affolée. « Ils sont partis !

— Qui ?

— Tous ! se lamenta la vieille. Lord Alben, les soldats, tout le monde, à l'exception de quelques domestiques. Qu'allons-nous faire ? »

Nalia gagna la porte d'entrée. Pour la première fois, personne ne se trouvait là pour l'empêcher de quitter ses appartements. Un sentiment d'irréalité s'empara d'elle lorsque, comme dans un rêve, elle descendit l'escalier sans autre escorte que Tomara. Elles enfilèrent de conserve les corridors déserts qui conduisaient vers la grande salle.

Il n'y avait personne d'autre en vue que les limiers abandonnés de Korin. Ils trottèrent vers elle en gémissant et en agitant la queue. Nalia sortit dans la cour et trouva la porte nord entrebâillée. Pour la première fois depuis qu'avait débuté le cauchemar de sa captivité, elle la franchit et s'offrit un brin de marche sur la route, émerveillée de sa liberté.

« Il nous faut déguerpir, la pressa Tomara. Descendez au village avec moi. J'ai des gens, là-bas. Ils vous cacheront, vous emmèneront dans un bateau de pêche...

— Et pour aller où ? » fit observer Nalia, tout en contemplant le ciel. Il paraissait aussi vide qu'elle avait l'impression de l'être elle-même. « Je n'ai plus personne au monde, à présent. Faites comme vous l'entendez, moi, je resterai. »

Elle se retira dans sa tour. Ce n'était plus sa prison, et c'était l'unique lieu de toute cette gigantesque forteresse qu'elle eût jamais qualifié de sien.

En début de soirée, le guetteur du mur sud lança un cri d'alerte. À travers l'obscurité grandissante, Nalia réussit à discerner sur la route une sombre masse de cavaliers qui survenait au galop. L'énorme nuage de poussière qui les surplombait l'empêchait de supputer leur nombre, mais elle voyait le miroitement sinistre de heaumes et de fers de piques.

La peur l'empoigna alors, tandis que s'ancrait plus avant en elle la conviction que sa posture était sans recours.

Il n'y a plus rien à espérer, maintenant, se dit-elle. Elle lissa ses cheveux et sa robe puis descendit dans la grande salle à la rencontre de son destin.

Tomara ne décolla pas d'auprès d'elle pendant qu'elle gravissait les degrés de l'estrade et, pour la première fois, s'installait dans le fauteuil qui avait été celui de Korin. Là-dessus entra à toutes jambes un petit palefrenier. « C'est un héraut, ma dame, et Lord Lutha ! Je les laisse pénétrer ?

— Lord Lutha ? » Que pouvait bien signifier cela ? « Oui, amène-les-moi. »

Lutha et Nyanis s'étaient préparés en vue d'une résistance mais certes pas attendus à trouver la forteresse abandonnée et sa porte ouverte devant eux. Arkoniel jugeait cela tout aussi suspect, mais il n'avait pas repéré le moindre indice d'embuscade.

Le gamin effaré qui les avait salués du haut des murailles revint annoncer que Lady Nalia leur souhaitait la bienvenue.

Lutha laissa sur place Nyanis et les Aurënfaïes,

n'emmenant avec lui qu'Arkoniel et le héraut dans la cour peuplée d'échos par leur arrivée. Elle était étrangement déserte, elle aussi.

Nalia les attendait dans la grande salle, assise sur l'estrade à la place de Korin. Tomara était seule à l'assister.

Nalia accueillit Lutha avec un sourire incertain. « Je suis heureuse de vous voir en vie, messire, mais il apparaît que vous avez changé d'allégeance. La nouvelle de la mort du roi nous est déjà parvenue. C'est Lord Alben qui l'a apportée, avant de s'enfuir.

— Korin est mort en brave », lui déclara Lutha. Tamìr ne lui en avait pas dit davantage avant son départ. « La reine Tamìr m'a envoyé à vous sur-le-champ pour assurer votre sécurité et pour vous annoncer que vous n'avez rien à redouter de sa part si vous ne vous élevez pas contre ses prétentions.

— Je vois. » Elle jeta un coup d'œil du côté d'Arkoniel. « Et vous, qui êtes-vous ?

— Maître Arkoniel, magicien et ami de la reine Tamìr. » En voyant ses yeux s'agrandir à ces mots, il s'empressa d'ajouter : « Altesse, je suis seulement venu pour vous protéger. »

Lutha déplora de ne pouvoir rien dire ni rien faire de plus pour la rassurer, mais il savait qu'elle avait de bonnes raisons de se montrer méfiante.

Néanmoins, elle conserva sa dignité et se tourna vers le héraut. « Quelle est la teneur de votre message ?

— La reine Tamìr de Skala envoie ses respects à sa parente, la princesse Nalia, veuve du prince Korin.

C'est avec un immense chagrin qu'elle lui envoie la nouvelle de la mort du prince Korin. Elle vous offre, à vous-même et à votre enfant à naître, sa royale protection.

— Et néanmoins, elle envoie une armée avec le message. » Nalia était assise très droite, les mains cramponnées aux bras de son fauteuil.

« La reine Tamìr présumait que Korin vous avait laissée mieux protégée. Elle ne s'attendait pas à vous voir abandonnée par vos défenseurs », répliqua Lutha, tout en s'efforçant de ne rien laisser transparaître de sa colère.

Elle balaya l'espace d'un geste circulaire. « Comme vous pouvez le constater, ma cour s'est singulièrement amenuisée.

— Nous avons ouï dire que Lord Nyrin était mort », intervint Arkoniel.

Nalia releva un brin son menton. « Oui. Lord Lutha, de la main de qui mon époux a-t-il péri ?

— La reine Tamìr et lui se sont affrontés en combat singulier. Elle avait offert des pourparlers, mais il les a rejetés. Ils se sont battus, et il est tombé.

— Et vous portez les couleurs de la reine, à présent.

— Tamìr, qui fut le prince Tobin, est mon amie. Elle nous a tous recueillis après notre évasion d'ici. Barieüs et moi servons avec ses Compagnons. Elle m'a envoyé en avant, pensant qu'une figure familière pourrait vous rassurer. Elle prend les Quatre à témoin qu'elle ne vous veut aucun mal, ni à vous-même ni à votre enfant. C'est la vérité, je le jure.

— Et qu'en est-il de Lord Caliel ?

— Il est retourné à Korin et s'est battu à ses côtés.

— Est-il mort ?

— Non, seulement blessé.

— Je suis heureuse de l'apprendre. Et maintenant, quoi ? Que va-t-il advenir de ma personne et de mon enfant ?

— J'ai pour mission de vous conduire au camp de la reine. En qualité de parente, Altesse, pas de prisonnière. »

Cela fit rire doucement Nalia, mais sans qu'elle perde son air affligé. « Il semble que je n'aie pas d'autre solution que d'accepter son hospitalité. »

M'y revoilà, songea Nalia plus tard cette nuit-là, tout en regardant de son balcon les nouveaux venus s'activer dans la cour. *Du moins est-ce de mon propre choix, cette fois-ci.*

Si fort qu'elle désirât faire confiance à Lord Lutha, elle redoutait le lendemain. « S'il te plaît, Dalna ! » chuchota-t-elle, pressant ses mains sur le léger ballonnement de son ventre au-dessous du corsage. « Fais qu'on épargne mon enfant. Elle est tout ce que j'ai. »

Tomara était descendue aux nouvelles, mais elle revint précipitamment, blême de peur. « C'est ce magicien, ma dame ! Il demande à venir vous rendre visite. Qu'allons-nous faire ?

— Laisse-le entrer. » Nalia se planta près de l'âtre, arc-boutée contre le manteau de la cheminée. Était-ce ainsi que serait exaucée sa prière, en définitive ? Allait-il la tuer sans tapage ou bien la faire avorter ?

Maître Arkoniel n'avait pas l'air bien menaçant. Il

était plus jeune que Nyrin et avait une physionomie ouverte, amicale. Elle ne vit pas une once en lui de la fourberie de Nyrin, mais elle s'était déjà laissé tellement abuser...

Il s'inclina, puis demeura debout. « Altesse, pardonnez mon intrusion. Lutha et les autres m'ont un peu parlé du traitement qu'on vous a infligé ici, et il ne m'en faut pas davantage pour deviner en vous une femme qui s'est vu gravement maltraiter. Nyrin était une créature infâme, et nombre des agissements les moins nobles de votre époux doivent être imputés au compte de cette canaille.

— J'aimerais le croire », murmura-t-elle.

Ils demeurèrent quelque temps ainsi, face à face, à se jauger l'un l'autre, puis il sourit de nouveau. « Je pense qu'une bonne infusion pourrait vous faire du bien. Si vous me montrez où se trouvent les ustensiles et les ingrédients nécessaires, je la confectionnerai moi-même. »

Aussi abasourdie que circonspecte, elle le surveilla de près pendant qu'il faisait chauffer la bouilloire et dosait les feuilles. Avait-il l'intention de l'empoisonner ? Elle ne remarqua rien de suspect dans ses gestes et, une fois le breuvage prêt, il leur en servit à tous deux et avala une bonne gorgée. Non sans hésiter, elle trempa ses lèvres dans le sien.

« Est-elle à votre goût, Altesse ? Ma maîtresse m'a appris à la faire plutôt corsée.

— Votre maîtresse ? » interrogea-t-elle, se demandant s'il voulait dire une amante.

« La magicienne qui fut mon professeur, expliqua-t-il.

— Ah. »

Ils retombèrent dans le silence, et puis voici qu'il reposa sa coupe et se mit à la considérer d'un air pensif.

« C'est vous qui avez tué Nyrin ?

— Oui. Cela vous scandalise ?

— Pas vraiment. Je sais de quoi il était capable, et, sauf erreur de ma part, vous aussi. »

Elle frissonna mais ne souffla mot.

« Je perçois quelque chose de sa répugnante magie s'attarder sur votre personne, ma dame. Si vous daignez m'y autoriser, je puis le supprimer. »

Nalia accentua sa prise sur sa coupe, écartelée entre la répulsion que lui faisait éprouver l'idée que subsistât le moindre vestige des manigances de Nyrin et l'appréhension de quelque duperie.

« Par mes mains et mon cœur et mes yeux, dame. Je ne voudrais pour rien au monde vous faire du mal, pas plus à vous qu'à votre enfant », lui protesta Arkoniel, devinant une fois de plus ses pensées.

Nalia lutta contre elle-même encore quelque temps mais, en constatant qu'il ne la bousculait nullement, elle finit par consentir d'un hochement de tête. S'il s'apprêtait à la trahir par le biais de ses manières affables et de ses paroles rassurantes, mieux valait le savoir tout de suite, et bon débarras.

Arkoniel exhiba une mince baguette de cristal qu'il inséra entre ses paumes en fermant les yeux. « Ah oui, là », fit-il au bout d'un moment. Il posa une main sur la tête de Nalia, et celle-ci sentit un chatouillement chaud se répandre dans tout son être. La sensation que cela lui faisait éprouver ne ressemblait en rien à celle que procuraient les sortilèges de Nyrin ; c'était comme la lumière du soleil comparée au gel.

« Vous êtes délivrée, ma dame », lui annonça-t-il en retournant s'asseoir dans son propre fauteuil.

Nalia se demanda comment en tenter l'épreuve. Ne sachant que faire d'autre, elle lâcha : « Nyrin m'avait séduite.

— Ah, je vois. » Le magicien ne se montra pas choqué par cette révélation, seulement affligé. « Eh bien, il n'a plus aucune prise sur vous. Aussi longtemps que vous serez sous la protection de la reine Tamìr, je veillerai personnellement à ce que personne n'abuse à nouveau de vous de la sorte. Vous avez mon serment là-dessus. »

Des larmes montèrent aux yeux de Nalia. « Pourquoi faites-vous cela ? Pourquoi Tamìr m'envoie-t-elle des êtres de votre sorte, alors que je porte l'enfant de son rival ?

— Parce qu'elle sait ce que c'est que de souffrir, et parce qu'elle a aimé Korin très fort, même à la fin, quand lui ne l'aimait plus du tout. Lorsque vous ferez sa connaissance, vous verrez par vous-même. » Il se leva et s'inclina. « Reposez-vous bien cette nuit, chère dame. Vous n'avez plus rien à craindre. »

Après qu'il se fut retiré, Nalia demeura longuement assise au coin du feu, prise entre l'espoir et le chagrin.

31

Lutha revint une semaine plus tard avec Lady Nalia. Conformément à son statut, Tamìr était assise devant sa tente sur un tabouret drapé d'un manteau, ses nobles autour d'elle et son armée massée en deux vastes carrés formant une avenue qui traversait de part en part l'immensité du camp. De nouveau sur pied mais encore défiguré par des ecchymoses impressionnantes, et son bras soutenu par une écharpe, Ki occupait la place qui lui revenait aux côtés de la reine.

Caliel avait poliment refusé le baudrier qu'elle lui avait offert, et ils n'avaient plus rien eu à se dire. Il se tenait à l'écart avec certains des nobles, Tanil près de lui, comme toujours. Tous deux étaient inséparables.

Tandis que s'approchait la force de retour, Tamìr fut étonnée de voir qu'elle s'était prodigieusement accrue. Le mystère fut résolu quand Lutha et Nyanis s'avancèrent, encadrant un troisième cavalier.

« Tharin ! » Jetant sa dignité aux orties, Tamìr se leva d'un bond et courut à sa rencontre.

Il sauta à bas de sa selle et la prit dans ses bras, non sans étouffer un grognement.

« Tu es blessé ? » demanda-t-elle en se reculant pour l'examiner de pied en cap, à la recherche d'une trace de sang.

« Rien de sérieux, lui assura-t-il. Lord Nevus nous a offert une bonne bataille avant que je ne le tue. Cela s'est passé le jour même où nous avons reçu la nouvelle de ta victoire ici. » Il baissa les yeux vers l'Épée qu'elle portait au côté et en toucha religieusement la poignée. « Enfin, voilà qu'elle bat le flanc d'une reine authentique. »

Ki les rejoignit en boitant, et son aspect fit s'esclaffer Tharin pendant qu'ils se serraient la main. « Semble que tu en as toi-même quelques-unes de bien bonnes à nous raconter !

— Plus que vous ne vous l'imaginez, répliqua-t-il avec un sourire chagrin.

— Je suis heureuse de te voir, Tharin, mais qu'est-ce que tu fabriques ici ? » demanda Tamìr, tout en l'entraînant pour regagner son trône improvisé.

« Après que nous eûmes battu Nevus à plates coutures et brûlé les navires envoyés par Korin, j'ai poussé vers le nord, pensant que je te rencontrerais arrivant de l'autre côté. Nous avons atteint l'isthme à temps pour opérer notre jonction avec Lutha et Nyanis, et j'ai décidé de t'apporter moi-même les nouvelles. Atyion ne court aucun risque, et les derniers des lords du nord sont en train de jurer leur loyauté d'une voix tonitruante. Je n'ai eu à en trucider que quelques-uns sur mon parcours. Ki, ton frère t'envoie ses amitiés. Assiégé, Rilmar a tenu le coup, et ta famille se porte bien. »

Quand les Compagnons et les généraux de Tamìr eurent achevé de saluer les nouveaux venus, Lutha renvoya un messager mander Nalia.

Elle arriva, montée sur un beau cheval blanc et escortée par Arkoniel et par les deux commandants aurënfaïes. La description que Lutha lui en avait faite permit à Tamìr de la reconnaître d'emblée. Elle était en effet dépourvue d'attraits, et sa tache de vin très marquée, mais Tamìr fut aussi frappée par le mélange de crainte et de dignité que révélaient son regard et son port de tête.

Arkoniel l'aida à mettre pied à terre et lui offrit son bras pour la conduire à Tamìr. « Reine Tamìr, permettez-moi de vous présenter Lady Nalia, l'épouse du prince Korin.

— Votre Majesté. » Nalia lui fit une profonde révérence et resta sur un genou devant elle, toute tremblante.

Tamìr se sentit sur-le-champ de tout cœur avec elle. Elle se leva et saisit la main de la jeune femme pour la remettre debout. « Bienvenue, cousine. Je suis peinée de faire enfin votre connaissance dans des circonstances aussi tristes. » Elle adressa un signe à Lynx, et il s'avança avec l'urne qui contenait les cendres de Korin. Nalia parut décontenancée et ne fit pas un geste pour les prendre. Au lieu de cela, elle serra les mains sur son cœur et lança à Tamìr un regard implorant.

« Lord Lutha et maître Arkoniel ont fait preuve envers moi de la plus grande gentillesse, et ils m'ont prodigué maintes assurances, mais il me faut les entendre de vos propres lèvres. Quelles sont vos intentions envers mon enfant ?

— Vous êtes enceinte, alors ? »

Nalia était encore très mince. « Oui, Majesté. La naissance aura lieu au printemps.

— Vous êtes Parente Royale, et votre enfant a part à mon sang. Si vous voulez bien me jurer de soutenir mes droits au trône et renoncer à toutes prétentions aux vôtres, alors vous serez bienvenue à ma cour et dotée des titres et des terres conformes à votre position.

— Vous avez mon serment, et de tout mon cœur ! s'exclama Nalia tout bas. Je ne sais rien de la vie de cour, et je ne désire rien d'autre que de vivre en paix.

— Je souhaite la même chose pour vous, cousine. Lord Caliel, Lord Tanil, veuillez vous avancer. »

Caliel lui adressa un regard interrogatif, mais il fit ce qu'elle demandait, entraînant Tanil par le bras. « Messires, consentez-vous à devenir les hommes liges de Lady Nalia et à la protéger, elle et son enfant, aussi longtemps qu'ils auront besoin de vous ?

— Oui, Majesté », répondit Caliel, qui commençait à comprendre. « C'est on ne peut plus aimable à vous.

— Alors, voilà qui est réglé, dit Tamìr. Vous voyez, ma dame, vous n'êtes pas sans amis à ma cour. Lord Lutha vous tient en haute estime, lui aussi. J'espère que vous lui donnerez également le nom d'ami. »

Nalia lui fit une nouvelle révérence, les yeux brillants de larmes. « Merci, Majesté. J'espère... » Elle s'interrompit, et Tamìr vit à quel point son regard s'égarait vers l'urne funéraire. « J'espère qu'un jour je pourrai comprendre, Majesté.

— Je l'espère également. Demain, nous nous mettrons en marche pour retourner à Atyion. Dînez avec moi tout à l'heure, et reposez-vous bien. »

Ce soir-là, Tamìr fit ses adieux aux Aurënfaïes, échangea des serments et des traités avec eux devant ses nobles et ses magiciens. Après qu'ils eurent pris congé, elle reconduisit Nalia à sa tente puis, en compagnie de Ki, se dirigea vers celle qui était la leur. Arkoniel remarqua la combinaison mais se contenta d'en sourire.

Pendant que le reste de l'armée s'apprêtait à marcher, le matin suivant, Arkoniel et Tamìr retournèrent à cheval jusqu'aux falaises qui dominaient la rade. Immobilisant leurs montures, ils contemplèrent en silence l'horizon marin. Ils pouvaient tout juste discerner les voiles des vaisseaux gèdres qui, dans le lointain, cinglaient vers leur patrie sous un ciel limpide.

« Ce n'est pas un mauvais site pour un port de mer, si vous entendez essentiellement commercer avec les 'faïes, observa le magicien. Mais qu'en sera-t-il avec le reste de Skala ?

— Je trouverai un moyen, musa-t-elle. Il sera plus difficile aux Plenimariens de nous surprendre ici. J'ai pas mal patrouillé pendant votre absence. Mahti avait raison. Il y a de la bonne eau, de la bonne terre aussi, et de la pierre et du bois à foison pour bâtir. » Elle jeta un regard alentour, l'œil brillant d'anticipation. « Je puis déjà la voir, Arkoniel ! Elle sera plus belle qu'Ero ne le fut jamais.

— Une immense ville brillante avec en son cœur un château de magiciens », murmura-t-il en souriant.

Enfant, Tamìr l'avait trouvé très laid et balourd, et souvent plutôt fou. Elle le voyait avec des yeux tout différents, maintenant, ou peut-être avait-il changé autant qu'elle-même ? « Vous m'aiderez à l'édifier, n'est-ce pas ?

— Bien sûr. » Il lui décocha un coup d'œil et sourit en ajoutant : « Majesté ».

Il pouvait dès à présent voir, lui aussi, s'élever les murailles, et il imaginait déjà le havre de sécurité qu'ils créeraient pour les magiciens errants et pour tous les enfants perdus semblables à Wythnir et aux autres. Il sentait contre son genou la pesanteur du sac taché par les voyages qui pendait encore à l'arçon de sa selle comme il l'avait fait à celui d'Iya. Il réaliserait aussi un abri sûr pour ce fardeau. Il ne s'en tracassait plus autant, désormais. Tout dangereux et déroutant qu'il persistait à demeurer, le vilain bol maléfique le reliait à Iya et aux Gardiens qui les avaient précédés... comme à tous ceux qui leur succéderaient, d'ailleurs. Peut-être que Wythnir lui était finalement échu tout exprès pour ce faire, assumer sa relève en tant que Gardien ?

« Je vous servirai toujours, Tamìr, fille d'Ariani, murmura-t-il. Je vous donnerai des magiciens tels que les Trois Pays n'en ont jamais vu de pareils.

— Je sais. » Elle redevint silencieuse, et il devina qu'elle était en train de se concentrer en vue de quelque chose. « Ki et moi allons nous marier. »

Il gloussa de sa timidité. « Je devais sûrement l'espérer. Lhel serait tellement désappointée si vous ne le faisiez pas.

— Elle savait ?

— Elle l'a prévu quand vous n'étiez encore que des enfants. Elle avait un gros faible pour Ki. Même Iya a dû admettre qu'il valait mieux qu'il n'en avait l'air au premier abord. » Il se tut un instant puis gloussa doucement. « Navets, vipères et taupes.

— Quoi ?

— Oh, juste un truc qu'elle disait. Ki était le seul garçon qu'elle jugeait digne de vous.

— Jamais je ne l'ai comprise. » Elle s'arrêta court, et il devina que lui parler d'Iya la mettait mal à l'aise.

« C'est très bien comme ça, Tamìr.

— Vraiment ?

— Oui. »

Elle lui adressa un sourire de gratitude. « J'ai si souvent rêvé de cet endroit ! Ki se trouvait avec moi, et j'essayais de l'embrasser, mais je tombais toujours du haut de la falaise ou me réveillais avant d'avoir pu le faire. Les visions sont des choses bizarres, n'est-ce pas ?

— Elles le sont, effectivement. Les dieux nous montrent un futur possible, mais rien n'est jamais fixé. C'est à nous de saisir ces rêves et de leur donner forme. Il y a toujours un choix à faire.

— Si c'est vrai, alors j'aurais pu choisir de prendre la fuite, non ? J'y ai pensé tant et tant de fois...

— Peut-être l'Illuminateur vous a-t-il élue parce que vous n'en feriez rien. »

Elle fixa pensivement la mer pendant quelque temps puis hocha la tête. « Je crois que vous avez raison. »

Elle jeta un regard à la ronde une dernière fois, et

Arkoniel vit l'avenir dans ses prunelles bleues avant qu'elle n'éclate de rire et ne talonne son cheval pour lui faire prendre le galop.

Arkoniel se mit à rire, lui aussi, d'un rire sans fin, puis il la suivit, ainsi qu'il le ferait toujours.

Épilogue

Aujourd'hui il n'y a plus que des moutons qui vaga-
bondent sur le Palatin, et Atyion même a perdu son
éclat. Remoni est devenu Rhíminee, pour coïncider
avec les idiomes skaliens, mais le sens demeure le
même. Bonne eau. Rhíminee, la source de vie de l'âge
d'or de Skala.

« Nous autres, magiciens, nous sommes comme des
rochers dans le lit d'une rivière, attentifs aux flots
torrentueux de l'existence qui s'écoule en tourbil-
lonnant. »

Je songe souvent à vos paroles, Iya, tandis que je
déambule dans les rues de la brillante cité de Tamìr.
Du haut de mon balcon, je puis encore suivre le tracé
des murailles qu'elle construisit cette année-là. La
ville ancienne repose comme un jaune d'œuf au cœur
des adjonctions réalisées tour à tour par ses succes-
seurs. Je sais qu'elle se plairait à voir s'en poursuivre
la construction. Là était sa véritable vocation, en
définitive, bien plus encore que celle de guerrier ou
de reine.

Au nord, à l'endroit même où se dressait la for-
teresse de Cirna, passe le grand canal que nous
frayâmes pour elle, premier présent fait à sa nouvelle

capitale par la Troisième Orëska. Sculptée quand elle était plus âgée, sa statue le garde toujours. Que de fois n'ai-je levé les yeux vers sa physionomie solennelle ! Mais, dans mon cœur, elle aura pour jamais les seize ans du jour où, debout avec Ki sous des tourbillons de feuilles d'automne aux couleurs rutilantes, ils annoncent officiellement leur union devant le peuple, entourés de tous leurs amis.

Tamïr et Ki. Reine et consort. Amis intimes et guerriers hors pair jusqu'au bout. Vous êtes tous les deux à jamais enlacés dans mon cœur. Vos descendants sont vigoureux et beaux et gens d'honneur. Je vous aperçois encore furtivement tous deux dans des prunelles bleu sombre et brunes.

Rhíminee a oublié les autres – Tharin, les Compagnons, Nyrin, Rhius et Ariani. Erius et Korin sont des noms voués à l'ombre dans la lignée, une fable morale. Même toi, Tamïr – Tamïr la Grande, comme on t'appelle désormais –, tu n'es qu'une fable à moitié contée. Tant mieux. Frère et Tobin sont les ténèbres jumelées au sein de la perle ; la seule chose qui importe, c'est son orient.

Le cri bref poussé par un nouveau-né persiste à hanter mes rêves, mais ses derniers échos s'éteindront avec moi. Ce que Tamïr a construit continue d'exister, transmettant à l'avenir son amour et l'amour de ceux qui se tenaient à ses côtés.

Extrait d'un fragment de document découvert par le Gardien Nysander dans la tour est de la Maison de l'Orëska.

Postface

Certains d'entre vous, lecteurs pointilleux, risquez fort de vous demander, juste après avoir tourné la dernière page : « Mais alors, et ce maudit bol à propos duquel Iya faisait tant d'histoires ? Que venait-il faire dans tout cela ? »

Arkoniel aurait été bien en peine de vous le dire, parce qu'il n'en sut jamais rien. Au lieu de s'en préoccuper, il se contenta d'assurer sa sécurité, comme il avait été chargé de le faire, et laissa se dissiper au fil des années la connaissance qu'on avait de lui. Il n'en était après tout que l'un des Gardiens, mais pas le dernier. Ce qu'est effectivement le bol et ce qu'il advint de lui, c'est à quelqu'un d'autre qu'il appartient de le relater, longtemps après l'époque dont les événements faisaient l'objet de ce récit.

Vous trouverez ces réponses dans deux de mes autres ouvrages, *Les Maîtres de l'ombre* et *Stalking Darkness*[1]. J'espère que la quête vous divertira !

LF
19 janvier 2006
East Aurora, New York

---

1. À paraître aux éditions Mnémos.

Remerciements

Merci, d'abord et surtout au Dr Doug, ma principale muse et mon meilleur ami. À Pat York aussi, Anne Groell, Lucienne Diver, Matthew et Timothy Flewelling, Nancy Jeffers, au Dr Meghan Cope et à Bonnie Blanch pour leurs remarques secourables et leur patience, ainsi qu'à tous les lecteurs qui m'ont si fort encouragée au fil des années.

*Composition et mise en pages réalisées
par ÉTIANNE COMPOSITION
à Montrouge.*

Achevé d' imprimer par GGP Media GmbH, Pößneck
en Mars 2009
pour le compte de France Loisirs,
Paris

N° d'éditeur : 54884
Dépôt légal : Février 2009
Imprimé en Allemagne